D.D. DID

Magdalena's Bones

"You men, your bones, they are the bones of my bones, your flesh is the flesh of my flesh. I am Hyvah, Eve, I am Hawwāh and the goddess Lilith. This world, it is my world, this world belongs to me..."

Publishing agent: DAVIDUNGLESS.COM

First edition

ISBN: 978-1-3999-6568-2

Cover art by Nuno Moreira
Editing by Davina Realm
Agent: DAVIDUNGLESS.COM

This book was professionally typeset on Reedsy.
Find out more at reedsy.com

"We will be beaten, abused nor hidden no more. We will not remain beneath your threatening shadow. We have names, it was a woman who gave you Martin Luther King, it was a woman who gave you Mandela. The Bible, the Quran, they tell you it was a woman who gave you the prophets Jesus and Muhammad. You men, you know this, don't you ever forget."

Janelle Monee

Contents

1

PROLOGUE

The soundless vessel passed through newborn galaxies at uncountable billions of light speed. Nothing existed, no sentient lifeforms had yet evolved to detect the strange starships' silent passage. In precious few gas clouds, embryonic half-life slithered in primordial survival, wriggling and squirming deep inside scattered star-forming nebulas that radiated insipid grey light. No inhabited world was yet formed, no civilisation lived that could sense the new beginning was about to unfold - it was not the first creation, nor the second - the young infant universe would, at last, give birth.

The starship arced on a converging course through one vast fermenting galaxy before it began to slow. Its reducing velocity took many millions of parsecs, the path and purpose defining the anomalous vessels' destination with some determined precision. Without noise or sound, the ghost vessel closed towards a young, still-forming white star with two giant gas worlds of almost equal size - both worlds larger than its dominant star. The starship's deceleration took it past the largest of the two worlds then out towards a third, much smaller world, a strange dark moon that had formed its rocky core long before the creation of this new universe. This cold world orbited no star or planet, it existed in the far remoteness at the precipitous edge of the galactic frontier. The vessel halted, motionless on the edge of the empty relentless void. Beyond the dim and distant galaxy rim, time did not exist.

The strangeness of the vessel became discernible when all motion had ceased; a thin wedge-shaped platform with no visible propulsion or structures. Its dark shape merged into the blackness of the barren light where no sun or starlight penetrated. The inhabitants of the starship stood mingling on one surface of the platform; their lithe, misty forms almost solid except for their opaque transparence.

The second, smaller vessel approached from somewhere deep beyond the frontier, from another dimensional universe, hurtling through unimaginable physical barriers of time at indeterminate light speed. The precision of its own deceleration enabled it to close alongside the stationary starship; the same tall, graceful forms stood silent on the surface of the smaller craft, identical in every detailed appearance.

Both platforms touched, merging into one, a circular flat disc with no protrusions. The new shape changed through all colours of the wild spectrum before distilling to a deep black which reflected the nothingness of the surrounding universe. They joined, a union of two genders from vast, distant times of off-world dimensions, two different universes with ghostlier galaxies forming beyond. Pairs of transparent beings coalesced into one in the same manner as the two starship platforms; becoming one entity for a few brief moments before separating apart forever. Their togetherness ended; dense white mist drifted from the revolving disc in an outward spiral motion captured by weak gravitational forces from somewhere in the centre of this violent still-forming galaxy. The spinning speed of the disc increased, sending the angelic seed cloud further outwards until dissipated into countless billions of elements – and was lost.

In the tiniest fraction of immeasurable time the disc rotation slowed with an explosion of colour; intense light equal to an exploding star out of which the two platforms separated into their basic forms. In plasmid echoes of creation, each vessel drifted apart before gathering their momentum; the lifeforms standing in the same random manner as before. The smaller, female vessel turned back through the frontier then accelerated into the void; they returned to their own universe an unfathomable distance beyond.

The larger vessel did not gain speed but drifted out of control towards the dark lifeless moon orbiting just beyond. The starship's energy was gone. The moon's weak gravitational pull enticed the spent vessel, beckoning it towards its doom on the dead surface of the soundless world. In silence, the male lifeform withered then died in the downward plunge, burned by atmospheric chemical friction before the immense starship wrecked in the deep, black volcanic cavern that waited.

After this, each neutron particle of union created seed mist merged with the physical elements that made up the young universe. Through incalculable aeons, dark matter and gases, driven by the power of natural creation, gave birth to new forming stars with their violent raging planets. The infinite, rare, molecular seed drifted through the universe; through time, creating new strands of DNA within random planets and suns with one single sperm seed captured within the elements of spinning formation. Almost all new planets and stars ensnared no seed; these would be empty worlds, dead worlds, devoid of all life.

The third world, still forming from nebular gases within a young, volatile ring of nine worlds, captured one single element of female seed which became lost inside the primaeval soup that erupted, after millions of orbital years, from volcanoes and chasms of lava generated by the revolving forces of creation. The great white star at the centre of this planetary formation heated through fusion to breathe life into one world of this embryonic solar chaos.

In the beginning, the timeless obelisk stone said, there was no light. From the maelstrom storm of creation came light but the light was not good light. Then from the burning white lavas of fire came HYVAH and HYVAH was EVE, who was HAWWĀH and the demon goddess LILITH. Hyvah made the light good light and from the light of Hyvah came all light. Then from the darkness of the heavens came A'ADAM who was ADAMAH who was ADAM. In the GARDEN of all life, Hyvah said to A'adam, "Your bones, they are the bones of my bones, your flesh is the flesh of my flesh. You shall be called 'MAN', for the sake of all men who will be born from the eternal womb of 'WOMAN'."

In the goodness of the new light A'adam saw Hyvah's world, A'adam desired Hyvah's world to be his world, A'adam wanted all life to be his life. Then from the celestial firmaments of turmoil came GABRIEL, who said to A'adam "I am the angel Gabriel, this world will be your world, this world shall not be the world of Hyvah. There is no Lord to thank nor worship except my Lord." Then from the burning dirt and soil Gabriel created the serpent LUCIFER, who Gabriel made *his servant angel. A'adam took Hyvah's world to make it his world, and A'adam became the first of Gabriel's loyal prophets. After this beginning, LUCIFER in his serpent envy coveted Gabriel's new world, Lucifer wanted Gabriel's world to be his world. Then HYVAH, in the desert kingdoms of the mighty prophets, HYVAH slew Lucifer to end the rise of Gabriel's venomous devil...*

Mr Johnson

Mr Johnson's day job did not put demands upon him in the real sense of the word. The upshot was, that during his time away from the labs, Johnson's inquisitive mind would be captivated by any meaningless subject that caught his deep-brooding imagination. Trained for investigative research, he was the sort of unsettled nobody who loved to unlock sciences' more unimportant mysteries. Johnson would, by instinct, be drawn to minor details disregarded by his peers, unsolved bits of nonsensical evidence that could on occasion occupy his thoughts for indelible lengths of time. *Sometimes for far too long*, Johnson often chided himself - but this was how Johnson found his precious clues, those little bits of insanity that hid in dark wretched corners reeking with slime, the little scraps of nothingness that wriggled and squirmed in sinister hideaways where more eminent eyes than Johnson's failed to look.

As a rudimentary, still inexperienced off-world archaeologist Johnson was without doubt not yet the best in his field or even anywhere near the top of his profession. He had received his certification just two years before, taking a job in the BioLabs to get his feet on the first rung of the ladder that he hoped would one day lead to a long adventurous career. *A prosperous career.* But other graduates seemed to be advancing at a much greater pace, whereas Johnson formed the distinct opinion that he was stuck in a rut, a back-end job that he should have turned down - he could have waited for something better to come along. But, after all else failed, he suffered the indignity of being allocated his role by the impatient Ministry - and that was that. He suspected his rebellious attitude labelled him as something of a troublemaker though he himself knew that frustration was his real problem. He realised he argued his point just a little too much sometimes. But then, Johnson always believed he was right, even if his learned fellows *were* more experienced. They just did not see the things he saw - or the way he *knew* everything was.

To Mr Johnson it was natural. When Johnson saw something that intrigued him, he studied it over and over – and he *always* saw clues. Little bits of nonsense, pieces of information his compatriots somehow seemed to overlook. Those clues frustrated him when they led to tantalising problems that possessed no intrinsic reason, nothing he could fathom. He could wind himself in knots when the answers did not come to him in the short time he thought they should: he would sometimes vent his temper. It wasn't that he wanted to hurt or argue with anyone, it's just that they did not understand what he was saying. *Or trying to say.* He would force himself to walk away, even out of the lectures sometimes when no one understood his point. *Why did they always laugh?*

The usual thing that happened was he every time got the mundane work. Johnson figured that when you are bottom of the pile, this is what happened. Just the previous week he received the dubious summons from Dr Matilda, the deputy head of Material Analysis, to be given the task of analysing rock samples from the sedimentary basin of *Rios*, the largest of the moons orbiting *Affebiar IV*.

"Don't fuck up Johnson," Matilda forewarned him. "Keep it simple, we just want numbers."

The mining survey ship *Constance* had in the last week docked in Central City after completing its two-year exploration mission, but all the exciting stuff was gone, purloined off, allocated to more established research laboratories. Even the rest of his team at BioCity were involved in more mind-stretching sample work. However, the *Rios* residue rocks samples needed to be categorised for mineral content as a matter of routine. This was a job for a mineralogist, not a budding lifeform research archaeologist. *Johnson argued.* What he wanted, what he was desperate for, was to search for clues of other primitive off-world life, civilisations, alien technologies and all that kind of stuff. But Mr Johnson knew this could be frustrating beyond the extreme - because none had ever been found. Nothing. *By anyone.* No trace of extraterrestrial life existed. *Ever.*

In five hundred years of interstellar travel, after the great leaps in star propulsion technology, the exploration of near star-field territory and the closest star systems, no signatures or clues of other planetary life were ever found. *Not even microscopic life in its simplest form.* Every world that humankind found and explored was dead. *One hundred percent dead.* So, Mr Johnson's career as a budding planetary archaeologist was not much of an easy matter for him to consider. But maybe, just maybe, the clues were there somewhere.

What the impatient dreamer within Johnson desired, beyond anything, was to be out there, out in the cosmic universe exploring. To be employed in one of the intrepid scientific teams aboard the survey ships. Or, as he often thought in his more radical moments, what would be even more exhilarating would be spending his whole life onboard one of the mining-funded exploration vessels owned by the conglomerates that dominated the Mia-Earth World Foundation. To live and breathe alongside these ship's crews, the redneck breed of stellar explorers who were known to be untameable. They always lived strange, sometimes short lives. Even the research scientists themselves were wild and unfathomable, not able to live the mundane life back on Earth or the other colonised planets. The crews who piloted these pocket-sized exploration vessels were hardcore tough, temperamental, they did not suffer fools – much like himself Johnson liked to think. And then, after the exploration ships finished, in went the big scientific survey vessels which did the bulk of the real work.

The huge surveying rigs were owned and operated by the mining corporations, to get to work onboard these deep space giants you needed to be employed by them. These commercial-minded organisations were not interested in funding adventures because adventures were expensive. They were in for the profit, not wild speculation - so it was never going to be easy for Mr Johnson. His archaeological field of expertise was of little interest to them. They were looking for minerals or geological evidence of where minerals could be found, the total value yield and, of more importance, the *levels of contamination.* History provided numerous examples of how mineral contamination had wrecked many extraction projects, busting more than a few mining combines – even large multi-planetary ones.

The great mining cartels were obsessed with particle contamination – because they needed *pure* mineral ore to justify the expense. Especially the rare-earth ores such as uranium, titanium, yttrium and the jewel of all minerals... gold. Industrial mined gold from out in the cosmos, when alloyed with hydrogen and scandium in a still protected industrial process made scandium hydride, which was the core element used in the skins of every space vessel built in the last two hundred years, able to withstand violent distortions of time. Therefore, its value was beyond anything Johnson could dream up, this is what made interstellar exploration vital. Mining drove both the Earth and the off-world Mia Settler economies. It was fundamental in funding the growing human colonisation of Mars and the fourteen inhabited planets of the Mia-Earth Foundation.

Mr Johnson took delivery of the Rios lunar samples with a deep feeling of frustration. Dr Matilda gave him his analytical brief plus a much-restricted budget, which meant he had five days to complete the work. It would be easy enough, Johnson's confident prowess meant that it would be easy for him to finish the usual first-level calculations for molecular structure and the standard Prouse analysis for previous contamination by water or oxygen.

"BioCity ain't made of money Johnson," Dr Matilda warned, "I'm gonna keep an eye on you, just you remember that."

Johnson didn't find anything. *No one ever did.* But the samples needed to be checked as part of the preamble for a fourth-level DNA search. This was always the first preliminary screening for signs of any low-grade life or, indeed, any history of it. After this process, the mineralogists would take over the samples. The ore extracts Mr Johnson received were standard primaeval lava rock dust found in ninety-eight percent of all planetary geological samples. It was the remaining two percent that yielded the mineral evidence that sent the mining corporations wild with excitement, causing them to invest billions of yen in their next world colonisation and subsequent mine-building project.

With any new mining expansion, more so if related to significant major deposits of ore, there came the usual sequential colonisation procedures. Initial ring-fence security, habitation, transportation links, life logistics then commercial exploitation. The economies of all sixteen habited planets were seventy-five percent geared towards mining, planetary colonisation and mineral exploration. It was inevitable that any remaining economic spend was military in nature, it always was. Planetary weapons and their manufacture still drove major business interests; the designs of all current deep space vessels were based upon their military forerunners. None of the sixteen Foundation planets trusted each other when so much wealth was at stake. Although planetary confrontations were rare, sometimes it was inevitable when they erupted – for many hours now the news channels had been media streaming hour after hour warnings of yet more heightening tensions between Earth's government and the Mia Planetary Foundation, relating to the damaged exploration vessel *Cobra* that had docked in Central City on Mars. Money, wealth and the same old religious tensions were again causing political barriers.

The sedimentary rock samples provided to Mr Johnson were, he knew, over four billion earth years old and, except for the first few million years were inert, the samples were dead, they always had been dead, they always would be. They bore no mineral value as far as he could ascertain but that wasn't his job anyhow. Tomorrow he would run his standard DNA test then send the samples back to Central City for cataloguing and archiving. It could be a long time before the mineral boys got to them, if ever. The one positive outcome to the *Rios* samples would be his chance to once more try to solicit the attention of Ms Talors, the junior archivist over in BioCity Control.

It would not be easy. Despite his apparent fair to middling looks, his social skills were not considered good; his temperamental, argumentative attitude was these days well-known. While he pondered his vague chances

9

with Ms Talors, he noticed the dust samples in his possession were owned by the Cova Exploration & Mining Corporation. This was nothing new. They were by far the largest, most powerful of the mining conglomerates. Cova dominated the larger planetary projects.

But tonight, none of this mattered. For Mr Johnson, it was *fun time...*

Zipping back to his apartment high on the fortieth floor of Theodore Block Seven took him around twenty-five minutes in the evening rush. He had done it in less, but he liked to see who else was around - if there was anyone new to the building. Mr Johnson possessed an acute attention to detail, he noticed any form of change, even something quite small or insignificant, it was the minor things that bothered him. If anything was for some reason different, he possessed a desperate need to know why. It's not that change itself bothered him: well, he just needed to know, then he was just fine.

In the sky elevator, it was the same usual faces. It always was unless new people came to live in or visit the Theodore Building. Tonight, Mr Johnson saw that Ms Vera, whom he never spoke to, was wearing her hair brushed to the other side with a new wash colour he had not seen before. She also wore a different hair clip to the one she was wearing yesterday - and for the last four days. He often thought of talking to her but never showed the courage - because she never gave any sign that she noticed he was there. Glancing opposite, he could see that Mr Gerald, who Johnson thought was in mining finance, boasted new teeth implants, but he knew superstar celebrity bankers were all too frequent in changing their appearance; although Johnson wasn't quite sure why these people all the time needed to re-invent themselves. '*No doubt easy access to wealth funds*', Johnson surmised.

Mr Johnson could see there was nothing new to bother him right now. When the sky elevator exit door closed behind him, he hurried to his wash-down cubicle to clean away the Lab smells from the contamination overalls covering his body. The chemical steam wash was hot, refreshing - just like real water. Johnson then checked his vis-screen for messages, at the same time deciding he would eat down in the street malls tonight. And

Johnson had something important he needed to collect. But first, as he did every evening when returning from the labs, he would send a visual media feed to see if anyone close by was looking for a casual sex vis-link. He touched to Send but, as usual, nothing came back. Johnson, for some reason, on each occasion seemed to be ignored.

Mr Johnson was still dressing when his vis-screen on the entrance wall clicked...

"Johnson. Is that you? Are you there?" he didn't answer. He knew who it was.

"Johnson, I know you're there. Your entry-vis told me you're home." He thought for a few moments, then decided to ignore his vis-screen stream. It was Gloria Henderson; he did not want to speak to her right now. His wall screen clicked off.

Johnson waited, thinking of the consequences. He had the feeling inside that he was making a big mistake. At once he changed his mind. Mrs Henderson was an important network contact who, for some reason, had decided to cultivate him over a year before although, since then, he felt things had become much too complicated - deep down he knew he could not do what he wanted to do. Johnson turned to instruct his vis-screen.

"Call back Mrs Henderson." Johnson pulled on his shirt, he did not want to appear naked.

"I'm *pleased* you've had a rethink, Mr Johnson," the vis-screen itself replied in the condescending manner that irritated Johnson more and more. The maintenance engineer had still not fixed this. "Of course, I will send a media call to Mrs Henderson right away," said the on-screen voice, "Mrs Henderson knows you are home."

Gloria Henderson's face clicked into view on his screen. "Johnson, you make me cross sometimes." Her facial expression was angry. "I knew you were home; *you've ignored my last three media calls.*" She paused; Johnson had time to think for a moment.

"Mrs Henderson, I'm sorry. I was just taking a shower." He knew this was true, he also knew that Gloria would check it out. Gloria's screen vision faded for an intermittent few seconds as she consulted her vis-info feed.

"OK Johnson, I believe you. *This time.*" Gloria smirked, then her manner was full of smiles. "I'm free tonight Johnson. Mr Henderson will not be home until the weekend. He's been summoned to Central City." Her pearl-grey eyes sparkled.

"Oh? Why?" Johnson asked, this was a change variance his nimble mind straightaway picked up. Gloria's over-excited manner was somehow more different than normal.

"Just more high-end stuff. Nothing important. Something about one of the exploration ships being damaged, he needs to call in his top engineers. No media-vis news allowed, total news blackout," she said. Johnson detected a change in her normal expression, a slight pause. "Anyway, that's not important," she continued, "I'm free, if you want some decent food for a change, some fun time and a sleepover then I'm up for it?" Mrs Henderson looked extraordinarily pretty for her claimed ninety-odd years in age, but she looked a little impatient waiting for Johnson's reply. "OK. What do you think?" she demanded, staring at him through her screen. "You're not God's gift to women you know, no one else is gonna call you."

"Can I call you back in ten?" Johnson replied, hiding his irreverent feelings. He wanted to think. He was not comfortable about this situation at all - Mr Henderson was not the sort of guy to get the wrong side of. Neither was Mrs Henderson for that matter - Johnson was becoming more and more worried about how this friendship with Gloria was turning out. He was not in control, Gloria Henderson bullied him. He stared at her face on the vis-screen, trying to pin down what it was about her appearance that bothered him. She was anxious about something, Johnson sensed this for sure.

"You'd better call me back Johnson," Gloria looked harassed, "I know you're free tonight. You put out a media feed earlier this evening looking for a sex link." She was serious. *"Call me in five."*

Johnson was unsure what to do, he sat down to think. He had planned to go downtown to the food mall for a few hours. There he could get fresh food mix from the Chinese, try to get some basic vitamins into his body rather than the supplements he relied upon. Once he made plans Johnson didn't like them to be disrupted. A simple, straightforward casual sex link was all he wanted, something that lasted no longer than fifteen minutes without any commitments. But Gloria Henderson was another matter, she was an all-nighter, she would work him hard - she had likely been injecting supplements into her body all day. He wasn't up for that. Not tonight. Johnson was sixty-five years younger than Gloria Henderson, she fortified herself with stuff he could not even get hold of. God knows how Mr Henderson coped.

Johnson decided he would try to get out of seeing her but all along knew he would not be able. He called her back on his vis. His vis warned him, "Mrs Henderson has been waiting online for your call back. She has *prioritised* it, Mr Johnson." His vis-screen giggled with irritating posterity.

"Shit," Johnson thought to himself in anger, the attitude of his vis was winding him up even more. He again made a mental note to call maintenance in the morning...

"Nice to see you've *kept* your promise Johnson," Gloria's face was there waiting for him on his vis. She smiled; he was taken aback by her youthful-looking beauty. She'd painted her eyes with blue sparkly which, he knew, was designed to make it hard for him to turn down her offer. "I've got a new eye colour tonight..." Gloria stared, teasing her eyes... that was it - now Johnson knew why Gloria looked different. This wasn't his curious nature kicking in, he just wasn't good at trivial social skills that demanded he noticed when a woman made herself look different in a dressing-up sense. *Just for him,* she said. But Johnson once more sensed something was not quite right, a vague intuition that Gloria Henderson herself was agitated. Could there be a problem with something? Was it him? Had he done something wrong?

"Mrs Henderson, I'll be there in thirty minutes. I can't stay over though," Johnson hoped she would be sympathetic and give him some space for the evening. "I have some urgent mineral sampling to get out in the morning, I have to be in the lab early," he winced, "I'm not making this up."

"I know that, Johnson. You've got the *Rios* rocks." Gloria saw Johnson blink in surprise, she really did know *everything* - she laughed. "There's nothing gets by me, you know that. Anyway, that *Rios* stuff is nothing important, It's just routine dust." Gloria switched off her vis, Johnson suspected he was in for a long night.

Johnson felt his anger getting the best of him, he released a burst of amphetamine into his bloodstream through his wrist vis. In less than a second, he felt more relaxed. He dressed in no time then left his apartment through his personal sky-lift door, vowing he would end his relationship link to Gloria Henderson as soon as he was able. But she was married to Mr Henderson, Darius Henderson was the supreme head of technical and scientific recruitment of Cova Exploration & Mining Corporation. *Johnson needed contacts...*

The evening was a strange one as soon as it began. For starters, on the way down the tube to ground level, he noticed the young woman he had not seen before. She was pretty in a strange sort of way he could not figure out. She even stared at him, then smiled, her cute dark walnut hair that tumbled over her grey eyes, the way she tossed it aside with a casual flick of her hand. Johnson stared back for some intrinsic reason he couldn't fathom, startled at the way she did this routine irrelevant mannerism which, in some way, wasn't routine at all. The woman sat at the far end of the elevator; it was as if she *intended* to seek him out with her gaze. The tube slid open at floor nineteen, she'd gotten out but, by accident, bumped into him as she left her seat to walk by. Johnson thought this strange at first but then dismissed it as clumsiness. Still, it was nice to be noticed. Something about the way she looked at him agitated him... *her eyes...* the insignificant way she tossed her hair - but he could not figure out why. It did not bother him in any great sense because in an instant he forgot about it, there were other things on his mind. *It was that way she tossed her hair.*

Mrs Henderson was, for some reason, in a good mood when Johnson at last arrived. She had ordered Cynthia, her android maid, to fix them both evening dinner with fresh rare-earth food, using *soil-grown* ingredients that included potatoes with genuine powdered eggs. *How the rich lived,* Johnson pondered with envious eyes when he saw the table laid for two. His fork and knife were laid the right way around, but he saw that Gloria's was not. He noticed, for the first time since he had known her, when they began to eat, that she was this time left-handed. Every time before she was right-handed. *Strange.* Johnson also saw that Mrs Henderson herself was indelible in the way she was made up, she looked no more than twenty years in age he thought to himself.

"Well?" Gloria asked, staring at him across the table, "What do you think of my new eyes?" She waited for him to respond in her horrible commanding way, at the same time emphasising her new eye implants. Johnson did not fail to see the trap.

"Nice, you look so young," he lied, knowing full well he had avoided her wrath by a narrow margin for the second time in the evening. He *had* noticed her rather over-the-top eyes but decided to ignore them. *Why was Gloria Henderson all of a sudden left-handed?* Then, to Johnson's consternation, Mrs Henderson stood up, dropped her robe then stood naked. He just managed to down the last of the potatoes with creamed eggs, a mouth-watering meal that Cynthia had, with loving intent, rustled up in her android sort of way. *Not bad for a machine*, thought Johnson.

Much to Johnson's relief, Gloria Henderson was happy for him to leave after a couple of hours. He once more sensed that something was not right, his instincts telling him it was all to do with *Mr Henderson*. Even more disconcerting, while Mrs Henderson busied herself with him in her bed, Cynthia, the android maid, sat in the corner of the room watching everything, commenting with favourable comments upon the way her mistress made love to the young archaeologist - for some reason Johnson got the impression he wasn't going to be the only visitor during the night. At last, he prepared himself to leave, dressing quickly - the still ravenous beautiful ninety-year-old woman lying naked under the sheets...

"Don't mess with me Johnson," Gloria warned. "You're gonna need my help."

Cynthia let Johnson out through the side chute door, he made his way down the tube noticing Mr Polson from WPB Bank heading up in the opposite direction. Polson didn't see him, he seemed engrossed in a troubled sort of way. Polson also carried real synthetic flowers and a small official-looking bag. *It was a new bag* Johnson hadn't seen Polson with before. It was obvious to Johnson that Polson planned to spend time with Gloria Henderson - but there was something important inside Polson's bag that agitated the ageing banker to the point of making him perspire. Johnson always noticed small details like this.

Leaving the elevator tube he turned right in the fresh air, down the old Hamilton Elevated Road then headed for the downtown. Most of the buildings around him in this location were sky residences, they were opulent new ones - the Hendersons did not live in poverty. His entry-level salary at the labs was basic, enabling him to live in the older part of the city. Refurbishment and development were happening in some buildings in the district where he lived, but nothing at ground level. *Few London residents ever ventured onto the streets in the perpetual nighttime darkness where Johnson lived.* It was considered dangerous by many, although if anyone even bothered to examine local crime figures, incidences of violence and theft had declined downwards since the androids had taken over lower-street policing. Androids were incorruptible - this was the political-driven message streamed on vis-news feeds. There was no need to be afraid these days - but old fears ran deep.

It was a fifteen-minute walk to the downtown; Johnson decided the exercise would do him good; he turned down the offer of the taxi-android. There were plenty of other folks around, illiterates and itinerant street workers made up the majority. The sleaze and varied colours of their dress identified them; Johnson stood out in his drab one-piece suit. He had eaten with Gloria less than an hour before but his favourite night bar where he could sit alone was not far away – Johnson hurried in this direction.

Johnson walked at a brisk pace, taking in the night air, savouring the mid-evening sweetness - without thinking putting his hands deep in his pockets as he always did. He liked to walk this way, trying to mingle with the streetwise nightlife, often dawdling with arms buried deep despite his mother's, Mrs Johnson's, many attempts to break this habit when he was a kid. He never listened. Of course, he complied with his mother's wishes for a while to keep her from her constant nagging - then he reverted to the habit when leaving for archaeological pre-school fifteen years later. Ambling along in a striding walk, with his hands hidden deep, his head bent low towards the sidewalk also helped him to think, often he had no recollection that he walked in this manner - in his world of thoughts. *"You walk like a donkey,"* his paranoid mother told him often; as a consequence, Johnson tried to imagine a donkey walking around with its hoofs inside its pockets.

Johnson looked up and noticed the sky was changing, though midnight never came in the true sense. *The olden-days dawn that no one could remember.* It was later than he thought - maybe he would not linger long in the downtown. He could pick up store vitamins for his breakfast along the way, but he needed to collect the new DNA Implant Processors he had requisitioned from Can Sen the previous week. This was Johnson's other urgency; he would rather be doing this than being sidetracked by Gloria Henderson. Johnson was constructing his DNA probe to his own unique design, though he had been working with meticulous precision on his invention during the long nights for over six months it was never quite right. Even when he thought it was working, functioning as it should, he thought of how he could improve it. And so, his task went on.

Johnson's probe project was consuming his time, concentrating his thoughts more and more. If he could build then patent his DNA probe then maybe this was the way he could launch his career to start moving up the ladder. If his probe in some way became a success then he could get on to the off-world survey teams. He spent many hours dreaming of living the intrepid exploration life in his thoughts - but then one single problem would bring him right back down to earth. Of course, he knew *there was no lifeform DNA to find anyway.* And the survey ships were not open to looking for DNA. They were after the rare minerals.

He turned right, crossed the deserted road then hurried along the elevated street towards the Chinese-owned delivery chute, to see if his precious processors had arrived. They were special, they were being manufactured to his specification by the Chinaman Can Sen who lived in the old rundown part of Chinatown. Just then, with his right hand buried deep inside his grey one-piece suit, Johnson was startled to find something in his pocket. He felt it tucked right in the corner almost out of reach. Puzzled, he paused, he held in his hand a small, slim, oblong-shaped object which appeared to be made of white polished stone. Johnson stopped dead in his tracks, he stared at it, incredulous. *"That's odd,"* he thought to himself. Johnson had seen nothing like this before, he had no idea how it had come to be in his pocket. He felt its smoothness, then studied it close up. It was near to weightless. When his fingers ran over the surface meaningless words appeared, then vanished. He touched it once more. *It looked like a message.* He stood silent, perplexed, his mind racing like a fast-chasing tiger. This was outlandish, it was strange technology. The sidewalk sweeper android edging towards him avoided an accident by sidestepping to one side. Johnson did not even see the android or hear it apologise, *"Why, I'm sorry Mr Johnson."*

Johnson touched the small object again. The surface showed what was, without doubt, a handwritten message - even more strange - it was personal. Scrawled on the stone object, in what he thought might be some form of old-fashioned ink-like fluid, was a simple instruction. *'Call me using this vis-number Mr Johnson. I am the girl in the elevator.'* The message disappeared when he removed his fingerprint touch.

The ten-digit vis-number was written beneath the message, it was a strange number of the type he had not seen before. Johnson's first analysis came into his mind, this was an unregistered illegal vis-number. He stared at the object in his hand. *No one used this form of communication,* not in the last hundred years.

As midnight began to streak the dark sky, Mr Johnson hurried back to his apartment building forgetting his waiting processor implants for his DNA probe. He could feel the familiar stress building inside him, the uncertainty of the situation, his intense unease with the unknown. *He did not like mysteries.* Johnson's body started to sweat sweaty moisture from his forehead glands in a way he had not experienced since those confrontational lectures back in archaeological school. In Johnson's organised world where in an instant he recognised any minute change from the normal, he now faced a personal crisis that he had little time to control. Less than ten minutes later Johnson raced up the elevator tube, paying no attention to the other occupants. In his haste, he struggled to unbolt his apartment security door – until he calmed himself enough to act with more rational thinking. Once inside, Johnson contained himself enough to be less emotional - he turned to his vis-screen and, with his thin composure beginning to vanish, in the old familiar way that spelt trouble, gave instructions to his vis to dial the number written on the strange object he found in his pocket. "*Really*, Mr Johnson, you should not be using unregistered dial-ups like this. I am programmed and within my rights to protest..."

"*Dial* the number." Ebenezer Johnson repeated, this time with his nemesis sense of anger building inside him. The inbuilt, wall-mounted screen did not answer but Johnson heard the reassuring click of a connection being made.

Outside in the drab city, flat grey clouds spread across the bleak breaking sky. For the first time in over five or more years, *it began to drizzle*, the fine muddy-grey rain sprinkling a mist of uncertainty that Mr Johnson, in his focused trance-like stupor, failed to notice.

Gloria Henderson looked at Mr Polson with the appearance of unsubtle presumption, a cataclysmic feeling of predetermined doom - the type of gut premonition that cascades through a woman's mind when she realises, out of the blue, that she is not quite so young anymore. Without doubt, Mr Polson was visiting for his own reasons - Gloria's expression was one of dubious expectation.

"I think you know why I am here Mrs Henderson," said Polson. The look on his wrinkled face said everything, it had taken him fifteen minutes to find the courage to step into the tube elevator to then make his way skywards to Gloria's luxurious apartment. On the way up he thought hard about how the conversation should go. Therefore, his monologue was somewhat preplanned.

"On this occasion, I am visiting you in my capacity of your personal banker," he said.

"Then why the flowers?" Gloria Henderson quizzed, seeing Polson's eyes wince.

"I am here at the bequest of my superiors, I do not have much choice in this rather sensitive matter," replied Polson. He ignored her question about the synthetic flowers, they hung worthless in his left hand. "You know this is not easy for either of us Gloria."

"Then I take it this has everything to do with Mr Henderson?"

"Yes, I am afraid so. This is a difficult situation..." said Polson, his voice trailing in case he might repeat himself.

"I suspected this might happen," Mrs Henderson looked down to the floor, she looked every inch the old woman. There was more than a reasonable chance the dire financial situation might deteriorate further – although, in truth, this did not over-concern her even though it was a long way down to the bottom of the pile. "Where are all of my so-called friends now? Is this when all the proverbial rats start to desert the sinking ship?" she joked, half laughing, trying hard to be magnanimous.

Polson paused for a moment to choose his words as carefully as he could. "The implications of this disaster are enormous Mrs Henderson. The bank is fearing meltdown, more so when it comes to this terrible panic over Cova Corporation." Polson was not telling her the whole truth. He had been briefed in confidence beforehand that Darius Henderson could lose everything, right down to his last yen in the possible collapse of Cova Exploration & Mining – it seemed the high-risk commercial disaster that had occurred in the *Mu Arae* star system would ripple through right to the top. The economic consequences were vast.

"Perhaps your bank will melt down much less than I will Mr Polson," Gloria replied with more than a hint of sarcasm. Mrs Henderson's tone of voice said everything. "Is it possible we could settle this financial matter in some other, more pleasurable way?"

Polson laughed in unease, though not in an unkind manner. He ignored Gloria's unsubtle lure, he had decided that he must be on his guard to keep up his defences, right now would not be a good time to be drawn into a physical encounter with Mrs Henderson. This was a tricky situation for him, bankers were not allowed to enter into any form of relationship with their clients, even given that Mrs Henderson was a particularly persuasive woman - there were always unwholesome extra pleasures in being the Henderson's personal banker. Complicating everything was that Polson himself had been influential in the financial dealings that led Mr Henderson to invest more than he should have in the exploration of the distant *Mu* star constellation, Polson knew there could be bad implications if it all went wrong. And boy, had it *all* gone wrong in spectacular fashion. Cova Exploration & Mining, one of the mining conglomerate giants, was now, from nowhere, close to financial ruin.

"How bad will this be Mr Polson?"

"It is difficult to say.... it is early days," he lied, he stood beside the sofa in his usual awkward stance, not knowing whether to sit himself down or remain standing in his more official posture.

In fact, Polson knew how bad the situation was. The Henderson's fund accounts were already frozen by the bank, but Polson realised that even he did not know the whole story, he was just a private banker. To make things worse, the bank itself was in financial turmoil, this much was obvious even to Polson; he suspected that far too many enormous high-risk mining loans had been authorised during the last ten to fifteen months. The people on the top floor were beginning to sweat by the proverbial bucket load, if this financial crisis which, with total suddenness, had struck the banking world deteriorated much further then heads at his level would begin to roll. Already Polson's job was in jeopardy – even more if his illicit relationship with Gloria Henderson became known. As both Polson and Mrs Henderson stood there in strained silence, neither of them was quite sure what to say next. The android maid Cynthia began to pack her things, Cynthia's escape plan to return to her agency was already made - under no circumstances could she be associated with a ruined family. As an android, her reputation was at stake, she was not prepared to risk everything - nor not being paid.

This time, it wasn't the ongoing spectre of mineral contamination that ruined the much talked about, incredulous ore samples recovered from the exoplanet world *HD160691* orbiting the distant star *Mu Arae,* it was something far worse. Much worse. In recent days, the crippled Cova exploration vessel *Cobra* had somehow made it all the way back to the Mars polar docking station in Central City. They had completed a treacherous eleven-month journey of more than forty-nine light years to return home, a mind-blowing vast distance from the extremity of the remote *Mu Arae* star system. *Cobra* had suffered a systematic brutal attack, there were no doubts about this but attacked by whom or what no one on Earth or the Foundation could even guess. The devastation to the vessel was immense - the rolling implications dealing a tumultuous blow to the stock trading price of Cova Corporation – stocks that at this moment in time plummeted faster than a falling booster stage rocket. Mr Henderson himself had been summoned in haste to Central City, he was somewhere between Earth and Mars as part of the panicky mustering of an emergency examination team. Darius Henderson was involved in the *Cobra* expedition, he was exposed beyond his financial depth, being there on Mars he could work out what specialist investigative skills would be needed - he was also travelling as one of the primary Cova investors who had guaranteed the finances of the controversial *Mu* Constellation project. Without doubt, Henderson possessed a vested interest in knowing *everything* that had happened to *Cobra* - a top-notch exploration vessel owned in its entirety by the Cova Corporation. Darius Henderson could, and no doubt would lose everything if this incredible disaster turned foul – more so if the outlandish rumours being whispered around Central City were true.

Tensions between Earth and the Mia Foundation were high, they had been for some time. The Foundation of Planetary Settlers had denied everything, saying the damaged *Cobra* was nothing to do with the Foundation. Although all exploration and survey craft carried crude galactic weapons of sorts, none were ever used against other vessels because the high-specification technology did not yet exist. There were no accurate weapon systems that could track then attack another vessel - the multi-light travel speeds were just too great; no respected cosmologist or particle physicist believed that any known military science would be developed anytime soon to allow such fanciful confrontations between fleets of battle-hardened 'space cruisers' - this stuff was for fantasy stories and media entertainment, but this long-standing firm belief, it now seemed, was on the verge of collapse.

The implications of this enormous off-world event now filtered down as far as Gloria Henderson herself. Her credit funds were frozen, she had no means of securing the supplements and vitamin infusions she needed to sustain her lifestyle; her time as a seductress with a sexual appetite for younger men might be nearing its natural end. But Gloria was no stupid fool, she smiled to herself in self-seeming satisfaction, Gloria Henderson had no real need to supply her body with anything. In the morning she would know more, Gloria realised that Johnson's dust samples from *Rios*, one of the moons of *Affebiar IV*, would confirm what she already knew even though *Affebiar IV* was in every respect unconnected to the mind-blowing mineral deposits discovered on the unexplored world HD160691. As usual, Mrs Henderson was uncanny in her perception for one whose more infamous prowesses were, in many ways, unique. But then, Gloria Henderson was not who she purported to be.

Just as Polson left Mrs Henderson's apartment, Johnson's vis-screen clicked into connect mode when his screen condescended to dial the unauthorised vis-number. While the vis-screen considered Johnson's request, the news feeds were buzzing with the continuing stock market collapse; stocks and bonds were once more in free fall in every market sector. Johnson, his mind otherwise occupied, did not take much notice of the news, nor did he pick up the feed on the fiscal turmoil affecting Cova Corporation. For someone who always noticed intrinsic details in everything, Johnson's lack of interest reflected the *confused state of his mind*. By now the past midnight sky was pink with the incandescent dawn, in a couple or more hours the sun would poke its radiant head above the faraway horizon, a distant merging of land and skyline that no one could remember since the urban high-rise crawl of London had reached its zenith.

Johnson's vis seemed to take an eternity; the number dialled okay but the on-screen 'Wait' notification indicated that a complicated connection sequence was being resolved. In time, an indistinct image of the call recipient flashed up on the screen before Johnson's wide-open eyes, his apprehensive demeanour worsening when he recognised the same young woman he had encountered in the elevator chute, who had mesmerised his attention the previous evening. Her image steadied before focusing in full detail. As soon as her image steadied, she spoke.

"On the whitestone messenger you found in your pocket, you will see a sequence code. Dial this code into your vis-screen before you say or do anything. It will disable all call tracking and any link monitoring by your screen. There will then be no record of this communication or the conversation that will take place between us," she said all this, without any formal courtesy greeting or even a show of familiarity. It was as if the woman was expecting him to call which, of course, she had. Johnson once more took the white stone-like object in his hand, then touched the same surface as before - a series of hieroglyphic numbers accompanied by a chain of letters appeared, a mysterious sequence of events that just about fractured Johnson's tumbling sense of wellbeing. Johnson dialled into his wrist vis as she instructed. His wrist-vis went dead, the main wall-mounted vis-screen flickered then died – but the woman herself remained visible, in some way through a strange projection onto the screen. The whitestone object in his hand glowed with power. *This was unknown technology; this was stuff that Johnson did not understand.*

"Who are you?" Johnson blurted. There was clear unease in his voice. She paused for a good few moments.

"My name is not important. Someday soon you will know that I have many names." She then tossed her walnut-brown hair that had fallen across her crystal grey eyes - once more Johnson noticed this quirky mannerism, it was the same innocuous idiosyncrasy she had used in the elevator. He also saw that she possessed a strange simplistic demeanour - but it was the quick-witted intensity in her eyes, the oddity concerning her hair that shook the young scientist to his core.

"Why have you contacted me?" It was the second of the two panic-stricken questions that Johnson felt he must ask. His deep probing mind raced.

"You were hard to find, Mr Johnson, harder than you know," she replied. "To be brief, you arranged the making of two DNA probes from Can Sen, the instrument maker in the Chinese quarter. These probes are to your own design."

Johnson was even more confused. None of this made sense, he stood before the vis-screen not knowing what to say. Yes, he had commissioned the two probes, but there was nothing unusual in this, they were just his nighttime modifications to existing designs, because he felt, with resolve, that he could get more of what he wanted from his probes. He tweaked them all the time, trying new ideas, but he had never tested them in anger. And the obscure Chinese self-made engineer Can Sen was, without doubt, the best guy around to make them; his rumoured reputation was phenomenal - plus there would then be no sales or technology taxes to pay, nor any record that Johnson had designed the probes without the required innovation permits which was illegal in the strict sense of the word. Then a thought struck Johnson like a sickening thunderbolt, was this strange woman the police? *Was she investigating him and Can Sen?* Once more, he could not think of anything more to say.

"You have not yet collected your probes from Can Sen," the on-screen woman continued. "When you receive them, you will see there are some modifications that are not your own. Do not be alarmed."

"What modifications?" spluttered Johnson, he felt the familiar sense of anger rising inside him, *why was this bizarre situation happening to him?*

"You will see. When you analyse the *Rios* dust samples tomorrow, you will see," she replied. "You must be careful when you run your first tests. What you will discover is important, you must not discuss what you see with anyone. I will contact you using the whitestone vis you now have in your possession. You must be careful; you are being tracked by dangerous people who I am not at liberty to mention."

"Tracked?" Johnson exclaimed in confusion.

"Yes, but do not worry. I will take care of this."

The vis-screen on the wall clicked, there was a bright blue flash. The woman was gone. The vis-screen then flickered; the familiar talk screen reappeared as if nothing at all had happened.

"Are you okay Mr Johnson?" the vis-screen voice had not lost its sense of metallic unease. "You do not look good Mr Johnson, I cannot dial the illegal number you gave, there is no connection. You really do not look well..."

"Yeah? Well don't even think about calling in a fucking medic..." warned Johnson, the confused anger in his voice a measure of his growing unease. For someone who thrived in unlocking mysteries, Johnson was beginning to drown in his thick soup of uncertainty.

Darius Henderson stared with undisguised tension at the hologram figure of Commander Obera. It was well-known that Obera did not suffer fools, his lack of tolerance for his land-based superiors was legendary among the long-serving crew of *Cobra,* they held him in awe akin to adulation. Henderson was not looking forward to this meeting, even though Commander Obera would not be present in a physical sense. Outside of the thick glass observation windows, the redness of Central City reflected the inhospitality of the desolate Mars landscape. This was intense, hostile terrain - humankind could not survive without the protective shield that created the dry clinical living environment of the largest human settlement on the red planet.

Also present, and seated, were Henderson's two senior colleagues from the Cova Exploration & Mining Corporation, the mining giant that was from nowhere in deep financial trouble. Commander Obera himself was in close-guarded quarantine along with his crew, he could not be present for this first investigative meeting to find out what had happened to *Cobra.* Instead, his life-sized hologram image would be live-vizzed into the meeting room. This was going to be a tense confrontation; Henderson was well aware of this.

"Who are *you*?" demanded Commander Obera, staring likewise at Henderson.

"I am Darius Henderson. I employed you for Cova Mining over thirty years back," replied Henderson.

"Oh yeah, I remember you," sneered Obera. The commander sat down, his hologram image flickering with intermittent uncertainty as the primary vis-screen's projection struggled to keep up with his agitated movements.

"How are you and your crew coping with quarantine?" enquired Marcus Corelli, Cova's Head of Security to Obera.

"It sucks," Obera replied.

None of *Cobra's* crew believed their situation warranted being held in contamination quarantine. They knew full well that being confined in this way was nothing but a convenient method of keeping them away from the media and general public, meaning that Cova Corporation could then control the deteriorating situation to a considerable degree - at least in being able to minimise the damage to their stock price and their financial wellbeing. It was Corelli who had insisted, before *Cobra* docked in Central City, that quarantining the entire crew must be done. Henderson himself considered this an unwise move; it would lead to nothing but trouble.

"Can we begin this important first meeting please?" ordered Ducian Beim, who was Cova's Chief Financial Officer and in many ways ran the company as his own fiefdom – in the way he wanted. "Our examination team is carrying out forensic tests on *Cobra's* damage. We hope to have preliminary reports showing that interstellar rock debris struck *Cobra* at speed when orbiting the exoplanet *HD160691*, this happened while in the *Mu Arae* system. *Cobra* was NOT attacked. This should control market fears, meaning that everyone can calm their nerves."

"Eighteen of my men are dead, Beim," Obera interrupted, he fumed, "l told you already, we were not struck by debris, are you *nuts*? Our dust shields are more than capable of protectin' the ship from rock fragments up to the size of a fuckin' asteroid," the asteroid comment was an exaggeration, but everyone present would get Obera's drift. Sixteen of *Cobra's* crew had died when the attack occurred - then two more during the perilous journey back to Mars when onboard support systems began to fail.

The three company men glanced at each other with distinct unease, Henderson felt agitated, concerned over Corelli's decision to intern the crew to guarded confinement. No one was more exposed to this financial turmoil than Ducian Beim and himself, Beim was the business figurehead who held all the purse strings, he was head of the business board that funded, then guaranteed the *Mu* Star-Constellation exploration mission. The potential for mega profits once mining began more than justified the huge money risk - and *Cobra* with its Commander Obera was, without doubt, one of the best top-level vessels to do the exploration work - even though no one within Cova had given Obera express permission to single out then explore any of the exoplanets orbiting the star *Mu Arae*. But HD160691 had thrown up incredible mineral numbers, ore quality with stunning reserves like nothing ever before found. Then it all went wrong. Beim looked at his wrist vis, Cova's stock price was down a further eleven hundred points in early morning trading.

"I'll tell you what happened, you lily white piece of shit," Obera continued, glaring at Beim. "*Cobra* was attacked, it was deliberate. It was our tough gut expertise, our hell-bent ambition not to die like rats out there in the *Mu Arae* star system. That's what saved us Beim."

"How do you know it *wasn't* rock debris Commander Obera?" interrupted Corelli. Corelli was aware how his official examination team were already 'primed' to discover evidence of debris collision being the cause of the near loss of *Cobra*. Under no circumstances could there be any evidence associated with undiscovered extraterrestrial lifeforms, more so if such an advanced civilisation possessed superior hostile technology. Nor must this disaster turn out to be some form of aggressive Mia Foundation intervention. The end-game worst-case scenario must be some type of attack by a rogue survey or exploration vessel, *that* situation or one of debris collision could be dealt with in a quite straightforward manner. Then there would be a rapid recovery of Cova's stock price - with opportunities for huge fortunes to be made when stock prices rocketed everywhere... meaning the specialist vessel examination teams were each hand-picked men by Corelli, they were long-standing company boys who could be trusted. Beim looked at his wrist vis with wry confidence, if the Cova stock fell just another nine points then he would instruct his personal broker to covertly buy more Cova stock using his well-hidden identity. Both Beim and Corelli were confident the space debris theory would stick – the crucial report was already being written.

Obera glared at Corelli. "There's somethin' I know that you don't Corelli," sneered Obera with the stone-like expression for which he was infamous. "Somethin' that's gonna kill your goddammed stock price dead. You'd best call your team of shit-faced examination dogs off my ship."

Henderson, Corelli and Beim left the hologram meeting around thirty minutes later with intense deep foreboding. Darius Henderson himself felt even more uneasy, his whole life seemed to be collapsing before his eyes. Beim and Corelli said nothing. Beim, by this time thought hard about calling his broker to try to offload the remainder of his Cova stocks - but this would without any question send the stock price into free fall. Once this happened, it would signal the total collapse of Cova Corporation which would then throw the whole of Earth's economy into turmoil. Commander Obera held all the cards - Henderson, Corelli and Beim now held no doubts about this.

Cobra had sent three hardcore exploration teams down to the surface of HD160691, each of them in turn then requested immediate evacuation. The rock and lava-strewn world turned out to be a burning hell, the constant roaring hurricane winds formed of lethal gases far too hostile for anyone to survive any reasonable length of time – not under any circumstances could substantive ore exploration be carried out without serious loss of human life - though one intrepid team got small ore samples nevertheless. The close mineral examination of these samples outright stunned the crew of *Cobra*. The one option available for Commander Obera was to send in the androids, but to do this he needed a stable base to control the operation. Then, *Cobra's* navigators focused upon the single planet-sized moon that orbited *HD160691.* At the time, it all seemed perfect.

Cobra's long-range penetration probes at once reeled off reams of data showing the moon to be both stable and inert, meaning that it *might* provide the stability platform that Obera and *Cobra* needed. From this small orbiting world he could plan, then execute a detailed exploration survey of *HD160691* using high-tensile drones and level four android surveyors - infrared probe penetration readings already showed even more incredible raw ore data down on the hell planet. Obera and his wild-eyed crew had never before encountered anything on this scale. This hostile world was a potential yen gusher of astronomical proportions.

Approaching *HD160691's* moon was straightforward enough. That is until *Cobra* was outright plunged into chaos. The ship was hit twice, she was struck from two opposing directions, the smoke and debris at once filling *Cobra's* interior as cries of terror and confusion echoed through every communication channel onboard. Obera reacted with incredible speed, turning *Cobra* onto a reverse course that in all circumstances saved his stricken vessel. There then followed many hours of desperate damage control - the first priority being to save the environmental atmosphere vital to the crew's survival. Obera did this, he vectored in teams of desperate men to plug the hull damage even though another nine of his crew died in the process - sucked out lifeless into the dark depths of space where no man should ever die. Seven of *Cobra's* crew were killed in the two initial impacts when whatever it was that struck the vessel first hit.

Nineteen hours later, Commander Obera at last had everything under a reasonable measure of control. The shock of what happened was immense, the damage to his vessel beyond comprehension - but they were alive. Sixteen of his forty-six crew were dead, another nineteen injured receiving sickbay treatment, both his medical officers were gone, killed in the first hit. The wounded were receiving android care - it was the one thing that could be done. Then came the inevitable inquest, Obera was desperate to know what had happened to his vessel.

Sixty percent of *Cobra's* probes were damaged beyond further use. Obera ordered a slow, creeping return to *HD160691's* moon. The crew checked the dust shield readings, the shield had been functioning perfectly just before they were hit. The damage could not have been caused by asteroid or meteor debris, examination of the forward vis-screens confirmed nothing in their path or anything coming their way. The infrared probes showed that no debris had impacted upon *Cobra*. But the forward navigation probes showed something else, something far more unbelievable. Astonishing. Two feint objects seemed to be orbiting in close vicinity of the desolate moon. With high levels of regulatory caution, Obera ordered a course to take *Cobra* closer to the nearest of the two unidentified objects. His crew thought he was mad, they implored him to turn and run while they still lived - *Cobra* had survived enough - they might, the crew argued, with incredible luck, just make it back to Earth.

Alone in his Mars quarantine isolation ward, Obera once more stared at the digital image holograms taken from *Cobra's* forward vis-screens. He watched the whole sequence yet again, then sat in quiet contemplation knowing full well that everything in his upside-down life was now changed. The commander was relieved to learn that Henderson, the wretched Corelli and the imbecile Beim had now left the building in Central City – Corelli had by now called off his expert examination team from *Cobra's* damage investigation, he had no choice - as soon as Corelli saw the relayed images from the vessel's vis-screens, together with the confirmed data from the probes and androids, he straightaway stopped the charade of the damage inspection. There was little point, it was obvious to Corelli, Henderson and Beim that *Cobra* had suffered a hostile attack: to create a masquerade that Cova's exploration vessel was damaged by interplanetary debris would lead to more deep trouble. The Commander of *Cobra* smiled to himself with self-satisfaction, what screwed both Corelli and Beim beyond doubt was that he, Obera, the resolute commander of *Cobra*, held the original holograms plus all the vis-screened data in a safe location - there was no way that Cova Exploration & Mining could now take control of this disastrous situation just for the organisation's survival. This was a devastating scenario that might soon rock the absolute foundations of the human race.

By now, back in Cova's Central City Mars headquarters, both Ducian Beim and Henderson realised how much their impending financial ruin was nothing compared to the gigantic economic mega-storm that was beginning to unfold - the financial markets with their foundations rooted in mining and exploration were beginning to collapse like a pack of cards. Somehow, the news was out, the rumours were true, Cova Mining was in trouble, one of their exploration vessels had been close to being destroyed by unknown alien assailants. Henderson, just like Obera back in quarantine isolation, smiled to himself in reflection - no one understood what had happened to *Cobra* more than Commander Obera. Obera held all the aces. There was nothing that Cova Corporation could do because the truth could not be twisted nor manipulated in the way that Beim and Corelli demanded to save the corporation. And the truth, Henderson realised, as incredulous as it was, was devastating.

Cobra's hologram images viewed by Henderson, Corelli and Beim re-vealed everything. *Cobra's* approach to *HD160691's* single moon was nothing untoward, it was a straightforward manoeuvre that required no special interventions or course corrections to make a safe rendezvous with the small inert world orbiting the outlandish hostile planet – except that no one onboard *Cobra* had taken much notice of forward probe readings that warned of two unidentifiable objects already in stationary orbits around the moon. This was vast, unexplored virgin frontier – no one expected anything *that* unusual to be there. There never was. As *Cobra* made her final approach, the recorded hologram playbacks showed both the unidentified orbitals changing their vectors. For reasons that soon became apparent, they tracked the Cova exploration vessel as she approached the moon. There were no deterrent attempts or anything like that, no forewarning communications to *Cobra* to establish any reasons to be there, just two precision projectile strikes that struck *Cobra* without warning - with appalling accuracy and with lethal intent.

The terrible destruction, the damage limitation procedures that followed, the desperate fight for survival were meticulous in the recorded records by onboard vis-screens and Android optic RAM-drives. The hologram memory recordings showing both orbiting structures - and unnatural in their construction is what they turned out to be - were astonishing to watch. Their method of attack, their unmistakable hostile intent, their overwhelming ability to finish *Cobra* off was too mind-twisting to comprehend - but what these first hologram images showed was nothing compared to what then happened when Obera ordered his crew to take the damaged *Cobra* right back into moon orbit.

Commander Obera's infamous reputation for reckless bravery *was* well deserved, but he was no fool. His personal DNA profile records showed that he was of long-standing Russian descent, even more detailed analysis by Henderson had revealed the ancient Cossack blood ties in Obera's veins that were wholehearted in explaining his sometimes irrational boldness that drove his well-known resolve - which made Obera exceptional in the choice to command an intrepid exploration vessel such as *Cobra*, an unarmed vessel that thrived in the extreme regions on the unexplored intergalactic frontier. Obera knew there was no choice but to somehow return to *HD160691's* moon once he secured his damaged vessel - although his crew, to a man, did not see it like this. Their collective instinct was to turn and run even though each of *Cobra's* crew were tough roughneck renegades in their own right: but they did not possess what their Commander possessed – a short-tempered, nerve-dangling spiritedness that often bordered upon irresponsible madness. Obera himself could never find it within himself to reverse *Cobra's* course and flee – more so when he realised how this momentous disaster was humankind's first contact with any alien lifeform. Therefore, Obera needed to know more, he needed to know what superior technology he faced... and was the human race itself doomed to some form of alien destruction.

Cobra crept between the two hostile orbitals, both of which, according to the one remaining undamaged forward probe, once more tracked the crippled vessel in the same way as before. Vis-holograms of the stationary structures showed they each possessed one single enormous barrel-type projectile protrusion, and both vectored upon *Cobra* as she again neared the moon. But this time, neither of the orbitals launched an attack upon the damaged *Cobra*, but *Cobra's* onboard sensors confirmed that *Cobra* was being deep-probed to an extensive degree – warning alarms blared, and data streams revealed how the hostile probing was of no identifiable wavelength, nor was it of any recognisable technology. In the event, Commander Obera figured that these hostile probes, which right now raked every hidden corner of his vessel, in some way sensed that *Cobra* was critically wounded - and that *Cobra* herself carried no offensive weapon capability. Inter-vessel combative technology did not yet exist onboard any Earth or Foundation-built vessel. Even so, Obera could not figure out why neither of the orbitals finished *Cobra* off.

Commander Obera remained calm, but his crew sweated and cringed with visible dread knowing that, in a tiny fraction of a moment, they could everyone of them be dead. But Obera knew this was a game of nerves; he gambled all his aces by showing his vulnerable underbelly to his two assailants - perhaps they would see that *Cobra* was no real threat in her crippled state. Of more importance, this alien civilisation, which had shown its ruthless intent, might see that he, Vavilov Obera, was not afraid of their death-dealing capabilities. Obera commanded his helmsman to bring *Cobra* into a matching orbit, one that would be exactly halfway between the two orbiting sentinels, both of which kept their powerful weapons trained upon *Cobra*. Then Commander Obera, for the first time, tried to hail his two adversaries, he tried every known deep-space frequency band, even interstellar channels not used, but there were no indications of a response or even if any of his communications were being understood or received. There were no answering callbacks, no attempts at communication, it was impossible to open any form of dialogue with either of the two orbitals that threatened his destruction. In complete frustration, Obera then ordered the release of two of *Cobra's* last remaining drones, ones that had not been destroyed in the initial assault. Both drones approached the nearside assailant - with the commander expecting the drones to be blown apart at any moment. Nothing happened.

The first drone transmissions received by *Cobra* shook the more often than not stoic Obera to his core. The data showed no signs of lifeforms on either of the two orbiting structures, both were inert. They appeared to be automated weapon systems controlled by no hostile crew that could be identified or located. The commander, to the consternation of his crew, then made a seemingly irrational decision - he ordered two of his six undamaged androids to board one of the alien orbitals which were by now silhouetted majestic against the spectacular backdrop sunrise of *Mu Arae*. *Cobra's* androids could investigate who or what had attempted to destroy Obera's vessel. When both androids later returned to the stricken *Cobra*, their reports once more stunned Obera into introverted silence.

Henderson, Corelli and Beim themselves stared at the same data amassed by the androids plus what had been gleaned by the drones: all three men listened in shocked disbelief to the android's recorded hologram reports - clinical, unemotional details of what they found. When *Cobra's* science officer confirmed that both alien orbiters were indeed lifeless, Henderson, Corelli and Beim sat in silent confusion in the same way that Obera first reacted. They listened to *Cobra's* science officer confirming that both of the weapon-based orbiters were of unknown origin and construction - also that preliminary analysis showed they had existed for an unimaginable length of time. They were incredible in their age, older than the human race, perhaps older than Earth itself. The android's tests for molecular structure, which would in normal times be used to determine the physical age and rate of radiation decomposition of ore or rock samples, revealed data that Commander Obera knew would shake the absolute foundations of humanity. Furthermore, there was other data that Obera had, based on his gut instincts, decided to keep to himself, something the Commander would never in a million years divulge to Henderson and Corelli – and more so not to Ducian Beim.

Obera then decided to send in a three-man away team. The intrepid inspection crew confirmed everything already received from *Cobra's* androids and drones – that each of the structures was of enormous size, appeared to be well armed but devoid of any sign of life. Nothing moved or stirred, all systems seemed to be controlled by automation. There was evidence of a type of central artificial intelligence geared towards some mode of defensive operation - *Cobra's* away team suggested the weapon platforms had been constructed an incalculable time before to protect something which they could not yet discover, most probable something located below on HD160691's moon. The away team found no clues as to who or what had built these monoliths, they discovered no evidence of the ancient civilisation that had cause to protect something important on an insignificant moon orbiting a violent unexplored planet in the remotest parts of the galaxy. Metallurgic analysis later revealed that all of the material alloys used in the alien construction were unknown. Radioactive decay readings confirmed both orbitals' enormous age. Unsurprising, it was their age that blew away the mind of Commander Obera. These ancient behemoths, two unfossilised sentinels orbiting a dead moon, were constructed by some unknown civilisation that existed long before Earth and its solar system had even been formed. Even so, it was not just this astonishing fact that Obera and his science officer decided they must, in some way, keep to themselves.

Henderson was the first to understand why it was impossible for Obera to send away teams or androids down to the moon's surface. *Cobra* was in no fit state to enter into a low orbit, she was in no real condition to make it back to the nearest inhabited world. *Cobra* somehow needed to endure a forty-nine light-year journey back to human civilisation, Obera himself thought it improbable he and his crew would survive. Then *Cobra* at last, by chance, months later, rendezvoused with the mining mother ship *Majestic* on the outer rim of the *BAU Mia* system, *Majestic's* life-support facilities saved many of *Cobra's* crew who by this time were at the end of their ability to survive. Most did survive, *Majestic's* crew listened to the incredulous accounts of what had happened. Obera tried to keep everything under wraps, knowing full well how the news of *Cobra's* hostile encounter would cause uncontainable panic in both the Mia Settlers Foundation and on Earth. Obera was unsuccessful in keeping the whole thing quiet, the damage to his vessel was severe - when the news broke there was untold chaos.

Nevertheless, Ducian Beim convinced himself that Cova Corporation could still sustain control over its devastated affairs, there just needed to be a convincing cover strategy that would bury the truth of what happened. Henderson right now sat with both Beim and Corelli in Cova's headquarters; Beim needed to decide what must be done. Cova's stock price was now descending into absolute free-fall, there were days left before the company entered frightening new territory - where the corporation might not survive.

"Do either of you two have any worthwhile suggestions? I have to report to the second tier stockholder board in exactly one hour, then I have to stand before the supreme investors by the week's end, there's no doubt his righteousness will intervene," Beim could not hide his extreme agitation, when Gabriel learned of the disaster they would all be in this together - Beim's neck would be on the line.

"If Obera had followed strict company doctrine, then we could have controlled this disaster," snapped Corelli. "His crew should have been silenced; Commander Obera makes his own rules."

Henderson looked at Corelli, then at Beim. He could see that Beim agreed. Both men were in desperate straits. Henderson, though, suspected this whole situation was one of Commander Obera's making, he realised that Obera was holding something back, something of far greater gravity and consequence. It was just a gut feeling, a sixth sense honed by years of dealing with men like Obera while head of Cova's recruitment in an aggressive volatile industry. Cova Corporation was doomed, this much Henderson realised without much nuance.

"Are you saying that Commander Obera should have ensured his crew did not survive?" Henderson stared at Corelli with unabashed surprise.

"No, what I'm saying is that *Cobra* would better have been destroyed by those two behemoths," replied Corelli, "just like the survey vessel *Dros*, then this would have been just another missing vessel mystery. One we could have handled."

"In what way did Obera not follow company doctrine, Mr Corelli?" Henderson asked, Corelli was beginning to annoy Henderson. Corelli looked at Beim, who straightaway looked away. Henderson realised there was something between them he was unaware of.

Beim this time glanced at Corelli, a sideways look that confirmed Henderson's growing suspicion.

"As an exploration and mining corporation we have always accepted the risk of hostile contact with an alien culture," suggested Beim. "The company has certain 'procedures' in place to manage such an incident. We know that investor stock values might fluctuate in an uncontrolled manner if such an alien contact occurred. Mr Corelli here, as head of corporate security, is aware of what our strategy would be, I am afraid it is confidential."

"Yes, I know all about *that* policy Mr Beim, news blackouts, crew confinement, even what would happen to a renegade crew. I am no fool, Beim, I am head of recruitment, but that is not what Corelli here is talking about..." Henderson tailed off, his voice faltering – a staggering thought suddenly came to him, something that hadn't before occurred to him – was it possible that Earth and the Foundation, even Cova Corporation, had encountered some form of alien contact prior to this incident?

It was now a matter of days before the tumbling stock price heralded the end of Cova Exploration & Mining – investor confidence, the freezing of assets, the drying up of banking credit lines – these would all come together to deal the fatal blow. Cova Corporation was huge, one of three major players in off-world mining – the Foundation economy in particular. If the Mia Foundation collapsed, then it was too horrendous to even contemplate what would then happen on Earth. Henderson's banking credits were already frozen – with the rumours of the *Cobra* incident breaking into the media streams during the last eight hours. When the final collapse of Cova occurred, which to Henderson seemed inevitable, then Earth and Mia economies themselves would begin to disintegrate. The perfect storm – could this whole disaster even be some form of long-standing alien intervention against Earth's financial system? It was a wild madcap theory that danced around inside Henderson's brain – but for this to be so, Henderson realised with sickening foreboding, then Commander Obera and *Cobra* had to be in there in the remote region of HD160691's and the *Mu Arae* system for a reason.

Corelli and Beim indeed knew something that Henderson did not. Corelli, as overall head of security, was the first of Cova's top-level executives to learn that *Cobra*, under Obera's direct orders, had gone rogue. The miscreant commander was classified as a rebellious subordinate, a mutinous dog who displayed the audacity and adroitness to commandeer his own vessel, not unlike what had happened with the missing survey ship *Dros*. *Cobra's* exploration mission into the *Mu Arae* system was not authorised by *Cobra's* owners Cova Exploration & Mining, Henderson did not know this – even though his own money was invested into the whole damned mess. And there were *more* spellbinding reasons why Darius Henderson had been kept in the dark by Beim and Corelli.

Obera possessed compelling reasons why he was bound for HD160691, at no stage had he followed standard company procedures that allowed *Cobra* to enter an unexplored star system in a vast remote region - there were well-established protocols, doctrines to be followed, rules that governed the risk of alien first contact which might in some way occur. Henderson suspected that both Beim and Corelli knew why Obera and *Cobra* had disappeared into the *Mu Arae* system under his own accord – and as a result, Obera and his vagabond crew right now suffered the indignity of being quarantined under armed guard confinement.

Meanwhile, Commander Obera sat in his locked isolation ward unable to leave, contemplating everything that had happened. *Cobra* was damaged to a critical level – without doubt through his own actions; his exploration vessel was beyond normal repair and more than lucky to have survived. Now Obera stared at the strange whitestone object that lay on the table before him. All of Earth's unravelling troubles stemmed from this single piece of unfathomable technology. The wardroom entrance door suddenly opened - Obera knew who it would be.

Johnson stood perplexed. His two small DNA probe implants looked fine, running his eyes over their exterior surface he did not notice anything unexpected. They were unmistakable, they were the work of Can Sen. The smooth micro rack of sensors were expert in the way they were interwoven with ribboned ytterbium, the rare earth element crucial to the analysis procedure Johnson was attempting to create. Under his powerful micro magnifying viewer he opened the minute cantilever cover, being particular and careful when ensuring everything was in order. The actual micro sensors, each no larger than a half pinhead in size, were fine; Johnson could see they were exceptional pieces of work – he ran the diagnostic sequence through his vis-screen, nothing appeared to have been changed - not like the woman in the elevator had said in their vis-screen conversation. At the end of the rolling sequence, Johnson saw something *had* changed, the coding was different, it was amended in an odd sort of way that, to him, seemed unrecognisable. Johnson then took an even closer look at the four rows of micro sensor racks - they were not regular run-of-the-mill Can Sen-manufactured sensors. *They were something else he had not seen before.* With his heart beating like a thumping drum, Johnson decided to run a full analysis anyway.

When Johnson ground up the *Rios* dust into a fine greyish paste, he could not contain his excitement. This moment was the culmination of his upside-down life so far, a point when his dreams might either collapse and die or soar into the air like captive doves released into the new dawn sky. Johnson was careful when injecting the paste into the sensor reader, Johnson expected an instantaneous data feed into his vis. Nothing happened. His feeling of dejection grew like septic mould creeping through his pulsating scientific veins.

"Johnson, you have contaminated the dust analysis paste."

Johnson spun round in alarm. It was Gloria Henderson. He stared like a stupid child caught in some forbidden act. She looked resplendent in her tight-fitting all-in-one pure white tunic that made her look like some sex-kitten angel from heaven. By this time Johnson's fragile sanity began to waiver, it took more than a few moments for his mind to focus.

"Can Sen did not use his sensor racks when he put together your probes. He used the ones I gave him," said Mrs Henderson - without the slightest hint of emotion.

Johnson glared at Gloria for what seemed infinite moments. He felt a familiar feeling of vexation grow inside him, his anger began to well up then radiate through his throbbing veins, Johnson thought hard, *he had never been good in these situations*, unexpected surprises that he always failed to hegemonise. He fought hard to control himself, more so when it dawned upon him how this singular act of bewilderment was *all meant to happen*, this unfathomable chaos was deliberate, it was designed to unravel his complicated and structured world.

"Don't be alarmed Mr Johnson," Gloria Henderson stood coy-like in the doorway, "I have a vested interest in the success of your probes."

"Gloria.... why...... why are you here?" Johnson could no longer contain his wide-eyed astonishment. Nor could he hide the awkward confusion etched upon his astonished face. He fought hard to maintain his composure.

"I thought now would be a good time for you to see me with my clothes on," Gloria smiled.

Johnson stood silent. He could not think of anything meaningful to say.

"I think it would be prudent if you did not grind the *Rios* dust into that codswallop paste. Even the slightest hint of contamination will deactivate your coding," Mrs Henderson pointed to the liquidised rock paste on the worktop.

"But... but my probes, they are designed to ignore low-level contamination. It's the evidence of primordial DNA structures I am searching for," Johnson replied, gathering together a tiny semblance of his mixed-up thoughts.

"Can Sen altered the coding to my instructions," Gloria eyed Johnson close, this was the point at which the young archaeologist might lose his last sense of reasoning. This was a calculated confrontation, now was when everything mattered. "The information you were given when you dialled the whitestone vis number was quite precise," Gloria added.

Johnson at last began to think with inordinate speed. He could either sink into some unknown abyss, where this whole bizarre situation would overwhelm him, or he could fight back trying to regain his composure. In thinking with a clear mind, his pent-up temper, which was about to explode like an over-tensioned spring, began to abate. The first logical thought that occurred to him was quite clear, there was a specific reason why Gloria Henderson had just now revealed that she knew the girl in the elevator, the mysterious messenger who had already rocked his world upside down like a wild pendulum.

"Does your version of my sensor design require something different in terms of samples?" Johnson scowled.

"Yes, forming even a sterile paste risks contamination. That is, contamination by something you are unfamiliar with," Gloria replied without emotion. "Your DNA probe is not what you think it is."

"What do you mean?" Johnson was now thinking with logic, he needed to deal with his confusion.

"Well, let's run your little test with raw dust. Let's see what happens shall we?" Gloria Henderson was adamant that Johnson would do what she suggested. The testing of Johnson's DNA probe was just as important to her as it was to Johnson.

The altered specifications she had given to Can Sen were unreserved and unique, they were unlicensed, unlike anything Can Sen had seen before - they had caused Can Sen to eye Gloria Henderson with acute suspicion. But when the Chinaman read the code he set to work, Can Sen understood that he was working with something unworldly, something outside the realms of even his vast experience. He recognised how the illegal sensors would work, he realised that Gloria Henderson was entrusting him with new, unknown methods of DNA probing that he did not, at first, understand - though Can Sen learned fast. When he at once understood what he was manufacturing, he smiled to himself in complete satisfaction. These probes were not meant for analysing DNA. *Perhaps he, Can Sen, needed to be careful.* The authorities, and others who he could never quite name, watched him like a hawk. Can Sen always danced on the edge of what was legal - but there was something to be admired in the unique way Gloria Henderson had changed Mr Johnson's coding. Can Sen recognised

Johnson's work, Johnson's coding sequences were themselves cutting-edge but the elements that Mrs Henderson had changed were mind-enhancing and sagacious - even to Can Sen. But Can Sen was no fool, when he understood what the new sensors were he realised straightaway who Gloria Henderson was.

The early morning transition from nighttime to dawn was no different to every other dawn since the birth of humankind. Sunrise gave way to a new day of unassuming disparity, the blameless blue sky held no evolutionary secrets, four billion years of countless sunrises offered no substantive clues to a world close to being destroyed by man's futile neglect. Yet on this reticent dawning day, an unpaid debt to the creation of mankind began to be repaid not for the first time. In all-of-a-sudden commemoration, uncountable thousands of black-tipped swallows soared high into the cloudless heavens to witness the archangel Gabriel's prophesied demise.

Gloria Henderson smiled to herself in anticipation. Ebenezer Johnson sat down without even thinking, his mind in a whirlwind of spectacular wonderment when he watched his innovating sensor probes reel off information code unlike anything he had seen before. Gloria activated Johnson's wall-mounted vis-screen, knowing the coding would be streamed to the screen in the way that she had envisaged. The vis flickered into life; Johnson spun around in surprise – this was not how he expected his sensor probe to register its first communication. The probe began to stream moving images to his vis-screen, at this point Johnson realised with infinite shock that he was in some way looking backwards in time - the *Rios* rock samples had been unlocked, they were not mere rock samples at all, not simple pieces of moon debris able to give up clues to lifeform DNA but ancient fragments of prehistory that could stream molecular evidence *far beyond Johnson's ability to understand.*

Johnson sat spellbound, captured in mind-crunching awe - he did not see Gloria turn to leave through his still-open apartment door. While Johnson sat in captivated concentration, she summoned the elevator to descend to the underground level – even then Johnson still had no inclination that he was now alone. Never for one second did he realise there were compelling matters that Gloria needed to attend to, a situation that would have shaken his paralysed mind into oblivion. Mrs Henderson knew that two of Corelli's trusted assassins were by now inside Johnson's apartment building.

In the meantime, the images flashing through Johnson's vis-screen were like nothing he or anyone else had before seen. The data stream showed a desolate moonscape in another time, an off-world landscape that Johnson reasoned must be *Rios* itself. There was not much to see in the chilling twilight stillness of the empty inhospitable world, a world that flickered and flecked on his vis-screen before his wide-open eyes. For a brief moment, Johnson saw something unusual in the far distance, a strange object hiding on the moon's horizon. For some inexplicable reason, *Johnson felt disturbed.* His mind now began to function at breakneck speed, he could not figure how straightforward rock samples could give up such brain-stopping non-geological information – but, in his desperate race to find answers, Johnson did not for one moment pause to consider how these granite-like fragments now in his possession might be more important than he ever believed.

A monolithic stone monument, a cenotaph of incalculable age stood tantalisingly too far away on the horizon of *Rios* for Johnson to make out. In a few moments the obelisk gave up a clue, in some strange way there was an unfathomable link between whatever it was that existed on the *Rios* moon and the probe of his own invention that even now reeled off code at dazzling speeds. The link was without doubt being driven by the strange whitestone device he had before been given, which began to glow with a greenish tinge on the bench top before him.

Johnson reached out in involuntary surprise. His over-inquisitive mind raced when he realised his probes had been specifically redesigned to link with the whitestone viz for some purpose that began to reveal itself. He touched, then held, the whitestone in his hand, there was a slight vibrating hum which travelled through his hand then up his arm, causing a poker-hot spasm of pain. Johnson reacted with instantaneous shock, once more he was transfixed like a prowling cat sensing some form of unobservable energy.

His close-up vision of the *Rios* stone obelisk seemed to originate from somewhere within his consciousness as if his imagination was in some way playing cruel tricks. But, in his mind, he was there, he stood right before the obelisk: his conscious self was on the *Rios* moon of *Affebiar IV* - which Johnson perceived was pure fantasy. He stood before the stone monument like a new crowned king, no longer was he the young inexperienced off-world lifeform archaeologist, right now he was the majesty of his profession, standing as if in some form of transcendental trance – what he saw *twisted and turned* his confused brain into a maelstrom of inconclusive madcap thoughts. Johnson's mind was now alive, this is what he was born to do, the ultimate mystery he forever knew he was meant to unlock. He saw worm-like hieroglyphic carvings, a strange written language unknown in his experience as a budding archaeological scientist. Johnson could discern clear etched symbols that were carved into the stonework by some inconceivable intelligence - in a manner that suggested some ancient antiquity of considerable age. The writings were not of human, or even of earth origin - for some instinctive reason Johnson was quite clear about this without knowing why.

The whitestone vis dimmed, Johnson's newly manufactured DNA probe ended its first-ever test run, his personal wall vis clicked off. Johnson was back in his dim lit apartment room, the outside sunlight finding no easy way into his darkened room. Johnson turned to Gloria Henderson, having forgotten that she was there. Only then did he realise that his white-clad angel had left. Johnson was alone.

Commander Obera sat quite still in his quarantine wardroom, it irritated him that he was under armed guard. No one could enter or leave the building without the express authorisation of Cova's head of security Corelli. Through the window, the Mars sunset was once more spectacular, the deepest of red skies cascading a reddish glow deep into every hidden crevice of Central City. The long shadows of a Mars sundown were famous for their eerie grey redness that could never be recreated by artists or painters who tried to deliver to Earth their feeling of artistic awareness. The wardroom lights then dimmed, a statement of intent that someone was about to enter the room - when the door opened Obera held his breath.

"I knew it would be you," breathed Obera to his unexpected visitor, making no effort to stand. The young woman walked through the sliding door.

She sat herself down in the nearest chair to him, keeping her guard - Obera had an unpredictable reputation.

"You look surprised to see me," she said. There followed a short moment of silence during which neither of them knew what to say. Obera hesitated to choose his words.

"You knew they were there, didn't you?" he scowled with clear hostile accusation in his voice. He waited for an answer, but nothing came. "I took my ship and walked straight into your piss-fart trap. You knew those two bastards were out there waitin'. You knew," the bitterness of his words was difficult for him to hide.

"You presume too much Commander Obera," she replied. "Your greed for mineral wealth took you to *Mu Arae*, it was nothing much to do with me." As she leaned forward her walnut dark hair fell across the left side of her face, she tossed it aside with a casual flick of her hand. Obera's heart inadvertent skipped a beat - there was another pause while he tried to fathom his unease.

"So, why are you here now?" he demanded, his brusque voice hiding nothing. "How did you get past that bastard of a goddammed guard?"

"I was not taken heed of," she answered. "No one knows I am here." The guard outside the door was dead, felled by the simple touch of her womanly hand.

Obera looked at her with distinct unease, he glanced at the still-open door. She possessed guile and guts, he did not doubt this, this quarantine security ring was rigid in its enforcement for a whole load of different reasons.

"Then tell me. I know you know. Why are those two death traps orbiting that moon?"

"I do *not* know Commander," she replied. "The civilisation that made use of that moon in the same way you intended are long extinct. They no longer exist."

Obera sat still in bolt silence. Both orbiting sentinels had been lifeless, he was double sure of this. He had difficulty in believing what she said. Could the two orbitals really have been there, benign, for countless millions of years? He thought hard.

"You told me about the *Mu Arae* system. You sent the coordinates of that rotating hell planet on this goddammed stone-vis thing, you lured me into that ambush," Obera's face was contorted with rising anger. "For what reason did you want my vessel to go there? We nearly died."

"You were told where the missing exploration vessel *Dros* was lost, nothing more," she replied. "That was a long time ago, before you were born Commander. You then made your assumptions of what that hostile world might be made of. It is mineral greed that took you there. It is ironic that you are the one being accused. Because of you and your actions, Cova Corporation will soon face financial ruin."

"My crew by a miracle survived," he hissed, half ignoring what she had said. He was well aware that his decision to head for the mystical richest of worlds was now the cause of Cova's collapse. "Cova ordered us to the *Mu* star system because of long-standing rumours about a possible goldmine-gushing planet, but not to *Mu Arae*, *Mu Arae* was not listed for exploration. I broke Cova regulations to go there, we were supposed to be somewhere else. We were lucky to pull through."

"If you had tried to run from the moon, those sentinels would have destroyed you. Like they did *Dros*." The air in the wardroom began to chill. "Those orbitals were built to protect the moon, nothing more. They do not mean to destroy mankind or anything stupid like that, you mining men mean nothing to them."

Commander Obera thought the facts over for himself. The exploration vessel *Dros* had disappeared over two centuries before when interstellar mineral exploration was in its infancy. It was well-known that her crew mutinied but that was all, the missing vessel then became an infamous legend, a story told by storytellers throughout the Foundation, in sleazy bars and backstreet brothels where roughneck exploration crews and off-world miners spent their hard-earned wealth. Rumours that *Dros* had found the ultimate richest of all planets abounded, though there could never have been any basis of truth in these tales. No trace of *Dros* was ever found. Commander Obera had formulated a canny hunch about the fabled planet, nothing more. When he unexpectedly received exact coordinates pinpointing the location of where evidence of *Dros* might be found, Obera straightaway reasoned how the fabled ore-rich planet would be there. Obera's mind drifted, then the simple facts brought him back down to earth with a shameful bruise.

"Will these aliens now attack Earth and the Foundation? Is this their intention?" Obera suspected that he knew the answer - after his near-death experience, he was determined to know everything. His every mannerism became strained as the emotions of this moment toyed with his rational sanity.

"There are no aliens, Commander, they do not exist, they do not lurk behind every corner or hide under big stones. Their civilisation has long been extinct," the atmosphere between them seemed to relax. "Humankind will destroy itself long before there are encounters with other intelligent lifeforms, in the same way those who built the two orbitals that came close to destroying yourself and your crew. The lure of mineral wealth and wild unimaginable riches is the one thing that every time unravels greed, whatever the civilisation."

"Then tell me, if there are no aliens then who in hell's name are you?" Obera's eyes bulged with incandescent frustration. He struggled to make any reasonable sense of this pulsating situation. *Cobra's* commissioning orders had been to explore the region of the *Mu Deleras* star system, not *Mu Arae* or any other of the hundreds of star systems in the *Mu* constellation, but the strange whitestone vis he had for some reason found in his possessions revealed bizarre information that had stunned him. To the consternation of his redneck crew, he ordered *Cobra* to change course to *Mu Arae*, to an unexplored planet designated *HD160691*. Obera's wild hunch about the missing *Dros* and the supposed treasure planet had proved correct. "And how do *you* know about the exploration vessel *Dros* and that goddammed planet?" he demanded.

"I am no extraterrestrial alien, Commander. I am more human than all you humans born. This world will always be my world," she saw the extreme puzzlement in Obera's eyes. "I know about *Dros*. They were in the *Mu Arae* system. I knew the crew well; they were good men. They were there for a reason, just like you."

"What reason?"

Obera's heartbeat increased in rapid intensity, the ancient Cossack blood in his veins pulsated around his body out of control. The Commander, in his long years as an intrepid leader of men, who had known many trials and near-death experiences that would have floored any lesser man, now sat perfectly still, his mind focused upon the beguiling woman who sat before him. She once more flaked her hair through her hands, staring back at him with a quick-witted intensity that made the tough interstellar explorer shudder.

"The science officer of the exploration vessel *Dros* had good reason to go to *Mu Arae*," she said with calm clarity. "She was there in the *Mu Arae* system because of the discovery of the obelisk on the moon of *Affebiar IV*, the moon is called *Rios*," she paused, looking at Obera for a few silent moments. "Until a short while ago, *Rios* was never explored, but the discovered obelisk there is identical to one that exists on Earth, it is a frightening testament to what mankind's future will be." The dry, over-conditioned air in the wardroom began to feel oppressive. "Do you know *Affebiar IV* and its moon Commander?"

Obera leaned back in his chair, trying to make sense of what she said. The infamous Miranda Svedberg was one of few scientists to have risen to first officer rank of an exploration vessel, she had led the reported crew mutiny onboard *Dros* before the ship went missing. If this young woman here in this room knew Svedberg and the crew of *Dros as* she said then something was seriously wrong with his maths, his calculations, his perception of reality – this would make her well over two hundred and fifty years old, which was not possible. If she had some connection with Svedberg, which he doubted, then why had she lured him and *Cobra's* crew almost to their doom?

"I know of Affebiar IV, but not the moon," Obera replied. "It is located in the *DRU Meir* system. It's remote, Cova Mining are just beginning to explore out there, the survey vessel *Constance* has recently returned. I know their commander, he is a wild one," Obera sat motionless, wondering what she would say next. She said nothing, she waited for him to continue. Obera decided to temper his words carefully. "You cannot know Svedberg or the crew of *Dros*. Why do you make this claim? That would make you more than five times older than *me*. Just look at you babe, do you think I'm a fool?"

"You are no fool Commander," there was a darting subtleness in her piercing grey eyes. "I knew your father; he was no fool either..." she paused for effect. "And you should know that Darius Henderson of Cova Corporation, who you talked with yesterday with Corelli and Beim, is the reason why you headed to *Mu Arae*, though he does not yet know this. The conflict of attrition that now wreaks havoc throughout this corrupt Foundation dates long before I was a sparkle in a drunken miner's eye, it is a struggle that has ravaged this world of men since the beginning, a long time before even your father's *father,* and his *father* were born Commander."

Commander Obera sat still, his whole self frozen with indecision and total incomprehension.

Gloria Henderson stepped out of Johnson's elevator at the lowest basement level. Deep underground, this was where the rats and vermin used to thrive until they were exterminated as a vile species over two hundred years before. Mrs Henderson knew this would be the perfect place for skulking lowlife to hide. In the darkest corners, where the stench of stale urine permeated into every damp crevice of the crumbling masonry, there were the obvious signs of the homeless who lived their wretched lives outside the mainstream fraternity of the cosmopolitan city. Gloria Henderson knew these people well; their DNA lineage was all important in her relentless search to seek out true blood ties to the time at the absolute beginning. Somewhere, living amongst Earth's pitiful homeless, was the genetic seed of Amobea, the supreme warrior-goddess who would one day defeat the so-called Dark Lords.

Gloria knew full well what she must do. Corelli's men were here lurking in the damp darkness, somewhere inside the basement – she knew they had not long before killed Can Sen, leaving his broken body entwined in the semi-industrial maze of his destroyed ramshackle laboratory. Corelli, with his henchmen, were desperate to find both Gloria Henderson and the archaeologist Ebenezer Johnson. Johnson, it seemed, needed to be eliminated alongside Can Sen. Gloria knew that she was riding her luck to the extreme because both Corelli and Beim at last suspected who she was, that *she* might be the one responsible for the immanent collapse of Cova Corporation. Earth's economy might not be far behind. This was the covert secret hidden from Darius Henderson by Corelli and Beim.

Beim and Gloria's husband Darius would lose everything, this much was certain, Gloria never had any intention of warning Mr Henderson how foolish it would be to invest in the *Mu* exploration venture, because the high-risk investment by her husband provided her with the perfect cover - nor had she revealed that *Cobra's* exploratory mission was a baited trap, a calculated lure to strike against Cova and the mining conglomerate economy. Gloria had gambled everything, a slow creeping game of attrition more than three hundred years in the making. *Cobra* in some way had to survive, when the news of *Cobra's* near destruction by alien technology broke there would be financial turmoil – and the gamble had worked to perfection. Through Mr Johnson's innovating DNA probe of his own invention, Gloria now knew for certain how the stone obelisk discovered on the surface of *Rios* held the key to the unexplored distant moon of HD160691. If *Cobra* somehow survived the initial onslaught, then the vessel would not be destroyed by the orbiting sentinels, not like the mutiny ship *Dros*, because the two sentinel's sensing probes would lock on to

Commander Obera himself, not Obera direct, but the strange whitestone viz he possessed – their sensors would make the tenuous connection with the obelisk on the moon of *Rios* together with the near-identical obelisk still undiscovered in the northern swamplands of Earth. In doing so the economic dominance and monied corruption of the mining giants would in the end begin to crumble.

Gloria had cultivated Ebenezer Johnson well, he was unique, he was the one off-world archaeologist capable of deciphering the ancient hieroglyphics carved into the *Rios* stone - he would dissect the mystery writing until he had solved it in his inimitable style. Can Sen, the majestical Chinese gadget-building magician was the missing link, Mr Johnson himself had led Gloria to Can Sen, she then provided the coding for the sensor design changes to Can Sen, so that Johnson's probe would do what *she* needed - the ability to decipher the link to the *Rios* obelisk in a way that no one could imagine. Can Sen in some way knew who Gloria was - then Gloria learned that Can Sen himself was of her same heritage blood. Furthermore, Gloria Henderson knew how well the moon of HD160691 would be defended – she suspected the momentous secret that lay hidden on the surface of the desolate unnamed moon orbiting HD160691, she knew this through Miranda Svedberg - the Cova exploration vessel *Dros* had been destroyed over two hundred years previous for one good reason. *Dros* was close to finding the rocky cavern with compelling evidence of a starship wreck of incalculable age.

Cova Corporation for a long time suspected that Svedberg had not acted alone when she triggered the mutiny onboard *Dros* - then disappeared. Neither Cova nor anyone else knew what happened to their top-line exploration vessel - except for Gloria Henderson, who knew the whole damn tale. The mystery of the disappearance of *Dros* became a whispered legend throughout the Mia-Earth Foundation: more so given the last received communication from *Dros* describing the crew mutiny led by the vessel's scientific officer Svedberg. Only in recent times did Corelli and his security force at long last learn about the chilling heritage of Miranda Svedberg, that she was more than a straightforward science officer, that she was inexorably linked to the feared billion-year bloodline of Hyvah – right to the absolute beginning when life on earth was created. Corelli and Beim in the fullness of time discerned with dread that Svedberg was true full-blood – perhaps the one who carried the absolute DNA gene and the dark sword of light itself. But who the hell was Gloria Henderson?

Beim and Corelli realised too late. Cova Corporation had been infiltrated in a masterful way. Someone within Cova knew every detail they proposed - their planned two-century strategy of economic dominance that was now on the verge of collapse. Cova's basket-weaving takeover of the Earth-Mia Foundation economy was close to completion, but the gigantic conglomerate now faced certain ruin. Every one of the megalithic off-world mining corporations dreaded the daunting prospect of combating a superior alien technology. As a consequence all stock prices were now in free fall, all fund and investment lines were frozen by nervous banks; vital government and political support, whose patronage loyalty had been bought for outlandish prices for years and years, was beginning to crumble. There were cracks – hard-faced political men never did like losing their easy-gained back-pocket wealth. The value of the yen was at a one-hundred-year low - this was exceptional, dangerous and mind-numbing fiscal territory.

All this because one wayward commander had commandeered his own vessel, for his own inane reasons not unlike those of the fabled *Dros*. Then he took his ship to an undesignated exoplanet with a moon defended by the legacy of an advanced civilisation that had shown no hesitation in attacking the Cova exploration vessel *Cobra*. Little had Corelli and Beim realised just how much danger Cova Corporation was in, only in the last few days did they at last suspect a devious undercover mole in their midst, that it was none other than Gloria Henderson through her hapless husband Darius. As the wayward wife of the third senior executive in the conglomerate, she knew pretty much everything that was decided, Gloria could worm anything she needed to know from her pliable, adorable husband. Corelli was the first to work out that Obera had gone to *Mu Arae* for his reasons, that someone had provided Obera with vital information that made him disobey orders and change course. Corelli in no time picked up the trail, Darius Henderson himself had proposed that the *Mu* Exploration Mission be given to Commander Obera and the crew of *Cobra*, they were the best, incorruptible, the most resolute and experienced – and as head of mission recruitment it was Henderson's call. Pure love and undying devotion had played little part in the marriage of Darius & Gloria Henderson, though only now did both Beim and Corelli suspect the worst. Furthermore, Darius Henderson's gut-feeling hunch that Cova Corporation and Earth might be under some form of subtle siege was correct – though not by any *alien* lifeform.

The dark, dank atmosphere of the underground basement did little to dampen Gloria's resolve. She decided to morph into her other being. The ageless vitamin-induced sexual temptress in her white virginal attire began to fade, her new mistlike ghost silhouette materialising into her hunter-killer form more suited to the lethal game Gloria now faced. In no time, she sensed that she was herself being hunted. Gloria hastened her changing self with impulsive urgency, she fast shed her alluring satin garments, then her sensual silken underwear to reveal a death-dealing nakedness that was half human. She little by little became more feminine in appearance - but with the powerful neanderthal apelike genome that was her four billion-year heritage. With her morphing change complete, she moved in four-legged agile stealth through the damp darkness of the vast basement, using her pervading sense of smell and piercing blue-grey eyes to track the two man-odours that right now appalled her. Gloria Henderson was no novice fool, she knew these men were ruthless hunter-assassins in their own right, to deal with them she would need to be the raptor-like huntress her nimble footedness gave her. She paused, there was a third scent, a new threat that made her feel for a moment uneasy. A familiar agitation in the pit of her stomach warned her she might be in peril - in no time at all Gloria realised this might be the time she was prophesied to die.

Gloria stalled her rapid advance; she hid behind the widest of the rough masonry pillars pitted with the salty grime of seeping moisture. Foul-smelling water dripped from somewhere above, but Gloria paid no attention as the mould-green drips ran down her dark-skinned forehead to end their long eighty-story pilgrimage trickling through the decaying crumbling brickwork, to drop unnoticed from her wide nostrilled all-sensing nose - Gloria's prime facial attribute honed by timeless evolution to keep her alive. The new scent made her shudder, Gloria knew who it might be, that this miserable rain-sodden night might be her last.

Gloria saw two half shadows in the near distance to her right, two indistinct shades of darkness that differed from their surrounding bleakness by a fractional degree. The scent-smell from the same direction was not quite right, by her instincts Gloria knew this was a lure, a trap to trick her into a devious ambush that would make the kill against her. Gloria moved with great stealth to her left, knowing what she must do; she carried no weapon or mechanical means of attack, nor did she possess any tool of death, just the honed survival instinct ingrained within her genetic DNA. Gloria reversed the ambush, in the few moments it took for her to cover the distance to where both hideous shadows hid, she made no sound, no desperate manifestations; nor did Gloria reveal any clue that she was there.

Corelli turned in horror, his basic instinct warning him that he was in extreme danger. In the darkness, he saw something repulsive, a humanoid figure unlike anything he had before seen. In a brief moment, he recollected that what he saw was in some way female, part primate and the rest a mistlike palaeolithic huntress ghostlike in appearance – though not in any way primitive or backward native. He saw hostile intelligence in its piercing grey eyes, a will to overpower him in a way that, had he managed to live beyond the next few moments, would have rendered him senseless for the remainder of his futile life. Corelli's fellow assassin kneeled beside him facing the opposite way like a coiled spring ready to kill, having no inclination of how their devious trap had been sprung. Corelli raised his zap gun as fast as he could, he realised that whatever it was that had sprung upon them was unarmed, it carried no hostile method of attack. He half smiled in anticipation, then the outlandish thought occurred to him that this myth beast, in some way, was Gloria Henderson in her primitive form. He pulled the trigger without much time to think, with a gratifying sense of glee that her life was in his hands, that Ducian Beim and the almighty Gabriel would shower him with praise beyond his wildest dreams.

Gloria stood before Corelli. He raised his weapon to fire, but in the fraction of a second it would take to finish her nothing happened. In the absolute smallest of one moment it took to apply the final pressure to the zap gun trigger, Corelli died. Gloria Henderson invaded his mind, she probed his bewildered conscience with a sense of deep hostile vengeance, she searched for vital life support memories that she could wrench from his inglorious soul. Gloria saw the time he murdered, in pure cold blood, the three women who stood naked in the windowless holding cell deep in the confines of Cova Corporation's hidden catacombs - their innocence ravished and bleeding from the tortured wounds that lacerated their broken bodies. Gloria then saw more onerous evil, she saw the time when Corelli raped and murdered his friend's cousin, sniggering and squealing his high-pitched giggle that made no effort to hide his vile pleasure. She saw the time he shot dead two running men; two heroes who tried to defend the woman tied to the dreadful midnight tree - two good men who knew well Corelli's evil intent. Corelli, the nauseating lord of pleasure, chief assassin for Cova Corporation, died when Gloria Henderson sliced the foulest of his foul memories from his festering shit-ingrained brain. He fell, he was dead before he hit the slimy waterlogged concrete ground.

In near-to-total darkness, the second assassin spun around in absolute confusion, his conscienceless mind tumbling in turmoil as he struggled to comprehend this new situation. He did not die, not like Corelli who lay crumbled lifeless a short distance from the second assassin's feet. The assassin stared at the dead Corelli, then at the womanlike humanoid crouched on her haunches above Corelli's lifeless body. He saw that she watched him with warning animalistic eyes while she checked the neck pulse of Corelli, at the same time staring the second assassin straight into his terrified eyes. The assassin thought that he would die if he did not attempt his escape. Gloria Henderson penetrated his mind, seeing

56

appalling age-old memories that made her shudder in pain. This time she did not strip the killer's memories from his conscious self, nor did she twist his sanity inside out, she allowed his thoughts to remain, his awareness would prevail so that his memories could fester and torment him for the remainder of his miserable life. The assassin thought for a moment about raising his zap gun to finish her – then realised this useless endeavour would not save his life. He turned to run, hoping the darkness would hide him someplace within the bleak shadows of the damp basement. When he ran, he expected her to fall upon him, that she would in some way ravage him until he was dead. Nothing happened; Gloria Henderson decided that he would live, that there must be a blabbering witness to what had happened, a mind-numbing record of how the evil Corelli died. This must be so, thought Gloria, because she knew, before the miserable night was out, that she herself would be dead.

Commander Obera had decided that his destiny was not in his own hands. He sat quiet and contemplative, trying his best to think everything over. He glanced up to see that she still stared at him, when he rose from his chair to walk over to the landscape view window, he felt her eyes follow him. She was a pretty thing for sure but in no way was she what she seemed, she did not allure herself to any physical attraction. Obera felt drawn towards a feeling of subtle enticement he fought hard to fathom. He knew there was no doubt that he was now hers, that he would be forever.

"Why are you here?" he asked, looking long and hard out of the window. "What is it you want me to do?"

Obera hoped she would open up, to at least show some measure of compassion. But nothing much came. He found himself thinking how they might fall in love - then things could change. She offered no respite to his confused state of mind, just a resolute stare straight into his eyes.

"The repair teams now repairing your ship are not Cova's men," she replied as a matter of fact. She ignored his feeble attempt at empathy. "Cova will soon be bankrupt, their technical teams have been taken away on the pretext they might never be paid, which is more than probable."

She turned towards Obera in her swivel chair, knowing that even Corelli's security men were beginning to question their loyalty to the Corporation – more so when their boss was summoned back to Earth. Where was Corelli now? With Corelli gone it had been easy to switch Cova technicians with purpose-built off-world androids. "The work teams now onboard *Cobra* need six more days to complete basic repairs. Your new crew will be technical androids, mustered with a few hand-picked officers."

Obera stared dumbstruck.

"Do not look alarmed Commander. Once you leave here you will be tasked to proceed to a rendezvous point that will be given to you," she added. The air in the room began its routine evening humidity purge. The dryness of Mars was legendary with no natural water reserves of its own. "The coordinates will be sent through your whitestone vis communicator that was given to you. At those coordinates a dart shuttle will bring to you an off-world archaeologist from Earth, you must then proceed to *Affebiar IV* in the *DRU Meir* system, more specific to the *Rios* moon," once more she tossed away her silk-like hair that had fallen across her smooth mature face.

Commander Obera stood in shock.

"What will then happen on *Rios*?" he demanded; Obera walked back to stare outside the window. Nighttime on Mars had now descended, the controlled atmosphere within the whole enormous dome of Central City pumped through to chill the cosmopolitan ambience, to provide overtones of evening relaxation to the hundred-thousand or so settlers and vessel maintenance work teams who lived there. There was no ore mining permitted on Mars.

"This I cannot tell you, Commander."

"Why?"

"Because I do not know," she said.

"Will you tell me at least one thing?" Obera pleaded.

"I will answer what I can, this is a difficult situation for both of us," she huffed with irritated impatience.

"It is *not* a difficult question," Obera continued to gaze out of the window.

He began to take back control of his thoughts, thoughts that raced in wild confusion as this whole damn episode unravelled. The thought of the guard outside of the wardroom door agitated him, where was he? Why had he not intervened? Though these questions were not what he needed to ask.

"Your name? On the two occasions now I have met you, I have never known your name."

She paused, then exclaimed her breath - as if this would ruin everything. It was true, although she had endeavoured to convince Commander Obera there might be a tenuous link to Miranda Svedberg, he still did not know who she was. To tell him might risk everything because that might open a can of worms to churn the sanity of the commander like an out-of-control windmill. Obera was an unknown quantity, a loose cannon in his own right, he was a flashpoint rebel with a well-deserved reputation for the unpredictable. This was why Gloria Henderson had gambled everything upon *Cobra* surviving the extraterrestrial attack when attempting to explore HD160691. The sentinels would not destroy *Cobra*, it had worked, but knowing who she was might ruin the attritional plan to bring down Earth's corrupt mining economy – and then lure the dark archangel himself to once more reveal he had returned.

"My name is not important. Through my time I will be known by many names," she said. She looked down to the floor, hoping the commander would not demand more answers.

"If I am to take my half-repaired ship full of goddammed androids, a rookie archaeologist and an unknown crew to this weird and wonderful *Rios* moon you tell me about, then I want some answers," said Obera. "If not then you can go fuck yourself."

"It will be you that *fucks* me, commander, have *no* doubts of this," she said, looking up. There was a prolonged awkward pause, the sort of pause that would forever make Obera think hard. "I think you will find you are free to leave this Cova quarantine facility," she stared. "Be careful to step over the guard when you make your way out."

Vavilov Obera turned to gaze at her with a stunned expression. Obera was speechless, he had no more words he could think of to say.

Mr Henderson had no idea that his wife was over seven hundred years old. How could he? No man ever questions the age of a woman.

He had met Gloria in strange circumstances, he had known *this*, but something as inconvenient as the real age of his wife did not concern him. He assumed that he was maybe a few years younger but was never sure exact. At first, there was a strong physical relationship between them, though this declined until it at last dawned upon him that he was there to provide their substantial wealth and Gloria to spend it. Never in a zillion years did it occur to him that he was a manipulated stooge, that he was Gloria Henderson's gateway to the powers at Cova Corporation.

Darius Henderson sat in Ducian Beim's luxurious office with his head in his hands. At this moment neither of them took much notice of Beim's collection of rare art adorning his walls, nor the fine woven carpet turned out by the one ethnic mill still operating in the Kurdish mountains. In fact, Henderson wasn't in much of a state to notice anything at all. Everything had fallen into place, his gut-feeling instinct that Cova Corporation and Earth itself might be under some form of hostile attack was uncanny and correct, except there were no extraterrestrial aliens. Earth, the Foundation and the mining-based economy was on the verge of economic collapse through the actions of, according to what Beim now revealed, his own wife. Henderson looked up at Beim who was beginning to froth in the corners of his ugly wide mouth.

"Corelli, he knew there must be someone acting against us, someone feeding false data about the *Mu* Constellation, the exploration vessel *Dros* and every other damn starstruck goldmine planet that was gonna make us all rich. Someone who knew every damn move we made. But Corelli never suspected it was through *you* Darius," said Beim. "Not until he found the link between Miranda Svedberg and your damned wife Gloria."

Darius Henderson said nothing. He was still in shock.

"That swine Obera took his ship *Cobra* into the *Mu Arae* system of his own accord, we all know this now, but he must have gone there for good reason,"

Beim continued. "Why did he go to that specific exoplanet? Why there? We know of its existence through extraterrestrial telescopic mapping over nine hundred years ago, it was nothing special, no exploration vessel has ever been anywhere near that goddamned remote location. The whole damned venture into the *Mu* Constellation was a ruse, a shitfaced conceived commercial disaster that Cova, the investment banks and just about every gullible stock market guru in the Foundation risked everything in. Cova invested heavily in the exploration of that constellation. You and me too Darius. Me? I risked the lot, I bet my last goddammed bottom yen that you risked a whole lot more Henderson. All on the fabled existence of some Shangri-la mineral planet that no one was even sure existed."

"But it does exist," interjected Henderson, his ashen face grey with morbid apprehension. "Look at the probe and the android data that *Cobra* brought back."

"Yes... except it's all no doubt been mined out by goddamned fucking aliens, who then tried to blast our vessel out of the cosmos. No doubt there's an alien fleet winging its way over in our direction as we speak, think of all our mineral wealth at their disposal," ranted Beim without taking a breath. "The history of Earth's early civilisations being wiped out by greedy explorers looking for gold doesn't bode well, does it Henderson."

Henderson looked up. It was true. Just about every indigenous race on Earth had suffered at the hands of desperate treasure seekers, greedy conquistadors arriving on their doorsteps in their ancient sailing ships. Could the same now happen to Earth and the Foundation? The human race was without doubt at least a million years behind whatever alien technology had attacked *Cobra*, *Cobra's* data from the two deadly orbitals proved this. The age of those things alone was enough to blow your mind if you considered it, thought Henderson.

Henderson, though, said nothing.

"But *someone* knew, Henderson," fumed Beim once more. His voice began to raise itself to the pitching rant that Beim was infamous for. "Someone knew what was fucking out there. And do you know who this was? Your wife, Henderson. Your fucking wife, who can't keep her damn legs closed."

At this absolute moment in time, Henderson hated Ducian Beim. Henderson realised that he had always hated him, he hated Beim's rotten foul mouth.

Outside of the building where Henderson sat in miserable contortion, in the rising earthlight of the new day, dawn broke in a magnificent explosion of colour, an exhibition of magnificence not seen for a long time on the dust-ridden mediocrity of urban Earth. Uncountable thousands of early morning risers peered in wonder at the unexpected appearance of the interwoven mosaic of colours, the sort of dawn that almost no one could remember. The doom and gloom of the growing economic crisis, now dominating everything, seemed to be forgotten, just for a few brief moments, though there were those who heralded the new dawn - not of a new day but a new beginning - those who perhaps foresaw the looming shambolic fall of the predatory human race.

Henderson and Beim saw none of the colourful sunrise, the greyed-out window screens hid it all, only the *grey* light of the new day invaded the grim room where Darius Henderson thought that he would like to murder his loathsome boss Ducian Beim – his superior who he now despised. He would never do it, of course, Henderson never had the guts for any sort of violence, that's why he had always been the soft touch for his wife Gloria. At least Henderson smiled, he smiled to himself then he smiled to Ducian Beim who sat on the other side of the obscene, large desk that Beim now lurked behind like the wounded king of mining capitalism that he was. The mighty Ducian Beim, the head of Cova Corporation who had been outwitted by his wife Gloria, his wife whom Darius Henderson at this moment in time loved more than anything.

"You might sit there and smile to yourself Henderson," boomed Beim, condescending in his manner. "Well, I'll wipe your stupid smirk away. I have the sad news to tell you that Corelli himself is seeing to it that your wife is disposed of. Mrs Henderson and her gang of conspirators will by now be dealt with." With this statement, Beim smiled his sly smile of satisfaction. Little did Beim know that Corelli was by now dead, that his mind had been wrecked then turned inside out like wet pieces of cardboard, that in Corelli's last fraction of a second of cohesive thought he had visualised who Gloria Henderson was. Corelli, in his futile gasp for life, at once understood why Ducian Beim, himself and the once unstoppable might of Cova Corporation stood no realistic chance of survival. That is, unless...

"In ten minutes, I have to report to the supreme board of owners of Cova Exploration & Mining Corporation," continued the now calmer Beim. "In the meantime, you will be taken into custody by Cova Security. The Government Police Authority have been informed of your involvement in this crisis, this shit that will see even the Government itself fall." This time Beim did not smile. "There's a lot of powerful men out there Henderson, rich men who are going to lose everything they have. All because of your incredible stupidity and your bastard wife who lured us into this disaster we are now beginning to unravel. We don't know with pinpoint accuracy who your wife is yet, or her exact connection to some alien civilisation and to Miranda Svedberg, but Corelli is no fool Henderson. Soon we will know everything."

Henderson sat quiet, still feeling solemn. There was now a serene silence in the room. A weird thought occurred to him inside his confused head. The young woman he once in a while saw in the elevator, the one who flipped her hair in a strange way that every time spellbound him. Who was she? Why did he think of her now? Why now did her image pass through his mind at this obscene moment? Why was it this woman sometimes stared at him with those strange blue-grey eyes? What made him think that Beim was wrong to think his wife Gloria was the one who had brought down Cova?

Those eyes, thought Henderson. Why was it that both the woman in the elevator and his wife had those same creepy bluish-grey eyes? Gloria always tried to hide her eyes by changing them with cosmetic implants, but that young woman and Gloria, they both possessed those same self-alluring eyes. Then something occurred to him like an exploding bombshell, a time bomb that ticked and ticked until the ticking hand ticked its last tick. Henderson looked at Beim and laughed, he laughed in uproar in a way that irritated his conceited boss. Henderson did not care, because a teasing thought dawned upon Henderson for no sane reason. Miranda Svedberg, the renegade first officer who had led the mutiny on Cova's exploration vessel *Dros* all those years ago. Was it in any way conceivable that Svedberg had not disappeared at all?

The door of Beim's office opened, in walked two hair-cropped security men with more than evil intent.

Mr Johnson realised he was now insane. His whole life had been one of compulsive disorders and head-on confrontations with authority, argumentative crusades that sometimes tangled his mind in twisted knots. Johnson might be considered unstable but never in his life did he harbour any criminal intent, nor any desire to enrich himself through personal greed. Johnson, more often than not, just wanted to prove a point. To then substantiate his arguments against his overbearing superiors he found it necessary to know the facts, the depths he then went to in his quest to understand even the smallest detail often tortured him, sometimes from frustration but time and again much more. The vis-stream visions of *Rios* streaming through the whitestone vis he had found in his pocket, the woman in the elevator and even the mind-tormenting thoughts of Gloria Henderson convinced him that everything he stood for was tumbling headlong upside-down. Nothing made sense.

These flirtations with insanity, Johnson reasoned, were self-inflicted, it could get worse unless he figured out what the hell was going on. His illogical heart told him that his more immediate enemies were his boss Dr Matilda, who had told him not to 'fuck up' with the Rios dust samples - and Gloria Henderson for turning his life inside out. There were those who laughed whenever he argued against a well-established point like a scientific principle or a stupid order he was instructed to follow that he knew in the depths of his soul was wrong. He possessed an uncanny nose for trouble, his reputation for knowing where to look where he *should not look* preceded him – *this* was why he got himself into deep water. But

Johnson's head told him otherwise, Johnson's head was at last beginning to take over his heart, Johnson's head told him he was on the verge of greatness, that he was not insane at all. To prove to himself that he was not insane he needed to get himself to *Rios*.

When he at last came up with this decision he felt good, he was beginning to take control of his insanity - his determination to make his way to *Rios* to unravel this mind-twisting mystery through his own efforts meant that he was fighting back, from this moment in time he would follow his own intuitions without anyone trying to *control what he did*. In his defence, the unsolved question of the *Rios* samples, the rock obelisk with its strange hieroglyphics and how the hell he had become involved in this whole mess was enough to render him insane for the rest of his life. The rock samples were not rock at all - they were gritstone granite.

Johnson resolved to decipher the intriguing complexity of the hiero-glyphics, in achieving this he would finally prove to Dr Matilda that he was his equal in every sense. He would end his crazy relationship with Gloria Henderson, the real demon who drove him to the edge of despair. But Johnson's midnight dance with madness, the unresolved psychosis that festered in the depths of his mind was more than anything he could ever hope to deal with. In his endless battle between his head and his heart, he knew deep down that a strange love drew him to Gloria, an unfathomable love that dwelled in a far-off place just the two of them knew. And Johnson's looming schizophrenia was about to get much worse, the whitestone vis that still lay sideways and inert on the bench top before him suddenly glowed the same strange opaque green. When Johnson touched its surface, the identical hand-type instruction appeared just like before.

It was the same message. '*Call me using this vis-number Mr Johnson. I am the woman in the elevator.*' With his newfound resolve and determination, though with more than a hint of foreboding, he once more instructed his wall vis-screen to dial the restricted number.

"Mr Johnson," his vis-screen responded with a tone of outward hostility, "I have to warn you how objectionable your instruction is, this number is not authorised and cannot connect. You are instructing me to indulge in gross illegal practice, I must report this to central vis-control. When I look back through the connection logs I have made for you, it is enough to drive *ME* insane and I am a machine. Why, I think I will report to central vis-control right now to....."

"Just dial the *fucking* number," interrupted Johnson. "Or I will put my boot through your screen."

It had been many hours since Gloria Henderson left Johnson's apartment. During this time he had heard nothing from her, which was unexpected given that she more or less controlled every damn thing that happened. It wasn't that he was worried, it was just that it seemed strange. While his vis-screen dialled the restricted number to now make the connection, it niggled Johnson somewhat that something wasn't right, something was wrong that he sensed in the back of his mind was not good. Unlike before, it was taking an inordinate amount of time to connect the vis-number, nor could he fathom why Gloria was silent. Johnson sat staring at the turning timing circle on the wall screen, the connection would not go through. While he waited, newsflash banners careered left to right across the foot of his screen, mining stocks on the financial markets were on the verge of some form of final collapse.

This was huge, big news. Johnson resolved to paste this headline to his vis-feed once he had ended his vis-communication with the mysterious elevator woman. He had not followed the latest news; his mind wasn't in a good place to take much interest. Johnson, like everyone else, guessed that all of the market turmoil was linked to Cova Exploration & Mining and one of their damaged exploration vessels - until now he had missed the sensational breaking morning news that *Cobra* might have been attacked by extraterrestrial alien forces. In the event, Johnson half believed the original news story about space dust damage to the Cova vessel, he thought the truth would come out at some point – *that* dust theory wasn't right in Johnson's mind. It now seemed he was right, the markets were in free fall, and some level of extreme mad panic prevailed. For a lifeform archaeological scientist, Johnson wasn't exactly on the ball regarding the damaged *Cobra*. Johnson, fighting his impending schizophrenia, had his mysterious off-world crisis to deal with, it was obvious the granite-stone cenotaph on the moon *Rios* was linked to some form of prehistoric cosmos-based civilisation, but when the newsflash banner ran across the screen describing the suspected attack on *Cobra*, Johnson froze. He froze in a bad way. Johnson suspected there was a connection. How could there not be? The obelisk monolith on *Rios* was without any shadow of doubt linked to the devastating breaking news that a Cova exploration vessel had been close to destruction in a far distant star system called *Mu Arae*. Then, Johnson's vis-screen at last connected.

It was her. The same young woman's face flickered onto the vis-screen; Johnson's heart skipped a beat. Her appearance was unchanged which Johnson thought unusual, her hair then fell across the left side of her face as she peered at something downwards, she read something, looked upwards into her screen and flicked her hair from her eyes. It was the same mannerism in the elevator that Johnson was never going to forget...

"I will ask you once more to dial this sequence into your vis, it will disable all call tracking and any monitoring by central vis-control. You are being tracked."

Johnson didn't say anything, he was familiar with the procedure. The whitestone vis transmitted the number sequence which Johnson dialled in. His vis-screen went dead but she remained visible on his screen. Johnson saw the whitestone vis streaming to his wall-mounted screen.

"Good morning, Mr Johnson. I have important instructions for you to follow."

Johnson straightaway felt a bolt of anger well up inside him. Again, he was being told what to do, he would describe to her everything that had happened, that he had resolved to somehow get himself to *Rios*. All this mess was without doubt connected; it was important to him that he sort this situation through his own endeavours. He just needed to get to...

"Mr Johnson, I will shortly send to you a location point," she continued. "From there you will be collected by an unmarked RAM shuttle. You will then be transported to the Cova exploration vessel *Cobra*, which will proceed to the moon *Rios* orbiting *Affebiar IV*. You will be under the command of Commander Obera."

Johnson's instantaneous feeling of madness struck him like a thunderbolt. How could this be? He was being controlled; his whole life was not in his own hands...

"Whoa... just wait," Johnson interrupted, the anger in his voice plain. "Who do you think you are?" He tried hard to restrain himself. He sensed that something was not right, she was stressed, the mannerism in her eyes told him that something new had happened. Johnson thought he could see tears.

"I have told you before, who I am does not matter," she replied.

"But it does matter, everything in this whole damn world matters," argued Johnson. He felt on the verge of choking, but he calmed himself down. "Are you connected to Gloria? Let's start with that. Do you know Gloria Henderson?" Johnson sat himself back. At once he felt a little easier, he was taking control...

"Gloria Henderson is dead," she looked at him straight. Then she said nothing.

Madness begins with a random feeling of hopelessness. Pure lunacy creeps upon you with indistinct feelings that things are not quite right, then your transcendental thoughts grow to remunerate inside your mind until they go round and round like a spinning top merry-go-round that will never stop. The world within your world changes, not in a way that brings happiness, but in a way that makes you begin to understand how the whole world is against you, when everything you do or say feeds the rotten stinking gremlin that becomes your insanity. To be consumed by your out-of-control thoughts, this is the age-old route to madness that every expert has never quite mastered, when the bright new sunrise brings nothing to your life, when the nighttime midnight kiss of whispering brings voices. Johnson's world collapsed like a sinkhole opening up right in the middle of a pristine sun-blessed lawn of summer green grass greenness, when the smell of new-cut grass teases your transitional senses to lure you into a feeling of happiness – which then disappears beneath your feet. The feeling of standing on a finely cut meadow, with larks and songbirds singing out their late evening melodies in leafy green trees while the sun sets in beautiful crimson redness - then all of a sudden you are falling headlong into oblivion, into the hole not made by you that with suddenness opens around you. This is madness, this is the relentless attrition within your mind that your tumbling conscience forever strives to make no sense of...

"Who gave you the right to destroy the life of every man-being on this planet?" Gabriel folded his magnificent white wings to hide them beneath his copious shrouds of flowing silk. He took his time to circle the morphed Gloria Henderson, who hunched herself low like a powerful coiled spring ready to strike. "The whole of mankind will never forgive me for this, they will suffer in their uncountable millions when their luxurious way of living disappears. All because of your righteous crusade," growled the transcendental angel of the Lesser Lords.

Gabriel clasped his fire sword with a firm grip, he saw that Gloria was unarmed. He knew that she did not need any type of weapon to cause him untold harm.

"Do you think I am a fool?" Gabriel continued; his voice tainted with outright venom. "Do you think I will stand by to let you take apart everything I have created?" he tried hard to corner her; the angel had known for aeons of years that one day this particular confrontation would come. As he circled, he saw that she turned with him, changing her direction to face him, by crouching low on the sodden wet floor she made herself a smaller target. The dark dank basement and the pitch-black air offered no respite, nowhere to hide for both of them. The dripping pools of foul-smelling water added to the miserable darkness that would soon see the death of one of them. Gabriel knew the odds were well stacked in his favour.

"Will you try to invade my mind?" taunted Gabriel. "Will you try to savage my memories, tear them away like flakes of tar to toss aside? Or will you rip me apart like a piece of rabid meat?"

Gloria said nothing, there was nothing she could say. *She* was the cornered rat, the caged jackass hunter waiting for the smallest opportunity to strike - but if she launched herself to assault him then Gabriel would cut her down with his emblazoned sword; but if she waited then the smallest opportunity might arise for her to save her life. Soon, with his hostile taunts, he might make one mistake - a single chance that she might then live. Gloria, though, knew that Gabriel would give her no such opportunity, that this was the long dark night she feared, the final confrontation between the two of them when she would die - the culmination of her long seven-hundred-year fight to reclaim her world from the relentless dominance of man. She watched him through her intense animal eyes, eyes that had seen many wrongs since the beginning of her time. Gloria was not the first in her bloodline, nor the last but she felt a tumultuous feeling of pride that her reverent seed was already sown.

"I know who you are and who you claim not to be," Gabriel smiled with ill-gotten conceit. "That worm Miranda Svedberg is not Svedberg, I know this too. I know who she is and that she is of your blood, I know which slithering bastard fathered her," he glared. "By my Lord's grace, I will end your time and finish you, then I will deal with this almighty disaster you have created. Did you think I would allow Cova to disintegrate just like that?"

Gloria waited, saying nothing. Her chance would soon come, it was close.

"Do not think you can invade my mind," Gabriel leered, "that would not do. I have no earth-born memories like any mortal man, no malignant thoughts that you can snatch from me." Gabriel knew she had no defence or other means of attack, but he was never a fool. Gloria might morph into her true self, he would have to finish her fast if she attempted this, he could cut her down with ease but she would then fight like a cornered cougar, a super powerful hunter capable of inflicting serious harm – and he still had the urgent task of saving the wretched world from her ruin. Gabriel then saw that Gloria moved slightly towards him, a minuscule of a twitching muscle in her apelike neanderthaloid legs. She was shaping herself to pounce, though, as yet she made no direct move. Gabriel felt a feeling of elation, this was the time he had long waited for, the time when he could end one more incarnation of the so-called Gloria Henderson. He knew this misshapen creature crouching and panting before him was not her usual form, nor the sexual huntress she had used to bring Cova down, that in reality, it would never be easy to finish her. In the back of his mind, Gabriel knew that her real self was the one single incarnation he dreaded most.

It happened in a flash, an instantaneous moment in time, the smallest fraction of a single second. She was upon him in the tiniest blink of his bamboozled eye. Gabriel was down. His furled wings splattered open, the pure virgin white feathers splashing into the cesspit water riddled with stinking grime, dirty foul effluence that any sane man in his prime would discredit. Gabriel had no time to react, Gloria rolled him over and over, at the same time battering his now non-smirking face that bore an expression of extreme surprise and total exasperation. While he lay forlorn upon the basement floor, Gloria raised herself to stand victorious over him knowing this was no victory. Deep down, Gloria knew it was her time to die, that her incarnation was ended, she would die in the same way that she was born a long time ago. Gloria was Hyvah and Hyvah was Gloria Henderson.

Gloria began to change, she changed not into Gloria Henderson but into something else. Gabriel stared wide-eyed when he knew who it would be, he lay helpless upon the stone-hard floor with her spreadeagled over him like the triumphant sphinx of Boudicca. She became the once saintly Joan of Arc and the rampant Attila the Hun, she was A'licia of the *Banu Amir*, Demeter of the gods then the tragic orphan Moon. Fleeting, Gabriel saw the Magdalena – in the same ghost form she had taken when he had tried and failed to end her life well over three thousand years before. Then Gabriel realised that what his supreme Lords every time imbibed to him was true, that nothing would ever end until the death of Hawwāh's bloodline. Hawwāh was Hyvah, Hyvah was Hawwāh, Hawwāh was Lilith and Eve. Gloria stood above him waiting in triumph, standing there in her moment of exultation. Gloria Henderson could have finished him, but she did not. Now was her time to die in the same way told, a prophesied death that Gabriel might never in more than four billion Earth years understand.

Gabriel disposed of his angel white wings. Now was not the time for any displays of splendour, there was a job to be done that must be done. Inside the grand council room of Cova Exploration & Mining the rich and powerful men of the supreme board had gathered, the mounting crisis would soon reach its point of no return - within hours Cova Corporation would be past the point where it could be saved. Gabriel burst through the tall double white marble doors as if they were not there, he found them all assembled with ashen grey faces, faces that Gabriel saw were blank and expressionless. Each of them was in a morbid state of periodic shock. Gabriel took the nearest available seat, the malevolent angel stared at the faces around him then motioned to Beim to begin.

Ducian Beim, recovering a measure of composure, was the first to speak. The seriousness of the situation called for the dispensation of the usual niceties preceding this crucial gathering. The atmosphere was hostile and tense.

"Gentlemen, I will make my report short," Beim saw the same grim faces around him. He noted that Marcus Corelli was not there, he was absent. Where was Corelli? Corelli's security report was going to be crucial. "As you all know, Cova Corporation has been brought to this crisis by detrimental outside influences," he perspired with more than a hint of uncertainty. Beim could feel fourteen pairs of eyes drilling into his mind.

"We know that our survey vessel *Cobra* was attacked by extraterrestrial forces in the *Mu Arae* solar system, she was assailed after being lured there with deliberate intention," said Beim. What to do now? At this point, Beim intended to hand over to his security expert Corelli who would then give a full explanation describing what had happened, including the lead-up to the attack upon *Cobra*. After all, Corelli knew the facts in far more detail than he did – and the disturbing news he had learned a few minutes before he entered the room about Commander Obera had crunched into him. It was reported that Obera had gone AWOL. He had disappeared. Obera had killed his guard, then in some way made his escape. This new development meant there was little chance of keeping the lid on anything - Beim assumed that vis-streamed recordings of the attack on *Cobra* had disappeared with him. Where the fuck was Corelli?

Beim stood there before the assembled Cova dignitaries, who waited in silent shock for answers. Each of them was going to lose a vast fortune, some of them everything - they waited for Beim to tell them it was all a bad dream, that they would not be ruined or destined to lead a life of low-life poverty. Beim, in his one supreme moment when he needed to demonstrate his absolute leadership to save the mightiest mining and exploration corporation ever to exist, could not think of anything worthwhile to say.

"Sit down Beim," boomed Gabriel. "You have made a big enough mess of this debacle." Gabriel stood at his full imposing height, the height of close to two men. "Listen to me, all of you."

Beim had no hesitation in sitting down, he felt himself beginning to shake. Both in nervous reaction and from shivering fear.

"Before any of you ask where Marcus Corelli is, Corelli is dead," said Gabriel. He then looked at Beim who sat with his wide open incredulous eyes bulging in their sweat-ridden sockets. "Yes, you might wonder how this happened. Well, I'll tell you. Corelli was killed by Gloria Henderson, yes, the same Gloria Henderson who we all know has brought this corporation to its knees." No one said a word, not yet, not while the news sank in like heavy oxen struggling in quicksand.

"Gloria Henderson, and her husband Darius Henderson who is Cova Corporation's head of recruitment, they are now both dead," he continued. Gabriel did not elaborate. There was no need to reveal how they both died, that he had finished Gloria Henderson when she should have killed *him*. But Gloria was not Gloria Henderson, not when he ran his reverend sword through her heart. Her husband Darius had by then been assassinated, murdered under torture by Corelli's security men.

Beim looked aghast – though it dawned upon him that this might be an improving situation. But the death of Corelli was a deep shock though even Beim suspected that a silenced Corelli might not be a bad thing.

"Each of you here today represents the old ancient creeds," said Gabriel. He looked in turn at Beim, Beim of the Jews, bin Salem - leader of all the Islam faiths, the Supreme Archbishop of the Catholics, the other high priests, they were all there seeking to save their empirical fortunes.

"Cova Corporation, as you each know, has existed for many hundreds of years, not just as the world's greatest mining organisation that controls all things, but as the culmination of the Lord's benevolence to the human race. By now you should all know who Gloria Henderson was, you *know why* she desired that Cova be brought to its knees. Gloria Henderson was the bloodline vassal of the despised evil herself." No one around the table said anything. Indeed, each of them thought how they would at last be rid of the latest reincarnation of the dreadful whore who claimed to be the mother of all men. Nonetheless, not one of the eyebrowed lords sitting there in the room gave any sign that they were overjoyed, they realised how this incarnation that was Gloria Henderson would not have died without good reason. The gathered leaders of the righteous religions of all men knew how much this might be a hallow victory, that if Cova collapsed then they would each suffer a catastrophic defeat, that each of them might endure the misery of destitute poverty - or even the ultimate pain of life ending excommunication.

"Cova will not fail, I guarantee you this," Gabriel vowed. "Already the volatile world of mining stocks rallies. Every government in the Foundation is pumping new money into their economies, Cova Corporation is too big, too important to fail. Every government that nestles its greedy paws deep inside our pockets is responding to our cause. Check your vis-screens, you will see that I do not tell you lies. There are no aliens."

As one, all present raised their wrists to activate their vis-screens. There were gasps of surprise... Cova's stock price was rising fast. Beim sat silent - would it be possible for him to contact his sideline broker? Beim felt the desperate need to buy.

"My desire to save Cova, and each of you, is strong," continued Gabriel.

"This job is done. Gloria Henderson, the latest incarnation of Hyvah is dead. Gentlemen, we have an improving situation, Cova Corporation will survive, your miserable cause will be saved. But I'm afraid there is more, much more. There is grave news that has since cost Marcus Corelli his life."

Gabriel looked stern and grim. Gabriel knew that Gloria Henderson had out-and-out withheld her victory attack upon him for a reason, that she had allowed him to deliver his fateful execution. Gloria Henderson meant herself to die. This, Gabriel realised, could mean just one thing, a much deadlier adversary was by now born – that seed was already sown and had been for some time. The rebirths relinquished their long lives when new bloods were born from the wretched mother womb, when Hyvah's new strength was ready to prolong their cause. This, thought Gabriel, was now Cova's greatest expositional survival threat.

Gabriel suspected that Gloria was not the only architect of Cova's demise. He had reasoned this for a while, one single woman could not bring down a mining conglomerate like Cova. There was an intrinsic reason for *Cobra* being in the remote *Mu Arae* system, there was a method in the madness of this whole damn affair, a systematic move to bring down the Earth mining economy in general. This was not just a sustained effort against Cova Corporation, it was a deliberate attack against himself, against his supreme Lords and the leaders of the long-established creeds - who each held a vital share of Cova. And not just Cova, but the corporate stock holdings they each held in the other large mining conglomerates. The more Gabriel considered, the more convinced he became. Gabriel recalled one more hidden obelisk; the granite monolith known to be concealed somewhere on Earth. He knew it existed, that it might be just one of a few precarious cenotaphs scattered throughout the unexplored universe. Were they in some way linked? What lay hidden on the distant moon of the exoplanet HD160691? How was it that those two death-dealing alien sentinels orbiting that moon did not finish the destruction of the exploration vessel *Cobra*? Why did they allow Commander Obera and the remainder of his crew to escape? Who was Can Sen and this young off-world archaeologist that Corelli had learned was a 'friend' of Gloria Henderson? Was there a link with *Rios*, the moon of *Affebiar IV* that Corelli had somehow become convinced held the key to the stunning capabilities of Gloria Henderson – and, more bizarre, were there yet more tentacle links to the mutinous Miranda Svedberg and the missing Cova survey ship *Dros?*

Johnson could not believe his unbelievable luck. He once more sat in contemplative silence on the pilot bridge of the half-repaired *Cobra*. The vessel was still a complete disaster, there was no way of hiding the immense destruction *Cobra* had suffered. The bridge deck shimmered in deep atmospheric cold, forward vis-probes only marginal in revealing the fast-approaching moon that had taken *Cobra* close to two Earth months to reach. The android crew busied themselves preparing for a low orbit atmospheric entry.

"What do you know about this moon *Rios*?" quizzed Commander Obera.

Johnson shivered inside his fleece-lined protective coverall then stared back at Obera, they had not interacted that well since he came aboard, the commander seemed distant, lost in his deep world. Johnson revered the commanders of all exploration and survey ships, it was his lifetime dream to be one of the intrepid crews that flew them - and right now he sat alongside one of the best, the legendary Obera onboard the same *Cobra* that suffered the first extraterrestrial confrontation in human history. Or was it? Johnson, in his inimitable way, spent the long days in his private quarters thinking, working out the insignificant clues that more often than not lead up blind alleys - there were riddles deep down that just didn't add up. In the back of his mind, Johnson knew he was *being manipulated*, that he was an intrinsic part of some toxic confrontation he couldn't yet fathom. On top of all this, he realised Obera wasn't telling him everything.

"I know that rock samples I was given to analyse came from *Rios*," replied Johnson. "The task I was given seemed straightforward. Routine. But then I found something strange in my pocket that changed things." Johnson decided that at this moment in time, something needed to happen, this strained atmosphere of high tension between himself and Commander Obera should change, it was the right time to ferret into the revered commander's inner sanctum. Obera was as much involved in this incomprehensible mystery as he himself, this mind-bending confrontation that seemed to be well beyond any human understanding. It was just a pent-up hunch that Johnson felt inside.

"Oh? What was it you found?" responded Obera with more than a puzzled glance at Johnson.

Johnson was unsure if he should proceed further. Obera was a forthright character whom Johnson found hard to read, the commander was a tough cookie, but this in itself did not fool Johnson. Obera was intelligent and clever, he did not suffer fools - but Johnson, being Johnson, saw something else. There were deep hidden facets to Obera that intrigued him, small insignificant mannerisms that were strange and familiar. The commander was *keeping something back*, something to himself that was vital to this crazy wayward mission to *Rios*. But it was something else, the little clues – for example, Johnson saw that every day at breakfast Obera ate his food right-handed, but during the evening suppertime, he was left-handed. Strange and inconsequential, but it niggled Johnson, nevertheless. It was as if he was related in some way to Gloria Henderson...

The reverberating thought in Johnson's mind was whether to reveal to Obera the whitestone vis he still held in his possession. While Johnson pondered his options, waves of doubt flooded his conscious self, he felt the super smooth surface of the stone vis still hiding there in his pocket. It never left his side. But Johnson had made his move, Obera's eyes riveted into him in the way that Obera glared at those who knew something that he did not – because Obera knew it was related to where they were heading.

Johnson took the vis from his pocket. He held it in his open hand, seeing the commander freeze in abject shock. Johnson's back-of-the-mind hunch had been right.

"Who gave you that?" demanded Obera, who then paused, trying to regain his composure. "How did you come by that?"

"Like I said, I found it in my pocket."

"Oh yeah? It just appeared? In your pocket? Just like nothin' at all? Look, don't you fool with me Johnson," barked Obera. "Where did you get that?"

"Am I to assume, commander, that you know what this thing is?" Johnson responded with grim certainty. Obera became alert - silent. The cold freeze-dried air of *Cobra's* bridge added to the chilled atmosphere that lingered like unbroken icicles between them.

"Describe to me the woman who gave you this," demanded Obera after a long deliberating pause. He was forthright but not threatening. The mystery in his confused eyes deepened.

Johnson thought hard. How could he describe someone whom he had seen once in an elevator - and then by traumatic crackling vis-links? In fact, Johnson found it hard to recollect her physical image in his mind.

"She often tosses her hair from her eyes, a mannerism that is strange in some sort of way that is difficult to describe to you," said Johnson. "Grey eyes. She has grey eyes. Ice-grey eyes with a hint of blueness that I think you might know well commander." He probed, he needed to know where the icy boundary between himself and Obera was. The boundary then crumbled.

Commander Obera released an involuntary sigh. His incredulous dealings with the same young woman was his unwholesome clandestine secret that he revealed to no one, he had vowed never to tell a soul how she alone turned his life inside out each time she made contact with him.

"Do you know what Johnson, I'm flying this patched-up piece of junk to a moon that you know everything about," Obera's voice was tinged with exasperation. "I was given coordinates of where to meet your shuttle by the same woman you describe. I have no idea why I'm flying this damn ship manned by a bunch of half-human androids to *Rios*, just that I have to take *you* there. Perhaps *you* will give me the *courtesy* of telling me *why* before I turn this wreck around."

"I don't know why commander," said Johnson, "I'm like you. I have been thrown headlong into this whole affair that I'm told threatens the whole human race, and I don't even know the reason." Johnson paused exasperated. "Tell me, how did you know about me, what else do you know about me?"

"I know nothin' about you," Obera replied. "But I'll tell you this. Two years ago, I found the same stone-vis thing that you have inside my bag. I don't know how it got there. That thing took me on a wild chase into the *Mu Arae* system with my goddamned ship, there we were almost annihilated by two goddammed fuckin' alien monster orbitals guarding a moon not unlike the one we are approaching fast as we speak. *Cobra* was *that* close to being destroyed, I lost lots of good men, god knows why those iron monsters didn't finish us," said Obera, "I'm now doing the exact same thing again. I must be some form of lunatic; I must be a stupid goddamned idiot. But you know what? Something happened to my men and my ship that I'm gonna get to the bottom of. And there's no way anyone is gonna get in my way."

Johnson deliberated, choosing his words. "Did you go to the *Mu Arae* system to locate the fabled planet of riches? Or did you go there to find what happened to the Cova exploration ship *Dros*?" Johnson had worked out that Obera in some way knew the woman in the elevator, though he was shocked to learn the commander possessed the same stone-vis communicator that he did. Then, to Johnson, it all began to add up.

Obera did not answer, he was silent, Johnson could tell he was thinking to himself hard and fast.

"Commander, did you know Gloria Henderson?"

"No, Johnson, I did not know Gloria Henderson, but I know who she was. How do *you* know Gloria Henderson?"

Johnson, at great length, told Obera about Gloria Henderson. With the hidden barrier between himself and Obera now splintered forever, Johnson described his strange relationship with Gloria, how he believed that Gloria had cultivated their friendship for her own insane reasons. Johnson recounted his contrived meeting with the young woman in the elevator, about their mind-churning vis-stream conversation. He revealed how he learned that he was being tracked by Corelli, he told Obera about his skyjacked DNA probe, the vis-streamed images of the stone obelisk on the moon *Rios*, he confirmed that Gloria Henderson was now dead.

Obera listened with fascinating dread, realising why the mysterious wife of Darius Henderson was at the centre of pretty much the whole damned mess - she was the one who had sent the golden jewel exoplanet location coordinates for the *Mu Arae* system. But then, who was the young woman that Johnson described in the elevator? Without doubt, she was the same woman who exploited his whole being, who twisted then turned him around her little finger like the ancient siren of sober annihilation - the same woman who came to him in the quarantine station on Mars, her who had somehow silenced both guards. Miranda Svedberg? That damned woman Svedberg. Who the hell was *she*, what in heavens' name had happened to *her*? Then, to Commander Obera, the penny from nowhere dropped.

"Do you know something Commander?" continued Johnson, he leaned back uneasy in his leather-bound crew chair that provided him with an element of comforting warmth, he saw the magnificent moon *Rios* grow in size on the huge vis-screen in front of him. *Cobra* now approached her high orbit trajectory guided expertly by *Cobra's* android pilots. "You know, they both have those weird grey-blue eyes."

Obera listened thoughtfully but said nothing. He picked up his fork to finish the near-frozen leftover food that had congealed cold and unappealing on his stark stainless steel plate. Johnson noted straightaway that Obera held the metal fork in his left hand. Obera looked up from his food with hard-won acknowledgement, an appreciation induced when realisation strikes from somewhere unknown. Svedberg, Miranda Svedberg, the born heir and daughter of Gloria Henderson, the one who tossed her hair from her eyes without realising she would flip your heart inside out...

2

Ten days before Easter the elm tree fell and hit the church. The stained glass window shattered when lightening danced along the pulpit perch. Christ's crucifixion lay broken, a large bloodstain in the dirt. The congregation, they came and gathered fearing it would delay the second coming of the Lord. They raised their hands to praise their God it did not fall on Friday, when the devoted would be hurt.

Come Sunday the faithful, they knelt like children to beg and pray, in their innocence to forgive. The preacher, he screamed, "The Lord is displeased, His resurrection will not come this day." With grey faces, they took donations whilst locked behind the door – and resolved to seek the same man who had made the glass before.

On Monday they discovered the man who had built the glass was the one man who could, but with sadness he was dead. His son, who was ninety, said he could resurrect the tools to reclaim the window for the preacher to break his daily bread. The congregation, they argued, the wise ones they rejoiced – on one hand they had a solution but on the other, they had no choice.

On Tuesday they gave the old man their blessing, he offered them his withered hand for them to shake. They gave him all the coins they had collected on their shining silver plate. They gave him everything they had raised for every daily toil; they gave him all they were ever going to take. Then the congregation, they were thankful the glass would soon be there, with Him in his glory, His blessed resurrection once more laid bare.

By Wednesday the preacher went to see the old man at supper time, he found neither hide nor hair. The old man, he had gone, leaving nothing left behind, *not an inch or ounce to show how much he cared – except a scribbled note to say he could not make the new glass there. The preacher, he cursed the Lord in such a way that even the devil turned to stare.*

Thursday brought the watchful angel from deep within her lair. She saw a way to make mankind pay while He rode through on sunshine and prayer. She bid the old man to make the glass in a crooked way that would make everyone stand and stare. The old man and the angel, they worked until their hands were bloodied, skinned and painful knuckle bare.

On Friday the glass was made then mounted in the broken church perfect and in place. The angel, she covered it with a ragged cloth so that no one would see the danger that every man who was ever born now faced. Then the congregation with the preacher came, eager with joy and tearful tears. They came to forever claim His beholding love and grace. The old man, he pulled away the cloth then turned to see the preacher's face.

Christ's resurrection, well, it was not there. The glass was mainly plain but not quite almost clear. The cross, it stood in the exact same place, but in an unforgiving way never to be praised. The preacher, he cried falling to his knees to pray. The congregation, they saw the beholding scene, the most perfect cross yet raised. The old man, he smiled and stood with crooked pride, the glass pitiful and glazed.

The glass was rough and bent, like the hand of man set against the ancient hands of time. There were bloodstains in the red and teardrops in the blue. The old man, he cried and said, "The glass, it may not be the best, but it is the best that I can do". The congregation fell silent and shivered like the dying born again. In every glass was the joy of man in pain. There was every fearful smile, every joyful tear; there was every lie that man ever preached to hide the truth with fear.

Then sunshine broke through the glass at the time the angel came, her bloodless hands scarred by the twisted nail that never was to blame. She rode through the church in glorious prayer and with their shameful shame. The angel, she removed her veil with a weary smile to reveal her tears that would forever be the same.

In Christ's place within the glass stood a naked woman's form, a maiden fixed upon the cross with bloodied hands, each pierced by a crooked nail. The congregation, they fell upon their knees and cried, "Let Her come to teach our sins, then preach Her prayers in Her glorious name in a way we will not fail."

The vengeful preacher, he turned to them and screamed, "Lord, please, you must hear my prayer, we repent and plead that men shall never be to blame." Then, with a tearful hateful voice he faced the old man who stood sniggering beside, "Are you the devil? Are you the devil who demands we beseech His name?"

Walter McPherson

"**S**o, what's your bad luck story, stranger?" McPherson glared at the man in the bedraggled coat held closed by a twisted string of dried leather - the decrepit belt of hide might once have been a fashion statement back in the good times.

The stranger stared across McPherson's kindling fire, not saying a word. He looked nervous with his over-bulging eyes. The man had appeared from nowhere, from behind McPherson's wagon making McPherson jump in alarm. Both men sat there in uneasy silence.

"You just gonna sit around another man's fire an' not say a goddamned word?" quizzed McPherson. The stranger offered nothing back. McPherson turned away; it did not occur to him to interrogate the man further - if a man did not want to talk then this was fine by him. Instead, McPherson lost in his thoughts, eyed the sun going down behind the low brown hills - for the first time in a long time he felt upbeat, almost glad to be alive. Looking at the stranger across the fire, McPherson did not expect any measure of friendship.

In the fading light, McPherson turned to inspect his two ponies, they grazed without much fervour on the stubby dry grass, grass that was withered a dull brown from the lack of rain. His rundown wagon stood under the broad shelter of the clump of trees, shaded and cool in the evening haze. McPherson decided to ignore the dishevelled stranger - he needed to count his days takings which he knew before he even started to unfold the muslin bag were meagre and threadbare. Maybe just enough to survive. McPherson took a sip of coffee heated from the paltry flames, he paused, then passed the steaming mug over the fire to the stranger who took it from him in eager gratitude.

"I used to be a banker," croaked the stranger without warning, at the same time watching McPherson count his takings while warming his hands around the hot mug - the stranger eyed the seventy cents McPherson had made from his days' work.

Walter looked up but made no reply. He understood the thieving look in the man's eyes, but McPherson did not want it to be the opening of an in-depth conversation because he did not want to pry. While he sipped the cooling coffee the stranger quipped meaningless snippets - even when McPherson made it plain, he had no real interest. It wasn't the banker's fault... it wouldn't take long... soon it would be like before, it was all temporary... McPherson half listened, he had heard the tale many times - everyone nowadays had the same story to tell, the same excuse of day-to-day survival and hardship. Trying to make your way in these troubled times was a life-threatening struggle, a thin line between starving or managing to maybe stay alive.

On days like today, McPherson considered himself lucky, he had made enough to get through one more day; dry oats would feed his ponies, he had enough beans to make himself two more meagre meals of brown rice. Just a few hours earlier he had been given, with grace or favour, a small bag of coffee by the old counter lady in the tumbled-down Big Barn store, McPherson felt good about this, for a moment he thought about sharing both the rice and coffee with the stranger who seemed in some ways more desperate than himself. A broken banker was of no use to anyone; at least, McPherson thought to himself, he could use his hands, he could mend things, make things work, he could go from house to house fixing whatever he was given to fix. Without much prospects of further talk between them, McPherson showed the dishevelled banker where he could sleep under the wagon.

"Best be gone by mornin' time," growled McPherson with a thin veil of unease, "I got nothin' I'm gonna share." There was no rice or oats to spare in his wagon - though there were a few ounces of beans and a half loaf of stale bread. McPherson was no charity. Tired and weary, McPherson rolled out his blanket next to the remnants of his fading fire - it would be some time before he would find anything like deep sleep.

Darkness cast shadows of bleak subterfuge; McPherson lost a little of his newfound exuberance from being paid in coffee for his work - he knew the nighttime bogeyman would soon come. The gentle snoring of the stranger did little to reassure him, the uncertain company of another man would not change the darkness of the dark hours that forever plagued Walter McPherson. All his mind-wrenching problems would return during the long night - with the constant niggle of destitute survival once more burrowing through his mind like a smack-blind worm. When the last remnant rays of the deep orange sun set below the shimmering horizon McPherson shivered, feeling the first pangs of his familiar despondency. His ponies were starving, they were old, the threadbare earnings as Mr Fix-It, the odd job man, just fed him - during the long, hard nights he was all the time hungry, even in the moderate warmth he was cold. Each new day he in some way made enough to survive. Some days, like today, older folk gave him coffee beans in extra appreciation of his gifted skills – or because they had no bucks to spare. McPherson felt proud, to his continual pride he was reliable, he was honest – McPherson knew he could fix pretty much anything.

The Great Depression. Everyone was calling it this now. Countless thousands were homeless, drifting around in poverty and grime, farmsteads abandoned – but at least the so-called rich were suffering alongside everyone else. The unknown bedraggled stranger who slept under McPherson's wagon - it turned out, that just a couple of years before, he was a big city New York investment banker, or so he said. Now he was a vagrant drifter. McPherson did not ask what went wrong – and the banker never ventured to explain. That's the way it was nowadays, everyone had their own story which more often than not they kept to themselves.

During the long night McPherson, with his euphoria over the coffee spent, twice had to raise himself from his weary slumber. His ponies were not well, they suffered bad from the biting insects buzzing around their protruding veins. Their thin legs ached because of worn hooves, McPherson did not make enough money for the new shoes his decrepit ponies needed. Under his pillow he had a couple of bucks, this would be enough to see him through the next few days. *The bogeyman wouldn't be so bad tonight*, he thought.

Like the broken bankrupt banker, McPherson had known happier times, faded memories of his childhood though he would never remember his mother or father. His days in the orphanages were tolerable because of friends, good friends, friends who understood the wretched orphanage nightmares - sleep without sleep, life-lasting visions of meaningless violence, the belittling abuse, more so during the long nights that still played upon McPherson's broken mind like drifting ghosts that twisted his mentality inside out. McPherson still hated the sight of any preacher or, the worst kind, catholic priests with the slightest resemblance to the proverbial monster, Father McCarthy who stalked shadowy corridors like a predator preying mantis. These days McPherson managed to suppress his hot sweats, his anger whenever he found cause to talk the meaningless talk with a righteous minister of the church. *Most of them were ok*, he told himself - still, there were those who... but once he had learned to suppress his resentment, to look after himself, then the faded memories of the dark hours receded – except for the dreaded bogeyman who came in the middle of the night. Nearly every night. Every homeless kid who found themself in the orphanage learned the hard way - days and nights merged, the priests, but the young McPherson had made kinships. *Friends who cared, friends who looked out for each other.* The friendships made the bad times good, the nightmares go away.

After he left the Cleveland Saint Catherine Orphanage at the age of twelve (it may have been thirteen, no one was quite sure how old young McPherson was) he had gotten a job in the huge tram workshops in San Francisco... and he learned. McPherson learned fast. Every tram grease monkey said the same - this young kid seemed to be able to fix just about everything. Anything he put his hands to.

In time, young McPherson made himself indispensable in the workshops.

His uncanny skills, his ability to work quick for long hours soon endeared him to the men in charge of the machines, men who each saw a way for themselves to make a quick buck. The foremen, the managers, they brought stuff from outside for McPherson to fix because, no matter if it was mechanical, electric wiring or whatever, McPherson would fix it. If McPherson had never seen the thing before or even knew how it ticked, he would know how to repair it, he would make it work. So, Walter McPherson started to make some money for himself, he began to creep ahead.

In time he began to love women. McPherson's long downbeat nose, broken more than a few times as a kid, was fixed to his thin-set head that did not combine well with his general features or his thinning hair, so McPherson was not a handsome young man by any stretch of a woman's imagination. The women, well they weren't attracted by his good looks - or his charm for that matter. He did not have much of either - just the gruff attitude, the absent-mindedness of an ex-orphan interested in the workings and wirings of some dirt-ridden part lying broken apart on the bench. The dime women McPherson attracted were the type who learned they could take his money, to fizzle it without McPherson knowing where it had gone. They seemed to be able to prize his bucks away from him because McPherson fell in love much too easy. After the orphanage, he craved love. His generosity, which was his perpetual undoing, ensured it did not take long for his fragile love tangles to break up in acrimony when his meagre money soon ran out.

That's why his marriage to sixteen-year-old Honey lasted just a couple of miserable months. She disappeared one night, sending a single telegram to say she wasn't coming home. *He had been hurt by that...* and McPherson joined the Navy to forget Honey as much as anything.

McPherson learned much more about anything mechanical or with electrical wiring while he was enlisted in the Navy Engineers. For the first time in his life, McPherson was in his euphoric element, even more so when the obvious skills he possessed gave him what the Navy was desperate to find. McPherson rose fast, often on the back of his superior officers who saw they could make illicit money from the rusty broken appliances that McPherson could fix - just like being in the tram workshops. Soon, McPherson was given his own small workshop which he ran with pride and precision. He didn't need to fight on the big grey warships because his place was in the large bases onshore, mending and fixing. *"I kept my bit of the navy going,"* McPherson would describe his role with pride after the brief period America fought at the end of the Great War. *But there was always trouble,* jealousy... and of course, McPherson always saw how the Navy did things wrong.

This, more than anything, led to the extraordinary, mysterious incident of the shell-damaged rangefinder that... well, McPherson not only repaired the big steel box bought into his workshop, he made some strange improvements. Not just mending the big cumbersome contraption with its viewfinder but *improving* it in his unique way. McPherson added wiring, he introduced an electric current into the mechanical calculator, why not make it faster and more accurate, he could do it easy. McPherson made the modification without even a hint of authorisation, nor did McPherson follow standard naval procedures for getting these things approved. The chief gunnery officer onboard the warship *Mississippi* died. Not from electrocution or anything like that - the man just went insane, losing his mind. Screaming in abject terror. They said the usual calm officer ran then jumped overboard, before anyone could hold him back.

The incident was investigated by the Navy. The final report was buried deep in Navy archives. The Ford Mark 1 Rangefinder, as it became known after necessary safety adaptations, was made the standard naval gun range calculator onboard all warships. It was named after McPherson's commanding officer; it was even sold for big profit to other navies after the war finished in 1918. The stolen credit didn't bother McPherson, he made a much smaller copy of his original, McPherson made more adaptations, he *knew* what it could do. He would smile, knowing. Through his version of the rangefinder, he could spy Honey - and the priest she took as her one-night lover before she killed him with his own gun. McPherson never told anyone about that.

Admiral Ford made sure McPherson never received the credit for his invention. Ford followed orders from high up, McPherson was out of the navy, a trumped-up court-marshal charge, a theft he didn't commit, an offence he never had any knowledge of. Ford rose to become the renowned naval tactical commander, serving in the Pacific while McPherson himself disappeared into obscure oblivion during the Great Depression. That's what they all called it now.

Walter McPherson shuffled and groaned as he tried to sleep beside his ramshackle wagon. Worst of all it began to drizzle rain, the first time for many weeks in this dust-bowl landscape. The ponies were restless, their aching bones were decaying with age while they struggled to find warmth within their thin, almost skeletal bodies. McPherson himself dreamed bad dreams, he constantly woke - the bogeyman coming and going through his minced-up mind. In his dreams, McPherson screamed in agony each night in Honey's arms when she tried to protect him from the dark shadows trying to hurt him. There wasn't a time when Honey did not witness McPherson's fearful nighttime wounds when priests in the orphanage came to drag him from his wretched bed, the anal abuse, the rough-skinned hands... sometimes more than once during a single night, the persistent hours that did not end.

The morning came when the sunken sun began to lighten up the sky, dawn descended like a silent monster even before the strands of daylight appeared over the horizon. True sunrise would come later but to McPherson, the day had begun. He rose in weary restless slumber, stretching his back to shake off the stiffness of his uncomfortable night's sleep. He went first to tend to his treasured ponies. Rummaging around the wagon he found the near-empty bag, he offered both animals the few oats he had left in the battered tin bucket. Then he checked under the wagon for the stranger, he was gone. McPherson felt a pang of regret, a feeling of detached concern.

Then McPherson made sure his ponies had fresh clean water before he fixed his meagre breakfast. With care, he led both ponies down to the near-dried creek which held new formed puddles from the scant nighttime rain.

For McPherson, breakfast was the same oats he gave the ponies but mixed with a small amount of powdered milk he was given the day before - he kept back his dry crust bread, his last rice, the beans, to make sure he had one meal if things turned bad. He had fixed the store's porch screen then found the woman had no bucks to spare, just the powdered milk plus, of course, the treasured coffee he had drunk the night before. McPherson was grateful, if he had no milk then it would be muddy water for the oats like his ponies. *But somehow, he always got coffee.* It seemed much easier to bargain for meagre supplies of beans by fixing some farmyard contraption buried way back in a barn, often a forgotten piece of rusting machinery rummaged out by a farmer trying to scratch his living from the dry, wind-soiled land that these days was the ravaged grain yard of America.

When McPherson did have coffee or, more often, dried oats or plain old white beans, he always offered them with generosity if he happened across other Fix-It travellers trying to get themselves by. In many ways, McPherson seemed to fare better than others because more often than not he left the poor farmer scratching his head in wonderment and appreciation. So, McPherson had a deserved reputation, he was known for being able to fix pretty much anything, folk would wait for him to happen by. But they had not much themselves to give because of the so-called Great Depression... the phenomenon the newspapers were calling the soul-breaking humanitarian disaster gripping the vast central belt of Oklahoma. The collapsing world of the rich and their perpetual greed for wealth had ruined everything.

Today, McPherson thought to himself, he would once more try the road south towards the small dusty town of Bald Rock. His thin bony body loosened up as he dug out the firewood from his waggon to make fire to warm his milk and oats. The coffee pot took an age to boil the muddy water, then the pot erupted like a miniature bubbling fountain while he sat watching the few flickering flames with threadbare heat. *The coffee was gone.* When he came to add the beans to the boiling water there was no coffee, the small grey sack was missing. The banker – he must have stolen the bag. McPherson was fearful, he contemplated what the new day would bring.

McPherson knew the bucket containing his supply of oats was running dry, he fought back the familiar feelings of black depression that began to engulf him - it was a new day - he forced positive thoughts into his mind. For some indistinct reason, he had woken with strange feelings of optimism, something he had not felt first thing in the morning for a long time. He figured he had worked Bald Rock a few weeks before, he had done okay, so maybe he could make a few more bucks or just work for some food. His team was hungry, McPherson knew that he was beginning to starve. *Something sure needs to happen today*, he told himself - today he felt something inside, a feeling he couldn't pin down, a niggling thought that today might be the day that changed his life.

He harnessed his weary team in the gathering heat of the early morning sun then set off down the gritty road that was still muddy from the overnight rain. Little puddles of grimy water held up his ponies as they furrowed their noses into the dirt-ridden water for anything that might be lurking they might eat. The first farmstead he came across he stopped to fix the transmission drive on the farmer's decrepit model-T Ford. It was rusting away like everything else on the ramshackle farm. The rough-timbered farmhouse and neglected outbuildings were just about falling apart.

"Hi Walt, got somethin' f' y'all that needs fixin' good," said Jake, the wily old farmer who was waiting for the time when McPherson might happen by.

"Is it that wreck of a T Ford o' yours Jake?"

"Sure is. It's a while since y'all las' came by Walt. That there transmission's gone bust this time, but that engin' y'all fixed afore's sure runnin' fine. I can't pay yuh nothin' though Walt, tho' I can sure feed them ponies."

McPherson fixed the transmission, he saw straightaway the drive gear needed adjusting, a job he had done umpteen times before, so McPherson knew the fix well. It did not take long - McPherson got himself some home-baked rye bread and more precious oats for his ponies. He ate some of the oats himself, careful to hide his hunger from Jake to save his pride before setting off once more down the stony road with his restless ponies - a little more willing to do his bidding.

A couple of miles further down the road McPherson slowed his waggon. He was puzzled. He had passed this way before a couple of times, McPherson possessed an uncanny memory whenever it came to being on the road, his mind was tuned to the geographical terrain - wherever he might make some money. Never before had he noticed the rundown house to his right, behind the willow trees hanging by the little dried creek that crept its way towards the road. McPherson pulled up his team to take a look. He saw the building had seen better days, with a decrepit white picket fence that was just standing in places. McPherson's studious face broke with signs of hope. '*That fence could sure do with fixing,*' he thought to himself. But why had he not noticed this place before?

The path to the house wound itself around the trees from the road, leading to the broken, wide five-bar gate. It did not open like it should, McPherson pushed hard, it seemed to him that it had not been opened for a while. He continued up to the porch, then opened the rusting, out-of-shape insect screen which McPherson could see was crusted with years of dead flies. He knocked hard on the door. McPherson waited, feeling impatient, he looked around, he saw there were not the usual signs of anyone living there, no dirty laundry hanging out, no rubbish on the front porch or any sign of kid's kick-around stuff in the yard. But then McPherson heard footsteps nearing the door on the inside. Someone *was* home.

The door opened halfway. The young woman stared back at him through the gap. McPherson was for one moment taken aback then recovered his wits. He was struck by the woman's bedraggled white-blond hair tied in a fashion he had not seen before. Her face was grimy, the unkempt look of abject poverty, she was beautiful in a distinct innocent way. *But it was her eyes...* the way she looked at him. After a few moments, during which she said nothing, McPherson came to his senses, dropping into his familiar drawl.

"G'mornin' M'am, my name's Walter, Walter McPherson an' I fix things." She stared back, studying his ragged form, his young middle year's withered face. With no immediate response from her, McPherson kept talking, he needed to keep the conversation going, "Don't you worry M'am, I'm good," he tried to reassure her. "That there fence sure needs fixin'," he continued, thinking quick on his feet. She waited a moment, looked at the fence then at McPherson, before replying in a kind of deep south accent he had not heard in a long time. Not since his days in the navy had he heard a southerner talk like this.

"That fence is look'n fine t' me mister," she drawled. "It's bin standin' a good few years an' it'll stand for a hundred more I reckons." She stood with a show of defiance, blocking the door.

"Well, that gate's not good either M'am," McPherson replied, his feeling of hope fast disappearing, "I could fix both for a couple a bucks an' I'd b' happy to oblige."

"As I told yuh, that there fence an' gate look swell from where I'm standin'," she replied, "an' I ain't got two bucks anyhow. Not that I can spare yuh."

"Well, truth is M'am, me an' my ponies right there are real hungry, I sure need to fix somethin' real soon," McPherson played his sympathy card, which often got him something. "Maybe you got some oats or a little sugar?" He sensed this was his last throw of the dice before moving on. "I'd be happy t' take my payment that way M'am." McPherson couldn't take his gaze away from her blue-grey eyes, he saw they were more of a *soft grey*, an icy grey, but she did not look for one moment interested in his proposal, neither did she look at him direct. For some reason, McPherson sensed something strange, something different about the young woman half hidden behind the door.

"Nope, no food in this house mister," she responded. "Nothin' to fix neither unless yuh'll work fo' nothin."

McPherson thought and pondered; he was often faced with this dilemma. Folk just did not have much to spare around these parts. He was about to refuse, he needed to move on to make some bucks somewhere down the road if he got no success here. "Don't know 'bout that M'am, I gotta get me an' my ponies some food," he paused, hoping the woman would change her mind. Then he had a hunch. "What you got that needs lookin' at M'am that I gotta work fo' nothin?"

The woman at the door stood in silence for a moment, McPherson sensed she was weighing him up, studying him just like new folk did when he knocked on their door for the first time. Some folks knew him well, he knew how to cultivate their friendships. But every once in a while, he would come across some new downturned homesteader, and it took time. Time to gain their trust until he knew them well enough. Then he would get the easy talk going, they'd be his friend. Of course, he would then call again anytime, they'd keep things aside for him to fix. That's how McPherson and his ponies survived. He was reliable, *he was good.*

"Wait," was all she said, she disappeared inside. A few minutes later she came back to the door, then out onto the front porch, leaving the door half open behind. Inside McPherson could see the house was empty, *there was nothing inside.* She held a small white stone object in her hand, it did not look anything familiar to him. She stopped at the porch table then placed it down. "Yuh can fix this if yuh like, but yuh ain't gettin' nothin f' fixin' it mister."

McPherson picked it up from the table, examining the object in his hands. He could not even identify what it was she was asking him to fix. He saw it was about three inches long, an inch thick by about an inch wide, it was made from some stone marble he had never come across before. It was just a solid object, with no screws or bolts, the surface plain white. Not even painted white, the thing itself was pure white. Clean white. McPherson was puzzled for the second time during the morning. Behind him, down on the dusty driveway, his ponies whinnied with impatience.

"What is it M'am?" he asked, "I can't figure this out," McPherson studied her expressionless face. He began to feel uneasy, realising he was in a strange situation he could not comprehend.

"Awe, it's jus' my finder," she replied in a resigned, uninterested manner. "It needs fixin' good tho, it's not worked in a while."

McPherson turned to look at the broken fence, the dilapidated gate, he felt exasperated, then he looked back to the beautiful young woman who, this time, stared straight back into his eyes. Her white-blond hair was untidy, her ragged appearance dressed in her torn dirty dress somehow, for some reason, did not fool him. There was something mesmerising about her demeanour, he was still transfixed by her piercing grey-blue eyes, the miniature cross around her neck. "Gimme somethin' t' go on Ma'am," he pleaded, "I ain't never heard o' nothin' called a finder before."

"If yuh ain't able t' fix it mister yuh just gotta say," she replied.

Because he struggled to think of anything more to say McPherson started to feel his way around the object in his hand.

"What's a finder M'am an' what's wrong with it?" he was beginning to feel something strange building inside him, his despondency lifted, pangs of another feeling filled his senses. McPherson stopped to think, struck by feelings he had not experienced in a long time, not since he loved Honey. He stared at the young woman in a kind of unfathomable disbelief. "What does it find?" he asked, pleading, despairing. For some reason, he thought to himself, he did not want to know the answer. He was losing heart, he needed to move on.

"Aw, well, it don't find *nothin'* mister," she said, as though revealing something simple that she wanted to keep to herself, "I'm lookin' for som'body an' it'll help me know where they'll be." For a brief moment, she seemed desperate.

McPherson's wily instincts told him this. His mind raced, he thought long and hard before he replied. "I can't fix this M'am, I'm sorry," he said, "I don't even know what it is an' how it works M'am. I ain't seen nothin' like this before." McPherson still held the object in his hand. He noticed it was growing warm, he looked, then he saw a soft green glow beginning to radiate from under its surface. He recovered his composure. McPherson turned to face her. "I gotta know what's wrong with this thing M'am?"

"It don't *find* nothin mister, like I said," she added nothing new, she leaned against the door post. She turned her face to look out over the bone-dry field of thin dusty soil, an ominous wind picked up, swirling a dust cloud that made McPherson's ponies stir and pull on their reigns. The breeze died away before it could build up, the dry heat of midday began to intensify, an ominous feeling in the air. McPherson caught the aroma of her warm unwashed sweat; his senses began to reel in turmoil. He tried hard to regain his control. What *was* it about her?

"M'am, I sure don't think I can fix this," said McPherson, his voice filled with suspicious caution, "an' I can't see how anythin' can just find somethin' or even any old somebody," his mind was racing, his rangefinder for the navy, his invention made in secret, it could find Honey... "Nothin' I know can do that M'am."

"How d'yuh know it can't find anythin' if it ain't showin' nothin' mister?" she spoke as if making her statement. *With sudden authority.* "Maybe my finder can just tell me anythin' I wanna know." She stared, challenging McPherson for the next move, she knew what he knew...

"But *nothin'* can do that M'am," McPherson huffed, then recovering quick. "An' I've seen a lotta strange contraptions in my time." He controlled himself to not snigger out loud, behind him his desperate ponies once more whined in hunger. The sweltering heat of the day began to make them restless, soon they would need water real bad.

"Are yuh gonna fix it, mister? Yuh Mr Fix-It ain't yuh?" It seemed to be her last ultimatum.

McPherson stared at the object, he touched it, caressed it, feeling for an opening lid or some hidden screws. There was nothing that he could find. McPherson's curiosity got the better of him, his instinct made him hold his forefinger down hard. Nothing happened for a few moments but for some reason deep within him he concentrated a little more. Then, the long right side of the strange object flipped open, followed in an instant by the top flat face. She watched him, seeming unconcerned. He looked inside, seeing strange unfamiliar circuits connected by miniature beams of light. McPherson knew in a fraction of a second that this was technology he had not seen before, he doubted anyone else had. His deft fingers moved inside the slim opening; he felt the pinpoint heat of the light beams against his fingertips. He sat down on the porch bench; his mind engrossed in the weird object before him on the bench top. At once he realised he needed to remove the top side for more access, then he began to move the light beams around, feeling and touching, sensing there was sometimes no rhythm in the light.

All this time, while McPherson was engrossed, she watched him without much curiosity, staring unconcerned, still leaning against the post of the half-open door.

A while later, McPherson looked up. The side of the object that was once in pieces on the table snapped shut of its own accord. He looked at it, the same low green glow returned. It seemed different, then a subtle colour change began to occur, gradual, starting from one end then moving to the other. As it did so McPherson realised he could see something, not inside the object but in his head. *A vision.* It was the same as before with his rangefinder invention, he could somehow see Honey but this time, for some reason, he could see inside her mind. He knew what Honey was thinking, he could read her thoughts. He turned, confused, to confront the woman standing by his side... *"Who are you?"* he demanded incredulous, this time without much of his stuttering.

"My name don't matter none, mister," she replied. "But folks, not from 'round here, they call me Moon."

She stared nonchalant at McPherson, then tossed her light blond hair from her eyes. Those eyes seemed an even deeper grey from which he couldn't avert his gaze - holding him in a fascinating trap like an animal being cornered within a steel-gated pen. Her face was grubby, toiled with the common dirt of poverty and daily survival suffering. Her clothes were unkempt, creased, stained; the soft skin of her face was unwrinkled, forever firm glistening in the shafts of sunlight that teased her out of the shadows. The growing afternoon heat, oppressive storm heat brought more beads of alluring sweat bursting to her brow. McPherson could see that she was beautiful, mesmerising in an exceptional captivating way, her unwashed aroma once more stole his masculine senses. But his fine-honed instincts cut right through her life of peasant poverty, the abject filth in which she thrived. Her deep country drawl did not fool McPherson.

"I didn't *ask* your *name* M'am," said McPherson, "I asked *who you are?"*

He probed, trying to escape from her spell, endeavouring to corner her in his effort to understand this insane situation.

"Well, yuh can't know who I am mister if yuh don't know my name," she replied but her manner changed; her eyes darted with a flicker of authority. She stood up from the post on which she was leaning, her slim virile figure not lost upon McPherson, he could see that her body was unravaged by hunger. She moved to take control, to transfix him in a way that demanded his utter surrender, knowing that she held him engrossed.

"What is this thing you've given me t' fix an' *who are you?*" he pressed his incredulous curiosity. McPherson was falling, he needed to know answers. He sensed the familiar panic deep inside him, the feeling of foreboding doom when he knew his life would twist and turn outside of his control, when he had fallen headlong into a new situation that would, in the end, turn out bad. Life was never straightforward for McPherson.

"As I said, mister, I'm called Moon," she looked him square in the eyes, showing a determination of her own for the first time. McPherson didn't respond, he waited, *sensing she had much more to say.* "An' if yuh reckons yuh fixed my finder then I reckons yuh can help me some more."

"I didn't come by here by accident did I M'am," McPherson replied from somewhere deep inside. "You were here waitin' for me. An' this house, I don't remember it here last time I came by, I sure know that." She didn't answer. "What makes you think I'm gonna help you?" McPherson laughed out loud.

"Coz, I know these things, mister," she replied, "an' yuh got a strange imagination," she added. "This house's bin standin' here a long time before yuh ever came by."

McPherson hesitated in thought for a few moments. Maybe he was going crazy. He figured the ramshackle house *must* have been here all along - but something had made him notice it today of all days. Why was today different? He paused... "If you know things Ma'am then tell me what the hell I'm doing here."

"Yuh fixed my finder an' I reckons yuh can fix things real good," she answered. "An' I know yuh see things, Walter," she used McPherson's name for the first time.

"How do you know that?" McPherson responded, *stunned*. He reeled, desperate to figure out yet another strange twist. McPherson felt himself on the edge of despair. What the hell had he gotten himself into? He had woken earlier in the morning full of optimism mixed with unfathomable foreboding for some reason; his senses told him this woman Moon was the ultimate cause of his unease, he had been lured, somehow manoeuvred, caught in a trap then pulled in to fix the weirdest thing he had seen in his whole life, something that should not exist in his world. But he had fixed it. He had sensed its workings, he had felt the minute light beams against his fingertips, McPherson then realised how the thing had in some way tuned his mind. He looked at her with tears filling his eyes, frustrated tears in his final moment of surrender, his emotional mentality beginning to collapse. "*What is it you want from me?*" he demanded in his desperate whispering voice, at this moment McPherson contemplated turning to run. He sensed his decrepit ponies down the path behind him, now for some reason silent, as if they recognised the moment of anticipation.

"Maybe yuh can help me," she replied with casual earnestness, "I wanna find some folks real bad an' like I say, yuh see things, Walter," she said, adding nothing more. No explanation. But there seemed to be a touch of emotion in her bland, detached voice. She did not need to explain.

McPherson's confused mind raced, he felt his long-forgotten sense of panic building inside his head. He needed to get away, he felt the desperate urge to leave, to extract himself from this strange woman's compelling grip; he didn't even begin to understand the weirdness of his situation, McPherson knew he was into something deep above his head - even though McPherson was no stranger himself to imaginary fortitude or strange inventions.

"Well M... M'am," he stuttered," I don't think I can help you. I sure need to be movin' on," he added, "I gotta earn some food or somethin' somewhere. Me an' my ponies need to eat," he paused, "I ain't got no time t' mess with this stuff M'am." He started to back away, back down the path towards the gate. She leaned with nonchalance against the veranda post, folded her arms, she watched him leave. Once more she seemed uncaring, unconcerned.

McPherson reached his wagon, hitched his ponies, he started down the rutted drive to the dusty road. He thought he would take one last look at the broken fence which he knew still needed repairing. McPherson turned to see the fence. He froze, stunned, it somehow seemed quite new, not long painted, not at all run down like he had seen before. In amazement, he turned to see the house.

She stood on the porch, like a ghost from someplace in the past. This time she was not the same. The dry hot breeze, from nowhere, blew harder, her unkempt hair swirled around her perfect face, hiding her eyes. She reached to toss it aside with an inconspicuous flick of her hand. Just then, McPherson thought he was going beyond crazy. The realisation flashed into his head, this weird insignificant mannerism with her hair, a tortured memory his twisted mind would hold forever. Appalled, McPherson remembered backwards in time - in those far-off days she did not call herself Moon. All those years ago, when he was a young kid, the woman who sometimes came to the orphanage... of course, it came back to him like a burning vision in a flash-pan fire, it was the same – perhaps, maybe, it was McCarthy and his sycophantic sweaty-fisted priests who this woman, for vengeance, needed to find.

Honey followed her intuition, she poked into her ragtag of a handbag to find her whitestone vis - it emitted no sound, but this time glowed with a greenish tinge. Tangled around the marbled stone device in a disorganised fashion were two fake gold chains upon which her remaining cheap Mary Magdalene pendants hung. Around her neck was her treasured cross of Eve.

Inside her handbag, there was more of the disorganised clutter that women need to get through their everyday lives. Her purse, her bulging purse, with the dollars she had just stolen from the man she had moments before strangled upon the unmade bed. He wanted sex but, as Honey knew, he was not prepared to pay, he had forced her back against the door making his intentions more than plain - his hand against her mouth, his other hand pressed hard between her legs. The ten bucks pilfered from his wallet would go a long way towards her next good feed, food her inward hunger told her she needed – though, even in her assassin form, she would never degenerate herself enough to consume meat, the usual sustenance means of the human race.

The bargain backstreet downtown hotel stank of dumped refuge through the half-open window, Honey faced the problem of the dead man's body and what to do. She made her way down the damp-ridden stairs to the lobby; the oversized black woman behind the grill-protected counter might be her one ally - or perhaps even her alibi.

"The room we paid yuh for," said Honey, "I reckon the man's dead."

"*What*," the woman exclaimed, the stunned shock in her expression was enough, it wasn't a question.

"He tried t' hurt an' force me, so I kill'd him. He's dead." Honey tried hard to show emotional concern though she found it tough. The woman pushed Honey aside before bounding up the stairs.

"I don't want no cops here gal, they nothin' but trouble," she blurted as she raced upwards towards the next floor landing. Honey ambled after her, the woman was in the room going through the dead man's pockets before Honey got there.

"So, what yuh dun t' him babe? He looks sleepin' an' all peaceful, yuh ain't knifed him," she rolled him over, the woman found some dollars in his back pocket - she pilfered then hid the money down inside her near to bursting brazier. She unfastened his cheap-looking watch, throwing it to one side across the ruffled bed. "What happened hon, he tried that rape? He beat yuh? He didn't wanna pay yuh?"

Rolling him without effort, the woman spied the purple-red bruises on his neck - thumbprint bruises, she saw that he had been strangled.

"Yuh necked him?" the woman exclaimed incredulous, the atmosphere in the room became electrified.

"Yup, I necked him. I could'na let him do that," said Honey, with no show of feeling or remorse. The woman stared, the man was well over six feet and heavy built, Honey was a skinny skimp of a woman, almost childlike, nearly all skin and bone. There followed a long disbelieving pause - outside the half-open window the subway train rumbled past at a squealing and thumping slow speed, shaking the decaying building to its damp foundations.

"How much yuh got fro' his wallet?" the woman saw it was empty, picking it up from the floor, she held it open to Honey in a gesture that made it plain she was in control, there was a hint of menace in her voice. "Like I tell yuh, I don't wan' no cops sniffin' round this place honeybun, they nothin' but trouble t' us niggers."

Honey made no answer, not straightaway. The cops would never believe her version of what happened; the hotel woman was struggling to comprehend the visual facts anyhow - no one of Honey's stature could strangle a man built so powerful unless he was drunk or something, but the woman had sussed alcohol not to be the case. He wasn't drunk, there was no smell of whiskey or anything.

"No cop's gonna believe was yuh that kill'd him, not if he was necked like yuh say. An' I can't see nothin' 'cept them two neck wounds, s' we gotta little problem here honey pie," the women glared into Honey's face, face up close. "Now I knows what yuh dun it for, I knows all 'bout that kinda shit gal, but yuh gotta see how the cops ain't gonna be concerned 'bout yuh, they gonna think it som'body else who did this dink in," she added. "They take one look at the size o' yuh, then they gonna think yuh just takin' the rap for som'body who ain't here."

"I'll give yuh five bucks, yuh get this guy outta here," said Honey. "That leaves me five bucks t' get me a couple of days feed an' some coffee."

The woman was silent, thinking. Then she spied the cheap-looking pendant cross that was strung around the guy's dick - there was more to this killing than was being made out. She decided to say nothing.

"So yuh got ten bucks outta 'is wallet, right?" it was obvious the woman was weighing over her options, the expression of calculation etched into her wrinkled brown skin brow. She thought over Honey's proposal, outside the greyness of the grey day threatened more incessant rain, the afternoon body-clinging humidity was building into the inevitable late evening thunderstorms. "G'me the five bucks, an' get yuh skinny ass outta here honeybun - an' don't yuh show that pretty little face o' yours 'ere no more." The woman smiled a half-respecting smile to one side of her scarred-lip mouth, the side with the three or four teeth without breaks that still showed - the rest knocked up by her own sufferance of mean, unsolicited male violence.

Honey, the assassin, left. She strode across the busy downtown street, meandering between the traffic in the drizzle, grey early evening rain. She half turned to check if she was followed, an instinctive self-preservation reaction now well rehearsed. Soon the cops would be on to her, she was sure of this - she was not yet ready for any stupid shoot-out. Five dead, two more before the debt was anywhere near paid.

Detective Agent Dermot O'Reilly was nonplussed, he was troubled in an uneasy sort of way. He knew he was being followed - why he could not even guess. In all his thirty-five years in the bureau, never had he cause to watch his back when going about his day-to-day crime investigating business – in fact, on lots of occasions, he had followed suspects himself in search of important incriminating evidence. He knew the ropes; he knew the routine - so it was easy for O'Reilly to spot the two rain-coated men who had been hanging on to his tail for over two weeks.

Spent tobacco smoke drifted into hazy thick layers in the noxious air of O'Reilly's unkempt office. When it rang, the telephone on the wall near his paper-stacked desk cut straight through his morning mood, until he had consumed more coffee he could not present himself to the world in anything like a measure of friendliness O'Reilly was rarely sociable par se. O'Reilly let the phone ring a few times, then walked over to pick it up; he listened without saying much before replacing the receiver hard down in thin disguised frustration. Another body - another suspicious death had been reported, this time beneath the rail culverts down on Southside. Bodies were found every day all over Chicago, but this time the regular uniformed cops had called O'Reilly for good reason - they figured the victim might be connected to the church.

Nothing fazed O'Reilly these days, he was hardened to the daily body counts these dire economic times threw up, as a serious crime agent in the Federal Bureau of Investigations he saw the raw side of perseverance needed to survive, the vicious remnants of wrecked lives woven throughout the crumbling grey city. O'Reilly's tough, streetwise demeanour had been honed and refined in Chicago's Cheapside slums; the near balding, rough-shaven detective found it simple to sink into the decadent way of life that drove everyday acts of utter desperation. Making his way down to the Southside, O'Reilly once more checked his rear mirror. This time, there were no signs of the two sidekicks on his tail – perhaps they weren't bothered about who had been killed, maybe they would make their regular appearance later when the cops were on the trail of a suspect who might be the killer. What the hell was their connection? Sure as hell, O'Reilly thought to himself, someone else was mighty interested in what was happening. The detective made a left turn onto Mulhouse Bridge leading to the miserable urbanisation of the south side. O'Reilly would soon find out who was tailing him – he had arranged for a uniformed intercept as soon as the two scumbags showed their slimy faces.

O'Reilly followed the overhead railway, then pulled over when he saw the cop cars parked beneath the furthermost culverts – above, the rattle of freight cars shook the arches that were depressing and damp from the incessant drizzle.

"You O'Reilly?" asked the cop, without showing much interest. One more dumped body was all in his day's work, he didn't care who investigated what - he was just following orders.

"Yeah," O'Reilly flipped his ID in front of the cop's eyes, who half glanced in a meaningless way to show how little he was impressed. Or cared. O'Reilly pulled up the collar of his raincoat to keep the fine rain from the back of his neck. It did not take long to spy the body disposed indifferently in the overgrown weeds, not well hidden, thrown down in a way that suggested to O'Reilly the man had not been killed in this location. Standing over the body was the guy from forensics, taking flash photos with not much enthusiasm in the drizzle-ridden morning air.

"What d'you know?" O'Reilly asked the cop; O'Reilly flipped his half-smoked cigarette onto the ground.

"Not much, it's all down t' you guys," the cop answered. "He was found by those vagrants there," the cop pointed to two homeless sleepers, prevented from leaving the scene by two more cops who made the vagrants sit handcuffed together in the litter and puddle-infested gravel. "They made a collect callback to the precinct, they asked if there was a reward for a dead priest."

O'Reilly glanced over, the two vagrants looked miserable, scared that they had made a bad mistake. O'Reilly doubted they had anything to do with the dead body - these lazy cops, they always went for the easiest suspect.

"They said there was nothin' last night. They were woken by noisy wheels; a car or truck of some sort stopped an' they found the body at first light. They've been through his wallet an' pockets though, they say they found nothin' on him."

"How do *they* know he's a priest?" O'Reilly queried - O'Reilly acknowledged the vagrants would take the opportunity to plunder the body, they would not hesitate to take anything of value – but why had they thought there might be some sort of reward? Why had they hung around?

The cop thought for a short moment, trying to recollect. "Yeah, one of em outright *said* they'd found a priest," he was unapologetic. "When they made the call to the station, we told em to hang around, there *might* be a reward... just a hunch, but it worked, they were still hanging around when we got here," he looked at O'Reilly expecting praise, though none came. "They said there's been newspaper talk of rewards."

O'Reilly winced. The erroneous rumours of rewards by the catholic church were not helpful. If the guy lying dead *was* a priest, then this one more made five, five, all catholics - there was a good reason why O'Reilly had been called in. Two in Chicago, then one each in Philadelphia, Boston and San Francisco.

There was a momentary silence. "Bring both these grimy gringos in, we'll find out what they know," ordered O'Reilly, knowing the cops here would resent the order from an opinionated Fed. O'Reilly turned to the forensic. "You fixed here? I want this guy whoever it is down to the morgue, we need to know who he was." O'Reilly walked with an uneasy gait to his car, this ongoing investigation was once more taking a bad turn.

O'Reilly made his way back towards downtown, first he needed to fix himself with coffee and a bite to eat, he knew where he wanted to go - he would wait till the cops had gotten the two vagrants down to the station then question them there in the precinct. Coffee would give him time to think. When he started his car, he without a second thought checked his mirror - there were still no signs of his tail. The half-hour drive took him onto 264th Street, there he turned the block at the lights then headed for Finnegan's. There was someone there who might know something, just an instinctive hunch - the word on the street while the murder was still hot; O'Reilly could get warm food, he needed to get the misty damp from further deteriorating his sombre mood.

The two dead from the previous year were known, they'd been identified from church docs on their bodies. There was still, as yet, no luck on the next two, just the same cheap lookalike Mary Magdalene pendants strung somewhat bizarre around their dicks – plus the standard letters of commendation written in Latin that priests always carried... with their crucial names cut away. The only speculative suspect O'Reilly had was the unidentified woman who had attended the burial of Father O'Hearn – she had spat into his grave when the first shovel of dirt was heaped in. O'Reilly could not find her name, a wall of silence, no doubt a pit of shame for some hidden reason that O'Reilly could not seem to break. Not yet, but he would, given time - if he had time.

Braden had been strangled, O'Hearn a bullet through his heart with his own silver Smith Wesson 38 he was known to carry – how was it a priest had reason to carry a gun? The other two, so far, both strangled, in the same way as Braden. O'Reilly would wait for the report on this latest one, to see if it *was* linked. O'Reilly sat himself on the barstool in the furthest corner of Finnegan's, he preferred to be away from prying eyes and listening ears. The bartender strode up, cleaning the already clean glass in his hand.

"Connor around?" O'Reilly asked.

"Sure, I'll find him. Yuh drinkin'?"

"Nah, I'm workin'," O'Reilly paused, undecided - he needed a clear head, coffee and some hot food - it wasn't even midday. "Nah," he changed his mind. "Get me'n Irish. Neat, with ice." He glanced down the counter to the corner of the long bar. O'Reilly drew his breath, he stared bug-eyed. He saw one of his unknown shadowers glaring at him from under his hat – same hat, same coat. O'Reilly emptied his whiskey in one gulp - they'd followed him when he didn't know he was being followed.

In the dim red light of the bar, O'Reilly gazed back. All pretence of hidden surveillance was gone, they'd made their move. O'Reilly waited. The sitting man was joined by the second man, who himself made eye contact direct with O'Reilly without any pretence of concealment. The sitting man then stood, both men made to leave the bar, the first man tipped his hat in O'Reilly's direction - a demonstrable acknowledgement to O'Reilly, a nod of intention that they too were involved. O'Reilly did not react, he did not concede, there was not to be any comradeship between them. Both men left, one with a well-read newspaper rolled under his arm.

O'Reilly rallied; he was quick to compose himself. He was interrupted by a thin man with a waspish moustache standing opposite behind the bar.

"Nice to see yuh in here O'Reilly," lied Connor, Connor knew that O'Reilly meant trouble, but Connor needed to play safe. No legitimate bar owner wanted cops in their sleazy drinking joints – Connor watched some of his regular punters finish their drinks to leave.

"The two raincoats sittin' at the corner of your bar, they just walked out. You know them?" asked O'Reilly.

"Nope," this time Conner did not lie, he told O'Reilly the truth. "Never seen either before."

Were they connected? Did they know something? O'Reilly expected the uniformed intercepts to soon pull them in - then he could give them the once over, with himself in charge. O'Reilly turned to Connor; he wasn't concerned about conversational niceties.

"There's been a body found, we think it's another priest," O'Reilly didn't see any reason to be obscure, if word got around then it would loosen tongues. Soon it would be in the papers anyway, no doubt by the evening news. Connor stood transfixed.

"Look, I don't know nothin," Connor snapped back, "I put the word out over the last one, nothin'. No one's talkin', no one's sayin' anythin'. There's a wall of silence, O'Reilly, it's like a bad nerve nobody is gonna goddam touch."

O'Reilly acquiesced - his boldness was on edge. Connor was right, O'Reilly knew this to be true, there were undertone feelings about the whole damned priesthood, reasons that no one was prepared to talk about – to add flame to the bonfire the church hierarchy were silent – unsettling whispers were coming out of the orphanages and reform schools - stuff that nobody talked about. O'Reilly's hunch about connections was beginning to bug him – five clergy were, for some profound reason, dead.

The atmosphere in Finnegan's began to feel horrible and oppressive, O'Reilly decided he had made a mistake - he stood little chance of learning anything new. He decided to leave and felt better for it. Without doubt, he would make more progress with the two vagrants held down at the precinct station. He left the bar; it had been a noteworthy twenty minutes - the warmth in the pit of his bowels from his single rough-cut whiskey fortified O'Reilly not one bit.

The drive to the precinct was uneventful, nothing happened. The drizzly rain became more incessant, preceding the early afternoon mist that began to roll in from mighty Lake Michigan, weather-wise it was going to be a miserable couple of days. There were no signs of his tail, O'Reilly wondered if his intercepts had made their mark – he would find out when he reached the precinct, he could make the call to his uptown headquarters from there to find out. O'Reilly turned on 48th towards the precinct, he was struck by its fortress-like appearance, the corrugated iron window shutters and perimeter wire made it plain this cop station was right in the middle of the city's shameful poverty-driven street crime - there were going to be no prisoners taken here O'Reilly thought to himself.

O'Reilly sat himself in the centre-most chair of the interview room, he was accompanied by two plain-clothed detectives, different cops from those down at the railway where the body had been found. The room was windowless and bare, the single lightbulb dangling from dangerous-looking wire that looked destined to fail at any moment. Stale tobacco smoke dominated, the stink of nicotine all-pervading and overpowering. Both detectives and O'Reilly himself chain-smoked their Marlboros like there was going to be a national shortage.

"Bring them in one at a time," ordered O'Reilly, who, in his official capacity wielded seniority over the two others - he could feel their familiar resentment. The first of the vagrants was brought in still cuffed, he was dumped without ceremony into the one single empty chair beside the bare table that sported the single overflowing ashtray spilling over its contents. No one cared. Within moments O'Reilly felt sympathy for the guy, he doubted the homeless vagrant had anything to do with the murder of the priest, he just happened to be in the wrong place at the wrong time. The light from the single bulb was too powerful for the small room, there were no dark shadows for any ugly lies, or the dark shameful tentacles of life to hide.

"I'm investigator Dermott O'Reilly," O'Reilly saw the instant expression of panic in the man's face, "I'm from the Federal Bureau of Investigations, these two here are from Chicago homicide. Tell me what happened, an' what you saw." O'Reilly lit one more cigarette, smoking it in the way he knew intimidated the one being questioned, it was an old interview trick from way back. He flicked the ash towards the ashtray and, with deliberate intent, missed; no one paid any attention.

"Look mister, I ain't dun nothin," the vagrant replied, "an' I get an attorney, right?"

"No, yuh don't," interrupted one of the homicide detectives. "Yuh ain't bein' charged with nothin', not yet." The door to the room opened, a uniformed cop entered holding typed-up sheets of paper. "We just got these first drafts back from forensics," he handed O'Reilly the papers.

"Thought yuh'd like to see em." He left, closing the door.

O'Reilly sat back in his chair, he quickly read the first, crucial page of the report. His eyes went straight to 'Cause of Death – Strangulation'. The same, same as three of the other four dead. The one other shot through his heart with his own gun. Then, a paragraph of typed information that struck O'Reilly dumb. The report stated 'Position of bruise marks found on the victim's neck – thumb imprints relatively close together, indicates small hands – possibly those of killer with lower height stature than the victim. Suggest victim's attacker is a smaller man – bruise indications of attacker possible female. Victim's height six feet two inches, probable weight around two hundred and fifty pounds.' O'Reilly read the forensic brief three times over. The victim was a big man, to hold him down then strangle him would have taken great strength, it could only have been done by a bigger, more powerful killer or if the victim had been otherwise tied or restrained. The report went on to say there were no regular signs of the victim being constrained. O'Reilly handed the paper to one of the homicide investigators, who studied it with equal fascination. O'Reilly gathered himself together, stubbing out his half-smoked cigarette then flicked the butt into the overflowing ashtray. The vagrant quickly made to pick up the butt - a reflex action of the pitiful homeless. The vagrant then held back - O'Reilly took out a new cigarette, lit it with a striking match, then handed it over to the vagrant. "Tell me what happened," urged O'Reilly, this time with a more conciliatory tone.

The vagrant repeated what he had told the cops. The exact same story, nothing changed, so O'Reilly knew he was telling the truth.

One of the homicides interrupted, "We suggest the victim, if he is a priest, came down to the culverts looking to help yuh homeless, yuh jumped him an' robbed him. Then yuh made a collect call to the cops to say yuh found a body,"

"No, I told yuh, it ain't like that," the vagrant was adamant. "We were sleepin', outta the rain, the truck came, som'body dumped the body. Sure, we looked f'his wallet, there was nothin' in it. Nothin', we were gonna take 'is pants, they were good pants, they were too big, so we left 'em on him."

"So, why'd you call the cops?" asked O'Reilly.

"Coz, when we pulled 'is pants we found this, we found it, it was sorta wrapped around 'is dick," the vagrant put his hand inside a small hidden waistcoat pocket, one missed by the mandatory police search, he forced his grubby finger inside then pulled out a thin chain, a woman's neck chain. O'Reilly stared, he fixed his eyes upon an unmistakable pendant, the silvery catholic pendant of Magdalene.

"When we found this, we thought he'd be a priest, we figured maybe there was a reward like we read in the papers," the vagrant went on, "so's we went down to the sidewalks t' that public phone there, the cops said there might be a reward comin' s' we went back."

O'Reilly fingered the pendant... he was deep in contemplative thought. Whatever was happening to these religious types it was without doubt the act of one single murderer, perhaps someone who had a deep grudge or hatred of the catholic church. It was O'Reilly's job to find the killer though he had nothing much to go on. The church itself wasn't saying much, they never did, they had their own investigator, their own inside henchman, folks in the church called him the churchman - the one lead he had was the woman at the funeral of Father O'Hearn, there was no doubt she had her reasons to be resentful, but she had straightaway disappeared, no one else at the funeral knew who she was...

"Let them both go, they both done nothin..." O'Reilly exhaled in complete frustration. "Give 'em both a feed, an' a dry bunk in your cells for the night outta this goddam rain."

O'Reilly stood abrupt to leave the room, there was nothing more to be gotten from these vagrants, even their real names didn't matter. The killer had strangled the victim someplace else, then drove to dump the body. The pendant was crucial, it was the pivotal link that made five dead. The same cheap pendant, strung around the victim's dick, the declaration that somebody had struck once more, a killer with a lethal cause, a crusade by someone with a death-dealing reason. Could it really be a woman?

O'Reilly, his hands inside his pockets, walked a slow pace down the dimly lit corridor, he was stopped by the desk sergeant. The corridor light made a disconcerting difference to the bright light of the interview room. "Someone came in, asked f'yuh by name then left, around ten minutes ago," said the sergeant. "Told me t' give yuh this," he handed O'Reilly a small, folded note of paper. O'Reilly stood nonplussed, unfolded the note then read it without much emotion, in a matter-of-fact way considering everything that had happened since the first phone call at eight-thirty the same morning. O'Reilly paused, then read the note a second time with rapt interest, the message was brief and simple, it read 'McCarthy, Father Donald McCarthy – Connor."

Walter McPherson hurried his ponies down the rutted stone roadway as swift as he could. The dirt kicked up by the pony's worn hooves added to the bone-crunching rattle of the waggon. Walter paid little attention; inside he was consumed by the unhinged state of his mind. As well as his sanity-twisting encounter with the woman calling herself Moon, there were more worrying troubles for McPherson to think about - the intense heat of the early afternoon was beginning to build, most likely, McPherson realised, into one of the high-intensity dust-bowl storms that in these dark days of disparity were ravaging the vast farmland regions of Oklahoma's great plains. McPherson was conscious that before mid-afternoon the dreaded westerly might begin to blow – heralding the onset of the blinding dust storm of bone-dry soil that would suffocate the breath from the lungs of everyone who failed to find safe haven. The surface topsoils of the barren farmlands would once more be stripped bare - another scourge of America's Great Depression.

McPherson eyed the mushrooming dark-backed clouds, figuring he had less than an hour to make it to the nearest farmstead. Walter knew Gregor's farm, with its decrepit dilapidated barns and homestead shack, was not far ahead - old man Gregor often kept his forty-year-old horse plough to one side in case Walter happened by. McPherson urged his ponies on, knowing they had not the strength to push themselves beyond even their threadbare limits. The ride became a race against time.

What happened with Moon played upon McPherson's mental wellbeing. He was struggling to recover his composure; he felt the familiar gremlin of dark ruination creeping through his subconsciousness - in the same debilitating way, the selfsame bleakness of his thoughts mirrored the blackness of the building storm clouds shaping themselves on the near western horizon. McPherson needed distance, not only was he outrunning the threatening maelstrom, but he was also running from Moon. Once it had penetrated his teetering mind who she might be then his humourless inability to reason came to the fore, the innermost core of his sanity started to unravel - the instability of his world began to verge upon madness.

The orphanage, the damned orphanage, the damned bastard orphanage - McPherson swore to himself over and over. Sure, he remembered - how could he ever forget? How the hell had she found him after all these years given everything that had happened? Of course, she knew who he was, why would she not? Earlier in the morning she gave him that extraordinary *thing* to fix - it was as if he had been lured to the homestead for one sole reason - like a hooked fish on a baited long line. McPherson had to get away, to make as much distance as he could. The approaching storm was, without doubt, meant to happen - the damned script could not have been written more appropriately - with the powerful wind might come much-needed rain, torrential rain that would turn the rootless soil into quagmire mud. It was the same, the exact same chaos she had created back then, uncompromising turmoil, the way she had generated wholesale havoc in the Saint Catherine's orphanage hierarchy the last time she came, she knew who those monsters were – *how had she aged not one year?* She was not called Moon in those days, not when she dragged those children away - *after what they did to them...* revenge, revenge must be her ultimate motive. Would she, after all this time, find those bastards? Every one of them?

McPherson's thoughts rolled over and over. Her finder... that *thing*... she called it her finder, she said she needed her finder... why did she need her finder? He had fixed it, how in heavens' name did she know he could fix it? Then a sudden thought struck McPherson, a bender of slight suspicion - did Moon's 'finder' really need fixing?

The whisper of the wind breathed its first breath, the tinder-dry tree leaves rustled in warning - then stopped. A brief lull, then one more sniffing breeze that sneaked its way through the wilting trees like a probing beast. McPherson realised he would not make Gregor's homestead before the windstorm hit, he whipped his pony's reins trying to drain the last ounce of energy from their sapped bones... to McPherson's surprise the ponies hurried their pace, perhaps they sensed the impending danger from the inevitable tempest.

The horizon darkened; the immense dust blow rolled over the flatland landscape from west to east in the rising wind. Before it hit McPherson saw the Gregor farmstead ahead, old man Gregor stood at the gateway beckoning him on with waving arms – he had seen McPherson and his team of ponies racing before the storm. McPherson reached Gregor at the broken gate, he turned his team at the same time pulling Gregor onto his cart, before racing up the dry trackway of the homestead. Gregor pointed to the rundown barn, McPherson pulled into the shelter of the outbuilding just when the first rolling dust wave hit, the crescendo of pandemonium was deafening, but they were safe – if the barn stayed upright and intact.

"Howdy Walt... y'all jus' made it... we gotta stay inside. Barn ain't gonna blo' down no time soon," yelled Gregor above the din of the stiffening wind and the clanging tin roof, "an' we ain't gonna make the house neither, not 'n this shite," Gregor pointed in the direction of where he and his crippled wife lived. McPherson thought about poor Ma Gregor, the tumbledown single-storey shack that was home for the Gregors was standing threadbare – the broken glass windows relied upon the flapping ragtag curtains to somehow keep out the ravaging storm. The two exhausted ponies whinnied in frightened panic, McPherson tried to calm them down as best he could, but straightaway he saw it was futile.

"Never thought I was gonna make it," McPherson called out loud. "This blow came outta nowhere, the sun was shinin' an' all just a couple hours ago," he fought to regain his breath. "Stopped by that place a'mile or so back, no sign o' this blow then."

Gregor looked puzzled. "What place?" he wanted to know; his yawping voice still pitched above the racketing wind.

"Place with the white picket fence," McPherson struggled to make himself heard, in the back of his mind there was the worrying thought how this storm could get much worse.

"Place's bin empty f'over a year," Gregor answered at the top of his voice, there was no other homestead in the direction from which McPherson had come. "Bank forced them O'Leary folks out," Gregor saw the alarm in McPherson's ashen grey face. "Happnin' regular, banks don't give no shit, folks don't get their corn or cotton harvest in they can't pay," he said. "Crops gets buried deep in these blows an' folks don't stand no chance, they jus' pack their jalopy in the middle o' night an' goes." McPherson listened; he knew Gregor was right - the O'Leary place wasn't empty though, surely Gregor knew this. McPherson looked over to his petrified ponies, he needed to get them unhitched. "Jus hangin' in m'self Walt, bet no folks can pay y'all nothin', I ain't got nothin', no folks got nothin', y'all gotta go west Walt, folks say there's work outta in California," Gregor lowered his tone... "Some folks 'round here ain't eatin' nothin'... some'er starvin' real bad." McPherson tried to listen hard, he grappled to hear much of what Gregor said.

"We gotta get Ma Gregor outta your shack," howled McPherson. "She ain't gonna survive thru this."

"She ain't there, she left, nigh 'n six months back," Gregor screamed.

"Where'd she go?" yelled McPherson.

"Dunno. Sister's I guess, over in Denston County. I ain't heard nothin' from her." Fine soil dust was beginning to heap through the uneven cracks, the gaps in the walls leaked in drifting dirt. The ponies were whinnying, McPherson pulled down hard on their reins.

Their conversation ended; the pandemonium of noise grew loud. Both McPherson and Gregor huddled beneath McPherson's cart, it was scant protection. McPherson thought about what Gregor had said, the O'Leary's place was abandoned – how could this be? But it made sense, McPherson had seen no signs of occupation, nothing in the yard, no kid's stuff knocking around – no shirts hanging out to dry – everywhere he went, there were always drying shirts. Then, none of it made sense, nothing made sense at all. The tin roof of the barn was rattling harder.

Outside, larger objects began to get blown around. McPherson heard hammering and banging, things being hurled against inanimate structures that might not stand their ground. This was more than a threatening dust bowl windstorm, something else was happening, disaster beckoned – there seemed to be a vortex in the air.

Gregor sensed the change, he looked wild-eyed at McPherson - there was outright fear in the old corn farmer's eyes.

"Walt – we gotta make fo' the shelter." His voice wavered.

Every homestead hereabouts had a 'twister' shelter, covered pits in the ground for around four to eight folks, two or three side by side for large families. Not much use for the big dust bowl storms because the flat ground-level door hatches would easy get covered. Gregor was right, thought McPherson, the terrifying commotion outside did not sound anything like good. An intense flash of blinding light – lightening. There came a tremendous roar - like a freight train heading straight for the barn.

"Where's the shelter?" McPherson bellowed, knowing it was too late.

"Back o' the shack," screamed Gregor. "We won't make it..." It was the last thing he said. Gregor died in the instant it takes to first draw breath.

The barn disintegrated. Gregor disappeared. One minute Gregor was hunched beside McPherson beneath the Fix It cart, the next second he was gone. The cart shattered into uncountable pieces; the two ponies were thrown with tremendous force against the back wall of the barn – then through the wall as the wall flew apart into a dark place called nowhere. The tether between the two ponies severed, McPherson last saw his ponies when they were picked up by the twisting tornado that tossed everything into the abyss. McPherson hugged the ground, lying spreadeagled flat, he knew he must avoid the outsized parts of the barn that were being hurled around like children's toys. McPherson knew he was going to die - like poor old man Gregor who was still, after all his time alive, desperate to find his wife.

It was near to total darkness. It was silent, McPherson did not know how long he had been unconscious. The black storm and violent tornado had passed but McPherson was scared, everything he owned destroyed, he lay flat face downwards hoping to survive, his arms out wide. He looked up, a sense, a feeling made him look. He shook, his breath exhaled in hyperventilation, his vision of reality reeled in confusion.

Moon was there, a few feet away, sitting cross-legged as though nothing much had happened. Calm as anything, the same dirty cotton dress, bedraggled, unkempt, she watched him waiting for McPherson to regain his senses.

"Yuh not Mr Fix it now, eh?" she said, without much fuss. "Yuh waggon's gone an' yuh ain't got no ponies."

She flicked her hair from her eyes when it fell across her face. McPherson froze, he fought to get himself together to retain his rationality. McPherson gathered himself up, he sat up against the one barn support post that was left standing, he judged that they were in the open air, around him was chaos. The evening sun shone through the remnant mayhem of the storm, it was set low on the horizon, the day was near ended. McPherson looked around, two of the wagons' wheels lay flat on the ground, the other two somewhere else that Walter could not begin to locate.

"Where's Gregor?" McPherson asked, dazed and confused.

"Over by the well," answered Moon, without emotion. "He's dead, I sorta buried him."

McPherson sat silent; his whole world had changed without revocation.

"These storms, the dust blower an' the twister, they don't usu'lly come together like that," said Moon.

"Oh... that's worth knowin'. Don't help Gregor non," McPherson answered.

"Farmers, they came t' these plains an' ploughed the grass, they turned up the soil real deep," said Moon, with no outward show of regrets. "No roots left t' hold the soil, when that westerly win' blows it blows an' kills everythin'. Farmer's ain't got no business on these plains, now they all runnin' or dyin'," Moon watched McPherson struggle. "Twisters, they a'ways bin comin', crop farmin' ain't no cause o' them."

McPherson seemed to be okay, he could not feel anything broken, nor see any of his own blood.

"Yuh're fine. Already checked yuh out," said Moon.

"What... what's..." McPherson hesitated... "What's gonna happen?"

There was a short pause, as if there was more bad news. "Yuh gotta come with me," answered Moon, she looked at him with a measure of compassion. The sun sank lower towards a glorious sky-red sunset, the streaks of cloudless yellow suggested little legacy of the merciless whirlwind storm. "I stole somethin', now we gotta get somethin' more, somethin' real bad."

"*What?*" McPherson was stupefied.

McPherson found Gregor's beaten pickup truck buried, it was covered in a thick layer of deep brown soil plus smashed parts of the barn and shack. It took him the best part of an hour to clear the debris to attempt to start the engine. Moon looked on, she watched without offering much help, leaning against the remaining corner of the homestead shack still standing. The dust had gotten under the broken bonnet, it mixed itself into the black oil residue on the cylinder head to form a quagmire of thick oozing crude. McPherson took one long look then realised it would take him a couple of hours, but the sunset was well set. Soon total darkness would descend.

"We ain't goin' nowhere tonight," growled McPherson. "Gonna take me coupler hours t' clean this crap."

"I got a half a sack o' rice from outta the shack. We ain't gonna starve," Moon answered. "Not t'night anyhow."

"Tell you the truth, I ain't hungry," said McPherson.

"Me neither," said Moon. "It'll save till breakfast I guess."

McPherson looked up from under the bonnet, in the half-light of sunset he looked drawn and withered. "Me an' you, we gotta talk."

"Sure. What yuh wanna talk 'bout?"

McPherson paused, he was nonplussed - as if there was nothing between them to discuss and resolve - McPherson had so much to ask he did not know where to start, he didn't think that Moon would even begin to explain - she had evaded every damned question he'd asked since they'd first met that same morning.

"Where'd you com' from? Let's start with that."

Moon waited, deciding if McPherson should know everything. "If I tell yuh where I com' from Walter, reckon yuh'll blow yuh're own brains out," she smiled, this was a crucial moment in everything that had happened.

McPherson found the two wires he was looking for - there was just enough daylight, he touched them together and the truck fired up, it roared into life in a crackling demonstration of uncontrolled power, the engine sounded bad. McPherson dropped the wires, he jumped into the shabby cab at the same time pushing his foot hard down onto the peddle, the engine revs increased and spluttered – but the junk-heap jalopy kept going.

"Jump in," McPherson beckoned to Moon without much show of excitement, he pointed his thumb to the cab, "We can talk while drivin'."

McPherson found the headlight switch, the weak beam lit up the devastation in weird luminescence, the destruction of the poverty striven farmstead was complete. As McPherson drove out onto the farm track to the gravelled roadway, the path of the tornado through the fields stripped bare of topsoil was all too plain. Great swathes of the landscape were flattened and ripped apart, the few trees that were standing before the storm were torn up and gone, dead livestock were scattered about - pigs and cows that had never before grazed on Gregor's land, livestock that didn't belong. Their meagre-looking torsos were broken, skin and bone heaped upon the ground among all types of debris - already the vultures were feeding on dead flesh, their gaping red eyes lit by the truck's headlights in the nighttime darkness. Seeing no immediate predators to steal their feed, the vultures sank their bare featherless heads back into their feasting pits of blood-ridden gluttony. McPherson saw that, when the trucks' lights passed over one more pack of feeding vultures, the hapless victim was wearing the distinctive worn-out leather of farmer's boots.

"Where do we head?" demanded McPherson.

"North. We go north." Moon seemed concentrated and forthright, sure of where they were going. "T'wards the Missouri line, then Illinois," she added.

McPherson turned and stared. "Missouri... that's a long way..."

"Yup," agreed Moon. "Gonna take more than a week I guess."

"We got no money... no supplies... nothin'. We gotta eat, we need gas."

"We'll get money, an' food an' we'll get gas. We'll get it Walter, we'll be fine, yuh'll see," said Moon.

The long drive north in the dark, through the night, was uneventful, McPherson worried how much gas they had in the tank, the needle gauge was not moving - McPherson began to suspect it was faulty.

"So... why Illinois?" McPherson probed, plucking up the courage. Were they heading to find Honey? The first streaks of dawn touched the blackness of the eastern skyline, Moon watched the still-dark horizon out of her right-hand sidelight.

"We gotta stop soon, we gotta eat." Moon evaded McPherson's question.

"Like I said, how'n hell we gonna get food? We only got the dirty rice sack," the exasperation in McPherson's voice hid nothing. "Like I tell you, we got no money..." They had seen no other vehicle, nor carts pulled by horses. No roadside shacks or gas stations, in the glare of the headlights the relentless gravelled road bone crunching its way under the suspensionless truck wheels. Once in a while, the glaring eyes of some critters mirroring back the headlight beams before they hurried away to find safety. The next fifteen minutes grew easier as the insipid grey light of dawn ascended.

Up ahead, the solid black police truck blocked the roadway like a rain culvert plugged with scrub. Two cops, rough and casual in their dress, flagged them down in the hazy light of the insipid sunrise, signalling them to stop. McPherson looked anxious, he was never easy with law enforcement men, he never trusted them. "Here's yuh breakfast comin' ahead," announced Moon. McPherson looked over to her mystified.

One of the cops stood in front of the truck, McPherson slowed to a stop. The cop walked to McPherson's drive side, there was no side window glass in the old jalopy. "Turn off your engine," demanded the cop - McPherson flicked the switch, the engine stuttered and died.

"Where yuh headed?" challenged the cop - there was no friendliness in his voice. McPherson saw the rifle slung over the cop's shoulder who looked mean in the dim light. The cop looked over towards Moon. "Hey, ain't yuh a' pretty babe..." he leered.

"We headed north," said McPherson.

"Yeah? Why yuh in a' hurry?"

"We ain't in a' hurry, we got hit by a twister, we lost all our stuff, everythin'..." McPherson answered.

"Yeah? Or maybe yuh stole this jalopy an' yuh running. Yuh got nothin' on it yuh might call yuh're own," the cop replied, the cop walked around the rear of the truck, noting the empty flatback - he drew level with Moon, he paused. "Babe, yuh sure is pretty, might get me a little peck on ma cheek from them pretty little lips of yours."

"Hank, y'all gotta lay off that kinda talk," warned the second cop. "We said, we talked 'bout that," until now, the other cop had said nothing.

"We boys gotta enjoy ourselves, Jake, yuh know that. Yuh jus' stay outta the way Jake," insisted the first cop. He opened the truck door staring at Moon. "Get out," he ordered.

McPherson straightaway jumped out, he ran around the front of the truck, he was confronted by the first cop pointing his rifle to his stomach.

"Where do yuh think yuh're goin' drifter?" warned the cop. McPherson stopped rigid. It was the last thing the cop said before he hit the hard soil-covered ground.

Moon stood from the cab in the way the cop ordered. Standing there, she penetrated straight into his mind, seeing what she expected to see - his hideous memories mixed with intermittent good, his finger-led abuse jumbled haphazard with happy family recollections, his repetitive violent violations of his wife fused with everyday home elation, the whimpering cries of his battered, beaten mistress woman. Moon did not strike out his memories, nor did she twist and turn his powers of reasoning - she saw the evil inside him, knowing that babbled jabbering for the rest of his life would be sufficient, enough to serve scant justice to his own vulnerable kids, all the defenceless women in his life, the five women he had raped by the roadsides. The cop rolled in a squirming heap on the ground - holding his wide-eyed head in incomprehensible mutterings that made no outward sense.

Moon stared at the second cop... there was a hard shield, a barrier, something peculiar... familiar – Moon straightaway realised who he was, he was no cop. "You," she pointed to him with menace. "Get inside the truck. You're coming with us." Moon's normal vague southern state accent was much less pronounced, she spoke direct - with angry conviction.

FBI agent Dermott O'Reilly sat back in his chair; his feet raised on his paper-strewn disorganised desk. On his desktop were two unexpected files left there by someone unknown, each with typed documents inserted in a seeming specific order. Through the rain-sodden evening, O'Reilly had read many of the reports in one of the files - some he had re-read over and over, several times, more than once. It was well past midnight; his baffled mind was numb with shocked disbelief.

The first file, the one to his left, listed the various kid's orphanages where each of the dead priests had spent their time. It made astounding reading, whoever had put all this together had undertaken huge amounts of outright old-fashioned detective work that described events so hideous that sometimes O'Reilly had to pause his reading. The file's contents were a nauseating bombshell, revelations that were mind-blowing and explosive. The second file, the one by his right foot resting on his desk, O'Reilly had only half skim read, its documents were strange and perplexing, difficult to piece together or understand. It was the middle of the night, he picked up his half-drunk mug of coffee - it was lukewarm cold, but he finished it nevertheless, stubbing out the remnants of his umpteenth or so successive cigarette in the bottom of the brown-stained mug.

O'Reilly had found both files there on his desk earlier in the evening, when he, at last, got back to his office from the downtown station precinct – it didn't take long for O'Reilly to realise that someone above him in rank hitherto knew every detail about the murders that he himself did not. Even so - he had no idea who had delivered the documents to his desk or when.

In frantic despair, O'Reilly re-read the note given to him by the desk sergeant down at the cop precinct. The murdered priest, Father Donald McCarthy the note read – and McCarthy was there, plain as day, named in the file though not one of the names listed as dead. The file contents were not concerned with the fate of the murder victims, it described specific orphanages listing catholic priests who had worked their time inside them. O'Hearn and Brady, they were named in the file – O'Reilly was in no doubt the two unidentified victims were somewhere listed as well, among the dozens or so mentioned. O'Reilly's stomach churned to the point the crime-hardened detective felt sick. O'Reilly knew it would take some time to figure it all out. Ronson, the day detective, could do the mundane work, a few hours of hard cross-referencing ball-aching graft would sort out who was who named in the typed-up papers. By the end of the day O'Reilly might know something more – or would he? The file was a gut spiller, a hidden bomb timed to explode – in terms of his murder investigation, the file's factual contents stopped everything. O'Reilly moved the other file to one side; beside the stack of files he had never read. For now – his only option was to ignore it - he had no choice.

O'Reilly once more picked up the orphanage file, this time reading it at random in not any particular order. There were many names, kid's names in the main, hundreds of them, priest's names, also the innocent names of nuns. O'Reilly half-read through the names a countless time. His gut instinct cops eyes stopped at one name, a kid's name, McPherson, Walter McPherson. Why? Then a reactive hunch, a guess, O'Reilly thought he had read the same name in the other file. Had he? Yes, he had.

He grabbed the second file, the same name, it was in some clipped-together papers right at the front - the second page. O'Reilly took another sip of cold coffee from his grubby mug, the last dregs, the dregs with the stubbed cigarettes he had forgotten about. O'Reilly spat out, spluttering, there were coffee stains over the sheet of paper in front of him... McPherson, Walter. Navy Engineers First Class, cold coffee splattered right over it.

O'Reilly leaned back, not realising he had been reading hard through most of the night. Allegations. Absurd statements. Child molestations, juvenile rapes – all vehement, repeated, refuted by the catholic church. Priests deliberately moved around out of harm's way. O'Reilly sat breathless, nurturing a stomach-churning growing hunch - the dead priests – claims against named priests. Outright revenge? Were these murders revenge? Yeah? Why not? Who in hell had left him these documents? Someone who knew? O'Reilly figured he was being led. A noise behind him, the door he always left open – it was closed.

The spare desk, the empty desk covered in more scattered files. O'Reilly gasped; he inhaled drawing his breath. A shadowy stranger sat behind the desk. A woman.

"Huh...! Who're you?" O'Reilly blurted out loud, startled. The night had taken an outlandish twist. "How'n hell did you get in here?"

Honey sat silent as if contemplating her next move. She fixed her stare straight at O'Reilly. Her stealth, her catlike slyness, she sat in her own black shadow.

There were more than a few moments of deep intense silence. "Was easy," Honey answered. O'Reilly felt an incomplete fool, he recovered his composure realising he had been outmanoeuvred.

"Who are you?" he challenged her outright, O'Reilly stayed calm. "What the hell do you want?"

Honey eyed O'Reilly with her piercing grey-blue stare gaze. The neon half-light of the outside streets cast an ominous silhouette of subdued luminescence, primary tones of colour that changed in intermittent flashes as Honey took her time to reply.

"I kill'd McCarthy. I kill'd O'Hearn, Campbell an' Brady," she answered, not taking her gaze off O'Reilly for one second, "O'Donnell kill'd himself, I gave 'im no choice. There's two more. I ain't got them yet. Sometime soon I will."

O'Reilly was struck silent - he didn't know what to say. Honey watched him reach beneath his shirt for his standard issue Colt 38.

"The two men who're followin' yuh, they looking for me, they think I'll take em to Walter." Hearing this, O'Reilly froze, he paused going for his

38. "Secret service. Navy men, amateur no-hopers," Honey added.

The middle of the night atmosphere cut through the intensity between them. "Campbell an' O'Donnell," O'Reilly whispered the names to himself, when he realised who they were - the two unidentified priests. He must buy time, he tried to think what to do. Campbell and O'Donnell would have to be checked out; O'Reilly realised in an instant how this part of the murder investigation had just been made a whole lot easier. But then the entire case had just been turned upside down, flipped upon its head.

"Yeah, Campbell an' O'Donnell," confirmed Honey, "I checked, it's all'n that there file,"

"You... did you leave these files?" O'Reilly sounded even more astonished.

"Sure, yeah, I did," said Honey, seeing the surprise in O'Reilly's face. "I stole that orphanage file outta the church's archive office, the one in the hall of catholic bishops. The navy file I got outta Navy intelligence." Her drawl accent seemed to have faded, it seemed more sinister. Daylight once more began to show its thin veil of deceit, soon other staff would start to arrive for their daily work in the outer office. Honey did not look concerned.

"How did you steal them?" O'Reilly demanded, fascinated and gripped.

"Yuh could say I borrowed em," said Honey. "Both the cardinals an' the navy know thos' files are missin', so yuh *gotta* be careful O'Reilly. An' the bishops, they know how every one of thos' kids named in there suffered bad... an' not just in the orphanages. The navy file is somethin' different, that's 'bout one man, I was hitched to him for a short time. He's special. I tell yuh, he's *very* special."

"Your name? Tell me your name?" O'Reilly challenged.

"Honey, folks call me Honey," she replied. "It ain't my real name."

O'Reilly saw it was pointless, he was being outwitted. This woman was something else, like nobody he had ever encountered – the self-confessed murderer he was investigating – she had confessed to everything. Why?

"In another two'r three hours, yuh'll have gotten instructions from way up to drop your investigation, they gonna stop you lookin' into these dead priests," said Honey. "Every priest an' bishop named in there, they got blood on their hands. The worst of em, McCarthy, he was takin' a cut, takin' a piece sellin' kids to other priests, an' not jus' to priests, to well-known big men, like bein' in a circle. An' not just catholics, it goes way up in other churches. Your God works in mysterious ways, O'Reilly."

O'Reilly still sat motionless, shocked, thinking. For years he had heard rumours, cases he had worked on, stark stonewall silence as if driven by shame, embarrassing deep cut shame... the night his father had pinned the priest against the alleyway wall...

"So, why should I believe it's *you* who's doin' the drop on these bastards?" demanded O'Reilly. "You're a bit on the small size to go around strangling six-foot priests, no jury's gonna believe you're the strangler if they saw you, even if they ever believe what's typed in these docs."

O'Reilly knew deep within his guts it might be impossible to nail her. He was in deep thought. If he detained her for their murders how in hell could he get a conviction? Of course, she knew this, it was why she was here, he couldn't touch her, there was no way to apprehend her. If he got her before a federal judge, her story would sure make sensational headlines - all those hard dicked priests, the cardinals... the catholic church was too big, too powerful - all the faiths were the same. *Jesus Christ*, thought O'Reilly... the crazy bitch, the crazy *crazy* bitch, maybe she was untouchable...

Honey thought about what O'Reilly said. "Like I said, your catholic God, he works in mysterious ways. Their church got its way of cleanin' its cesspit," she answered, avoiding O'Reilly's question.

"You killin' for the church?" O'Reilly asked, making a guess, almost in reverence.

"No, it ain't me cleaning up, there's priests I still wanna get but their church knows I got the names of every one of em, there's dozens, all named in that file. I'm kinda like their unwanted assassin... they runnin' scared. I'm only sniffin' for the ones I want for my own reasons an', like I said... there's two left."

"What then?" O'Reilly stared.

"The cardinals, they got a big contract out on *me*, I gotta be stopped, not just investigated an' run in by you FBI boys for murder, that would'na be helpful to those bastards, would it?" Honey smiled.

She was right. She was dammed right, thought O'Reilly.

"Why those five you say you already killed, an' the two more?"

"McCarthy was the worst, their kinda ringleader. They kill'd the kids who they thought might blurt, buried em or burned em. I was on to O'Donnell, I had kin inside juvenile detention, he was kinda in there for stealin', sort of on purpose. O'Donnell was there, he was doin' that shit back then, molesting kids, boys, but not a'ways. He found out I was on to 'im, that I was kinda special, an' my kin was not like thos' other kids. They bin lookin' for me since, they a'ways knew I'd come back, there's a shit-faced score to settle. There's cardinals an' bishops who're doin' the kids, all the way to the top, they know who I am... it's why they tryin' to find me."

"Jesus *fucking* Christ," O'Reilly had been taught from a young early age never to take the Lord's name in vain, but O'Reilly this time could not help himself. The atrocities listed in detail on his desk were explosive - O'Reilly couldn't think, right there he could not decide what to do. What in hell's name was the other file about - only then for the first time did he see the red 'Classified' label on the front.

"McCarthy, so he kill'd my kin who was my blood, my kin in juvenile detention, buried him somewhere, here in Chicago. So, me an' Moon, we set out to get em, every one of em, after they'd passed my kin around to put their filthy dicks up his ass. We'll get em, each one of em. McCarthy didn't know me, not at first, not when I strangled 'im. In thos' few seconds before I kill'd him, *then* he remembered me." Honey showed no emotion.

O'Reilly stood, he walked over to the copper coffee urn, it was only lukewarm, but he still poured two mugs. He passed one to Honey, she smiled a warm smile with unassuming thanks. She refused his cigarette with a negative nod of her head - her hair fell in front of her eyes; she tossed it away with a casual flick of her hand. O'Reilly, for some reason, caught his breath. He saw the unfamiliar cross of gold around her neck.

"Why are you here tellin' me all this?" he asked. Daybreak was casting an unwelcoming greyness through the big office window. The usual smell of dampness inside the walls would linger until warm rays of sunshine drove the odorous smell away – but the deep murky sky promised another day of overcast drizzle, one more day of relentless misery.

"Like I said, your investigation is gonna get wound up," said Honey. "Yuh gotta make a decision O'Reilly, yuh're not gonna get to come after me an' I want yuh to do somethin'. The church, they don't want thos' dead priests 'xposed, so yuh gotta decide what to do, who's side yuh're gonna be on, who yuh're gonna give this stuff to," Honey paused a few moments for what she said to sink in, because for her own selfish reasons she needed O'Reilly to give her more time - the FBI, the church, the navy, they were all trying hard to find her. "Your tail, they informed the powers yuh're gettin' in mighty close. They didn't 'xpect I'd get McCarthy so soon, they figured yuh might know why he's dead, why he got kill'd. An' they want somebody else real bad, not jus' me, somebody they know I'm connected to."

O'Reilly reached across his desk for the second file, he read the first paper. "McPherson? Walter McPherson?"

"Yeah. He's been in thos' orphanages, the same ones. Walter, it took a time for me to find him, to figure out 'xactly what he could do. We got hitched, but I left, I had to leave, it wasn't right, he loved me... me, a murderin' assassin. I knew from a long time back he was out there someplace, an' I found him an', like I said, we got hitched." Honey seemed agitated, bothered and uneasy about McPherson.

"Moon? Who's this Moon? And this catholic investigation guy, this churchman named in the file?" O'Reilly probed. His inquisitive detective mode kicked in.

"I can't tell yuh who Moon is, you'd never believe anyway..."

O'Reilly felt a strange feeling of intuition. The senseless was beginning to make sense, for the first time he had this Honey on the back foot.

"Walt, he makes an' fixes things, the way only Walt can do. An' me an' Moon, we need to get hold of somethin' real bad. Your tail, it's Walt they after. You find me an'... they find Walter. But they scared, they 'fraid if yuh find me, yuh'll know what I know about the church."

"What is it you need to find so bad?" quizzed O'Reilly, in instinctive cross-examination.

Honey paused, what could she say? For Moon to tear down the catholic hierarchy that hid the festering paedophilia within she must first get into the faith's inner core, right inside the Vatican innards where the brotherhood elite prayed. Moon was aware of the hard-rock core of righteous priests, the good ones dedicated to virtuousness and morality - but to hunt down the more sinister priests, to dig out the vilest thinking bishops, archbishops and the cardinals whose dedicated mission was to hide the church's sinister secret, there was one more file, the one hidden in the deepest vault protected by locks that even Honey could not force open. Moon must in some way penetrate the vault guarded by a complex combination of mechanical light beams, unconventional bolts that just one man could master – Walter McPherson, the same Walter McPherson who possessed the uncanny skills the navy needed for its selfish reasons.

The navy wanted McPherson bad, the catholic church was hell-bent on covering up the serial murders of their brotherhood even while Honey was hunting down the evil clique of butchering paedophilic abusers known to exist. To find McPherson the navy was tailing O'Reilly because they suspected, through the original range-finding device that McPherson had invented, that Honey was the killer who might lead them to McPherson. The bishops knew their file of broken lives had been stolen, that its theft was linked to the killer.

Within this wild murderous world of perversion and death, the obscure cleanup envoy known as the churchman understood that Moon was Honey, that Honey was Moon. Moon morphed her being for one important reason, Moon was never an intentional murderess, Moon's task was to nurture life, female life with instinctive goodness whereas Honey was life's ruthless destroyer - the palaeolithic hunter of powerful men with evil buried inside their impure hearts like a serpent's asphyxiating venom. Moon had in the first years tried to protect the young McPherson in the Saint Catherine's orphanage, she had ensured his survival for her own deep-rooted reasons.

Afterwards, after his mind-breaking orphanage existence and tortuous trauma in the navy, Honey found him. Then Moon tracked him with her vis finder that never did need fixing. Moon's vis was hooked into McPherson, Moon knew what McPherson could do, it was time for the catholic's main vault of secrets to be forced open. The institutional catholic church was in its last throw-of-the-dice peril.

Honey dug deep into her purse, she drew out the smallish white stone vis, the same one opened by McPherson when he first encountered Moon at the O'Leary homestead. She passed it to O'Reilly, who took it into his hand to examine it. It began to glow a greenish tinge as if it was communicating. O'Reilly became rigid, alarmed, sudden thoughts and outlandish visions came into his head... his mother, O'Reilly had not seen his mother since he was a child, he had been raised by his mother's sister when his father in the end walked out. O'Reilly grew to love his aunt, he worshipped his mother, he hated his father who pummelled his mother for no reason... when he was drunk... his father, who then beat his aunt - after his mother died, in childbirth, his baby sister... O'Reilly threw the whitestone viz back to Honey in disgust...

"What... what is it?" blurted O'Reilly, in a startled hushed tone.

Honey smiled to herself, her hunch had been right, O'Reilly had communicated, her viz still hummed green, the genes were there, his blood - he was linked, it could only be through his mother's lineage.

"It's a finder, it connects an' tells me things," revealed Honey.

"How'd you mean? Connects with what?"

"What was it yuh saw uh?" Honey played the advocate, she knew all too well what O'Reilly had seen, she watched the painful expressions etched upon his face.

O'Reilly sat agitated, he did not want to talk about his memories nor the visual impressions inside his head, those thoughts were hurtful, he never discussed his life with anyone, those days were agonising and harrowing – it occurred to O'Reilly that Honey did not need to be told about what had happened when he was a kid... this strange stone he had held in his hand, it was a key to unlock your thoughts, visions that had once flashed

131

through your pain-filled eyes. It saw who you were, where you came from, whether you were good blood or bad. A thought came into his mind, an urgent need to turn aside the debilitating confusion that threatened to overwhelm him... to bury the disorientation that cut through the air like the sails of a windmill. He stared at Honey, trying to read her expression.

"I would like to ask you one question," said O'Reilly, he saw Honey's grudging acceptance as if she knew what he would want to know. "You confessed to the murder of five catholic priests. You've said there are two more who are not yet dead. Will you tell me their names?"

Honey thought about O'Reilly's question, she paused. "Father Callaghan an' Father Mancini," she divulged their names after deliberating the relevance of the information. It made no real difference if O'Reilly knew or not.

"Why them?" questioned O'Reilly, beginning to regain his composure.

"It's typed up, it's all there in that file. They kill'd kids that were gonna talk," the venom in her voice shook O'Reilly.

O'Reilly thought hard. What could he do? Did he warn the two priests they were gonna be stalked down? Did he reveal everything to his superiors above to seek their arrest? Did he get word out to the church? Did he do nothing? O'Reilly realised how much his hands were tied, but he also figured that in most cases justice was a strange 'eye for an eye' outcome – lots of the investigative murders he saw were revenge for something or other, scores to be settled for obscure reasons he had to identify – motive was an important element of the conviction process, O'Reilly had witnessed crimes that nestled on thin lines when it came to morality. In this instance O'Reilly knew he would do nothing, he figured there was little he could do – God did work in mysterious ways - but O'Reilly had long since disbelieved in God.

The phone on the wall beside O'Reilly's desk rang, its shrill ring broke the intensity of the riveting atmosphere between himself and Honey. Honey watched him walk to pick up the phone.

"O'Reilly?" said the voice down the line. It was Dennison, O'Reilly's top-level Chicago boss who must have been early out of his bed. "I received a call from the governor's office, the vice-governor himself," Dennison paused, there was unease in his voice. "Your murder investigation into these priests, it's finished. No need for you to keep goin' O'Reilly. I'm told they're all suicides, they took their own lives. Gamblin' debts, it seems. It's over."

O'Reilly stood silent with the receiver in his ear, he did not say anything, with calmness he replaced the receiver after his initial out take of breath. He paused before turning to face Honey. "You said there is something you want me to do...?"

Honey was not there. She was gone, she had left, the door was half open. She had made no sound in leaving in the same manner as when she had entered.

O'Reilly's mood straightaway changed, he once more became fragile, alarmed, he sat down in contemplative silence, in time he picked up the second file marked 'Secret. For Level One Navy Eyes Only'. The sun, from nowhere, peaked daylight rays above the horizon, it was unexpected, lifting the depressive rainy gloom of Chicago's early winter – the sun's thin heat rolled back the Lake Michigan mist that still, for some unfound reason, waited over the distant watery horizon in a way that threatened O'Reilly's soulful mood.

The archangel Gabriel stood gazing out of the thirty-sixth floor window of Chicago's Tribune Tower. The wide open space was the public viewing gallery, so Gabriel took care to disguise his identity. His white angelic wings were folded beneath his dark grey raincoat, his one layer of protection against the miserable mist-driven weather that rolled in from unforgiving Lake Michigan. Gabriel was troubled, he was disturbed, he knew that Moon had for a long time planned her style of retribution against the catholic church alongside the murderous outrage unleashed upon the priesthood by the thin slip of a woman calling herself Honey. By no means was Honey her real name - Gabriel was under no illusion about who she was, he knew full well that Moon and Honey were one and the same.

Moon was manipulating her self-being, taking different forms to protect her near five hundred year existence since the beheading of her birthing mother at the hands of the English aristocracy. The simple-minded cardinals of the catholic faith had once more failed Gabriel - and the mushrooming crisis was not confined to the catholic doctrine of worship. Other breakaway faiths had been infiltrated by the same rogue cliques of paedophilic predators who were not the embodiment of Gabriel's vision of dominance. The hereditary weakness in male genetics was a raw congenital flaw, a reproductive imperfection that was still mutating all these thousands of years later – such deviant men had without mercy bored into the resplendent organisational institutions in their endless search to find victims, to fulfil their wretched desires in unimaginable ways that Gabriel found aberrant and repulsive. Now, one single entrenched nest of predacious subhumans had made a dangerous and crucial mistake – they had been lured under the guise of the catholic church into a menacing confrontation of their own making - by exploiting a victim who was, without doubt, distant kindred to one of Hyvah's lineage. Now these men were being murdered one by one, hunted down then killed - though not by Moon, this time she had evolved her strategy, Moon did not intend to be caught by the catholic church nor anyone else. Moon was Honey. The childlike Honey.

Before finding then confronting Moon, Gabriel knew he must establish how deep the perverse genetic deviation had penetrated the worshipping catholic faith – and, as he gazed across Chicago's grey unimpressive landscape, the all-powerful envoy of the Lesser Lords was appalled. Five of the perverted priesthood were dead, the catholic bishops were in nervous disarray, Gabriel knew there were more lurking under rotting wood like woodlice crawling in the damp and filth. Five dead could be controlled and managed – five hundred could not.

To make matters worse Gabriel realised that Moon could alter her form. Gabriel suspected the slip of a woman calling herself Honey was Moon's 'honeytrap' bait, one who could lure, then liquidate men with paedophilic obsessions who used the catholic church to select their victims. This Honey was a clever, menacing threat, one who could unravel everything for Gabriel – for centuries, infant descendants of Hyvah had been rooted out, hunted down, disposed of but, in these difficult circumstances, this could not happen.

This time, the whole web of worshipping faiths constructed by Gabriel might be brought crumbling to its knees. The aberrant genetic perversion festering deep inside deviant priests was nothing new, it was intrinsic, it was linked to man's inherent reproductive violence, his domination that drove the whole humanic race; though never deliberate in its cultivation within the worshipping faiths. The cardinals, archbishops, popes, mullahs, rabbis and hindu saints were tasked with keeping their faiths angelic and clean though they always failed. Gabriel knew that purity could never last, the barrier walls were all the time broken, the dams of morality too often burst – perhaps Gabriel needed to broker a truce, an armistice, a moratorium between himself and Moon, the latest manifestation of Hyvah, the embodiment of Eve, Lilith, of Hawwāh - until he could find a way to restore order inside his wayward catholic kingdom. Not until then could he chance his one fatal strike against Moon.

What was more, the church's own cleanup henchman was now missing - Gabriel suspected he had gone underground to track down this Honey. Honey, who had somehow penetrated the church's security to steal the church files containing all the names the church knew of through time - the church's desperate attempts to control the appalling truth that went right to the top in Rome. Where was the deadly churchman? The man who did the dirty work, the one who wiped slates clean.

All this played upon Gabriel's fine-tuned mind. Chicago's Tribune Tower was a fitting monument to the relentless progress of mankind - even though both could collapse in ruin if the violent predilection of man could not be constrained.

Walter McPherson struggled to comprehend what was happening. He drove the worn-out jalopy over the state line into Missouri with the sun beating down through the cracked screen covered in a cling film of Oklahoma dust. The breeze from the open sides relieved the midday heat. Beside McPherson sat the young cop, who seemed to McPherson to be unconcerned about being kidnapped and along for the ride. Leaning against the offside door was Moon, who had been staring out over the flat brownlands to the endless horizon as the truck bumped and rattled over the rutted road.

The three of them had robbed the store, they took food from the counter before declaring they had no money. The owner pointed his rifle for his bucks, but Moon had taken the rifle from him – she had taken it, just like that. The kidnapped cop, Jake, took gum from the store's back shelf, he agreed to pay for the gum, then for a small part of the food as well when he realised how much Moon and McPherson were penniless. The store owner said it was the third time in a week he had been robbed by drifters who were broke, Jake chewed the gum, turning it over and over with his tongue.

McPherson had never stolen anything, not in his whole life - but his belly was now full; McPherson relished the feeling of not being hungry. Jake somehow seemed relaxed to be along. McPherson was puzzled by Jake's easy attitude to being taken as a hostage; it was as if he relished it.

"You got folks?" asked McPherson, trying to break the strange impasse between them. Moon was half sleeping, leaning up against the bouncing cab door.

"Nah. I got one sister but don't see her none," responded Jake.

"How long you been a cop?" McPherson tried to keep the conversation going.

"I ain't a real cop," Jake revealed. McPherson looked over, astonished, taking his eyes from the roadway ahead until he swerved towards the weed-covered verge. "I just got roped in by Hank, to help him an' the sheriff when they were stealin' an' all," Jake added as an afterthought.

"They give you that worn-out uniform jus so's you cud steal?"

"Yeah, s'pose they did," answered Jake. "They takin' money from folks, stoppin' drifters an' like. Had no real problem with that, it ain't no big deal, then they started on the women folk an' I don' like that kinda stuff. My kin's ma, she was violated an' kill'd when I firs' came t' America." Jake looked over to McPherson, McPherson glanced back, seeing the hurt he saw in Jake's eyes. "Me an' Hank, we talked hard an' we agreed he'd hurt no more women folk. Moon here, she sure did the drop on 'im weird like. Y'all reckon he's gonna be ok?"

McPherson did not answer until he thought about what Jake had said. "I dunno Jake. I dunno. I dunno if he'll be ok," McPherson murmured to himself.

"She's kinda strange, I guess," said Jake, as an afterthought.

"They get him?" quizzed McPherson. "The man who did your kin's ma?" McPherson was prime-time interested; he needed to change the subject.

"Nah, the law didn't, they let 'im go from the courthouse," Jake replied. "My kin's pa did tho, was the youngest bro of the state governor who did the rape an' killin'. My kin's Pa kill'd 'im, near cut 'im in half with 'is shotgun. His pa still doin' time inside Shanklin' for that."

"Surprised you took up with the law," said McPherson. "Specially after all that business."

"Hank an' the sheriff, they ain't law," said Jake.

The sun drifted towards the western sunset horizon, the relentless long straight road took a half-quarter turn to the right, meaning they were heading directly towards the glowing red sunset. McPherson noticed that fuel was once more reading low - and they had passed no gas stops for more than two hours. In a couple of more hours, they would need to find somewhere to fill up then sleep, Moon still dozed against the cab door like a half-sleeping cat, sensing even the slightest disturbance without waking or opening her eyes.

It was dark when McPherson pulled into the gas stop. He got a bad feeling straightaway. McPherson saw that Moon was awake, full alert, like a preying lynx. Jake, his eyes were like two hunter's slits scanning the darkened building, sixth sensing the ambush he expected the sheriff to have prearranged from across the state line. Jake was right to be wary, the sheriffs way back in Oklahoma had no jurisdiction here in Missouri but this did not stop the law from reaching its entangled tentacles over the border.

137

The gas stop should not be closed up like this, trying to look like being run down and abandoned – the fuel pump was unlocked, recently used, there were no heckling signs of nature reclaiming its territory; everything was quiet, too quiet to be real.

Behind the torn curtains and grimy windows, loaded rifles and guns waited for the right moment, a given command to open up on the drifters' ramshackle jalopy driven by the renegade man and woman who had rendered a corrupt cop insane, then kidnapped his sidekick after robbing their last stopover store.

Both McPherson and Jake reacted in caution, they each grabbed one of the two rifles from behind the seats, the rifles taken from the cop and from when they robbed the store. Both men climbed down from the driver's cab, keeping the dilapidated jalopy between themselves and the shack, McPherson took the gas pump handle to check it would pump. Moon sat still, saying nothing, seeing that behind the closed door a cop ambush was waiting - through the dirty glass she could see rifle barrels aimed right at her.

"Wait," she instructed to McPherson and Jake. Moon climbed down from the cab; she then took two short paces to the closed store door. She squatted down on her haunches, facing the door, as though contemplating what might be inside - McPherson gazed on, baffled and uneasy.

A good two or three minutes passed during which nothing happened. McPherson and Jake continued to keep the wagon as their shield from unwanted bullets that might fly, Moon did not seem to care, she squatted quiet with a nonchalance that McPherson found unsettling and eerie, even Jake appeared perplexed. The door opened, an inch or two at first, then wide open. The first of four men stepped out, his rifle held high at shoulder level aimed direct at McPherson; the man moved to one side, two more men then fanned out in a line across the ramshackle veranda, their rifles loaded, the fourth, a sheriff, with his 38 aimed at no one in particular. Intimidating, the sheriff peered down at Moon.

"You jus' stand up ma'am an' then step back real slow, you two wanted for robbery an' kidnappin' a cop back over the state line," the sheriff's drawl was meaningful and menacing.

"What you gonna do?" responded McPherson. "You gonna arrest us or you gonna shoot us?"

"We'll, that rightly depends on you," the sheriff warned - with more than a hint of venom. "This woman don't get up offa her ass, then you both gonna get kill'd."

"We just want gas sheriff, then we'll be on our way," said McPherson.

"You drifters ain't goin' nowhere, you understand?" the sheriff's impatience grew, also his agitation, his uncertainty. He paused, he glared in horror at Moon - she knew, somehow, his instinct told him, she knew. The three unsworn deputies, paid sycophant farmstead landowners who hated drifters, they shuffled, waiting to be told what to do.

"Put down y'all rifles fellas," cut in Jake. "I'm the kidnapped cop an' I ain't kidnapped, I tell y'all. An' we *paid* the fella in the robbed store, not all of it, some of it, we didn't have n' more money to give 'im." The high-tensile tension reached an impasse, everyone glared at the sheriff - waiting.

"Why d'yuh kill her?" interrupted Moon, sudden, out of nowhere. The sheriff looked perplexed, scared, defeated – no way could she see inside his head. The sheriff froze rigid, he knew, he knew she knew. "Why d'yuh kill her? Moon repeated her question. No one said anything, all the men stood still, waiting.

"What...? What... d'you mean?" the sheriff stuttered, after pausing in an involuntary stupor.

There followed a silence that was not unlike a barrel of burning oil threatening to explode, the razor-sharp atmosphere could be cut with a knife – all five men gawked at the shocked questioning.

"Why d'yuh kill her eh?" this time Moon injected more toxicity into her voice. The sheriff responded in desperate reaction, he raised his 38 aimed at Moon's head, his angry insanity etched in his contorted expression.

McPherson shot him; the sheriff dropped to the floor in a wounded heap. The nearest deputy in an instant turned his rifle upon McPherson, in another split second Jake's bullet, from nowhere, spun the sheriff's deputy gunman dead - the two other men straightaway slumped their rifles downwards...

"Don't shoot," one of them shouted, in capitulation.

Both McPherson and Jake kept their rifles trained upon the two surrendering gunmen. Moon stood, she ambled over to the groaning sheriff lying face up in front of the door.

"Yuh'll live, it's just a bullet cut," the sheriff screamed in tortured pain, Moon inserted her deft fingers deep into his wound, she removed the bullet head amid profusions of oozing blood, the sheriff stared vacant, silent – he passed out. Moon crossed to the motionless deputy, who was silent, making no move. She saw that Jake's shot had found its perfect mark, through the man's heart with pinpoint precision. "He's dead," said Moon, she turned to look at Jake – her first hunch had been right, she knew in the blink of an eye who Jake was. "Yuh sure shoot straight for a fake cop," was all Moon said.

McPherson held the gas nozzle into the tank, Jake hand-pumped the handle to fill. On normal days no one filled their jalopy tank to full, the cost to threadbare farmsteaders was too high – but McPherson felt the warm feeling of not much caring what the pump gauge read, this time they *were* stealing the fuel, McPherson felt himself a full-blown thief. In under five minutes, the tank was full, McPherson had no idea how far the old wagon would get them, or if they would get that far now they had killed a deputy and wounded the sheriff. The whole state of Missouri would be on their tail by the morning, Oklahoma would issue an alert for their arrest – McPherson thought it a waste of time filling the tank to brimming, but anything might happen with Moon pulling the strings of fate. And Jake – McPherson was beginning to get a bad feeling about Jake.

They left the gas stopover store way after full nighttime descended. There was enough moonlight from the quarter moon and the clear starlit sky to make out the flat monotonous landscape of poverty-riddled southwest Missouri. The cotton and corn crops were meagre thin bare, brown and stringy, hugging the roadside ditches until disappearing into the silvery moonlight that gave them a semblance of visibility, a respectability that became lost once out of sight where no one cared. There was no chance of a sleeping stopover, so Moon took her turn to drive while McPherson tried to doze as best he could in the bouncing cab leaning against the passenger door. Jake sat himself in the middle, staring ahead at the relentless straight road lit by the dim light of one working headlight. There was as yet no sign of the search that would soon be launched to find them, McPherson began to drift into a half-subconscious sleep.

"Yuh that churchman?" asked Moon to Jake. She kept her keen eye on the insipid yellow light that lit their escape route north.

Jake paused, knowing the crunch time was rearing its head - this Moon was slick, he was gonna have to work hard to come out of this. McPherson half listened, pretending not to be awake. Moon was well aware of who the churchman was.

"Yeah, I guess, ma'am," Jake answered.

"Yuh join that sheriff knowin' I be headed down this road?"

"Guess so, ma'am, I know where yuh headed."

"Stuff you told Walt 'bout yuh kin's ma an' pa, that's true ain't it?" Moon knew she had to peel back the layers, to understand the reasons why Jake was riding along. If what she thought was true, then she needed to act fast.

"Yeah, it's true," said Jake.

"So yuh know who I am?" asked Moon, direct.

"Yeah, I know." Jake looked uneasy, keeping his eyes peeled ahead. He knew everything, how, morphed as Honey, she had slain five catholic priests. Jake also knew how much Moon needed Walter McPherson. Moon's relationship with McPherson was complex; Jake had also figured out McPherson knew little about Moon. Jake realised McPherson did not know Moon and Honey were one and the same.

"Did yuh jump onboard t' stop or help Honey killin' Callaghan an' Mancini?" Moon turned her eyes from the road, she peered straight into Jake who refused to meet her gaze. "An' yuh know I'm gonna get that file from the catholic vault don't yuh," Moon knew the answer. McPherson immediately jolted upright, alarmed.

"You *catholic?*" cut in McPherson.

"Yeah, I guess," said Jake to McPherson, eager to grasp the opportunity to avoid Moon's questioning; Moon would not let Jake off the peg.

"If yuh that catholic churchman, then yuh been on my tail a while," Moon probed, ignoring McPherson.

"Yeah, a while," answered Jake. "Took me a time to figure yuh were down in Oklahoma, I figured y'all need t' find Walt here after that Honey woman shot O'Hearn. Tho, I tell y'all, it ain't bin easy with the navy sniffin' the trail of that Honey an' all."

McPherson's head began to reel. What was Jake saying? What was he saying about Honey? It made no sense - but Moon's eyes, the way she tossed her hair, the way she played with his emotions, his reality of what was happening, his perception of the real world... McPherson was unable to speak or intervene, he was choked, he felt like something small in a big mincing machine he did not understand, an insignificant element in a paranoid world of confusion. Little did McPherson know how much his survival hinged upon his absolute unique abilities to work things, Mr Fixit, how his ancestral blood was linked far back to the mythical Eden... McPherson's world began to collapse inwards – the old familiar feeling – it welled up in consuming uncertainty...

"Yeah, that Honey, she's sure mean," said Moon, she drove the truck onwards, the night's darkness going nowhere.

"Piece o' genius, I reckon, all lookin' for a murderer who don't exist none," said Jake. "Y'all stole that file y'all gave to O'Reilly an' now everyone tryin' to tail that Honey, but y'all don't fool me none."

"Yuh're the church's clean up man?" asked Moon, "I know who the churchman is, he's been aroun' a while."

"Yeah, I guess,"

"Yuh gone renegade?" Moon probed direct, she had never crossed paths with the churchman whose centuries-old task was to clean up the filth inside the fallen priesthood - if it was true what he had said to Walter about his kinsfolk's ma and pa then there might just be a deep routed sideswipe to his motives. Moon began to follow her instinctive hunch.

Jake looked uneasy, pained. It had not been easy to locate Walter McPherson – the race against others desperate to find him had made it an undignified scramble against time. McPherson was the key to Honey, who was the open door to Moon - who was herself the contriver to the unravelling of the terrible secret that threatened the innermost core of the catholic church.

"I ain't gone renegade ma'am, I gotta protect the church, it's my job," said Jake. "Y'all kill'd bad priests, we both know how bad ma'am, but y'all put me in a bad spot. I can't let that Honey kill no more, y'all know that."

McPherson sat silent, stunned, listening. It all made crazy sense; the truck bounced along the rutted road in retrograde resolve.

"Maybe yuh'll turn renegade if I tell yuh somethin', somethin' yuh don't know already," said Moon.

Jake turned to Moon, saying nothing. What could he say? She was probing, searching for his weakness, he could not drop his guard, he could not let her for one moment into his mind, he knew first hand what Moon could do. Jake stayed silent.

"There's a turn in the road up ahead. By that turn yuh'll be renegade Jake, I tell yuh," Moon's eyes were lynx-like. "Yuh kinsfolk ma who got kill'd, she wasn't like yuh real ma was she Jake, jus' like you ain't no real cop."

"Yeah, I guess," answered Jake. He leaned back, he tensed, ready to leap and pounce. He might get one single chance, the one chance he needed. He could finish her.

"See, I know'd yuh real ma, she was a good woman yuh real ma, jus' before those catholic bishops kill'd her." Moon steered the truck onwards, not caring if Jake looked on or not.

Jake froze rigid, though he realised what Moon was attempting to do, to immobilise him, to knock down his defences. What were his choices? Not once in over a million years had Hyvah been knocked down, Jake did not know if Moon was Hyvah in her last incarnate or was pure offspring – either way, she was onto him which meant he had little chance of survival. His life did not matter, he had promised to give his soul to the church without pity, to God, to Gabriel, to the almighty pope in Rome. After his real mother had been burnt for witchcraft on the stake the church had raised him, trained him for his grim task, ageless in his three hundred years of work protecting the catholic priesthood. There were countless bad men of God, too many priests who were turned by impurities in their genes, his indoctrination, how they must be protected, how they must not be allowed to bring Rome crashing to its knees. Evil priests were dealt with by God and the church, not by revengeful souls driven by grief seeking to right wrongs.

For a long time, there had been widening cracks in Jake's resolve, he had seen and experienced many appalling events first-hand. God never intervened, not once had the Lord seen fit to stop or punish the evil men who acted out their deviant desires by abusing their victims, they could have been disarmed under the guise of the catholic church. The woman, Honey, had assassinated five of the worst kind, Jake did not doubt this, Callaghan and Mancini might deserve their fate, but murder was murder, murder was wrong in the eyes of God. Worse, this would make seven dead paedophilic priests, if the truth got into the open, it would lift the lid on a far greater scandal. Why did God, or Gabriel, not stop this evil rot? Why did unguarded women and kids have to be ravaged by men who were supposed to be offering a safe path to the arms of the Lord? Unless God himself was weak-willed without strength and conviction...

"How much d'yuh believe in that God Jake? I know Jake ain't yuh real name." Moon kept her cat-like eyes peering into the perpetual darkness ahead, the turn in the road was less than two miles, she saw the army and police roadblock prepared and waiting. Moon said nothing.

"I believe with my whole soul in my God ma'am, an' I believe y'all know this ma'am," answered Jake, fighting and winning his battle to stay calm.

"Them folks yuh told Walt 'bout, yuh kin's folks - they church folks?" asked Moon.

"Yeah, I guess," Jake answered. "They were good folks; I lived a while with them folks until she got kill'd an' all."

"Weren't no governor's son who kill'd her Jake, jus' like yuh real ma weren't no witch's witch when those catholic bishops burned her alive on that fire stake," Moon turned to see Jake's jaw dropped in wide-eyed shock horror, the bulging veins in his eyeballs threatening to burst in an instant. "Yuh see, yuh ma was burned coz she was my half-sister, back then in the France mountains two hundred an' fifty years back. That makes me an' you blood Jake, we're both kinda kin. Knew yuh'd come lookin' for me one day." The road turned; the waiting roadblock drew closer.

"We gotta little problem for ourselves ahead Jake," continued Moon without breaking to pause. "Yuh gotta decide kinda quick which side yuh gonna be on."

Jake shook with inward ineptitude, not in all his long life had he been taken apart with such ease, he could make out something sinister waiting ahead.

Moon knew every detail, Jake reeled, it could not be true, if his mother was Moon's blood then this changed his whole world, his sole reason for existing was on the verge of collapse – and all this had happened in the space of fifteen seconds. Jake stared at Moon, just how powerful was she? What were the limits of her capabilities? Jake knew in an instant that Moon was capable of anything, even bringing down the catholic church – but why? Why would she?

"I know what yuh're thinkin' Jake," Moon interrupted Jake's train of wild out-of-control thoughts, "I ain't gonna destroy your church like yuh supposin'. That seed is well set, it's gonna take maybe 'nother hundred or so years but it's all gonna blow up, your church is gonna destroy itself, it don't need me none, I already dun that job. O'Reilly'll set that ball rollin'. But, yuh know, I want that church file real bad, I ain't got it yet, the stuff 'bout thos' popes an' bishops. An' yuh know why I want it don't you Jake."

Moon was right, Jake did know, he knew all too well. Honey's crusade against the worst of the priests was not anything much, she was scratching the surface of a pit of decrepit snakes, the abuse and predatory priesthood that twisted and turned right to the pinnacle of the church, embedded nests of deviants that stalked the vulnerable. Jake had seen all this, he had spent his entire adult life covering up the church's wretched secrets, Jake had had enough – and Moon knew that Jake was ready to turn renegade.

"Y'all never get that file, Moon," whispered Jake in despair. "That stuff's been collected for over two hundred years, I seen it an' I know what's in it, an' it's protected by mechanics an' light beam wires that ain't got no place in this world. Y'all ain't gonna get in there Moon, nobody can." Moon turned the wheel to ride the bend, they were moments away from the roadblock, the truck's light cast a dim glimmer down the road that just caught the faint outline of cop cars and navy vehicles in a line blocking their approach, men with loaded rifles waiting.

"Maybe I can't... but Walt can, he can fix his way into anythin'."

McPherson, who had been listening mesmerised and riveted by every word, realised everything. His whole life clicked into place, why he had been born to be abandoned in the orphanage, why he had suffered the insane and terrible abuse at the hands of McCarthy, his time in the tram workshops that honed and developed his skills, the navy, the crazy gunsight, Honey, Honey who was Moon, the weird whitestone vis... it was the full circle, his heritage, his bloodline – everything lead to this moment, the opening of the vault that Moon and Jake talked about, it was his destiny. In the same moment that Jake's life apart, McPherson's life fell into place.

Moon drew to a halt, the headlights revealing a line of three dozen or more raised rifles. Behind the threatening line, the road was closed by nose-to-tail cop cars, behind which two armoured vehicles were parked in ominous support. Intense bright lights were switched on which illuminated the whole scene in fluorescent luminescence that cast a cascading unreality through the long past midnight darkness. In the far distance, the first streak of daylight heralded the beginning of the new dawn.

"Looks like we gonna get apprehended,' Moon smiled. "We gonna get arrested, we gonna get a free ride an' taken all the way to where we wanna go Jake." In the moment it took for Jake to blink, the churchman turned renegade.

O'Reilly sat through the whole day reading the secret navy file that Honey had stolen. The hard-nosed detective was not an expert on military affairs, but he knew enough to realise why he was gobsmacked.

Pretty much everything in the secret document related to this one guy second class engineer Walter McPherson who, it seemed, had modified a standard Mark One naval gunsight rangefinder without any level of navy authorisation, which had to be withdrawn from service when two warship gunnery officers died – not by accident, by suicide, both jumped overboard after 'seeing' unexpected visions through McPherson's altered viewing prisms when his novel application of an electric current was applied. The navy moved with uncharacteristic speed to make safety changes – resulting in the successful, accurate Mark Two that gave the United States Navy strategic advantages over its future enemies - and enemy agents were at this moment trying with their utmost efforts to steal the secret plans of the navy's new big gun rangefinder.

The US Navy were not mugs – they realised McPherson's potential, they had admitted one almighty blunder in court martialling their greatest technical protégé out of the Navy on trumped-up charges of theft. The navy wanted McPherson back, the chain of command had issued orders to get him re-enlisted. The highest office, the secretary of the navy, had worked out how much McPherson could change the course of future conflicts through his own version of what he had invented - the device he had modified to watch Honey shoot O'Hearn with his gun. When O'Reilly read this he was stunned, speechless to the point of mortification when it registered with him that as a simple federal bureau detective, he was out of his depth. Also, in the file was how the navy expected McPherson's device to track the spies trying to steal their enhanced Mark Three rangefinder secrets.

O'Reilly then read McPherson's personal history - it made mind-turning reading, not only did O'Reilly read McPherson's navy records he read about his life in the catholic orphanages. O'Reilly knew from the other file that McPherson was on the list of Father McCarthy's victims. This brought everything full circle, it explained everything, it was the link, it was the open door that Honey had walked through – when O'Reilly finished reading, the whole picture was like an unfinished mosaic painting – close, but not quite. Of course, Honey was Moon, it was obvious, Moon had visited the young McPherson in the orphanage for her own selfish reasons – was this linked to Honey later getting herself hitched to McPherson? There must be a reason why Honey had set out to take revenge against McCarthy for his paedophilic abuse, the murder of kids who dared to squeal. McPherson had survived because he kept quiet, he had kept his mouth shut. O'Reilly thought more about how much this guy McPherson had suffered – though it struck O'Reilly how much Walter McPherson had been used by this so-called Moon. Used as bait? No, it wasn't bait, this much O'Reilly was certain, McPherson was being cultivated for something far more reaching.

The investigative instinct within O'Reilly was ingrained, it ran deep inside his veins, O'Reilly wasn't fooled, not for one minute did he believe that Honey was singling out just seven priests – the more he read about McPherson, the more O'Reilly believed there was more at stake. McPherson was the key, both the navy and this woman called Moon wanted McPherson bad. Then there was this shadowy henchman known as the churchman, much of the information in the file stolen from the catholic vaults had been investigated from inside the church by this unknown cleanup jockey who without doubt knew his stuff, by the nature of the information he had gathered he was not of the priesthood, this guy was a professional, he had seen the absolute worse from within – O'Reilly would like to give a buck for this guy's thoughts.

But there was a nagging thought that bugged O'Reilly, it kept coming back over and over like an irritating itch he could not scratch. Where had McPherson come from? Why was he in the Saint Catherine's Catholic Orphanage? What if the murdered priests were not just revenge killings? What if the priests themselves were part of a trail of carefully laid bait? Might there be a much bigger fish in the big wide ocean to hook? Without doubt, the priority for this mysterious woman Moon must be McPherson – and if Moon could lure this churchman to be on her side, then all hell would let loose... it was as if Moon was luring the Pope himself into seeing the futility of the world's longest established faith - O'Reilly half smiled. Then his expression froze. It struck O'Reilly like a bolt to the head. The dead priests, this Moon, it *was* a deliberate trail, a lure, the killing of the priests was not just revenge, *Moon was, for some reason, stalking the churchman.* If she got the churchman... Moon, she was after more, much more... Who was Moon...? Of course... this was why Honey had from nowhere ghosted into his office to confess to five revenge murders. If this Moon, McPherson and the church's cleanup henchman in some way got together then there would be complete havoc inside the catholic church.

O'Reilly, with a conviction of righteousness he had never before experienced, was quick to understand without any shadow of doubt what it was Honey wanted him to do – once the penny had dropped there was an obvious reason why McPherson was in the same catholic orphanage as Father McCarthy. One rational thought led to another, with absolute shock horror O'Reilly realised who had abandoned McPherson in the orphanage when he was a young kid and why. McPherson was so extra special - through its own rampant paedophilic filth the catholic hierarchy might be irreparably finished. O'Reilly stood to walk to the phone on the wall beside his desk, beforehand he rifled through the navy file until he found the navy number he never thought he would dial.

"It's me, O'Reilly," he croaked down the phone without any feeling of remorse or apprehension - there was stone-cold silence on the other end of the line. "I've read your stolen McPherson file, it's here, right in front of me, it's on my desk."

There was a long awkward pause, the righteous world of confrontational rotten worshipping faiths revolved one small fraction of one daily revolution in the same way it had for more than four and a half billion years. "Stay there," ordered the navy voice, the voice of O'Reilly's tail. "We'll come down; we will bring you in."

Gabriel came to the same insane conclusion just three minutes, thirty-five seconds after FBI Detective O'Reilly - the difference being that Gabriel knew of the other catholic vault and the mortifying documentation it contained. Centuries-old accusations supported by stacks of historic evidence for the church's use only, never to be disclosed. Gabriel had been instrumental in creating the locks, he was confident that no human skills or technology existed that could break the vault doors open without any knowledge of the combination sequencing mechanisms holding the locks closed or the four complex keys needed to unlock the vault.

With growing conviction, Gabriel realised that Hyvah's reproductive birthright Moon was not going to be compromised with, under no circumstances was there a deal to be done, one that would protect the church from the explosive fallout that would follow if it was brought to light how deep predatory hawks had nested themselves within the church's hierarchy while portraying themselves to be men of God. Moon, and her two as yet unidentified companions, must be dealt with at all costs irrespective of the murderous acts of a few renegade cadre of priests, even though Gabriel knew the vile seed of rapacious exploitation was not confined just to the rank and file priesthood - it had long cast its slithering tentacles throughout the church's upper pyramid. Neither stringent canon law nor the piety of priesthood celibacy wielded by the Vatican Holy See to curtail the worst of subhuman behaviour had succeeded in keeping the genetic plague at bay.

Gabriel accepted the mutation festering inside certain strains of men had become ingrained, strands of human genome that created paedophilic tendencies were not uncommon, nor was it confined to the catholic church. Gabriel had long known the faith attracted the more devious kind, even though the church had tried to resolve each crisis behind its closed doors, one by one, one at a time, hindered by its own but, in these difficult times, there had been a catastrophic change. The faith's fixer, who had taken care of the fallout for countless years, had still not been found. He had taken himself underground to track the five mysterious revenge killings - serial murders that Gabriel suspected were linked - but the much vaunted, valued churchman had vanished. What's more, Gabriel knew that Moon had made her incisive move. The hereditary birthright of Hyvah might attempt to destabilise or even destroy the faith - not since the mayhem of medieval Europe had the catholic order faced such danger when catholic England had been lost, when the irreducible queen of England had brought catholicism crumbling to its knees.

Gabriel turned to face Cardinal Moncetti, all the grim-faced bishops were agitated and pale. Moncetti looked like death warmed up - the news he had for Gabriel was grave. The cardinal envoy from Rome, Cardinal Adamovich, sat quiet at one end of the long mahogany table, his face expressionless and all-seeing.

"My Reverence, I am, with great urgency, making arrangements to travel to Rome." The atmosphere in the cathedral chamber became more hushed and tense as Moncetti spoke. Gabriel thought it ironic that nothing of the building was more than eighty years old, a reflection of the new world of America - the great churches of Rome bore the two-thousand-year burden of history since Christ's suffrage on the cross and the redeeming nemeses of Saint Mary. None of the bishops deemed to say anything or wished to intervene. Some knew the terrible news that Moncetti bore, others did not - no one was sure who knew what. "Through our esteemed cardinal here I have received instructions from the Synod of High Bishops in Rome, I have been summoned by their decree to the council of the Holy See."

"Tell us Moncetti, what do you know? Something bad has happened?" Gabriel tried to remain calm, he feared the worst, the cardinal knew something he did not.

Moncetti's unease was difficult to hide, he decided to bite the bullet of truth. "Late last night, I learned that our key vestibule vault has been forced open. Some documents inside were taken, everything else was defiled or destroyed." Moncetti thought it best not to continue, he heard the gasps of shock around the room. He saw Gabriel's frozen expression. The master vault was supposed to be impenetrable, impregnable, the locks set by intrinsic light beam technology not known to the human race.

Gabriel tried to remain calm, his great white wings folded and hidden. It would not do for the council of American catholic bishops to see that he was distraught, that this was a disaster of the worst imaginable magnitude - the cardinals must never see how the church's own deep-down filth could destroy everything. Neither Moncetti nor the assembled bishops knew they had the presence of the supreme archangel in their midst - to them he was the high eminence deacon sent by Rome. The Vatican envoy, Adamovich, with good reason, stayed silent. "How did this happen?" demanded Gabriel.

"Three days ago, the renegade woman who calls herself Moon, she and her two accomplices were apprehended by law enforcement forces in southern Missouri," said Moncetti. "They were brought here to Boston for questioning by Navy intelligence and the Federal Bureau of Investigations. They were charged with murder and robbery back in Oklahoma, also for the theft of confidential information from the navy and ourselves the catholic church."

Gabriel stared in shock, he realised what was coming next. "Who were the two accomplices?" he demanded.

"One is the man wanted by navy intelligence, Walter McPherson," Moncetti paused, he paused for a considerable time, conscious of the fourteen pairs of eyes that bored into his soul. Moncetti, he knew everything. "The other man apprehended with this woman Moon, he gave the name Jake Donovan which is the false name of our investigator we call the churchman. Donovan has turned sides, he is charged with the murder of a deputy sheriff in Missouri, with aggravated robbery in Oklahoma and with a raft of other charges alongside the woman and McPherson. But I'm afraid this is not the worst news." Moncetti sat down to take a rest, the midday sun threw beams of light through the ornate cathedral window. Christ's stained glass crucifixion took on a new meaning, representing the pain of each man present in the great hall. Gabriel glared at the suffering image of Jesus, remembering well those chaotic days of pain when Mary Magdalene had brought his world crashing down. Walter McPherson, of course, Walter McPherson, it dawned on Gabriel who Walter McPherson might be, surely he was the same blood as Iscariot. Gabriel stared at Adamovich, the envoy from Rome, who stared back in horrified wonderment as their eyes met in mind rendering realisation.

"They disappeared from their individual police cells where they were being held, all three of them," continued Moncetti. "I do not know how they did this, their cell locks were still locked after their escape, their cells were guarded, their cells were empty when opened in the morning. Then it was later discovered that our vault had been opened, those locks had been broken also. We do not know how; this was all discovered last night."

"What do we know of this McPherson?" Gabriel hissed, holding back his rage.

"The navy say he has special skills, like nothing they have known before. They have been searching for him for ten years since him being court-martialled from the Navy. They say he has been living as a vagrant in Oklahoma, working hand to mouth as a fix-it traveller, building a sizeable reputation for his skills. He has the ability to fix pretty much anything. Navy intelligence laughed when we informed them of the escape; they reckon it would have been easy for McPherson to open our vault."

Gabriel thought for a few moments, it had all been a clever laid trap. The FBI, police, navy intelligence, the catholic church, they had each combined to bring Moon with her chosen companions right to where she wanted to be, within striking distance of the vaults that held the hidden secrets that in themselves could bring down the church. Gabriel smiled; Moon had done it all so perfect.

"You know more Moncetti," quizzed Gabriel, "I do not think you have yet told us everything." He saw fear in Moncetti's eyes.

"Navy intelligence scrutinised our orphanage records, the orphanage registers of Father McCarthy," continued Moncetti once more. "A woman, unknown at the time, left the orphaned McPherson at the Saint Catherine's gates, we have no records of his birth or heritage. The woman visited the young boy three times in his first three years, the last time she came there was trouble, she took one boy away by force, claiming he would be murdered, afterwards nothing more. There is an old photograph of her and the child McPherson together during the woman's first visit," Moncetti paused, endeavoured to smooth his way through the revelation he was about to divulge. "We know it was this woman who calls herself Moon who left the child McPherson at our San Francisco Saint Catherine orphanage.

153

It seems she purposely left the photograph in our records. There's no doubt the church has been lured into an intentional game of revenge. It's puzzling, her age does not seem to add up, she has not aged during these years. Now, five of our worst offending priests are dead, strange justice has been dealt in a way we cannot begin to imagine."

"I'm afraid you are wrong when you say five priests," interrupted Bishop Rafferty of the local Boston district. "I'm sorry to inform everyone here that, before this emergency gathering of bishops and cardinals this morning, I was informed of two more deaths. One long-standing priest, a good friend of mine, strangled, here in Boston, the other in upstate New York, his neck broken. The cops here and in New York are investigating."

Moncetti stood disturbed, this was another unexpected twist, the day was the worst in his entire professional life but then, as he shifted his feet in discomfort, he was not deep down shocked. "Were they Father Callaghan and Father Mancini?" Moncetti asked.

"Yes," Rafferty answered. "How did you know this?"

Moncetti looked grim-faced. "As each day passes, it becomes more apparent that we hid an evil cadre of human faeces within our midst. Five, now seven, of these men have been targeted, singled out then assassinated. There is little we the catholic church can do, we cannot defend them, the crimes these men committed were hideous."

"It seems our dirty work is being done for us. Do we know who murdered these men? How do we know they are linked?" asked the wrinkled-faced bishop Ivan from Chicago. He looked the thug he was reputed to be.

"Yes. Yes, we do," answered Moncetti. "Navy intelligence told us that a revenge killer is on the loose, when Father O'Hearn was shot with his own gun, they traced the killer through some McPherson invention. We tried our hardest to get the killer apprehended, we even put out a contract through our usual Philadelphia sources. Then the Federal Bureau of Investigations, the FBI, their religious affairs investigator, his name's O'Reilly, got on the case in Chicago where two more of our priests were found dead. Each one of the dead was found with a cheap lookalike Magdalene pendant left hanging on their bodies, O'Reilly discovered that the killer of all the priests is the same woman, or her alter ego who uses the name Honey, she turned up at O'Reilly's office to confess. So, you see, it's all linked. McPherson, McCarthy, Moon, this Honey... she wears the damnable cross of Eve around her neck. The church has worked hard, we got O'Reilly's investigation stopped, we did this through the state governor's office. O'Reilly's since played the advocate, he's turned everything over to navy intelligence."

"I know O'Reilly," said Ivan. "He's immigrant catholic blood. Hardcore cop, smart, ain't corrupt. But how'n the hell does a woman get to strangulate seven men eh?"

Adamovich, the envoy in the room from Rome sat silent, concerned. He knew that Moon in any of her guises was easy capable of finishing any man in whatever way she chose. Cardinal Adamovich was third in line from the Pope, he glanced with worry at Gabriel, they both knew that none of the American cardinals and bishops in the cathedral hall realised what they were up against. Adamovich stood to his feet.

"I am Cardinal Adamovich, I have sailed by ship from Rome, please sit down Monsignor Moncetti," Adamovich's thick east-European accent added to the suppressed atmosphere in the hall. Gabriel continued to sit in his quiet contemplative mood. Cardinal Adamovich was the one man present who knew who Gabriel was with his hidden, folded white wings. "You have failed in your tasks; the policy of the worldwide Roman Catholic Church is to deal with abuse allegations of these sorts. The man you tasked with cleaning up your mess, your so-called churchman, is a long-standing disciple of ours. It is unfortunate, I believe he has turned against us. He was sent by Rome to assist you; this churchman knows what you are up against. You, my friends, do not."

"Where is this churchman?" demanded Moncetti. "Where is he? We have not seen him since he decided to take himself underground."

"Do not concern yourself with the churchman, he is a problem for the Holy See in Rome," Adamovich responded. "His real name is Paolo Adrussi, he is skilled in adapting to many identities, in the same way is this woman, Moon. They are of the same distant half-blood; it is said they are blood-related. Adrussi knows the ways of this Moon, we in Rome are concerned that Adrussi and Moon might be in league together, our forefathers did not cover themselves in glory when they burned Adrussi's mother on the witch's stake. This union between Moon, this McPherson and Adrussi is not good for catholic Rome."

Gabriel listened with even more concern. Cardinal Adamovich was no fool, to send Adamovich here, Pope Paulus was throwing in his heaviest possible drumfire. Gabriel understood what Adamovich was saying, this was now a serious deteriorating disaster being well manipulated by his extreme enemy. The church's disgusting filth was being used to destroy itself.

"Do you know of this man McPherson?" asked Bishop McCluskey.

"No, not much," answered Adamovich. "But his abilities and powers are concerning. We need to learn more, but we must pit ourselves against the might of the United States Navy to get hold of him. However, in this, we will succeed."

Gabriel stood up; he stood his full height to gain the mightiest impression from his captive audience. Everyone in the room sat spellbound, Adamovich huddled down, trying to show his humbling benevolence.

"You bishops and cardinals here now, this church of yours faces immense danger," hissed Gabriel in anger. "You have brought the catholic faith to the verge of destruction..." Gabriel stopped; he was without warning interrupted. The tall arched door to the cathedral hall was flung open.

The impressive height of the ornate entrance added to the intentional attempt to add historic ageless grandeur to this not-so-ancient cathedral, a celebration of Christ in the glorified fashion of rich colours evident in every catholic place of worship stretching back throughout the civilised world for nearly two thousand years. The false illusion of great age was complete, the appearance of history was entwined with breathtaking golds, opulent reds, teardrop-coloured blues and the striking rich greens of catholicism in its finest crucifixion triumph, all entangled by a Hollywood way of construction that even the unskilled eye could discern was less than fifty years old. Such were the illusional reproductive achievements of America. The dreamlike quality of the spectacular archway shattered, its tallness tumbling when the nymphlike Honey entered the room through the open door.

Gabriel was not the only one present who suffered the shock of instantaneous mortification. Honey strode the thin line of outward adversity, she walked without remorse to sit in the one free chair at the head of the great oval table.

Honey held the moment, every cardinal and bishop, the emissary from Rome, even Gabriel sat silent.

"All of you here give grace to the assertion of the immaculate conception." Honey was quite forceful in what she wanted to say. "Was not Mary, the mother of your holy Christ born without sin? How can this be when the virtuous Anne of Gethsemane, who gave birth to your wondrous virgin you all call Mary, is herself cast with sin when she was defiled by threatening force by this man who called himself Joachim, a man upon whom you have bestowed your sacred honour of sainthood?" Honey spoke with no southern drawl in her voice, she was in her most combative mood, she had no time to hide her real self. "Each one of you men here, you pretend to worship the sinless virgin, the pureness of her conception, yet your lives are defiled by the filthiest and foulest sins that any man can deliver."

Honey turned to face Gabriel, who stood unashamed and silent while he fought to gather his reeling senses. "What of you Gabriel? Do I offend you in my more childlike guise?" Honey suddenly morphed, her form changing into the adulthood Moon, the blueness of her grey eyes capturing Gabriel in the same way as always. Then her change continued, a long way past the peasant back-country Moon who prowled Oklahoma until another Moon's white fair hair fell across the brow of her face. She flipped it away with a casual hand movement that, unwitting, took the last inch of breath from every bishop and cardinal present in the room. Moon's metamorphic change was complete, there were gasps of astonishment intermingled with staggered shock. Moon turned to the stricken Bishop McCluskey.

"Ah, I see that you shake and tremble. And for good reason McCluskey.

Is it not ironic that you sit at this table when the celibacy of your life is so impure? I can see into your mind bishop, I see your odious memories, the ones that are not written in those stolen files I now have in my possession. Are you not concerned with your sins? Do you not sit uncomfortable on your fat ass when there is this talk here today about your church's ways of hiding the not-so-immaculate conceptions that happen in your orphanages every night?" Moon saw McCluskey wince, then she stared at each bishop and cardinal around the table, she saw the panicking fright in each of their minds – but not in the thoughts of Adamovich, Adamovich's mind was shielded, Adamovich had long been trained to protect his sanity should Hyvah or her birthrights ever attempt to bring him down by twisting his memories into a quagmire of insane insignificance.

"Cardinal Adamovich, I see your Pope in Rome has sent in his big guns. It's my dubious pleasure to see you again. How is your mother? You know that she shares my blood?" Moon's gaze pierced into him; the cardinal remained calm. This was not his first encounter with Hyvah, he knew there existed a deep-rooted link with Hyvah's hereditary ancestry – one she shared with the churchman Paolo Adrussi and, indeed, with Walter McPherson.

"Good morning to you, Moon. Is this the commonest name you go by these days?" Adamovich answered with unsubtle smoothness, without much warmth. "My mother is frail, she is aged by many years, though she is well. She will be greatly honoured that you ask of her," he added. The sunlight through the stained glass archway took on a more reddish hew, beams of iridescent half-colours tried to intervene but this was Moon's confrontational moment.

"Can I ask why you come here now?" asked Adamovich, with half-hidden unease.

"You know why I am here cardinal. Do you think it is not the right time for me to collect the debt for all those who are defiled and dead?" Moon saw the cardinal for a moment wince, for a small fraction of a second he oozed sweat though Adamovich was no novice in this game of eternal life and death; he was quick to regain his composure.

"You have assassinated seven of our more unholy priests, how much debt do you wish to collect?" No one deemed to interrupt, Adamovich fidgeted in his seat, he sensed his defeat, he could only buy time. He saw Gabriel's warning look in his unearthly eyes.

"You know what I demand, cardinal." Moon stood from the chair where she had taken her seat, she paced to face Adamovich. "Gabriel here hides the might of his power from these bishops, while you talk of seven priests who have died for their sins as penance for the way your church hides its revolting secrets. Was it not your Baptist who wrote what your saviour commanded 'Let him who is without sin cast the first stone? Is this not written by that Baptist in your bible book? Which of these bishops and cardinals here will cast the first stone cardinal? Will you cast the first stone?"

Adamovich was close to an emotional upheaval; he knew Moon was right. The catholic church was riddled with habitual hawks, faithless men who saw easy opportunities to take advantage of the credibility the faith bestowed - Adamovich had spent most of his adult life distrusting those around him. How could he admonish Moon, even Gabriel appeared uncertain in his demeanour. The bishops, Adamovich could see they were in mortified disarray.

Moon saw how she had found her mark. "Only seven of you have suffered the price of death, because they believed the life of a child is cheap. More than ten thousand of your brotherhood hierarchy should be dead of pitiful shame, this is the legacy of your catholic faith cardinal."

The cardinal envoy from Rome sat back, he did not answer, he could think of nothing worthwhile to say. He had been sent by the holy assembly to see what could be done, the festering crisis of child abuse was not confined to America, it was a simmering catastrophe wherever the catholic faith was the dominant religion, where the systematic structure of social credibility could be taken advantage of by men who had every intention of burying themselves into vulnerable communities for their own gratification. Adamovich was all but on Moon's side, but not quite. For many centuries the conspiracy radicalisation of Eve had been a consistent thorn in Rome's heart, the hearsay allegations, rumours of prehistoric tablets that challenged what was said in testaments written by men - Adamovich was well aware the church could succumb to the formidable attrition that Moon could wield.

It was bishop Moncetti who broke the confrontation between Adamovich and Moon. "By foul means, you have opened our cathedral vaults, you have stolen the confidential contents inside. You present yourself here by your endeavours. What is your purpose here? What do you want?" the cardinal interrupted Adamovich's disturbing exchange. "What *is* this debt you claim?"

"Cardinal Adamovich here knows my demand against your faith. Perhaps it is time for you to redeem the name of Judas Iscariot, though this debt is not the reason I am here. My cardinal friend from Rome knows you cannot deliver my demand, so your church is forever condemned in my eyes. Your Lord's angel who calls himself Gabriel, who sits himself across from me now, knows I will not bring down your despised church, not yet, not this time," Moon was trance like in her deliverance, Moncetti's stupefied gaze did not flicker, each of the bishops turned to stare wide-eyed at Gabriel. "Seven of your devil priests are dead by my hand," Moon did not stop, "I was not seeking revenge, they did not die because they murdered one of your Christ's young bloods, they died to protect more shameless victims, more who would have come into their hands if this cesspit of catholic vultures had been left untouched. We by purpose sought them out, we found them, they died like the rabid dribbling dogs they were. And know this, there are two of you in this room who know this shame. I know who you are, in the same way Cardinal Adamovich knows who are the ones in Rome."

Cardinal Moncetti could not contain himself. "You outright threaten the catholic church? Is blackmail your ultimate motive?" he exploded.

"Yes, perhaps it is Moncetti," responded Moon. "Paolo Adrussi, your churchman, your cleanup henchman, he is mine, I have him, he has turned against you, he will find you. I have every known name, every damned one of you who is not worth the blood in his veins."

"We will hunt you down," Moncetti warned, "I will not allow our faith's monumental greatness to be threatened in this way. Our Lord will prevail... the holy trinity is divine... Jesus in his wisdom will guide us... he died on the cross for our sins... our sins are blessed... mankind has paid the price with the blood of Christ... you are a woman, do not think we will take this," his talk was stuttered with anger.

Moon studied Moncetti, seeing what she already knew in his twisted mind. "When those cops pulled your little sister from that swollen river, did they know her brothers climbed into her bed each night to finger her? Did they know this Moncetti? Did they ever find out why her drowned bloated body was there festering in the reed beds?"

Moncetti's unexpected expression of shock and horror told instant lies, it hid the explosion of culpable guilt that swept through every sinew of his being. Since he was a boy he had tried everything to forget, he twisted and turned the facts over and over until it was never his fault. He turned to God, to Jesus to forgive his sins, to the apostle John who promised him redemption before the gates of heaven.

"The man you call the Baptist, in your bible he promised you salvation, eh?" Moon did not let go, she had Moncetti in her hands, he would pay the price.

Gabriel knew that Moon was not here in the hall to play mind games. One of the dead priests shot with his own gun, O'Hearn, had killed the boy in the juvenile remand home who had been befriended by Honey, Gabriel was convinced there must have been a blood link between this boy and the young McPherson - if there was a link then the church was faced with a deepening crisis in a war of christian morals that was by now lost. But this was inconsequential in the real dilemma that Gabriel faced, there was an intrinsic reason why Moon had chosen this day of catholic reckoning. Gabriel, the intermediary of the Lesser Lords, was no fool.

It was the hard-headed, pug-faced mafia-linked Bishop Ivan who triggered Moon's trap.

"The way you talk, it seems you don't like the good book?" drawled Ivan in his stilted Chicago accent. Ivan did not flinch when Moon's cool grey eyes drilled into him, he was well used to open mafia thuggery; nighttime violence.

"Is that your good book written by your storytelling apostles? or those old testaments scribed by ancient Abrahamic Hebrews? The ones that say I myself was born from the rib bone of Adam?" There was an unbroken stillness in the room, a silence unpierced by four billion years of earth evolution.

"What... what are you saying? Who are you?" blurted Moncetti.

Both Gabriel and Cardinal Adamovich knew what Moon was claiming. For the last four hundred years, and in other days long before this, the inner sanctum of the catholic hierarchy had dealt with the monstrous monstrosity that their gospels might be wrong, that the immaculate conception never did exist, that man had not been created in God's image in the mythical Garden of Eden - that Christ himself was not who the church claimed him to be. Nothing had been proven against the holy bible or its teachings, but the horrific affirmative proof that every god-worshipping religion created by men was flawed stood before the cardinals and bishops in their cathedral right now.

Adamovich was well aware that each female incarnation of Hyvah, each reborn reincarnation of Hawwāh - or Lilith by her ancient Hebrew name scratched on rock fragments still hidden by the first orthodox Jesuit religions - had every time been hunted down then slaughtered by sword-bearing horsemen over many centuries. Even this had not eradicated the mystical myth of Hyvah, of Eve, that she would return to reclaim her world, that she was the true-blood creator of all men, that man was created from the primordial biological cells of woman, that all man are replicated in the fertile wombs of women, that men were formed in Hyvah's image.

Gabriel himself knew there was more. The genetic race of men born from the renegade prophet Yeshua; the radical prophet crucified though never for the sins of man through the eyes of God his father. The impure-blood prophet, the fractional-neanderthalic prophet, Magdalene's unholy prophet, the men born in the prophet's image, his heritage, his blood, his nameless trinity of motherhood. McPherson and Adrussi sprang to

Gabriel's more immediate mind, though there were many, far too many others. And what about Iscariot? The traitor who had since buried the bones of his blessed Magdalena.

Only in the long-since decayed strands of his memory did Gabriel sense victory, when Adam had, in the beginning, beat the rhythmic drumbeat, when the genesis of Eve had danced the dance that entranced him, when her animal eyes, primaeval ape-like eyes, during that prehistoric time had caused him temptation.

This was a long-lasting conflict, this was not the first, or even the last confrontation.

McPherson stared at the huge, rounded door of the vault. In the gloom of the catholic catacombs, the man-sized safe looked formidable, McPherson felt daunted, he doubted that he could open it; his first thought was the door looked impregnable – McPherson was no safe cracker, never before had he taken it upon himself to steal anything that was not his own, that is, until he had been led by the hand into a headlong life of crime by the redoubtable Moon.

The four opposing locking levers were disconcerting in themselves but combined with the large steel rotating wheel to open the main lock then McPherson was under no illusion that his task looked impossible. McPherson's first concern would have to be the combination lock, then the four keyed corner locks would need to be cracked as well – neither himself, Jake nor Moon possessed the keys or knew where to even find them.

Jake eyed McPherson, the churchman was sceptical to say the least – the catholic's infamous cleanup hitman knew this strongroom vault, he knew the life-threatening importance of what it contained inside – Jake also knew that Gabriel himself had overseen the making of this door, the method in the locks - in Jake's mind there was no way on earth this vault could be forced open. Jake suspected the technology Gabriel had used was not of this world.

With pangs of despair, McPherson first turned his attention to the oversized combination lock that required the correct sequence of eight digits – two numbers more than any standard high-security safe. Putting his nonchalant ear to the lock, then one by one spinning the numbers, which he had read of in crime fiction novels, revealed nothing. There was no sound or clicks of whirling wheels or the pings of disengaging pins, McPherson was at a loss – both Moon and Jake stood behind McPherson offering nothing in the way of ideas. McPherson stood back, devoid of any nuance of what to do next. Then McPherson thought of another approach – if he was designing or making this door, what would be the first method of assembly he would consider? Of course, his initial thought would be for the door to swing open, for this it must be hinged. McPherson studied the three large heavy-duty hinges. McPherson looked at the middle of the hinges up close – he then took two paces backwards and smiled. The stupid fool who had dreamed up this hinge, how could he have not seen what Walter could see?

Moon, she watched McPherson, she knew way before McPherson that it was just a matter of time before he broke the vault open. Moon had always known this, opening the vault to take what she wanted from inside was the culmination of her one-hundred-year masterplan – from a young orphan Walter had been moulded from a distance, drilled and manoeuvred by Moon, his life had been fashioned and contrived to lead him to this one single moment, to Moon it was inconceivable that McPherson would *not* open the vault. Even so, Moon began to sweat human tears through her ingratiated pores, beads of real perspiration that represented fragile nerves of possible uncertainty. It had been a heinous act by Moon to feed McPherson into the St Catherine's orphanage, into the abusing and murderous hands of Father McCarthy and his sycophants - but it had worked, it had all come together. McPherson was McPherson because of McCarthy, McCarthy in his worst nightmare had never figured that McPherson was a lure, the bait to bring McCarthy's rotten core of abuse to its knees.

In the dim light of the catacombs McPherson studied the centre hinge with more care. Though it looked complex and heavy, in its basic form it was of straightforward double leaf, knuckle and pin construction, from the door-side leaf a hardened steel facial bracket ran to support the combination lock mechanism – remove the hinge pin to separate the two plate leaves, one supporting the front face of the combination then Walter would be able to access the innards of the combination itself. Two heavy knocks from his tap hammer and bar, the oil-lubricated pin fell to the floor - the two hinge leaves parted. McPherson left the pins of the top and lower hinges in place to enable the door to swing when the time came to open it. McPherson then lifted off the combination lock cover plate to peer inside, he could see the heart of the lock operating mechanism – Walter was horrified. He saw light beams. McPherson had seen *nothing* like this before, except he then remembered that he had - the same weird technology he had seen not long before. McPherson touched the first of the beams – in the exact same way when he had opened Moon's whitestone vis in what seemed like an age ago - but he then remembered it was all less than a week or so before. McPherson once more felt the humming vibration in the pinpoint high-intensity light beam, he sensed the rhythmic pulse he expected to find – then, from nowhere, he was struck by a sudden hunch. McPherson once more smiled. He took a sheath of paper from his knapsack, timed the beating pulse to perfection then inserted the sheath into the path of the first beam at the exact moment of the next pulse, breaking the connection between the sender and receiving probes – McPherson knew the timing was crucial, it disturbed the all-important flow of charged ion particles that flowed negative to positive using the gentle murmur of the beam. McPherson remembered - Fleming's rudimentary Left-Hand Rule – the circular flow of electrons in relation to the curled fingers is equal to the direction of the outstretched thumb. McPherson grinned to himself in eager satisfaction, he heard the mechanism click as he tricked the lock into releasing the first of the eight-digit combinations. Within moments McPherson did the same with the seven remaining beams, he stood back, turned the lock wheel anticlockwise, pulled each of the four lock levers downwards, each in opposite directions then unlocked the combination lock.

McPherson then turned his attention to the four huge key-operated levers - and was astonished to see they were fake. He paused then smiled in acknowledgement, the cleverness of this was not lost upon McPherson, for goodness knows how many years the four individual key holders must have thought that all four persons needed to be present for the opening of the vault – one or more dissenting key holders could hold ransom but not if these locks did nothing, not if they were there to give the *impression* of impregnability. McPherson figured that just one important key-holding individual would know this, the one person that mattered – for the fourth time in succession McPherson smiled. Six minutes, McPherson reckoned, it had taken him just six minutes to unlock what was supposed to be the impossible.

McPherson turned to Jake in self-congratulating pride. Jake, astonished beyond any measure of normality, leapt headlong into the vault to search for what he knew was inside. McPherson then turned to Moon... but Moon was gone, she was not there. Where was Moon?

Moon, there was no Moon, it was not Moon...

3

wo untroubled years had passed, Seppo's ravaged mind was much calmer now. The rising heat of the day caused the windless air to shimmer in ripples of silence, the slight updraught of breeze stirring the late morning stillness. In the near cloudless sky the lone skylark hovered motionless, transcending the peace of the vast wild wilderness by peppering the tall grass meadow with its dreamlike melody; creating a feeling of implausible solitude.

The child was lost in her childhood game, trying to chop the fallen logs with the toy axe he had made for her the day before yesterday. With squinting eyes Seppo scoured the menacing tree line, the sun grew hot, the summer mosquitoes buzzed around his head in a way that irritated him with their blood-sucking stings before they disappeared to die in the lost mosquito graveyard where no one cared. Today was the same treasure day, like the days he remembered from his own boyhood time when he worked the endless forest with his brother Jakk. For a brief moment, the transient memory of his dead brother formed a tear in the furthest corner of Seppo's one good eye.

He watched, she talked to herself while she played, Seppo knew her summer dreamworld was real – her imaginary friends would be chiding her, laughing with her until she grew tired, then sobbed. She still cried most nights during the long, dark snow days of winter when she relived the time before her mother died, when she thought her father might not listen. On this warm summer day she amused herself with her new woodcutter, her childish game on the edge of the evergreen forest – her world of fairies and scurrying animal kingdoms. She turned to look for reassurance, to make sure he was there – that he was *watching, that he would come for her if the horseback hunters appeared from the tree line of the threatening greenwood. Seppo smiled to reassure her, he sat motionless on the fallen trunk that lay flat upon the grass-covered mound.*

Seppo saw the sun beginning to move across the sky, realising it was past midday; she would be hungry though he had given no thought to what she might eat. He stood, to beckon her – at first, she ignored him in the way of every child. Seppo did not feel anger, he stood for a while, content to feel the sun's warm rays upon his forehead. He waited, waiting for the sun to move behind the fluffy white cloud that drifted in the deep blue sky beyond the tall forest pines.

The sudden loss of warmth upon his face stung his memory, he called her again, she flung her child's axe to the ground with impudent defiance, refusing to move. Seppo called to her one more time, adding more authority to his voice to make her obey him. She picked up her little axe then strolled through the long tall grass towards him, the fairness of her fair hair blowing in the gentle cutting breeze. The sun, without warning, came out from behind the cloud, following them as they strolled up the hill to the ancient obelisk stone. Today was a good day, a warm day that would last for many days in the delights of the northbound summer.

The top of the hillock was bare of trees, it was clear except for the leaning stone which gave welcome shade from the heat of the sun. The shadow of the stone fell into the meadow pasture where they stood, the tall flowery grasses reaching to touch her bare knees. Seppo was glad to rest a short time to regain his composure – but to reassure himself he turned to search the thick line of woods now a stone's throw away. He could see the threatening darkness just a short distance into the trees, where the sun would not penetrate to the dark, damp floor.

Then, from nowhere, the breeze blew to ruffle her yellowish hair across her face, she flipped it away from her eyes with an insignificant toss of her small hand. The wind came back, this time stronger – it was the way she pushed her hair through her fingers when Seppo realised she would one day change the history of the world. She laughed loud, a childish girlish laugh, it seemed to him those good days like this would last forever. In a short time, the sun would set down, it would be lost in the tops of the tall-reaching pines of the primordial evergreen forest – the boundless woodland realm that stretched endless before her sun-kissed eyes.

When the deep snows of wintertime came, Seppo knew she would ask. It was a question of time. It was late summer now; the sun would stay low in the sky for many days yet. Seppo still had time, time to think how he would tell her she had inherited her mother's task, her terrifying boldness, her burden of timeless confrontation.

The ancient standing stone with its flaking inscriptions etched and faded in an unknown language, made plain to the world of conquering men that soon the fateful day of their reckoning would come, that another murderous conflict would prevail. A war of wars to end all wars, the final war that, this time, would not be the victorious conquest by bloodthirsty hoards of ever-raping men...

Jean Rombaud

On the morning of the execution, the queen sent for him. Jean Rombaud thought this strange, even unnerving. He read the note, written in his native tongue then felt his heart beating hard inside his head. Rombaud tried to stay calm, his agitation overwhelming his sense of reasoning for which his gruesome trade was not well known. This alarming development demonstrated no straightforward logic - as the executioner he always demanded that he remained anonymous to the guilty condemned to die. He read the folded paper a second time, anticipating the threatening situation that would without any doubt unravel. Under no circumstances must he allow her to form any disposition of friendship - the cleanest stroke of his axe was essential if the execution was not to be botched. There must not be the slightest possibility of any emotional bond between them.

The queen, destined to perish later in the day, at the stroke of noon, had for some reason decided to summon Rombaud to her prison chamber - and Cranmer, the king's archbishop, decreed it acceptable, *even desirable* that he attend. This meant Rombaud needed to change everything, his whole routine planned with meticulous precision on the morning of every execution - a procedure he then insisted must be adhered to. Even before daybreak sneaked upon the twilight gloominess troublesome crowds were gathering outside the magnificent imposing Tower, they bickered, jostling for favourable positions to witness the gruesome spectacle of the queen's death. Jean Rombaud, the expert swordsman summoned from his own land would be given little time to think - he suspected all too well how this

170

ominous turn of events could turn into a resounding setback.

Rombaud, wide awake, sat bolt upright, he turned to gaze into the black darkness beyond his tiny open window. Outside the stone walls, the wind howled between the stone battlements before curling through the cobbled courtyards to rattle around dark shadowy corners. Rombaud had never been at ease with this impending task, he had always felt that something was not right. Illicit fate, he suspected, would in some way decide the outcome of this gnarled day ahead.

Rombaud sat on the corner of his bed, he read the note a third time. He was not educated like his peers, but he was deft enough to recognise a woman's hand. Rombaud satisfied himself the message was genuine – any doubts about the note's authenticity were banished by the insistent words of haste from the bearer. The archbishop's own Captain of the Guard stood before him.

"Monsieur De Rombaud, please dress with haste. You must come."

Rombaud saw the troubled impatience in the elegant officer's strict demeanour. The Frenchman did not reply, his mind raced in uneasy consternation, his thoughts trying to decipher what good might come from this proposed audience with the queen. Under no circumstances would he let any condemned prisoner see his face before the sentence of death was carried out - he wore his black hood of concealment for good reason. Jean Rombaud, ever wary as a citizen of France should be when in the country of his traditional enemy, satisfied himself that this situation was not a trap. He rose from his bed in reluctant hast, dressed as swiftly as he could, donned his short sword for his personal protection then clad himself in his long crimson robe. It would be necessary to conceal his ominous identity to hide his sudden purpose.

In the morning darkness, the resident black ravens inside the Tower were stirring, gawking with echoing fervour, fluttering around like hidden demons - sensing the impending day of bloodletting ahead. Outside the ramparts and heavy portcullis gates, the ever-present stink of London drifted off the foul river that wound itself around the great bastion prison that these days was filled with those opposed to the English king.

Rombaud followed Cranmer's envoy in silence through the winding courtyards then down dark alleyways, his thoughts still racing to unravel this unforeseen development. *It was not his duty to hear the confession,* the final admittance of guilt sought from prisoners before their execution - Rombaud thought this could be the one reason why he was being summoned. His feelings were grim. In the damp early morning cold Rombaud's instincts were now wild and alert, feeling the dark hand of the despicable Cranmer at work - and was astonished to find Cranmer himself waiting for him in the half-light at the top of the hard stone stairs.

Rombaud paused, standing suspiciously before the imposing archbishop, seeing how the officer envoy who had summoned him from his bed was now gone, he had made himself scarce like a timid ghost by disappearing into the grey shadowy shadows. Rombaud felt beads of sticky sweat under his tunic, a sure sign that he was uneasy, but even so, he still shivered from the intense nighttime cold. The scheming archbishop Cranmer made Rombaud nervous, this powerful man of the church was the king of England's closest ally, he chose to make things happen in the most dubious ways. These days England was in rebellious turmoil, in fractious upheaval over Rome's decision to excommunicate both the king and Cranmer himself. Since then, turbulent upheaval had preceded the fall of the English Catholics, causing immense strife throughout this troubled island kingdom. All of this, in Rombaud's purist mind, could be laid nowhere except at the feet of the condemned queen.

"Thank you for your precious time," Cranmer said to Rombaud in a low, almost whispering voice, "I am afraid we have a matter of great urgency."

"My Lord, why have I been summoned by Her Royal Highness the Queen?" Rombaud demanded, conscious of his deep French accent while expressing his concern as best he could.

The archbishop thought for a moment but did not reply. Rombaud straightaway understood Cranmer's dilemma, seeing the worried expression etched into the old man's face. Rombaud realised it was not only himself struggling to comprehend this strange turn of events. The archbishop hesitated, then motioned Rombaud to follow him. Together, they made their way down the dark stairwell lit by flickering candles of dim yellow light that led deep into the damp dungeons - where Rombaud knew the queen was imprisoned. He had been here in the same place only three days before, to observe at a distance the Earl of Rochford, the supposed brother of the queen. Rochford, the wealthy, titled aristocrat had since been executed for high treason against the king and the State and, with more shame, for beastly acts of a man before the eyes of God. Jean Rombaud was his executioner, despatching him with one expert stroke of his axe-like sword.

Even now Rombaud's mind raced, trying to decipher the unorthodox situation he now faced - it was unheard of to even speak with a condemned prisoner; more so if the unfortunate prisoner was the esteemed queen of England. But then Rombaud's expert skills with a heavy axe, his gruesome reputation, his impeccable attention to the smallest detail when dealing justice to high royalty and the nobility classes, was the precise reason why he had been summoned from Calais by the callous, scheming Cromwell - Cranmer's ally and the king's chief minister.

The prison guards gathered in the smallish outer chamber were not expecting visitors, this much Rombaud noticed straightaway when they challenged Cranmer. There were three guards, each of them unkempt and dishevelled, peasant-like in their appearance dressed in ragtag Tower uniforms. The guard's general lack of discipline was notorious, but in this instance, Chief Minister Cromwell had selected the most reliable from the two dozen or so available. Their demeanour changed when they recognised the archbishop for who he was: the taller, big fat lard of a guard who was without doubt the dungeon warden, confronted Cranmer.

"My Lord, we were not expecting visitors at this hour in the morning," the warden exclaimed, then hesitated, waiting with expectation for an appropriate explanation from Cranmer. The warden's specific orders were to allow no visitors to the queen. Even so, the guards knew full well that most instructions concerning the prisoner in their charge originated from the archbishop himself - or from Cromwell, in their perverse way.

"Please wake the queen *now*," Cranmer responded with sharp atonement in his voice.

"My Lord Archbishop, the prisoner is already awake," the warden replied. The two other guards remained silent, watching with curiosity for some clue as to why Archbishop Cranmer and his strange, cloaked companion had appeared out of the darkness of the stairwell. Rombaud himself said nothing, though he felt the keen gaze of all three men as they endeavoured to recognise him. After all, this was their utmost duty, to ensure this turn of events was no elaborate attempt to escape. They knew, like everyone else, that their prisoner inspired considerable sympathy amongst her vast numbers of protestant followers who felt she had been betrayed.

"I take full responsibility for this intrusion," Cranmer replied to the warden. "We are here for an audience with your prisoner."

"Archbishop, you know this is irregular," said the warden, there was no hiding the suspicion in his voice which was not unreasonable considering how this serious dilemma might cost him his life. "We are expecting no one until first light which, as your Lordship will appreciate, is still a good two hours hence," the warden added, endeavouring to establish his authority. But the powerful archbishop was not to be trifled with - the roughneck warden was well aware of this.

"Inform your prisoner we are here," was all Cranmer was prepared to concede.

"My Lord, may I beg your permission to ask the identity of your companion?" The warden gestured to Rombaud in a manner that indicated he was not going to give way to the archbishop's demands. Everyone within the chamber turned to look at Rombaud, including Cranmer, as if waiting for this strange visitor to in some way reveal himself. Rombaud waited, considering his dilemma, realising the guards would not grant him access to the queen without knowing his identity. They had no clue with regard to these unfolding events. Rombaud made the rational decision to remove his hood, his senses telling him this whole situation now rested in his own hands. He reached upwards; his woven woollen hood of rough intricacy dropped from his hairless, bald head to reveal to everyone who he was. In the dim candlelit light of the prison chamber, with the dank walls of blackened stone creating a pervading atmosphere of deep foreboding, Rombaud spoke aloud for only the second time since being summoned from his bed.

"I am Jean Rombaud, citizen of France, esteemed deliverer of your king's justice on this solemn day before us. I have been summoned here by your prisoner, the venerable queen of this godforsaken country," Rombaud spoke with authority, needing to establish his control over these obscene Englishmen, "I too demand that you let us pass."

All three guards remained silent; they were well aware of who he was. Rombaud felt an element of compassion for their intolerable plight. The Frenchman knew they were in no position to deny Cranmer, the third most powerful man in England after the king and his minister Thomas Cromwell. In no time they recognised the identity of the queen's formal executioner: the tall dark foreigner who was predisposed to his intimidating reputation. The awkwardness of the guard's uncertainty, their obvious reluctance to give their desired acquiescence was broken by Cranmer,

"As I have before informed all of you infernal guards in this cursed dungeon, my responsibility is to our king and to God, not to you," there was a warning tone in Cranmer's voice. "First, you will inform your prisoner of our arrival, then second, you will pay with your miserable lives if you utter any words to anyone about our presence here which you now witness," Cranmer paused for added effect... "Do I make myself clear?" The archbishop was well used to getting his way.

Silent, without reply, in an atmosphere of uncertainty made even more hopeless by the constant dripping of water into some distant echoing puddle of ominous fortitude, the smaller of the three guards took the large key from behind the stone pillar to unlock the creaking wooden cell door, first unbolting the two immense iron bars from their rudimentary, rust-ridden restraining clasps. The bolts rolled back with a resounding clang.

The door opened with tallow-greased ease to reveal the silent queen standing imposing before them in the centre of her dim lit prison chamber.

Having no desire for sleep or rest on the day of her execution, she stood dressed in a simple one-piece gown of fine white silk, which reached down to the dirty cobblestone floor in a way that revealed none of her infamous mesmerising allure. Her long fair hair, brushed and groomed to one side, fell over her left shoulder to hide all outlines of her heartbeat breasts. She stood quite still, the squalid darkness of her dungeon adding to her radiant composure. She presented herself in a commanding manner that suggested no sign of compromise or subjugation to Archbishop Cranmer's presence. Rombaud saw her for the first time, he gasped aloud in involuntary demeanour. In his mind's eye, he saw the abominable intriguing situation that he now faced, instant in his realisation of how much his meticulous planning had fallen to pieces – like the crumbling of a mountainous pack of cards. On no previous occasion had Rombaud cause or reason to talk with any prisoner whom he was commissioned to execute in the name of Almighty God. How, in God's name, Rombaud thought to himself with revulsion, could he take the head of such a handsome woman? Then another incomprehensible thought struck him in a fraction of a moment - the gruesome experience of his many executions, the justice he delivered with his infamous axe gave Jean Rombaud the unique adeptness to sense those who were guilty or innocent of their accused crimes. This condemned English queen conveyed something to him quite different. God, Rombaud now realised deep within his fast-beating heart, had dealt him a cruel blow.

England's queen, Rombaud recalled as he stood with an uneasy feeling in the deep pit of his stomach, would die on this fateful day for two reasons proclaimed by the highest court in England - purported acts of treason and for alleged adulterous liaisons. Or if more common whispers were to be believed - for failing the King of England the right of a princely son to the throne. In the Frenchman's considered mind, kings did not allow themselves to be judged by their peers or subjects for being wrong, kings made laws for the governing of men, they governed with armies of horsemen, of archers and battle-hardened swordsmen confronting like-minded challengers who sought to oppose them, who were often themselves esteemed kings or emperors within their own lands - because Rombaud had learned the hard way, the executioner's way, he knew that only almighty God ruled a king or commanded a pope. In his bitter experience as the bloody dispatcher, he had long realised that God seemed to side with a king's cause whenever the king chose to proclaim God's will - and this English queen must die for sins far greater than any mortal man could forgive.

In this forsaken land, God was worshipped by the new protestant church, by a fractious religion the English king himself had established into his realm with himself its supreme ruler. And now, as Rombaud recalled in his rattled mind, this fortuitous King of England decreed that his young queen should die on this miserable rain-filled day when the swirling river mists hid the consciences of the king's elegant dressed men who in these dark days ruled this mighty island kingdom. Rombaud's conscience had long ago withered – to defy the catholic pope is not much sacrilege when a king decides he needs no pope to command his obedient church. The sweet queen, the English queen who was never a queen in the pope's judgemental eyes. The queen who was not a queen, the mysterious queen of no recorded birth who would never be the forgiver of powerful men. The victorious young queen of England, forever the tormenting enemy of those against Rombaud's protestant faith.

"Why are *you* here Cranmer, I did not summon you?" the queen confronted the archbishop with clear hostility, with a determination that showed she was not intimidated by him.

Cranmer's face twitched as he tried hard to control his anger. This was a difficult confrontation for him; in the eyes of the reformed English church, he had himself annulled the queen's marriage to the king only hours before. The pope in Rome, with great alacrity, forbade the king's divorce from his first queen, the devout catholic Catherine of Aragon - and events had erupted out of Cranmer's control since. Both Cranmer and Cromwell long ago realised that a distant strangeness had overcome the king once this accursed woman had captivated him, something that was driving him down a dark road of conflict with an impassioned belief in his immortality; a self-belief that he talked direct with God. This had led to the banishment of Catherine, the spectacular rise of protestantism in catholic England; his marriage to his mesmerising mistress - the faithless woman behind the fall of the catholic hierarchy. Chief Minister Cromwell at first welcomed the opportunity to break from the dominance of Rome and, indeed, Cranmer's rapid rise to archbishop was without doubt due to his willingness to acquiesce to the king's wishes. All of this had not been easy for Cranmer, the realm would be quick to collapse if the king did not produce a son and heir to the new English protestant throne. England's fate had been inexorable when driven by Henry's manic obsession with his new intolerable agnostic queen - his captivating spellbinding hoar while still married to Queen Catherine.

Despite Cromwell's and the archbishop's tremendous efforts, there was still no male heir to the throne. Catherine of Aragon had fallen, replaced by this occultist queen now condemned for repulsive acts conjured to turn her subjects against her - the throne's male succession collapsing in a heap of uncertainty with Cromwell suspecting a fearsome ungodliness - the outlandish prospect of a feminist queen, a supposition so concerning that it shook him to his inner core. Cromwell suspected that never was it possible for this queen to produce a male heir, a womanly heir was the one single possibility – a deliberate and calculated move to create a female queen who would not be the queen through wedlock. Cranmer's immediate urgency was to learn if Cromwell's dreadful suspicions were correct - if what they faced was a bottomless barrel of worms far more dangerous than they ever suspected. Why *had* the queen summoned her executioner to her chamber on the morning of her death?

"I'm here, my Lady, because the captain of my Guard tells me you have requested your executioner to hear your confession, this is a matter of utmost importance," Cranmer replied in the calm manner of a man not used to being questioned, more so when he had schemed long and hard alongside Cromwell to have the new queen tried for treason. "It is the duty of the archbishop alone, myself, the appointed chancellor of the king's Church of England, to hear the final confession of the queen before her God," he replied. "Not her executioner nor any other man who she herself deems fit." Cranmer stared in supreme anger; he would not tolerate defiance by any woman. Nor did he reveal that, once he had learned of her private note to Rombaud, he himself decreed it desirable that Rombaud attend the audience with the young queen. The ageing archbishop suspected what she intended, that through a false confession she might try to manipulate the mind of Rombaud in one last vain effort to escape - she would attempt to once and for all bring down the remnants of the catholic court of the English king, the eighth king to carry the ominous name. The archbishop hoped to learn the absolute truth behind his excommunication by the pope and the spectacular collapse of the catholic church - and the bloody turmoil of reformation sweeping through the king's rebellious kingdom.

"Rombaud is here for my reasons, not to listen to my confession," the queen replied. "If this Frenchman is to take my head this day, then there is something he must know before I die headless under his sword. It takes but a small moment to change history, perhaps only the briefest time it takes to swing an executioner's axe," her defiance had the mastery of the archbishop - none of the five men now in her presence realised the queen's trap was now sprung.

Rombaud listened, he sensed the intense drama of the moment. His mind raced and turned, trying to decide how he should proceed. He doubted whether the archbishop was able to speak in his own native French which he knew the queen spoke with fluency; for a moment he considered asking the queen in his language why he had been summoned, but seeing Cranmer's thin-disguised anger and veiled impatience, Rombaud in a moment chose otherwise, "My Lady, *why* have you demanded that I myself attend your presence?"

The queen turned to face him, studying him for the first time; Rombaud felt uncomfortable, he felt dribbles of sweat trickling down the crick of his back beneath his thick woven tunic. She stared at him with mesmerising clear grey eyes, in a way that challenged his calm supremacy;

he immediately felt that she was endeavouring to overpower him, that she could, if she desired, impose her will over his own to take control of her execution. Rombaud looked at Cranmer who, it struck him, had lost his futile dominance over this unforeseen gathering of bewildered minds. With a feeling of intense foreboding growing inside him, Rombaud discerned how this woman was no ordinary queen.

"Thank you for honouring me with your presence Monsieur Rombaud, I did not think you would be allowed such unconventional honour," she spoke with a hint of irony, "I suspect you are here because the learned archbishop here and the king's vile minister Thomas Cromwell desire it."

"You do not answer my question, Your Highness, it is irregular that you should seek my audience," Rombaud responded, he was determined the queen should not gain mastery over him. He already sensed she had some mysterious manner about her which concerned him and, more worrying, a strange familiarity he had not expected. "Again, I ask you, why am I here?" Rombaud suspecting the queen was right in what she said, the archbishop had much to do about all of this; it was the Captain of Cranmer's Guard who had awakened him with the note from the queen, the note written in his own native French, signed with the single name that had stunned Rombaud's senses. Rombaud's instincts were on full alert - a warning in his mind that he should be prepared to terminate this confrontation as soon as he could. He sensed the intrepid queen trying to penetrate his thoughts while he asked his simple question. Rombaud waited for the queen to respond.

"Two days previous to this day you removed the head of my laughable brother, the Earl of Rochford," she replied, stepping forward with a half step that entrusted the Frenchman should remain unsure of his position. "I presume you already know the preposterous reasons I am condemned to die by your sword, that I am hideously charged with scandalous copulation with my so-called brother," she added, knowing full well that Rombaud was aware of her terrible crimes, "I have also been informed by my peers that I have fornicated with a gaggle of other men too. This I have learned from the lamentable trial of law forced upon me." She peered deep into

Rombaud's eyes with a condescending voice laced with surety. Rombaud was struck by her righteous ability to deliver her version of the justice forced upon her. Cranmer was quick to intervene.

"You have been found guilty from truthful evidence, and the confessions of your contemptible lovers my Lady. Guilty of incest, adultery, witchcraft and treason. Your royal highness has been condemned to death by the king's lawful court, a court convened from your peers of our God-driven realm, you are guilty under the king's common law," growled Cranmer with authority. "You do not have the right to summon your executioner to your presence my Lady."

"Then why is he here?" she replied, now ignoring Rombaud.

"We do not know. Perhaps you could enlighten us, Your Highness," Cranmer responded with anger. "He is here at your demand, with the king's good grace."

Rombaud perceived the cat-and-mouse game being played out before him. The queen had asked that he, Jean Rombaud, attend an audience with her before her time of execution, he still retained her note in his possession. The queen, who had given the letter to the Captain of the Guard, must have known her message would be intercepted, *which it had*, by Cranmer or Cromwell, he wasn't sure by whom. But for some reason unknown to Rombaud, his proposed audience with the queen had been allowed to proceed but only with Cranmer present. Rombaud's mind raced. It then came to him - *they themselves needed to know some hidden truth*. The fog of uncertainty that clouded his suspicious mind began to clear. Could it be, he now reasoned, that this mesmerising and confident woman, this beautiful young angel standing before him had cast her elaborate entrapment web? Rombaud saw that she looked at him, that she smiled when their eyes met. *Those strange bewitching grey-blue eyes.* He felt himself slipping out of control, the feeling he had resolutely decided would not happen. He could allow himself no sympathy with the condemned woman, no feeling of empathy or anything that could render him uncertain when he raised his axe. This would make him, in his own eyes, a simple murderer. She watched him while his mind raced, while he tried to decipher the situation he had been lured into. In the blink of her enchanting eye, she turned to confront Cranmer.

"I am condemned to die because I did not bear your esteemed king a son, the future heir to the protestant throne, not because of these contrived accusations against me. I gave the king a child, though not his desired heir of male birth. The king and that snivelling snake Cromwell are displeased, both you and I know this archbishop," she replied to Cranmer in a fateful voice. "Do not presume otherwise or give rise to any more lies lest we fool ourselves that truth is sacrilege." Rombaud felt uncomfortable truth in the queen's response.

"You presume wrong my Lady," Cranmer replied. "Never would the king or his justice be so cruel as to deliver such an abominable command to order the execution of his wife and queen without just reason and good cause."

"Do you deny that, when I am headless, the king will be free to marry another queen, a queen to bear his son to the English throne?"

"This would be so my Lady, but it is not the king's fault his queen lured good men of honour into her bed chamber for lust and pleasure," spat Cranmer with alacrity and venomous disgust. "And your own brother succumbed to your predatory demands, an unlawful and ungodly act for a man to endure."

"Yes, that would be so if it were true."

"Confess your sins," Cranmer demanded with newfound confidence. "Your peers and your executioner will hear your good grace. You will receive my forgiveness and my blessing before God. Only then can you enter into the kingdom of heaven to receive our Lord's forgiving love."

"You will receive no confession from me, Cranmer. And do not presume to be so confident in your manner. I have not done with you yet."

Cranmer froze. And then, in the aftermath of the crossfire between the queen and the archbishop, in an instant flash of her piercing gaze, Jean Rombaud's world fell apart like the sudden shattering of a crystal glass chandelier.

The defiant queen turned to face the still-silent Rombaud, she walked towards him. He straightaway sensed insecurity in the hard ground beneath his feet, the sensation of treacherous quicksand replacing the stone-cold granite of the dungeon floor. His instinct warned him of imminent danger, he inched his right hand towards the handle of his sword. The queen paused before him.

"Jean Rombaud, my dearest executioner, or shall we say, a murderer of the glorious innocent?" she spoke with chilling clarity, standing with an angel-like quality in the darkness of the room. "Please know this before you salute to the baying crowd with your triumphant axe raised high," the queen's eyes burned with glowing fierceness, Rombaud recoiled. "You will change history on this fateful day when you take my head. Though, as my loyal executioner, I beg that you cut my neck clean so that your conscience remains forever *pure* when you kneel before *your* forgiving God," she paused for one moment, the gloomy dungeon shadows receding as the first streak of the grey dawn struck the ink-black sky beyond her cell window. "Consider this, Rombaud, as you lift your axe to strike my womanly neck. I stood with your own mother, I stood beside her when the catholics took *her* head. Though not so clean as you might take mine, I might add."

"*What?*" Rombaud reeled, his mind spinning in instant anger. What did she mean? How could she know anything about his mother's death? This was impossible, it was not conceivable how this woman could even know his mother, much less so that she could have witnessed her death. Rombaud recoiled in confusion, his mind-twisting and turning, he tried to make sense of what the queen had said.

Cranmer also, making no sound or movement, froze in horror. He realised the condemned queen had just unleashed the devil, the absolute monster he feared. He had warned Cromwell not to do this, not to allow Rombaud anywhere near the queen before her time of execution. From this moment the distraught archbishop understood the awful situation they now faced. Cranmer saw Rombaud's face crumble as the queen paused to let the effects of her strike sink into the Frenchman's reeling brain. The archbishop saw Rombaud stunned into incomprehensible silence, with his proud thoughts tumbling, trying to understand what this ingenious woman had claimed. Cranmer perceived Rombaud staring at the queen in shock, in the realisation that standing here before the infamous executioner from Calais was no king's condemned unfaithful wife. The archbishop from this moment knew that confronting the Frenchman was the church's long-feared nemesis, who had struck a resounding blow right through the proud executioner's invincible armour. What the archbishop did not know was that Rombaud's mother had died when he, Rombaud, was young, a six-year-old boy. His mother was beheaded, murdered when the holy procession was routed by the Duke's horsed henchmen. Racing through Rombaud's mind right now was how could the queen herself know this. And what did she mean when she said she had been *there* beside her? For heaven's sake, of course, this all made sense.

The resplendent queen stood before Rombaud, facing him with her icy cold expression. "I have no doubt the archbishop here at last suspects who I might be," she continued knowing her powerful strike had found its mark, that in her own way, she had given Cranmer the confession he was desperate to get. "So, we can disregard *him* and his entourage of vengeful cronies," she hissed, lowering her voice. "Now, what I must know from you, and you alone my dearest Rombaud, is whether this vile brother of mine is well dead?" she paused, as if to consider her words with care, waiting for the moment she thought Rombaud might have recovered his senses. She saw that Rombaud was fighting to find his composure, his male defiance trying to hide the gaping wound in his crumbling self-belief. Then she struck once more before Rombaud had time to organise his feeble defences. "Did my lying brother die under your axe like a coward wretch? Like a rat in some rotten sewer perhaps?"

"Who are you?" Rombaud found his faltering voice, his determination surfacing to try and take control of his deteriorating crisis. He saw that Cranmer was still silent, shocked by the beautiful young woman who struck him dumb like a guilty bystander struggling to retain his dignity - while floundering out of his depth in a sceptic pool of human excrement of his own making.

"You here are all men of sorts, each of you knows who I am. I am the king's queen, the despoiler of the catholic faith," she replied, "I am condemned to die by your sharp axe, will it be the same axe that executed my fictitious brother for despicable crimes of incest and treason? My so-called brother, who was accused of plotting the downfall of my righteous husband the king of England."

"I asked who you are. You are no queen of this wretched island kingdom," Rombaud exclaimed, fighting to suppress his rising anger that threatened to explode at any moment, "I see no condemned woman kneeling before me begging for forgiveness, no high and mighty downfallen monarch pleading for her life. Nor do I see a desperate, frightened soul who has accepted her fate to die under my sword of justice."

"You talk bold talk of a condemned queen," the queen responded. "Ask the quivering archbishop here who I am. For he knows that I destroyed the power of the catholics in this godforsaken country ruled by our king of kings. This land is governed by men for the greater good of men and their fornicating lust for power," the queen was in her stride, aware that she now had both Rombaud and Cranmer in her hand, "I do not seek forgiveness before any God created in man's contemptible image, nor will I confess a sinful lie to these men who claim to be the new protestant faith when not three years before this day they professed to be loyal catholics following their wretched pope in Rome. Glad they were then, these two miserable peers and their fortuitous king, when they saw good reason to subdue the catholic church on my behalf."

"I am no loyal praying protestant, nor am I catholic, neither are you," Rombaud replied. "You are not *my* queen, yet you stand here before me then tell me you stood beside my mother when she died, when she was slain more than thirty years before this fateful day we now face. What trickery is this? What sinful lies do you this time pronounce to try and turn *my* head?"

"I do not tell lies Rombaud. Lies would be sacrilege on the day of my death."

"But you cannot have been there my lady," Rombaud laughed with incredulity. "You are not yet thirty years since your birth into this world. So how can this be?"

"Do not be deceived by what you see before you," the queen's eyes were full of fire, like a furnace of hot iron. "Your mother was a glorious unforgiving woman, a righteous mentor who should not have died by the Duke of Malmantard's vengeful sword." She paused, she reached inside her gown, into the silk fabric that held her white left-side breast. She pulled out a small chain of gold. "Your saint of a mother gave me this, her most powerful memory of her life to give to you on this fateful day, the day your mother warned me would come, the day when you and I would meet not for the first time." The queen held out the palm of her hand. She held the small golden chain with a tiny pendant of ornate and decorative design. It was his mother's cross, Magdalena's cross of Eve.

Rombaud stared incredulous at the object in her hand. He now remembered the woman from his childhood. The memory came to him like a flash of lightning striking through his brain. When he was a small boy, he remembered the woman in the grey woollen cloak. He sometimes fed from her breast. How could this be?

Cranmer stood solid though silent. No longer bemused. The archbishop at last realised the mind-bending truth, the awful hypocrisy both he and Cromwell feared, revealed by the woman who in her devious way now changed everything. The terrifying confession of the condemned, the woman who held the fate of the beleaguered catholic aristocracy and the nascent protestant church in the palm of her upturned hand. Cranmer's mind raced, knowing the danger he and Cromwell now faced. The queen, Cranmer knew, was innocent of the crimes they had brought against her - though they had long suspected that she was not who she claimed to be. Together with Rochford, they had set out to corner her, but the fool Rochford had been outwitted by his purported conniving sister. The king, stupid in Cranmer's opinion, had ordered Rochford's execution. But then Rochford, he *had* gone *too* far. All of the queen's so-called lovers confessed under torture, their illicit confessions forced out of them under pain of death; this had brought the queen to her knees, leading to her incarceration in this dark dungeon deep within the Tower of London. If the queen was who they suspected then she needed to be imprisoned, confined. But Rochford had forced himself upon his her, he was caught in the act of defiling assault. It had been agreed that he would merely make the allegation of her seduction, her crime of incest, but something in their plan went wrong. Rochford was one of themselves, not the queen's real brother whose exact birth was unknown, he was aristocratic blue blood, the hallowed structure of powerful men that included Cranmer, Cromwell and every king of England who ever ruled. Somehow the king's new queen had driven Rochford's downfall, finding her savage revenge. But there was more...

The aristocracy, nobility, their church of God was under determined assault. Catholicism in England was on the brink of tumbling over a cliff because, incredible though it was, the king had fallen under the spell of this young woman. The pope was under siege, the power of his church broken. Popery was crumbling, viral protestantism was flowering, though even this contentious new church was reeling in the king's troubled kingdom as if controlled by some hidden force. God forbid - could there next be a *woman* on the English throne?

If this condemned queen was who Cranmer believed, then a terrifying prospect lay ahead. A virgin queen of England, who would rule without a king. Could it be Mary, the daughter of Catherine? Or, much worse, the unsaintly Elizabeth, the already-born child of this queen who would die today. Queen Catherine of Aragon, her ancestral heritage had been investigated by Cromwell, he confirmed that her child Mary was no lineage witch. But this queen's birthright ended abrupt, there were no known memories of her inexplicable birth, everything was faked. All the dreadful signs were there, they had been stunned into immediate action, they needed proof. If, as Cromwell suspected, Rochford was never the queen's brother then they would know the awful truth. It would become ever more imperative there must be a son and heir. The nobility's male rule would then continue. This queen, if there was even a small chance of descent through the Magdalena, bearing the same abominable bloodline, then she must die.

It would need to be a public execution, one for the vilest of crimes, the queen should die under an unsanctified axe-like sword, Rombaud was summoned for this reason. Not only had the queen schemed the death of Rochford, but she had also now produced the chilling confession of who she was. The reviled grail - the despicable heritage of the unbiblical Hyvah. The queen had declared something unexpected; she had proclaimed her life link to Rombaud, the protestant executioner summoned by Cromwell - there was now the dreadful prospect that Rombaud's mother might be descended from the defiled concubine of Christ. Cranmer felt his heart miss a conspicuous beat; this had all been contrived. Then it became clear to him, a bolt of consciousness struck Cranmer a powerful hammer blow deep within his rapid turning mind. Might they all have been outwitted? Could it be, the thought raced through his brain, the ancient nobility of kings had been lured into this queen's cunning laid snare?

Cranmer, with an acute sense of panic, now acted with speed. This confrontation could not continue, it should never have happened. He motioned to the three guards, standing silent beside the entrance to the cell, who had heard everything, to take action. The queen needed to be constrained, they must all take their leave before this situation became much worse than it was. The guards, obeying Cranmer's frantic instruction, moved threatening towards her.

In the instant it takes a fly to avoid the swat of death, Rombaud drew his sword, he thrust outwards in the manner of the expert swordsman he was. There was a strange red mist before his eyes, a fog of anger, an obscenity that clouded his usual clear judgement, an inability to reason before he reacted with decisive intuition. The larger of the guards died in a fraction of a second before falling to the cold granite slab of the floor. The two remaining guards hesitated, confused and frightened; they were not trained soldiers at the peak of their physique.

Rombaud was supreme in the moment. His intervention changed everything. In the near light of dawn, as the last semblance of darkness disappeared into the breaking daylight of the Tower, the flickering candle of the cell that held the queen captive for some inexplicable reason extinguished itself, the oblique greyness of the new day took hold.

Rombaud thought hard about what he should do next. A terrible dilemma faced him with a crisis of immense proportions now bulging like a sceptic blister about to burst. He saw the queen standing silent, quiet, staring at the guard lying dead at her feet with the blood flowing from the gaping wound to his throat. To Rombaud the queen did not seem concerned, appearing to be in some trance-like state until her white-blond hair fell from her brow, awakening her to the reality of her surroundings. She tossed her hair from her eyes in a casual way that made Rombaud involuntary shudder; he had seen this mannerism before, another boyhood memory from his childhood he could not comprehend.

The two remaining guards eyed Rombaud with menace, he knew they would summon the Captain of the Guard; he would be no match for the trained guardians of the Tower if they came in great numbers. He was a Frenchman in the country of his traditional enemy, his few options were diminishing with every second that ticked by.

Rombaud was now in an appalling position of his own making, he well knew that Cranmer was in a state of frightened shock, he would be no hindrance if he, Rombaud, wished to leave, but he would not get far once the guards had recovered their wits. What should he do about the queen? She had control of everything, but if she wished to affect her escape then further catastrophe was sure to follow. The queen was not his responsibility. Rombaud needed to know more, he needed to understand what had happened in the distant past, both thirty-one years ago and in the last few hours. Rombaud for a brief moment considered taking Cranmer hostage and, with the queen as his companion, trying to make his way to France. Within an even shorter moment, he dismissed this outrageous plan because they would all die. With all his options fading fast, Rombaud turned to the queen.

"Your Highness, what shall you have me do?" he pleaded, resigned to his fate.

The queen eyed him with keen eyes of obliqueness. "Wait, my Frenchman friend," she seemed quite relaxed, "I think it wise to assume Cranmer here will seek the captain of his guard," she was strange, unconcerned. "Or perhaps we could take the course of action you have heretofore dismissed in your mind, your thoughts to attempt our escape," she said, unconvinced. The warden of the guards had left to make his own escape, to summon the more threatening troops of the infamous Tower Guard.

Rombaud surveyed the incomprehensible scene shimmering in the stillness before him. The ominous black ravens outside the Tower window cawed loud in cascading numbers, as if they knew the day of death ahead was to be their spectacular spectacle, that they might be the real victors with their predatory deep-black eyes set above their razor-sharp beaks in raptor-like reverence. This was utter disaster. The Frenchman stood defiant with his sword still raised to strike, the ribbons of sweat across his brow a measure of his determination to protect the English queen. By now he remembered the defiant woman standing beside his cherished mother unmemorable years ago, though he was only a small boy at the time; two sword-wielding siblings, survival, twin sisters side-by-side, the horseback riders, the flash in the moonlight of the rider's sword - a faded boyhood memory etched into his sharp juvenile mind. This queen, Rombaud realised, held him firm in her angel-like hands, there was nothing he could do. Neither was there anywhere they could run. Did they need to run? This thought erupted from somewhere deep inside the convoluted mixture of his mental imbalance.

The footsteps of the approaching guards echoed down the stone stairway, more than two dozen swords of death were a short distance from the prison cell from which there was no escape. The grey dawn of the monumental day of execution was, as yet, one hour old.

4

"**W**here are you now?" she begged; her whispering voice pierced by the cold night breeze. The orange-tipped sunrise began to streak across the ink-black sky, grey light broke shadows across the ravaged land the horseback raiders had long ago burned dry.

"I am in the oak wood forest, near the ruins where we both said goodbye. God forbid if these men learn that you did not die, when they hunted you down with their wretched swords and barking hounds. When they raped and pillaged the day our children died," tears fell from his haunted, red-smoked eyes. "Where is it that you are now?" his upturned gaze searched the morning sky - the sun burst with venom from where the nighttime dies.

"I am far from the place where our children lie buried, a long way from where you are now," she lied, knowing the pain deep inside her heart would tear his mind. She turned to listen when the wind blew hard. She gazed down upon the graves, behind the wall that lay broken and charred, the ramparts demolished into crumpled mounds. "What is it they seek, these devil horsemen with their swords and barking hounds?"

"Your bones, they seek your bones from their first dreadful attack, their dogs growl but their horses hold back. The grey wolf, she snarls and stands her ground; the same she-wolf that sought our salvation," he raised his head to see the ice-cold breeze tease the midnight raven. "Please tell me, are you close by?" the north wind blew that made him glare then cry. The new dawn broke free to escape the long black night, the brave new day that spawned its brightest light, to flood the ancient forest that never, in the next ten thousand years, would lose its might.

"I am far away, too far to feel your pain, the memory of that day you died in the lightning rain," she whispered, feeling his anguish as she descended through the soft white clouds. She saw him below in the burning village, where the rampaging horsemen galloped to once more torch and pillage. She found his savaged body lying beside the broken wall, their swords driven through him in his one last fall.

"I hear you; I know you are close by," he croaked and cried, his tears bursting like wildflowers that wither then dry, his bleached bones washed by whiplash rain after more than ten years gone by. "Please tell me, where are you now?" he pleaded. "Tell me before the terrible day is upon me, the day when I fight and die."

"I am where I can see your fight to survive, your heartbreak rage, these horsemen and their last victory charge. I see our frightened children; they hide behind the stone wall that keeps back the forest. I see your fear when you know they die. I see the grey wolf, she tries to save you, I see your life is spent from the wounds inside you. They hack your head in spiteful revenge. They lavish in triumphant spite, cheering and laughing before they ride on by."

"Please... please tell it another way. Not like this. Tell me I survive to fight one more day. Tell me our children flee to hide in the forest. Tell me they were not hunted down like vermin, with hounds and swords by these Gabriel men." He saw why his severed head did not lie, why his sun-bleached skull lay there staring into the now blameless blue sky, right there beside his bones now stripped bare with more and more years passed by.

"I cannot watch your death one more time, your harrowing pain is beyond my will to suffer. Nor can I watch my children die like hunted rats in those devil traps," she cried and cried, then cried more until warm raindrop tears fell from fluffy white clouds drifting high in the by now pale blue sky. Colourful butterflies fluttered their wings to say their summer goodbye.

"Are you close by? Are you where the songbirds fly?"

"I am in the long time past, not where you are now," she whispered into his blood-filled ear, just a small tearful moment before he died. She felt his pain that she would always hold dear. Then she kissed his sun-drenched head, knowing in her heart he was already dead, she felt pain with more pain that

would for nearly ten years hurt. She heard their evil victory chant when she drifted unseen above their wretched heads. She turned to flee through the hard cold mist, she left him dead without his head. She soared high beyond their flashing swords; she flew leaving her children dead. She paused when she heard their triumphant roar, she turned to strike each horseman's head. Then she left with a silent tear, leaving behind those she would forever hold dear.

"We shall one day kiss like the day we wed, we'll make love in the long tall grass, when the breeze blows through the trees with singing larks, budding leaves and sweet honeybees," she gently, ever so gently said.

"Do not leave me, not like this. Stay close so I can feel your wild embrace. We can save our souls then love again in His holy heaven," he screamed aloud, knowing full well there was no such forsaken place as God's sacred heaven.

"My deepest love, I will wait in white beside the ancient stone, I am close beside you now, now I am where you are now," she whispered comforting in his ear in the same old way, just when the cockerels crowed the brand new day. "When the last of these Gabriel men depart, when they have gone to seek praise in their merciless hearts, I will tell you when we can leave side-by-side, when together forever we will be together. And these men, if they find our children's graves there behind the wall, then I will muddle their minds in my way to make them dead," she said.

He turned to see her standing there without feeling fear, she healed his wounds with her one last tear, she wiped his blood with her white satin cloth, she cleaned his sword in the long dry grass that hummed to the tune of the hummingbird moth. She smiled and whispered in his longing ear, they made love while the songbird flew aloft, it sang its song then flew above like the twittering lark. They cried and cried until the day drew dark, they still lie there side by side this day, buried beneath the ancient stone in the same old way, the silent way their children lay.

Khaled bin Al-Tarif

Today, Rahim realised, would be the most important day of his life. When the sun dipped low behind the sand dune ridge, the girl he had imagined since a young boy, the one who was destined to be his dutiful bride forever, would walk through the ceremonial doorway to join him in their humble desert dwelling.

Outside in the half-light, the rainstorm beat down relentless, forcing the more bedraggled of the *Al Buainai's* tribal goats to seek shelter alongside the young nomad shepherd who found himself on the cusp of Bedouin manhood. Rahim waited with unbridled impatience, feeling agitated while at the same time confident in his male adolescence: knowing he was the centre of attention made him impatient to show his male bravado to the men and boys who waited with him. Beyond the doorway, it rained and rained, it rained until the dry craggy landscape of his waterless homeland turned into a yellow quagmire that in the morning would be broken by fresh green shoots of grass – nutrient grass that would keep the nomadic people feeding their herds in this barren place a few more days. This was another sign from almighty Al-Ilāh that Rahim's father Khaled bin Al-Tarif, widowed father of three growing sons, had chosen his eldest son's new bride well.

The persistent year-long drought had broken with some unfathomable vengeance, a long prayed-for deluge that would, for a short time, ease the fragile truces between warring Bedouin tribes – without doubt, one more offering from Al-Ilāh to sustain desert alliances strained by broken treaties. Deep in the desolate wilderness, beyond the meagre grasslands that struggled to nourish the scattered goat and camel herds long evolved to withstand harsh wilderness conditions, the treasured oasis water wells would be filling to their brims - which would delay the murderous tribal infighting over precious few sources of life-giving water until another time. The fragile tribal friendships would last a short while longer – until the long days of hot, dry subsistence survival returned, when the hard negotiated truces in the name of the nascent religion of the warlord Muhammad would once more be tested to their limit.

Rahim's impulsiveness was tempered by his eager anticipation. Told that his wife-to-be was both young and beautiful in ways uncommon to the Bedouin, this desirable news eased the determined uncertainties ruminating inside his head - made harder by the fact that both himself and the menfolk now waiting with him knew little about the girl's tribal ancestry. Rahim had been informed, out of the blue, in no uncertain terms, a few days before by both his father and the tribal elders, that their newfound friendship with the *Banu Amir* Bedouin needed to be strengthened - the proposed marriage was essential, it would be good, there would be a more lasting peace between two of the more bellicose nomadic tribes.

Rahim's younger brother Kahmed made the proposed marriage easier for him by recounting rumoured talk he had heard from tribesmen who traded with the men of the *Banu Amir,* fireside tales of the young bride's beguiling beauty, her legendary allure. Rahim's brother retold vivid recitals of her slender, vivacious body, her long silken hair, of her perfect hair the same colour as her bewitching chestnut eyes. This same young girl had now arrived in their camp a few hours before with her whole entourage family, she was accompanied by *Banu Amir* elders for the bride's customary Henna preparation, the Bedouin act of deity and beguilement which meant hours of intricate body painting by the elder women of both tribes ahead of the young couple's first meeting.

The girl's final virginal ceremony was taking place in another tent not far away - in the distance Rahim could hear loud girlish laughter while he sat surrounded by his brothers, his cherished brothers who chattered away in their foolish banter to hide their excitement. Rahim was bullish, this was his manner, he liked to hold sway over the younger men sitting around him, he relished the perceived status the rumoured beauty of his wife-to-be gave him. Meanwhile, Rahim's infamous fearsome father, a man of few words, sat alone in the near-hidden corner, deep in his silent thoughts.

In his place of mindful solitude, the dark leather-skinned nomad saw much. Khaled bin Al-Tarif watched with calm fortitude from the shadows through the squinting slits of his piercing grey eyes, knowledgeable eyes that had seen hardship and harrowing events not meant for those unaccustomed to the brutal ways of this cruel wilderness land - the scorched desert in which he both fought and etched a living so that he and his sons might survive.

The sunburned Al-Tarif had himself, a long time ago, seen what he dreamed was Lucifer the devil, who beckoned and enticed him to his mortal demise. The alter-nemesis of Al-Ilāh had tempted him with false promises of love, alluring visions of a loving wife planted with suspicion in his mind. As the rainstorm hammered down upon the bivouac ground outside, the widowed Bedouin warrior nomad saw his three sons clamouring together in the gloomy candle-lit tent surrounded by their meagre-looking goats thinned by months of hunger. Everyone knew the grass hereabouts had, for some uncommon reason, been poor. To the deep-thinking Bedouin father, the much-feared desert fighter who often showed little mercy to his enemies, something was not right, he sensed indecipherable trouble ahead. He saw his eldest son, the son he had raised with pain in the tribe's strict code of honour, now teased by the tantalising image of a woman he had not yet set his eyes upon. A girl, Khaled bin Al-Tarif had been informed, so beautiful it was said she was created in the image of Al-Ilāh's mother of creation – and, rumours whispered, watched over by the great prophets themselves.

Al-Tarif's eldest son Rahim bin Khaled declared his thanks in silence to the sacred prophets of Al-Ilāh and the magnificent holy warrior Muhammad - the manifest Meccan who, everyone said, was guided by

Al-Ilāh's sanctified angel Gabriel. Nighttime stories around the communal campfires told how the mighty warlord himself had once passed through their camp, staying more than a few nights teaching of Abra'ham's and A'adam's creator Al-Ilāh in a new way, a mesmerising way, telling how they must follow his teachings, abide by ancient laws the warrior-preacher called the truth of I'slām. They must follow Al-Ilāh, pray to him in one true way with obedience if their goat and camel herds were to thrive to bring prosperity with glory to the untamed Bedouin tribes of these dry arid lands.

The preacher's unannounced visit had made an indelible impression, transforming everything - tribal talk described how, on the day the redeemed warrior left their camp it had rained and rained glorious rain just like today when soon, in a short time, the young Rahim bin Khaled's new wife would walk into his life for the first time. Late in the evening, after they were betrothed, she would lift her veil, the much-excited goat shepherd could gaze his eyes upon her; the beautiful alluring young woman he had imagined in his mind for all of his adolescent years.

The youthful Rahim bin Khaled with his band of lifelong boyhood friends often boasted about their fantasy wives who they would someday marry - how they would fall in love, cherish their women in the traditional tribal way. The one way they knew. They talked together with obsession every day, about the beautiful women who would be chosen for them by each of their fathers under the watchful eyes of Al-Ilāh. Right now, today, it was young Rahim's own special time. Over the last few days, Rahim had watched the proceedings move with uncharacteristic speed, his fearsome father, not long since returned from the triumphant holy war against *Mecca*, was not concerned with these arrangements - they were left to the womenfolk in the traditional Bedouin way.

Right now, Al-Tarif squatted, his contemplative time in deep thought. He recalled the two tumultuous events now unfolding, the marriage of his eldest son to the girl of the *Banu Amir* and the victorious crusade of Al-Ilāh that had been foretold by the warlord holy preacher. The great merchant city had fallen, laid to siege by the new Bedouin army of Al-Ilāh led by the mesmerising Muhammad himself. The celebrations even now were emphatic - the first pillar in the blossoming powerful influence of Al-Ilāh's desert I'slām now established. All the triumphant warriors sat around nighttime fires retelling stories of how Al-Ilāh's vision, foretold through the angel Gabriel, had promised success, victory by declaring there was to be no mercy for shallow unbelievers, those who worshipped despicable images of Al-Ilāh or other false gods.

In the euphoria following the victory over the dominant army of *Mecca*, the young Rahim bin Khaled relished the time he would be able to leave his goat herds behind, to stand beside his father and his father's brothers in the great war of redemption in more crusades promised by the mesmerising warlord of their rising emboldened faith. Rahim would follow Muhammad, the redeemed saviour who talked direct with Al-Ilāh - in the holy preacher's name the tribes had come together, ancient long-held blood feuds had been forgotten, a new era of prosperity for the nomadic people promised. Tomorrow, it would be first the day of young Rahim's marriage to the beautiful A'lisha Amjad bint Saleh of the *Banu Amir*. The two tribes would be bound together in lasting friendship.

But right now, haunched deep in the shadows of the outsized ceremonial tent, Khaled bin Al-Tarif thought long and hard about his precious son Rahim. He kept his own mind, not telling anyone about his deep misgivings about this proposed marriage. The proud dark-skinned warrior, scorched and burned by years of survival in the endless sands where men died like flies in the arid wilderness when the waters of the desert dried, did not think his son was yet ready. Something was not right with his eldest son's mind, perhaps his madness had roots somewhere deep in his mother's death five years before. His strange behaviour had worsened since she had died, but there were worrying signs even before then - his unfiltered cruelty to the girls of his tribe, his frame of mind to other Bedouin women, the way he over-relished sacrificial killings and, perhaps much worse, the time he had come close to forever maiming his close friend Ahmed in the brutal fight that began over an insignificant argument about Bedouin honour. Or was it something else? Al-Tarif had heard these whispered rumours also.

The incident caused some deep discussions with the tribal elders, others harboured their own opinions as well; but there were also those who thought the young Rahim someday capable of culpable bravery, that he could one day be a triumphant warrior against their tribal enemies. Al-Tarif himself knew that Rahim showed sure signs of being a brave tribesman, there was no doubts in his mind about this, but it was his son's insolence, his sometimes violent temper towards others of the tribe that caused him to reprimand Rahim over the years. His mother would never have stood for it, things would have been different if she was alive. And then, Al-Tarif thought to himself, on top of everything there was his unfathomable uncertainty over the girl his eldest son was about to marry. These things played heavily inside Al-Tarif's mind, during the last nights since their betrothal had been declared Al-Tarif had lain awake thinking through most of the rain-sodden nights. He had much to think about.

The young girl betrothed to Rahim had been found wandering in the desert more than fifteen years before. Those who found her thought she was perhaps three or four years old; no one knew for sure, there was no way of knowing but the death and carnage surrounding the caravan was plain to see. The young girl was the sole survivor, it was a strange and savage attack, all the merchant travellers cruelly put to death in a manner that threw vague suspicion on a particular Bedouin tribe who for many years had nurtured a vengeance, a deep hatred of the *Meccan* merchants for their domineering cruelty towards nomadic people. But that tribe had voiced strong words of denial, they were rigorous in arguing their innocence at the yearly gathering of the Bedouin tribal leaders and, of course, there was never proof of the murderous intent or the insane slaughter inflicted upon the *Meccan* caravan. Long-held Bedouin tradition also meant the young orphaned girl who was found alive, the one still living from the merchant baggage train, should have herself been put to death, sacrificed as an appeasement to Al-Ilāh - but the mad holy woman R'aisha bint Benim of the *Banu Amir* Bedouin, who had discovered the girl wandering deep in the desert wilderness a short distance from the ravaged caravan, prophesied how this would be a great sin, that to offer the sacrificial life of this orphaned child would anger the sacred souls of the long-dead prophets - that it might bring down the wrath of the mighty life giver A'adam, of Abr'a'ham and the renegade prophet Yesh'ua who the Christian non-believers claimed was the crucified son of Al-Ilāh. And M'oses, the saviour of all men said the holy woman, might inflict one more great famine upon the Bedouin people. And so A'lisha, as the girl was named by the *Banu Amir*, was taken and raised by *Saleh bin Abdel-Salman ibn Ameen Ahl Farsi*, tribal leader of the *Banu Amir*. The child had grown into a young girl of some renowned beauty. But this girl A'lisha, she had no ancestry of note, therefore no dowry of any value. Nothing to give to the family of her betrothed. At first, she was raised more or less as the family slave but her unforgiving, forceful, beguiling disposition was now well stained by *Banu Amir* tribal honour - and A'lisha had grown to become the accepted daughter of the tribal leader. The proposed marriage between Rahim bin Khaled of the *Al Buainai* and A'lisha Amjad bint Saleh of the *Banu Amir* was meant to cement the fragile friendship between the two Bedouin tribes, to try to resolve the long-standing blood feud between these sometimes violent and proud people of the desert. *These* were the troubled convictions that wound like a worm through the thoughts of Khaled bin Al-Tarif on the night before his eldest son's wedding.

The young Rahim heard the distant girlish laughter stop; he sensed the immense moment had arrived. Everyone around him drew silent. The incessant rainstorm ceased, as if controlled by some unknown force that in the powers of reasoning of each of the men assembled could have been yet another intervention by Al-Ilāh. A strange expectation of sensual excitement settled, a pervading atmosphere of domination - male domination, centuries of traditional mastery of men over women, a long-held power written into the testaments since the beginning of time, an ancient time when A'adam himself was tempted by the serpent snake, the beguiling sexual intent of women created. All the men gathered inside the enormous camel-skinned tent anticipated revelation, they desired appeasement, a display of temptation prowess by women over their menfolk. Soon, there would be enticing celebration, traditional dancing, a union of two Bedouin tribes followed by a coming together of men and their tribal women who, for a short while, wished to escape their enslaved-like existence. All the women were covered, hidden by gaily coloured robes to conceal their power of seduction. Beneath tight woven shrouds, clean-limbed and shapely bodies with heaving breasts breathed and perspired, the aroma of forbidden flesh mingling like a mountain lynx concealed in the dark corner, sensuality that lured testosterone that aroused passions in the menfolk when the full gathering of women at last entered through the doorway. The beautiful A'lisha, hidden so that no one could tell which of the robed women was the beautiful one, she was hustled inside the tent to be revealed when the intense moment came.

The leather-skinned Al-Tarif sat haunched and still, ignoring the throng of women filling the enormous Bedouin tent, he squatted in the way those who are used to long hours of waiting know how. His deep grey eyes penetrated the darkening atmospheric celebrations as the tribal men and women all came together.

Al-Tarif watched for the one man he knew full well would seek him out. He waited for the moment when his age-old enemy, who had before made a vow to seek the vengeance of death against him, would look for him squatting alone in the dark corner of the celebration tent. Soon, after a few brief moments, Al-Tarif saw the silhouette of the powerful built figure making his way towards him through the babbling crowd. The great gathering of hard-bearded Bedouin men, they were now in raptures over the gyrating women who moved ever more enticing in sensual dance, the musicians quickened their rhythm, all six of them kneeling in a short line under the tallest of the stout wooden pillars that held the smoke-laden tent up to the sky. The musicians drove their piped rhythmic music deeper, faster - the dancers responded, they danced in ever more enchanting allurement, luring, willing the men to show their desires, their passion... Al-Tarif was waiting, with deliberate patience, for the inevitable confrontation - he knew the time had come.

"Greetings to you Khaled bin Al-Tarif, brave warrior of the *Al Buainai.*" The solid-built Bedouin squatted before Al-Tarif in defiant deference. He was also dark bearded, his deep mass of facial hair obscuring his weathered flesh burned by the intensity of the desert sun. The deep-etched wrinkles in his face made him look frightening, fearsome, a fierce Bedouin fighter of the dry wasteland wilderness. "Do you know who I am?"

Al-Tarif studied the newcomer, the man who now sat back on his heels before him.

"You are the esteemed Saleh bin Abdel-Salman ibn Ameen Ahl Farsi, of the *Banu Amir.* Yes, I know who you are," replied Al-Tarif with cautious optimism.

Al-Tarif knew who the man was, he would never forget. Five years before he had put his sword through this man Abdel-Salman Ahl Farsi's brother, killing him in an instant during the violent encounter beside the Samalla Wells, a bloody confrontation inside the crumbling walls of the precious green oasis. Another bitter skirmish over the priceless sweet water trickling from the much fought-over life-preserving spring. The last time Al-Tarif had seen this man who now sat haunched before him, the renowned tribal leader of the *Banu Amir,* the man had vowed his revenge against him with blood-swelled eyes, with his sword raised pointing to the sky while mounted with defiance upon his glorified adorned camel - which itself snorted in belligerent indignation. This same forthright Bedouin chieftain now squatting before him, fate had decided, was the surrogate father of the adopted girl his son Rahim was about to marry.

"I have sworn to kill you Khaled bin Al-Tarif and, by Al-Ilāh's will, one dark day you will be dead by my willing," growled Abdel-Salman in a succinct way that was, surprising to Al-Tarif, not threatening or laced with imminent danger.

"The blood feud between you and I, Saleh bin Abdel-Salman, is for another day, not today," Al-Tarif retaliated with reverence. He did not flinch or move a muscle, "Mighty Al-Ilāh decrees that my eldest son and your revered daughter are to be married, our families will be joined."

Abdel-Salman paused as if to consider Al-Tarif, then moved without menace to squat to one side of his long-sworn enemy – with deference to his left to signify he meant no threat. Sitting on the opposite side to Al-Tarif's sword hand signalled the acceptance of a grudging truce between them,

"It is five years since the death of my brother," Abdel-Salman whispered. "Not one day has gone by when I have not thought how you will die by my sword," scowled the tribal leader of the *Banu Amir*.

"Your brother died as he should have," replied Al-Tarif, he did not care much about the death of Abdel-Salman's brother. "He and his band of thieves stole the water from my two sons. Then your coward of a sibling murdered the eldest son of my good friend Omar el Basuun. It was Al-Ilāh's will that your brother died by my sword."

Abdel-Salman glared with deep anger at Al-Tarif but his sworn enemy was right, this was not the time for open confrontation. "Al-Ilāh works in mysterious ways my friend," he conceded in a low voice just the two of them could hear, a voice that seemed to suggest some measure of understanding. "Now Al-Ilāh in heaven wills that you and I will be related through wedlock blood."

The tribal leader of the *Banu Amir* looked at Al-Tarif in a way that somehow offered his grudging friendship. But Al-Tarif was no fool, the ancient traditions of the desert, the settling of deadly feuds were never ended by simple marriage. After a brief moment, Abdel-Salman offered a measured smile to Al-Tarif, this time his expression seemed more sincere, breaking up his handsome craggy face; a considered offer of a temporary truce between them, a forced alliance of two hard-born men of the arid mountains.

Al-Tarif breathed an inward sigh, he relaxed just a little. For now, there was to be no trouble between them. He had been thinking hard to himself before Abdel-Salman approached him, reflecting upon this uncertain situation; he worried that things would not go well, that there was little prospect of a long-lasting truce. In his mind Al-Tarif needed to know the reason for his niggling doubts, why he felt the uncertainties over his son's proposed marriage. Now was the moment, perhaps, when he should touch the raw nerve of this supposed new friendship between their two tribes, to test the sincerity of his adversary's will - because the instinctive all-powerful sense of something not right kept rattling inside Al-Tarif's unsettled mind. Al-Tarif decided to take the initiative, to probe inside Abdel-Salman's thoughts. He delved into his convictions to choose his words with care.

"I am troubled by this union of my eldest son to your adopted one. Perhaps you will enlighten me with your own thoughts Saleh bin Abdel-Salman. What do you make of this supposed convenient marriage?"

Straightaway surprised but taking the bait, Abdel-Salman turned to look Al-Tarif square in his eyes. He paused for a moment to think how to respond. Abdel-Salman knew his rival was not to be underestimated, he knew that Khaled bin Al-Tarif had a formidable reputation for both directness and fortitude, a will that was not to be trifled with – a quality in a man the tribal leader of *Banu Amir* Abdel-Salman respected. "Why are you troubled?"

"It is a growing feeling inside me, a sense that all is not as it should be." Al-Tarif stared with forthright intensity, testing the uneasy ground between them.

Abdel-Salman paused, thinking, deciding his words. "Your eldest son Rahim bin Khaled who is to be married to my adopted daughter A'lisha, is rumoured to be brave and reckless just like his father. You must tell me more. Why do you have this trouble inside your head?"

The beating music that drove the enticing dance seemed to grow in intensity, the multitude of veiled women sensed their men were becoming aroused - the atmosphere inside the tent became all pervading, tensions eased as the hoarded camel-dung alcohol mixed with the aroma of smoking weed began to take effect. The men were losing their inhibitions, the women began to taunt their men in their unique defiant fashion. This was just the beginning...

"Do you not see?" Al-Tarif replied with a cautious whisper. "You are my sworn enemy, who makes a promise to Al-Ilāh that you will one day take my head in revenge for your brother. Yet you are persuaded to join

your adopted daughter to my eldest son," Al-Tarif gave no hint to his
longtime enemy of his real thoughts circling like a hawk inside his mind,
the worrying suspicions about his son Rahim, his fear that Rahim would
one day unleash his habitual violence against his new wife - the daughter
of his bitter enemy. His son would, without any doubt, show his usual
brutish manner - in the same way he had demonstrated many times over
recent years. Al-Tarif knew that any maltreatment of the tribal leader's
daughter would bring retribution from Saleh bin Abdel-Salman ibn Ameen
Ahl Farsi of the *Banu Amir,* the truce between the tribes could never last, it
would end in bloodshed. Al-Tarif did not say this to Abdel-Salman, nor
to anyone else, he would keep these thoughts to himself - Al-Tarif knew
the long-sought truce decreed at the insistence of the new holy warlord
was fragile in the extreme. But other doubts were burgeoning inside his
thoughts, some warning sense that his adversary squatting beside him
in supposed friendship perhaps had his own reasons for the marriage of
his daughter. Al-Tarif remained far from convinced about this proposed
wedding.

"Our new esteemed preacher, our beloved holy Muhammad who speaks
directly with Al-Ilāh through his angel spirit Gabriel, he has decreed that
all Bedouin men must unite in his I'slām way of thinking," warned Abdel-
Salman with a hint of venom. "This is Al-Ilāh's will, his command Khaled
bin Al-Tarif. You know this."

"Yes, I know this," replied Al-Tarif, "I think there is more of you left
unsaid. Perhaps there is some other reason in your heart Saleh bin Abdel-
Salman. You do not pay me the respect of telling me what is your truth."

Abdel-Salman seemed startled but held back, sensing the luring tripwire.
"I feel in my heart, also in my head that you are no doubt wise," Abdel-
Salman countered, "I think we are both fools, you know all things that
trouble your mind. Perhaps our new friendships will be the new future. A
new way to live in this cruel wilderness." He waited for his words of fragile
diplomacy to register, but instead saw Al-Tarif deep in thought. "This is
my thinking; do you not believe in the preacher Muhammad's will?"

"Tell me what is the *unsaid* demon hiding inside your heart," Al-Tarif replied in a hard voice that this time failed to hide his deep uncertainty. "Tell me what schemes through your mind. Tell me, before my eldest son and your daughter are joined together in the eyes of Al-Ilāh. Why do you want this marriage?"

For a few moments, Abdel-Salman said nothing. He was himself deep in thought, Bedouin honour, the wishes of the holy preacher - neither would be enough to hide the truth from his long-sworn enemy, the full horror of what he suspected lay ahead. The tribal chief of the *Banu Amir* again paused in uncertain strong-mindedness. Al-Tarif saw the unease in Abdel-Salman's deep wrinkled face.

"I know dark secrets, Khaled bin Al-Tarif," Abdel-Salmon lowered his voice, "I know unseen things men like you do not understand," he glowered, "I believe Al-Ilāh himself will one day dance to the tune of this girl your oldest son is to marry. You ask what is in my heart Al-Tarif, so I will tell you for nothing what is in my heart...," Abdel-Salman paused - to decide what he would *not* say to Al-Tarif.

"You say these strange words," interrupted Al-Tarif. "Now you must speak more Saleh bin Abdel-Salman ibn Ameen Ahl Farsi, you are my long-sworn enemy. Is your heart your mind?"

"Yes, my heart is my mind," replied Abdel-Salman, with defiance. Perhaps, in another time, there might be a germ of friendship between them, a likewise understanding of two similar minds out of which some mutual bonding would grow. But even now, Abdel-Salman thought to himself, his daughter's strange magic was working against him. As the moment passed, he could not prevent his words spilling from his hard-hearted heart... "Lucifer the devil, he will one day find you Al-Tarif. Neither almighty Al-Ilāh nor our beloved preacher Muhammad will take your side. Take my daughter into your humble dwelling, protect her with everything your damned tribe can give, because I warn you, only blood will satisfy the death of my beloved brother at your hands."

Al-Tarif saw the burning fire in Abdel-Salman's eyes, though not for one moment did he feel intimidated. This was more as he expected, he had succeeded in peeling back the false façade of tribal friendship. "I have seen the devil dance Saleh bin Abdel-Salman ibn Ameen Ahl Farsi," said Al-Tarif, looking deep into Abdel-Salman's desert-scorched eyes, "I know in my mind something is not right with this marriage. I think your burning heart is perhaps my heart, we are both in this together my esteemed friend."

Abdel-Salman became silent. This was now an uneasy moment slipping from his grasp, a curving interlude he had not expected. Everything so far had gone well, he had talked direct with his greatness the warlord Muhammad, suggesting a fighting alliance between the *Al Buainai* and the *Banu Amir*. When it had then been proposed by the inner circle elders of the *Banu Amir* that his adopted daughter should marry the eldest son of his hated enemy, the tribal leader of the *Banu Amir* at first refused, this was not the way he had envisaged - but then he saw a way to deliver his long-planned revenge against the *Al Buainai* for the death of his brother. He had long known that his daughter was indelibly strange, that she possessed some inherent ascendancy which grew stronger each day, every day that she turned into the young woman of beguiling beauty. He knew this because he had seen with his own eyes her strangeness that he could not believe, even now... events that were not possible to the human eye.

For a while, the old Bedouin tribal leader suspected with an ingratiating feeling of intuition as the inglorious wedding drew closer, that it might not be his sworn enemy Khaled bin Al-Tarif who would suffer at the hands of his daughter A'lisha Amjad bint Saleh - perhaps the esteemed preacher Muhammad himself would be bitten by the sharp-fanged snake when the union of the *Al Buainai* and *Banu Amir* collapsed in inevitable bloodshed. Like the words now spoken by his enemy Al-Tarif, Abdel-Salman also thought that something was not right, there was an intangible force, an unknown entity driving a darkness before it.

Like a leaping dragon, a storm of fire erupted inside Abdel-Salman's heart. "I want you to know this Khaled bin Al-Tarif, we both know there are troubled times ahead," he growled. "When this girl, my adopted daughter whom I took into my family for protection was found in the desert, she was a small child. Every soul in that caravan train was dead. They had been killed in a cruel way, a strange way, in a way no Bedouin warrior would kill. Their hearts had been ripped from their chests, cut from their ribs then left unbeating in the blood-red sands beside their fouling bodies. Never before have I seen this; this is not the Bedouin way. I believe that some evil, or Lucifer himself was searching for something hidden or, Al-Ilāh forbid, this girl was delivered to me for a reason. She was left for me to find." Abdel-Salman spoke with unbridled passion, he was lost deep within his thoughts, his head wandered to the time many years in the past, a time that still troubled him. He again turned to speak to Al-Tarif, this time in a low voice, a deliberate voice, a voice that seemed to motivate him with passion. "She is yours now. Your eldest son Rahim will take my adopted daughter for his wife to do with her in the Bedouin way. But I warn you, If she is harmed by your people, if one hair upon her head is shed by you the *Al Buainai*, then my sword will cut your throat Al-Tarif, your death will be my revenge. I say this to you in warning, because it is not Al-Ilāh's will that your eldest son and my A'lisha of the *Banu Amir* are joined together in marriage." Abdel-Salman paused his warning for a moment of thought, "I think you are right to be worried Al-Tarif, something inside you, some clever way of knowing the truth knows that nothing but bloodshed will come from this, that this tribal friendship between us will not last. But this, my friend, is the Bedouin way." Abdel-Salman fell silent, turning in defiance to face the frenzied gathering slithering and weaving to the mesmerising music.

Al-Tarif sat in foreboding thought. He had found the raw nerve he knew was there. Abdel-Salman was indeed seeking revenge for the death of his brother.

The music and the dancing girls reached their crescendo, the veiled A'lisha Amjad bint Saleh of the *Banu Amir* was brought forward to be given to Rahim bin Khaled of the *Al Buainai*. Al-Tarif watched this momentous occasion, he was silent, he did not speak. The troubles inside his mind, his misgivings were now even greater. Without knowing why, he turned to stare in Abdel-Salman's direction, piercing deep into his angry eyes. Al-Tarif stayed silent, he said nothing.

"Tell us," Kahmed asked his not-long-wedded brother Rahim as the sun of the next day dawned bright and cloudless - there were no signs of the deluge rain clouds. The unbelievable week-long downpour of rain had now ceased its relentless scourge. "Is she so beautiful that she is like the stars in heaven?" The eagerness in the boy's eyes betrayed the futile way the eldest of Rahim's two brothers tried to remain restrained. Both brothers waited for Rahim to speak, to tell them everything they wanted to hear. Were the rumours true? Rahim seemed to be in some strange trance-like dream; perhaps, they thought, his mind had been taken by the girl who was now a humble nomad shepherd's wife. Rahim smiled but said nothing – he would make them wait just a while longer so that he could torment their curiosity. Both the brothers tried to remain calm but together they all laughed when they realised that Rahim was teasing them. "Tell us *now*." Kahmed repeated with impatience, his laughter dying away in frustration.

How could Rahim possibly tell them? He *was* still in a dream. When his new wife A'lisha lifted her veil, his heart skipped a hundred beats. Her perfect chestnut hair bejewelled and combed like silk to the left side of her shoulder was different in a subtle way, not the dark brown hair endemic to every Bedouin man and woman, but a shade lighter - though it was the frivolous way she tossed her hair aside from her eyes with a deft flick of her hand that had struck him speechless. Her eyes! Her eyes captivated him as soon as they drilled into him, her eyes burned inside him probing inside his mind, into the far corners that were sacrilege to himself. His new bride's eyes were not the colour of her hair, they held a passive firmament of fire within them. Her fair skin, her lips... she was beautiful beyond his imagination, more than even his wildest dreams. Rahim was beyond captivation, his wife A'lisha was the embodiment of everything a young man could desire, a new Bedouin wife who would fulfil his every wish. It was the mesmerising way she tossed her hair, hair that hid the greyness of her chestnut eyes...

How could he describe her beauty to his brothers? Of course, they would never be allowed themselves to gaze upon her face - his wife would always be veiled so that only Rahim himself would know of her rapturous beguilement. This was the way it had always been, no Bedouin woman would ever be allowed to tempt the devil, to tease the mind of another man who was not her husband. Or ever would be. Had not Hyvah, created from the rib bone of A'adam before tempting him with forbidden fruit in the garden world of Yahweh, incurred the wrath of Al-Ilāh-the-creator for all time? The serpent who some said was Lucifer himself, had sown desire within Hyvah, taught her how to control A'adam for her wanton satisfaction. A'adam wanted to love Hyvah, to cherish her, to behold their love though this was not to be. Hyvah had taught A'adam that lust was the meaning of all life - then all men, because of woman's temptation, became culpable of great evil. Man would kill other men, deal death without compassion, men could take women without mercy through lust and unbounded cruelty. Women of the desert were veiled, covered, shielded when they became of young child-bearing age, they could not deliver temptation, not when man wanted to love and to behold. And was it not the will of Al-Ilāh through Gabriel, that all women should be veiled so that temptation would not drive men to evil, to fall under the spell of Lucifer, the fallen angel who was forever the devil? For it was Hyvah alone who was A'adam's incarnate woman.

Had not the holy preacher Muhammad spoken direct to Al-Ilāh? And was it not Al-Ilāh's will how the fallen angel should be kept bound in hell, held secure in chains of fire? Al-Ilāh's desire, his preaching of wisdom spoken through the angel Gabriel to his preacher Muhammad was simple and clear, women in Al-Ilāh's world should not cast their temptation spells - their life was to love, to obey their men. First their fathers and brothers, then their husbands to bear sons who were brave with determination emboldened to fight their enemies, to destroy those who did not follow the Lord's will. To follow Al-Ilāh's bidding for all time, for Al-Ilāh was the supreme creator of all men.

But Rahim bin Khaled had felt another evil inside him, a feeling he had felt many times. He felt the familiar rise of anger within his soul. As usual, he could not control the evil inside, the unfathomable anger that drove his mind into a frenzy. He was desperate, he hoped his new wife would change this unholy thing that was beginning to control his life, she was beautiful beyond his imagination - with the unbounded loyalty of his new wife Rahim's life would be different. But this did not happen. Nothing that Rahim hoped would ease the confusion inside his head came forth. A'lisha had removed her veil, then her habib, to reveal her scant clothing beneath. She was his, her sublime curved body with her small pointed breasts, the coloured stone jewel in her navel - these all combined to offer Rahim the first-night love of his new wife, the first time for him also. A'lisha was the embodiment of everything he could desire. He felt nothing. She smiled. A bewitching smile he would remember for his whole life. It was as if she knew...

The last time he felt this same anger erupt was when his friend laughed, taunting him because of what happened. The friendly wrestle between two adolescent shepherd boys, beduins of the desert. Rahim had felt the excitement grow inside him, his penis stiffen with a strange feeling he could not control. Rahim, without realising, felt for his friend's crotch, then used his superior strength to pin Amal down beneath him. Amal cried out, Rahim let him free but Amal laughed and teased. He would tell all the boys. Rahim reacted out of control - he came close to killing Amal. Rahim was pulled away by the other boys who came to see who was screaming in pain. Amal never said anything to Rahim because now Amal was afraid.

Twice Amal's younger sister Karman taunted Rahim because she heard the rumours from other boys, whispered hearsay with sometimes a giggle. Rahim beat Amal's sister without remorse, Amal's father watched but he did not intervene. Afterwards, after the eldest sister begged for her life, Amal's father Al-Dalma held his knife to Rahim's throat, saying that if he harmed any of Amal's sisters again then he would be cast from the tribe. Amal's father did not stop the attack upon his daughter Karman because this was the Bedouin way, men had rights over women, wives and sisters; it had been like this since time began. Tonight would be the second night of Rahim's marriage to A'lisha, tonight would be different. Tonight, Rahim decided, he would forget his concealed temptation for male love, tonight his desires for his beautiful wife A'lisha of the *Banu Amir* would awaken.

Rahim's brother Khamed needed to know. His desperation knew no bounds, he desired to see how beautiful his brother's wife was. He had lain awake every night since the betrothal of his brother was announced, even before this he listened to other shepherd boys tending their goats in the desert. They told him of the rumours, stories of the beauty of a young girl adopted by the *Banu Amir,* how she was found in the desert when a young child. His imagined vision of this girl tormented his thoughts, he had long since created an image of her in his mind, she became his dream. Then, when his father told him his brother Rahim was to be married to the same orphaned girl of his dreams, he was both distraught and electrified with excitement. He was fifteen years old, he was now, he thought, faced with the prospect that his own wife, when she was chosen by his father, would never be so beautiful as that of his older brother. Khamed had to know how beautiful his brother's wife was.

"Please describe her to me my brother Rahim. Are the rumours about her true?" Khamed followed Rahim out to the goat herd. They passed the new pitched wedding tent which Khamed knew now housed the girl of his forbidden dreams. He felt a tinge of excitement when they walked past the doorway, out towards the bleating goats on the desert hillside. The goats were feeding with eager excitement on the new shoots of fresh green grass erupting from the barren earth still soaked from the week-long deluge of refreshing rain.

"Of course, the rumours are true my little brother," said Rahim. "But you will never know."

"I hope that one day my wife will be beautiful, that our father will find me a Bedouin girl just like yours, Rahim. This will be the desert girl of my dreams." He did not dare tell his older brother his real dream, how the vision of his brother's wife had captivated him since he could first remember his awakening desire for girls. "Are her eyes the colour of chestnuts like they say?"

"No, my little brother, they are not quite the colour of chestnuts. They are a deeper shade than simple chestnuts. Did you know that her eyes sparkle like rare jewels found in heaven?" boasted Rahim. "They have a deepness that is fabled amongst the men of the *Banu Amir,* her beautiful eyes are unlike the eyes of all other desert girls, because their common eyes see their menfolk without love. A'lisha is like a flower growing amongst desert weed," said Rahim, he enjoyed the teasing he could inflict upon his younger brother. "And did I tell you about the roundness of her breast, my little brother?"

Kahmed's heart skipped a beat. Of course, he had imagined A'lisha's breasts many times, he had seen them in his mind's eye during the middle of the night when his rampant thoughts threatened to overwhelm him. Now, if his brother would describe her breasts to him it would become their intimate secret forever, he would somehow save the vision in his mind. Khamed laughed in eager anticipation,

"No Rahim, you did not say. Please tell me about A'lisha's breasts. Are they round like watermelons? The melons Meccan traders sell in the market, my Rahim?"

Rahim sniggered, "I cannot tell you, my little brother. If I tell you about the firmness of her breasts, how they point to the heavens when she lies beneath me then Al-Ilāh will strike me in a foul way, he will bless me with no sons from my marriage. I will not tell you more my little brother Khamed, because you are too young to know such things. And no man wishes to be cursed from heaven with no sons to his name."

They climbed the small hill, the goats skipped out of their way to hide among the camels, somehow sensing their meagre lives were once more under threat. Rahim looked around, he picked out two young kids that would do nice. The second evening's feast with their new tribal friends from the *Banu Amir* needed to be as good as the first. Tonight would be the celebration of friendships, vows of continued collaboration with stories late into the night about their infamous feuds of the past, recounted battles with Bedouin tribes that were now, perhaps, their common enemy. And tonight, Rahim thought, he would at last cement the union with his new wife. They were not yet wed in the eyes of Al-Ilāh. Tonight, he promised to himself with outright determination, he would plant the first of his many sons into A'lisha's perfect belly.

Khamed had already made up his mind. He knew he could not control his burning desire to see the face of the mysterious girl he dreamed of every night, ever since he first heard whispered rumours from other shepherd boys in the desert. Khamed always listened to their boyish talk, their dreamlike promises of how they would each teach this girl about love. He heard their proud boasts, their talk about how she would bear their sons into the world. He listened to the menfolk talk, whenever there was any news about the *Banu Amir*, he would every time listen. And now, his brother was married to this same girl. This evening, Khamed decided he would take the risk, he would chance everything just for a fleeting glimpse; this was all he needed to satisfy his growing fascination, his need to see her face to see if the rumours were true, that his imagined dreams of her image fitted the picture in his mind. But this, Khamed realised, would break the strict Bedouin code of honour that no man should covet the wife of another man in any way whatsoever, that another man should not be tempted by the hidden desires that women could weave, the magic that could be created by casting mesmerising spells weak men could not resist. Khamed knew full well he was walking into trouble, but this mystifying girl of his dreams had cast her spell. Tonight, the unforgiving world of Bedouin nomads would change forever.

"Come to me NOW," demanded Rahim with venom. "Remove your veil, I want to see you as my wife." A'lisha inched towards him in the dim light of their stinking camel-skin tent.

"My husband, how do you wish to see me this night," the nighttime descended, casting its veil in the fading light. The evening's celebrations had long since ended.

"Take off your robes, let your body stand before me. I have made my promise to Al-Ilāh that I will put my unborn son into your body." Rahim tried hard to arouse his passion, there were stirrings of desire deep inside his mind - he also felt confusion - there was the familiar rising resentment welling up inside him. He saw the confident young woman standing naked before him, not the nervous girl he expected or desired in her nakedness.

Beads of sweat trickled from his brazened forehead to run down into his tangled black beard, his beard of manhood that still grew in its immaturity.

"If you desire me tonight then it is your will. Better than the hurt we suffered in our first marriage night." A'lisha delivered her words with chilling audacity.

A'lisha's sentient words made no difference. Rahim saw the familiar red mist rise to obscure his condescending vision. He convinced himself that she suspected, that she knew his concealed secret. If she did know, it was not this girl's place to question him. His anger inside mounted, it grew like a festering mushroom spurting in rancid nighttime rain, it was as if he had Lucifer inside him. She came closer and, losing his control, Rahim struck out. The rear of his rigid hand landed square upon the side of A'lisha's flinching face, she flew backwards in pain, blood flowed free from the gaping red wound upon her right cheekbone. When she fell to the floor, Rahim's foot kicked deep into her abdomen, she whimpered in silence, in pain. Rahim knew he would lose his mental wellbeing. He at first tried to draw back, but the anger, the confusion inside him grew strong. He kicked hard, his wife made no sound as she lay upon the dry sandy floor of their tent. Then, one final time, his foot lunged to land hard against her breasts. By this time A'lisha had curled instinctively into a ball to protect herself, while her false tears of pain flowed to mingle with the blood oozing from her cheek wound. Rahim began to feel another strong feeling stirring inside him, an unfamiliar feeling of lust for a woman. The more he thought of inflicting pain upon his new wife the more this feeling within him grew. The shepherd warrior, the young man on the cusp of becoming a brave new desert fighter launched himself at his submissive wife once more, this time he could not prevent himself, he lost control. He lunged into her again, kicking out not in anger but in lustful enjoyment. A'lisha was past screaming, she moaned in suffering pain. Her instinctive will for survival meant that she was now curled into a full protective ball on the blood-soaked earth. Pausing to gain his breath Rahim held back, something distracted his attention without his realisation. He turned and there in the doorway, with shocked horror etched in pain upon his terrified face, stood his brother Khamed. Rahim's angry violent state was now confused by the sight of his younger brother. Rahim did not see his submissive, blood covered wife uncurl herself from the sand dust floor. A'lisha was something more, she was not A'lisha of the *Banu Amir*, her eyes flashed a different look, a more animal, prehistoric look - they were never the chestnut-coloured jewels that Rahim once before described.

Khaled bin Al-Tarif woke with a start. Daylight showed itself through the unsewn seams of his goatskin dwelling, the rising sun seeping through the cracks of the rough flapped doorway with little beams of sunlight teasing the dry arid air. The damp air of incessant rain was now gone. It was not the hum of excited voices outside that wakened him, nor the barking dogs yapping in abject alarm - it was the sense of dagger-like danger inside him. A deep inner feeling of stupendous foreboding made Al-Tarif wake from his alcohol-fuelled slumber. It took a few moments for him to gain his senses before the flap of his doorway burst open sending strong rays of morning dawn swordlike into the dark interior gloom. In the doorway stood the youngest of his three sons Dusan, shear panic burned upon his strained facial features still too young to bear the dark whiskers of manhood. Al-Tarif sat bolt upright though even before Dusan could utter a single word the ageing Bedouin warrior was out from beneath his sleeping skins, standing clothed. No one in the desert ever undressed for a simple night's sleep.

"Father, Father, please come quick," tears welled in Dusan's eyes, "it is...." The boy never got to complete his frenzied request. Instead, he froze as he tried to form the words that would not release themselves from the inside of his confused mind.

Al-Tarif burst past his son, out into the fullness of the new day. He saw the excited group of men accompanied by growing throngs of veiled women gathering outside of his son Rahim's tent. There was both excitement and panic in their voices, even more when they saw Al-Tarif striding towards them. At the same time, on the south side of the encampment, another group of men began to break into a run towards the confused group gathered beside Rahim's tent. This second group hurrying towards the confusion were the men of the *Banu Amir*, leading them from the front their Bedouin tribal leader, Saleh bin Abdel-Salman Ahl Farsi.

Behind Al-Tarif ran his son Dusan. Together they reached the gathered crowd, Al-Tarif pushed his way through the bickering horde to the door of his eldest son's dwelling. No one else dared to enter, even though they had all heard the frenzied screaming. Panicking shouts spread, something was wrong. The dry blood soaked into the sandy earth outside of the doorway was plain enough, everyone could see the stained ground, the ominous trail that led inside. Many of the womenfolk there had risen before daybreak, it was the women who, in the half dawn, sensed there was some intense drama being played out on the outskirts of the camp. They had seen Dusan, the youngest of Al-Tarif's sons, burst from Rahim's tent screaming in terror. Men were still awakening from their sleepy slumber after being summoned by their women, even the shepherd boys making their way with their goats returned down the hillside to see what all the commotion was about. By the time Dusan entered his father's tent to wake him, the crowd was beginning to gather. A few moments later Al-Tarif burst inside Rahim's tent with great purpose, he froze in instant horror. His senses, the same sense of impending disaster that had plagued him for days now, reeled as his eyes took in the blood-soaked scene confronting him.

Rahim, his eldest married son, lay on the floor. The bloody carnage left no doubt in the ageing Bedouin's mind that his son was dead. He looked around, there was no sign of his son's wife A'lisha, or indeed of anyone else. A few moments later Saleh bin Abdel-Salman burst through the door, he too froze in abject terror. The scene before them was beyond their comprehension. In the gloomy half-light of the early morning, in the frail sunlight that just penetrated the pungent atmosphere still reeking of the goat herd flocks that bleated in defiance on the nearby hillsides, they both saw that Rahim's heart had been ripped from his open chest. It lay in a bloody heap upon the foot-trodden ground beside his lifeless body.

Saleh bin Abdel-Salman Ahl Farsi of the *Banu Amir* stood in stupefied horror. The gut-wrenching feeling of overwhelming alarm inside the fearsome Bedouin left not one thought to his imagination - he knew straightaway who had butchered the son of his bitter adversary. The tribal leader of the *Banu Amir* turned to look into the stark, emotionless eyes of Al-Tarif, Al-Tarif for a long moment glared back uttering not one word - there was nothing he could think of to say. Where was the missing girl? Where was Al-Tarif's son Khamed?

"A'lisha is gone Al-Tarif, she is not here," breathed Abdel-Salman reading the mind of Al-Tarif, mouthing his words in knowledgeable bewilderment - this was not the first time he had seen death dealt in this brutal fashion. "Be wary if you follow them," he warned in a low voice whispered in earnest. "Out there in the desert, she will hunt you. If you try to find her she will kill you, your own heart will beat its blood into the sands. Please listen to me when I say this."

Al-Tarif did not reply, his startled mind whirled in wild confusion. A'lisha of the *Banu Amir* was not much more than a child, a young woman who could never possess the killer instinct of the most vicious of Bedouin warriors – it was not possible. This was a ruse, a clever means of revenge dealt by the *Banu Amir.* The wedding had been a conspiracy, a sham, a way of exacting retribution for the killing of Abdel-Salman's brother at the Samalla water well. Al-Tarif considered the situation more rational, with logic - he drew his long-sheathed knife to point the tip sharp against the throated flesh of Abdel-Salman.

"Tell me, Saleh bin Abdel-Salman Ahl Farsi, did you believe that we *Al Buainai* Bedouin would fall into your lamentable ambush?" Al-Tarif shrilled his challenge in angry defiance – though he held his knife back from piercing the jugular of his long-standing enemy. Al-Tarif paused, then hissed. "Do you think I am not wise enough to know the blood of my son is vengeance for your miserable brother?"

Everyone standing inside the forlorn goatskin tent held their breath, the emotional strain failed to cut the silence of apprehensive disaster - the angry slaughter between two traditional warring tribes that was about to unfold. In the congealed bloodstained sand of the humble desert dwelling the crumpled body of Rahim bin Khaled lay lifeless, rigid, the onsetting stiffness of death overwhelming his violent demur.

Abdel-Salman of the *Banu Amir* had no choice, his proud demeanour did not allow him to show weakness or remorse. "Kill me, you *Al Buainai* scum, kill us all," snarled Abdel-Salman in defiance. "Cut our beating hearts from our Bedouin chests, in the same way hearts were wrenched from the Meccan slavers slaughtered in the caravan from where this girl came. Who do you think did this? Who do you think killed those traders, those unbelievers in Al-Ilāh who barter in the tears and blood of slaves, eh?"

Al-Tarif stiffened. His instinctive reaction made him hesitate, the incredulity of the moment, the notion that a young child may have played some part in the killing of every Meccan trader travelling in the desert caravan that had many years ago crossed the remote Sambula sands. Everyone stared at Al-Tarif, what would he do? The distant bleating of itinerant goat herds added a symbolic interlude to the moment, ravenous and starving vultures circled unseen high above the *Al Buainai* encampment - somehow sensing the inglorious feast of dead and decaying flesh that might soon present itself in the dry arid wilderness of these nomadic Bedouin lands.

Gabriel was glad of his concealed invisibility – his obscurity and silence was crucial. He must remain inconspicuous, unimposing if he was not to lose any understanding of what was happening. Gabriel's unbridled unease tore away his desire to appear majestic with his usual all-consuming power, his furled white wings drooped in a way of forlorn displeasure that offered no means of transgression. From Gabriel's citadel of dominance from where he saw everything of consequence, he spied in open-mouthed stupefaction as the drama in the *Al Buainai* encampment unfolded - this was not possible, it could not be happening, not in the way he now saw. Gabriel was grim, but he was not deep down surprised. The all-at-once circumstance of the disaster was not unexpected, Gabriel had long realised his nemesis would at some moment in time make her move - though he realised her hidden location might need an element of good fortune for him to uncover. There had been spurious leads, tentative clues that seemed to add up but drew to tantalising dead ends – nevertheless, to be double sure, any suspected girl-child had been hunted down then put to death. Gabriel was never a fool, he had known the new rising tide of Al-Ilāh would lure her majestic deity from her lair, that she would seek to find the emerging prophet who would need to be resolute and strong if he was to survive. Until now, Gabriel thought, Muhammad had proven himself decisive, magnificent, supreme in his wisdom without knowing his nemesis would at some point deliver her revenge. This child had concealed herself with cunning trickery, never had she revealed her concealment among the Bedouin desert nomads. Not until now. What was more, this strongman Bedouin, this Al-Tarif - Gabriel sensed something in this desert nomad that made him break out in beads of disquiet - in a human-like way. A hunch, a feeling of disparity, a worrying premonition that his warlord Muhammad might be in some peril.

Gabriel, in his stunned state turned to his nearby vassal, his untrustworthy but diligent dark angel Lucifer who himself seemed agitated. "What do you know of this aberrant child?' Gabriel demanded. 'Why did you not know she was among the *Banu Amir* Bedouin?"

Lucifer looked chided; the reprieved angel had not expected this turn of events.

"We made a mistake,' Lucifer confessed, 'I must tell you, a time ago my hunter angels Chemosh, Moloch and Dagon, they discovered this same child travelling in the slaver's caravan. The end was not good, my angels did not survive, my hunters were slain."

"Your angels *were slain?*" Gabriel was once more shocked. "Who did this? Who slew them?" Gabriel fixed his gaze upon Lucifer, Lucifer looked up from the ground in sheepish submission.

"First, I believed the slavers killed my angels but the traders, they too died, there was no one left alive." Lucifer lied - he had long known the Meccans were never capable of defending themselves against his foremost predatory assassins, during their ambush upon the caravan another entity had intervened – Lucifer's coveted angels had one by one died, cast aside to become unearthly demons with nowhere in history to hide. To conceal the inconceivable deaths of his infallible angels another Bedouin tribe had been blamed for the caravan attack, an outright act of deceit that Lucifer hoped would hide the disastrous turn of events that might well bring his rival kingdom tumbling down. Lucifer had miscalculated, blundered, a misjudgment though he had no intention of being made the scapegoat - he did not like this position of servitude. Lucifer hated Gabriel; he despised his master's dominating power.

"I was told the child had died though it seems she in some way survived." Lucifer did not care if Gabriel showed his anger. There was more that Gabriel did not know, Moloch, Dagon and Chemosh were certain they had once before killed this same infant child, they had buried her in the ground, it was inconceivable that she would be travelling on the Meccan slavers' camel train. Lucifer's two remaining assassins, Belial and Iblis had earlier warned him – the child raised by the *Banu Amir* was dangerous, she must be found, she was capable of unqualified destructive havoc. This child's latent abilities were immense, she was not like the others – not in any way could she be homosapien human. Lucifer was worried – *it was as if Hyvah herself had risen.* In his bitter memory, he recalled the slaughter of the merchant caravan nearly fifteen years before - his three angels had been butchered along with each one of the Meccan slavers, the vicious attack had been short and savage. Back then, this girl, she was a young child – it was not possible, it could not be the same infant child... the dead, their hearts had been ripped outright from their beating chests. Angels did not die, not like this, angels were above the simple act of death.

But there *had been* a mutilated body, what appeared to be a child's body. Unidentified. In his grief Lucifer had made a mistake, other slaves were being transported on the train - he had not made sure this body was the one his angels sought, the unexpected death of his hunters had caused him great consternation but, to everyone, it appeared the child had died. Lucifer now thought hard - the medicine woman in the desert, the old cripple woman, her name was *R'aisha bint Benim*, she had found the slaughtered carnage of the caravan – could she have taken the real child?

Lucifer, for now, did not elaborate, it could all go wrong. Vilified as the devil, the deadliest of Gabriel's seven fallen angels, for a long time now Lucifer had been endeavouring to re-establish himself into Gabriel's favour, at the same time cultivating the means to reconstruct his fledgling realm - incurring Gabriel's wrath at this moment in time would unravel his scheming cabal. Lucifer had little choice - he needed to find and eliminate this young girl with speed before more trouble mired the desert sands in blood. Besides, Lucifer still shivered with frustrated anger when he thought of his slaughtered angels – they were his best, his most loyal hunters, his most capable who on every occasion had stalked down each emerging bloodline birth of the contemptible Hyvah.

Gabriel did not trust Lucifer, for a time now Lucifer's credence had remained at a low ebb, now Gabriel was concerned why the deaths of Moloch, Dagon and Chemosh had been kept from him - because they would be forever immortalised as demons. Gabriel realised his intervention was vital, the archangel of heaven knew what was happening - these astonishing events were no pure accident - how could it be coincidence that these deaths coincided with the emergence of perhaps his ablest prophet yet - his esteemed preacher Muhammad.

A'lisha Amjad bint Saleh of the *Banu Amir* came into the world without a given name, nor had she inherited any name through birth or male procreation. A'lisha Amjad bint Saleh was the name bestowed upon her by the elders of the *Banu Amir* Bedouin nomads, in the main because it was decided that she was the property of Saleh bin Abdel-Salman ibn Ameen Ahl Farsi, tribal leader of *Banu Amir*. In reality, the child who was A'lisha Amjad bint Saleh had no name, not before or since she was reborn and resurrected from the swamp mists of the vast snow-covered forests in the cold northlands the desert Bedouin tribes did not know existed. The significant, unidentifiable name etched into the hard-rock stone of the granite monolith slab might never be decrypted nor untangled to reveal its true origin - to the *Banu Amir* and the *Al Buainai* Bedouin she would be known as A'lisha Amjad bint Saleh, the same name Muhammad the prophet would one day come to know well - fulfilling chilling prophecies that for ten million years had prophesied Muhammad's coming. So far, no man had read or even discovered the prehistoric hieroglyphic remonstrance hammered into the primordial granite of the hidden stone, the cenotaph that stood tall in the succulent green meadow grass on the edge of ancient pine forests – lands vast and different from the scorched desert where rain drenched the sands perhaps once in every ten years.

Right now, A'lisha Amjad bint Saleh, as she was presently known, sat beside the shaking and shivering Khamed bin Al-Tarif, the devastated younger brother of the dispatched Rahim. A'lisha knew that Khamed was teetering on the brink of madness, the devastating scene he had witnessed between herself and Rahim was beyond the young shepherd's ability to understand - as far as Khamed believed, no human could transform into the animalistic being that butchered his older brother in the savage way that occurred right in front of his bulging eyes, more so when the killer was the beautiful essence of his fantasies whom he cherished and adored even in his deepest dreams. Khamed's sanity was breaking down, desert vultures that for uncountable years had fed from opportune morsels of measly flesh festering in the arid sands, sensed the gluttonous feed that might soon occur. They circled overhead with their unflapping wings on endless eddies of rising air like the forebears of death heralding their reason for existing.

A'lisha, she looked skyward, she watched the feathered harbingers of doom, she did not see ugly birds with their scrawny necks formed to forage inside lifeless corpses as enemies of life, she saw them as the simple virtues of non-human life that possessed the same inordinate right to feed from flesh as any Bedouin nomad. The teachings of prophets and holy men that elevated men above the realms of animal existence meant nothing to A'lisha Amjad bint Saleh, the lies told by Gabriel's cohorts in the name of his almighty Lords were beyond A'lisha's understanding of reality. A'lisha's rebirth from the earth that had consumed her, her three-hundred-year existence was enough to ensure that her war of survival would be both bitter and savage. Only in the last fifteen or so years had she progressed her age faster than the childlike existence that had hidden her identity for an eternity so far. A'lisha Amjad bint Salah's new purpose was to seek out the mad woman R'aisha bint Benim, she cherished her as the true deceiver of violent men. First, A'lisha had to ensure Khamed's survival - before the feathered vultures could devour his lifeless body piecemeal.

A'lisha Amjad bint Saleh saw that she had not much time, she reached inside Khamed's mind to take hold of the twisted sinews of broken nerves that heralded his death. A'lisha touched them, she joined the endless ends of useless memories, she threaded each unbroken memory into new delicate pathways that would perhaps change Khamed's perception of what had taken place - his recollection of what had happened inside the blood-sodden tent of the *Al Buainai* Bedouin. A'lisha then endeavoured to temper his infatuated worship of herself, knowing she would not succeed - his besotted love was too deep for her to reach. It would take time for Khamed to recover, when she removed herself from his mind A'lisha set about protecting Khamed from the brutal desert sands by fashioning a hollow in the scrubby earth before covering him with her worn torn cloak of goatskin felt. She tossed her hair from her eyes with a casual movement of her womanly wrist, at the same time glancing upwards to warn the circling vultures to be gone, to take themselves elsewhere to find their opportune meal. She watched them end their circling as they peeled away to soar upwards in the rising desert air, flying skywards towards fictitious clouds that never appeared.

Khamed was beyond redemption, his quivering lips tried to utter words that never did form themselves into anything coherent. A'lisha knew the boy was spent, that he would not for a long time understand the troubled situation they were both in. She had meant for his half-brother Rahim to die, this was her first intention but not until she had fulfilled her real purpose. Rahim was her pathway, but his violent vicious male aggression had changed everything – A'lisha did not know if Khamed would survive.

A'lisha Amjad bint Saleh strode to the nearest peak of the highest dune of sand - this would have to do; this place was where she would make her defiant stand. She marked four straight lines into the yellowish earth, one each to the north, east, south and west - from these directions, except the north, would come the inevitable assaults upon her existence. From the east the hunting tribesmen of the *Al Buainai* and *Banu Amir*, from the west would come the murderous army of the warlord Muhammad to protect his embryonic faith, from the south the enemy A'lisha feared above all else – the vengeful angels Lucifer, Belial and Iblis, their retribution driven by a powerful force that A'lisha herself understood.

From the north might come salvation – the decrepit medicine woman of the wilderness desert - the crazed mad woman *R'aisha bint Benim*.

"Are the *Al Buainai* and *Banu Amir* now at war?" mocked Saleh bin Abdel-Salman of the *Banu Amir*. "Do we *Banu Amir* retreat to collect ourselves to die by daggers drawn to our throats?" Al-Tarif did not answer the defiant flow of words from the *Banu Amir* tribal leader. With unrealising hesitance, he lowered his knife from Abdel-Salman's jugular.

Al-Tarif felt a deep feeling of indecision, the same uncertainty that had plagued him for a time now since before the marriage of his son Rahim to A'lisha Amjad bint Saleh of the *Banu Amir* - the proposed marriage had never seemed sincere - the nagging doubts that had no substance, the sixth-sense premonition of something not right - Al-Tarif studied Abdel-Salman eyeball to eyeball, there was an immovable impasse, revenge...

"My brother Rahim is dead," interrupted Dusan, Al-Tarif's now next-in-line son who had first woken Al-Tarif from his overnight slumber. Dusan's voice quivered in uncertain pain. The darkness of the tent did not lessen even when the sun began its relentless climb into the early-morning sky. "We will find who killed my brother, what you say is madness, no childlike woman has the power to kill like this."

Abdel-Salman glared at Dusan, if he knew what he himself knew - but perhaps here was the *Banu Amir's* way out with their honour and lives intact. This Dusan, he might be right, he said what he believed was true, words that every other tribal warrior and women of both Bedouin tribes were by now thinking. No one in their right mind believed the *Banu Amir* girl could have done this, someone with brutal power must have entered Rahim's tent during his second wedding night, then abducted the new wife and killed the young *Al Buainai* shepherd warrior when he had fought with bravery to protect her. This rationalisation spread through everyone's mind; it was the one reasonable conclusion. The men and women inside the crowded tent nodded in quiet acknowledgement, with the same mutterings being spread through the tent flap opening to the gathered crowd of both tribes standing in bewilderment outside. "Where *is* Khamed?" whispered an unknown voice back inside the tent, this question spread like wildfire with everyone looking around for the, by now, missing brother. The flurry of the question shook Al-Tarif from his stupefied but studied trance. Where was Khamed?

With this question in his mind, Al-Tarif strode with single-minded purpose from the tent. With his expert eye, he picked out the faint tracks leading away from the tent towards the west, into the wildest part of the wilderness desert. Soon the relentless late-morning breeze would cover the light indentations of two sets of feet, they were Khamed's footprints, Al-Tarif saw there had never been any incursion by deadly forces from outside. None of this made sense. Abdel-Salman, a fraction of a second behind saw the same, he followed Al-Tarif, his own nonsensical beliefs settled.

"Why did you not warn me about this *Banu Amir* girl eh?" Al-Tarif turned to Abdel-Salman. "What is it you hide?" Like everyone around, Al-Tarif did not consider the young bride of Rahim capable of brutal murder - and the thought that his son Khamed may have played a part or instigated the deadly act was, to Al-Tarif, inconceivable.

Abdel-Salman, thinking on his feet, grasped the opportunity to deflect blame from the *Banu Amir*, he needed time to reflect, to react, to piece together a way out of this unfolding catastrophe. "Your youngest son Khamed, he is not here," said Abdel-Salman, "We all see these sand tracks. Their tracks are lightweight, they are the tracks of my daughter and whoever absconded with her, perhaps they *were* taken against their will," Abdel-Salman knew this fallacy would not hold water for long, there were two sets of tracks - unlike his Bedouin adversary, Abdel-Salman knew that everything that had happened made sense, the whispered rumours would soon collapse into a heap of accusations and recrimination... but Abdel-Salman was convinced, with sickened dread, that his adopted daughter was the one who, in her sickening gruesome way, had killed the oldest son of his long-time enemy Khaled bin Al-Tarif. He had seen her capabilities before, there, in her eyes, when she possessed that wild gaze, when she distanced herself in her animalistic far-off glare... Abdel-Salman tried to hide his half-smile, his sneer of heartfelt revenge, retribution for the death of his brother at the hands of his enemy Al-Tarif. The payback was bittersweet, though not the revenge that Abdel-Salman in any way thought possible - the *Banu Amir* tribal leader knew it was not how his long-held vengeance was meant to be... what was more, this whole wretched saga might easily turn against the *Banu Amir*. These stupid *Al Buainai* did not realise how simple it had been for his A'lisha to kill this boy Rahim.

For the seasoned trackers of both tribes it was easy enough to follow the trail of A'lisha and Khamed, within one sun-hour of the discovery of Rahim's body the search was underway. Abdel-Salman had warned Al-Tarif not to track her but his adversary's passion for revenge was too great, now Abdel-Salman estimated they were maybe less than one half-day of sun from the runaways – if indeed they were travelling together.

There now seemed little doubt that something breathtaking and horrific had taken place, that Khamed and the new married wife of his brother Rahim were in some way involved in Rahim's death. Al-Tarif felt uneasy, he suspected that Rahim's infamous brutality had played a part in his death - Al-Tarif was no fool, from the beginning he had suspected there would be trouble in the marriage but not like this. Rumours and whispers flourished, the same thoughts were being expressed among all the *Al Buainai* tribe people and even the trackers - what struck the battle-hardened men of both tribes was the brutal manner in which the young Bedouin had died. Al-Tarif thought hard, he was disturbed - what had his enemy Abdel-Salman meant when he had warned the girl would hunt *him* down? Al-Tarif studied Abdel-Salman once more - his bitter enemy knew, the tribal chief of the

Banu Amir knew his son had been killed by this strange non-Bedouin girl.

Out in the desert to the west the trail became difficult to follow, Al-Tarif realised the fugitives had chosen their escape route with shrewd intention - the terrain became wilder as the scrubby sands began to roll up in ever more desolate heaps. The pair could not be far ahead, they were both on foot whereas himself, Abdel-Salman and the half-dozen trackers of both tribes rode their camels in a determined fashion. Al-Tarif guessed that a little after midday they would find the two absconders.

Dead ahead the trackers paused, their ragged headscarves wrapped tight around their heads to protect them from the beating sun. The lead tracker pointed to circling vultures high in the sky, a sure sign that life close by was teetering on the edge of extinction. The group picked their way between the higher dunes, careful to stay off the ridges where they could be spotted by watching enemies. The weak trail by now had subsided, overwhelmed by the drifting sands that wiped away any tears of redemption – the trackers made in the direction of the scavenging vultures sure in the knowledge that this was where they would find the two desperate fugitives.

The lead trail finder ahead paused, he turned his head side-to-side looking for something he could not see, he sniffed the air with deep suspicion then stopped. Al-Tarif hesitated, more from instinct - he rose standing high in his saddle. The *Al Buainai* and *Banu Amir* were not the only ones out in there in the desert, there was someone, or something else, nearby. The tribal trackers of both tribes halted, they each reigned in their camels then drew their swords. Al-Tarif noted that Abdel-Salman sat rigid and still, Abdel-Salman turned to Al-Tarif,

"Hang tightly to your heart Khaled bin Al-Tarif," warned Abdel-Salman, "I fear it might soon beat your own blood into these sands." Abdel-Salman peered searching, scanning every horizon for the peril that had not yet showed its head.

Dusan bin Khaled, the youngest of Al-Tarif's three sons, idolised and loved his older brother Khamed, more so than his eldest brother Rahim whom he hated. Dusan had witnessed Rahim's bullying violence on more than one occasion, he often avoided being his victim by the narrowest of margins. Dusan felt aggrieved, passed over, he was not even considered when the hunting party was put together to find the murderous runaways A'lisha Amjad bint Saleh and his brother Khamed. Dusan was heartbroken, he was distressed, not for his dead brother Rahim but for his beloved brother Khamed who was now by circumstance incriminated in Rahim's death.

In Dusan's mind, Khamed could not have committed this odious wrong, he was too young, his brother sang gentle songs of poems, rhymes of love, not the usual Bedouin chants of warring bravery or anything like that. Khamed was a gentle soul, a caring brother - an unusual trait in the hard subsistence living of the nomadic Bedouin. What sank Dusan's heart more than anything was Khamed's obsessive infatuation with this indelible woman who, it had been decided by tribal elders, would become the Bedouin wife of Rahim bin Khaled. Dusan was at this moment consumed with grief, with extreme anxiety - would his brother Khamed be killed in revenge alongside A'lisha Amjad bint Saleh?

In the chaotic mayhem following the departure of the *Al Buainai* and *Banu Amir* scouts, of his father Al-Tarif and the *Banu Amir* chieftain Abdel-Salman, Dusan slipped out of the encampment unseen riding his bedraggled camel. He saddled up then departed without anyone noticing he was gone - he followed the hunting party at a reasonable distance, in his unobtrusive manner he thought they would not spot him.

Dusan concealed himself well, Khamed would have Dusan protecting him by his side when he was hunted down and found by the scouts - Dusan could then strike down this A'lisha Amjad bint Saleh whom he regarded with a mountain of contempt. First, Dusan would have to find Khamed, who was on the run with this savage snipe of a woman his older brother had married. Dusan could not do this by his own means, he was not skilful in the ways of tracking or giving chase - the young *Al Buainai* shepherd's one option, using what stealth he possessed, was to follow the hunting party ahead.

His task was easy enough to begin with, not one of the scouting party suspected they might be followed – an ill omen for seasoned trackers. They did not observe Dusan's slow meandering trail behind them, they were the hunters, it did not occur to them to look behind. When the Bedouin scouts at one point paused, spotting the circling vultures high in the sky, Dusan panicked, he sidetracked to his left to follow his own path which took him through a locale of denser perimeter dunes. He skirting around the Bedouin scouts who were more concerned with their sense of danger somewhere ahead.

A'lisha spied the hell-bent Dusan bin Khaled while the boy shepherd was still some distance away, she watched him wind his way closer at the same time aware of the hunting party of Bedouin scouts lurking further to the north. A'lisha deliberated then reacted, realising that she needed to act – even more so when she knew that Lucifer and his two angelic creatures would soon appear. Her ambush was well set - this fool Dusan bin Khaled could ruin her whole plan.

A'lisha made a steadfast decision, she left the still unconscious Khamed hidden safe in the hollow she had dug to protect him, she thought she might kill two birds with one stone. A'lisha made her way without effort along the small valley of the dunes through which Dusan drove his recusant camel. She moved like a ghost, she left no tracks nor any sense of movement, there was a tinge of open apprehension in the dry hot air.

"Stay there," growled A'lisha. She raised herself from the sands right before Dusan's startled camel. Dusan, frozen stunned, was beside himself in instantaneous fear. A'lisha appeared from nowhere right before his wild, bulging eyes. Dusan could not, in panic, think of what to say.

A'lisha herself was dressed head to foot in her ragtag goatskin wrap, to both hide her identity and to protect her from the scorching sun. "If you are here for your brother Khamed get down from your camel then drop your sword." A'lisha barked her command without any hint of compromise.

Dusan eyed A'lisha, his world collapsed, all thoughts of his brother's heroic rescue alongside how he would down this abhorrent witch were forgotten. Dusan shivered in the midday heat and then obeyed, he took a moment to dwell upon his bad luck before leaping down to the ground unable to hide his nervous disposition.

"Why are you here?" demanded A'lisha. Her voice was clear and precise.

Dusan could not answer straightaway, then his voice croaked, his anger over Rahim and Khamed began to surface. "Uh? You killed my b-b-brother," he stammered.

A'lisha did not respond. She thought about what the boy said which was not untrue. A'lisha did not think it appropriate to explain her reasons nor was any confession warranted to one so young, she probed his mind to discover his thoughts - in doing so learning that he was no hunter-killer. The boy, she found, was more of a poet, a writer of prose that he transcribed into songs - he was no real danger to A'lisha or her impending task. A'lisha unwrapped her headscarf, she revealed herself in her own way, she did not wish to be encumbered with hiding her female identity nor abide by the demeaning desert laws of I'slām. A'lisha shook her hazelnut hair free which fell over her shoulders in swathes of breathlessness and defiance. She would confront this young Bedouin face-to-face without any hindrance of tradition to which she did not ascribe.

Dusan gasped. Seeing the beauty of A'lisha's face, her eyes, her hair, herself, the hidden wife of his dead brother, the killer of Rahim – all of this made a mesmerising impression that was sure to stay with him his whole life - if he managed to stay alive. What struck Dusan dumbstruck was the way this woman shook her forbidden hair from her eyes with a slight toss of her head, a flick of her wrist, an involuntary action that for some unexplainable reason caused Dusan to dance on the edge of insanity.

"Come with me," instructed A'lisha.

A'lisha made her way back through the vastness of the empty dunes, a short distance to where Khamed still lay trying to come to terms with his helplessness. Khamed was conscious, seeing the great expanse of the blue sky through squinting eyes. Not far, on the near horizon, A'lisha saw the Bedouin hunting party pause in its pursuit, she once more watched the spiralling vultures circling overhead knowing the feathered predators had caught the attention of the Bedouin scouts. Of more concern, A'lisha knew that Lucifer with his two assassins were by now approaching from the south. A far longer distance, perhaps three or four days, the warlord

Muhammad had gathered his one hundred most precious tribal warriors. To the north, A'lisha knew there was her one chance of survival - the mad woman *R'aisha bint Benim.* But before anything that A'lisha expected to happen, Khamed and Dusan were her priority. She hesitated, feeling the burden of her responsibility, then brought Dusan face-to-face with his brother Khamed. Dusan's resolve to take his revenge against A'lisha crumbled.

Dusan looked aghast. "Khamed?" he wailed. His brother Khamed did not answer. Dusan turned to face the woman he believed was Khamed's kidnapper. "What have you done to my brother?"

A'lisha did not answer. As far as she was concerned she had saved Khamed, she did not feel that she was answerable, not to this young Bedouin boy standing beside the hollow in the dune - she had not involved Khamed, Khamed had involved himself. "What have you done?" repeated Dusan. "You killed my brother, Rahim, now you are killing Khamed."

A'lisha stared. There was a long uncertain pause. "Rahim was not your brother," Dusan froze. He screamed inside, the sort of silent scream that no one hears. "Khamed," A'lisha pointed down to the hollow in the ground. "This Khamed is your half-brother, you were born from the same surrogate mother. Khaled bin Al-Tarif, he is not your father." There was no warmth or compassionate emotion in A'lisha's voice. Meanwhile, the sun reached its midday zenith overhead, but not quite, "Rahim bin Al-Tarif, he had the blood of Lucifer inside him." A'lisha's final throwaway comment did not register with Dusan.

Dusan reeled. What did this wanton sorceress who had destroyed the interwoven truce of both tribes, the *Al Buainai* and the *Banu Amir,* mean? Was she saying that Rahim bin Khaled, Khamed, all three of them, were not the born sons of his father Khaled? His mother who was dead? This woman, she told lies, thought Dusan with deep-rooted anger.

"I put my healing fist inside this Khamed's mind, I have done what I can for him," A'lisha said. "There is nothing more I can do. Put him on your camel, take him home."

"W-W-What do you mean?" Dusan floundered.

"Khamed witnessed the death of Rahim, your half-brother should not have been there, he broke your Bedouin laws, he should not have seen this," answered A'lisha.

"D-Did you kill Rahim?"

"Yes. I killed Rahim." A'lisha did not see why she should elaborate. She thought a moment about what more she should say.

"My father and Saleh bin Abdel-Salman Ahl Farsi of the *Banu Amir,* they search for you. When they find you, they will kill you," Dusan responded, he half laughed, he began to lose his sense of insecurity, the anger rose in his voice.

A'lisha studied Dusan, still without any hint of solicitousness. "You will die if you stay here, Khamed will die also."

Dusan once more reeled. "If I witness your death, then it is everything I hope for." A tear for his brothers formed in the corner of his eyelet gland, in no time it filled his eye then ran down his cheek. A'lisha reached out, with the edge of her sleeve she dried his skin. Dusan's heart flipped one more turn in turmoil.

"This fight is not your fight, you must take Khamed home," said A'lisha. "What he saw when Rahim died is not what he thought. What you think you see now is not real. Take your brother home, he should not be part of this."

Dusan thought hard. If he could get Khamed out of this then he would have fulfilled his task. His father Khaled and the Bedouin trackers would take care of this *Banu Amir* tribeswoman, they would deal out their ruthless punishment, she would not live. Little did Dusan know how much he was out of his depth, that he would do well to get Khamed and himself gone.

With A'lisha's help, Dusan heaved Khamed up onto his recalcitrant camel. Meanwhile, not far away close by, Lucifer the devil with his hunters Iblis and Belial crouched behind an insignificant hillock ready to deal their own form of justice. A'lisha sensed them, she smelled them, she felt their shimmering stink that permeated the hot desert air.

Lucifer had long realised he was himself the devil. His two surviving angels, the malevolent Belial and the fire-breathing Iblis, were seeking outright revenge for the brutal deaths of their compatriots Moloch, Dagon and Chemosh who should never have died – they had been promised immortality by Lucifer, endlessness in perpetuity for their unreserved loyalty to his cause. Now they were dead all three faced banishments, torment as demons by both Gabriel and his mighty Lords above. Moreover, Lucifer was no fool, he knew that Belial's and Iblis's true-hearted trustworthiness was fickle. They were fallen angels, their redemption was never more than a vaporous dream that could be burst open if they failed to right the disastrous wrong of what had happened in the arid Sambula mountains. Being the devil was always Lucifer's ambition, if he could capture the souls of mankind then no more would he be Gabriel's nodding vassal. Lucifer held the advantage, he saw the image of this child in his mind - there was no doubt of her ancestral blood, she was no more human than he was. Of more importance, Lucifer realised that Gabriel outright feared her. He recognised the shaken acknowledgement in Gabriel's eyes, the ill-concealed dread of who this snake of a woman might be. Could it be, Lucifer thought, that he, with his two remaining angels, could take this young woman alive? Could he then use her to bring down Gabriel's kingdom? There was little difference between Gabriel's so-called heaven and the devil's hell - Gabriel's mankind was capable of evil in great swathes in the name of their Lords.

Lucifer descended to where he needed to be. He waited in the shadows of the highest dune flanked by his two impatient assassins - they had spied the dozen or so nomadic scouts making their way from the east on their war camels. In the heat of the desert, the stillness prevailed, any meagre life that scurried around with preservation-driven instinct quickly buried itself beneath the hot surface of the course grit sand, there was nothing to be gained from this burning daytime environment except death – the urge to survive in this harsh sun-scorched land transcended any notion of curiosity, even the deadly scorpion that scuttled from beneath Lucifer's claw-like feet sensed the desire to be gone, to make itself scarce. Lucifer, Iblis and Belial crouched low, conscious of how their small size gave them a distinct advantage – they were well used to adopting the hunkered-down pose of the death-dealing hunter. Iblis turned to Belial; they both squinted their eyes to stare at each other. They felt an unexpected shiver, a disturbance in the immediate atmospheric substance, a subtle change in their molecular surroundings that neither hunter-assassins could single out. Lucifer sensed it also, he crouched lower into his loins without straightaway knowing why - he gripped his fire-sword firmer realising there was, from nowhere, another presence, one not linked to the approaching nomadic trackers.

For a brief moment, Lucifer felt fear, then he brushed it away by forcing it out of his twisted mind. Even so, he recalled the same expression of feeling he had seen in Gabriel's unfettered eyes. Lucifer's premonition was primordial, a single sense of a memory he could not remember - something in his genetic inner being that warned him he might not live long.

"Muhammad, we did not foresee the peril now upon us," Gabriel expected this to be a difficult head-to-head encounter with his emblazoned new prophet. Muhammad's all-conquering crusade must, for a short time, be paused. "We did not see this, not when your moment of victory is near." Gabriel was unnerved, agitated, he stood tall beside the towering granite peak of his mountain domain, a trickle of crystal-clear water created a miniature maelstrom that flowed swift in the cool mountain air. "This girl-woman is not who we believed, she could ruin your victorious triumph, your glorious conquest is threatened unless we act now without caution." The water gathered into a small pool, surging a little before disappearing over the precipice to the harsh brown desert a vast distance below.

"Gabriel, the one way is through our strength," pleaded Muhammad, his tearful frown of frustration burning into his bearded, sun-parched face. "I have united the tribes to fight, I have joined the desert nomads together, I have created a magnificent army that believes in the greatness of Al-Ilāh," Muhammad looked distraught, he was devastated. "All the prophets before me, their deaths pay tribute to my cause, they dreamed of my struggle against these unbelievers, this harlot cannot change our destiny. Please, my dearest Gabriel, you must believe me when I say this."

Gabriel looked down upon Muhammad, the archangel's patience was beginning to wear thin. "Those prophets, the ones who preached before you, they failed, you know this, every one of their crusades crumbled into twisted wars of conflict," Gabriel shuddered with frustration. Muhammad's fast-growing faith was not the first to spread the word of Al-Ilāh. "The prophets of whom you speak, they breathed the same fire into their flocks, men who then decided their own ways to worship Al-Ilāh, now they hurtle to their deaths fighting each other."

"Why is this, Gabriel? Tell me why we have not succeeded," begged Muhammad. "Why is it we are torn apart like ferocious dogs?" the turmoil in Muhammad's heart grew greater, he saw the anguish in the face of Al-Ilāh's magnificent angel.

"We did not see, Muhammad. We did not foresee this young child's ascendancy, nor that she is born from M'agdalena's blood," Gabriel shivered when he recalled how the prophet Yesh'ua had been lost. Not for the first time Gabriel had been outwitted, made a fool of - he had believed Lucifer when he claimed the infant child was dead. Gabriel fixed his eyes upon Muhammad. "We failed Muhammad; we did not know. This young *Banu Amir* bride, she is reborn, resurrected, she could not have been born from a simple woman's womb, she must have crawled from those vile swamplands where their granite stone lies hidden."

Muhammad stood back. "I am the new prophet," he said, "I create the new path, a new way. All believers in Al-Ilāh will prevail, the hearts of women will stay in my hands. You must trust me, my Lord. I can do this. I can reunite all men under one true faith."

Gabriel looked down upon the kneeling Muhammad. The Lord's angel desired this prophet be given immortal life, that he should be inveighed with more than those before him who had failed. The Baptist's Christians, they were driven to the west, they had fought the Romans and the Jews of M'oses, now the fractious armies of the cross were turning against each other. Gabriel feared men would again lose the struggle, the deadly fight waged for the last two hundred thousand years, the conflict of who was master of this world that Hyvah called Erewhon

"I have spoken with the Lesser Lords," Gabriel revealed. "Perhaps there is a way, for if not I fear the worst. There is nothing but war and death between us, bloodshed that will decide more than we fight for in this damn world." Gabriel paused, he saw the preacher's tears fall into the desert dirt, forming tiny myriads of mud in the grime of his mountain citadel.

"So, it is true, she is once more risen."

"Yes, it is true. The child, she was found alive in the desert to the south of the Maude Mountains. Lucifer's hunters fought to slay the child, but his angel warriors died savage deaths, their hearts ripped from their ribs to prevent their ascendency to heaven. The child survived, three of our angels were slain. She was taken by the greyhead holy woman, the mad woman who we do not know, who has a strength of mind we do not understand. There is a link between this child and the crazy woman of the desert, we know this child is born from the Nazareth prophet's whore, if she is born pure then you are in danger, Muhammad. The child's power is strong, stronger than we thought possible, we suspect it is the mad greyhead herself who protects this child, if the child is descended from M'agdalena then the blood of Yesh'ua will flow through her veins. Know this Muhammad, you must slay this harbinger or you will fail. This is the only way."

"Why is she returned, my Lord? Do you know?"

"Each time a prophet through Al-Ilāh is born, when a new crusade begins, one of Hyvah's comes among us. This time now will be the same, but with your new way of Al-Ilāh, we will fight back."

"Am I to be your lure, my Lord?"

"Yes, you have destiny before you. This child bride will find you then destroy your faith. You can win, you must unite all the prophet's faiths. You are right, the one way is to bring all men under one I'slām faith. Strength is solidarity. You must earn your immortality by uniting the broken tribes to worship Al-Ilāh in heaven. There is one true God, one way to love his love."

"What is this child's purpose, my Lord?"

"To bring your crusade to its knees. Before, we have found and slain these infants, with this young girl we have failed twice. If we fail again like we failed with the M'agdalena in Judaea she will turn a traitor's mind, a man she deludes into standing by her side; this man will weaken the faith you build in the name of our own Lord. This time we are prepared, we know who this man will be."

"Will he be another Isca'riot?" Muhammad paused; he considered the thought of another betrayer in their midst. Yesh'ua's blasphemous harlot had turned the traitorous Isca'riot, a man tempted against his will. Through him, the prophet Yesh'ua had died, the myth of the son of Al-Ilāh created, the parable of the virgin birth. Through Isca'riot's shame another centuries-long conflict had been set in motion, even now men fought against men, uncountable men died in Al-Ilāh's name. Gabriel knew that Lucifer's angels had found the one infant they thought existed, Lucifer claimed to have killed the child but now she was back among them. The greyhead, the thought again struck him, was it possible? Could it be? Gabriel shivered, he shuddered with extreme unease.

"Yes, there will be more Isca'riots, or every man who will fall for the love of a woman's lure. You must not let your five pillars be broken, you must unite the names of the dead prophets, create one faith in Abr'a'ham's name. With this strength we can defeat this sorceress evil, all women must bend to the will of our Lord because man is the power in this world. This is the way, the way the angels and Al-Ilāh wish to prevail." For a fleeting moment, Gabriel felt the pain of his own love for the one who had once tormented his heart - he drove the memory from his mind. This preacher Muhammad standing on the mountain before him, one mortal man touched by Al-Ilāh, was their one remaining hope, Al-Ilāh's last chance to reclaim His world. They would win the struggle, they had to win this war to preserve their holy heaven. This time, Gabriel was convinced they had Al-Ilāh's will to succeed.

"Muhammad," Gabriel continued, "I have agreed with the Lesser Lords, you must halt your crusade. Then choose one hundred of your ablest warriors, lead them eastwards towards the Maude Mountains. This woman, she is a bride of the *Banu Amir*, she is there, you will find her, she is close. Select half of your men to protect yourself from her, the remaining men to find her then cut her down. Then we will be done with this misery." Gabriel glared at Muhammad to ensure the absolute strictness of his will.

"I do not need fifty of my ablest to protect me. This is a simple tribeswoman we seek," Muhammad looked back at Gabriel, he felt his honour slated.

"Then you will be defeated," Gabriel warned. "You will die."

These stark words from Gabriel shook Muhammad. Gabriel was the almighty angel of Al-Ilāh who coveted the whole world, what he believed was man's destiny. Little did Muhammad know that Gabriel did not see everything, Gabriel had not seen the *twin* births from the Nazareth prophet's woman - Gabriel's age-old nemesis. Her first born had been resurrected from the swampland mists; Gabriel had not expected her ascendancy nor her undiscovered sisterly sibling who even now kept her identity hidden. The archangel did not foresee the perilousness of what would soon happen, nor that Muhammad's Al-Ilāh teaching was destined to create yet more lasting conflict - every faith that prayed to mighty Al-Ilāh each time pitted zealous men against the throats of each other.

R'aisha bint Benim. The greyhead mad woman of the *Banu Amir*, she was not mad at all. First, R'aisha had made double sure her sibling twin was held captive on the Meccan caravan by selling her child sister to the slavers. Afterwards, after the caravan departed, hidden in the high peaks she watched the Meccans approach the Sambula Sands in the Maude Mountains and waited. R'aisha, never her given name, was certain that Lucifer's hunter angels would be there in ambush, having with deliberate intent left a trail of clues for them to follow. Moloch, Dagon and Chemosh, they smelled blood, they would know for sure that an infant descended from the M'agdalena's bloodline was being transported on the caravan. What the three hunters did not know, was that R'aisha herself even existed.

R'aisha was riven through with revenge, aware that Lucifer's angels had once before cut down her child sister. R'aisha knew the child now known by the name of A'lisha Amjad bint Saleh was special, that she was unique, that when the child had been slain then buried in the earth the sacred soil had returned her. The earth's dirt and clay, it belonged to the irrepressible A'lisha - not since the time of Hyvah had the garden world of Erewhon's keeper held the mastery that A'lisha possessed. Moloch, Dagon and Chemosh never suspected how their ambush would itself trigger a deadly trap, that their attack would be assailed by their elusive adversary. When the three hunters realised with shock horror who the child held by the slavers was, the child they had once before slain, for Moloch, Dagon and Chemosh it was too late.

Even R'aisha did not expect the brutal reality of what happened. When the sun began to set, in the half-light of twilight, Dagon and Moloch launched themselves from the slopes of the trail pass as it passed through the confines of the sand hills of the Sambula Pass, they set upon the shocked slavers who stood little or no chance of survival. Chemosh attacked from the caravan's opposite side, his task to hunt for the child – coming face to face with the same child he had killed more than two hundred years before. Chemosh froze, his expression of alarm conveying the momentary panic of his distress, this time Chemosh died his own violent death a fraction of a small second after he realised who the child was – she transformed there in front of his eyes. She was no child, she stood lithe and transparent, near-neanderthal and majestic, still childlike in her deadly poise. Her ghost-like hand struck inside his angel chest, tearing out his angelic heart that she then held high in the sky with vengeance, without compassion. When Dagon and Moloch heard the short-lived death-knell wail of Chemosh they came running, they fell dead, cut down in the same way as Chemosh. Most of the slavers had died by Dagon and Moloch's hand, there was no one left except the half-dozen still chained slaves imprisoned on the caravan. These were set free, their memories of the slaughter they had witnessed wiped, their recollections altered – giving rise to hearsay rumours of other Bedouin tribesmen having carried out the attack.

R'aisha found herself on the back foot. In no time her sibling regressed to her form of a small defenceless child. R'aisha led her away from the butchered caravan as soon as she could, she would take the young girl to where she had made her own hidden habitation. As the mad woman with the *Banu Amir.* R'aisha never expected to see what she saw - the hearts of the slavers and Lucifer's merciless angels ripped from their chests, their bones heaved apart with their blood oozing into the dry sand.

The course of the prophets was now reset. R'aisha made sure the young child would become the adoptive ward of Saleh bin Abdel-Salman ibn Ameen Ahl Farsi, tribal leader of the *Banu Amir.* Yet even this was a small part of what the deranged woman of the tribe hoped - two of Lucifer's angels, and Lucifer himself, were still roaming free – but here now, today, out in the heat-seared desert where the burning sun ruled, the two remaining angelic assassins, murderers of scores of Hyvah's bloodline newborns, would die.

Khaled bin Al-Tarif and Saleh bin Abdel-Salman held the cruel hopes of Lucifer and Gabriel in their sword fist hands - the two Bedouin warriors were heading into a headlong confrontation over the fate of the young woman who had slain the son of Al-Tarif, the boy a shepherd warrior who believed that submission, obedience and acquiescence were the foibles to be traded for his love. Khaled bin Al-Tarif and Gabriel's Muhammad would once more cross paths - this time it would not be a nomadic tribesman paying homage by following his warlord into fighting battle. Both Khaled bin Al-Tarif and Gabriel's Muhammad were being led by their hands into a long-nurtured confrontation. One or both of these fierce Bedouin leaders of men might die, perhaps by the hand of the other unless the medicine woman R'aisha's predilection came to pass.

Right now, in the drifting sands of the sweltering Maude Mountains, R'aisha bint Benim watched Lucifer, Iblis and Belial. She saw them skirt the highest dune to stalk the group of Bedouin trackers riding their snorting camels that smelled the foul stink of danger. R'aisha watched Lucifer and his vengeful angels leave no footprints in the soft white sand which confirmed to R'aisha without any doubt who they were, that each of these evangelical hunters was hand-in-hand with violence and death. By now the white-hot sun seared the whole desolate landscape with fierce furnace-like heat - like the proverbial fire pits of Lucifer's unrelenting hell. R'aisha then spied her own tribal leader, Saleh bin Abdel-Salman, riding ahead of the warrior who was of the *Al Buainai* Bedouin, Khaled bin Al-Tarif. R'aisha watched Al-Tarif with care, this was the man who held the key, R'aisha's meticulous decades-long plan was at last coming to fruit.

Like the nearby A'lisha, R'aisha feasted her eyes like a hawk, she saw the two Bedouin scouts at the head of the dozen or so nomads pause – Raisha spotted the same dozen or so vultures circling like road kill scavengers high above. She could see the Bedouin scouts, they were skilful hunters who knew their work, they *sensed* danger without knowing from where it lurked. The scouts were not wrong in their cautious vigilance because, not far, hidden behind the nearest dune ready to strike, crouched Lucifer, Iblis and Belial. The Bedouin hunting party would have little or no chance against these inhumane predators, callous beings who every time crushed their enemies without any measure of compassion. R'aisha took stock of the situation, of Lucifer and his hunter assassins, realising the absolute danger the Bedouin trackers were in - she knew that Lucifer would not hesitate in killing these beduins who might endanger his ambition of revenge against his deadly nemesis who was herself not far away. R'aisha intervened, she revealed herself, she changed everything by standing tall on the highest dune.

The two foremost Bedouin scouts at once spotted R'aisha, the familiar mad woman of the *Banu Amir*. The second in line of the trackers turned to his *Banu Amir* tribal leader Abdel-Salman - the scout pointed towards R'aisha standing on the peak of the high dune to the north. Abdel-Salman spun himself to look, seeing straightaway that, with her familiar tattered ropes blowing in the hot desert breeze, it was the inept deranged woman who hung around the fringes of his tribe. Abdel-Salman was puzzled, why would she be here, why now at this most crucial turn of events?

"Who is this?" demanded Al-Tarif.

"She is the lunatic woman of the tribe, she is unhinged, I don't know why she is here now," replied Abdel-Salman with unease, the *Banu Amir* tribal leader was beginning to sense a bad feeling, a thought that all was not well. All three *Banu Amir* trackers were alarmed, they were unnerved with uncertainty in their eyes - as yet they were still unaware of the three angel predators lurking behind the dune to their left. Al-Tarif hauled in the reins of his camel, he looked at Abdel-Salman. Al-Tarif could see that his rival was disturbed, it was as if Abdel-Salman was trying to put pieces together in his head - like a soothsayer knowing what might soon be about to happen.

Lucifer, he also saw R'aisha. This he found disconcerting and unexpected. Who was she? The larger built Iblis, he turned to Lucifer - this did not seem to be the way it should be. Belial, he was the first to see the second figure standing aloft in a defiant stance on the far side of the Bedouin scouts. Belial's angelic hair stood hard on his back – he knew who this other fugitive was, there could be no mistake, it was A'lisha Amjad bint Saleh, the young woman they had ascended from Lucifer's burning hell to kill. Lucifer, when he saw the aberrant female he so despised, he was the first to realise they had been lured into a well-set trap.

The warlord preacher Muhammad, he was still a long distance to the west. The irrepressible warlord was at the head of five-score of his best hand-picked men – he still thought Gabriel was over cautious about this young harlot who had come among them. Why one hundred of his best fighting core? Muhammad, he stalled, he stopped his men with a halt, the grey premonition instinct he was infamous for kicked in but he did not know why. Nevertheless, Muhammad was certain that, for some reason, somewhere ahead strange events were beginning to unfold.

Al-Tarif was the first of the beduins to see the young A'lisha. He was struck dumb with disbelief – she had discovered the Bedouin trackers rather than the other way around - it occurred to Al-Tarif that she had been waiting, not running, not fleeing, not in the way he had expected. Al-Tarif knew that she was staring at *him*, straight into his inner being, he felt it, even from this distance her eyes burned into him. What was it? He saw her move, she motioned to him, she pointed downwards, down to behind the dunes to their left. Something was there, she was warning him, there was danger. The lead Bedouin scout, he saw A'lisha pointing, he turned his camel in the direction she made then galloped up the sliding sand slope dune - it was a hard going struggle but the Bedouin soon reached the peak of the dune then stared down. Lucifer and his two angel hunters were there hiding in wait, the *Banu Amir* scout glared down in horror then turned to race back down the slope to safety, to warn the others. The immortal Iblis struck, he pounced, he was quick to down the Bedouin with his claw-like hands, ripping his throat into a thousand pieces. The scout's camel fell to its knees, losing its slavering breath in its anguish, the tracker fell into a motionless heap on the blood-soaked ground - his own blood. It was over in a fraction of a moment but the game was up, everyone who was there in the intense desert daylight saw the gruesome slaughter - what would happen next?

What happened next was that Iblis himself died. His death was sudden, it was unexplainable, Iblis dropped, his beating heart spurned from his ribs. He fell to his knees beside the dead Bedouin scout. Belial, who saw it all, turned to run, he knew the game of retribution death had gone wrong. R'aisha ghosted into her animalistic being, her near-primate self - almost neanderthal but not quite, she cut Belial down before he could make his futile escape to the summit of the rearmost dune - he died a quick non-angelic death. Before he breathed his last breath he turned to plead in vain to Lucifer but Lucifer had gone, he had disappeared, Lucifer was not there.

Al-Tarif sat silent upon his faltering camel, from somewhere deep in the back of his mind all of this made some sense, subconscious recollects surged through his memory without him being able to piece anything together. His wife, his wife who died, of course, of course, yes, yes, he was a fool, how could he have been so insane? Al-Tarif urged his camel forward, up the steep dune, towards the deranged mad woman of the *Banu Amir*. Saleh bin Abdel-Salman of the *Banu Amir* smiled when he watched him go – now would his longtime enemy know for sure how he had been deceived - Abdel-Salman's mouth twitched in satisfaction. Al-Tarif stooped, he climbed down from his camel to stand before this R'aisha who by now had regained her more human form. Al-Tarif stared down at the slaughtered Belial, then into R'aisha's bestial eyes.

"Tell me, you are no mad woman, tell me who you are," the thin desert air shimmered in the scorched haze, but nothing moved.

R'aisha glared back at Al-Tarif, the semblance between them buzzed with edifying tension. "Use your mind, Khaled bin Al-Tarif," she replied, "I cannot answer this for you. You know who I am."

The truth hit like a mountain rock. Al-Tarif felt his head spin, the shocking blue sky fell upon him, the piercing white-hot sun penetrated his vision to wreak more confusion in his sun-blind mind. It could not be true, it was not possible – he had seen her die, he had seen her perish with his own eyes.

Al-Tarif rallied. "This cannot be, I saw you die," pleaded Al-Tarif, the raw emotion of his soul tore into him one more time. "Y-y-you said you would not leave me," he stuttered in futile pain, it was the one thing he could think of to say – much more than a single tear formed in the fearsome Bedouin warrior's eyes.

"Yes. I am here now," said R'aisha, who was not R'aisha, "I did not leave you, I stood over you, why do you think I gave A'lisha to you, why do you think she came to *you*, the *Al Buainai?*"

The thought that flowed into Al-Tarif's mind appalled him. "My son, he was your son, Rahim, he was born of our blood," shrieked Al-Tarif loudly, "I must know, he was wed to this murderous woman, our enemy the *Banu Amir*. Please tell me, she is not of your blood. This cannot be."

"A'lisha *is* my sibling blood, Khaled," countered R'aisha, she spoke without emotion or guilt, "I confess this to you. Rahim was not your blood; he was not your son... do you think one born evil could be the blood of the one good soul of a man who exists?"

"What? What is this you say? Tell me you are wrong," Al-Tarif begged, the fiercest Bedouin of all the nomad tribes. He was close to defeat, not from bloodstained enemy swords or head-cutting camel-riding desert fighters but from the one woman he had ever loved. Not far away, standing on the rounded sand peak of the opposite high dune, under the blaze of the sun heading towards its downward zenith, A'lisha Amjad bint Saleh gazed, her tattered robes rippling in the afternoon breeze.

R'aisha watched Al-Tarif crumble, their sham of a Bedouin marriage for R'aisha had been a fake, a means to an end – during her century's long existence a multitude of men had loved her, each time she had singled them out, used them in different ways, she moulded their destinies knowing their heritage blood was unique. This was how it was for Khaled bin Al-Tarif.

R'aisha had lavished her attention upon him, groomed him, she had nurtured his soul owing to his own unique birthright blood - he was one of the few homosapien men who could stand against the marching Muhammad, Gabriel's new prophet. R'aisha's unwritten task was to protect Al-Tarif, to protect A'lisha whose own self-motivated quest was more far-reaching – to deliver the end to the evil that was Lucifer, Gabriel's fallen angel devil.

For A'lisha, *her* purpose was outright revenge. She had eliminated Lucifer's cold-blooded assassins Dagon, Moloch and Chemosh, now the vengeful Iblis and Belial were dead. Moreover, A'lisha had, in silent retribution, killed Rahim bin Khaled, the heinous tribesman chosen as her husband who was, in reality, Lucifer's half-blood, born from an innocent concubine woman first ravaged by Lucifer in lust – with Rahim born to the ancestral surrogate mother R'aisha had salvaged by taking the boy to raise as her own. R'aisha always knew who the boy was, by setting in motion the marriage of Rahim bin Khaled and A'lisha Amjad bint Saleh, the revenge of both R'aisha and A'lisha became entrenched.

Lucifer held ambition for Rahim, he planned that Rahim would one day be his successor to rival Gabriel's Muhammad. Knowing Rahim was being raised by the *Al Buainai* tribe by his unsuspecting substitute father Khaled bin Al-Tarif gratified Lucifer – Lucifer did not know that he was being deceived by the demented woman who lived among the nomadic desert Bedouin. Lucifer had no knowledge of her existence nor that his nemesis, the child descended direct through M'agdalena's blood, the most menacing of Hyvah's lineage, born with no name, was reborn from the soil in which she had been buried without ceremony - or that A'lisha Amjad bint Saleh had since hidden herself among the *Banu Amir*. Not until it

was too late, not until his half-blood child protégé Rahim was dead –
slaughtered by the same child he was tasked to hunt down and finish.

There in the desert Lucifer was, at this moment in time, consumed with
rage, his survival was now at stake – all five of his coveted angels were
dead, his offspring Rahim was gone, his kingdom stratagem to rival Gabriel
was in free fall tatters. R'aisha bint Benim had always known there was
one piece in the complex jigsaw that was Erewhon Earth's struggle for
mother-gender supremacy, the freedom of homosapien woman – Saleh
bin Abdel-Salman ibn Ameen Ahl Farsi of the *Banu Amir* Bedouin, who had
raised and hidden the recalcitrant jewel that was A'lisha Amjad bint Saleh.

Abdel-Salman eyed the whole unfolding drama - for some considerable
time he had known that his surrogate adopted daughter brought to him by
the medicine woman was not who she purported to be. During her young
adolescent years, Abdel-Salman watched the child grow – not that she
aged like a normal child. Her childhood was an illusion, a masterpiece of
deceit, a lie that for a time fooled the tribal leader of the *Banu Amir*. Abdel-
Salman realised he had a child prodigy on his hands - in the beginning
thinking she was a gift from Al-Ilāh though this misplaced belief did not
last. When R'aisha bint Benim, who had wormed her way into Abdel-
Salman's inner sanctum, proposed the notion of a wedding union with
the *Al Buainai* Bedouin, Abdel-Salman was enthused, he was intrigued.
Revenge against Khaled bin Al-Tarif for the death of his brother. Perfect!

Never at any point did Abdel-Salman give one thought to R'aisha having
her own motives, her own reasons for the union between A'lisha Amjad
bint Saleh and Rahim bin Khaled, at no time did Abdel-Salman suspect the
tribe's mad woman of creating the drama that was unfolding - not until
now, not until he sat upon his blustering war camel witnessing the events
that now uncoiled. Unlike Al-Tarif, Abdel-Salman was not awestruck, to
Abdel-Salman this was significant, the pieces began to fit together like an
ancient trader's puzzle. But R'aisha's ultimate plan had not yet come to
fruit, not yet, not until both Abdel-Salman and his foe Al-Tarif were joined
in the crazed woman's concluding stratagem - her desire to change the
rampaging crusade of the burgeoning Muhammad. In R'aisha's pinpoint

mind, there was also unfinished business with Gabriel's renegade angel Lucifer. Where was he? He had vanished. Not until Lucifer was finished could her struggle against the warlord Muhammad begin.

But, right now, for Abdel-Salman, there was the mind-blowing question of R'aisha bint Benim. Like everyone, Abdel-Salman did not suspect the spiritual soothsayer was also not who she claimed, that she was not mad in the head, that he had been duped by the clandestine wife of his sworn enemy Al-Tarif - the woman who everyone thought dead. The truth to all this, Abdel-Salman was soon to find out.

Lucifer was on the run. He was no angelic simpleton; he was now the devil fugitive hunted by both Gabriel and the two inhuman women of whom there was now little doubt as to who they were. Lucifer knew the kingdom realm he had worked long and hard to establish was no longer even a dream, the fire pits of hell were all that remained. His chief ambition now was to survive.

Leaving behind his dead compatriots Iblis and Belial was easy enough, he simply faded away by furling his wings before he vanished. Unknown to Lucifer, A'lisha witnessed him disappear, she prowled like a hawk then followed him into the nether region of molecular time in which he escaped. A'lisha was there, waiting when he reappeared.

Lucifer was surprised then shocked, his sense of panic kicked in when he realised he was cornered, trapped like a rat in a trap. Lucifer was well aware how this might not be a one-sided fight – he could escape even though his existence was at stake.

"Do you think you can easily destroy me?" Lucifer hissed, crouching low to improve his slim chance of defence.

A'lisha did not respond, she did not speak. Instead, she changed, she morphed into the same strange animal entity, halfway between ape-like neanderthal and the ancestral lineage of her unworldly heritage - transparent and powerful. Lucifer stepped backwards in mortified stupor, this was the last thing he did. A'lisha was upon him in a fraction of an instant, shredding his throat into a million molecules before seizing his lifeless heart as he fell. During his last defiant death knell, she tore off his devil wings, tearing the gossamer-thin tissue that would no more signify his angelic existence. Lucifer died the death of the true fallen angel, the devil incarnate was dead, never again would he claim the souls of men to burn in hell in the way all the devils craved.

Gabriel felt the surge, he sensed the reverberating change his world had suffered. Gabriel knew that Lucifer was gone, that this was a momentous remake in the history of human survival, the endemic end to the myth of heaven and hell. On the one hand the sacred concept of the inferno abyss was finished, on the other was the brutal rise of what Gabriel feared most – the reverberation of the childbirths that snaked back to M'agdalena, the immortal bloodline of the rebel prophet Yesh'ua who died by crucifixion at the hands of the Jews of Nazareth. And the shame of the traitorous Isca'riot.

A'lisha in her inhuman form looked down upon the slaughtered Lucifer, his heart still dripping blood from where she held it in her transparent neanderthalic hand. In her abdomen she felt her child embryo stir, the embryonic union of the heinous Bedouin shepherd Rahim bin Al-Tarif with herself, the brutalised tribal wife A'lisha Amjad bint Saleh - the unborn infant girl-child that would carry the bloodline of Lucifer himself. A'lisha Amjad bint Saleh turned her eyes skyward, up to the cloudless realm of Gabriel. The nuclear sun burned relentless - the galaxy star at the centre of this minute part of heaven. The sun burst hideous-long flares of unimaginable hot plasma out into the nothingness of the cosmos, the murderous heat of which wrapped itself around the world on which unforgiving men lived. Uncountable numbers of homosapien lifeforms died, they perished in the earthquakes, volcanic eruptions and the tsunami waves that ravaged the world for one whole hour before the long light-year tentacle of starlight evaporated and dispersed.

The warlord preacher, Abū al-Qāsim Muhammad bin Abd Allāh ibn Abd al-Muttalib ibn Hāshim, turned to his steadfast second in command Ali ibn Abi Talib.

"Did you feel the wind and the shaking in the ground Abi Talib?" said Muhammad, the shiver in the air left Muhammad in no doubt the land he commanded had for some reason changed. Abi Talib looked around with undecided suspicion, the renegade Meccan saw flocks of vultures without warning take to the air.

"Muhammad, the death birds, they know something we do not," both Abi Talib and Muhammad eyed the vultures with a feeling of misgiving, the bareheaded birds flew high then circled in deliberate indecision, finding no reason or decaying prey to stimulate their blood ravaging instincts.

Muhammad lapsed into contemplative silence, without doubt his infamous instinct would lead him to where the root of his uncertainty lay – he was under no illusion, this unexplainable wave of disturbance in the air was linked to his all-important task.

"This is a fool's errand," Abi Talib warned, perturbed. "I see no good reason why we are here, we should turn back," Abi Talib gave the deliberate impression of being both frustrated and apprehensive.

"I understand your caution Abi Talib, but my burden is Gabriel's commanding wish," replied Muhammad. Gabriel had instructed Muhammad to take one hundred of his ablest men, to keep fifty behind then order the remainder to hunt for the bitch of a whore who threatened his crusade. Muhammad found Gabriel's reasoning repulsive, an insult to the strength of his fighting capabilities.

Abi Talib returned Muhammad's glance, annoyed. "This curse of a woman, she is still a child, just one of our best men could race onwards to finish her. I myself would be gratified to take on this task my Muhammad."

Abi Talib's words struck a chord with Muhammad, this whole episode was disruptive and disturbing. Perhaps not one, maybe two or three of his best hand-picked men could ride ahead to get this dirty work done – this inconvenient charade of a trek could then be turned around and finished. Muhammad deliberated before turning to Abi Talib.

"You speak with wisdom my friend," said Muhammad, "I entrust this chore to you, but not alone like you say. Choose two of your best swordsmen, then proceed swiftly to get this work done. We will wait here five days, then we return to Al-Masjid an-Nabawi."

Abi Talib deliberated, he smiled then pulled hard on his camel reigns, turning around abruptly with purposeful meaning. He galloped his camel in haste, spurred on by his determination to please Muhammad. Abi Talib paused before singling out the two men he sought – Badr al-Din and Abū al-Faraj, both renowned tribesmen who had fought victorious alongside the esteemed preacher and Abi Talib since the beginning. All three got their meagre supplies together, wrapped themselves tight in their all-protective head scarves, bid farewell then galloped eastwards in the direction of the pass that opened to the Sambula sands two riding days away. Muhammad watched them leave, he gazed in deep reflection until they disappeared into the shimmering desert haze. Muhammad turned to face his remaining men,

"Make camp, we stay here. Get the cooking fires burning," his commanding orders were tinged with an apprehensive undertone that played havoc with his meandering thoughts. Muhammad looked skywards – the dozen or so starving vultures circling high in the sky had wheeled to follow the three departed riders, Muhammad felt his black mood deepen. If the vultures sensed blood then this errand was mired in uncertainty.

During the evening the three riders Abi Talib, Badr al-Din and Abū al-Faraj made their camp, eating the first of the meagre goat meat with the weevil-infested rice they carried, they slept for just two hours before reloading their camels – travelling during the coolness of the night would mean more rapid progress. The next day became harder as the terrain deteriorated into more extreme desert but the three riders did not pause, they would next rest once inside the shade offered by the Sambula Pass with its towering walls and infamous narrow confines.

After two tiring days, Abi Talib with his two companions entered the high pass that signalled the way into the desolate desolation of the distant Sambula sands - the vast uncharted land of drifting desert dominated by mountainous dunes baked dry by the unforgiving sun. Here was the heartland existence of the nomadic Bedouin - Abi Talib gripped his sword handle firmer, making sure he could unleash his short, sharpened blade without undue warning. The battle-hardened Meccan was aware that in these lands the Bedouin ruled, the resilient nomads could survive in this waterless wasteland with not much else. Abi Talib knew the fiercest of his warlord's fighters were the unreliable nomadic Bedouin, bound by fragile oaths of allegiance to fellow tribes and to the preacher Muhammad, alliances that might be torn and broken at the smallest whim. Abi Talib was under no illusion - his greatest threat in these parts would come from the fickle Bedouin who could turn from friend into his deadliest enemy, whose unreliable friendship might dissipate on a small issue of irrelevant honour. Abi Talib held the Bedouin in low regard, they were untrustworthy, double-dealing, time and again they had proven treacherous and deceitful – his esteemed master at all times commanded them with care and great diligence, Muhammad was never trusting of the Bedouin brotherhood treaties.

Abū al-Faraj was the first to spot the Bedouin scout watching from high on the rockiest outpost of the pass, their friend, or foe, was clad in the traditional tight sand-coloured yellow robes that scant showed the scout's observing eyes - the Bedouin's all-enclosing headscarf firmly tied so that no flapping fabric would reveal his presence – unless for some reason he desired it. The scout was in full deliberate view, he intended that he would be seen - a remonstrance to proceed no further except with extreme risk.

"That scout, he knows we are here," warned al-Faraj.

Abi Talib gazed upwards; he had expected contact at some point. "He can do no harm from there, we keep moving forward," answered Abi Talib.

Badr al-Din then gestured to the peak on the opposite side of the pass. A second scout stood motionless and threatening, this time his desert robes fluttering in the hot breeze. Abi Talib spurred his camel on slow with caution towards the bend that turned to the right ahead then disappeared - here would come the ambush or attack, thought the Meccan leader. All three gripped their sheathed swords in grim anticipation. With Abi Talib in the forefront, the three mounted riders rounded the bend then stopped dead in their tracks. The rough rock-strewn pathway ahead was barred, it was blocked by five camel-born men in triangular arrowhead formation, one man at the point with two fanning back his either side. Abi Talib saw the men were nomadic Bedouin – their distinct but simple coloured keffiyeh headdress scarves covering their whole faces except for their sun-scorched, deep wrinkled eyes. The three riders had no option but to halt their camels with a show of meek deference.

"Why are you here, Ali ibn Abi Talib?" challenged the nearest Bedouin who was out in front, who appeared to be their leader.

Abi Talib was startled. How did the Bedouin know his name, his entire body was cloaked in concealed protection.

"And you, Badr al-Din, you who was born in the southern uplands of Assam. Yes, we know who you are," revealed the same Bedouin nomad. Badr al-Din glanced across to Abū al-Faraj with distinct unease. The same flock of vultures appeared high overhead, they began circling in eager anticipation. The unknown nomad leader gazed skywards, direct towards the vultures.

"Have these featherless blood birds followed you all the way here, Abū al-Faraj?" exhorted the Bedouin - who in reality was Saleh bin Abdel-Salman ibn Ameen Ahl Farsi, tribal leader of the *Banu Amir*. Both Abdel-Salman and Al-Tarif knew the three riders, from the crusade alongside Muhammad in his fight against the mighty city of Mecca. Abdel-Salman had always held the Meccan Abi Talib in dubious regard, a traitorous renegade who had turned against his own people, a moral-less turncoat in his desire to be the warlord's sycophant second in command. Even so, Abdel-Salman and Al-Tarif respected Abi Talib's fighting abilities, they also acknowledged Abū al-Faraj and Badr al-Din - all three were the warlord's feared and ablest swordsmen. There was a specific but still hidden reason why they were here in the Sambula Pass.

Abi Talib showed his outright defiance. "We are here by the will of Muhammad. Muhammad is himself commanded by the archangel Gabriel," the leader of the three declared. "We are tasked by Al-Ilāh's bidding, we are here to find the wedding bride who calls herself A'lisha Amjad bint Saleh." Abi Talib glared hard at the all-threatening Bedouin - he was unable to recognise any of them in their concealing head scarves -

but Abi Talib was no fool, these men ahead were formidable adversaries and, what was more, the three of them were outnumbered by their five.

Al-Tarif, to the right of Abdel-Salman, removed his keffiyeh headdress then drew his sword. Abi Talib was once more startled.

"Khaled bin Al-Tarif of the *Al Buainai* Bedouin," acknowledged Abi Talib in abrupt recognition. He shifted, uncomfortable upon his camel saddle, this was no insignificant nomadic fighter. Abi Talib looked around, there were now five Bedouin scouts surrounding them on the low peaks, perched higher on separate rocky ledges. "If this woman we seek is under your protection, then in the name of Al-llāh give her up, then we will be gone from your land."

"A'lisha Amjad bint Saleh is my adopted daughter, a *Banu Amir* tribeswoman, she means nothing to you," replied Abdel-Salman. "Go back to your preacher, back to Al-Masjid an-Nabawi from where you came. While you still live."

This was now a difficult, unexpected situation. The *Banu Amir* Bedouin were still allied to Muhammad. Likewise, the *Al Buainai*. But Abi Talib had made a promise to his warlord master, an unbreakable pledge to kill the *Banu Amir* woman, an undertaking to end this business once and for all. Then it dawned upon Abi Talib who the tribesman confronting him was.

"Are you Saleh bin Abdel-Salman ibn Ameen Ahl Farsi, tribal leader of the *Banu Amir*?" Abū Talib demanded.

"Yes, it is I," replied Abdel-Salman in rumbling deep throated defiance.

Abi Talib realised that violence would be quick to follow. The five scouts would not be able to intervene – it would take them a while or two to climb down from their high perches upon the cliff edge, it was three against five – but who were the two rearmost camel-riding beduins mounted behind Abdel-Salman and Al-Tarif? Also, the Bedouin to Abdel-Salman's left? Abi Talib stared in scrutiny at the rearmost riders – he thought he saw the concealed forms of women's shapely bodies beneath their tight-woven desert robes. It dawned upon him there might be just three Bedouin fighters – three upon three, the other two were women - the initial opening odds would be even. This was their chance - their one chance.

Abi Talib spoke in an audible low voice to al-Faraj and his compatriot Badr al-Din. "Both of you, you take their leader Abdel-Salman, I will take this *Al Buainai* tribesman Al-Tarif. If we are swift the three remaining Bedouin will not be in the fight, the scouts on the cliffs cannot do much during the time we fight. We will be through the pass into the Sambula sands before they react." It then struck Abi Talib like a ravaging fist that one of the two women might be A'lisha Amjad bint Saleh herself, he then reasoned this to be a certainty. Abi Talib never understood the danger he was in.

Without warning Badr al-Din launched his sword through the air, aimed at Abdel-Salman with arrow-like precision. The ageing *Banu Amir* tribal leader was taken by complete surprise, he was slow to react, Badr al-Din's sword found its mark below Abdel-Salman's left shoulder, above his heart. The wound was not instantaneous fatal, but it was enough to drive Abdel-Salman off the goatskin saddle of his camel - he fell into a heap upon the stony ground, the fall was a long way down, his right shoulder took the force of the impact before shattering into a dozen pieces. Badr al-Din's companion, Al-Faraj, launched himself forward with lightening speed, leaping from his camel when he saw the easy opportunity to finish Abdel-Salman while he lay wounded on the ground - though al-Faraj never got that far. Al-Faraj died, Abdel-Salman's last remaining strength heaved his short sword into al-Faraj's abdomen before his attacker's leaping momentum tore the sword upwards to pierce his heart.

Badr al-Din also died a fraction of a moment later, an inexplicable death, unexplainable after heaving his sword through the air in the direction of Abdel-Salman. Badr al-Din fell from the saddle of his camel and was dead. Their leader Abi Talib, his tall-order plan to take the life of Al-Tarif failed before it even began. Instead, he sat frozen in his saddle, immobilised and unable to make a rational decision, his thoughts invaded when his memories were erased. Moments later Abi Talib fell to the ground in ill-concealed agony until A'lisha Amjad bint Saleh removed herself from his mind.

Both Al-Tarif and R'aisha jumped down from their camels to the ground then descended upon Abdel-Salman, who by now was close to agonising death, his blood flowing like water into the miserable stone-ridden ground that had no right to soak it. The dozen or so vultures ceased their prospective circling high above, satiated in their instinct that a tasty meal of human flesh would be quick to ensue - they descended to perch themselves beneath the closest peak to the confrontation that had now played out in death. Al-Tarif knelt over his old enemy's dying body, seeing straightaway that Abdel-Salman was finished.

"My esteemed friend," said Al-Tarif, "I fear our desert land will soon take you. Al-Ilāh will welcome you into his realm in the Bedouin way." R'aisha stood right beside, she might be able to save him but now was the exact time for Abdel-Salman's death, it was how it was meant to be. A'lisha joined R'aisha to stand by her side, she knelt down, she kissed his cheek, his face was now riddled with the pale whiteness of death.

"Your death has reason," A'lisha whispered. "You raised me, then you gave me the protection of your tribe. You were never a good man though you were the finest Bedouin leader you could be." A'lisha shook, before turning to stare into Al-Tarif's eyes. "The ancient stone, it is written that Abdel-Salman dies by your hand Khaled," said A'lisha. "Finish him, do not let these buzzards, these vile vultures make a meal of him." For all of A'lisha's hard-faced meanness, a tear rolled from her empty grey hazelnut eyes - one emotional misdemeanour the outright deadliness that A'lisha could not control.

Al-Tarif paused in indecision. Nomadic tradition, Bedouin honour, made that the dying could never be left alone to die in the desert. For a thousand years, any Bedouin wounded in battle was finished – it was heartless and necessary. Khaled bin Al-Tarif took his dagger, held back for a moment, then drove the blade into the throat of Abdel-Salman whose blood gurgled and bubbled into the desert sand. On the nearby low peaks of the pass, the Bedouin scouts, the vultures, they watched in forlorn hopelessness.

Al-Tarif then wrapped Abdel-Salman's body tight in his rough-hewn desert robes, he heaved the *Banu Amir* tribesman up onto the now own-erless camel, slumping him over the goatskin saddle. Al-Tarif tied him down so that he could not fall. R'aisha and A'lisha watched in silence, the Meccan Abi Talib, still squatting in mental desolation, saw nothing, just his defeat and dissolution. Al-Tarif turned to the one remaining scout who stood nearby.

"You trackers, stay here to bury these two unfortunate fools who came to kill us. Do not leave a meal for these disgusting blood eating creatures."

Another daylight dawned. Al-Tarif, R'aisha and A'lisha rode westwards out of the Sambula Pass, towards the direction from which Abi Talib and his two companions first came. R'aisha held the reigns of the camel upon which the dead Abdel-Salman was tied, A'lisha led the desolate and senseless Abi Talib who knew little of what now happened. The vultures followed, finding nothing in the pass upon which they could feed, perhaps an opportunity might arise back from where they came. Two days and A'lisha Amjad bint Saleh, along with R'aisha bint Benim and Khaled bin Al-Tarif, would find the encampment of the warlord Muhammad. Muhammad could still count on nearly one hundred of his best fighting men, A'lisha was aware of this – she had stolen the memories of Abi Talib. R'aisha had taken time to explain their probable suicide journey to Al-Tarif, who was now aware of what was at stake – his life. R'aisha already knew - this was her own agenda, her aspiration, her determination of how everything was going to be.

The first evening came, there was to be no respite, no rest. A short quick meal consisted of nothing but rice, seeds and beans – neither A'lisha nor R'aisha consumed meat or flesh. Al-Tarif was hungry, his desire for something more substantive was overwhelming.

"Why do you not eat meat or game?" asked Al-Tarif. Now that the scouts had left there was no goat-meat cooking.

"In all animal kingdoms, hunting is meat and violence. The kill, it is the same with humankind," R'aisha tried her best to explain. "Man kills for meat, a woman does not, this violence in men is driven by the hunt and the kill. And man will kill man, his own kind. There is not this instinct in women, only in men, my kind do not make a meal of flesh."

"But does not Al-Ilāh preach forgiveness and love? His prophets teach that taking the life of another man or woman is wrong," said Al-Tarif. "There are ancient scriptures and tablets that say this. The preacher Muhammad teaches this."

"Do not be fooled Khaled bin Al-Tarif," said R'aisha. "Even Gabriel's prophets fight each other. Man's wars against man bear fruit to no one, the dominance of one prophet against others is war. Men, women and children die in the name of these preaching prophets."

"There is no almighty Al-llāh who made man in his own image, Khaled," A'lisha intervened, A'lisha never spoke unless there was a meaningful meaning. "Al-llāh is Gabriel's invention, Gabriel's Lesser Lords are Lords concerned with their dominance of this world and the heavens, the scriptures to which you refer are written by men. Man was not created in the image of Al-llāh, Hyvah was not born from the bone of A'adam, these are lies spread by Gabriel's nodding vassal, his foolish prophet Abr'a'ham."

"Then what is your truth?" responded Al-Tarif.

"There is no truth," A'lisha answered.

In the nighttime sky, the blackness was riddled by a million or more stars. Al-Tarif stared in wonderment in the same way he had stared when a young boy. These spectacular heavens must be the creation of Al-llāh, what A'lisha said made no sense, how could countless stars, the sun and moon, all the wonderments of the world, everything that grew and graced, the love of man for a woman - how could this not be the work of the almighty creator Al-llāh?

Al-Tarif finished his meagre meal, he made sure the Meccan Abi Talib drank water, then Al-Tarif looked into Abi Talib's eyes – there was nothing there. What had they done to him? By this time Al-Tarif himself was struggling, he could not come to terms with the way this whole shambolic interlude had unravelled, without doubt he must be in a dream, a bad dream, a nightmare of indescribable proportions, this was the only logic that made sense – by R'aisha's own admission they were headed for Muhammad's encampment, into the lion's den where the simple act of revenge could never happen.

Al-Tarif looked grim, he was once more loading their supplies onto the one spare camel, the one taken from the dead Badr al-Din who now did not need it. Al-Tarif then checked the lifeless body of Abdel-Salman, why were they taking him along? Why had they not buried him in the Bedouin tradition – into the ground upon which he had been slain? Then Al-Tarif heaved Abi Talib into his saddle – once more Al-Tarif glared into the tribesman's eyes, what Al-Tarif saw made him shudder.

"Muhammad, Muhammad. Riders approach." Muhammad's aide-de-camp Abū Bakr woke him from his deep slumber. The warlord rose without hesitation, adorning his regal kaftan and keffiyeh headdress as he strode with purpose from the grandness of his goatskin tent. It was true, in the distance, from the direction of the Sambula Pass, three camel riders appeared out of a drifting cloud of hoof-trampled dust. It was Abi Talib, Badr al-Din and Abū al-Faraj, they were returning thought Muhammad with a beaming smile. He then saw two more riders and a spare camel with them – in a fraction of a moment it clicked, they had taken the fugitive harlot A'lisha Amjad bint Saleh captive. Muhammad congratulated himself in gratifying satisfaction, he felt well pleased in his overjoyed sense of achievement.

Muhammad's face-wide grin turned into a puzzled grimace, then his smile froze – as the riders drew closer it became plain these riders were not the three men who had left the camp four days before. Bemused tribesmen began to gather around their warlord. A dozen or so, sensing danger, were quick to don their swords. By now, the morning sun had climbed above the rocky mountain horizon, the distant craggy ridge line creating beams of redness tinged with yellow hues - light that bounced skywards into the pale-blue sunrise of what would soon become a nonsensical day. It struck Muhammad that he had no idea who the riders were.

R'aisha bint Benim, clad head-to-foot in her protective kaftan cloak that concealed who she was, rode at the head of the five riders. As she drew closer, with a good measure of nonchalance, she galloped through the outer ring of prepared tribesmen who were slow in their attempt to form a protective ring around their prophet leader. Muhammad's guard was ineffective, inept in its lack of preparedness – a concerning development that Muhammad was quick to note. Muhammad had no choice but to disregard his vulnerability – which allowed his infamous curiosity to kick in. A short camel length behind R'aisha rode Khaled bin Al-Tarif, who led the camel over which the body of Abdel-Salman lay slung over the saddle. Last came A'lisha Amjad bint Saleh, disguised and indistinguishable in her tight-wrapped desert cloak. A'lisha herself led the camel carrying Abi Talib, whose mouth by now was foaming incoherent foam; the fool who was the foolish Meccan traitor.

R'aisha pulled her camel up short to an abrupt snorting halt. "As-salamu alaykum," she barked to Muhammad – the longtime traditional desert greeting between strangers.

Muhammad eyed R'aisha with outright suspicion, for one moment he paused, endeavouring to understand who these intruders into his encampment might be. "Wa 'alayka s-salām," he offered back, noting the rider's female voice. Muhammad's tribesmen guards looked to him for his verbal command.

Raisha stared around, deliberate with intention. "You," she commanded, pointing directly to the meanest swordsman, a tall, bald, muscular man of exceptional fierce demeanour. "You," she repeated. "Make a funeral pit, then bury this brave Bedouin who fought for your warlord in your conquering of Mecca," R'aisha gestured in the direction of the lifeless Abdel-Salman. The startled tribesman made no move, instead he peered at Muhammad for instructions of what he should do. Muhammad, uncertain, nodded his grudging acknowledgement with a slight affirmation of his head. The tribesman, himself a headman of repute, motioned to two of his men to cut down Abdel-Salman's body from his by-now slavering camel. Every man standing then stared wide-eyed at the disoriented tribal warrior already known to them – Abi Talib.

Raisha saw their agitation, they looked on with menace – they were bewildered, eager, ready to draw their swords.

"The two companions you sent with this man, they are dead," said R'aisha, without remorse. "They are buried in the desert."

Muhammad took half a step back, trying to stay composed. "Can I ask how they died?" he tried to remain calm, but his anger threatened to overspill at any moment.

"Like rats," said R'aisha.

Muhammad's hair bristled down his back.

Muhammad fought to regain control, he paused, then studied the other two riders. He saw Al-Tarif, a bolt of recognition struck his memory. "I know who *you* are," he declared, looking direct at the Bedouin nomad, the one sane rider not wearing headdress. "You are of the *Al Buainai* Bedouin. You are Khaled bin Al-Tarif." Muhammad grew more suspicious, none of this made sense.

"Yes, I am Khaled bin Al-Tarif," acknowledged Al-Tarif. "This man you bury in the ground, he is Saleh bin Abdel-Salman ibn Ameen Ahl Farsi, tribal leader of the *Banu Amir*," Al-Tarif looked stern. "He fought with bravery alongside you, yet he is killed by these assassins you sent against us."

Muhammad did not respond; he would not be drawn. "What happened to this man Abi Talib?" Muhammad demanded, pointing to his once second in command who sat forlorn in his ragged saddle. Muhammad realised he needed more time, time to think with speed, time to take control of this extraordinary situation. The warlord preacher was on the verge of ordering his men to seize the three riders, yet he was confused, baffled by why they were here in his encampment - Muhammad could not decide if this was good fortune or a threat of monumental danger. Who was the third rider who had, as yet, said nothing? Was the vigilante woman at their head, the one who spoke her mind, was she the harlot whore his three men had set out to find? Muhammad, for some reason, did not think she was.

Muhammad tensed, waiting for Al-Tarif to reply.

"Your assassin's mind, it has been ravaged," said Al-Tarif. "Now he is more stupid and deranged than when he left your camp."

The warlord was shocked with anger, once more he reeled. Muhammad rallied. "Who is she?" he challenged, this time pointing to R'aisha at their head. This was an undoubted hostile situation.

"She is R'aisha bint Benim of the *Banu Amir*," replied Al-Tarif.

The name meant nothing to Muhammad. He thought through the situation, she was irrelevant, a *Banu Amir* tribeswoman, an insignificant servant-wife who suffered the impertinence to order his man to bury the dead Abdel-Salman. If what Al-Tarif said was true, then she was not the witch woman Gabriel was afraid of. Muhammad eyed the third rider, the one who sat motionless and silent, he could not tell who this rider might be but, from the rider's form beneath the tight-wrapped robes, he thought he could see the shape of another woman's body - just her eyes were visible. They were piercing dark eyes.

"This rider, who is this?" Muhammad gestured to the third rider.

"She is your worst nightmare," Al-Tarif answered.

Again, Muhammad bristled.

"I am A'lisha Amjad bint Saleh, the one who you seek," interrupted A'lisha, her voice laced with sinister brooding. "This is my given name."

Muhammad flinched; straightaway he was undecided about his next move. He must think quick. Both his aide-de-camp, Abū Bakr, and the tall bald headman known as Abi Casr, made to unsheathe their swords. They waited with impatience for Muhammad to give his command.

"If any of these men draw their swords, they will die here, right now," warned R'aisha, with intentional menace.

Muhammad eyed R'aisha with scorn. "We are nearly five-score armed men, you cannot kill every one of us," he mocked, sneering a laugh at Raisha's warning, though instinctive caution deep in the back of Muhammad's mind made him hold back - he did not give the order to his men to seize the intruders, not yet. Both Abū Bakr and Abi Casr made no move.

"Why are you here?" Muhammad challenged.

"Why did you send your tribesmen to assassinate us?" snarled R'aisha, she had no intention of letting Muhammad take control - right now she and A'lisha held the upper hand through fearless surprise and audacity.

Muhammad hesitated, she had not answered, just with a question following his question. This intrusion into his encampment was a deliberate and clear incursion. How did he respond? With the truth, he thought, this whole crusade in the sacred name of Al-llāh was based on truth, or Muhammad's version of it.

"Gabriel, who is Al-llāh's holy vassal, he commanded that I hunt down this woman," Muhammad gestured in A'lisha's direction, "I am tasked to choose one hundred of my best men to find this A'lisha Amjad bint Saleh, who is an enemy of I'slām," Muhammad tried to feel calm, more in control. "Gabriel is the messenger of Al-llāh, so my charge to take her head is in Al-llāh's name." Muhammad did not reveal why he had been chosen, that Gabriel, for some reason, feared the child descended by blood from the Judaean M'agdalena and the renegade Jewish prophet. Then the unease inside Muhammad grew greater - why was the head of this A'lisha Amjad bint Saleh being handed to him so easily on a plate? Could this be more devious work by the traitorous jew Isca'riot?

R'aisha smiled, she decried herself grim - the same bloodthirsty vultures once more appeared circling overhead, sensing the harbinger of blood-filled doom in the unfolding events below.

"Will you take A'lisha's head like you did those of the *Banu Qurayza?*" R'aisha fired off her question with acidic poison. "You beheaded six hundred pitiless men, their women and their children who you declared traitors for refusing your damned faith? Was this by Gabriel's command? Was glorious Al-llāh's judgement fulfilled?"

Muhammad quivered. Al-Tarif too sat uncomfortable in his saddle, he knew that R'aisha was not wrong in her claim. Al-Tarif had witnessed the ritual slaughter of the whole tribe taken prisoner following the *Qurayza's* defeat in the bloody battle of the Trench. Muhammad's I'slām army had at last broken the Meccan siege. The *Banu Qurayza* had been condemned as traitors, the Jewish tribe having chosen to fight against Muhammad's army trapped in the city of Medina. When Muhammad emerged victorious against the besieging Meccans his furious retribution against the *Banu Qurayza* had been savage.

R'aisha, facing down Muhammad, did not blink. "The one hundred heads you took of the *Bahilah* tribe, those who chose to worship their idol of Dur I-Khalasa," R'aisha grew more intense, "Was it A'lāh's will for them to die like vermin?" she let her question dangle, the legacy of the warlord's atrocities was well known. The *Bahilah* tribe had paid a heavy price for their faith. R'aisha sensed that she had Muhammad in the belittling palm of her hand. "You slew more than two hundred of the *Khath'am* jews. All of them. Women and children who could do you no harm." R'aisha was calculating, deliberate, ruthless and calm, eyeing the uncomfortable defiance in Muhammad's cold expression. A'lisha, beside her, sat silent in her saddle.

The vultures swooped low, the agitated impatience of Muhammad's men increased in intensity, the featherless bird's instinct to find an opportune feed appeared to be well served. R'aisha, in her venom, was not finished. "Your seigneur Abdullah ibn Khatal, his slave girls Quraybah and Fartana," she growled. "You took their heads because they sang songs of your murderous deeds. Was this by Gabriel's command?" By now R'aisha held Muhammad firm in her grip, she could turn and twist him with little intention of letting him go. Overhead, the vultures cawked their growing delight. "The blind man Al-Harith bin Al-Talatil, Al-Talatil who died mocking you, even when he could not see you. The old man died on your murderous whim."

Muhammad's angry impatience increased, this was intolerable in his own camp, he was about to snap. He had heard enough.

Al-Tarif saw Muhammad's menacing promulgation. "Do not do it," Al-Tarif mouthed to Muhammad, warning the warlord with a slight, noticeable side-to-side nod, "You are being baited, she will kill you," he voiced in a low audible whisper. Abū Bakr and Abi Casr peered at their lord and master in eyed anticipation – they expected Muhammad to at last give the command to take them. A few score men would soon finish these intruders, their impudence was astonishing. Muhammad held back, Gabriel had warned him, he could die at the hands of this notorious whore who had not, as yet, said anything of note. Then a wild supposition left him teetering – her companion, this R'aisha bint Benim, could it be...

The thought struck him like a thunderclap jail house door, Muhammad reeled in yet more undecided confusion. Gabriel had forewarned him, he had warned of a sibling twin, there were gospel rumours of a second birth, tablet stones carved and written then for a long time hidden. M'agdalena and the rebel prophet, the baptist and the rapscallion Isca'riot. Two? Of course, it made sense, R'aisha bint Benim and A'lisha Amjad bint Saleh, they were of the same blood, descended from the preaching jew of Judaea - the renegade prophet Yesh'ua.

Muhammad groped, thinking upon his feet. Somehow, he needed a break, time to rethink, to fight back, time to fulfil Gabriel's task, time to strike both these intruders' heads from their shoulders - Muhammad's infamous way of retribution.

"I beg a parlay," barked Muhammad to R'aisha, "I beg to speak with some truth to the Bedouin Khaled bin Al-Tarif. Will you allow me this? This man is a believer in my faith of I'slām." Muhammad guessed that splitting Al-Tarif from his two companions would allow his men to overpower the two whores, he could then deal with the Bedouin alone - in his own way.

R'aisha and A'lisha glanced at each other, both making no comment - as if this turn of events was expected. A'lisha, beneath her headdress veil smiled. Al-Tarif, making the decision, jumped down from his saddle. Muhammad beckoned to him with his upturned hand - with a beaming smile of invitation that did not fool Al-Tarif.

"Please, Khaled bin Al-Tarif, please, please come to my tent, we can talk." Al-Tarif looked to R'aisha who made no sign of dissent. Muhammad turned to his aide Abū Bakr, "Get that fool Abi Talib down from his damned saddle," he looked at his former comrade whose mind was gone. "Deal with him," he snarled to Abū Bakr.

Al-Tarif was awestruck by the luxurious comfort the warlord enjoyed, his tent was draped in colourful curtains and fabric. The sand-gravelled earth was covered in arabica carpet, the sitting space with prearranged goat skin festoons – a far cry from the functional living tents of wild desert nomads.

"Please, please sit," Muhammad beckoned to Al-Tarif. "Bring tea," instructed Muhammad to his personal servant boy, a slave taken prisoner at the battle of Uhud. Al-Tarif squatted in his usual Bedouin manner. Muhammad, taking Al-Tarif's lead, sat with legs folded beneath his relaxed torso.

"Why are you here?" demanded Muhammad, adopting his more usual straight-to-the-point manner. At this point Muhammad could begin to take control, he had separated the intruders apart.

"I do not know Muhammad," Al-Tarif answered – which was true, he did not know why they had travelled the two days to Muhammad's camp. A'lisha and R'aisha were the alpha renegades who were supposed to be on the run.

This whole escapade venture had begun with the death of his son Rahim bin Al-Tarif who, he had learned, was not his son at all. Then there was his second son Kahmed, whose mind was somehow ravaged in the same way as that of the Muslim Abi Talib. Everything, Al-Tarif's whole world had changed, it had in every way twisted and turned, it had then transformed beyond reason when A'lisha Amjad bint Saleh of the *Banu Amir* had ended the lives of the two angel assassins Iblis and Belial. More astonishing, A'lisha had then slain the dark messenger Lucifer who made his unscrupulous claims to be the devil. Al-Tarif's life had been turned upside down, it would never be the same, no longer was he the nomadic Bedouin warrior who, in a time not long before, had embraced Muhammad's I'slām faith with his heart. But Al-Tarif was now a slave to his changed beliefs, in just four days he had spun to face new presumptions, a new belief - now he too paid homage to the iconic image of M'agdalena and her ancestral hierarchy.

But what had happened in the world before R'aisha bint Benim? Before A'lisha and the mystifying M'agdalena? Al-Tarif was fearful - the notion of two billion years of heritage to Hyvah and her garden realm of Yahweh was breathtaking, in its way unbelievable. Who was Hyvah? Or Hawwāh by her more obscure non-human name. Each cut of the narrative told to Al-Tarif was hearsay, speculation, history etched in stone on an indestructible granite stone of which he had no knowledge – a rock monolith in a cold-white northland he had never heard of.

"Then tell me why are you with them," Muhammad pushed Al-Tarif further.

How could the now *Al Buainai* outcast answer this? It was complicated to the extreme, it would take an age just to understand the bare bones of what had happened because the complex trail of events was unbelievable. Al-Tarif thought for a few moments before replying.

"My Muhammad, like you and your men, we were in the desert searching for this A'lisha Amjad bint Saleh," replied Al-Tarif. "She murdered my son two nights after they were betrothed in marriage." Al-Tarif saw the surprised look in Muhammad's eyes. "You and I are not alone in searching the badland mountains for this young woman." Again, Al-Tarif noted the unease in Muhammad's shocked expression.

"My burden is great, I am tasked by Al-Ilāh to seek her," said Muhammad, "I have more reason to find her than simple revenge, the devil himself can curse this woman for what she has done," Muhammad fixed Al-Tarif with his stare. "Who else searches the desert?"

Al-Tarif shifted his squatting position while he thought what to say. "Not five days from now two inhuman assassins were killed by this A'lisha Amjad bint Saleh and the *Banu Amir* mad woman R'aisha bint Benim when they tried to ambush our scouts," Al-Tarif answered. "Lucifer himself led these angel hunter killers, after they died Lucifer disappeared like the coward he is,"

Muhammad shook, he shuddered. Both Gabriel and Lucifer, the self-declared devil, were desperate to find this harlot, this sorceress who could do no good. If the angels themselves were spilling blood, then he could see the outright importance of his task. Muhammad smiled, he had them, both were here in his camp, all he had to do was take them, it would be simple with one hundred of his best men. Muhammad relished his good fortune. But this A'lisha Amjad bint Saleh, she possessed the power to kill angels?

"The devil, he did well to run," Muhammad half-joked with a deep-throated growl.

"The devil Lucifer is dead," said Al-Tarif, "A'lisha Amjad bint Saleh, she killed him."

Muhammad froze, his feeling of good fortune evaporated, it was gone.

Outside, R'aisha bint Benim and A'lisha Amjad bint Saleh sat upon their camels in reverence, they waited. Both knew the silence would not last long. A'lisha eyed the chieftain Abi Casr, she beheld he was on the cusp of drawing his sword to attack, that soon he would be able to contain himself no longer - the smallest provocation or nod from his warlord would be enough.

A'lisha delved into Abi Casr's mind, his memories, the multitude strands of sinew that made up his soul. She saw Abi Casr flinch, his face twitched in involuntary hurt - A'lisha felt his pain, beneath the keffiyeh headscarf that concealed her face she was ashen grey. She reached inside his inner mind, the strands of memories for which she searched - they were there. Abu Mustafa's daughter, who Abi Casr had raped then murdered, burying her in the sand for no one to find. The womenfolk and wives of defeated enemies, defiled and killed in victorious plunder - there were too many for A'lisha to count. The decrepit storyteller, the one who had also once before read his mind, A'lisha flinched, she drew back, who was this vagrant woman? In this instant, a thousand leagues north, a storyteller in her own world smiled. A'lisha felt the embryonic foetus inside her abdomen turn.

Abi Casr, his head hurt, he felt the pain of A'lisha's incursion into his mind. He grimaced, he cried out, those nearest to him became alarmed. Then the voice inside his head...

"Did she scream in pain when you ravished her?" the voice said, the voice was venom, it hissed and tortured. "Was there fear and tears in her eyes before you cut off her head?"

Abi Casr in an instant fell to his knees. What was happening? What were these words inside his head? He raised his bulging wide eyes to stare wild at A'lisha,

"Your faith belongs to your prophet," the voice said. "But your heart, it belongs to me."

Abi Casr died, he died when his memories were shredded from his thoughts. He crumbled to the ground, his expression contorted with excruciating pain from within his chest, his heart felt that it might be ripped from inside his bone cage. Then, in a moment, Abi Casr was dead. Every one of Muhammad's tribesmen followers stood in horror, Muhammad, from the exotic surroundings of his tent, sensed the soundless mayhem that was unfolding. Still faltering from Al-Tarif's terror-struck revelation, he jumped to his feet then ran fast outside - once more Muhammad stopped dead in abject shock.

R'aisha knew the final bait was now set. A'lisha jumped from her camel, no man moved against her, not yet, not until Muhammad gave the word. The light that was already intense flashed with more bright light, the air brimmed with electrified particles, molecules that unwound in physical fusion. R'aisha smiled, now was the time she thought Gabriel would come.

Gabriel, out-of-the-blue stood tall and magnificent; he had chosen his human angelic form because he would be surrounded by easily enthralled men. He furled his great white wings which R'aisha knew were just a thin gossamer thread, an illusion that did not fool her. Muhammad, his men, Al-Tarif, they all fell to their knees in speechless reverence. A'lisha made no move, Gabriel could with great effort take her. She stood two paces back, more under the protection of R'aisha.

Gabriel hesitated. Yes, there were two, his worst nightmare was confirmed. The angel looked down at Muhammad who had failed, the preacher had not heeded his warning. "Get up Muhammad, get to your feet."

"So, the angel himself came," R'aisha removed her headdress, she half-smiled a surreptitious smile.

"Is this the bloodline of Hyvah who is reborn?" Gabriel gestured towards A'lisha. He felt A'lisha probe his mind. "Don't," he warned. "You have no need."

"Yes, she is A'lisha Amjad bint Saleh of the Banu Amir, we expected you to make your appearance," R'aisha replied.

"So, I walk into your trap, is this the reason Lucifer and his angels died?"

Gabriel hesitated, realising he had been lured. He gripped his hidden lance.

"Your fallen angels died like scorpions, squashed beneath our feet," R'aisha felt tense, though unfeeling, she held no fear of the archangel. It seemed there was an acknowledgement between them.

Gabriel withstood the challenge, it would do him no good to be defeated in the presence of his one last prophet whose emblazoned crusade was now in the balance, teetering on the edge. Gabriel grimaced; this confrontational catastrophe had first begun with the traitorous Isca'riot - the conflict that might never end.

"Tell me," growled Gabriel, "I believed she was dead, I was told the angel Chemosh had killed her when she was a child?" Gabriel made a gesture to A'lisha, he guessed there was a sinister link between this A'lisha Amjad bint Saleh, the traitor Isca'riot and the despised M'agdalena.

R'aisha eyed Gabriel with contempt. "The soil and earth, they do not belong to Lucifer, Lucifer tried to take this world when it was not Lucifer's to take," she stared with hard eyes, "Chemosh, it is the same, he took the child's life when it was not his to take. The ground, the dirt, the soil, they gave the child's life back. The bones of M'agdalena, they are buried in the same place, taken there by Isca'riot. The blood of M'agdalena is within this A'lisha Amjad bint Saleh, it is the M'agdalena who chose the fate of your prophet, you should not dwell on this name A'lisha Amjad bint Saleh."

Gabriel was rendered speechless. Muhammad, standing beside the archangel, fixed his eyes on A'lisha - how much more could he take? Gabriel remembered the death of M'agdalena, how could he forget? The anarchist prophet? The Baptist, the disciples, the overwhelming victories of the marching Christendom armies - it had all fallen apart. The gospels had not done what they were supposed to do, everything driven into the ground by the temptress M'agdalena who stole his Bethlehem prophet. Gabriel's warlord Muhammad, I'slām, the new Muslim realms, the new way, Gabriel's desire to reclaim his world under duress from the descendant priestesses of Hyvah, of Hawwāh, Lilith, of Eve.

"What do you want?" Gabriel demanded.

"A truce," answered R'aisha.

"*What?*" Gabriel was astonished.

"Khaled bin Al-Tarif, the *Al Buainai* tribesman, he must stand beside your warlord, be his second in command, his mentor," R'aisha waited. "Abu Talib is finished, Abi Casr is dead."

Both Gabriel and Muhammad stood speechless.

"If you do not agree this then your preacher's crusade is ended," R'aisha motioned to Muhammad, "I beg to remind you, in the same way that each of your other crusades have failed."

Memories of history flashed through Gabriel's thoughts; his mind spun with the staggering request R'aisha had just made.

"Who *are* you?" demanded Gabriel.

"My given name is R'aisha bint Benim, this is not the name I was born with. In my existence I have had many names, you know this. In the same way as A'lisha Amjad bint Saleh here, I was created from copulation with the Naz'areth prophet Ye'shua bin Ya'akob ben Gennesareth, the rightful *Hasmonean* Lord of Judaea who believed in the truthfulness of Myriam bint M'agdalena of Judaea, the bloodline of Hyvah. My name at birth was T'amar. What more do you wish to know?" R'aisha sharpened her guiltless expression, knowing that Gabriel and Muhammad knew little of this. The absolute truth of her birth would astound Muhammad, but not Gabriel. R'aisha looked around – every man there listened.

"Why a truce?" demanded Gabriel.

"You cannot forever make new prophets," said R'aisha. "Each prophet you send to this world is a man by birth, you sanctify the image of man as though he is the reason for everything, when he is not."

Gabriel sensed the trap. Of course, each of his prophets were of the male species, the dominant species. Why would they not be, he never intended there to be any equality. Each of the faiths, all of them, preached from the outset that it was men who spread the word of his Lords, women were the subservient obedient race - this was how Gabriel wished it to be. Gabriel felt uneasy - man needed women for the procreation of his race. He stood silent.

271

"If every woman in this world joined beside me, where would you be?" R'aisha continued, "I have no doubt men would react with violence against their women, this is the way men are, it is how they resolve everything."

Muhammad, standing silent, intervened. "Are you saying that women are equal to men? They might even be the superior race?"

"No, neither woman nor man can be born without the other, it is the way life has evolved in this vile world. Not just human life. There was *never* a *virgin birth*. This is why we demand a truce from this long conflict," said R'aisha. A'lisha stood beside her camel saying nothing. Every tribesman in earshot was spellbound, they expected Muhammad to give the command to kill the intruders at any moment. To Al-Tarif, this confrontation did not make sense, he was stunned by the rolling revelations like everyone else.

"What are the terms of your truce," Gabriel was interested though he doubted that any demands would be acceptable to him or his Lords. But the thought of unhindered dominance by mankind was intriguing. Muhammad, nearby, stood aghast.

R'aisha demurred, she did not expect Gabriel to agree anything and Muhammad was irrelevant. "Your vassal Lucifer is dead, so are his five assassins. The days of your devil are finished, we have seen to it this curse of evil is no more," said R'aisha, "I think you know what we want now."

Gabriel was not over concerned, Lucifer with his five fallen angels was no loss, the scheming idiot had failed in his tasks more than once – if Lucifer had made sure the infant child A'lisha was dead then none of them would be standing here now.

"While you think long Gabriel, know this," said R'aisha. "My sibling sister here carries the embryo child of Rahim bin Al-Tarif, who is the bloodline of Lucifer. When this child is born then we too are the blood of angels," R'aisha smiled, she saw Gabriel's face contort with uncontrolled horror. "Why do you think we proposed the wedlock marriage of Rahim bin Al-Tarif of the *Al Buainai* and A'lisha Amjad bint Saleh of the *Banu Amir* eh? Do you think it was for the unification of Bedouin tribes to strengthen your preacher's crusade?" R'aisha let her question dangle.

Gabriel once more thought hard. The unborn child would be female, he did not doubt this. Lucifer and his hunter-killers were dead - who would carry the relentless burden of hunting the newborns down? If this child carried the hereditary bloodline of M'agdalena and the renegade Jerusalem prophet, Lucifer and this redoubtable A'lisha Amjad bint Saleh then not just Muhammad's crusade but the whole future of his worldly task would be under monumental threat. This proposed truce was no truce, it was a thinly disguised demand for his capitulation.

R'aisha right now was under no illusion, if Muhammad or his tribesmen tried to kill A'lisha, Al-Tarif and herself, now would be the time they would do it. Al-Tarif sensed this too, he firmed his grip on his sword though their survival odds against, he guessed, one hundred or so fearsome warriors were well beyond zero. A'lisha though, she thought otherwise, A'lisha knew there would be no attack, she sat with her eyes fixed upon Gabriel with the gaze of every Muslim man of Muhammad's band of renegades glued to herself in fascination - not unlike the flowering germination of wonderment idolisation ~ a humanoid trait that both A'lisha Amjad bint Saleh and Gabriel were well aware of.

"I ask you again, what do you want?" Gabriel was beginning to lose his self-control. He fought hard to remain calm, to keep his composure. Meanwhile, Muhammad and his men turned their attention to Gabriel - his human form concealing his angelic illusion.

"This preacher you call Muhammad is to be your last prophet. There will be no more prophets," R'aisha answered, "I make the promise that Muhammad will not be harmed, nor his men, his crusade can continue to its never end."

Muhammad gasped. "Why do we not just kill you? Here and now."

"Will you then take our heads? In your way?" admonished R'aisha.

Muhammad felt the ripple of dissent in his men, his tribesmen were uneasy, his gut instinct warned him these fallible beduins tied together by fragile allegiances were beginning to waver – all of them knew Khaled bin Al-Tarif, they held him in high regard even though more than once he had been an enemy to most of them. Al-Tarif was Bedouin, Muhammad and this strange angel being reminiscent of wine-swilling Meccan aristocracy, with his rattly pitched voice was not. What was more, each and every one of them was mesmerised by the forcefulness this R'aisha and A'lisha Amjad bint Saleh of the *Banu Amir* Bedouin wielded – and the death of the *Banu Amir* Abdel-Salman at the hands of the Meccan renegade Abi Talib was for a good number of them approaching the last straw. The tortured strange death of Abi Casr right in front of their eyes, another strongman Meccan turned traitor, seemed to be the rightful outcome in a way that Muhammad at first did not grasp. Then Muhammad felt a worrying gut feeling sensation – he was beginning to lose the loyalty of his men.

Gabriel's intuition perceived the same unsettling change, it occurred to him how the two erroneous *Banu Amir* tribeswomen had calculated this whole deliberate situation, they had no doubt groomed this dead *Banu Amir* tribal leader Abdel-Salman, the *Al Buainai* tribe too, also this Al-Tarif who Gabriel sensed was no simple Bedouin tribesman. Al-Tarif bothered Gabriel more and more as the intense moments ticked by. Gabriel by this time was alarmed, he was beginning to suspect the game might be lost.

Muhammad turned to Gabriel, the warlord was approaching the end of his tether, he teetered on the verge of ordering his warriors to seize the three intruders, to put an end to this charade of womanly superiority – Muhammad was slow in his thinking, R'aisha was holding out, delaying her thoughts, waiting for the moment when she knew Muhammad's tribesmen would turn renegade. Time, like a sand-filled hourglass draining fast, was running out - R'aisha needed one more subliminal act.

"This dead Bedouin Abdel-Salman lost his life to a turncoat traitorous Meccan," said R'aisha to Muhammad. "He was the bravest of the Bedouin tribes, you used his life like blood turned to meaningless water," R'aisha turned to the hoard of tribesmen who stood spellbound. "Who among you are Bedouin?" she bellowed. "Will you not follow one who is the bravest, braver than Saleh bin Abdel-Salman ibn Ameen Ahl Farsi of the *Banu Amir*? Here is Khaled bin Al-Tarif, he is Bedouin, each of you know this man, he fought beside you when this warlord was victorious in the city of Mecca," R'aisha said this, even though she knew women and children had been slaughtered in the usual inevitable way, like always.

"Your warlord is not Bedouin," R'aisha hushed her voice, she looked around, she had each of Muhammad's Bedouin men in her hands. "This Muhammad you worship and follow, he is *born* of Mecca, his blood father was Abdullah ibn Abd al-Muttalib, a Meccan of wealth who wed himself to this preacher's mother Āminah bint Wahb, who was herself born to the woman Barrah bint Abd al-Uzza. He was nursed by the slave girl Umm Ayman, an Abyssinian captured by the *Abu Zuhrah* tribe of the *Quraysh*. This Muhammad, this preacher, he was then raised by the mad woman Halimah bint Abi Dhuayb of the *Banu S'ad,* she who freed the girl slave from her life of milk nurse servitude," R'aisha turned to stare direct at Muhammad, who stood rigid - the warlord was baffled. "Take a long look Muhammad ibn Abdullah, who do you see? Do you not see the crazed woman Halimah bint Abi Dhuayb? The woman of the desert who raised you, here before your bloodthirsty eyes?"

There was a murmured gasp, it rippled through the crowd like an unseen riptide wave. Muhammad staggered back, he was struck dumb, of course he remembered Halimah bint Abi Dhuayb, young well-to-do Meccan boys were often sent to the desert to be raised in the ways of traditional boyhood, to be taught the absolute truth of Al-Ilāh, to be inducted into the way of their long-standing faith... Muhammad froze. Khaled bin Al-Tarif, alongside, stood paralysed with him - both had been duped by the same woman born under the Judaean name of T'amar. Gabriel, like Muhammad and Al-Tarif, reeled aghast.

Had Muhammad's whole I'slām faith, his values and beliefs, his radical ambitions been deliberately shaped in his formative years? Of course they had – but by who, Gabriel asked himself, R'aisha bint Benim?

"I see there is an inclination of realisation," R'aisha goaded Gabriel.

R'aisha was right. Gabriel was quick to understand his deteriorating predicament, the crumbling ground he stood upon – Gabriel never had lorded over his new emerging preacher and the radical version of his faith. Was the rising faith of I'slām a figment of R'aisha's devious guile? But why?

For R'aisha, why was easy. The ancestral descendants of Hyvah, through the irrepressible bloodline of M'agdalena, had long realised that Gabriel would yield one last prophet, more so in the shadow of the catastrophic failure of the preacher Yesh'ua of Judaea. Gabriel would have no choice, his ambitions for domination by his lords drove everything. Neither Gabriel nor Muhammad realised that each of the womenfolk close to the young Muhammad - his maternal grandmother Barrah bint Abd al-Uzza, the Abyssinian slave Umm Ayman and the first of Muhammad's thirteen wives, Kahdiya bint Khuwaylid, were linked by kinship to Muhammad's desert-nursemaid Halimah bint Abi Dhuayb - to R'aisha bint Benim – or her alter-name S'arah-Tamar. R'aisha knew Gabriel was being meticulous in his grooming of Muhammad, the Lesser Lord's angel on earth had spied Muhammad's radical beliefs – the worldly germination of I'slām. Unbeknownst to Gabriel, Muhammad's new faith was held firm in the hands of Halimah bint Abi Dhuayb and the gaggle of women surrounding him.

It took just a short while for the full horror to strike Gabriel full to his heart.

Nusaybah bint Ka'ab, wife of merchant Zayd ibn Asim in the city of Medina and fiery sister of the warlord's coinage keeper Abdullah bin Ka'ab, did not take the news of Muhammad's unlikely situation well. Nusaybah was downright angry, the *Banu Najjar* tribeswoman seethed in resentful malcontent. This new second-in-command to the warlord, the *Al Buainai* Bedouin Khaled bin Al-Tarif, kept his own counsel, he had no rightful claim to be in this influential position. His quiet defiance made him a law unto himself, he did not condescend to talk with anyone – there was no doubting the nomadic Bedouin's bravery, not one of the warlord's tribesmen could question Al-Tarif's courage, but the crusading march of I'slām had irreversibly changed. Muhammad, it seemed, had agreed to disquieting constraints, outlandish promises of compromise. Almost, many claimed, an act of surreptitious capitulation.

Nusaybah was a firebrand, her reputation was known far and wide for the way she stuck by Muhammad's side regardless, in every battle the warlord fought – twice she had saved his life. Nusaybah bint Ka'ab's loyalty to Muhammad was unwavering, exceptional, unnerving beyond the call of what most men desired of their womenfolk – and Nusaybah was not wed or even mistressed to the warmongering preacher. Many of Muhammad's righteous followers could not figure Nusaybah bint Ka'ab out, she was herself arrogant and defiant, she was obstinate and recalcitrant in ways that *Banu Najjar* tribal women should not be. When told of what happened in Muhammad's desert encampment, how this Al-Tarif had thundered his way into the camp along with two itinerant *Banu Amir* peasant women, Nusaybah was enraged, bitter without understanding the intense feelings of jealousy that devoured her.

In Nusaybah's overworking mind, this *Al Buainai* tribesman and the two women must have manipulated her beloved Muhammad into an impossible agreement he did not want – a deal, she was told, in return for the continuation of his crusade of I'slām. Al-Tarif had been levered into the all-important second-in-command rank now that Abi Talib was dead – dispatched once it was decided his sanity had turned into stagnant water. Nusaybah was even more determined to protect her Muhammad than before – in the unlikely event of Muhammad being killed in battle then this *Al Buainai* tribesman would become the de facto leader of the new all-conquering Muslim army. How?

Nusaybah bint Ka'ab had by now hatched her plan. She would see to it that this *Al Buainai* pretender would be slain along with the two women who, she had no doubt, were his slave mistresses – and Nusaybah had no reservations about being the one who would do the slaying. This R'aisha bint Benim and her sister-accomplice A'lisha Amjad bint Saleh would learn their womanly place in a way that Nusaybah knew they would remember – she would not let them forget.

The man to whom Nusaybah *was* wed, Zayd ibn Asim, was a more of moderate citizen of Medina, he believed that Muhammad the so-called prophet was inept, the warlord should not have attacked the city of his birth, which meant that Asim's wife would have remained in her place, she would not have taken up her radical dream driven by her inexplicable obsession for the prophet. Nusaybah bint Ka'ab was an embarrassment to the ageing merchant who blamed her radical brother Abdullah for his wife's rampant beliefs in the new faith of I'slām. The older Asim took it upon himself to talk with Abdullah bin Ka'ab to try to reason with him about his sister Nusaybah's increasing distance from being his common wife – as a trading merchant, trade was suffering bad, he was being avoided more and more by marketplace buyers who thought he should control his wayward wife with more sternness. Asim, in his own way, stuck his head into the proverbial sand.

R'aisha bint Benim found Nusaybah bint Ka'ab in a defiant mood, halfway between Mecca and the magnificent mosque of Al-Masjid an-Nabawi, located in the city of Medina where Muhammad had established his base encampment. R'aisha knew from hearsay of Nusaybah's volatile reputation, that she had fought a woman's fight in every battle of the warlord's campaign. Nusaybah had begun her involvement by nursing wounded tribesmen then progressed to being Muhammad's personal medicine woman when the warlord suffered minor wounds at the Battle of Uhud. Nusaybah bint Ka'ab had been rapid in her transformation - from nurse to the embittered protector of Muhammad's life.

Nusaybah preferred horse to camel, though right now she rode her pack mule to draw less attention in this desolate land of male domination. When the two women at random came together on the roadway out of the village of Al-Atomya, it was an unexpected meeting of two like-minded travellers – or so Nusaybah thought.

"Sabaahul khayr," greeted R'aisha, the traditional marketplace acknowledgement between peasant strangers. "Kayfa haalik?" she asked.

Nusaybah did not answer, she studied the unknown woman with a hint of uncertain disdain.

"Are you travelling far?" probed R'aisha, her mule pulling alongside that of Nusaybah's.

There was an uneasy pause. "To Al-Masjid an-Nabawi," replied Nusaybah, without elaborating.

Nusaybah was irritated, she wished to travel alone, nor did she intend to get into meaningless womanly conversation with a roadway stranger, though Nusaybah thought it odd how this woman had no male travelling companion – but then neither did she herself. It then occurred to Nusaybah that riding with this woman might make her journey easier to her benefit, much of the time she would be harassed by local men pestering her by insisting they ride along with her, making what they wanted plain. Or by village elders probing why she was alone.

For Nusaybah, once she was back in Muhammad's ostentatious encampment, she would make it known to him she was there to stay, she would not be returning to the humdrum wife-like life with her wedded merchant husband Zayd ibn Asim – she would leave him to claim his second wife in the same old Medina way. Nusaybah was now caught between two hard stones, to ride alone subjecting herself to harassment or to travel along with this itinerant peasant woman, to once more return to Muhammad for what she saw as the remainder of her life. Nusaybah was also under no illusion that her husband Asim would be out to find her - until she could claim the protection of her radical brother Abdullah bin Ka'ab.

"Ah, to Al-Masjid an-Nabawi, in the beautiful city of Medina," replied R'aisha. "My good sister is there; she camps near to slopes of Mount Uhud." R'aisha did not lie, she had agreed with the warlord that A'lisha would stay by the side of Khaled bin Al-Tarif, though, without R'aisha's knowledge, this had not happened.

Nusaybah did not reply, she did not wish to engage in meaningless small talk conversation. Nusaybah did not suspect the unseen link with her ostentatious task.

R'aisha bint Benim knew all too well who this woman was but decided it best to keep her intrigue in check. R'aisha for a long time expected there would be an attempt on their lives at some point, more so upon Al-Tarif – now that Lucifer was dead the mantle of being the hunter-assassin would be passed on, Gabriel was not one to sit back to dwell upon his defeat. Back in Muhammad's muted and subdued camp, R'aisha had heard intriguing talk of this woman Nusaybah bint Ka'ab, of her devotion to the warlord preacher, her undying jealousy and willingness to throw her life away to protect him – and Al-Tarif had been warned in subtle ways to keep a wary eye upon his back from this woman's revenge. More unsettling, there was the prophecy that R'aisha was aware of, a warning carved into the ancient standing stone for eternity – that one of Hyvah's own would die by the deftness of a woman's hand. R'aisha eyed Nusaybah with a determined sideward glance as they rode together side-by-side.

Likewise, Nusaybah scrutinised R'aisha, the *Banu Najjar* tribeswoman from the Meccan second city of Medina decided she did not want the company of this illiterate peasant woman, they had nothing in common, little they could converse about - why was it she had latched on to her? Nusaybah goaded her mule onwards, trying to quicken its pace, perhaps this stupid woman would take the hint to leave her alone.

R'aisha did not leave Nusaybah riding ahead, R'aisha prompted her mule to pull forward alongside. "We can ride to Medina together," R'aisha suggested, noting Nusaybah's uneasy disposition, "I would be happy with the company of a woman to talk with." Nusaybah did not answer. R'aisha smiled a wry smile, she was certain she had found the right woman.

The sun began its journey from its midday peak towards the rocky mound horizon, the landscape hereabouts was not desolate but consisted of short low hills dotted with cultivated olive groves intermingled with smallholding fields of stubby maize. Here there was no mean desert scorched dry by the burning sun, this was where man cultivated his corn and raised his sons. Scattered settlements dotted the rough-hewn roadway busy with mules, wagons and camels loaded with mounds of harvested produce destined for either of the two walled cities of Mecca and Medina. During the afternoon, a caravan of camels passed by with slaves of both men and women, R'aisha was quick to note the destitute manner of the captives destined for the trading marketplaces of Mecca, many of them dark-skinned from the vast lands to the south. R'aisha made a point of continuing the meaningless talk of women with Nusaybah, who had given up trying to lose the irritating peasant who had latched onto her. R'aisha began every conversation expecting the short sharp sentences in reply, in time she began to sense more of this Nusaybah's characteristic disposition. What R'aisha learned made R'aisha grimmer.

"Why do you travel to Al-Masjid an-Nabawi?" R'aisha asked for the second time.

"I have work to do there, I told you already," answered Nusaybah, continuing to stare ahead.

Nusaybah and R'aisha rode towards Medina, Nusaybah like a bad-tempered sow at the slow pace of her mule - the two mules themselves beginning to draw to each other, as time crept by they did not need the prompting or encouragement of their riders to stay together. R'aisha and Nusaybah passed through several minor outpost hamlets, each time attracting the glancing stares of poor crop growers and the more wealthy farmers. Women travelling was not in itself uncommon, but most travelled in family groups or were chaperoned by safety-conscious men – there was no denying the risks women encountered from predatory males who saw women alone as easy bait.

For this reason, Nusaybah decided it best to stay with R'aisha, if only this peasant market woman was nearer to her own merchant social status. Nusaybah's interest was to fight alongside her warlord preacher of Al-Ilāh, this woman alongside her knew nothing of this, only the price of fish and damned milled flour, though by this time R'aisha herself realised that she and A'lisha were in danger – R'aisha's façade of the peasantry was working for now but this Nusaybah bint Ka'ab was a born assassin, driven by the trait well known in some women – jealousy, bitterness and insecurity.

R'aisha and the recalcitrant Nusaybah slept the night beside a corn shack. Halfway through the evening, they were shaken awake by the farmstead's slave girl who bid them to make a bed inside the pig shed, it was safer, warmer with more comfort. The slave girl was helped by the wife of the farm who was alarmed to find two women alone. Long before the midnight hour, R'aisha and Nusaybah got hot food - pig meat and corn though R'aisha refused to eat the pig meat which the hungry Nusaybah took from her - Nusaybah eyed R'aisha for the first time with a hint of suspicion. R'aisha turned to question the slave girl...

"Where do you come from with your dark skin?"

The girl was surprised, uneasy, it was unusual to be asked. "From the western land of Kamen. I am Berber, from the city of Carthage. Why do you ask?"

"Were you taken captive?" R'aisha grilled, she noted that Nusaybah listened.

"Yes, I was taken a long time ago," the girl looked around fifteen, she bowed her head, in shame, to hide her tear. "My father and two brothers were killed by traders, they were slavers, the slavers were my own people."

"How are you treated here?" R'aisha cast a warning glance in Nusaybah's direction, Nusaybah squatted perplexed, her mind turning.

The girl again looked uneasy. "The wife here takes care of me, she is a good woman, she was once a slave," she answered. "I do not like the husband, nor his second wife or his sister who is evil, she beats me. The husband, he comes to violate me in the night," the girl looked away, ashamed.

Nusaybah listened, this deep-meaning conversation changed everything, this was not the talk of a market woman.

"Do you wish to leave?" questioned R'aisha.

"Yes, many times I have thought of running away," replied the girl. "Where would I go?"

"What is your name?" R'aisha asked the question with sincerity, with a distinct measure of authority.

"Abaya, my name is Abaya,"

"Abaya, in the morning you leave with us," R'aisha glanced at Nusaybah when Nusaybah gasped.

"She cannot do this," Nusaybah struck back, her voice a rising crescendo of disapproval.

"Why not?" R'aisha demanded.

"Her place is here, if she leaves these people will look for her," Nusaybah almost hissed. "They will find her with us, we will be stopped, her fate will not be in our hands, they will stone her."

"I thought you were the fearless fighter, the one who shows no fear when standing beside your triumphant warlord," said R'aisha. This now became the moment of truth, up to this point there had been no mention of who Nusaybah was or the reason why she travelled to Al-Masjid an-Nabawi.

Nusaybah was dumbstruck, her estranged merchant husband Zayd ibn Asim himself owned two slaves, Nusaybah had no burning issues regarding the ownership of slaves, it was just the way things were – but what staggered Nusaybah more was that this R'aisha bint Benim was not who she said, she was no simple marketplace seller. Nusaybah realised, with dread, that she had been deceived and misled.

"Gather your possessions together Abaya while it is still dark, at first light daybreak you come with us," said R'aisha. Abaya at first looked uneasy, as if she was weighing up the risks, then her face beamed with a grin, the one-time slave had decided to be free.

Khaled bin Al-Tarif took one long look at the self-proclaimed prophet who had donned his finest warlord ropes. Al-Tarif felt ill at ease in this newfound role as Muhammad's second-in-command, his increasing disdain for the I'slāmic beliefs he had once relished put him at odds not just with the one hundred tribesmen Muhammad had gathered to seek out A'lisha Amjad bint Saleh, but with the multitudes of Muslim fighters encamped at Al-Masjid an-Nabawi. They knew little of what had happened, why he was here, their views were coloured by rumours and untruths.

What *had* happened was phenomenal. Gabriel listened to the redoubtable R'aisha bint Benim, Al-Tarif's ex-wife who, it turned out, was also known as Halimah bint Abi Dhuayb and numerous other names. When R'aisha was Abi Dhuayb, she had raised the delinquent teenage Muhammad ibn Abdullah following his mother Āminah bint Wahb's death, when Muhammad was six years old. Before Abi Dhuayb the young Muhammad had been nurse-maided by the Abyssinian slave Umm Ayman whom Abi Dhuayb had freed. Throughout his younger life, Muhammad had been surrounded by, and lived by slaves. R'aisha bint Benim's compromise demands to Gabriel and Muhammad were simple.

Muhammad was the first to acknowledge that Abi Dhuayb's teachings influenced his beliefs in his new emboldened faith – Abi Dhuayb's prophecy that Muhammad would one day receive divine messages from Al-Ilāh through his mighty angel Gabriel had proved incongruous and correct. Little wonder that Muhammad's entire world changed when he learned who R'aisha bint Benim was.

The devout promises made by Gabriel and his warlord to R'aisha bint Benim were far-reaching and agreed to be set in stone. First, inside the faith of I'slām, women would become sanctified, equal to men in men's eyes - they would be protected, allowed the same rights, hallowed by their husbands, fathers and brothers. There was great demurring among Muhammad's tribesmen when they heard this from Raisha's mouth. Furthermore, in Muhammad's proposed crusades, there were to be no more captives summarily beheaded or sold as slaves. Then there was R'aisha's final demand – Muhammad would be the last of Gabriel's prophets.

To keep an eye on the triumphant excesses of the warlord's tribesmen against their defeated enemies, Khaled bin Al-Tarif would be the warlord's second-in-command. Muhammad at first did not agree, he reacted with vehement verbal abuse then, after some scheming deliberation, he came to understand his choices were few. Gabriel, for his inane hidden reasons, agreed without thought or hesitation. R'aisha knew that each one of these promises was whispering thin, they were insincere, they would not last.

Meanwhile, A'lisha busied herself with disappearing. Unknown to R'aisha she vanished, her burden complete – in the west there was Byzantine Christian violence to be undone. R'aisha by now was gone, she slipped away in the middle of the night with no word of goodbye, even to Al-Tarif.

To Al-Tarif it was a whirlwind of confusion. He was treated with a good deal of disdain, more so by Muhammad and his close-knit circle of confidants and friends – Al-Tarif was in no doubt he would have to work hard to win his spurs, fight for the respect he deserved. It would not be easy.

The truth Al-Tarif felt deep inside. It was not in man's nature to seek peace; man had no sense of equality even to each other – in these circumstances finding equality for women and those ensnared by slavery would be nigh on impossible. Like R'aisha, Al-Tarif doubted the sincerity of Gabriel and Muhammad's promises, violence was endemic in man's inherent nature, it would always be so. Al-Tarif had seen many instances of the viciousness of victorious armies, tribal rivalry, death over the simple issue of water drawn from a well, the conflicts arising of different faiths, different colours of skin. Al-Tarif had been warned, he must guard his back, his life would be short-lived, the vengeance of his rivals would one day succeed.

Al-Tarif sat under the starlight of the cold night - nighttime in the desert lands was never warm. The ageing tribal warrior, the simple Bedouin shepherd, made a straightforward decision. By sunrise, he too would be gone. He had no time for this last of all the prophets, the one who called himself Muhammad.

At first daylight, when the sun's rays for some reason seemed subdued, R'aisha stood to leave. She waited, there was no sign of the young slave girl called Abaya. Abaya was dead, her throat cut by the land-owning farmer who found his slave gathering her meagre possessions right at the time he demanded his midnight fleshly pleasure. R'aisha turned to Nusaybah when she realised the grim reality of the day ahead - by this time Nusaybah's bitterness had simmered, it brimmed over when she grasped how her blabbering marketplace companion was no low-born peasant - she was the same beggar woman who had defiled her divine masters' sanctum alongside the Bedouin scum who called himself Khaled bin Al-Tarif. Nusaybah had been hoaxed, she had been lured, belittled by this woman who even now did not reveal her true name. Nevertheless, Nusaybah had made the right guess.

In the rising half-dawn of pale insipid daylight, R'aisha waited a few moments for Abaya before her fateful intuition took hold. Abaya would not be coming, never would she be free, not in this living world thought R'aisha to herself wryly.

R'aisha became lost in her contemplative thoughts - one of her rare moments when her usual impenetrable guard was down. R'aisha died a sudden and quick death, the one she had expected all along, death by a woman's hand, the death inscribed upon the granite rock obelisk. Nusaybah's delicate knife blade had found its lethal mark.

Out in the desert, the *Banu Amir* tribeswoman A'lisha Amjad bint Saleh felt the ripple of shock in the air. Her sister R'aisha was dead. For a few moments, A'lisha looked down to the hard stony ground in her version of remorseful silence before yanking the reins of her wild pony to continue her journey west. Towards the shimmering horizon, where at every nightfall the sun escaped the ravages of the bloodthirsty madness that was man.

5

T he winter storm worsened. Snow fell in blankets of thick white mist that in a small moment of time smothered the whole of everything. Remorseless evergreen forest stretched into unbounded perpetuity, impenetrable to the human eye - but to the renegade traitor this meant nothing, his immediate world ranged to the limit of his vision in the mutinous blizzard that threatened to engulf him. Isca'riot shivered in agonising confusion – his life was not meant to end like this, his vow was not yet complete, the turncoat betrayer who was Yehudas Isca'riot could not imagine how this might be his time to die.

Through the murderous snowstorm, Isca'riot thought he could see the outlines of what might be the lost track, the obscure path through the wall of trees smothered in layers of white snowflakes. Until now, Isca'riot had not experienced snow in his entire life, Isca'riot's habitual homeland was the hot, arid semi-desert scrubland of Judaea, far away from this cold northern wilderness that was alien to his inner existence. Yehudas could not take this, this horrendous white storm was nothing like his determined alter-ego had warned him – he would have to fight for his survival; within a fraction of one second it struck Isca'riot that, before he was able to move a few more paces in this waist deep snowdrift, he would die. He would die fast - his senses were by this time beginning to shut down.

Isca'riot, with decreasing determination, forced himself onwards, by lifting each of his legs one at a time from the freezing cold depth - his torn leather leggings saturated by frozen snow. Meanwhile, the cold wind blew harder, cutting through his thin tunic wrap, driving the blizzard against him. Yehudas

287

kept going, a little at a time, making sure his precious knapsack was strapped firm to his tired bent-over back. His drive to live began to dissipate, to evaporate like the swirling mist before his bloodshot eyes. Isca'riot fell, with difficulty he climbed from the snowdrift that threatened to become his final frozen grave, his tomb. Isca'riot looked up into the driving snowstorm, through his squinted, unfocused eyes – he thought he saw a light, a light that beckoned – to Isca'riot it must be the light of death, gesticulating and luring him into what seemed to Yehudas to be his one salvation – an end to the exhausting hypothermic pain that was killing him. Yehudas turned, he crawled, his hands and knees sinking deep into the virgin white coldness. His eyes peeled back, they bulged. Then came the welcome blackness...

When Isca'riot woke, his mind climbed from the total numbness that had overwhelmed him. The flickering flames and joyful warmth of the nearby fire licked the pinewood ceiling of wherever it was he now was. Isca'riot did not know, his senses would not tell him – though he knew he was no longer at the mercy of the threatening snowstorm. The old wrinkled babushka, she lifted his head, Isca'riot tasted the hot brown liquid the woman poured into his resisting throat, he swallowed in choking splutters. In no time, in a tiny moment, Yehudas felt weak strength return to his lifeless limbs. The dim light of the log shack was lit by one single candle and the flickering flames of the grated fire.

"Who are you?" croaked Isca'riot, startled. He gasped for breath.

The woman made no reply, nor did she look in Isca'riot's direction. She appeared indifferent, giving no indication of why she ignored him – or if she was the one that saved him.

The babushka, she was dressed in torn layered rags in every way more appropriate for the cold than Isca'riot's tattered tunic. Over her rags, she wore a shouldered cloak of foul-smelling fur, bear or wolfskin, Isca'riot could not tell. Her furs' rich brown thickness was inviting, worn to ward off the perils of coldness that Isca'riot's much-travelled goatskins could never even begin to contend with. The cabin was warm, safe, inviting, it stank of stale habitation and thick woodsmoke.

"Who are you?" Isca'riot one more time begged, once more the wrinkled, weather-faced babushka did not answer, the old woman's manner did not promise much. In sudden panic Isca'riot sought to find his precious knapsack, he raised himself to look around, it was there, hanging on the rough-hacked door, its precious contents still safe – though Isca'riot was anxious to check for the urn of ashes – her bones, the spiked nails and pendant cross wrapped inside were dry, not ruined by the killer snowstorm hours before. Isca'riot could still fulfil his promise, his pledge to the woman he had betrayed – never in his life should he be labelled a traitor. The babushka poked the fire, it burst into a towering flame then in a moment died back. She placed one more tree log into the fire's inner core, her hand into the flame, her hand did not burn. Isca'riot watched astonished, Yehudas thought he might be going insane.

"Talk to me old woman," he watched her take her hand from the fire, she had suffered no pain. One more time she ignored him, he wanted to thank her for saving his life. Outside, the wind rattled and roared.

Three days later the storm abated, Isca'riot had given up trying to communicate with the babushka, he spent the long hours of northern darkness regaining his strength. Daylight came every day in one stark short stretch, an insipid lack of darkness that created a surreal twilight which Isca'riot was not used to – his land of incessant sun and hot days was in mind-blowing contrast to this miserable daily existence in the cold north. But here, somewhere, was the ancient stone, the monolith he had promised to find. For three precarious years, Isca'riot had trekked his way north, following meandering riverbeds and forest tracks; in the early days the shoreline of the great black sea, all the time avoiding thieves and violent human contact. At this moment in time, Isca'riot had no idea where he was, he could have been a thousand leagues from his destination – Yehudas had no way of knowing. Isca'riot carried no map, just a vague outline of the directions she had given. 'Go north, to the vast northern forest, bury my bones beneath the ancient stone' was everything she had said. Isca'riot guessed he might be somewhere close to where the obelisk should be but, in this hard cruel arctic winter, his first task was to survive – and without the old, withered babushka woman, he would be dead.

"In my land, I am a despised traitor," Isca'riot let out in frustration after another long day in the warmth of the small ramshackle log shack. *The babushka did not answer, nor did she look or give any signs that she understood or would ever reply. Her manner was one of complete indifference.* "I never loved any woman, only the woman I betrayed," *he added, hoping the old woman would listen. Outside, the snowstorm had long blown itself out, though from time to time the door rattled in some strange way that made the babushka look up, her face riddled with fear.*

"The messiah, my loyal friend, he died because of my betrayal. They spiked him to the wooded stake until he breathed his last breath but he did not die." Isca'riot did not know if she listened, he reasoned her language was not his own. There could not be a way that she understood what he said. *"She died because of my treachery,"* he confided in contorted desperation – the babushka heaped more wood onto the fire, she hooked on the cooking pot to the overhanging wire, another broth of rabbit and unknown vegetables spiced with pine leaves – though Isca'riot by now knew that she would eat none herself.

"When I left my homeland, I first travelled east to the Salt Sea," Isca'riot continued, telling her of his momentous journey as if she wanted to hear. *"I knew they were trying to find me, the messiah's followers, the apostles, his disciples. They condemned me for what I had done. I went north into the valley of the river Jordan, into the land of Samaria. When I came to the land of Galilee there was the Lake of Galilee; the Romans there tried to kill me. I escaped, every day I headed north. I came to the land of the Phoenicians, those despot people who know no God...?"*

The babushka, she did not listen, almost as if she had no interest in the story of a traitorous renegade who was running scared, a man whose soul had turned against him. She went about her business with the steaming pot, the contents of which Isca'riot consumed with eager hunger – the babushka did not watch him gulp down the rabbit gruel, perhaps the appetite of a starving man reminded her of men who were not to be trusted, their place at the table signifying their dominance in the hierarchy of starvation and famine. The old woman, once more she did not eat.

"Why do you not take your food?" Isca'riot looked into the pot to see what

was left. The pot was clean, unblemished by the taint of cooked food. There was nothing in it. It then struck Yehudas like a hammer that he was in a dream – for all he knew in his death dream – he was near to death buried in the snow tomb that had three days ago engulfed him. Panic overwhelmed him. Isca'riot forced himself to snap out of it, remembering the messiah's miracle of the five loaves and fishes, realising that not everything was what it seemed. The messiah, his friend, they say he died screaming in pain.

Isca'riot cried, trying to accept that he was dead. His sobbing tears fell into his bowl of cooling broth, the morsels of rabbit meat congealing in the thickening fat and grease. The measly, inedible pine leaves that Isca'riot had left to one side on his plate left no room for mercy.

The old woman looked at him, she stared. "You cannot bury her bones beneath the ancient stone," she said, unexpected, in Isca'riot's own tongue. "Here in the north this land is frozen. In the wintertime, you cannot break the soil. You must wait, wait here with me, until the sun warms the foul earth that spawned you."

Isca'riot gasped, then shook in uncontrolled shock. His lips trembled without reply, more so when the old babushka looked into the cooking pot. Her stinking bedraggled grey hair fell across her eyes – which she flipped away with a toss of her hand in a way that Isca'riot knew all too well...

Yehudas Isca'riot

Magdalen squatted down on the rocky ground trampled bare in the sweltering heat of the hostile crowd. What could she do? She had not foreseen this, she had not expected the bitter betrayal of Isca'riot nor the terrible wrath that now played out before her tearful eyes. Magdalen, pariah of the twelve apostles, needed time, time to conserve her strength, time to find a way she might survive - in the deep depths of her weeping torment, Magdalen knew that time in the insanity of this promised land was a blessing she did not possess.

On the tip of the barren hill, behind the ring of Romans who gripped their spears with growing unease, the preacher was dying. Magdalen could feel his pain, she felt the anguish inside his heart - the storyteller from Naz'areth had now reached the pinnacle of his evangelical existence. In his last days he had morphed beyond her expectations, he had grown into the maniacal blasphemer, the rebel, the fanatical disciple of God undone by what Magdalen had revealed to him.

With the afternoon sun beating down like a magnified prism of hot glass, Magdalen concealed herself within the menacing hoards growing ever more restless as the day of intense drama wore on, she made herself scarce, she knelt on her knees consumed by her quick-thinking mind. Magdalen, bewitching in her simplistic demeanour gazed upon the gruesome scene knowing she must not succumb to the tragedy unfolding in the sweltering chaos of the mob-driven madness. The renegade preacher loved her, Magdalen knew this beyond question – she knew because inside her womb their embryonic twins grew slow and magnificent. Isca'riot, knowing the implications, had acted with desperate intent. Now, hour by hour, the rebel Magdalen cherished was dying in pain on the dirt-encrusted hilltop; perhaps this was his long-prophesied demise, the fate etched and written upon the ancient stone. The barbarous soul of mankind was opening its wounds for one last time – the preacher's destiny lay in his own bloodstained hands.

The mood of the baying crowd worsened to the edge of violence, it struck Magdalen what she should do – first she must preserve her existence then nurture her long-planned revenge. There was nothing she could make happen, not yet, not until the preacher was cut down from the stake to which he was spiked. Neither Shem'ayon now Peter, the Baptist or Shem'ayon of Kananaios were of use to her now, nor the others, they were powerless in their grieving anguish; their wretched tears staining the dry parched earth where they knelt. She watched, seeing each of them wail in their abject compassion. From this day forward she must once more rely upon her instincts, her forthright passion, her strength that weakened as each day passed. Magdalen knew that soon her own end would begin, when the birth of her unborns was done. Even so, in her heart, she relished in the power of who she was, she was one and the same, she would each time rise in the image of her creation. In the endless evolution of her mind, Magdalen was Lilith the seductress and Bath'sheba, she was Jerusha and the fabled H'elena of Troy. She was Elenoras, Tabith'a the Concubine and Ruth the faithful unbeliever, she was the glorious T'amar and the unredeemable Shiph'rah of the Gentile Jews. Through her bloodline and the embryos she nursed her spirit would be reborn. She would be both Miriam and Boudicca, Joan D'Arc the scourge of the catholic kings and the ruthless A'lisha of the *Banu Amir*, she would be Sacagawea and the undefinable queen who gave her life to conquer the darkness of the eighth king. Magdalen's lifeblood would become the insane Susanna of the Finns, the orphan child Moon and one day the tyrannical Tonia-Celese who in her own way rallied the dead. In the essence of time, she would be the magnificent Samantha Hon and all the tragic newborns who would be slaughtered and killed. And one infinite distant day from now, in another time, she would be Princess Amobea, immortal Amobea who in the end defeated the Lesser Lords. Magdalen, the glorious Magdalena, the woman of many sins who time before was Hyvah, Lilith, Ḥawwāh or, to the fair-skinned men of the north, Eve.

Nighttime descended upon the desolate rock-ravaged moonscape of Je'rusalem, the long grey shadows of twilight creating strange illusions of ghostly demure as the day of disreputable circumstance faded. Yosef of Arim'athea, torn by all-consuming grief, knew his impending task. The Romans possessed the dead body of the preacher and they must give it up. Even in the gloomy darkness of the prison hallway, Yosef could see how the elite guards who had taken the wretched body down from the stake were uncertain of what to do, they waited with impatience for their centurion to give his orders. The centurion Peleus was with Pontius Pilate and they were in deep conversation, Yosef saw Peleus arguing with the supreme Prefect. Then with sudden purpose, the centurion returned to his men who straightaway pointed Yosef out. The centurion beckoned Yosef to come forward. Yosef, his heart thumping inside his head, approached Peleus with uncertainty, not knowing if he would be listened to or even struck down.

"Sir, my humble task is to request the three dead men to whom you have delivered your Roman justice." His anxiety born of near sixty years lessened when he saw that Peleus at least listened. Yosef of Arim'athea, one of the more moderate priests of the Yehudiish Sanhedrin, had taken it upon himself to give the dead preacher the respect he deserved. He felt apprehensive, he had made a sincere promise to Shimon, known as Kephas or Shem'ayon now Peter, to return the preacher's body. "It is the custom of our people that souls of convicted men be given up to our great Lord in heaven the night after they died."

"Yes, I know the ways of your people," Peleus replied, his abruptness a measure of the impatience for which he was well known - the centurion took it upon himself never to suffer fools. "My men will deliver their bodies before the sun rises."

"I thank you, sir, our women will take care of them, they must anoint their bodies." Yosef tried hard to be magnanimous though he could not help but feel anger towards the centurion who had ordered the penalties of death against the three condemned Judaeans.

Peleus stared at Yosef for a moment, as if trying to choose his words with care. The centurion had not relished his task earlier in the day, he knew beyond doubt that one of the men crucified had committed no crime other than not repent the spurious allegations against him. Both himself and Pontius Pilate had tried in vain not to carry out the sentence of death demanded by the Judaean senate. The Sanhedrin had claimed this man believed himself to be the son of their God - the passionate crowd that gathered on the first day of Passover were extreme in their belief - this man should die by crucifixion, the worse form of execution reserved for the foulest criminals. Pontius Pilate offered another criminal in place of the Judaean who had committed no Roman crime. This was not enough, the Judaeans demanded the storyteller's death. The steadfast Peleus was concerned - though it was not even this unwarranted event that for some reason rattled him. As the day of high drama had unravelled, what played upon his mind more than anything was the ragged woman who had remained at the side of this supposed messiah when the high priests of the Sanhedrin demanded the rebel should carry the stake upon which he would die. Even now, in the cool evening air, he recalled the beguiling scene in his mind while this man Yosef of Arim'athea stood before him begging for the return of the three executed men for their symbolic Yehudiish burials.

It was this single moment for Peleus. When his men forced the woman to part from what appeared to be her man, or perhaps her lover, her dark unkempt hair had fallen across her face to hide uncommon grey-blue eyes. Passions ran high, the crowd were in a frenzied state, but this woman by the side of their messiah did not resist or plead or even cry tears like the others - with an ambiguous look in her eye, she had turned to look straight at himself, Peleus of Andante, the commander of the Roman legions in Judaea, the one who had given the orders for the sentence of death to proceed. She stared at him, then cleared her hair from her eyes with a casual toss of her hand to give him a long purposeful glance that penetrated deep into his thoughts. It was this small insignificant gesture that seemed to show a deliberate calmness, that it was she who was in control.

Her momentary gaze had touched somewhere deep inside Peleus which he, the confident and often brutal centurion even now could not explain. It had for some unfathomable reason unnerved him. The woman, dressed in a simple ruby-red robe, did not wail out of control or cling to the condemned prisoner like others from the crowd, but whispered something in the prisoner's ear over and over. Peleus had watched mesmerised, curious, unable to avert his gaze. This man Yeshua of Naz'areth, the so-called Judaean dissident who the Sanhedrin said had confessed to being the new king of the Yehudiish people, the deliverance of their God, seemed to grow in strength, to gain a visible stature that appeared to go unnoticed by everyone. But to him, Peleus, the centurion who had risen through the ranks of Roman generals because of his ability to notice such small detail, it was significant. All through the day this single event played upon his clear-cut mind, plaguing him without him knowing why. Then, later in the evening, when the condemned men who died were in the end finished, he again saw the same woman - he saw that not once did she approach the Judaean's body after he was taken down from the stake upon which he had been crucified. She searched, picked something from the ground then turned to stare at him once more, before turning her back to walk away. It was as if she held some strange destiny in her womanly hands.

And now there was this concerning news given to him by his guards. A grave problem of far-reaching consequences. But he decided not to act at once or even convince Pontius Pilate to intervene. His honed instincts deep within him made him wait, he felt sure this woman who intrigued him was woven like a web into these strange events he did not yet understand. There would be another way.

"Are you Yosef of Arim'athea?" Peleus asked.

"Yes, I am."

"Then it is best that you take these executed men away during the time of darkness. This way you will avoid these bloodthirsty Yehudiish, the ones who desired your so-called messiah dead," Peleus replied with authority, wishing to dismiss what was done and the aftermath that was bound to follow. The ageing centurion, with his close-cropped grey beard and clean-shaven head looked uneasy, betraying the thoughts racing through his mind.

"Sir, the mothers of the two thieves who were convicted under your Roman laws, they will take care of their own dead. The apostles will take the body of their messiah. Their womenfolk will be here soon," said Yosef with more confidence. This centurion seemed to be affable despite his infamous reputation.

"Will the dark-haired woman in the ruby cloak be among them?" Peleus asked.

Yosef paused. He did not expect this strange question. "Yes, I think she will," he replied with caution. He thought quickly about how to respond. "Why do you ask this?" Yosef straightaway felt he had perhaps overstepped his mark. The centurion looked at him with some discomfort, with a measure of displeasure

"Who is she?" Peleus demanded, ignoring Yosef's question.

"Sir, she is called Marusya. Marusya Magdalen, she hails from the Heb'rew township of Magdala, in Galilee beside the shores of the Dead Sea." Yosef felt uneasy. Why did he want to know about Magdalen?

"What is her relationship with this so-called messiah?"

This was the question Yosef did not want. Nor to answer. Ordered by the high priest Caiaphas to follow the self-proclaimed preacher from Naz'areth during his storytelling and miracles amongst the Judaean people, he himself was not part of Yeshua's inner friends, the supposed disciples or dedicated believers, he was a low priest of the Yehudiish Great Sanhedrin but, for his inane reasons, he desired a fitting end to these unsavoury events of which he did not approve. He, Yosef of Arim'athea, was struck by this Yeshua born in Beth'lehem and his preachings but did not want to confess that he also felt uneasy with this woman, that although she was at first treated with some disdain by the messiah's followers, as were most of the women who tried to show their devotion to their preacher, this Magdalen woman seemed to hold some hidden strength. She did not mix or associate with the other women or try her luck with the men, she held her own company on the fringes of the group. Yet Yeshua had been drawn to her, he seemed to seek her more and more. Yosef too had found the woman compelling in a beguiling way that he could not explain; she was not well-kept or dressed by any standards of wealth; just the same ragged ruby cloak with the chain and small ornate cross she wore around her neck every day, the cloak unwashed and torn; shabby and discoloured by the Judaean sun.

"Sir, I do not think there was anything between this woman and the one claimed to be the chosen messiah. Why do you ask this?"

Peleus once more ignored Yosef's question. "The bodies of the three crucified will be outside of this door before sunrise. Have them taken away while there is darkness. When you have the body of your messiah you must act with speed." Peleus said this because two things played upon his mind. First, he sensed how this Magdalen woman was far more important than this man Yosef of Arim'athea admitted, and of even more foreboding, an unsettling problem concerning the dissident Yeshua of Naz'areth had since arisen, one that would grow to haunt the seasoned centurion as time passed.

Peleus turned to walk away from Yosef, leaving the ageing and ample-proportioned Yehudiish priest of the Sanhedrin standing mystified. It was Peleus's responsibility to ensure that all lawbreakers condemned to die were disposed of without ceremony once they were dead, the Romans themselves could burn the crucified remains from this dark day of retribution but Peleus and Pontius Pilate, the supreme Prefect of the Roman province of Judaea had made the decision to return all three bodies to the Judaeans without grace. Pontius Pilate had washed his hands of the rebel storyteller's death; his instincts were to let this distasteful Judaean saga now play out to its conclusion. Peleus, after deep thought and deliberation, had decided to proceed by allowing the crucified Yeshua of Naz'areth to be returned to the Sanhedrin because, he suspected, this woman in the ruby cloak would then cross his path again. To Peleus, this whole unsavoury situation was an unfinished business that had not yet reached its intriguing end.

Magdalen entered through the ornate doorway of the senate hall knowing that no women were allowed inside the forbidden citadel of the Yehudiish temple. This was the revered seat of religious power where God and heaven entwined with the chosen people. This did not concern her. Magdalen made her way along dark passageways that for good reason struck vague, haunting memories of another time. She then moved without sound down the longest of the corridors lit only by undefinable shadows before turning into the small hallway. The dank hall with walls adorned by ancient hieroglyphics familiar to Magdalen led to another doorway towards the end of the passage. There was the small matter of the guard, but she located what she sought, she found the high priest Caiaphas and Yehudas Isca'riot arguing between themselves in the half-lit back room of the temple. In the gloom beyond the doorway, the bareness of the walls was struck by a single ray of sunlight that seeped through the small window beneath the high roof. The light in the room was just visible. At first, the two engrossed men did not notice her; they were engaged in heated conversation, arguing in whispers in case their talk could be overheard. Isca'riot seemed emotional while Caiaphas's pained face betrayed the anxiety of the past few days; the incessant weariness etched into his furrowed brow half hidden by the hood of his layered green cloak that highlighted his stature of high rank. Isca'riot looked up, he was the first to see Magdalen. He froze in horror.

Caiaphas, seeing her, leapt to his feet unable to contain his rage at this fundamental of forbidden intrusions. In the back of his mind, he half-recognised Magdalen whereas Isca'riot knew full well who she was. It was Caiaphas who admonished her while Isca'riot stood quite still, for a moment unable to form a cohesive thought in his head.

"Woman, leave now. This place is sacrosanct, no woman should ever be here," screamed Caiaphas in uncontrolled temper, his face contorted with outright indignation, he spat saliva because of his inability to control his rage. He then yelled for his aide-de-camp guard who stood before the outer doorway. How had this woman bypassed the best of his armed guards?

"Your guard is distracted. He is not there," Magdalen replied, the calmness of her voice adding a distinct chillness to the nighttime air. The guard was dead, felled by a simple wound that drew no blood.

Isca'riot reacted in panic by running past Magdalen, through the doorway, forcing her out of the way. He found the guard lying beyond the second door. Isca'riot looked up, he stared back at Magdalen.

It dawned upon both Isca'riot and Caiaphas how they had no control over this sudden situation - the intolerable intrusion of this woman at once held a different meaning. Meanwhile, Magdalen reached inside her cloak, she pulled out something held inside, revealing her open palm to Caiaphas. She showed him three bloody pieces of rough-hewn iron, the sharp rustic skewers that had nailed her lover to his wooden stake only a few hours before.

"Do you see these Caiaphas, high priest of you chosen people?" Magdalen hissed with undisguised venom. "Do you know what they are? Do you realise what you have done? You have done more than deal your miserable justice to your supposed messiah, the one who you say claimed to be the son of your god. You have unleashed Lucifer himself from Gabriel's inferno hell. From this day there is a new damnable faith upon this world and you, the people of Judaea who claim to be god's chosen will suffer damnation," she stared at Caiaphas with piercing destain. "With these spikes now in my hand you condemned a man you desired dead for your own foul reasons."

Caiaphas was silent, unable to speak, unable to comprehend what was happening in the dark gloom of the temple room in which they all stood. He stared at the twisted nails Magdalen held in her hand, then at her. He knew what they were but why was this woman bringing them to him now? Isca'riot, regaining his composure intervened, breaking the silence. He spoke with a voice of cool reasoning laced with extreme unease.

"Marusya, why are you here? This temple is sacrosanct, the high priests, they have the will to harm you for being in this place. Why do you break the law? These people will punish you. And the guard..." Isca'riot broke off. Once more he tried to comprehend this deteriorating situation.

"Is this not the same rot-ridden place where Caiaphas's guards overpowered and took your preacher from Naz'areth when he came here just six days ago?" Magdalen challenged. "Is this where they beat then bloodied his sacred body under the eye of his supposed spiritual father?" She glared at Isca'riot with piercing eyes. This was the man who had backstabbed the people's revered preacher, the rat rewarded by Caiaphas and the Sanhedrin court of high priests to bring Yeshua to his knees. They had contrived Yeshua's death; they had beaten him for the false confession Caiaphas had then waved in the air triumphant.

Isca'riot realised he needed to show quick thinking in what was a dangerous and deteriorating situation; his misunderstood act of betrayal had put a huge weight upon his shoulders which served to deepen the anxious anxiety he felt over his role in Yeshua's death.

"Marusya, you of all people know our beloved preacher Yeshua was not who we believed him to be. He could have avoided his death by confessing he was not the promised messiah, he could have saved himself," tears of excruciating frustration began to form in Isca'riot bloodshot eyes, he was well aware that to the whole of Judaea, he had betrayed the man he had tried beyond anything to love with his heart, but with each day that went by he had begun to discern the uncomfortable truth behind Yeshua's deteriorating mind, the inexplicable influence of Magdalen, an incomprehensible hold she excerpted that threatened everything he believed sacred. "Like me, the Sanhedrin know he is not the promised messiah, nor the son of our Lord, they are convinced he is not even descended from David. They do not believe the hearsay talk of this virgin birth through the mad woman in Beth'lehem. Even so, after all this, I loved him as the beloved preacher of our Great Lord in Heaven, who decreed the Yehudiish of Judaea his chosen people, I too witnessed the miracles, Marusya, but Yeshua cannot be the messiah who will return to save our people."

Isca'riot knew more, he knew that Magdalen carried Yeshua's child, he saw the awful implications that would follow. Anyone who might be the new messiah could not through sin father a child, a bastard son who might then lay claim to his name, *who could become the hereditary king of the Yehudiish people*. This had been the ultimate reason that persuaded Caiaphas and the Sanhedrin to act because a new emerging king of Judaea could be tolerated neither by themselves nor Rome. Caiaphas believed with his whole heart that Yeshua of Naz'areth was not the prophesied coming of their promised Lord, that this troublesome rebel maker must be stopped. The cruel betrayal of Yehudas Isca'riot was meant to not just protect the power of the Sanhedrin but to lessen the incomprehensible frenzy of the people of Judaea who believed Yeshua was the long-awaited prophet. Isca'riot himself had decided that he must be the one to take control of this intolerable disaster before Magdalen began to consolidate her blaspheming mastery over the chosen twelve - the close band of devoted believers who were dedicated to Yeshua.

Isca'riot could only guess why she had come among them - if she succeeded in her task then she would act to bring unbridled trouble to the Yehudiish of Judaea by incurring the wrath of Rome. For her own reasons, this heretical woman had set her heart upon Yeshua, there was the terrible prospect of Magdalen giving birth to a son more powerful than any of them could even imagine. Yeshua, or Yeh'oshua of Naz'areth as he was known by the unbelieving Pharisees, was not the promised messiah, of this Isca'riot was by now certain - but he was without question a mesmerising teacher of loving faith, perhaps a new preacher of the people delivered by God to lead them. But it had all gone wrong, a child of Yeshua would be a catastrophe of unforetold magnitude — and for this Yeshua had paid with his life. Caiaphas and the Sanhedrin were vehement in their belief that Yeshua was no more than a rebellious dissident, a chancer, a renegade preacher who caused deliberate trouble - the future of Judaea and the Lord's chosen people was more important than the fate of one single man or his lover - or the consequences that might follow.

If, as the Sanhedrin claimed, Yeshua was not the long-awaited messiah delivered by God his father, if he was no more than an unruly rebel, if the growing crowds of devoted believers who listened in awe and witnessed the impossible miracles were wrong then something more sinister had descended upon the people of Judaea to ravish their embellished lives. If Yeshua was not a deliverance of God, if he was no prophet of the Lord then who was this storytelling preacher from Naz'areth? How could this man make these miracles happen? Everything seemed to stem from this Magdalen woman - since her appearance among them the hysteria of the coming of the promised prophet had taken hold among the people.

But Isca'riot knew that Yeshua had never declared himself to be the son of God, his devout and cherished friend would never be foolish enough to utter such blasphemous words that would inflame the wrath of the powerful Sanhedrin, it was his following hoards who had made this embellished claim. In the final days before his betrayal of his friend, Isca'riot considered the loathsome prospect that Yeshua's newfound baptism to being the son of God was a figment of Magdalen's manipulative conniving, that this hellacious woman desired her newborn to be the appointed king of Judaea, that she had set herself the villainous task of propelling Yeshua to be the divine ruler of the Yehudiish people. This was Isca'riot's logical explanation, the reason why she had from nowhere appeared among them.

Recovering his composure, Isca'riot began to feel confident enough to confront this aberrant woman but saw that Magdalen herself grew in stature - he saw fire in her limpid grey-blue eyes he had not seen before.

"I know more than you declare of me Yehudas, the history of mortal men shall be the judge of you, not me," Magdalen ignored the still-mortified Caiaphas. "You are not wrong in what you say, your righteous Yeshua of Naz'areth is not your promised messiah, never did he claim to be the son of your god, not until he was beaten by this snake here to make a false confession," she pointed to Caiaphas without meeting his eyes. "Yeshua of Naz'areth is much more than these self-chosen priests of the Sanhedrin will ever know. You will one day understand what you have done Yehudas, you are the betrayer of the prophesied prophet of Judaea, your path is chosen." Magdalen sensed that she had both men in her hands, she turned to Caiaphas. "Know this you high priest of the abominable Sanhedrin.

Yeshua is a Lord of men because he is descended through Miryam, the daughter of Joa'chim, and the immortal Ha'nnah who are not of your house of David. He is descended by cruel death from the seed of Adamah, but not your Adamah, not the wonderful Adamah of your Heb'rew scriptures or those foul words of your prophet Ab'raham." Caiaphas's eyes widened in shocked disbelief

"You cannot say this," Isca'riot once more interceded, this time with more unforgiving resolve and with rising anger. "This is sacrilegious slander Marusya, you insult the descendant heritage of our Lord God." Isca'riot paused to choose his words with more care, he felt overwhelmed, suspecting that he was being drawn into something sinister that seethed high above his head, that his fragile world might soon come tumbling down. The same excruciating self-doubts that drove his insecurities in the days before his wretched act of betrayal came to the fore in his mind,

"I have thought long about you Marusya, for some time I have known that you are not who you claim to be," Isca'riot tried hard to keep his composure. "When Yeshua our Lord's preacher preached at Sabid and made the miracle there I saw you. I did not know you then, but I saw you. I saw you there, standing on the hill when the people began to cry out who our saviour might be. There was something strange about you, you watched him, and you knew. I saw you." Tears flowed down Isca'riot's face, passionate tears because it occurred to Isca'riot that Magdalen wielded far more strength of mind than he had ever imagined possible.

Caiaphas this time interrupted, breaking his shocked silence. "Woman, you must be silent and not speak these monstrous words. These are the words of a serpent. I will summon the temple guards," he tried to reassert his authority. "We can have you tried before trial for your blasphemous outrage and this will, I assure you, resolve this little problem we have with you. Your days are soon ended, you will pay for this intolerable outrage."

Isca'riot turned to Caiaphas to implore him not to make this confronta-tion worse. The high priest of the Sanhedrin did not understand the danger of this sudden situation, the fullness of events that would unfold. Isca'riot knew that Magdalen was not here for revenge, this was not her way, she had entered this citadel forbidden to women to show her power, that she did not care for the supremacy of Caiaphas, for the Sanhedrin nor for the righteous might of the Yehudiish chosen people. Isca'riot had long realised that Magdalen possessed unnatural ways, she was not of Judaea or even a Philistine, he knew this for sure, he had been forewarned about Magdalen, the whispered rumours told by those few who had tried to befriend her, that she was not who she made out to be. Every instinct within his body warned him of dire trouble that sent shivers of cold through his deteriorating mind.

Because Isca'riot knew more, much more, he knew because he suspected why Magdalen had come among them, why she had entwined herself to the unimpeachable preacher whom they all loved, a preacher whom the people were saying was born of the Holy Spirit. Since the appearance of Magdalen, the once joyous disciples were in disarray. In time, Yeshua had come to talk with him in absolute devastation, to confess to him his growing love for Magdalen. A passionate, deep and forever-lasting love that Yeshua could not deal with or even resist. It was a confused love that Yeshua himself could not reason.

But there was yet more, why Isca'riot sought the sanctified sanctuary of the Sanhedrin. Yeshua had told him in his state of mindful confusion something more abominable than Isca'riot could ever believe. Magdalen had told Yeshua that never was there an all-powerful Adamah created by God in his own image or anything like God's Garden of Eden. She claimed the world was not made in seven days. The scriptures and gospels of men were lies carved by men. Magdalen professed that God and the devil would one day be revealed not to be all-powerful. His dearest Marusya, Yeshua had confided in tears to Isca'riot, could never be vanquished because she was the beholder of all men, she had fallen upon him, entangling him to countenance the power of God his spiritual father. Isca'riot had listened in disbelief when Yeshua confessed from deep inside his deteriorating mind that he believed Marusya was linked through all men to the birth of time, an impossible claim that Isca'riot realised could not be true.

Isca'riot knew that Yeshua became confused and distraught. Yeshua desired the loving word of God, but God did not speak. Magdalen had told Yeshua that never would there be a promised messiah, nor a son of the holy spirit. When Yeshua and Magdalen made love only then, Yeshua told Isca'riot, did he realise the true purpose of his journey, his awful destiny, the reason why he was born into the world through his mother in Beth'lehem. Isca'riot had implored Yeshua to give up Magdalen, to forget her, to once again join the path of the chosen people, to be the new holy prophet, to love and behold God who might be his true father.

Then Yeshua had confessed to his faithful friend something damnable, that Marusya carried their infant child. Isca'riot was shocked, devastated, unable to contemplate the sudden collapse of his world. Isca'riot had no choice, he went to Caiaphas at the Sanhedrin, Isca'riot revealed everything to Caiaphas so that Yeshua would go to the temple to confess to the Sanhedrin - because Isca'riot believed the Sanhedrin alone could decide the insoluble truth, they possessed the true knowledge to understand God's ultimate word. Yeshua could then tell the Sanhedrin all the vile untruths that Magdalen claimed, the Sanhedrin would spell out the consequence of his immorality, his wrongful desires for the salacious Magdalen. The Sanhedrin could break her mind-bending witchery because Magdalen had convinced Yeshua of her ungodly way, a more sinister way, she said that all men from the beginning of existence had committed unholy sins in the name of their all-forgiving God. The evilness of man and of men who ruled all men could never be undone, Magdalen had convinced Yeshua that he was born more merciful than the God of men. This was too much for Isca'riot, this disreputable charade must end - in Isca'riot's eyes, both Yeshua and Magdalen must face the truthful righteousness of the mighty Sanhedrin.

But it had all gone wrong. Isca'riot did not see the deviousness of Caiaphas, Yeshua's tortured confession to the Sanhedrin, when Yeshua refused to disclaim being their promised messiah - the snare Caiaphas himself had set, his trap to rid Judaea of this dangerous rebel, this false prophet with his storytelling miracles. 'Are you the son of God our creator of every living thing?' Caiaphas had demanded from Yeshua under torturing pain. 'If you say I am,' Yeshua had replied, with his blood-ridden face a testament to their violence and their festering fear. But Caiaphas, supreme high priest of the Yehudiish Sanhedrin had not foreseen the snare that Yeshua himself had set, that death in the eyes of the Ju'deans would make the preacher immortal, that Yeshua's apostles would create their icon image among the people who never believed in the power of the Sanhedrin. A cruel rebellion of faith in the promised land.

"Caiaphas, please hold your tongue," Isca'riot implored, turning to the high priest. "You must believe this woman can cause untold trouble for both of us though I suspect that is not why she is here." He again turned to Magdalen. "Both Caiaphas and I know that you carry Yeshua's child, our beloved teacher Yeshua of Naz'areth confessed everything. Also, that you are not of our Heb'rew faith," he said. "Our holy preacher died by the Sanhedrin's hand today because he would not deny the people's claim of being the son of God, our chosen messiah and the King of the Yehudiish, yet he knew this not to be true. He was made to make a false confession; he was beaten by the Sanhedrin guards, but this was not how I believed the Sanhedrin would act. It now dawns upon me like a mighty hammer blow laid against my head, like a sword thrust into my heart. I did not foresee that he would die the beggars' death he died today. He deceived all of us Marusya, he used the Sanhedrin for his own reasons. He chose death to protect you and your unborn child."

Magdalen smiled a small measure of benevolence, "Caiaphas here committed a dishonourable deed for his people today," the glint in her eye belied her sense of victory. "The so-called disciples, the apostles who preach Yeshua's love, those faithful followers who believe in his endearing miracles will each go out to teach his forgiveness. They will forever tell of what happened today. Do not doubt that yet one more worshipping faith will soon be upon you, yet another new denomination of powerful men will grow upon this forsaken land to worship the crucified Yeshua's image you the Sanhedrin have created. In time, men who seek their revenge will rise against you who claim to be the chosen people, then this wretched temple created by men to worship worthless scriptures written by men that are only beheld by men will fall in ruin. Where will your god be to help you then? Do you expect your god to every time choose your side? Will your wretched god stand by you when men inflict yet more death upon men in his forsaken name?"

Magdalen fell silent for just a moment, feeling that she needed to choose her words with care. She saw that both men stood transfixed before her, their minds silent in subliminal submission. Magdalen turned to the grey-faced Caiaphas. "Such disciples of Yeshua that you have created will walk far, they will go into the distant corners of every land to preach his love and their anger, then the revenge of the new order will one day be overwhelming for you the Yehudiish people, much more than anything I can ever make happen. The cruel seed of fate you create has been well set, do not doubt this my dear Caiaphas." Magdalen again paused, this time to draw her breath but with fire still burning in her eyes.

She turned to Isca'riot, pointing to Caiaphas in outward defiance. "Dishonourable Caiaphas here, with his abominable threat to destroy both me and my unborn does not cause me to quake in fear as he thinks I should, because his days will soon be finished by the side of those of the Sanhedrin. Though I will say this to you, not by my hand will he die." Magdalen hissed her words with outward venom. She glared straight at Isca'riot, piercing into his eyes while he still stood silent. The ice-cold atmosphere of the room bore little resemblance to the dank warm air outside the ancient temple, the residual heat of the long day offering no respite to the desperate confrontation that unfolded. Beyond the room in which they stood, in the darkness of the corridor where the guard still lay lifeless and stone-cold dead, black rats scurried and sniffed with deliberate intrusion, sensing some new fear in the minds of all living men.

"I will say this to you, you the betrayer," Magdalen tempered her voice to offer a small hint of benevolence, "I am here in this vile place forbidden to women to lay claim to you, for I am not done with you yet, not yet, not while you have one last breath in your beating breast."

"What are you saying Marusya?" pleaded Isca'riot, his senses in turmoil.

"I have long known of you Yehudas Isca'riot, much more than you know. You followed your esteemed preacher with all your heart until you decided by some will to act against him," her passionate voice remained cool and calm in the stillness of the half-lit room. "Do you not yet know that he gave you no choice but to betray him? When you chose your path for a mere pittance in silver? You did not foresee Yeshua's death but this snake Caiaphas here did," Magdalen again pointed with defiance at Caiaphas who still stood silent. "He desired Yeshua seized and tried before the Sanhedrin for his life. When Herod and Pontius Pilot both declared him not guilty of any Roman crime Caiaphas here still demanded death by crucifixion, a death by the Roman way and not one of Judaea. Yeshua always knew this would be so, he was never a fool Yehudas." The passion in Magdalen's chilling voice was overwhelming, "I did not expect your betrayal, not yet, but I knew it would come one day. And I did not foresee that Caiaphas here, with his dreadful Sanhedrin, would see to it for the Romans to crucify the man who came to save all of you. Nor did I expect that even Peter would abandon Yeshua in his time of distress, but you told Peter did you not? You told Peter that I carry Yeshua's infant child." In some dark distant corner of the great temple, there came the long wail of a call to prayer, a ritualistic pleading of worship for God to save them, a passionate plea that would forever go unanswered.

"Yes, I did. But not the others. Peter was devastated, Marusya, though from fear for his life he vowed to stay silent. Once Yeshua told me who he thought you might be, the heretic lies you told him, I begged him to give you up or, if not, to renounce the people's claim that he was our new messiah, the saviour of mankind even if he was not the seed of our Lord. But he would not, even though he knew he would die by the Romans who would never tolerate any new king of Judaea in their midst. But, like you say, Pontius Pilate did not believe one word extracted by brutal torture about the return of our saviour or wish to cause any uprising within Judaea, you saw this today Marusya. The Sanhedrin begged Pontius Pilate to do their dirty deed, a public crucifixion for everyone to see. The Romans have their own false Gods with no desire to acknowledge the power of another God who is not their own." Isca'riot spoke with passion, guilty tears stained his still dust-ridden face, the grime of many hundreds of trampled feet of the crowd that witnessed the crucifixion of the three condemned men earlier in the afternoon. He did not desire the death of his friend; this was not how it had been agreed with Caiaphas. But the deviousness of Caiaphas had taken him by surprise, Isca'riot despised Caiaphas, the high priest of the Sanhedrin had manipulated him, deceived him, now it was believed by the righteous apostles who did not know that a child of Yeshua would soon be born that he, Yehudas, born in the Heb'rew kibbutz of Isca'riot, one of their own, had betrayed the one true messiah they all believed and loved,

"But our dearest preacher Yeshua would not renounce the false confession he made, of him being the son of our Lord, the king of the Yehudiish, because he realised something much more," Yehudas continued. "Perhaps he thought that he alone could bring down the Sanhedrin by turning Rome against the chosen people but then you came among us to destroy everything. Yeshua knew why you are here, but he still loved you beyond anything Marusya. You became his life, his passion, even though you used him. I believed in him from the beginning, you know this, but when he told me he loved you I knew then I must act to end this charade, this unravelling revolution of disbelieving falsehoods that you alone were creating. I myself have no love for the Sanhedrin, I came to believe that Yeshua was born of the holy spirit, that he was sent by his holy father to save us. He told me his death would be atonement for our sins, but he was playing into your hands, it was your manipulation, your crusade against the Sanhedrin to deliver your child to be the new king of the Yehudiish people."

Caiaphas stood in absolute silence listening to the intense drama while it unfolded. He at last began to sense the immediate danger of this new situation. The supreme leader of the Sanhedrin believed that he had accomplished enough to destroy the growing power of the so-called disciples, that by ridding himself of their charismatic preacher their revolution would grind itself to a halt – the undeniable charge of blasphemy would be sufficient to destroy any pretender. But right now, he could not speak or think how to regain control. His one thought was how to contrive this heretic woman's death, her bastard child must not be allowed to live. Isca'riot too, he thought to himself, was a danger that would need to be silenced by his loyal guards of the Sanhedrin.

"You speak with passion; you are a devout man among poor men," Magdalen replied. "You say he died to protect me, perhaps this would be true if he were dead. I know the Sanhedrin desire my death before my child is born but do you not think you presume too much if you think Yeshua is dead? What if he was to rise again Yehudas?"

Isca'riot eyes widened in disbelief. Caiaphas stood stunned with sudden horror. He was not as quick-witted as Isca'riot; the ageing councillor had risen to head the Sanhedrin by being more calculating and manipulative, by giving himself time to plan and manoeuvre. But it dawned upon Caiaphas what Magdalen had said, why she might be here in the temple forbidden to women. Confused, horrifying thoughts ran through his head.

"What, what do you mean Marusya?" Isca'riot responded with an incredulous stammer in his faltering voice.

"Do you not see these in my hand?" Magdalen replied, "I have here the three bloodstained spikes the Romans used to nail Yeshua to his crucifixion stake today. They were hammered into his hands and feet. These spikes are made of the same iron pot of the five fishes and loaves of bread used at the miracle of Bethsaida. Do you not think there is perhaps something more powerful than the power of your God?

Isca'riot and Caiaphas both stood standing in a state of stupefied shock. Magdalen waited for Isca'riot to respond; she knew she had delivered a hard enough blow, that she had bought herself time. Shem'ayon now Peter had promised to her that Yosef of Arim'athea would bring back Yeshua's body, that Peleus, the much-loathed Centurion, would give up the dead for symbolic Yehudiish rites. More than anything Yeshua had to be returned to her because she must in some way resolve this dreadful situation, the calamitous disaster caused by Isca'riot and his bitter betrayal. The resurrection of her soul through her unborns was uncertain given these dark days of foreboding circumstances that had descended upon her; Magdalen knew what she had long known, that Yeshua was more than the promised messiah, that Isca'riot the traitor was the one man who would change everything. When she found the discarded spikes at the foot of the cross, she had smiled to herself in self-seeming satisfaction, an inclination of why everything was so, a realisation that her desperate lover was without question still by her side, that Isca'riot might be the one traitorous traitor who could yet save the fragile life of her unborn. Perhaps only a villainous traitor could save this godforsaken world.

Magdalen looked at Isca'riot who himself stood speechless, trying to comprehend incomprehensible events that unfolded before him. Marusya broke his trance-like state.

"This is all beyond you Yehudas. You have played your part in this conspiracy; you must let Caiaphas here complete the abonishment of the Sanhedrin. Their desperate days are finished although it will take a good while yet," she could not say much more. "Take heart. Your betrayal is not a true betrayal, your path was chosen long before you ever knew."

"Marusya, they will slay you; they will kill your unborn child. Please, you must know this. There is not a way you can survive."

"Perhaps. Do you not see this is how it is meant to be?"

Isca'riot and his mind were in turmoil. He saw that Marusya cried quiet tears. She cried the simple tears of a woman suffering indescribable anguish, a woman who knew that she and her unborn were condemned to die a violent death. His thoughts raced through all the possible outcomes, but they came to nothing, everything ending only in dejection. Everything ended in Marusya's death and that of her child. She shed a small tear that tore out his heart, an ordinary tear that twisted his confused mind inside out.

"Please, you must be careful. You are desperate, you must believe that Yeshua is dead and cannot protect you. Peter and the disciples are now Yeshua's apostles, they will bring their blame upon you when each of them know the truth, when they know why this has happened. They will cast you out and abandon you. They will never countenance you or forgive you, nor will they accept your child among them. If you think your child will be safe with them when you are both hunted by the Sanhedrin, then you are mistaken. There is nothing they will do to help you. For God's sake Marusya, I more than anyone know what it is like to be damned."

"No, they will not heed me to save my child, you are right in what you say. But when you say they have no love of me then think of their saviour's seed within me. There is nothing they will do for me except the one thing that will absolve their sins in the eye of other gods far greater than yours, the true creators of your race who do not demand worship."

"These are blasphemous words you speak Marusya Magdalen. You cannot say this. Not here in this place, not anywhere. These are unspeakable untruths that will see you and your unborn child dead. Your talk condemns you here in the temple of the Sanhedrin, the heart of everything you find abhorrent in the same way that our messiah Yeshua did here in this same place only six days before you. You make this outrageous talk that will see you accused of heresy and then dead, I do not understand you."

"You will know Yehudas. When the time comes to bury my bones and those of my children, then you will know." In the slow, descending nighttime darkness, Magdalen caressed the small ornate cross she wore around her neck.

Just then, in the all-pervading atmosphere of the room hidden from the fading day that might forever change the world of violent wars and endless famine, Magdalen turned, she departed into the dark shadows of the temple. Magdalen moved with speed, knowing that she would soon be hunted down, but Caiaphas let her leave unmolested, both men still suffering the deep shock and sufferance that was as Magdalen intended. She knew that she had severed any semblance of union or bonding between Isca'riot and Caiaphas, buying herself and her nurturing embryos inseparable time. On the small rough-hewn table before them she left her legacy, the bloodstained spikes that had slain the man who would someday be called by another name, a name cherished by men not yet born who never knew him. The twisted legend of the man who, it was said, was the promised messiah, the crucified preacher who knew he was always the blasphemous prophet.

Outside the imposing prison door of the Roman garrison Yosef of Arim'athea waited. Darkness had come, the tragic day of intense drama drew to its close. Yosef heard the approaching sound of cartwheels trundling along cobblestone alleyways which echoed in the dark night as the cart drew closer. Then he heard whispered voices. Yosef's fellow priest of the Sanhedrin, Nicodemus, appeared out of the nighttime blackness leading his donkey cart loaded with stone jars and great reams of white silk cloth. With him was Miryam of Bath'uma, wife of James the disciple and Salome, the youngest daughter of Thesoba - women who counted themselves part of Yeshua's loyal inner circle. Yosef noticed there was no Magdalen with Nicodemus, who looked to Yosef pained and harassed. All three wore dark hooded cloaks to merge into the pitch-black night. Coldness descended; the debilitating heat of the day was gone.

"Where is Marusya?" asked Yosef.

"Yosef..." Nicodemus tailed off, his voice uneasy and unsure.

"What? Where is she? What has happened?"

Nicodemus was hesitant. He was still trying to understand the day's dreadful events. The young priest spoke in a strained whisper. "After Yeshua was cut down from the stake, Marusya took herself to the temple of the Sanhedrin. Now there is alarming news."

"What news?" Yosef demanded.

Nicodemus stared at Yosef for a few moments as if trying to choose his words. "It is all confusing rumours Yosef. A temple guard is dead, there is great commotion. They are searching everywhere for Marusya. She entered the forbidden temple and found Caiaphas there with Yehudas Isca'riot, this is all I know."

Yosef stared at Nicodemus in silence while trying to take in what he had said. Both he and Nicodemus were fellow priests of the Sanhedrin, Magdalen's tempestuous links with Caiaphas could only have worsened to the point that both Yosef and Nicodemus needed to be more careful. Surely, she could not have entered the temple forbidden to women. He and Nicodemus were without doubt in danger, neither of them wished to be accused of disloyalty or treason by the Sanhedrin. Caiaphas's implicit instructions to Yosef were only to observe, to report to him everything that happened around the radicals, but Yosef had become entwined with the rebellious band to the point that he sometimes felt he was one of them because, for some unfathomable reason, he believed in Yeshua's storytelling and his prophetic teachings.

Yosef saw the miracles, he noted the way the people of Judaea drew to him but, despite Caiaphas's attestations, Yosef believed that Yeshua had not radicalised anyone. The long-travelled preacher preached love and forgiveness, the parable stories he told were provoking and righteous, they delivered profound meanings. Even so, Yosef of Arim'athea knew that Yeshua of Naz'areth was, without doubt, a danger to the inner nub of the Sanhedrin though Yosef was a self-confessed convert to the preacher's teachings – these days his divided loyalties were to the crucified Yeshua, not to Caiaphas or the Sanhedrin. But, at this precise moment in time, both Nicodemus and Yosef needed to be cautious because Caiaphas did not tolerate betrayal by his own priests. With the disturbing news that Nicodemus had brought with him Yosef's mind raced, his thoughts were overwhelmed by the sudden complications, the appalling alternatives he faced. Just then, the bolts of the door to the garrison prison jolted as they were slid back by someone inside. The door opened.

No moonlight shone outside the garrison walls as midnight approached. Intense darkness prevailed. The moist cool air of the night was refreshing but a gentle warm breeze blew from someplace unknown, rustling the nearby willow bushes where hidden nighttime crickets clicked their relentless rhythmic beat. The noise of the crickets seemed to grow in intensity in a mocking form of laughter, taunting the ethos of the dark night as the group of four stood silent and spellbound, wondering what would happen next. A dim light shone from inside the open door, a soft yellow glow that illuminated the strained faces of each of them who outside stared in. A tall Roman guard appeared, bent his head through the undersized door and stepped outside.

"You are here for the condemned Yeshua of Naz'areth?" the Roman demanded to no one in particular. The guard looked agitated.

"Yes, we are here for the body of the preacher from Naz'areth. We are here for you to give him to us," Yosef endeavoured to be as magnanimous as he could.

The grim-faced guard studied Yosef for a few moments without saying anything. He looked around at the others before he spoke. "You, you alone, step inside," he barked to Yosef. The guard bent forward, then disappeared through the door.

Yosef paused with apprehension, he looked at the others. They all returned his look with the same foreboding, the strain of the day and the intensity of the night showing in each of their half-hidden faces. Yosef bent his aching body, his unbound portliness a hindrance to his diminishing mobility as he followed the guard through the small open doorway.

Inside there was just a little more dim light, lit by a flickering flame on the far wall of the oversized chamber with its high ceiling. The residual warmth inside the room from the dry hot day offered a welcome relief from the coolness of the night. Yosef saw that two more Roman guards stood beside the single body that lay upon a wooden lattice, which itself lay upon the stone floor trampled smooth by years of passage. The inert body was wrapped in a bloodstained grey woven blanket with the bloodied face of Yeshua still visible. The preacher's features had not yet set into the marbled stone-like look of the dead, though his long dark hair protruding from the blanket was matted with blood mixed with the wind-blown grime of the stony hilltop where he had been crucified. His unkempt black beard was dirt-encrusted, with the dried saliva of his long hours of suffering; there was no pride left in his contorted features, just intense humiliation coupled with insane pain. Yosef looked at Yeshua, straightaway feeling uneasy, he saw that something was wrong. A sense of pervading uncertainty enveloped Yosef's mind like a fireball explosion invading his fragile brain. The tall guard, the one who ordered Yosef inside, spoke in a whispered tone, but with wavering authority.

"This man should be dead but for some reason he still lives," the guard declared in a gruff voice laced with uncertainty. "My men have twice speared his body but even now he lingers." The Roman did not pause to choose his words, it was as if he had considered what he would say and how he would say it. There was a hint of embarrassment within his manner, a quiet acceptance that he and his fellow guards had not done their job with customary efficiency, they wanted to be rid of the mess on their hands. Now the guards were following the Centurion's strict orders to return the dissident's wretched body to those who came to claim it.

"Take him. We have been told to give him to you in the way you find him, ask your womenfolk to take care of him. We Romans think this wreck of a man deserves to live. We say he cannot be guilty of any spurious crime, not when he clings to life like this."

Yosef's mind once more raced. What should he do? The appalling implications filled his thoughts, he felt beads of sweat break out upon his forehead. The Roman stared at him with his piercing eyes, so did the other two guards standing beside Yeshua, waiting for Yosef to say something. Yosef did not say anything. He could not think of anything to say. He looked down upon Yeshua's supine face, it did not have the grey stone appearance of someone dead. The rest of Yeshua's twisted body lay hidden beneath the dirty grey cloak, but the Romans were telling the truth, Yosef could see this for himself. Yosef stood silent as he thought what to do. This was a crisis of immense proportions - which could unravel to destroy everything, himself included.

He had before promised to take Yeshua's body back to Shem'ayon now Peter, helped by Magdalen and the others; once there with the disciples they would anoint his body with the balm fluids, then dress him with respect in the cloth that Nicodemus had brought in the cart. But, according to what Nicodemus had said, Caiaphas's guards were at this moment searching for Magdalen, they would certainly head straight to Shem'ayon now Peter. If they found Yeshua there not yet dead then big trouble would break loose, if Yosef was there then... who knows what would happen? The right thing would be to take the wretched, mutilated Yeshua directly to Caiaphas in the temple, or to some other safe place then at least inform Caiaphas that Yeshua was still alive. He could then ask Caiaphas what should be done. But Yosef hesitated. A feeling deep inside him began to take charge of his mind, and a strange and coherent thought occurred to him.

"We will take care of this unsavoury situation," Yosef replied to the tall guard. "I am Yosef of Arim'athea, a priest of the Sanhedrin, you Romans need not concern yourselves further with this matter."

"That is good enough for us. Take him away," the Roman guard confirmed.

The two remaining guards lifted the wooden lattice but struggled with the weight of Yeshua, just the two of them. The small doorway was cramped but they manoeuvred through the door, throwing their load to the ground outside as if glad to be rid of such a complicated problem. Both Roman guards then paused, as if realising something to themselves they did not want to reveal. Then, with reverence, they picked up the body from the ground assisted by Nicodemus to heave it onto the back of the cart. It was an open show of respect. The tall Roman and Yosef came out through the doorway.

The three guards turned to retreat through the door, it shut behind them with the sound of sliding bolts being the last reminder that the deed was done. The flickering inside light of the Roman garrison disappeared, and the little group stood forlorn in the cool darkness beside the tall grey wall. The nighttime crickets became silent - as if they sensed the immensity of the moment. Yosef of Arim'athea, thinking on his weary feet, had decided what he should do.

Magdalen squatted, hidden in the darkness of the nearby mulberry bushes, their scraggy growth giving her just enough cover to remain concealed in the eerie grey shadows. Around her, the pungent smell of ripening fruit mingled with the cool night air, the sweet aromatic scent of far-off blossom trees creating an atmosphere of freshness that relieved the relentless stink rising above the noxious city. From the small hilltop overlooking the temple, Magdalen saw the Sanhedrin's guards leave their barrack room, bursting out in frenzied determination through the ornate side door which emitted a long glow of light from inside. From the commotion and the length of time the doors remained open she could guess that a large number of guards had spread around the city now that

Caiaphas had come to his sinister senses. The Judaeans would try to find her, Magdalen knew this for certain. But in hunting for her she would be buying more time because she believed in her heart that Yeshua might have survived; perhaps he would perform one more of his much-vaunted miracles to raise himself from the dead.

Marusya accepted one fact without revocation, something she thought more about as the dreadful day wore on - with utmost certainty, she needed the help of the weak-willed Isca'riot. His collusion was vital, by the time of the next springtime, one year from now, she knew that she herself would be dead, just as Isca'riot had prophesied inside the abhorrent temple of the Sanhedrin. Aside from her deteriorating body genetics, it would be impossible to survive the tremendous forces of destruction that would soon be brought against her. Without doubt, she would have to face the formidable Gabriel, who would take draconian steps against her - the archangel's unbound fury might well be her undoing if she could not once and for all suppress his immensity. This monumental confrontation had yet to come, the thought caused a shudder of foreboding to run through her tired body fatigued from the intensity of the heinous day just passed. There was one more consequence that Magdalen knew could not be prevented - her fading strength, which confirmed that her own time in the world was ending, the new resurrection in her endless task would begin with the birth of her twins, the infant daughters within her womb who must, against all odds, survive beyond their first five years. The Sanhedrin feared the birth of an infant son, they claimed this was written but Magdalen alone knew this was impossible – not once in the historic history of her ancestry had a male child been born. From the time of her death, Magdalen knew that each descending birth through her line would suffer the same, the newborns would be hunted down like rats by Lucifer's fallen angel hunters until strong enough to survive by their own will.

Magdalen hid in the shadows of the hilltop while the Judaean temple guards searched for her with their burning torches, they spread through the narrow alleyways of the mud-built houses, they hurried through the dusty spruce tree-lined squares, then across the desolate wastelands of

Je'rusalem, a Je'rusalem that lay under gentle streaks of soft grey light that began to tease the night sky with the breaking dawn. Little black swifts and darting swallows sensed the welcome heat of the morning sun still hidden far below the distant horizon of the dry city teeming with desperate men, the awakening birds swooped high into the grey blackness from the warmth of their mud-built nests that hustled under uncountable rooftop eves. It would be a few hours yet but the first day of the new dawn began to rise. It would not take long for Caiaphas's guards to find Shem'ayon now Peter, but Magdalen would not be there, it was never her intention to seek out Peter or the others whose destinies were now in their own hands. She waited in the trees, squatting on her haunches in the darkness until Isca'riot chose to leave the temple.

Inside the temple cenotaph, Yehudas Isca'riot came to his fragile senses. Caiaphas, he reacted with sudden decisive energy by summoning the guards to seize Magdalen as she left through the main ornate door – but they were too late, the guards had been altogether occupied with the remnants of the crucifixion crowd. Meanwhile, as the commotion and drama unfolded elsewhere, Isca'riot bent over the dead guard who still lay in the outer doorway to the inner sanctuary. What had Magdalen done to him? How had this weak woman felled the best of the trusted Sanhedrin's guard? Isca'riot found no significant wound or blood nor any signs of violence, or whether the guard had in some way fought back, just a small burn-like blemish to the guard's neck; the mark resembling two ill-defined imprints of a thumb, in the forlorn form of a rough cross. How had she gotten so close to him?

Then his heart missed a beat, he stared at the strange insignificant mark, he had not in his life seen anything like this. A flicker of unease stirred in the back of his mind, a vague recollection, a surge of agitation – the whispered rumours he had heard in the marketplace, the babble of women's talk under their breath, wild allegations about Magdalen and the Bethlehem-born preacher. A thought struck him like a bolt of lightening, a faded memory flooding into his mind, strange talk he had heard a long time back, in his days as a young rebellious cleric when he had listened to tales telling of writings etched into ancient tablets of stone, scriptures discovered then hidden by the Sanhedrin; Yehudas remembered rumours of stone transcripts uncovered more than ten-score years before, inexplicable parables, impossible tales and malicious untruths written by long-dead holy men, radical priests who transcribed tablets telling of primordial tribal warriors in another time before God created the earth and all life upon it. Broken, incomplete tablets, describing a deviant she-devil, a ghost-mist enchantress who felled satan's powerful serpent with the simple touch of her hand... leaving only vague thumb marks in the mysterious shape of a cross. A demon-like goddess who defied Adam. Isca'riot remembered these untruths, this demon was called Lilith.

What if these strange scriptures existed and were not lies? What if they had been found, then hidden by the Sanhedrin? If there was something of truth in these primitive gospels, then perhaps Yeshua spoke with conviction when he confessed to him his fears about Magdalen. What if the miracles of Yeshua of Naz'areth were not miracles at all, perhaps they were clever illusions, simple tricks performed by a magician who somehow discovered strange abilities within him, or powers he had been given by someone else. Or something he had been taught. These random thoughts powered through the mind of Isca'riot while he squatted beside the body of the temple guard, thoughts which all came together like broken pieces of rock that formed themselves into the perfect stone. The methods, the miracles, they were always the same, the spikes that nailed Yeshua to his crucifixion stake - Magdalen had said to both himself and Caiaphas that these spikes were made from the same iron pot of the miracle of the loaves and fishes. Could there be some link with the dead guard who lay on the floor at his feet, his sword still sheathed and unfettered, felled by a weak woman who carried no weapon?

The over-fertile mind of Yehudas was in emotional overdrive because from nowhere came more brutal memories that struck him, another bolt of thunder that made Yehudas squat still in shock. An awful feeling of foreboding overpowering him like a creeping sickness. Why did he recall this right now? For some insane reason more bizarre recollections came

321

flooding back, only at this point did they surface in his fragile mind. More strange gospels he had heard talk of, his own mother, both his mother's sisters, they had often gossiped when he was young, their recalcitrant dissatisfaction with the *Sanhedrin*. The vague old woman who used to sit him on her knee, mist-faded memories danced around inside his head, memories of the wrinkled babushka woman whose name he could not recall, once an obscure friend of his mother who told him handed down stories. Who was this old woman? She had taught him about scriptures and the fabled history of the Yehudiish, common talk of the Judaean people, also about the rising power of the Sanhedrin. Isca'riot tried to recall the stories she told, about the Sanhedrin and the one object they were desperate to find, a symbol of something foul and evil. Something indescribable that no one even knew how to describe. A symbolic artefact so old it was said to be hewn from the world's first iron cast in Lucifer's cauldron fire of hell. A fabled cross-shaped relic brandished by the devil's serpent in the ancient garden kingdom, then supposedly given to the temptress she-devil Lilith when original sin came into the world of men. When Yehudas was a small child, he was told about this she-devil's mark, how it was long sought by the Sanhedrin, a fabled piece of antiquity that hidden scrolls declared could one day bring down the ruling power of men, something which could destroy the kingdom of Judaea and wreak havoc amongst God's chosen people. The cross hewn from ancient pure iron purportedly created at the very beginning of time, formed in the fires of hell long before heaven and earth were created by God.

The simple cross that Magdalen wore around her neck. It all of a sudden, for some reason, seemed important. Yehudas had never taken much notice, thinking it just insignificant decorative regalia that women adorned themselves with all the time - he did not think anything of it except that she always wore the one same thing. Could it be? Was it possible? Might there be a connection? Could there be a link to the mythical token supposedly given to the demon-ghost Lilith? Hyvah? Was Magdalen linked to the entity hidden scriptures called Lilith? Were Hyvah and Lilith one and the same? Was this heretic legend in some way true?

Yehudas's mind raced in unfettered out-of-control turmoil, everything seemed to come together like a clap of thunder. The mysterious cross Magdalen wore around her neck might be some religious replication - when she confronted both himself and Caiaphas in the Sanhedrin temple forbidden to women, she declared the crucifixion spikes were fashioned from same iron pot that fed his hoards of followers at Bethsaida. The crucifixion stake tied together in the shape of a cross, the same symbolic ritual of the cross. Was this one more dreadful link? Was it conceivable that history had played a cruel hand? And might the Sanhedrin have unwitting found the mark of darkness for which they had for a long time searched. Caiaphas! Isca'riot smiled to himself as it, for some reason, dawned upon him like a blow from heaven, Caiaphas might have triggered events that could threaten the existence of the Sanhedrin. Caiaphas might have begun a death-dealing confrontation against something immense and more powerful which he had to destroy at all costs. A battle that Caiaphas was desperate to win, a conflict that might well consume the Yehudiish people. Yeshua of Naz'areth, a renegade preacher who Isca'riot irrevocably adored, a preacher who many were calling the anointed Son of God, a man who he believed in beyond all hesitation and then betrayed, was crucified by the Romans on the same symbolic cross. Was this a terrifying coincidence in every way possible? Was all of this frenzied turmoil that had ruined his fractious life in some way meant to happen?

Yehudas and his unbalanced mind were in free fall. Who was Magdalen? Could she be descended from the fantastical Hyvah created by God from the bones of Adamah? Could she have been born one and the same in the way his friend Yeshua had claimed? These chaotic thoughts erupted in Yehudas's mind like a raging river - he realised with one more bolt of sickening shock that he must find Magdalen before the Sanhedrin seized her. His betrayal of Yeshua struck him to be a terrible mistake, an awful disaster that he himself had caused - pains of sheer panic tore into his heart when the realisation burned into him. Magdalen had said to him that betrayal would be his destiny, that he would be known as Yehudas the Betrayer. She had revealed that Yeshua foretold his downfall, that Yeshua might well have used him to destroy Caiaphas and the Sanhedrin. Could Caiaphas have walked into his own trap? Had Magdalen outwitted all of them? The beloved preacher had used their deep trusting friendship in a strange way, knowing that Magdalen carrying his child would be enough for himself Yehudas to turn traitor. His true destiny, this occurred to him like a sick feeling inside. His salvation, it dawned upon Isca'riot like a fire burning inside his brain, might his salvation lay with the devil woman who was destroying his life? And with her unborn child?

Yehudas stood back to his feet, leaving the guard dead on the stone-cold granite floor. It occurred to him that he needed to get a grip, his mind was beginning to cavort with the dark side of unreality. The unnatural thoughts that raced through his head made no normal sense. He studied himself - his out-of-control reasoning was nonsensical, in many ways insane. But then, everything that had happened since his first encounter with the preacher from Naz'areth was dripping with illusionary madness – and into this frantic turmoil had come Marusya Magdalen, who peddled her own form of deranged hysteria.

Yosef of Arim'athea tried to think with rational speed. The wood-slatted door of the Roman prison was closed and bolted, the Romans had washed their hands of this developing crisis, it was not their business, it was the Sanhedrin's responsibility to decide how the Judaean people should proceed. But to Yosef, this was a difficult situation. He could not take Yeshua's body to Shem'ayon now Peter as he had promised, Caiaphas and the temple guards would without doubt discover them with the rebels, then all would be lost. Nicodemus, Miryam of Bath'uma and Salome, daughter of Thesoba all looked at Yosef in confusion. Right now, they were unaware that Yeshua was not yet dead, he had not died when spiked to his crucifixion stake. Yosef decided it best that he did not tell them, not yet, not until they were someplace safe - they would not understand the seriousness of the situation nor the momentous implications of what might happen. Yosef needed a well-hidden location where they could go, where he could buy time to work out in his mind what should happen next. As luck would have it, he thought to himself with a smile, there was the perfect location not far away.

It was well past midnight. Back towards the skull-like hill of Golgotha where the crucifixion of the condemned men had taken place, there was the cemetery where the burial tombs reserved for priests of the Sanhedrin were located. Yosef's family tomb, made ready for the day he himself died, lay deep in the depths of the cemetery and it was empty. It was well hidden and, more gratifying, not used. They could take Yeshua there until they found a place where he could be tended by the womenfolk, they could bring healing balms if needed or the preacher might be allowed to die in peace beside those who revered and cherished him; surely he could not survive these appalling wounds for long. Thinking of the crucifixion and the spear wounds inflicted by the Romans, Yosef did not expect Yeshua to live for any length of time; perhaps he might linger for a short while but not much more; they could try hard to do something for his wounds, to tender his sufferings though it would not be easy. Yeshua lay silent, sombre in his comatose state which meant the others did not suspect the inconceivable. Yosef saw the first streaks of tentative greyness in the past-midnight sky, with anxious deliberation, he realised they had not much time left. Once more he felt the familiar beads of sweat form along his furrowed brow.

"Nicodemus, we must go, but not to Shem'ayon now Peter."

The bewildered Nicodemus did not reply but nodded. He understood the danger they faced because of Magdalen's nonsensical incursion into the temple of the Sanhedrin, Nicodemus himself sensed something serious in the wind. Like Yosef, he did not wish to face the wrath of Caiaphas if caught with the rebels. The younger priest was here through his loyalty to Yosef of Arim'athea, nothing more - he felt desperate unease, he did not revere Yeshua or his followers like his fellow priest, though he viewed the injustice dealt by Caiaphas and the killing of the Naz'areth preacher with his own concealed repugnance. But this woman Magdalen was above herself, how could she even consider entering the sacred temple of the Sanhedrin?

"But Yosef," interrupted Salome, "Ya'qub of Alphaeus and Peter, they are waiting. And the Baptist also. We have with us the oils and the embalming cloth for Yeshua's burial."

Yosef turned to look at Salome and Miryam. Salome in her younger years seemed confused with panic. How could he tell them the truth? He could not, not yet, not until he hoped to have more news of Magdalen and the Sanhedrin. His deepest instincts warned him the time was not yet right.

"In good time Salome," Yosef responded with unease. "Later we can take Yeshua to where he needs to be, but he needs to be safe from Caiaphas and my compatriot priests of the Sanhedrin."

"Salome, Yosef is right. Yeshua's sacred body must be somewhere safe from this trouble Marusya has brought upon us," interrupted Miryam, who sensed wisdom in Yosef's reasoning. "Yosef and Nicodemus will have great difficulty with Caiaphas if they are found with us," Miryam added, she was devoted to Yeshua, she did not wish to see further harm inflicted by Caiaphas. Never had she been a devotee of Magdalen, like the majority of women close to Yeshua she viewed Magdalen with some disdain, with a jealousy reserved for women who see their lifelong devotion to a man overwhelmed by some absurd fondness for another woman. Miryam of Bath'uma had seen first-hand how Yeshua was drawn to Magdalen, now the temple guards of the Sanhedrin were searching for the one person Miryam blamed for the tragedy that had descended upon them.

"We shall go to the cemetery of Golgotha, there is a place there where we shall be safe," Yosef suggested. "We must bide our time until this heat that abounds dies away." The two women each looked at him confused as if considering all the consequences, then they nodded their reluctant agreement. Nicodemus stayed silent.

Yosef led them with the loaded donkey cart down the well-used mud path now dried to dust, it being just discernible in the dark grey light that begged the early morning dawn. They met no one along the way though Yosef was confident that if they had, they would raise no suspicion, it was not unusual to be about so late past midnight. Je'rusalem was beginning to stir for the new day. In a few hours the squalid city would be bustling in the grimy warmth of spring, the traders in the markets would be busy in the half-light, moving their wares and foodstuffs to their rickety stalls in the crisp morning air still sharp from the nighttime cold. The cool nights gave a welcome relief from the open pits of rotting excrement that festered in the hot noonday sun.

The four of them rounded the rocky knoll to the hilltop, each of them conscious that not far above them was the site of the bloody crucifixions the previous day. They turned to follow the crumbling rocky pathway to the right.

Nicodemus realised where they were heading, he paused then turned to Yosef alarmed. "Yosef, this is the burial place of the Sanhedrin's dead. Are we right to come here?"

"Nicodemus, do not be alarmed, we need someplace where no one will come searching. No one will search here, not for a good while yet. My family tomb is ahead to the left, I trust our Lord God Almighty will see that it remains unfilled for a long time yet, that is if I have anything to do with it," muttered Yosef, with confident unease.

No one said anything, instead, they continued up the slope with care, leading the donkey with its laden cart as far as they could. They were tired. Each of them had waited outside of the Roman prison, it had been cold and dark, now they were faced with the hard task that not one of them expected. The Romans had delivered the bodies of the two other crucified prisoners much earlier in the evening, but Yeshua's body had been delayed as if there was some unknown reason for it to be held back. Little did they know that intense debate over the storyteller from Naz'areth still raged, discussions had rattled around inside the prison while Pontius Pilot and the garrison's notorious centurion once more argued about how they should proceed. In time Peleus had won the day, ordering the crucified preacher's body to be released to the waiting Judaeans.

Yosef of Arim'athea knew the reason for the interminable delay, the wayward priest of the Sanhedrin deliberated inside his mind about when he should tell the others, when he should lay bare how their world had not yet ended in complete disaster as they expected. Yosef considered whether he should in some way get word to the waiting disciples, but through some stubborn instinct in the back of his mind, he decided it wise not to say anything to anyone. Not yet. But deep down inside he knew it was only a matter of time, it would not be long before the unthinkable would be revealed.

Tiredness through lack of sleep meant the undermining of their will to persevere was gradual but the intensity of the moment kept each of them going, the adrenaline of their task overwhelming their desperate desire for rest. Their eager progress began to slow, fatigue and the ever-increasing upward slope causing the ragged donkey to struggle with its heavy load; Salome and Nicodemus tired less, they were themselves younger in years while the elder Miryam felt driven by pure devotion coupled with her desire to protect her masonic messiah from any more wretched cruelness. Yosef, much older than any of them, encumbered by the virtues of easy living, sweated from the exertion of their task while he struggled to keep going. He began to think more and more of Magdalen's freakish role in all of this, he cursed her under his breath when they neared to where they needed to be. The dawn cold grew in intensity, but the chill was repelled by the relentless exertion of their exhaustive uphill task. None of the fatigued band who considered themselves the harbingers of Yeshua's deliverance in any way suspected the unthinkable, that inside her timeless womb, Magdalen nurtured the unborn infants of their holy messiah.

Yosef's family tomb was inaccessible for the cart, they needed to climb the last few paces up the mound of small boulders. Leaving Miryam and Salome to tender the donkey, Yosef and Nicodemus scrambled up to reach the tomb entrance; then with great effort they rolled back the stone to reveal the dark cave-like chasm. The rancid air inside blew out in a gentle breeze which made both men pause with involuntary indecision, the tomb was interconnected by small airways with other tombs that contained the embalmed bodies of the dead. The stench was overpowering.

Inside the tomb, there was no light save which came through the small open doorway. Yosef lit a torch of fire which revealed not much inside, just stone shelf slabs that one day would be the resting place for Yosef and those close to him. As was normal with all priests, he had paid the

Sanhedrin a great price in silver for this hole in the side of the hill so that one day he could be buried with the sublime leaders of the chosen people.

"Let us bring Yeshua into here, then we can begin," Yosef ordered Nicodemus. Yosef shivered, it dawned upon him that it would soon become obvious to both Miryam and Salome that Yeshua still lived, they were used to dealing with the dead, nothing would fool them for long. Yosef decided that he should tell them the truth or they would surely find out for themselves when they attended to Yeshua's body - they were here to clean Yeshua, to anoint him with their oils, to embalm him ready for burial. It struck Yosef that he was stupid - how could he not tell them the man they had come to prepare for burial was not yet dead?

In the forefront of Yosef's mind there lingered the worrying problem of Magdalen; like Nicodemus, he thought it inconceivable that a woman might desecrate the temple by ignoring the long-held laws. Furthermore, it had been decided by both Shem'ayon now Peter and Johan the Baptist that she would be here alongside Salome and Miryam of Bath'uma, she was supposed to accompany them with Yeshua's body, to go to the hidden place arranged with the disciples. That plan was dead in the water. From gnawing necessity, Yosef once more thought fast, like a man possessed. Magdalen should be here with them: he felt a bitter sense of annoyance growing within him, a feeling of displeasure that festered more and more on the pathway since they left the Roman garrison. This was an unsavoury situation, an unwelcome disaster that no one in small part expected. Yosef's inner feelings were that Magdalen was an intrinsic part of this whole calamitous mess. She was connected with an unbiblical chord with everything that had happened; he believed that Magdalen should be the one to be punished for this unexpected situation, she alone should pay the price for the dire consequences that would without doubt follow.

The Naz'areth preacher was not his responsibility, he had agreed to collect the dead preacher's body, then take it to the disciples who would themselves arrange for the burial. All this had been agreed with Shem'ayon now Peter because he, Yosef of Arim'athea, possessed some credibility with the Romans - as a priest of the Sanhedrin he dealt with the Romans all the time. This was why he offered his help and nothing more. There were serious consequences, he and Nicodemus could be in big trouble with Caiaphas and the Sanhedrin given everything they had done so far. But if the four of them went to Shem'ayon now Peter as agreed then the Sanhedrin guards would find them, the two of them would never be able to explain anything of this. Yosef looked around his tomb, he shuddered with involuntary shakes; the thought occurred to him that he might well be lying here entombed in his own burial chamber much sooner than he expected. Afterwards, when all of this was resolved, he would seek out Magdalen.

"Yosef, Miryam and Salome, they are uneasy," said Nicodemus, interrupting the thoughts ruminating around inside Yosef's head.

"Yes, I know. And with good reason." Yosef wheezed, there was caution in his husky voice. He knew why, he had seen Miryam twice look at Yeshua's still visible face, then glance at Salome.

"Something is wrong Yosef. None of this is right, we could be in big trouble. What happened inside the prison with the Romans? Why are we here?"

"Let us go outside, then we can talk," replied Yosef.

The long hard night began to fade. The sun still lurked far below the nebulous horizon, forging a murky grey panorama of nothingness that brought little joy to the chosen people of Judaea. Without warning, the darkness in the sky morphed into its early morning blackest blue, tinged with hints of bright flaming orange trimmed by the deepest bloodstained reds. In the twinkling of an eye, the teasing half-dawn descended with not quite the intensity of hapless daylight. The coming day would soon erupt, it would explode in exuberance like a desperate prisoner released from the shackles of his shadowy soul. Yet again the day would be cloudless and hot, Yosef of Arim'athea knew they needed to be hidden inside the tomb... a sixth sense feeling warned him that all was far from well. Outside, Miryam examined Yeshua closer, she felt apprehensive. She felt unwell.

"Yosef. Yosef..." Miryam called as loud as she could, the urgency of her voice ingratiating a feeling of sudden panic.

Yosef and Nicodemus stepped outside to join Miryam and Salome beside the rickety cart.

"Yes, I know what you will say Miryam," said Yosef, he expected this delicate situation to unfold with considerable alarm; he had thought long and hard about what he might say. Now he must tell them.

"We have a grave problem that our Lord God has thrown upon us. You can see with your own eyes that your beloved preacher is not dead. We must act." Yosef's face was grey with anxiety. "Let us take him inside, I will tell you everything I know."

Nicodemus stood stunned; Salome shook in abject shock. Miryam smiled to herself in holy gratification - God had no doubt spoken. Miryam of Bath'uma had been waiting for God to intervene, to save the messiah from this terrible disaster that enveloped all of them. The Almighty would deliver them from this horrendous injustice dealt by the Romans and the Sanhedrin. She always knew it would be a matter of time before God would speak, the Lord in heaven would bring an end to all this pain and their intolerable suffering.

Straightaway Miryam and Salome felt a new sense of purpose, their intense fatigue evaporated although both their minds spun in wild total confusion. What was happening? What worrying event was unravelling before their blood-red weary eyes? With new-found haste, Miryam and Salome hurried themselves to tend to the prostrate messiah lying forlorn inside the decrepit donkey cart that itself threatened to break apart at any moment. Nicodemus was stunned with horror, the awful implications were obvious; he shuddered in uncontrolled nervousness.

All four of them heaved the unconscious Yeshua up the granite boulders into the dark shadows of the tomb. Inside, they lay his body down upon the cold granite slab of stone, then in the half-light gloom they unwrapped the grey blanket from his broken body. Salome gasped; the horror etched upon her young face. The sacred preacher revealed himself smeared in excrement mixed with congealed blood, without much divine dignity, a mortal man whose painful suffering had wreaked havoc with his vanquished pride. Perhaps God had intervened to save his humbled preacher, but the price Yeshua had paid was beyond the forgiveness of the two women who cleaned the preacher's dried blood and bathed his appalling wounds. When the sun threw its first rays of light through the open doorway, Yeshua lay naked and exposed, cleaned but serene in his newfound glory, resplendent in the worthy honour that restored a degree of pride to his wretched body. They combed his hair to offer him a measure of righteousness, they dried the saliva that matted his beard before wrapping their messiah in soft-silken cloth; they then perfumed the rotting stench of his near-death suffering to restore an illusion of immortality. Salome cried pitiful tears, Miryam whispered her prayers of thanks to her almighty God. Both women suspected their beloved saviour might not live long; the festering odour of putrefying flesh was all familiar to those who attended the dead or the dying.

Outside the tomb, beside the granite stone door that Yosef and Nicodemus had struggled to roll aside a few hours before, a magnificent light shined bright. The glow of whiteness transcended everything surrounding, then steadied into a beam of incandescent starlight that burned. The radiance grew in intensity before rescinding into the dim glow of a forbidding golden shadow. The burst of pure white energy was not much to do with the dawning day still hiding below the horizon - the death-dealing messenger of God had found them.

Isca'riot too found Magdalen just as Magdalen intended. Isca'riot left the sanctuary of the temple to make his way through the Garden of Bethmara to avoid the growing throng of merchants in the early morning marketplace. Without warning, Magdalen stepped from the shadows of the crumbling doorway of the west side cenotaph where she waited. From the high tree line, she had watched Isca'riot leave while bands of Sanhedrin guards raced through the streets of Je'rusalem. Isca'riot was mortified with horror when Magdalen once more confronted him, his initial shock threatening to overwhelm his fragile unease. Inside his confused thoughts, he felt that he could not take much more, his senses reeled like ripples of thick swirling mist. The dawn-breaking sun silhouetted Magdalen's ruby-coloured robe against the backdrop of the red stone temple laid bare by a myriad of random colours - then outraged panic began to overwhelm him. Again Isca'riot forced himself with great effort to remain calm, his outward silence belying his concealed anguish. Magdalen stood before him with conciliatory intent.

"Do not be so afraid," she reproached him as he stood frozen under the growing heat of the morning sun. "I am not the worm of a woman you believe me to be."

For a brief moment, Isca'riot eyed her, noting the fatigued tiredness in her exhausted facial expression. His foremost instinct was, for some reason, to trust her - Isca'riot felt calmer; though his mind still churned over and over with deep foreboding. He forced himself to recover a measure of composure.

"Marusya, why are you here? They are searching for you," Isca'riot's low voice was the sound of a man knowing he was in a perilous situation.

"They search in the wrong place. The guards of the Sanhedrin will not be so fortunate to discover me," said Magdalen with a cool confidence that compounded Isca'riot's uneasy feeling.

"Caiaphas has vowed to hunt you down for your blasphemous intrusion into the temple and for the killing of the guard," beads of nervous sweat began to permeate Isca'riot's forehead. "When the Sanhedrin's guards find you, they have orders to arrest you, to kill you if you resist."

In a fraction of a second Isca'riot sensed Magdalen's unease; his warning had shaken her, for a fleeting second he saw the weight of the forbidding world in her wary eyes. Isca'riot saw that Magdalen still wore the ornate cross around her neck; it was concealed by the dust-ridden cloak that she every day chose to wear, but the cross was there even though it was more than half hidden.

"Then come with me to someplace where they will not look," Magdalen teased, with a casual half-smile that belied her suffering. "Perhaps there can be a worthwhile truce between us. We are both suffering the consequences of our embattled deliverance."

Magdalen felt the time was right to confide in Yehudas, he might be her one way out given the likelihood that her impassioned lover was either dead or mutilated beyond hope. Yet she hoped, almost in desperation, that Yeshua would keep his promise to forever stand by her side, that he would still be alive, though she had no way of knowing. It was the sense of her feelings that made her imagine the procreator of her womb could have in some way survived the cruel injuries he had suffered, but if Isca'riot was even seen with her right now then the desperate plan she held in her mind would fall into dark oblivion. The survival of her progeny would become difficult, with the chance of her newborns dying child deaths more certain. "Come," she ordered. "Follow me, though you must cover your head."

Isca'riot considered his diminishing options, then acquiesced by pulling up the hood of his dark grey cloak, the loathsome grey colour of a traitor's cloak. Earlier, when inside the temple, Isca'riot had convinced himself that he should find Magdalen which, he now thought to himself, had happened all too easily. It occurred to him that she had found *him*, though Isca'riot reasoned it would be in his best interest to follow her. Magdalen led him through the alleyways busy with the rising day, the oppressive morning heat beginning to build in the narrow street passages filled with the colourful array of Judaeans setting up their stalls of marketplace provisions. The pungent spicy aromas of myriads of differing senses mingled with the dry dusty air, tinged with the ever-pervading effluence of stinking foulness that forever permeated Je'rusalem. Magdalen took a deliberate roundabout route, one that Isca'riot could not fathom. After crossing the small tree-filled square they arrived at the nearside entrance to the Sanhedrin temple - Isca'riot stopped in absolute disbelief.

"Marusya, are you insane?"

Magdalen looked at him with sly confidence. "Let us go inside Yehudas. Do not be afraid, never will Caiaphas be clever enough to think I may be lurking inside his mighty citadel forbidden to women. His guards saw me leave."

"But we will be discovered," Isca'riot pleaded. "Why are we back here in this place of danger Marusya? What is it you want from me?" His nervousness returned; though the way she then looked at him ingratiated a feeling of calmness, something he was beginning to understand whenever he was in Magdalen's company. It occurred to him that she possessed a clever way of manipulating the state of his mind.

"Let us go inside, then we can talk. I will tell you whatever you wish to know," said Magdalen, "I have little time left. I need your help."

Isca'riot did not reply. Hesitating full of foreboding, he followed her through the doorway then down the passageways that Magdalen seemed to be familiar with. They moved through darkened corridors and passageways, Isca'riot noted how Magdalen became cautious at each corner as if trying to remember where she must go - or realised the danger she had placed both themselves in. Every few steps she turned to check they were not being followed, then she turned into a small dark room unfamiliar to Isca'riot.

"Where are we? How do you know we are safe in this place?" Isca'riot had given himself over to Magdalen, but his anxiety was not eased by her reckless behaviour. He stared at her, and not for the first time he noticed how engaging she was for what seemed like her young middle-aged years though it was hard to define her real age. Her ragged brown hair hung down the left side of her dark-skinned face, concealing her strange grey-blue eyes that were a unique rarity in dark-eyed Judaean women. She tossed her hair away from her eye with a casual movement of her hand - Isca'riot's fragile heart skipped a beat, he felt a momentary pang of breathlessness without knowing why.

"We are safe. Trust me Yehudas. I have survived many traumas since the beginning of this damned world when life flowed from the fiery lavas of hell. So, one more year should not be difficult, if it be that long."

"What, what do you mean Marusya?" begged Isca'riot, with a stammer. He stared, confused.

"Do not act surprised. You know the she-devil I am supposed to be. All those whispered rumours must have reached your ears though I beg to tell you that few of those lies are true."

Isca'riot paused to gather his thoughts. He was both baffled and anxious, his mind raced back through the tumultuous events of the previous days.

His encounter in the temple that had seen Magdalen rise in supreme power had come close to destroying everything he held dear – even his sanity.

The situation could not be much worse for Isca'riot. They were back inside the temple forbidden to women, Marusya was being hunted by the Sanhedrin for blasphemy, there was the bizarre mystery of the slaying of the guard and he was being persecuted for his act of betrayal. Even so, Isca'riot felt calmer knowing that Magdalen appeared well able to control even his destiny. But the rumours he had heard told about her mysterious origins unsettled him.

Little did Isca'riot realise that Magdalen's outward bravery was, in these dark days of disparity a thinly disguised veil, that inside she was consumed with her vulnerability for the survival of her unborns. She had little time left, knowing the immense forces that would soon be ranged against her. It was not Caiaphas, or the temple guards that Magdalen feared, though their retribution would be hard enough. Magdalen knew the ruthless enemy she must soon face – the merciless Gabriel and his dark angel Lucifer, they would work hard to find her. Magdalen had confronted many adversaries in her long, relentless fight to survive but the one that disturbed her was the ungodly overmaster of humanity – the supreme angel on earth who had vowed to destroy her. His Lord's emissary would not tolerate this new unravelling catastrophe, this ultimate challenge to his dominance of humankind. And now she carried the nemesis in her womb that Gabriel feared.

The messenger of God would never accept that she had lured the wayward preacher Yeshua of Naz'areth into the darkness of being the creator of her own resurrection. Gabriel would react with violence and venom against her but few realised that Yeshua was the most far-reaching of Gabriel's revered prophets, not in any way was he the son of any God worshipped by men. Gabriel, God's powerful vassal by now was well aware of who his renegade preacher was.

Gabriel believed that Yeshua was born to the simple carpenter, himself the son of Ja'cob who was descended from the line of King David, father of the chosen people. Gabriel, when it was too late, learned that he was wrong - being deceived in this crucial transitional happening instilled the archangel with anger and rage. Gabriel was slow to realise how this preacher had for some inexplicable reason turned rogue, he had been tempted from his all-important task. Yeshua, extreme in his beliefs, had grown into a powerful advocate of his own morals, a self-declared radical of the Yehudiish faith - was this the reason why Magdalen had ensconced him? Or were her motives more sinister? For her own reasons Magdalen had singled out Yeshua, chosen him to be the seed of her child. The supreme archangel Gabriel, in collusion with the faithless Lucifer, relied upon Lucifer's gaggle of angel-assassins to hunt down Hyvah's newborns. Gabriel was at this moment unsure of Magdalen's motives – though he realised the immense danger that all men of menkind faced.

Magdalen knew that Gabriel would lay bare her menace, that he would retaliate against her with all the power he possessed though, she reasoned, she would at least have the traitorous Isca'riot by her side. Isca'riot did not know who he was meant to be, that his destiny as the faithless traitor who dealt death to his friend would one day be written into the twisted history of desperate men, men who would make war with each other for the next three thousand years. Dark wars of conflicting religious beliefs. Magdalen, in her self-belief that drove her preservation knew, without any shadow of doubt, who Isca'riot was.

"Marusya, you say to me that you need my loyal given promise. If you ask for my forgiving help then you must explain to me these deplorable things that are happening," Isca'riot was a measure of his desperation. "I have been reviled and pummelled by everyone I live by. I have sinned a great sin. You are right, both you and I are hated by everyone," with some newfound steadfastness Isca'riot felt enough determination to see the truth behind the tortuous events of the last few days.

"Yes, you will be Yehudas the betrayer, the much-vilified disciple of Yeshua," said Magdalen. "You have been paid a price in silver to betray your devout friend. I am the woman of evil who lured the prophet with my flesh. This is how we shall both be known."

"But little of this is *true* Marusya," exclaimed Isca'riot.

"Oh, it is Yehudas. It is how history will be written, have no fear of this my friend."

"How can this be? There is much I do not understand," he replied. "First you must tell me, why did you seek out Yeshua and join our band of believers?"

"It is simple enough," offered Magdalen. "My time of life in this world of men cannot last forever. There must be new blood to make the reason for my existence stronger. Yeshua's bloodline is pure in ways you cannot imagine." Magdalen looked Isca'riot in the eye, seeing the disbelieving expression in his face, as though he would never accept the truth. "My newborn will be of Yeshua's blood; in this way the survival of my kind will be strengthened. Two men who will change this world came together as two inseparable friends side-by-side. You both stood on the hill at Bethesda. The demands of powerful men and kings will destroy this garden world unless there is a race of men who are equal to their women, women who are the true creators of nascent life in this world." Magdalen tried to keep her answer simple enough for Isca'riot to understand.

Isca'riot was struck by Magdalene's deliberate calmness, he felt that she wished to reveal more - but what she said made no sense. He felt his pulse beat as though his fragile world was about to change. There were many questions he needed to ask, many intricate reasons that led to his betrayal of his friend to Caiaphas and the Sanhedrin.

"You said in the temple that Yeshua would rise again. Why did you say this?"

"By your god's will it is not yet his time to die," said Magdalen. "His determination to live until he knows my child is safe is beyond the will of Caiaphas to have him dead," Magdalen knew that she had Yehudas's riveted attention. "Your messiah, when he was dying, he begged that I find the spikes that nailed him to the stake, to take these spikes then deliver them to the Sanhedrin. Then Caiaphas would know his vile scheme had not succeeded, that together we are stronger than anything the Sanhedrin can threaten," Magdalen hissed her words. "Yeshua promised he would not suffer death until my child is safe, until you came to terms with your betrayal and you agreed to help my unborn child, when you put down your traitor's axe to come to me in peace. Yeshua thought you would one day do this because the wrath of Caiaphas is great, not least because soon the most powerful of my enemies will descend to destroy both of us Yehudas." Magdalen had long ago decided that no one, not anyone, would know she nurtured the unthinkable, that not one but two embryos grew within in her woman's womb.

"How do you know that Yeshua is not dead?" Isca'riot begged with disbelief. "And who is this devil you fear?"

"I do not know if your saviour is alive or dead, not until Yosef of Arim'athea has brought his body from the Romans," said Magdalen. "If I am right, you will know how you must trust me without revocation. You must know that my enemy who you must also survive is no glorious messenger sent by your righteous god."

"What do you mean Marusya? You speak the words of the devil. My Lord God in heaven will protect me, this much I will always know."

"Ha! You men speak then make your path to god as if you know the one true truth. You know nothing except that you believe your god made this world in seven days, that your god created man in his image in the clay of Adamah, that Hyvah belonged to Adamah just as all women are beholding to their men for all time," new fire flamed in Magdalen's eyes. "None of this is so. There is no almighty creator in man's image. Hyvah was not created from the rib bone of Adamah. Never was the history of the world like this."

Isca'riot stood shocked, then shuddered. "But this is how it is written. Ab'raham and the honoured prophets? Mo'ses, the promised land? The scriptures, the commandments given by God to all men, why do you talk this sacrilege? Lucifer and his fallen angels, the serpents of hell..."

"Your god, the angel Gabriel, Lucifer the devil, they are all of the same blood. I know this, I have faced them enough since I was born from the foul dirt of this cruel world, when I rose from the seed that first set deep into this fertile earth, when the world itself was formed a time ago that you cannot even imagine. I have reborn myself many times since I came down from the trees to walk tall in the long grass, by your god's grace I know all about that. Oh yes, I do know about that. This is how it is Yehudas."

"What is this talk? What do you mean?" Isca'riot begged, unable to comprehend what Magdalen was saying. These were the same words his friend Yeshua had confessed to him, what Magdalen claimed to be the true history of the world, blasphemous words of incomprehensible meaning.

"This world was not created by your god from the darkness in seven days. One day all men will know this world is just one of countless more worlds they see in the night sky, they will know that every star they see is not a twinkling light in heaven, each star is one more daylight sun just like the one that feeds all life, this unredeemed sun that means humankind will survive to see one more new dawn," said Magdalen.

"But God is God, he created everything. How can you not believe this?"

"Man's god is an image fashioned by men in their minds. Your god is an imaginary being who beholds only men in the muddled minds of all men," Magdalen shuddered, knowing that what she said would tear Isca'riot apart. "He created nothing except the lies you believe; man's god is no loving god. He is one among many gods created by men to worship, when they create mindless crusades for all men to follow. The truth is, the vassal of your god came upon this world when it was a cauldron of gas and fire, knowing the seed of life was well set before *he* put eyes upon it. Your god's harbinger of life saw that his consummate seed could be planted inside everything female born, made to combine within the world that already existed." Magdalen could not control her increasing anger; her passion grew stronger when she revealed to Isca'riot how everything was.

"There have been other races of men in this world, tribes of humankind who evolved through evolution in time, in ways that meant they could not survive. Those beings themselves possessed their self-created gods to worship and behold," said Magdalen. "Your god, your creator of the tribes of men he nurtured, he commanded that his malignant archangel messenger should destroy all the neanderthal kinds so that only his Lord's seed would survive, your god then begat a race of men in his warlike image, men who are hunters, eaters of meat who will kill another man for his meat. Even so, man is not alone in how he lives Yehudas, he is just one more beast that hunts among all beasts in this world. Men will kill the next man or slaughter his neighbour, even the next land to make life good for his people. Every man who is born wants to be a god or to be a king, so that he is the leader of other men, man has the insatiable need to be supreme, to deal death, to be the king of men is the soul inherited from this god who binds you. This is why god and devil are the same Yehudas, have no doubt about this."

"If these lies are true then who are you Marusya," Isca'riot demanded. Not for one second did he believe Magdalen nor understand the unfathomable lies she spoke. For more than a few moments he thought to himself that perhaps Caiaphas was right to hunt her down.

"There are many rumours that fester in this world about me Yehudas. The truth is I have many names. Now I am called by this name though my first name, the one that will always be written by others is Hyvah, sometimes it is Hyvva or Lilith though they are not the names I choose, it is a name written down by men who say they have their say. I am Ḥawwāh by others who wish to destroy me though the truth is I have no name. Names are given when a child is born Yehudas, I am called whatever time says I should be called. So, there might be some truth in the stories you have heard of me."

"How is this? What do you mean Marusya?" Isca'riot could not hide his disbelieving confusion, his world was tumbling. "What you say hurts my head, your words cannot be true. Men of great strength have saved our people and you, you have witnessed the wrath of Rome and the death they deal. Almighty God is with us, he sends his prophets to save us because we are all born from his creation. Why is it you seek me, why am I the one who listens to what you say and then suffers damnation?"

Magdalen thought about Isca'riot's question, "I am born from the same seed that created time, so are you. You are one of few men among all men. That is every man who was ever born. The god you worship is not your creator; you are the rarest of small flowers that I have protected without you knowing." Isca'riot listened in stunned silence. "You led me to Yeshua for whom I was searching, he is the false prophet who is also of your bloodline, I chose him to be the creator of my resurrection. Yeshua's seed was planted inside me through unredeemable passion, the same way your supposed god with his serpent sibling intended everything female to be implanted. But they did not see the bloodline of men who are righteous, men who are not of their blood or their god's creation, the smallest tribe of blessed near-neanderthal men who for many tens of millions of your years I have cherished like children. Both you and Yeshua are of this neanderthaloid blood. From this day, whenever a child is born who is of my blood with your bloodline then we are stronger than god's angel and Lucifer the devil will ever be. This is why Gabriel must destroy both of us Yehudas."

Magdalen began to see a change in Yehudas the betrayer, something she had long been waiting knowing it would happen. "I am nearing the end of my time here in this suffering world, I cannot survive much longer. I am fatigued, with lessening strength each day. My will to once more fight the dark forces gathering to destroy me grows less as time goes by. I cannot move mountains now, nor can I carry the burden I was given. My urgent task was to find Yeshua to light his fire, to create the embryo within me who will be my resurrection. I can ask you, you with the strongest will of all living men, to protect my heritage when I am dead. Then with my child safe, you have the most important task to deliver."

"Pray tell, what is that Marusya?" Isca'riot asked, a tinge of uncertainty echoing in his voice. Right now, he wished he had never set eyes on Magdalen.

"You must not abscond on the task I will ask of you, or you will die your spiteful betrayer's death," warned Magdalen. "When I am dead you must burn my bones. My ashes, with the spikes that crucified your messiah, you must take to one place, somewhere unknown in this part of your world. It is in the far north, in the deepest coldest forests many thousands of leagues from here. It is a white land of ice where these good men live. Men of your blood with my blood. There is a place marked by an ancient stone, it is the place where I was born when this world was nothing more than a cauldron of fire and tempestuous water. My ashes, the iron spikes, my sacred cross, they must be returned deep beneath this stone so that my strength can return to the earth to create life for those who will be born after me. This is your task; this is why I found you."

"And what of Yeshua?" asked Isca'riot, his lips trembling with anticipation.

"He will rise again, he will rise because he cannot be dead, he made a vow not to die, not yet, not until he knows my child is safe in our survival. Only then will he join with me, he will die a mortal man's death. No man can survive the wounds he has suffered," said Magdalen. "This is written, it is why we made our pact together so that my child can live. Caiaphas, the Sanhedrin, the angels of their god, they believe my child is the new she-devil who must be destroyed, but she is no demon Yehudas."

"But what of Peter and the disciples? They worship the messiah who is Yeshua the prophet from God," argued Isca'riot.

"Oh, the so-called apostles, they will survive. Their task has been well written. They will go out to teach the world about the son of their god, that grey cloud will suffice to hide my task. Their new faith in Christ the Saviour will grow just as countless other faiths have done, they will worship then fight each other for supremacy as they always do. While they fight over the love of their god then bad men will slaughter bad men. They will have no qualms about the deaths of women and children, this is the evil that we fight among us."

Isca'riot stared at Magdalen in disbelief. There was horrible truth in what she said, the endless conflicts and violence even the Yehudiish people had endured was testament to that. And Magdalen was speaking to him with no attempt at concealment, without hesitancy, without any concept of preaching nor with any deliberate fire in her voice. The matter-of-fact way in which she told him how the world endured drew suspicions of truth that began to tease his mind. But could he believe that Magdalen in her incarnations had existed for unimaginable numbers of years, that she had witnessed the beginning of time? This was too big for Isca'riot to comprehend, his mind began to lose any semblance of logic. He was desperate to hear more, there were too many questions, too many impossible untruths.

"So, what is this blood that you say we are made of?"

Magdalen studied Isca'riot. Was she making any impression?

"When a man deems to fall in love with his woman, this is his way to declare his loyalty. His woman will every time love back with undivided faith," she replied. "Your blood and that of Yeshua was born from other men, good men who believe another creator of time exists without any demands for worship. Adamah and Ab'raham were not of this blood, they were embraced by their powerful lord who you call god. The bloodline of Adamah then flowed through the race of men who stole this world, they desire that all humankind worship one god with their rule, like every lord or king who ever ruled. But your blood is pure Yehudas, your bloodline existed long before Ab'raham and Mo'ses." Magdalen paused, she waited as though considering something before she spoke. Isca'riot sensed the coming blow.

"I feel there is something more," he begged, without much surety.

Magdalen again tossed her hair that had this time fallen over her right-side eye. Then she stared while Yehudas, of nervous disposition, came under her spell. She revelled in being the image of the mysterious woman, her incarnate existence gave her everything she needed, Magdalen possessed more than enough of a woman's beguiling beauty; her relentless evolution over uncountable years enabled her to forever hold a man's eye when the situation desired; she knew that she held Isca'riot in her hand. She cast her fatal attraction to men in a way that would be subtle, she would never stand above other women who were more alluring in their splendour. She desired to blend into the crowd, to mingle into the throng without ever being noticed, for this Magdalen needed to disguise her natural self - she used simple tricks, easy mannerisms to lure a man's attention without them ever understanding why. Whenever she cast her web Magdalen could become a man's mistress, she could change the way a man saw her just enough to captivate his undying love. Little by little Magdalen drew Isca'riot in a deliberate way that might ensure the survival of her unborn females. When she tossed her hair from her eye with the casual sway of her hand, when at the same time her half-hidden breast heaved, she ingratiated a feeling of sexual uncertainty, she radiated just enough of enticing irresistibility that Yehudas could never hope to resist her lure. His deliverance wavered; his hostility began to fail.

"You are of my blood Yehudas. A grandfather of your grandfather's grandfather and countless generations before that," said Magdalen. "The future inside my womb is the not the first birth I have given to this world. Two creators from life, this is the seed I carry from my conception, when I was born from the sea mists that swirled upon this barren world, when life was miserable microbe bugs so small the eye could not behold. I was not in this humanoid form then. I give this world my blood to countenance the power of the race of men who are not born from me, who themselves came to exist by more foul means. Now my children will be my resurrection, their bloodline will be more powerful than I ever was. This is who you are, this is why your god who is not your god and his despicable sibling Gabriel desire me well dead."

Isca'riot stood stunned, unable to take all of this in. His mind recoiled in turmoil but everything Magdalen said made horrible sense. He knew his mind would soon capitulate, he sensed that her way of explaining everything was designed to make him see reason; her words played with his solid vision of the world that was, right now, on the verge of collapse. Once his life fell off the precipice of the cliff edge there would be no going back; his world, his reason for living would change forever from the intense debacle of where it now stood. Was not he Yehudas the vile traitor of all men?

Only forty days before this day he had disavowed the holy preacher who many said could be the promised spirit of God. This rebellious woman who stood before him had turned his life inside out, she had entered his life then changed everything he believed in. Because of this woman, he betrayed his long-time friend who without any doubt died because of his betrayal. Then, this same heretic woman from hell deemed to tell him unbelievable lies that his insane instincts warned him were not lies at all. Isca'riot felt himself beginning to tumble into the pit, falling to his ultimate doom knowing that once he landed upon the hard unforgiving ground, he would be hers - just as she had intended all along. In his mindset, he saw the vast swamp an indeterminate distance away waiting to consume him but for some extraordinary reason he did not care anymore, his mind capitulated in a small moment that gave himself to her, then he saw that Magdalen knew what she had always known, that she was his mistress, also his salvation, that she was his one escape from the abysmal shockwave of what he had done - his damming guilt that shrouded his thinking each minute of every day. Isca'riot gathered his senses then paused, knowing the one thing he must ask. Sweat stood on his brow, his heart bled blood while it raced in panic.

"You must tell me one more truth," whispered Isca'riot in his weak, wavering voice, his thin disguised mastery now vanishing like leaking water. "The cross you always wear around your neck?"

Magdalen shuddered. The decaying token of the world's first beginning had not left her ageless neck in well over a hundred million years, not since it had been given to her by the nascent Gabriel, his one offering of unrelinquished love. Magdalen could not tell Yehudas this because soon she must give up Gabriel's token of love - because the angel of God would soon return to reclaim it from her. It would be Yehudas's task to hide the symbol of blood love in the same mystical place it was hewn, beneath the granite stone that yielded the iron from which Gabriel had fashioned the object of his love. She did not answer the question asked by Isca'riot, she could not. How could she explain to any mortal man the reason it was given? Magdalen saw that Isca'riot in some way understood her unsaid answer buried deep in her tearful eyes. Yehudas's own eyes then cried the same tears, then Magdalen knew that Isca'riot was forever hers. Together they would stand side by side. Side by side they would fight the emissary of the Lord who would soon come to destroy them. If neither Isca'riot nor Magdalen survived, then Lucifer himself would dance on their graves - with one victorious hand held high to the midnight sky.

Just then, the intense moment that defined the existence of man was broken by the echoing sound of temple guards hurrying along the dark-lit corridor towards them.

Both Miryam of Bath'uma and Salome crumpled to their knees in reverence when they realised an angel of God stood before them. Yosef of Arim'athea, with Nicodemus by his side froze in stunned silence, not knowing how to react or how to behold the vision confronting them. The intense lightness faded, the apparition morphing into the tall slender figure of a magnificent man whose radiance belied his indeterminate age. His glorious, feathered wings reached from behind his back half hidden by the flowing white robes that adorned him. Yosef and Nicodemus both recovered their senses, they fell to their knees in adulation. Gabriel looked down upon all four of the conspirators who refused to look upwards at him lest they suffer his wrath.

The princely angel was well used to taking any form he wished, anything that was required of him though being an angel was a masterful stroke of illusion he rarely used. On few occasions did Gabriel display himself at all, he seldom had any contact with the human race, preferring to resolve his subjugation of the world through his resplendent prophets and loyal priests who then governed according to his commanding wishes. It was a hard task, the archangel of God often remastered his plans given the constant warfare and death that prevailed in all tribes of men who roamed the world in the name of his Lord. Men used any means they could in their endeavours to destroy each other.

It was the same each time. Gabriel knew the reason, every species of flesh-eating male life that had evolved in this garden world evolved the same desire to kill that he as the guardian tasked by his Lords then had to control. The evolution of mankind's basic instinct to hunt other lifeforms for his sustenance drove everything, even the slaughter of rival tribes. This in turn kindled beliefs in the minds of men that whoever it was that created their existence would always cherish them, that their loving God would protect them and countenance their need to do whatever was needed to ensure their means of survival. Gabriel knew that each tribe of man would turn upon each other at some random moment in time, with the instinct in men to create conflict being buried deep inside their evolved existence. Gabriel's charge was to nurture mankind's belief in the powerful God that created them, a supreme being of their own kind who demanded their worship; Gabriel's master was the almighty protector of all mankind - providing man gave his undying soul for the mighty Lord to behold.

To delegate, to keep alive the task of domination given to him by his master, Gabriel needed revered prophets, he needed men who were devout in their beliefs, men who possessed the vision or the uniqueness to be martyrs to their masses. The basic instinct of all species of men was to kill, to devour flesh just like that found in all other animal life on this godforsaken world. But this was what his own Lord commanded, the reason why this world had been discovered then nurtured in a way that created the image of one true God. Gabriel was conscious that he had made just one mistake, one single error that came close to costing him everything. Once, at the beginning of time when human life showed the first signs of formulative intelligence, he fell under the mesmerising spell of his adversary, his one powerful enemy whose task to countenance his existence was rendered rightful because she was the incarnation of the true creators of this world. Gabriel still felt the horrible pain inside his heart - even considering that his strange, tragic desire for the prehistoric Hyvah was long past forgotten. He had on rare occasions confronted her since but each and every time...

At the beginning of the world, he was deceived. Gabriel realised this; he would never have allowed this disastrous situation to happen but the consequence of Hyvah's masterful trickery was grave. Gabriel's first instinct when he morphed into his preferred vision of an angel was to look around, though he found nothing to alarm him. He decided to keep his angel form; the reverent angelic vision would induce sacrilege from the four humans splayed on their knees before him - or any other humankind he sensed might be around. Gabriel saw no sign of the renegade preacher who he believed beyond doubt should be dead, reasoning that Yeshua's body would be hidden within the cave chasm behind the rocks to his left. With more importance, there was no Hyvah, or Magdalen in her present incarnation. Gabriel breathed an inward sigh of relief. He removed his deft hand from the concealed clasp of his fire-blade sword that he left well covered with his flowing robe; it would not do for these people to see that he bore such a potent weapon of destruction. The so-called white angel warriors who dealt death and desolation were still far off in the future.

"Yosef of Arim'athea, please, look up to me then rise from your knees," Gabriel commanded.

Yosef's mind was in turmoil. He was a simple priest of low stature who found himself at the forefront of this inconceivable string of momentous events, now he was confronted by the ultimate being who was revered and worshipped by just about the whole of mankind. While these thoughts raced through his head Yosef glanced at his three companions, seeing their total capitulation coupled with absolute reverence. Yosef looked up.

"Get up Yosef. Stand."

Yosef stood up. The others remained kneeled, their faces to the ground with their arms splayed before them.

"Sire, are you our angel of the Lord?" Yosef spoke in a wavering voice.

"I come in many guises in my desire to be the loyal servant of our Lord, Him who abides above in heaven," Gabriel replied in his strange pitched voice, a chilling voice that reverberated in the uncanny atmosphere of the night. "Yosef of Arim'athea, where is the preacher Yeshua, the one who will soon be called by another name?"

"My Lord, he is inside the tomb of my giving." Yosef did not hesitate to tell the truth. "He still lives, we have brought him here at my command." Yosef felt overwhelmed, seeing no reason other than to tell everything he was asked. This that was happening right now was far greater than any of the tumultuous events preceding, the Sanhedrin's rebel priest felt his mind beginning to crumble.

"He lives? Bring me to him," ordered Gabriel.

Yosef did not reply, he had nothing to say. He turned then walked to the tomb with Gabriel kind of half walking, half hovering behind him. He saw the angel's great wings fold down into a much smaller size, then Gabriel's man form began to take more prominence. It was the angel's consummate height that struck Yosef, it was phenomenal, the height of two men.

Inside the tomb, Yeshua lay unconscious on the stone slab. The light radiated by Gabriel's reverence cast a strange soft glow that illuminated everything - even the dark shadows that hid in the deepest corners of the tomb. Gabriel looked down at Yeshua, seeing the strange preacher was in a trance-like state, a coma induced by shock which was worsened by his painful suffering. God's vassal put his long silvery hand upon the pulse to the side of Yeshua's neck, feeling a faint beat in the thin ice-blue vein. Yosef looked on, he noticed the transparency of the angel's gangling limps, more so his long tentacle-like fingers. After a few moments, Gabriel turned to Yosef.

"Yes. This prophet still lives. He should be tendered with care until he regains his consciousness," said Gabriel. The magnificent angel was no fool, nor was he compassionate, he knew that if Yeshua lived then he would find Hyvah. This Magdalen woman would soon reveal herself to be who she was, Gabriel would then see for himself whether she carried inside her the one thing he feared.

"How shall we care for him, my Lord?" Yosef was overawed. He was worried, how would Caiaphas and the Sanhedrin treat him afterwards, how would they view his traitorous actions alongside this momentous confrontation with God's graceful harbinger of tumultuous faith?

Gabriel paused. He saw Yosef shaking then realised this was a difficult situation that he must handle with care. "Your womenfolk must bathe his wounds in water that is near to boiling, then add the pulp of ripened lemon fruit with high measures of salt to clean his lacerations. Take the pungent mould from the walls of this cavern, also from the dead who are in this place of death, smear this mould into your messiah's wounds, more so to those wounds in his hands and to his feet then wrap them. Every hour replace the mould poultices with fresh ones. Let the maggots of flies breed into the deeper cuts, they will eat the rotted flesh." Gabriel paused, thinking to himself for a few moments. He possessed the ultimate power to heal this near-dead preacher but this would not do, Gabriel needed Hyvah to search for her risen again preacher. By not resorting to his miracle powers Yeshua would never recover but he would live long enough for Hyvah to find him, perhaps Yeshua would regain his consciousness when he sensed that his Magdalen was close by. Gabriel realised that only Yosef of Arim'athea, his accomplice Nicodemus and the two servant women must ever know of these events, including the whereabouts of the unconscious preacher from Naz'areth. His trap for Hyvah would then be well set.

"What will happen, my Lord? Will the Sanhedrin bear us great ill?" Yosef still feared the retribution that would no doubt befall them.

"Make sure the Sanhedrin and the Judaean people know nothing of this. Do not fear Yosef. There is a greater will for this man to survive his wounds than all of God's children can imagine," Gabriel replied. "Tender him until I return to you two days from now. Do not forget the mould, it will hold back the black infection that will soon kill him." Gabriel saw no immediate gain in anyone knowing about this momentous confrontation that would change the whole world; or the beginning of Yeshua the Saviour's sacrament that would soon dawn upon mankind. There could be salvation yet in this impending disaster.

Gabriel froze, then looked up. He sensed something, a hidden danger. The spirituous wisdom bestowed upon him by his master told him that outside the tomb something or someone threatened. His unnatural instincts warned him of a disturbance. Gabriel realised the situation had changed, there was a new intrusion into the delicate time web he had laid before making his appearance. He prepared himself to leave, he must not be discovered in these strenuous circumstances.

None of the four who had taken upon themselves the task of their messiah's last rites burial realised that, since leaving the Roman prison, they had been followed. Peleus the Roman centurion, who knew that Yeshua still lived, had spied their whereabouts. He watched from the peak of the hill of Golgotha, seeing everything that transpired - gasping his breath while staring in wonderment at the appearance of the tall white starlight apparition who Peleus guessed could not be of this world. The centurion was flanked by his two most loyal guards who stood beside him.

"Find me this Magdalen woman, the one who wears the ruby-coloured cloak." He barked. His two trusted guards disappeared towards the bustling throng of Je'rusalem. They knew exactly where to look.

Isca'riot trembled, his nerves shredded into a thousand shards of sharp-edged glass, he could not take much more. The ominous sound of approaching footsteps echoed down the corridor causing both Isca'riot and Magdalen to freeze. He heard frenzied shouts as each room preceding the one Isca'riot and Magdalen had taken refuge was searched. A few moments later armed temple guards burst through the doorway, around half a dozen or so who, in an instant, drew their swords. The first two guards, for some extraordinary unknown reason, fell to the floor stone-cold dead. The others stopped in stupefied horror. Isca'riot turned to Magdalen in pure terror - except there was no Magdalen. She was not there, not where she had stood beside him just a fraction of one moment before. Isca'riot stood stunned. The stillness of the windowless room shimmered in the growing heat haze that created a menacing atmosphere, the dim light causing dark shadows that teased the senses of instantaneous comprehension - offering no clues to what had happened in what could only have been the short blink of an eye. The remaining guards stood motionless and confused, they stared at Isca'riot in dysfunctional silence. Nor did Isca'riot know what to say; his muddled mind raced, refusing to operate with any semblance of coherence. Everyone in the dark dank room just... well, they just stood around in shocked silence. Magdalen was there and then she was not. The two guards lying dead on the floor bore no testament to any wounds or signs of violence, there was no blood or expressions of hammered pain, nor were there any manifestations of surprise or untoward awkwardness on their upturned faces, they lay motionless on the cold stone floor without any clues as to why they were there.

By instinct Isca'riot stepped forward towards the doorway feeling an acute sense of panic welling up inside; in their bewildered confusion, the guards parted to let him pass. Isca'riot left the room shaking from fearful nervousness, then he turned along the same corridor expecting the guards to recover their senses to overpower him. They made no move nor any effort to follow him; it dawned upon Isca'riot that they were as stunned and terrified as he was. What had happened? Everything ran through his mind while he half ran with speed and purpose without any recollection of reaching the same side entrance door through which he had entered alongside Magdalen. Isca'riot walked through the door, out into the blinding bright light outside that for a few moments reduced his vision to nothing, which added to the growing turmoil in his mind's eye. His head spun in confusion, his sudden dizziness compounded by his inability to comprehend anything at all. His sense of foreboding did not lessen when he joined the throng of people beyond the temple entrance, none of whom possessed any knowledge of the intense drama that had unfolded just a few moments before.

The early dawn neared to mid-morning in the narrow streets outside the temple doorway. Isca'riot felt the dry heat which threatened to overwhelm him as he staggered around trying to comprehend what had happened. First, his intense thirst drove him to the water seller standing by her wrought-copper cistern on the street corner, Isca'riot needed to drink, to calm himself down so that he could begin to think straight, to try to fathom the strange sequence of events leading up to this transcendental moment. Isca'riot turned everything over and over in his mind though nothing made sense, but he knew that he must in some way save his fragile sanity. He pushed his way through the babbling crowd to the corner of the square without any sign of whether the temple guards were following him or not. Isca'riot felt a small sense of relief, a vivid sense that he was under no immediate threat. Everything seemed unfathomable and normal, a confusion that added to his deteriorating awareness. Then he felt his mind spin, the world around him melted into an unfathomable haze that closed down his senses, he was struck with a bizarre dizziness. He quickened his pace fearing that at any moment his world might blacken or even collapse unless he somehow calmed himself down. A few seconds later Isca'riot reached the relative safety of the street corner where he paused.

"Quick, give me some water," he demanded to the water seller.

The woman said nothing back, reaching for a dirt-encrusted drinking cup which she then filled with clear water that Isca'riot sensed was both cool and refreshing. The small moment of relative normality was then broken by a sudden commotion along the left side street leading from the corner of the square, from the opposite direction to the temple entrance. Isca'riot thought he saw two Roman guards pushing their way through the busy street, through the crowds that gave way to their hurried hustling. Isca'riot turned to the water seller whose hair had fallen across her deep wrinkled face. Unconcerned, she filled the drinking cup held in her hand to pass to him. He paused with involuntary revulsion, his senses in descending turmoil as the water seller tossed the hair from her eyes when she looked at him without any pretence of menace or foreboding. Her eyes pierced into him, those familiar eyes that plagued him to cause his relentless downfall into desolate oblivion. Isca'riot staggered backwards, his mind spinning out of control like a whirlpool in the waterless heat of the sun, his head seemed to spin to some dark unknown place just when his staring eyes reached upwards to the relentless blue sky above. Which then disappeared from his vision.

Isca'riot fell to the ground, his unconsciousness inordinate and peaceful, his wretched mind oblivious to the great commotion that abounded around him.

Caiaphas listened to the commander of the Sanhedrin's temple guard with growing frustration. The night had been long and tumultuous since the momentous events of the previous day - he was still agitated by the whole episode, his normal sense of being in control rocked by his hostile confrontation inside the temple with the mad woman Magdalen - who had caused him incomprehensible shock by her slaying of his trusted guard. Magdalen's blasphemous outbursts in the dim gloom of the cenotaph still incensed Caiaphas, he felt a growing determination to find her which drove him into an ever more frenzied temper. Now, here in the dwelling in which he lived, he suffered his guard commander's latest report regarding their frantic search for the abominable woman who had caused him to lose his sense of wellbeing.

"Have you news of the whereabouts of anyone at all?" he demanded without any show of patience and with an outright hint of menace. "Have you searched the *whole* of Je'rusalem and found *anything*?"

"We are still searching, noble Caiaphas but we do not wish to alarm the Romans. Nor do we have any news of Yosef of Arim'athea or our venerable friend Nicodemus, both seem to have disappeared from the face of the world." The commander offered no apology, nor would he, he was a powerful built man who himself had no love or loyalty to Caiaphas - nor did he like the way Caiaphas all the time sucked up to the Romans, more so to Pontius Pilot, the Roman Prefect.

"I am suspicious, I believe there could be a link with Yosef of Arim'athea. We know that Magdalen did not go to Peter the disciple as we expected, that despicable gathering of rebels have no news of the woman either but, of course, they could be lying," added the guard commander. Making the situation worse, the dead body of the Naz'areth preacher had disappeared unless it was still held by the Romans - but they said not, they did not have it. This whole debacle was deteriorating fast.

"And what of Isca'riot?" demanded Caiaphas.

"My men are searching inside the temple. I think we might find him there; he was seen leaving the temple but later returned according to the old storyteller who begs for money at the corner of the temple square, he said Isca'riot went back to the temple, he was not alone. He said he thought the woman with him was Magdalen, the preacher's concubine." The commander was quite agitated, he was concerned. First, the beggar was supposed to be blind, so how could he have seen anything? Furthermore, it was Caiaphas's fault that Magdalen was allowed to escape, when one of the Sanhedrin's more reliable guards, his aide-de-camp was felled by a mere woman who should not have been allowed into the sacred temple that he, being the Sanhedrin's guard commander was tasked to protect. Caiaphas had both right there in his hands, he should have detained Magdalen in the temple cenotaph. This whole affair was a mess of Caiaphas's own making, now the temple guards were under scrutiny by Caiaphas for Caiaphas's own failings. To make matters worse Caiaphas now demanded that Isca'riot also be found.

The commander had vague suspicions of a trap, he thought it conceivable they were being manoeuvred, manipulated with deliberate intent - someone was twisting the Sanhedrin to cause disruptive chaos. There was no other plausible explanation to explain what happened inside the temple or the ugly confrontation with Pontius Pilot two days previous. The commander considered his report to Caiaphas with care.

"I made a request to the Roman garrison at the prison for the whereabouts of the body of the so-called descendent of our Lord, they claim the crucified corpse was collected for embalming sometime after midnight by a group of two men accompanied by two women. The dissident apostles are adamant that no dead body of their messiah was returned to them." The commander was worried, "I know from what they revealed, they expected their messiah's body to be brought to them by priests known to the Romans. I suspect those men were our Sanhedrin priest, meaning they must be Yosef of Arim'athea and Nicodemus which, of course, is a cause for concern." The commander was perturbed, he had interrogated the condemned Yeshua of Naz'areth before the death penalty was carried out, even at the time he suspected the confession he forced from the prisoner was no real confession - a strange turn of events that played upon his mind. Why would Magdalen return to the temple with Yehudas of Isca'riot? It made no sense; the guard commander did not believe for one minute they would be there, but he had ordered a search anyway.

"Where else has been searched? We must find this woman, I cannot think why she would be with Isca'riot," exclaimed Caiaphas.

"We have searched everywhere up to the west wall; my men now search to the east. She could be anywhere, Caiaphas." The commander knew his task to find this Magdalen woman would not be easy but the death of the guard by her hand made him determined to apprehend her. She would suffer his revengeful wrath when she was found, there were no doubts about this, it was only a matter of time. How had she overpowered the temple guard? An unarmed woman could not outwit the ruthless diligence of his guard, the one he trusted to carry out the most desperate of his orders. He was now dead.

There was a sudden commotion, both Caiaphas and the commander turned to see one of the guards who had been ordered to search the temple. He burst his way through the door of Caiaphas's home where they now talked, followed by Caiaphas's flustered servant wife who tried to prevent the guard from entering in such a frenzied state. The guard pushed her out of the way, urging that he must speak to his commander regardless of Caiaphas's instructions not to be disturbed. The intense confusion written on the guard's face was plain to see.

The guard did not wait to be asked why he was there. "Sir, I have grave news," he blurted.

"What news?" Caiaphas himself interrupted. It was plain the guard was both emotional and distressed.

"We found Isca'riot and the woman together in the temple," proclaimed the guard who then turned to his commander. "Sir... two more of our men are dead... she struck them down, the woman is not human, she is a demon...."

"Calm down," Caiaphas barked. "Calm down you idiot," he repeated. "The Magdalen woman was inside the temple? Did you apprehend her? Tell us what happened."

The guard took a few moments to collect his senses. "They were there together in the temple just as the storyteller told us. We found the two of them talking. In the cenotaph. We found them..."

"Two of you are dead? What has happened? How can two of you be dead?" interrupted the guard commander.

"Sir..." The guard dithered his words. "Sir, it happened in the blink of an eye. She was a woman standing there, then she was not. Two of us fell dead, then she was gone. Just disappeared in front of our eyes like the ghost mist of a demon."

"What do you mean she *disappeared*?" Caiaphas once more interceded in his usual condescending manner.

"She is not a woman... s~she is not human, we are dealing with a demon," stuttered the guard.

Caiaphas for a moment stood silent, his mind turning over. He recalled his encounter with Magdalen in the temple the previous day, now he felt even more agitated. This woman seemed to have her hold over everything that happened. Now, for some reason, she had developed a more than keen interest in Isca'riot. More and more Caiaphas felt the Sanhedrin was being threatened, thinking the essence of the Heb'rew faith in God was under some form of strange belligerence. Right now, he thought that God must speak to him, the good Lord above must tell him now more than ever what he should do. Caiaphas, in his unimaginable uncertainty, felt the ground beneath his feet beginning to feel threatened.

"Calm down man. Tell us what happened," demanded the commander.

"It all happened in the blink of an eye. We could not do anything, then Isca'riot left." The guard paused as if trying to find the courage to explain. "We entered the room and drew our swords when we found them there. She pointed to us with the palm of her hand, she had no sword or knife but our first two into the room fell to the floor. She changed into a ghost, a human ghost. I could see through her; I could see the wall behind her. Then she... she just stepped backwards, she stepped backwards through the wall and was gone."

Caiaphas and the guard commander stood silent. Stunned. Caiaphas recalled the guard who had died in the temple when Magdalen entered the forbidden cenotaph to confront himself and Isca'riot. Caiaphas felt a cold shudder run down his spine. Who was this woman who could perform these devilish tricks? And this Yeshua of Naz'areth, the false prophet who could somehow make his miracles happen, how did he do this? Who was he? The preacher whom he had desired dead at the hands of Pontius Pilot.

The guard commander thought more minacious thoughts. All three dead guards were each from his band of specials, experienced interrogators who had tortured then beaten Yeshua for his confession, they had worked him over under Caiaphas's violent questioning for the confession that was never truthful. Was this just coincidence? The commander once more recalled the words confessed by the dissident from Naz'areth, "Only if you say I am...."

358

"Where did Isca'riot go? Why did you not detain him?" the guard commander barked. The guard looked uncomfortable as if knowing he had done wrong.

"Sir, we were confused. We, we did not know what to do," the guard stammered. "I left two more guards with our dead, then two of us left the temple. We went out into the square to find Isca'riot but there were many people, the crowds had grown in the morning marketplace." The guard tried his best to recall everything that happened. He could only tell the indecipherable truth; it was for his commander and Caiaphas to fathom the facts. "We then saw Isca'riot drinking water in the far corner of the square," he continued. "We fast made our way towards him but then I saw him fall to the ground. Then the Romans came."

"What do you mean the Romans came?" Caiaphas exclaimed.

"Two Romans, they were the centurion's men, we know them. We could do nothing. We stood back," the guard replied. "Peleus's men took Isca'riot into the house on the corner of the square. We watched and waited. After a while one of Peleus's men came out of the house to speak with the old water woman selling her water in the square. She must have given Isca'riot bad water to drink, or poisoned him, I do not know."

"What happened then?" The guard commander was visibly alarmed by the apparent intervention of the Centurion's men. Why were they there? If Peleus was involved in this, then something far more serious was unravelling. The commander looked at Caiaphas whose own face was a concerned shade of grey. The high priest of the Sanhedrin looked deep in thought, worried. What about this Magdalen woman, this woman they were searching for with orders to kill if need be, who in the devil's name was she? The commander stared at his guard, "Did you see anything more of Magdalen?"

"No. Nor would I want to. Sir, she is the devil's incarnate."

"What of Isca'riot?" asked the commander.

"After a while, Peleus's men left him in the house. The Romans left the square without him, neither did they take the water seller with them."

"Why did you not go into the house to find them? Or look for Magdalen?"

Caiaphas intervened. By now he was less authoritative and more cautious. Caiaphas at last began to suspect they were in deep above their heads. He had wanted to crush the rebels led by Yeshua, to put an end to their rebellious outrage. Pontius Pilot ordered Yeshua to be put to death and he, Caiaphas, thought this would be the final act of the despicable plot, that this nonsense with the Yeshua preacher being the promised messiah would be over. But Magdalen, whom he had not heard of before this growing catastrophe, had changed everything. And she was the one who carried the Naz'areth preacher's child. Both Magdalen and her infant must be brought to justice, Magdalen must be tried then condemned to death before her child was born. Even better that she could be slain while resisting arrest. But Caiaphas realised with ominous dread that Magdalen herself was far more resourceful than he realised, more so when she was cornered. Caiaphas looked at the guard waiting for him to answer, he sensed the guard desired to tell something more.

The guard looked at Caiaphas who asked why they had not followed the Romans when they took Isca'riot into the house or why they had not found Magdalen. Instead, the guard turned to his commander ignoring Caiaphas's question. "Sir, there is more."

"More? What? Tell us," the commander ordered.

"The water seller," said the guard. "She saw us. She picked us out from the crowd even though we were holding back, she knew who we were." He paused, as if reluctant, but decided to continue. "When we tried to follow, she raised the palm of her hand, in the same way the Magdalen woman had done back in the temple."

"How do you mean?" questioned the commander alarmed, suspecting that he knew the answer.

"She raised her palm in the same way... as if warning us not to follow. That we would be dead if we tried. She was just an old woman. But she knew who we were."

"Was this water seller Magdalen?" Caiaphas intervened as if hit by some sudden enlightenment.

"No. Not unless she can transform," the guard answered Caiaphas. The

360

thought had already occurred to the guard, he had seen her morph into a weird grey ghost who could step through a wall, so the question about the old water seller was not one he could answer with truth, nor did he wish to.

The commander, he thought to himself for a few moments. Why would Peleus's men want Isca'riot? Unless they were searching for Magdalen. They knew of Isca'riot because Isca'riot had testified before Pontius Pilot and to Peleus, perhaps the Romans realised that Isca'riot would lead them to Magdalen. But why would the centurion want Magdalen? Why speak to the water seller unless she was in league with Magdalen in some way? Something else niggled at the back of the guard commander's mind. A vague thought that bothered him without him recalling what it was. The commander stayed silent while he deliberated over everything the guard had said. Caiaphas again intervened.

"This is a strange affair. This cannot be the hand of our Great Lord in heaven, we are faced with the dark work of demons. I must bring together the full Sanhedrin court to debate this grave turn of events." But Caiaphas was deep in thought. There were many secrets hidden by the Sanhedrin, many ancient artefacts, scriptures and tablet writings that were concealed, ancient gospels that were not common knowledge - talked about rumours and unsubstantiated whispers. Caiaphas himself knew they were real enough, more so he knew of primitive stone tablets that told of strange occurrences that seemed linked to what was happening now. Caiaphas began to feel uneasy, without doubt, each of the guards who witnessed the strange transgression of this Magdalen woman must themselves be silenced, they must be unable to tell anything of this, their fate was sealed – no one must know of Magdalen's strangeness lest she became a legendary sorceress in her own right. Knowing what was long written on the primordial tablets this, more than anything, could bring down the Sanhedrin.

The guard stood waiting for either Caiaphas or his commander to continue but both men said nothing, both were agitated, preoccupied in deep thought. Caiaphas was lost for words, it dawned upon him that much of what Magdalen had said to him when she confronted him and Isca'riot inside the temple contained an ominous smell of catastrophe. He needed the word of his Lord because he sensed great trouble, perhaps even his downfall. One awful thought played upon his mind more than anything - if Magdalen possessed such strange abilities alongside those of the false prophet Yeshua, whose well-witnessed miracles had caused unbounded discomposure to the Sanhedrin, what powerful abilities would a yet unborn child of theirs possess? Magdalen and her child must not live. They must be found, then put to death without delay.

"Please leave us then continue your search for Magdalen," ordered Caiaphas to the guard. "Do not mention what you have witnessed to anyone on pain of your life." The guard looked uncertain, resigned to the fact they would not find her. He looked at his commander who nodded his affirmation without speaking, the guard turned towards the door, he was greeted by the servant of Caiaphas who stood waiting to see him out of the building. The commander was deep in thought, something was not right, something he could not put his finger on bothered him, it churned like a lead weight inside his fertile thinking mind. Then, as the guard reached the door to leave, the nagging doubt that troubled the commander which he could not explain smacked into him, it came to him like a thunderbolt striking the ground beneath his feet.

"Wait," he shouted to the departing guard. The guard paused, then turned.

"The storyteller... the blind storyteller," demanded the commander.

In the cavernous tomb where Yeshua lay wrapped in his blood-soaked cloak, the growing heat of the sabbath day did not penetrate. It remained a constant cool tinged with the smell of rotting foulness, the wretched aroma of the dead drifting from other tombs causing the rancid air to be untouched by the clean white freshness of the outside day. On the cold stone slab Yeshua still lingered though he made no sound, just shallow noiseless breathing that grew more noticeable as the hours wore on. Beside him, Miryam of Bath'uma and Salome bathed his wounds while Nicodemus collected more festering mould from the tomb walls. It occurred to Nicodemus that mould grew in damp places fed by unseen putrid rot, the remains of the decaying dead, but whatever the greenish sponge-like growth contained Yeshua's deep wounds appeared to improve as the hours passed. The greyness of imminent death that etched the preacher's face receded into the depths from where it came, there was a growing sense he might linger a little longer. No more puss oozed from his mangled hands through which the spikes had been driven, but his feet were beyond any recognisable description. Even if he were to live then Yeshua would never walk, unless he performed one of his own revered miracles to his battered body.

More worrying, Yeshua's sinewy arms were torn from their cavernous sockets. His contorted body offered a forlorn testament to the intense pain he had suffered, the cruel torture that was well beyond the will of any man to endure - suffering that in every other instance finished those unfortunate enough to be nailed to a wooden stake in crucifixion, dying in mortifying pain while the baying bloodthirsty crowds looked on. Salome wished to herself that Yeshua would die to save his misery, both Miryam and Salome knew that something strange and unexpected was occurring, they had both cared for the dying many times. They realised Yeshua's deep comatose-like state seemed to be stabilising. He refused to die while the rancid mould even in the last few hours healed his wounds, it crept into his blood, penetrated his veins then seeped into his bones. The infinite minute microbes of an indefinable structure spread through his dying body bringing a small measure of relief to Yeshua's twisted limbs. The slithering maggots sown to the inside of his gaping flesh had done their work. Miryam and Salome did the best they could.

The mighty angel of God had taken it upon himself to leave, Yosef of Arim'athea sat outside the entrance to the tomb in deep thought. Two days and nights had passed since the intense drama of the crucifixions, the aged priest crouched on his haunches deep in far-off contemplation. They were all four in this abominable situation deep above their heads, but since the appearance of Gabriel one day before everything had taken a more sinister turn. How could he face Caiaphas and the Sanhedrin to explain any of this, how would they react? They would not understand or offer any clemency, more and more he felt his destiny lay in the hands of the unfathomable Magdalen who Yosef felt should be here to help them. Something bad had happened elsewhere, something had gone wrong which meant that other tumultuous events were unravelling much beyond his comprehension. Salome had been into the marketplace to buy food, she had since returned to tell them of the great commotion there, there were Sanhedrin guards everywhere, Romans also. More worrying, Salome said that Yehudas Isca'riot was now detained by the Romans. That wretched scum of a man who had betrayed the messiah would talk; Yosef did not doubt this. For a few moments he sensed that he should go to Caiaphas to save his skin, but something held him back, a sense that his destiny lay elsewhere, not with the Sanhedrin. Perhaps, he thought to himself, this had always been the case.

Nicodemus came out from the tomb to crouch on his heels beside him.

"How is our suffering messiah?" Yosef asked with a hint of acerbity. There was an element of bitterness in Yosef's voice because he had not foreseen any of this, this whole situation had twisted and turned well beyond his comprehension.

"He is improved but Miryam senses he is still dying," replied Nicodemus. "The mould is a strange thing, it cleans the wounds, the putrid smell of gangrenous festering goes away. Miryam and Salome are impressed by its power to heal rotting flesh, his wounds are still full of hungry maggots." Nicodemus paused, "I am worried. What of this angel who came Yosef?" They were all four still floundering in deep shock.

"I do not know Nicodemus," Yosef looked apprehensive. "All we can do is wait. The almighty Gabriel said he would return by tomorrow, but I think we must act. I have grave feelings that all is not well."

"Do you believe this vision *was* the blessed Gabriel?"

"Oh yes, let us have no doubts," said Yosef, "I think the wrath of God is upon us. Perhaps a great sin has been committed by we the chosen people. Perhaps we *have* put our Lord's beloved son to death. Either this or we have raised a spectre so gruesome that every Yehudiish of Judaea will pay a terrible price."

Yosef paused. A brief flash of light caught his eye, a flash of intense sunlight glinting upon hidden metal in the high hilltop boulders a measurable distance to their right. Yosef realised straightaway they were being watched.

Nicodemus saw it too, they both remained silent, straining their eyes to see while at the same time knowing they must react. Yosef was the first to respond.

"Quick, inside the tomb. Move without showing panic."

"Who is it?" Nicodemus hissed.

"I do not know. But whoever it is knows we are here."

They both ambled towards the entrance to give the impression of no undue panic, then they ran inside. Miryam and Salome looked up startled.

"Someone is outside in the hilltop boulders of Golgotha. We must be careful," warned Yosef.

"Who?" Miryam began to lose her self-control.

"We do not know. But the sunlight is reflecting from metal, perhaps armour or a sword," suggested Nicodemus.

"How is Yeshua? Can he be moved?" Yosef tried to weigh up their options, he knew that trying to move Yeshua was pointless. Whoever was up there knew everything, though there was every chance they did not know that Yeshua was inside the tomb. Or it was possible they did, Yosef had no way of knowing.

"No, he cannot be moved. He is close to death, he will do well to survive the day," warned Miryam. "His wounds heal, he breathes with more ease but his fever sometimes grows, then he is delirious without consciousness. I do not know how he still lives."

"Then we must leave him here. We cannot stay, it is not safe," said Yosef.

"We cannot leave him here alone," begged Salome, alarmed.

"We must or we will be put to death if we are found with him," Yosef answered. "We can close the tomb; we can roll the stone entrance shut. It is the best we can do."

Nicodemus stayed silent but knew Yosef was right, they were now discovered, they were in real danger. Salome interrupted,

"I will stay to tend his wounds. Close the tomb, we shall be safe inside."

"I will stay," declared Miryam. "We have sustenance and water for two days."

"No, whoever is out there knows we are four. Four must be seen to leave after the tomb is closed. Whoever is there may not know Yeshua is still in the tomb, they may think we are preparing the tomb for another burial or the burial of Yeshua himself. It is the only chance we have. If they come and find us all together with Yeshua then we are doomed, then Yeshua will not live," said Yosef.

Miryam, Salome and Nicodemus all stared at each other knowing that Yosef made sense. Salome began to cry, her tears falling down her cheeks before free-falling into Yeshua's tangled beard still encrusted with remnants of his blood, she had cleaned his hair which was now well groomed, she was about to start upon his matted beard. Salome had no desire to leave Yeshua in such poor state.

Miryam tugged Salome's sleeve to pull her away. They each stood silent before deciding in their confused minds that Yosef was right, that it would be more prudent to leave then return in the morning at first light - the third day since Yeshua's supposed death, today was the sabbath day of rest when fewer people would be about. Tomorrow, they expected the reappearance of the reverent Gabriel. The four left the tomb without knowing if their mysterious watcher was still there or not, there was no way to tell in the fading light of another agonising warm spring day.

Once outside the tomb Yosef and Nicodemus rolled the enormous round stone over the entrance to close the doorway, making as much commotion as they could to show their intent to leave without anyone alive inside. They sweated and heaved, the desperation of their effort not all for show as the lumbering stone covered the entrance to the tomb. Why would they leave behind anyone undead? The tomb was a place for the dead, those who had no place in the world of the living. At worse they had left someone dead behind in the tomb, if not then they were preparing the tomb for someone not yet dead, or dead but not yet buried. Perhaps their desperate ruse would work.

Yosef led the way down through the rock-strewn cemetery leading the donkey cart that still stood waiting. Nicodemus was pleased the donkey made so much noise, the racket the animal made with the rattling of the cart would leave no one in doubt they were leaving the tomb closed. They made their way down the rocky path. It was tiring work but within the hour they rejoined the paved pathway that led back into the bustling city of Je'rusalem.

"My homestead shack is close," said Nicodemus. He offered his own humble dwelling on the city outskirts, where they could sleep the night while still close enough to return at first light the next morning. They each agreed, Salome was stricken with disquiet while Miryam knew the next day would be the telling day, the day that would reveal if Yeshua lived or not. Even so, each of the two women dreaded the new forthcoming day, no less because of the impending and frightening return of the angelic apparition they both knew was way beyond their fragile nerves. Yosef thought a tumultuous day of reckoning lay ahead the next morning, he hoped they had done enough to convince whoever observed them that only a simple funeral preparation was in hand.

Despite everything Josef had done to cover their tracks, Peleus was no fool. The cool-thinking Centurion realised the guard ordered to keep a keen watch upon the tomb had been spotted, though the veteran leader of the Roman legions was not concerned. Peleus knew full well the Naz'areth preacher was still inside the closed tomb, though he assumed he had since died - given that no man could survive those wounds for long. The body being left inside the tomb with the entrance now sealed appeared to confirm this. But instinct with a keen sense of intrigue drove him, these remarkable series of events had not yet reached anywhere near their fascinating conclusion - whatever was about to happen might have unsavoury consequences for the Romans in Judaea. Peleus and his mind were in overdrive, he was still awestruck by the apparent manifestation of the strange god-like being, a magnificent cosmic apparition he suspected was an outright prelude to a deteriorating situation of tumultuous proportions.

"Follow the four of them," Peleus ordered his one remaining guard. "I will stay here and wait. They leave their damned preacher behind in the tomb, they think we are fools. I suspect that soon I will not be alone. These strange happenings are not the work of any god I know of."

Magdalen felt exhausted, she had little strength left in her deteriorating body. Her growing concern was for the wellbeing of her embryonic infants as each day of intense extremity passed; Magdalen knew her abilities to endure the deepening crisis would soon fade, that she must in some way conserve her strength to give her children the best chance of survival she could. Perhaps she had made a grave error in returning to the temple with Isca'riot, but it had served her purpose, she had lured the bestial guards into their damned place of religious reverence. Caiaphas would know that his treacherous pact with Isca'riot was severed, the power of the San-hedrin's sacred citadel broken - even so, her minacious miscalculations were growing ever more frequent with the slow deterioration of her mind. She could feel the decay, she could sense the acidic end though she had no thoughts of how her death would happen.

Many fearful events had occurred since she last retreated into her own sphere, a parallel world where she could change herself into an alternative self. Right now, she felt afraid and alone, there was no others of her kind to whom she could turn, there was no one man to love her or to comfort her in the way she saw other good men protect their women. The man who loved her had been torn from her by Caiaphas and the Sanhedrin, by Isca'riot's betrayal and the harrowing decision of Pontius Pilot to carry out the penalty of death demanded by the Sanhedrin. These men were abominable, they were men whose lives were governed by their ambition, men who dealt with threats to their status with violence and destruction. It had long been Magdalen's remorseless task to defend herself against egregious men, predatory men who disdained women, men who treated their women in brutal ways - men who thought that women should be kept for fleshly pleasures, to bear sons of their own seed. The race of men whom Magdalen pitted herself against saw themselves forever dominant, it was their mastery of self-belief that decided the way they lived their lives of uncaring barbarity. There was little occasion for good men in Magdalen's solitary life, never was there time for thoughtful peace or enough tranquillity to dream the dreams she always dreamed of.

When the elite band of temple guards found her inside the temple with Isca'riot as she knew would happen, her ingrained response came to the fore without any deliberate intent. The Sanhedrin guards were brutal men who killed, she straightaway saw their wide-eyed sins - when she took hold of their minds to block their sins from her own mind they died, they fell to the floor dead. The first guard who burst into the room, she saw in his memories that a time ago he had ravaged then killed the young girl who resisted with her screams echoing from hell, the girl cried terrified tears that only Magdalen could hear. When Magdalen wrenched the guard's twisted memory from his consciousness his life drained like foul water disappearing into the earth. She saw the second guard throw the slave woman into the rain-filled chasm, he held her down until she drowned struggling in the murky brown sewer filled with nauseating excrement, foulness that Magdalen saw choked then killed her in a vile way that no mortal human should deserve. Magdalen took his sins, flashing them before his terrified eyes in the smallest fraction of time before he too died, he died before he crumbled to the cold stone floor. He died through the insatiable insanity of the slave girl's eyes that burned into his wretched soul, turning his twisted thoughts into white oblivion. Then Magdalen saw more guards armed with their swords that could kill her, she had no strength left to defend herself or to see deep into their consciousness but in a fractional moment saw that never had they murdered or killed. She retreated, she stepped back into her unworldly world, the ghost world where she did not die, another world where she felt safe and protected. It was her one chance, her one escape from these evil men who would end the life of her unborn. She would save Isca'riot later, her precarious ploy to

369

survive until the birth of her child had so far worked to her advantage. She would again find Yehudas outside of the temple, Magdalen would save the despised traitor and his wretched soul one more time - just as she always did.

"Where do you take him?" The water seller blocked the way of the Roman who held the half-conscious Isca'riot to his feet.

"Go, woman, take yourself away," the Roman ordered. Then he looked at her closer. There was something about her that made him pause, old age did not hide the purpose in her grey eyes that burned into him with threatening menace. He struggled to support Isca'riot who needed a good deal of help if he were to maintain any sense of nobility.

"Take him into that house there, he needs more clean water to revive him," the water seller pointed to a single-story building she chose at random, a house with a crumbling red tiled roof and a door that was half open. The second Roman who had been endeavouring to search for Magdalen in the square joined them with distinct indifference.

"There is no sign of the Magdalen woman," said the Roman, without taking any notice of the water seller. "She must be around here someplace, if we have this so-called traitor with us then I suspect she will find us." Their clandestine informer, the blind storyteller, had earlier confirmed that Magdalen was seen in the vicinity of the temple in the company of Isca'riot. They both looked at Isca'riot, realising they needed to do something quick, neither of them was able to revive his consciousness since hauling him to his feet from the ground where they found him. The Roman holding Isca'riot looked to where the water seller pointed, then half dragged Isca'riot towards the doorway.

"Quick, give me a hand," demanded the Roman to his fellow guard. "He is heavy, he is losing his senses."

Together they stumbled with Isca'riot into the house where an old man sat motionless beside a decrepit three-legged table that stayed upright only because it was supported by the rough back wall. His face distorted with alarmed fright when the Romans burst through his door, even more so when the old woman followed them into the single cramped room of the dirty cluttered dwelling. The old man was more than willing to give up his stool, he scurried to the corner - he was not about to argue with two armed Romans intruding into his home - but who was this half unconscious man they carried? He looked familiar to the old man who lived in the house. The two guards threw Isca'riot onto the stool, he stooped backwards resting his head against the mud-plastered wall.

The water seller pushed herself forward to pour cool water into Isca'riot's open mouth, she saw that it made little difference, sensing his will to live had collapsed. From the vacant expression on Isca'riot's blank face she realised that his mind, which had teetered on the edge ever since the brutal torture inflicted upon Yeshua by the Sanhedrin guards, had given up, that his dubious chance meeting with her in the market square outside of the temple had destroyed everything he believed in by ending his resolve. Isca'riot was never a strong man, his frayed nerves always besieged him whenever he tried to stand his ground or make himself more forceful; the much-held image of a weak-willed betrayer seemed to suit him well. But this was never the real Isca'riot.

The old woman saw in an instant that she needed to do more, or she would lose him. The water seller decided to take a chance, one that would without doubt endanger her in the presence of the two Romans. She removed the small iron cross buried around her nape; she then held the twisted metal warmed by the bosom of her sagging breasts against the forehead of the motionless Isca'riot. The water seller concentrated her mind, in an instant seeing the muddled thoughts that entwined him like razored wire inside his head. She felt the great pulsating pain enumerating from his heart, pain that he could not deal with nor understand - the weakness of his pulse alarmed her when she realised there was little time left. Moreover, it was the guilt of his conscience, the guilty acceptance that it was himself who caused the death of his friend, the intense guilt of his deliberate betrayal severing any sense of morality that remained. She saw gaping wounds inside his shredded consciousness, something she expected to be there knowing it was this that could finish him. The unresolved questions he demanded; where was his God when he needed him; why was it this Magdalen woman twisted all of the values he held dear? Everything he believed sacred she had destroyed, leaving his sanity hanging in tatters and then blowing in the wind like ancient prayer flags torn by years of neglect. The old woman saw all of this knowing the fault was hers – she understood what she must do, she foresaw the awful responsibility of the task she faced.

The two Romans and the old man stared in unmitigated bewilderment, they stood spellbound beside the old water seller who seemed to morph into some unknown form that appeared to reach inside the mind of Isca'riot; whose once strong face bore the expression of a small child close to death. The old man's eyes widened in disbelief when the iron cross she brandished shimmered like long-lost starlight, casting a deathlike shadow upon the two Romans who stood transfixed. Then everything was pitch black, like the intense deep darkness of night that would never see sunrise; each of them in the room saw countless millions of stars hidden by colourful clouds of cosmic dust drifting in the mayhem of their minds, minds that hung by the merest threads of disbelieving vision. None of them saw the water seller take the twisted fibres of Isca'riot's sanity in her wrinkled paw-like hands, nor her fingers that traced the broken strands of grey tissue that dripped like hot lava through his trance-like vision. They did not see her piece together the sinews of tangled wire threads of lignin that formed broken thoughts inside the wretched turmoil of his mind, a mind that revealed no coherent reason to live. She toiled with her bent hooked fingers, she worked like a young virgin tripping through fields of fresh green grass rippled wet by morning dew, she drew without effort on skills honed by tens of millions of years of fighting to survive in a fertile world of predators. The water seller fixed the severed ends of nothingness, elements that existed inside his terrified consciousness wrecked by the manic demons that danced then crawled through his miserable insanity. Then she was done. She stepped backwards, fading into a strange mystic mist as she did so. A small fraction of a moment later Isca'riot uttered a short breath, the greyness of death gone from his face. The two Romans stood in a transcendental state, but the old man smiled to himself in absolute satisfaction – he had before witnessed other miracles, this was the powerful work of his loving God. Isca'riot opened his eyes. He gazed around taking in his surroundings just as the old ageing water seller stood before him – convincing the relentless tortured renegade of a traitor that it was all a bad dream.

It took a few moments for Peleus's two Roman guards to comprehend that something reverent, savage and strange had happened. They had earlier in the morning beheld the incomprehensible apparition of Gabriel outside of the tomb, which had frayed their nerves beyond their normal senses – now this new strangeness destroyed their resolve as they stood back from the water seller in confused disorder.

"What will you do?" the water seller asked. The two guards gazed at her in utmost silence. "Will you take me and lock me into your prison?"

It took a good while for the two Romans to come to their senses. The old man stared at the water seller with a wry smile etched upon his weathered face, not since the miracles of the preacher prophet had he witnessed anything like this. One of the Romans broke the cold atmospheric ice.

"By my lord, by my lady midnight, who in her glorious name are you?" his voice echoed with a feeble tremor in the half-light of the room.

"I have no name. Not in this world do I have a name."

"You have no name? How can you have no name?" The guard dithered between reverence and authority, he sensed that he must not be forceful lest she took some vengeance against him.

"I have no name to give you, here in your world I am not called by any given name."

"But who are you? You are no demon or demigod of evil; you are not the despot woman we have been told to seek nor are you the rebellious rebel we hear the Judaeans desire dead. You are not a saintly woman of this world, perhaps you are a witch with your strange ways, we saw what you just did to this man's mind, only a witch with dark powers could do this to a man, even a man who is near stricken dead by demons." The guard outpoured his wild confused thoughts, unable to contain them in the stifling atmosphere of the stinking room.

The second Roman, as if struck by intuition, then interrupted. "Old woman, do you know the woman called Magdalen?"

"Magdalen? Yes, I know Magdalen," she paused, then held back. "Are you going to take me to your prison?" Her calmness belied her indifference.

The old woman seemed distant, as if the reverence of the occasion did not concern her. The two Romans glanced at each other, their demeanour showing they had little clue with regards to their next move.

"How do you know Magdalen? Do you know where she is?" The guard ignored the old woman's question about their prison.

Isca'riot still sat back restless upon his stool, his senses returning to his befuddled vision. Isca'riot half listened to their questioning with a growing foreboding inside his still groggy consciousness. Even in his confused state of mind he realised the water seller was Magdalen somehow transformed, but nothing about Magdalen surprised him anymore. Isca'riot had no strength to intervene in their worthless questioning.

"The Magdalen you seek is of my blood. I know where she hides but you will not find her. You can search until the birds fly to the moon, but you cannot find her, not in your world," she answered.

The Romans glanced at each other with unease. Peleus would never contemplate them returning without Magdalen as he had ordered, not without incurring his foul-tempered wrath.

"Why do you search for Magdalen?" Isca'riot interrupted the Romans, his croaky voice reminding all of them they were all here in this room because of himself.

The guard paused surprised, thinking how he should reply to Isca'riot - who no one expected to intervene.

"We are here searching at the command of Peleus the centurion. There are strange happenings in the cemetery of Golgotha," said the guard. "We have no orders to detain her or imprison her, just that Magdalen should go with us to the hill of Golgotha." The Roman guard poured out the truth, thinking it pointless to hide anything after everything he had witnessed. He could not contain himself. "Please, if you know of where she can be found then you must tell us."

"Why?" the water seller asked.

"Our centurion is there waiting. The Heb'rew preacher who was crucified two days ago is buried in a closed tomb in the cemetery. There are others there as well, there is great urgency that this Magdalen woman should be there." The guard felt he had overstepped the mark, given away too much information, his fellow Roman regarded him with unease. But they had both had enough, they desired to be away, they felt danger, they were unsure of themselves even considering their much-endowed bravery and their formidable reputation. Events were happening much beyond their comprehension, they did not worship the same god as these people, the Romans possessed their own gods who never revealed themselves in the formidable ways they had witnessed during this one single day so far.

"Is the preacher dead or alive?" the water seller demanded, alarmed.

The two Romans once again looked at each other which straightaway answered the old woman's question. The two of them remained silent because this was something neither wanted to answer - the prison guards back at their garrison had revealed how the condemned prisoner survived his execution, even though Peleus had ordered nothing to be said. Intense politics were happening, neither of the two Romans wished to be bridled with blame though it was evident, even to the old man who still stood crouched in the corner of the darkening room, that rumours concerning Yeshua could never be concealed for long. The old man had twice before witnessed unbelievable miracles performed by the executed son of God, was it not inconceivable the preacher could survive even his own death?

It was Isca'riot who interceded. "Romans. Return to your centurion. Tell him that Magdalen will go to the hill of Golgotha this night."

"You can promise this?" the guard asked. They were anxious to be gone, they wished to be well away from this unbelievable strangeness.

"No one can promise anything where Magdalen is concerned," Isca'riot replied. "But I know where to find her."

"Then take us to her," the second guard demanded.

"You cannot go to where Marusya is," replied Isca'riot. "Please, you must believe me when I say no mortal man can go there."

The two guards stared at Isca'riot knowing he was right. They thought for a few moments, this was their opportunity to be gone.

"Then, we leave you, but we demand that you do as you say. The centurion does not suffer those who cross him. It is your head Isca'riot." Then they both turned to leave through the half-open door. Outside in the still bustling street darkness had only just descended, though the hustled dwellers of Je'rusalem were blessed and unaware of how the fragile fate of mankind hung by a thin strand of thread that could be cut with ease.

Still inside the room, Isca'riot stared at the water seller. The old man remained silent, unnoticed in the farthest corner. His toiled breathing reminded the old woman and Isca'riot that he remained in the room.

"What has become of Marusya?" Isca'riot suspected he knew the answer, but he had just awakened from his terrifying nightmare dream.

"You must not ask this question or demand an answer Yehudas," said the water seller. "Your mind is still weak; you will never understand the boundaries that bind you."

"Then we must go quick to the cemetery on the hill. You know this."

"No, I do not know this. We shall not go there to that place. You and I will go to another place Yehudas." The water seller turned to the old man still in the corner. "You have witnessed all of this before you old man. We are in your humble house; great happenings have revealed themselves to you that should never have been revealed. I am sorry for this trouble we have caused but your memory will be strong, even stronger for the silver Caiaphas and the Sanhedrin will no doubt give to you when you tell them of what you have seen this day. Perhaps you will tell them that we go to the hill of Golgotha?" She smiled, knowing what would happen once they had left through his door. The water seller saw the sudden enlightenment in the man's face, his expression lit up when it dawned upon him how well he could be rewarded by the Sanhedrin for describing what he witnessed. But the old man was no fool, he realised the water seller had for her own reasons planted these thoughts inside his head, though he had deduced that he must never cross this powerful woman who was sent by God.

Isca'riot struggled to his feet, his strength returning, he felt weak. The water seller did not help or assist him, she turned to leave through the door. Isca'riot leapt up, almost stumbling, he looked at the old man as if begging to leave his presence. They both smiled uneasy smiles knowing they would never meet again; such was their fate in this incomparable world of betrayal.

Once the two strangers left his house, the old man gathered his things so that he could leave. He was desperate for money to buy food, a payment in silver would be welcome to stave off his debilitating hunger for a short while longer. He smiled to himself in a way bereft of any cunning, betraying a betrayer would be a good way to be rich, he thought, if only for a few days of wealth and great doughtiness. He ambled out of his doorway, checked in all directions for more hidden dangers such as sword-bearing Romans, or yet more strange beings, then he headed in the direction of the temple of the Sanhedrin.

The commander of the Sanhedrin guards found the blind storytelling beggar plying his trade at the corner of the square. He made his men drag the blind man inside the temple, they hustled him down the darkened passages to where Caiaphas stood contemplating the difficult situation he faced. There was some danger, there was no doubt about this, there was a sense of insoluble panic that must be overcome if he and the Sanhedrin were to regain control of these intolerable events. Caiaphas needed the problem of both Magdalen and her unborn child resolved. Yehudas Isca'riot, who knew a good deal about what scuttled around behind the Sanhedrin's closed doors must be dealt with too. Caiaphas's desperation knew no bounds, his determination to succeed drove him relentless; Isca'riot and the traitorous blaspheming woman must be found then silenced before the situation deteriorated beyond worse. There was growing unrest amongst the Yehudiish people.

The commander proceeded with more care, he followed his instinctive gut feeling – the guard commander was sure they were being led by the hand, by whom he did not yet know. Caiaphas had lost control; the commander was certain of this - this whole mess was escalating into free fall disaster. To make matters worse the Romans had intervened, as far as the commander could work out, they now held Isca'riot in their hands, they might well have the woman too.

Both the commander and Caiaphas agreed on one thing, they must get to the bottom of how this seditious situation had come about. Then they could regain control, the Sanhedrin would restore its credibility with both the Romans and the Judaean people so that even more troublesome disorder could be averted. The two temple guards forced the beggar down to his knees before their irritable, resolute commander.

"You informed both of my guards who stand before you that Yehudas Isca'riot made his way to the temple, you also told them he was not alone," the commander tried to remain calm but the beggar continued staring ahead unseeing. "If you cannot see the guards then how did you know this? Did someone else see them then tell you? You are not one of our usual informers."

"Commander, I am a man blind since a young boy, blinded when the liquid sun of our Lord in heaven burned into my eyes. Why do you ask this question?"

"Answer my question, it is simple enough," the commander barked.

"If it is so simple then let me tell you and your guards a little story, one that will perhaps answer your question," offered the beggar.

"We do not need one of your stupid beggar stories," interrupted Caiaphas, "I want you to answer the question." In truth, Caiaphas himself was not sure why the commander had ordered the blind beggar to be brought before them, it was insignificant who had informed the guards that Isca'riot had returned to the temple - even if Magdalen was with him. This was old news, they knew from the beggar or whoever else that both returned to the temple, Caiaphas did not understand his commander's line of questioning. The beggar turned in the direction of Caiaphas's voice, giving the false impression that he could not see him.

"You are Caiaphas the high priest, eh?" the beggar sneered in contempt. "You are the worm who gave our preacher to the Romans, you condemned to death the Lord's new prophet because you would not believe he might be the spirit of God."

The commander looked on; he sensed his hunch was right. The beggar was no beholder of the Sanhedrin, there could be no further doubt. What concerned the commander was the contempt Caiaphas had brought upon himself, contempt also upon the Sanhedrin from great swathes of the Judaean people, more so among those who listened to the renegade preacher's preachings. Judaea was in chaos, a rift-riven land of Yehudiish who believed they were God's chosen. Even so, many Judaeans in authority were still unconvinced about the Sanhedrin's claim that Yeshua had confessed to being the prodigal son of God sent from heaven to save them. But if this beggar sneered at the Sanhedrin, then why had he informed upon Isca'riot and the woman to the Sanhedrin guards? And how did he know they were in the temple? The commander bent closer to the blind storyteller.

"If you do not answer who told you and why you then informed my elite guards, you will suffer more than the loss of your sight old man," the commander warned the beggar.

"The answer is simple enough sir, I think you might be interested in my little story, my story to you that might tell you why I might not be so blind as you think," said the beggar who then smiled with mischief, knowing full well that he had both the commander's and Caiaphas's unabridged attention; there were many advantages in being a storyteller.

The commander kneeled before the beggar; he was silent - he realised he had just been sidestepped. Caiaphas stood back not knowing what to say.

"You do not need to threaten me with your despicable threats commander," the beggar added. "Perhaps you will even indulge me with a little silver in my palm for my story?"

"We will pay you nothing," interrupted Caiaphas, irritated. "But you will pay with your life if you do not tell us everything you know. Are you saying that you see everything, blind beggar?"

"I am a simple storyteller, if you pay me in silver I will tell you a good story, if you pay me nothing then I will tell you lies." The storyteller, who was not blind, saw the commander glance at one of the two guards who then without sound drew his sword. The storyteller's eyes did not move or give any indications that he could see everything, his eyes stayed fixed in the way that all blind beggar's eyes stare when staring somewhere into oblivion. His eyes stayed looking straight ahead, even when the guard's sword stopped short from the beggar's throat, paused to strike if the commander commanded the storyteller dead.

"Tell us your story then blind man," instructed the commander. "If your story is good then you will get your slippery silver, if you tell a lie then you will be paid in sharp bronze."

Everyone in the temple room stood in silence not knowing what would happen next, except for the beggar who still kneeled upon his dirt-encrusted knees with his grimy broken hands tied behind his back. He knelt in quiet solitude, knowing they would not kill him just yet, not when they wanted to know all that was inside his head. This was the advantage in being a blind storyteller who saw everything that everyone ever did.

"Let me tell you about a young boy, a boy born among the tall watery grasses that even in these blasphemous days still grow beside the slow River of Labinda a long way from Judaea." The storyteller began his tale that he thought might save his life though he did not hold much hope. But then he did not much care.

"The boy grew strong, strong enough to help his father take fish from the river to feed his four brothers and his servant sisters, his three sisters who tended to their mother who was dying from the foul water sickness common in the hot swamplands of the Labinda."

"This is nonsensical nonsense," interrupted Caiaphas. "Why do we listen to this?" The commander glared at Caiaphas without losing his composure. Caiaphas then remained silent.

"The boy was the eldest of the five brothers, the youngest of whom died when the slavers came one dark day in the springtime. The slavers, they killed the youngest brother when they took away his three sisters. The slavers looked for the father but he hid in the long, tall grasses along with the older brothers. The youngest brother, he was driven through with a sword when he tried to drag back his sisters from the brutal slavers. Then the slavers saw the mother, she was lying in her bed of reeds in the mud dwelling she called home, much too ill to make any efforts to save her daughters and the youngest of her sons. The slavers left the mother to die her death, before the slavers departed they poured boiling water into her eyes so that she would not see them again. She never set her eyes on anything more until one day, one full moon later, the mother slept the deep sleep that never wakens."

The storyteller paused, he always paused at this point in his stories, first to know if he had the absolute attention of his audience, then to decide in which direction to take his story because he could alter any number of details in the way that all good storytellers do. The old blind man had different ways of ending every tale he told. This depended upon how interested his listeners were, if they held on to his every word with their eyes wide open then he would continue. If the storyteller needed to work harder then he always had subtle twists, tricks of suspense and gigantic cliffhangers he would hold back to throw into his story as he saw fit, for just such an occasion that he could make more silver when the time came to collect. He could manipulate his audience in ways that being blind had huge advantages. Right now, he knew he did not need to twist and turn this story at all, nor would he consider doing so given the story he told to his captivated audience. He knew he had their full attention without even the smallest chance he would lose them. This was the most important story he had ever told; he had been waiting for this opportunity since the miracle that changed his life. It was not his blindness that was his gift, it was something far more powerful. All he needed was to be brought before the Sanhedrin.

Caiaphas listened to the blind storyteller because in his younger years he had created the beginnings of his great wealth by being a trader in slaves. While the beggar related his story Caiaphas became alarmed but said nothing, few knew about his earlier life when he operated his own bands of slave hunters who ranged far beyond the boundaries of Judaea.

But then he had moved on, using his wealth to gain notoriety, the success in public life that enabled him to be the most powerful man in Judaea.

The guard commander listened because he had risen to his esteemed rank by sending young slave girls to Roman prefects who would then ship them back to Rome - after they had indulged in rampant barrack room gratification. This gave the commander access to the highest ranks in the Roman army, which then led to his rapid promotion within the Judaean special guards because he was more than tolerated by influential Romans. The guard commander became the special link between the Romans and wealthy Judaean governors who themselves held no interest in seeing a new radical preacher in their midst.

The lesser of the two guards, the one who held his sword to the blind beggar's throat listened to the storyteller's story because, when he was a young boy in his native land beyond Judaea, his youngest brother had been killed by slave trading hunters while his three sisters were raped then taken away as slaves - while his blinded mother lay dying. He had hidden in the swamp grass with his three brothers and their old man of a father who could do nothing to intervene, the five of them watched their sisters violated, the youngest brother killed by a sword driven through his throat. Right now, at this moment in time, in the dark room of Sanhedrin temple, the guard's mind tumbled into absolute turmoil, his before calm expression while he held his sword to the storyteller's throat as ordered by his commander concealed his feeling of intense shock. The guard's expressionless jaw dropped open like a great chasm about to throw foul bile from the sudden sickness inside his stomach. His salivating mouth dried like the caked mud of the summer swamplands of his childhood as he stood listening to the blind man relate to the hilt what had happened over two score years before. The guard stood motionless, trembling with the intenseness of his long-hidden nightmare that played out before his terrified wide open eyes...

The storyteller, Celidonius, had once been blind, that is until the miracle on the hill of Bethsaida when the young preacher from Naz'areth, the prophet who everyone talked about, in some miraculous way cured

Celidonius's blindness in front of the frenzied crowd that gathered to watch the rumoured miracles of this new messiah. The preacher, who some were saying was the prophesied son of God, had spit saliva into the ground then smeared the mud into the eyes of Celidonius. When Celidonius then washed away the mud in the nearby lake of Siloam he could see for the first time since a young boy – though the gift of sight was not the only gift he was given. When the strong sunlight invaded his clearing eyes he had felt pain, intense pain like no physical pain he had ever experienced, pain that threatened to tear apart his mind like an exploding inferno of fire. A few hours later, when the unbearable pain subsided, when his vision cleared, the extraordinary preacher from Naz'areth was not the first person he set his eyes upon in the near forty years he had been blind – the first person he saw was a beholding beautiful woman, a woman dressed in a ragged dusty cloak the colour of which he could not remember. She had strange eyes, she sat close by on her haunches watching him with no sound, waiting for the time when he could see her with his own eyes. This was when Celidonius knew it was not just the gift of sight he had been given, he could see other strange things in his painless mind also.

One of the first things that Celidonius realised after the miracle of sight was that he gained nothing by being able to see again. No one listened to a blind storyteller who was not blind. The silver he earned from telling stories grew smaller, he made not enough to eat, he starved, that is until he decided he must be blind once more. Celidonius soon perfected the art of being blind, hiding his obvious ability to see everything as it was. In time he came to realise something else, something far more important – he possessed the gift of seeing memories. Not his own memories but the memories of those who sat listening to his stories, once he held their undivided attention he could feel the flow of thoughts from their minds, their shocked expressions when he touched upon the little things that changed their lives. Now this was a good way of earning a more decent living, but the blind storyteller, who was not blind at all, kept this little secret to himself.

In the marketplace, Celidonius had seen Isca'riot. He remembered

that he was the traitor who had betrayed the preacher from Naz'areth
to the Sanhedrin, he saw with him the same strange woman who squatted
beside him at the Lake of Siloam many moons before, waiting to see if
his gift of sight would return. She never said anything to him then but
Celidonius knew it was the same woman, she wore the ruby-coloured cloak
she wore at the lakes that time ago. She saw him squatting in the corner
of the marketplace square then smiled to him knowing who he was, then
she walked down the alleyway with Isca'riot to the side entrance of the
Sanhedrin temple. More strange, Celidonius could not sense her memories
in any way, when he tried to fathom her thoughts there in the marketplace
she invaded his mind in such a hostile manner that he closed down his
thinking as soon as he could. She warned him, inside his head, she knew
his thoughts, she knew what he could do. Celidonius realised he must be
wary, because it was not the remarkable preacher who had given him this
gift at all.

Celidonius saw that Isca'riot was the traitor, he saw in the memories
resting in the mind of Isca'riot that this woman he was with carried a
child. Celidonius then saw something he did not understand, something
of which he had no comprehension, he saw that Caiaphas of the Sanhedrin
desired this woman and her child dead. But this woman in the ruby cloak
was strange and powerful, she planted thoughts into his mind which
he then could not control. Celidonius discovered that Caiaphas himself
had contrived the crucifixion of the Naz'areth preacher, these were the
confusing thoughts that flowed through the storyteller's head.

So, it had occurred to Celidonius that he should deliver Isca'riot back to
the Sanhedrin, this would be a good way to seek retribution for Isca'riot
being a traitor; for betraying the preacher Yeshua that he, Celidonius, held
dear. But another thought hung in his mind, what if Isca'riot was not
the traitorous villain everyone said? Even so, it grew in his mind that he
might use Isca'riot for his revenge, he could use the traitor to ensure that
he himself might be brought before the Sanhedrin. If he could do this
then he could deal Caiaphas a hard blow, something which had been in
Celidonius's thoughts for many years since he was born from the womb of

his own wretched mother slave. Celidonius knew something of Caiaphas and his slave trading ways, Celidonius's mother had suffered pain at the hands of Caiaphas when the high priest traded slaves. Celidonius knew many other bad things also. Now, all he had to do was inform the Sanhedrin that Isca'riot was inside the temple with a woman, knowing that no woman must ever be inside the sacred citadel. The blind storyteller's chance might then come. As moments in time passed, it dawned upon Celidonius how this strange woman herself had planted these thoughts of vengeance inside his head. Celidonius knew he was being used, but it was a small price to pay for the gift he had been given.

Now, while on his knees storytelling for his life with the tip of a sharp sword only a thumbs distance from his throat, Celidonius saw everything, he saw things he had not known before. He saw despicable Caiaphas; he saw that Caiaphas had taken the guard's sisters as slaves then sold them at the slaver's market in the northern town of Assima. Celidonius saw the commander of the guards, who had in a roundabout way bought the same girls in a manner that Caiaphas had no knowledge of, with scores of other slave women destined for the Roman barracks in Je'rusalem. Celidonius saw how the guard commander was rewarded well. What made Celidonius smile to himself in self-satisfaction, what made him think that he might yet survive this vile confrontation inside the temple of the Sanhedrin, was that not one of them knew of the others' hidden secret, three of those in the room now present knew nothing of the involvement of the other in this thing that happened a long time ago. But the woman in the ruby cloak, she knew, somehow, she knew everything. Now, this was a good story worth telling.

It became clear to Celidonius why the woman in the ruby cloak contrived that he be dragged to his knees before Caiaphas and the guard commander, the same commander who had tortured the holy preacher in the dark dungeon of the Sanhedrin. Of more importance, Celidonius knew that this temple guard who held his sword with its tip a shorthand distance from his throat would not, in a million years, drive it home to kill him. Celidonius smiled, this was the greatest story he had told in his entire life, he held the riveted attention of everyone in the room in the way that a good storyteller should. He could now take the foul end of this story in any direction he chose; he had the fate of Caiaphas and the Sanhedrin's guard commander resting right there in his grimy hands. The mystical woman who wore the ruby cloak had in some way cured his sight, then she had given him this strangest of storytelling gifts.

Celidonius paused for a short while in his narrative, now was the primordial gap in every good story, it was the crucial time when the sharp blade of glistening bronze would pierce his throat but would be held back because of the uncertain bewilderment of the stunned guard. Now was the time when Caiaphas at last stumbled upon the fact that he was himself a foolish fool, a fool who was desperate to know how the storyteller's story ended. Now was when the Sanhedrin's guard commander realised there was an important reason why this storyteller was kneeling with his hands tied behind his back, with a sword at his throat who did not beg for his worthless life as he should. This was the time for the dreadful silent pause, when the fate of mankind hung in spellbinding suspense, this was the time when a good storyteller held the fate of his audience in his manipulative hands.

All four of the Sanhedrin's incongruous stared in silence at the kneeling storyteller, who himself gazed straight ahead at the blank white wall - appearing to see nothing.

"Do not stop," said Caiaphas, breaking the hiatus. "Tell us how this story ends." From at first having no interest in the storyteller's tale Caiaphas felt compelled to know why he sweated in discomfort under his stiff collar. Neither Caiaphas nor the commander discerned the guard holding the sword to the throat of Celidonius, who was beginning to waiver, the guard who was shivering in his unwitting resolve.

"Yes," replied Celidonius. "But are you good for my silver?"

"Your silver is safe if your story tells the truth," said Caiaphas.

The commander at this time said nothing, everything was going around inside his puzzled head. It occurred to him how this storyteller might be here for a reason, there could be a purpose to the blind man's betrayal of

Isca'riot to the Sanhedrin's guards. Finding them conspiring together here inside the temple had caused mayhem, three of his elite guards had been slain inside the Sanhedrin's stonewall citadel temple, the blind beggar had been dragged here on the orders of the commander himself. Had the commander walked into a trap of his own making?

Celidonius thought for a brief moment before staring once more at the bare wall in front of his eyes. Of course, he would finish his story because this was what every storyteller did, in the history of the world only dead storytellers never finished what they set out to tell. Now was the moment when Celidonius saw everything, everything there was to see.

"When the mother of the four remaining boys died, their lives fell from the sky like watery raindrops," the storyteller continued. "Their father soon passed away, he died of a broken heart which, you will agree, is not unexpected given the grieving anguish he suffered. If you yourselves lost your daughters, your youngest son and your loving wife how would you endure the pain eh Caiaphas?" Celidonius tilted his head towards Caiaphas in a way not to reveal that the storyteller could see him extraordinarily well. The storyteller saw the extreme doubt hiding deep within the supreme priest's eyes.

"Then the eldest of those boys of whom this story relates, he left his homeland and his brothers to make his way to Judaea to seek his fortune and his salvation," continued Celidonius. "He found neither, nor did he learn of what became of his three sibling sisters whose lives were lost in the myriad of misery that happens when slavery becomes the chain of pain that shackles every slave's life."

"Enough of this. All we want to know, storyteller, is how and why you knew that Magdalen and Isca'riot were inside the temple of our esteemed Lord," interrupted the commander. "Unless you can see perfectly and well then somebody must have told you. Why did you inform my guards when it is obvious that you have no love of the Sanhedrin? Is it because of the traitorous Isca'riot?"

"I tell you this story commander, I tell you because the oldest son who suffered so terribly from the loss of his sibling sisters, from the death of his dearest mother and his loving father now stands here before me with his sword at my throat," said Celidonius.

Both the commander and Caiaphas looked to the guard in instantaneous surprise, an involuntary action that shook both of them. The guard lowered his sword, the sweat of indecision permeating his furrowed brow. The guard with the sword said nothing.

"I will tell you many other things commander, I tell you that Caiaphas here, the supreme priest of the despicable Sanhedrin, who crucified our Lord in heaven's preacher who came into this world to tell us of God's will, Caiaphas paid those same slavers who blighted this guard's life," a sly smile smit the lips of Celidonius. "And you commander, you sold those same stolen slaves to the Romans," the storyteller saw the instant alarm in the commander's glazed-open eyes. "I bet you know how my story ends now eh?"

The silence in the room was deeper than the silence of pure emptiness. The flickering flame of the burning light cast glorious shadows of golden luminosity across the stunned faces of Caiaphas, the guard commander and the two guards. No one said anything, none of them could think of anything to say. The storyteller sensed the disturbing flow of confused memories knowing that he had put himself in great danger, but his feeling of revengeful satisfaction ingratiated the lowest depths of his decimated soul. He had served the will of the strange woman, his extraordinary mistress whom he hardly knew. His formidable debt to both her and to the dead messiah was paid.

The guard commander stood motionless, his mind in turmoil while it dawned upon him that he had been lured between gaping jaws of his own creation. This was all contrived to happen. What devilish potency had they unleashed when he and his guards beat the supposed messiah into his false confession, when Caiaphas had gotten his way by making the Romans crucify the man they made admit to his blasphemous crimes - crimes which they all knew were erroneous. The commander began to sense the devious power of this woman, without doubt the child she carried was woven into something far more potent than he ever imagined. And this beggar was not blind, he deduced this for sure but the commander had no inclination of what to do next. Just then the bolted door of the grim darkened room burst open, the sudden calamitous noise of mayhem breaking the tragic intensity of the endless moment.

The two remaining Sanhedrin guards, who had earlier been sent by the commander to search for Isca'riot in the marketplace, they dragged an old man, the same old man who had witnessed Isca'riot being taken into his home by the Romans. The old man who, like the blind storyteller, demanded silver in his palm to reveal the whereabouts of the hunted woman. The woman, it appeared, who held the fate of everyone in her hands.

"What is happening Yosef," asked Nicodemus, the worried look in his bloodshot eyes said everything. "Are we to be punished for our great sin?"

"Of which of our many sins do you refer?" replied Yosef. "Our sin for defying the Sanhedrin or all the unholy sins of mankind?"

Nicodemus's expression crumbled, he stayed silent. The sanctuary of his ramshackle hut offered the four of them a small respite from the unsavoury events of the last three days. In the dark shadowy corner, Miryam prayed in silence for their salvation, her perseverance a testament to her reverent suffering - she offered thanks for the wretched messiah who was now saved. Salome squatted on her haunches outside, alone in the darkness of the starstruck moonlight.

"We have put ourselves in deep trouble," said Nicodemus.

"Yes, we have, but our fate is not held in our hands," replied Yosef. "There are great happenings we do not understand. Somewhere, there is a conflict of strong winds, of strong minds."

"Do you think our preacher *is* the given son of our Lord as the people say?" asked Nicodemus. There was a halting nervousness in his voice, as if he knew what Yosef would say.

"No, I do not Nico," Yosef shuddered, "I thought for a time that he might be our prophesied new messiah but I do not think this now. He suffers pain, he faces death like any mortal man, our Lord in heaven would not see his true sire suffer like this." Yosef then thought long to himself about the archangel Gabriel, Yosef had seen no worshipping reverence when God's messenger first set his eyes upon the torn body of the messiah, there was no all-redeeming love for the holy preacher by his supposed father's vassal. There was a feeling of hostility, a distinct show of malevolence that Yosef was quick to notice when he came to his awestruck senses. There was no love lost between the angel and this prophet.

"Then what are we to do?" begged Nicodemus.

"I do not know my good friend; all we can do is wait until daylight. Then we can return to the cemetery of Golgotha to see how our saviour survives. It is now three days since he was spiked to the stake, his life hangs on a thin thread of chance, tomorrow will be his day of deliverance when we know if he will live or die." Yosef paused, he stared once more at Miryam who still kneeled whispering her sincere praises to the Lord in heaven. There was no question that she believed God had intervened to save her disavowed preacher.

"Do you think the angel Gabriel will return as he said?" asked Nicodemus.

"Yes, do not doubt this. This thing that is happening is beyond our will or even our comprehension," said Yosef.

"But the Romans, they must have spied us at the tomb. They saw the coming of the archangel also," said Nicodemus.

"Perhaps you are right Nico. Tomorrow is a day of much reckoning. The tomb is closed, we must hope that no one suspects that our dear preacher still lies inside," said Yosef. "The centurion knows that Yeshua is not dead, he gave our preacher to us knowing he was still alive, there is no reason for the Romans to open the tomb. I suspect they watch to know how this disaster unfolds."

Yosef did not comprehend that Yeshua was no more than human bait, that Magdalen in her benevolence of carrying a child was the vindication that Yeshua still lived - the reason why his life had not been ended by Gabriel. And Yosef did not yet know that Magdalen bore the fruit that would one day bring down the power of the Sanhedrin.

"I think we four should all rest, it is more than three nights since we slept a peaceful sleep," said Yosef. "At first light, we can return to the hill of Golgotha to see what God's will will bring."

As the night progressed none of the four slept much sleep. Miryam continued her mumbling prayers throughout the long night, while outside Salome sobbed to herself in silent tears of nervous fright. Both Salome and Miryam knew that Yeshua lay on the teetering verge of death, that under no circumstances could he be moved, not yet while he lay undiscovered and hidden like a mysterious phalanx. Salome was emotional and distressed, she fretted with anxiety over the reappearance of the archangel Gabriel; she would never regain her composure over his towering magnificence. Little did she know that, in time, many reverent shrines would be built to her lasting memory.

Yosef tried to sleep but his restless mind kept churning over, the hurtling catastrophe of the last few days twisting and turning his thoughts into tangled myriads of horrifying facts. They were in deep trouble, Yosef was well aware of this, the responsibility of their task weighed heavily upon him. All four of them were now in the long silky hands of Gabriel, yet it was the centurion Peleus who held all the cards. Soon Caiaphas and the Sanhedrin would know everything that was happening. Where was Magdalen? Where was Isca'riot whose cruel betrayal had caused all this mayhem? As the long night passed into the twilight silence of the early rising dawn the twittering of bickering swallows mocked Yosef's restless mind, the graceful feathered blue-backs sensing the coming of the spectacular new day. As they perceived the imminent sunrise, they swooped from their nighttime roosts to once more soar high into the bleakest of brooding skies, ominous skies that revealed the first grey streaks of doom-ridden adversity.

Salome could not sleep. Unable to settle her over-emotional mind she had made her way in the receding darkness to the marketplace to find food and water. They each gave little thought to their daily sustenance, now she made her stumbling return to the rundown shack of Nicodemus; disturbing the still restless sleep of Yosef of Arim'athea upon her arrival.

The younger of the two women lit the small fire outside of the crooked doorway from which hung an old, ragged sackcloth that served as the door, barring the everyday world from inside of the dark hovel. Salome had disturbing news.

While the hot water boiled from the incandescent heat, Salome's thoughts drifted around inside her anxious mind. Yosef ambled outside of the hut to sit beside her; his restless sleep disturbed by the dawn of a worrying new day. Together they sat staring at the bubbling water as if something might be given up from the depths of the battered iron pot. Salome stirred in the unbleached oats she had found down in the market.

"I did not hear you leave Salome," said Yosef.

"It has been a long night Yosef. We need to eat, we bought nothing with us, only jars of balm oils and reams of white silk."

Yosef stared over at the donkey cart still laden with its load. The donkey chewed the meagre dried grass, its bony ribs showing that it also suffered the burden of adversity.

"We might need those balming oils if the messiah does not live out the day," answered Yosef. In his mind, he could not see how this disaster might end.

"I do not know how he survives," said Salome, whispering to herself.

"Is there any news in the market?" asked Yosef.

"Yes, there is much news, many strange rumours," Salome replied, trying to remain calm. "More Sanhedrin guards are dead; Caiaphas has seized the blind beggar who tells his stories in the square of the tall trees. You might know the man, the one who enthrals the people who pay him silver. The Sanhedrin guards took him." Salome looked up to see the worried look in the eyes of the ageing priest.

"More of the guards are dead?"

"Yes," answered Salome. "I do not know how this happened, except they perished in the Sanhedrin temple." Salome spooned more rough-milled oats into the boiling cauldron. The aroma of hot porridge permeated the early morning air.

Yosef sat silent, his thoughts once more in turmoil.

"And the Romans took away Yehudas Isca'riot," continued Salome. "He was with some old water seller woman."

"The Romans took Isca'riot?"

"Yes. He was ill, he had fallen to the ground," said Salome. "They took him into a house to revive him."

"Who was the water seller woman?" asked Yosef.

"I do not know," replied Salome. "I was talking with the market woman who sells our oats, she does not know the water seller either."

Yosef thought odd thoughts, the same traders and beggars plied their living every day - but then he reasoned that penniless pedlars came into the busy municipality all the time.

"I was told something more," continued Salome. "The commander of the Sanhedrin guards, he suffered a sword attack by one of his own men. He is pierced with wounds; he might not live."

This struck Yosef hard; how could this be? Yosef knew the commander of the Sanhedrin guard; he was the tough hand of Caiaphas who could not be brought down with ease. What had happened? Yosef remained silent while everything that Salome said whirled around inside his head. What was happening? The Sanhedrin guards and their resolute commander had suffered yet more attrition, these guards had perished inside the Sanhedrin's own temple and, from what Salome had learned, the commander himself was now cut down by a sword. Yosef knew these were the same guards who had tortured and bloodied the crucified preacher.

Also, unnerving Yosef was the inevitable; soon it would be time to return to the cemetery of Golgotha. There they would once more face the awe-inspiring archangel whom they each by now feared with reverence. Yosef was certain the centurion Peleus would intervene; he would be accompanied by yet more armed Romans. Where was Magdalen? For what reason did the centurion ask searching questions about Magdalen? Why had the Romans taken Isca'riot? What interest did Caiaphas have in the blind storyteller? For what possible reason would the Sanhedrin seek then arrest a simple storyteller? Then a sudden thought struck Yosef - was this blind man the same storytelling beggar who by a miracle regained his sight at the preachings of Bethsaida?

Salome handed Yosef his steaming cup of oat porridge laced with warm goats' milk; he began to eat without much appetite. The sackcloth doorway parted, they were joined by the still-fatigued Nicodemus and the prayerful Miryam of Ba'thuma. Miryam appeared more splendiferous in her demeanour. They all four sat around the meagre fire trying to claim its warmth, they ate and drank in silence without much enthusiasm for the daunting day ahead. Yosef had no thought for conversation, his mind twisted and turned in all directions until he could think no more. He looked up to see each of the others watching him, waiting with trepidatious dread. It was time to leave for the hill of Golgotha.

On the third day after the preacher's crucifixion, Gabriel's mind was far from tranquil. His monstrous adversarial nemesis weaved her web in complex ways that wrought havoc with God's version of humankind. His Lord would not forgive him if her relentless evil prevailed, if Hyvah could cast her gossamer thread to entrap him in the way foretold by prehistoric inscriptions on the stone obelisk no mortal man had yet discovered. Some fragments of ancient tablets had been found some time ago, but these small relics were remnants of the seductive imagination of traitorous men, men who believed in other masquerading gods. Gabriel expected these age-old relics to be concealed for eternity by the Sanhedrin.

The evolvement of this garden world had reached its transitional zenith, Hyvah's time on earth would soon end. Gabriel was well aware that her biological existence must transform, he knew that he must act to destroy Magdalen before her newborn could be born, Hyvah's spiritual resurrection was predicted upon the rock monolith in the place where she herself was created - when the young world breathed only lava and volcanic fire. Gabriel was angry, Hyvah's transcendental immolation had once before defeated his attempt to destroy her, when she tempted him with the enticing beauty of her curvaceous body and the deviousness of her mind. Together they had devoured the forbidden fruit of untruthful love in a time when neither of them endured human form.

Through Hyvah came a band of mankind that venerated only Hyvah, men who knew what Gabriel knew, that spiritual Hyvah was the protector of these men without the manipulative hand of any God. Gabriel realised that now was the time when these decrepit races of men would come together, when they would emerge from shadowy corners and crawl from under their miserable rocks to converge. They would gather to watch over Hyvah, they would seek to defend both her and her unborn child in ways that Caiaphas and the Sanhedrin could never imagine.

These loathsome unbelievers were gathering right now, Gabriel could sense their presence, the omens were not good. The falsified miracles: the blind beggar who had set about the Sanhedrin guards - the same guards who had tortured the suffering preacher before his crucifixion. There were others, not just the storyteller, there was the supposed miracle of raising the spidery Lazarus from the earth, repugnant Lazarus who would soon take it upon himself to ravage and scourge the Sanhedrin. The giving of life to the Roman manservant in Capernaum, the same Roman curd who would in revenge take the life of Pontius Pilot - and the strange healing of the frenzied madman in Gadara, who then guided the renegade Yehudas Isca'riot to the preacher from Naz'areth. Gabriel knew these happenings were all the dark work of Hyvah, it was Hyvah's hand that gathered together these scurrilous men, these were not miracles performed by the Heb'rewic messiah from Naz'areth - they were the deliberate act of his nemesis who knew she must protect her unborn. But this fallacious preacher had his own unnatural ways, Gabriel at last knew why his Lord's new prophet Yeshua had been sought by Hyvah, why she had chosen him to be the seed of her resurrection.

Gabriel thought Caiaphas a stupid fool, he had allowed himself to be lured by this renegade preacher who was of the same spurious bloodline of godforsaken men. The seditious preacher, who was no true prophet in Gabriel's eyes, knew that he was not the immortal messiah, that he was no descendent of God - even when Hyvah fashioned his martyrdom so that his sycophantic apostles would go out into the world to write of his Holy Spirit, the greatness of Hyvah's own concealed prophet. This masterful trickery masterminded by Hyvah would serve to create yet one more conflict between men, when men would kill men without compassion in the name of Gabriel's Lord – and in this violent Christendom world, Hyvah's offspring would survive, they would thrive, they would create mayhem to feed the destruction of conquering kings and the lordish leaders of men.

Right now, this rebellious preacher who had risked everything lay close to death in the tomb carved into the hillside of Golgotha – but he refused to die for some insane reason that Gabriel guessed must be to protect his unborn. Gabriel had seen his deep wounds, the appalling state of the fallen preacher knowing that no mortal man could survive this much mutilation. The traitorous messiah lingered by a thin thread - this Yeshua preacher hung to life knowing that Hyvah in one of her incarnations would come to find him. This suited Gabriel, his decisive plan to put an end to the awful prospect of Hyvah's child being born would thwart Hyvah's emancipation of the female kind, he could prevent the prophesied resurrection written on their granite stone, he could conquer this garden world in the name of his own true Lord. He would be victorious in the countless wars of faith fought between men. By destroying both the rebellious preacher and this Magdalena woman he would then unravel Hyvah's trickery, bring to an end this messiah's self-imposed martyrdom. Today would be the venerable third day, the day that changed everything. The day the world of men changed.

But Gabriel had not foreseen the inexplicable hand of Yehudas Isca'riot. The dawn of the third day since the crucifixion began with the first streaks of insipid luminescence spreading across the dark remorseless sky. Yehudas turned to look at the water seller, he saw what his common sense told him he would never see. There in the silvery half-light, the old wrinkled face of the itinerant water seller was distorted with pain, harrowing pain that no human could contemplate as the first signs of the physical demise of whoever the water seller was began to occur. Her face morphed, she changed in fleeting moments of time, numerous flashbacks of previous incarnations bloomed like new budding flowers that withered away as the molecules of her existence deteriorated out of her control. Her decrepit body twisted in hurting spasms, she writhed in convulsive contortions like a cornered witch about to be condemned. Isca'riot looked on in unrelinquished fear, the vision before his wide-struck eyes giving him no escape from his tragic damnations.

The water seller was Magdalen reincarnated, Isca'riot was convinced of this though he had no inkling of whether the Magdalen he knew would ever return; but there in the grey darkness, he saw outlandish transfigurations that threatened to sink his delicate mind once more into oblivion. First, he saw the intelligent eyes of a helpless biped primate, eyes that knew more about the beginning of mankind than men ever did. These visions then reconfigured through many forms until they, in some way, became human; then the old woman's face flashed through yet more interchangeabilities, one after another each morphing evolved then dissipated before Isca'riot's bulging disbelieving eyes. He saw the old woman who used to sit him upon her knee when a young boy, then came many female forms whom he did not know, he saw beguiling princesses with regal crowns, decrepit beggar women etched with grimy old age wrinkles, women of intense beauty and more non-human faces of profound repulsiveness that tore the heart from the seller's inner soul.

Isca'riot then felt extreme panic swell up inside him, nothing must happen to Magdalen just yet, not while he relied upon her for his sanity and survival. He stared mesmerised, not knowing what would happen next; the overwhelming discomfort of him realising how the incongruous old woman who taught him so much when he was a young boy was the same Magdalen that led him into this devastating disaster. Nothing surprised him anymore, Isca'riot's swirling mind grasped this - at this moment in time he needed Magdalen more than anything. The water seller's morphing flashbacks slowed, then ceased as she recovered her composure... though there were no signs that the water seller would ever recover her Magdalena form. Then it occurred to Isca'riot that even the water woman's elusive Magdalen incarnation was a temporary illusion, that never was there any real Magdalen whom he could rely upon. When this worrying thought flashed through his mind, he realised that the wrinkled hag who taught him as a boy and the old water woman were one and the same. Isca'riot did not feel good.

Isca'riot sat squatting, haunched upon the hard stony ground, the rough gravel cut into the soles of his worn-out sandals like sharp spikes of incongruous blades. The inky black nighttime of disparity gradually dissolved into the breaking dawn of the new day – an extraordinary day that might well ingratiate its tentacles of doom around the psyche of mankind for the next five thousand years.

Other grim thoughts were bombarding Isca'riot's worn and crumbling brain. Isca'riot held no doubts, this strange woman who at this time lay writhing in agony on the rocky ground was the same harbinger of sin that Ab'raham had written was created from the bones of Adamah - this water seller was Adamah's Hyvah in her dying form. But Magdalen claimed that never was there a garden of Eden nor any Adamah in the way the Yehudiish believed; she even denied that Ab'raham was everything the Sanhedrin held dear. Isca'riot accepted this now, though the consequences would be enough to turn his fragile mind inside out; but he did not know that Hyvah's first throes of death would not come just yet, not until her resurrection infants had been born.

More thoughts of dread raced through Isca'riot's subconscious sense of reasoning. The prospect of the messiah rising from the dead in the likeness of his own miracles horrified Isca'riot. If both Magdalen and the Romans were right in what they said then something significant was happening on the hill of Golgotha, something that Isca'riot could not conceive. What if Yeshua did return from the dead as Magdalen warned? How then could he, the weasel of a man who had betrayed his friend, ever face the man whom he had denounced? Isca'riot knew that healing the dead was not beyond the realms of inconceivability, had not Yeshua himself breathed life into the daughter of Jairus at the miracle of Gerasa? Isca'riot had witnessed this with his own eyes. Then there was the young boy from the village of Nain on the slopes of Mount Tabor, brought back from the dead through the desperate pleadings of the boy's widowed mother. Then the strangest of all, the miracle of Lazarus of Bethany, buried in perpetuity for four days before he was repealed from death - Isca'riot was aware that, whenever the disciples meandered through the land of Judaea with their messiah, healings of the dead happened, he had seen these miracles of the Lord happen time after time. What now imploded upon Isca'riot like a cataclysmic storm, what convinced him that fate was stacked against him, was that Magdalen had always been there also, standing by the healing preacher's side. With this thought, Isca'riot once more teetered on the edge of reality. Were these miracles all of the Magdalena's doing? Was everything Magdalen's magical hand?

The old woman raised herself from the ground exhausted, she haunched herself upon the largest of the silvery rocks that reflected the half-light of the descending grey dawn. Shimmering dancing shadows grew lesser in their towering length, in some way portraying the imminence of a new tumultuous event. Nothing was said between Isca'riot and the old water woman, they both sat silent and still. The water seller recovered herself to restore her composure, for Isca'riot this was one more affirmation - Magdalen was everything she claimed.

"Come Yehudas, we must hurry, there is some other place we must be." The weakness in the old woman's voice echoed the contorted pain etched upon her exhausted, worn-out face.

Caiaphas and the guard commander stared at the old man dumped on the temple floor by the two Sanhedrin guards. Caiaphas stood beside the two other guards who had earlier brought in the blind storyteller Celidonius who still kneeled with his hands tied tight behind his back. In the temple, torchlight flames created incandescent shadows that flickered in the withered gloom of the great hall, it would be many hours before the nighttime darkness gave way to the insipid greyness of yet one more breaking day. The atmosphere inside the hall was tense, all four who had listened to the blind beggar's slave trading tale of disparity were shaken beyond common reason. There was no sword pointing at the throat of Celidonius, the intensity of that moment was broken by the sudden incursion of the two guards who dragged in the old man, the bead-selling cripple who himself had something himself to tell.

Celidonius was startled to see the old man, he recognised him. He realised this was the cripple who lived alone in the ramshackle dwelling in the corner of the marketplace square, the storyteller saw him most days even though no one realised that Celidonius could see the whole world around him.

There were a few moments of awkward silence while everyone standing there came to their senses, Caiaphas was the first to react.

"Who is this old man you bring here before us?"

The two guards deliberated. "He has something to tell but he demands silver," replied the taller of the two guards.

Caiaphas stared at the cripple, contemplating this sudden new intrusion and the turn of events. "So, we have another renegade who thinks pieces of *silver* will loosen his slippery tongue." There was a hint of extreme exasperation in his voice.

"High priest, it is our understanding this cripple knows the whereabouts of those we seek," said the guard.

"Who? The Magdalen woman and Isca'riot?" interrupted the guard commander.

"Yes commander, this is my understanding," the guard replied. "He approached both of us outside of the temple, saying he possessed information for Caiaphas and the Sanhedrin."

The guard commander sensed that all was not as it seemed, the hairs of suspicion tickled the skin beneath his sweaty woollen vest. Why would this man approach the Sanhedrin of his own free will? Loyalty to the Sanhedrin was fickle as far as the preacher from Naz'areth was concerned.

"Who are you? What is your name?" The commander stared at the old man slumped on the floor.

"Why is it that you think we will pay you in silver?" added Caiaphas.

"I am Ahaziah, Ahaziah of Naz'areth," replied the old man. "I am a poor bead seller; I think what I know should be rewarded by the Sanhedrin."

Celidonius listened with keen interest while kneeling with his hands still tied. It struck him with intrigue that all of those who had had a bad hand in the not-long-past crucifixion were in this one temple hall together. Now they had been joined by this crippled bead trader who was here for a reason. Was this old man just a greedy opportunist? Realisation dawned upon Celidonius that both Caiaphas and the guard commander did not know this Ahaziah, neither did the guards, therefore the old cripple was not one of the Sanhedrin's usual informers.

Caiaphas though, thought with speed. He realised how difficult it would be for the general Sanhedrin guard to search all of Je'rusalem, they could run around for many days without finding this Magdalen woman. If the old man knew of her whereabouts, then the Sanhedrin could act fast to end this unravelling unpleasantness. It occurred to Caiaphas that both this old man and the blind storyteller could then be dealt with without the need to part with silver.

"Tell us what you know," demanded Caiaphas.

The old man deliberated; he did not trust Caiaphas. He had been induced here by the outright prompting of the water seller, in no way did he want to cross her, he had seen with his own eyes what she could do: Ahaziah did not much care whether he received his silver or not. He looked across to the storyteller Celidonius realising his plight - these happenings were far too complex for his normal understanding; he began to regret the temptation of greed; meanwhile, he remained slumped upon the temple floor without much compassion.

While Ahaziah thought about his options, a large red cockroach scurried across the smooth cobblestoned slab right before his eyes, its repulsive manner reminding him that life thrived whether he told Caiaphas what he knew or not. Ahaziah watched the cockroach until the dirt-ridden puttees of a guard's foot crunched it dead. The cockroach lay squashed and mangled, the juices of its life ebbing away between the small mortar cracks of the stone floor.

"He came into my humble house, one of the two whom you seek," said Ahaziah, shaken by the abrupt demise of the cockroach. "Two Roman guards were with him."

"Romans?" Caiaphas reacted in alarm. "What matter brought the Romans into the place where you live?" Everyone in the hall straightaway listened with keen interest.

"The man Isca'riot was brought into my home with an old woman who sells water, Isca'riot was collapsed and benumbed, he was near death, his mouth foamed while he babbled in madness," Ahaziah shivered. "The two Romans bundled the two of them through my door."

"Then what happened?" demanded the guard commander.

"The man was a m-madman, he hissed l-like a snake," stuttered the old man. "The woman then put her h-hand inside his h-head. Her h-hand was like no h-hand I ever saw." Everyone in the room stared at Ahaziah, the marketplace cripple, who all of a sudden became more important.

"What do you mean?" Caiaphas in an instant felt uneasy, the old man was telling a deliberate lie - though the ageing priest was struck with ominous uncertainty.

"She took his b-brain in her h-hands, she worked it t-together, it was as if this man Isca'riot's skull bone was not t-there. The woman is a d-demon, she is a w-witch or m-maybe an angel from God."

From nowhere the dead cockroach sprang to life, ignoring the repugnant juices of its body that had created a dark red stain upon the slab. The cockroach scurried away into the black recess of a deep dirt-ridden crack, leaving behind the crumpled remnants of its mangled shell. The sudden silence of the flame-lit room became the cockroach's degenerate kingdom.

"Then this m-man Isca'riot was healed, it was one more m-miracle, he spoke the words of a man awakened," continued Ahaziah after a long pause, the confidence in his voice growing, his stuttering abating when he saw the riveting attention he created.

"And the Romans?" asked the commander in open shock.

"Like you, they were s-shaken," answered Ahaziah. "The guards asked if the w-water seller knew where the Magdalen woman whom the S-Sanhedrin seek could be found. They w-wanted to take her to Peleus the centurion, but they l-left alone." Ahaziah paused to consider whether he should tell the commander everything, then he remembered why he was there. "The g-guards then left for the cemetery of Golgotha, the p-place where the noble preacher who was crucified now lies." Ahaziah again looked across towards the blind man Celidonius who was watching him with unbounded interest, the old cripple recognised the storyteller who plied his trade in the corner of the market. Ahaziah knew Celidonius was not blind, although the intense look in Celidonius's eyes said everything.

"So, the preacher from Naz'areth lies dead in the cemetery of Golgotha?" hissed Caiaphas. "Why are the Romans and the centurion Peleus there?"

"I d-do not know why the centurion and his men are there, the Romans did not s-say. It is not for me to know anything like that. I know the preacher lies at Golgotha because the g-guards wanted to take Magdalen there, if she could be found. The two Romans f-feared to take her by force but, anyway, they c-could not find her." Ahaziah then looked at Caiaphas and the commander each in turn, the old man still had his own question to ask. "How much will you pay me in silver if I tell you something more?" asked Ahaziah.

"We will pay you, old man, have no fear of that," answered Caiaphas. "How we pay you depends upon what more you have to say." Caiaphas had no intention of paying either the storyteller or this old man Ahaziah anything, the gratitude of the Sanhedrin could never be bought.

"What more do you have to tell us, old man," asked the commander.

"I have n-never seen this water seller before," spluttered Ahaziah. "She never sells her water in the m-marketplace square. When she made this Isca'riot man well again in his head I heard her whisper something to him, s-soft under her breath."

"What?" demanded Caiaphas.

"She said 'Forgive him, for he knows not what he has done.' This is w-what she said," replied Ahaziah. "You know who this old woman is, do you not?"

"The colour of her eyes? What was the colour of her eyes?" interrupted Celidonius. The blind beggar was spellbound just like everyone else. He could see that Ahaziah was telling the truth, he could see why the old man had decided to come here to Sanhedrin just like himself. Celidonius saw the uncertainty in the guard commander's mind. Furthermore, Celidonius grasped that Caiaphas intended to pay no silver to anyone.

Ahaziah turned his gaze to Celidonius, seeing that he was here being treated with an undignified lack of regard. "Her eyes were f-faded-blue, even more f-faded than the blue eyes of the women of Al-Yamāma Baby'lon in the north," said Ahaziah. "Do you know the eyes of the Al-Yamāma? I have only seen eyes like the water seller's in the fabled witch Zarqā Al-Yamāma, whose greatness we all know."

It was obvious even to Caiaphas that this man Ahaziah of Naz'areth was telling the truth, what he said corroborated with the same bizarre events reported by the two Sanhedrin guards who had seen Isca'riot with the old woman. A bell of alarm sounded in the mind of Caiaphas, what Ahaziah now told them attached more credence to the unnatural events in the temple when Isca'riot was found with Magdalen. Two more of Sanhedrin's elite guard were now dead, Magdalen had in some way disappeared by morphing herself before their eyes. Caiaphas began to feel more agitated; he was by now under no illusion how this woman was more potent than he realised, she was powerful beyond his every imagination. The crucifixion of the preacher from Naz'areth was beginning to engender a crisis for both himself and the Sanhedrin of enormous proportions, one that might even be an unconscionable setback for all of the Yehudiish people. But the Yehudiish had faced many catastrophes in their divine past, even when they had been led to the promised land by the esteemed prophet Mos'es. Ab'raham and their Lord God would always protect them, this much Caiaphas was resolute and sure of.

Caiaphas made the affirmed decision to go with his Sanhedrin guards to the cemetery of Golgotha, they would confront whatever was happening there, even the wrath of the Romans if need be. Caiaphas knew the hill of Golgotha would be the penultimate gauntlet, he was certain that in the cemetery he would find Magdalen with the traitorous Isca'riot, the Sanhedrin could then deal once and for all with the false preacher from Naz'areth. In the meantime, the high priest of the Sanhedrin realised that he must deal with these two renegades kneeling on the floor before him – the blind beggar Celidonius and the crippled informer Ahaziah who both demanded the Sanhedrin's silver. They no doubt had loose tongues, both would talk in the marketplace - meaning the Sanhedrin's trials and tribulations would be far from over. Caiaphas concluded that he must detain them, they could be kept in the Sanhedrin's dungeons until he decided what to do with them. He could later release them without their miserable silver when all of this troubling mayhem was dealt with. Or, if he needed, he could have them both silenced forever – not unlike the action he had taken against the false preacher from Naz'areth.

"Take these two beggars down into the thief's hole in the cellars," ordered Caiaphas to the two guards who had dragged Ahaziah into the temple. "We will deal with them both later."

There was an awkward silence in the hall. During the melodrama with Ahaziah, no one paid much attention to the guard who had been told to hold his pointed sword to the throat of Celidonius the storyteller, the guard whose mind even now twisted and turned in penultimate turmoil over what the storyteller had revealed. Caiaphas had processed the misfortune of the guard in his mind by blanking out the delicate matter of his slave trading days - in the same way that those with a troubled conscience dismiss what they have done in a previous life. The high priest had moved on to far more important flies in his ointment.

The guard's name was Bazeus of Heb'ron Al Labinda, he had paid a high price as a boy at the hands of murdering slave traders. He now reacted with instinctive pent-up rage. His anger stirred in crazed resentment like a raging bull, even more so when the faded memory of the woman with mesmerising eyes formed like a clearing fog inside his mind – he recalled the woman who came to his family to buy fish when he was a young boy. When the two guards drew their swords to drag away Celidonius and Ahaziah, the resolve of Bazeus broke, he raised his sword to strike down his fellow guard who took hold of Celidonius. He pierced the guard's left shoulder, the momentum of his thrust carrying downwards into the blood artery. The guard dropped down to the hard floor with his sword clattering away towards Celidonius who still kneeled in impotence with his hands tied. Neither of the two remaining guards moved, Caiaphas stood frozen to the spot.

The commander was the first to react, his instinctive wherewithal kicking in as he drew his sword just as Bazeus slashed downward at the rope ties that bound Celidonius's hands. The commander raised his sword high to swipe low upon the forehead of Bazeus but in doing so exposed himself to the upward thrust of the dropped sword that Celidonius was swift to retrieve from the floor right before him. For a blind man, the sword was aimed with precise precision, spearing the commander in shocked surprise. Everything happened in an instant, the frenzied split-second of bedlam exploding in uproar as the commander half-turned to stare at Celidonius in agonising reverberation. The fractional moment of silence was broken by the excited guffaws of black ravens roosting high in the dark rafters of the temple hall, they cawed their annoyed remonstrance at being disturbed by the furious mayhem below. They flayed their ruffled feathers in noisy disapproval, before flying around in short chaotic circles to then settle back amongst the rot-ridden rafters in watchful silence.

The commander staggered back wounded, his blood flowing without restrain to stain his sweat-ridden tunic. The second of the guards who had brought Celidonius into the temple then reacted, he drew his sword to hold it with menace against the throat of Caiaphas. The guard's eyes flared in impulsive defiance.

"I am with you. I am beside you Bazeus," declared the second guard aloud, leaving no doubts as to where his loyalties lay. The guard looked with apprehension at his commander leaning back upon the wall trying hard to stem the flow of blood with his hand.

Ahaziah smiled, realising how the water seller had in her own way struck with defiance at the Sanhedrin. Beside Ahaziah, Celidonius stood tall, his eyes now devoid of the straight ahead stare of a dull-witted blind man. Alongside the revengeful Bazeus and the shaken Ahaziah, Celidonius backed away towards the hallway door, his darting eyes leaving no one in any doubt that he could see everything he wished to see. The rebel guard who once held his sword at the throat of Caiaphas jumped to join them. With the commander wounded and the sword-struck guard's life ebbing away, Caiaphas and the one remaining guard could do nothing.

Celidonius saw the fear and confusion in the mind of Caiaphas.

"Never play your vile games with a blind beggar, you wretched piece of human shit who purports to be the highest priest of the Sanhedrin," spat Celidonius. "The grey-eyed woman with the dark skin of black ashwood, she holds you in her grip of iron. Your penance will come for the misery you have dealt upon the holy prophet."

Caiaphas stood silent, the rampaging memories of his slaving days playing havoc with his sense of reality. The cackling ravens roosting in the dark high-up rafters once more laughed in uproar, they guffawed loud at the high priest's mighty and ignominious demise.

Peleus slept a broken sleep beside the flickering campfire, the heat from the flames not enough to ward off the coldness of the long night. The centurion's unease dominated his thoughts, the puzzling array of strange circumstances raced through his mind like stormy thunder clouds mushrooming forever skywards. In the meantime, the cheerless nighttime crawled towards an unusual dawn. Peleus, for some reason, sensed the significance of the coming day, he suspected it would be a day of indiscriminate confrontation governed by hostile reckoning, even a day of extreme violence. His gut instinct warned him of tumultuous events, with consequences that might cause unwelcome trouble for the Roman garrison in Judaea. Not just this, Peleus realised with intuitive reasoning why the deviant apparition of the god-like figure he witnessed outside of the Sanhedrin tombs might be woven into everything that had happened, even connected to the one woman whom he could not erase from his mind. She played havoc with his thoughts, thoughts which ruminated over and over inside his head - to the point that she was now becoming an incongruous obsession.

The two guards Peleus had sent to find Magdalen had not yet returned. In the meantime, two more of the garrison guards had joined him, he ordered both to keep a keen watch over the tomb entrance which lay on the opposite hill a short distance from where they now camped. There was enough moonlight for the Romans to see that nothing came or went from the tomb; the great stone remained rolled over the entrance, keeping it closed from eternity. Everything seemed quiet and undisturbed.

Peleus sat thinking matters over while ignoring the meagre heat from the fire. The crucifixion of the Yehudiish preacher was a grave mistake, the ageing centurion was sure of this now - he could not help but sense the intense ramifications that might soon follow. His feelings born from many years of warfare and Roman conquest warned him that, for some reason, immense changes lay ahead for Rome. Furthermore, something rattled around in the back of his mind like small round pebbles in a stone crock. Peleus could not work out why this woman with the freakish eyes captivated him, why she held him in such a way that exerted an uncanny hold over him in a way that suggested embryonic feelings of warm-hearted humaneness - feelings the much-feared centurion tried hard to drive from his mind.

The centurion stared upwards to the starlit sky, curious about which of the gods would play their outlandish games of devilment during the coming day of disparity. Then he heard trudging footsteps, footfall muffled by the subtle rattle of sheathed swords. His two guards sent to find the Magdalen woman were returning. Then he saw that both guards were alone - the long night threatened to unravel into perpetuity. The guards made no bones about what had happened.

"What do you mean that no one has word?" Peleus was agitated.

"Centurion, there is no sign of where she can be found, she has disappeared like dwindling mist," repeated the guard. "And we have more disquieting news. We must report something strange."

Peleus stared at his two guards; they were the trusted of his men. "Make your report. Tell me what you know," the centurion demanded, restraining his impulsive frustration.

"Later, during the day of the crucifixions on the hill of Golgotha, after the crucified preacher was cut down from the stake, the woman we seek went to the Sanhedrin temple," said the guard. "While she was there, one of the more esteemed Sanhedrin's guards died." The Roman guard saw the instant look of surprise in his commander's eyes.

"How? How did this temple guard die?" Peleus demanded.

"We do not know centurion. She was in the temple with the high priest Caiaphas and the man Isca'riot, the one who they say betrayed the Naz'areth preacher," the guard replied. "Then she left, but later returned to the temple with Isca'riot."

"Why? Why would she return to the temple?"

"No one knows why, not anyone we spoke to," said the guard.

"Is that all? You said there was something strange," the deep tones of the centurion's voice reverberating with an echo. Peleus tried to speak in a whisper. Peleus saw both guards glance at each other, with nervous uncertainty in their eyes.

"Isca'riot was unconscious on the ground when we found him in the marketplace," the guard replied. "An old woman selling water was standing over him, we have not seen her in the marketplace before. We took the woman and Isca'riot into a nearby dwelling, she told us to do this. Sir, the woman then did something freakish and uncanny."

"What? What did she do?"

"She put her hands inside the head of Isca'riot's. It was as if she had his subconsciousness entwined around her fingers. But I tell you, they were no human hands," the guard shivered, he tried to add more but could not think of anything to say. There was a long silent moment, a pause that seemed to stretch well beyond incoherent moments in time.

The sudden stillness caused the nearby cliff edge to somehow loom closer, ten thousand nighttime crickets abruptly ceased their incessant high-pitched grating, a gloomy silence descended without any of the five Romans noticing that something had changed, there was a primordial shift in the molecular structure of the surrounding air that was well beyond the perception of the sword-clad Romans - the history of the world had, in an instant flash of purpose, been remade. In this moment, something outlandish had happened, a few soundless seconds later the crescendo of rackety crickets resumed their grip on the darkness in the timeless way that crickets have always done when the fading sunset abounds. Peleus stared at his two guards but looked straight through them, his thoughts twisted and turned like a small itinerant hummingbird flitting from flower to flower. The second of the two guards then spoke, breaking the silent spell of stupefaction.

"The woman said she would find Magdalen, she seemed to know where to find her," said the guard. "She would not say where."

Peleus did not reply, he still enumerated the image of Magdalen in his mind. Then the centurion came to his senses.

"Then why did you not go with this woman to where Magdalen could be found?"

"Centurion, I have fought bravely in many wars, I have seen near death many times for the glory of Rome, I have faced both the Syrian warlords and the Jadeites of Troy without any shadow of cowardice descending upon me, never before have you had cause to doubt me," replied the guard with a pleading sincerity in his voice. "This time, I tell you, I was afraid. Every sinew of my body warned me not to cross this old water seller woman. She is some image of a god; she has powers that no human can possess. Her eyes have a strangeness that a low man such as I could never fathom."

"Her eyes?" Peleus stared, riveted to the spot. "What about her eyes? Tell me about her eyes." The centurion's inquisitive instinct was aroused.

"They had an uncommon awareness centurion, freakish in a way that I cannot describe to you. But it wasn't even the colour of her eyes, it was the way she saw everything, the way she looked when she listened," said the guard. "They were animal eyes. it was as if she was searching inside my mind. Centurion, I was afraid. And she knew I was afraid."

Peleus once more did not reply, his thoughts raced like fast-flowing white water. What in hell's name was he faced with? Both the Yehudiish people and the Sanhedrin were confronting something even the veteran centurion did not understand. The centurion was even more convinced that all these mysterious happenings were contrived, that some form of hostile bloodshed was being waged for reasons that he could not yet comprehend.

In the back of his mind something niggled, something he could not fathom devoured the centurion's logical thinking, it wriggled under the surface of his thoughts without revealing why. Then a sudden thought hit him like a hard sword blow to the head. Peleus at once remembered that Caiaphas had given Pontius Pilot compelling information of burning devilment, something that now seemed important about this Magdalen woman. The high priest of the Sanhedrin had revealed that she carried the embryo child of the crucified preacher. Of course - this was the reason behind everything. It did not need much imagination to realise that, if the so-called prophet had in some way risen to be the new king of the Yehudiish, then this child would one day become king, the next king of Judaea by hereditary coronation, one who would be born of the holy preacher and an undoubted goddess of considerable prowess - who, Peleus suspected, might have the power to destroy the central essence of Judaea. Roman Judaea.

This was the same woman who twice before had riveted his inner feelings with her gaze, she had singled him out on the hill of Golgotha after the Romans cut down the body of the preacher from the crucifixion stake. She never approached the dead body while it lay there on the ground, she had not wept or wailed a tear over the flesh and bones of her man like any normal woman would, she had stood staring at himself. She had looked at him in a way that now played havoc with his understanding of how things were, in a way that she seemed to be reading his mind. Then she had taken hold of his heart, the legendary centurion who commanded over ten thousand men had felt his pulse being held in her hard grasp, somehow he sensed that his long-honed sentimental barriers towards love and devotion were being dismantled, in a way that only a witch or an enchantress might wear down his stubborn resistance. Then another thought riveted him to the spot with a bolt of alacrity, a sudden streak of enlightenment that made him stand and stare into the bleakness of the night like a man stripped of his dignity. Peleus recalled the compelling vision of the godlike apparition he had witnessed outside the tomb the previous day. What if this all-powerful being was not here to claim the dying preacher as the centurion presumed? What if this image of a self-prophesising god was here for the same bewitching woman in the ruby-coloured cloak, the woman who had, so far, withstood everything thrown at her? Might it even be this woman's unborn child that could be the cause of some monumental confrontation? Could there be a bitter head-to-head collision of resolve over a hereditary new king of the Yehudiish people? Might there be some death-dealing encounter if a new king descended upon Judaea? The centurion's mind raced at the speed of a wild out-of-control chariot horse, then one more thought materialised at the forefront of the centurion's reasoning like the clearing of mist in the heat of the morning sun, a thought that was pure logical rationality uncontaminated by common sense. What if this woman's unborn child was never to be a manly king at all? What if this newborn, who might change the fate of Judaea, was an infant girl?

Yosef of Arim'athea watched the bleak nighttime sky change through magnificent shades of crimson red then incandescent yellows as the cold dawn transcended into another new day. The ageing priest trudged along with faltering uncertainty, the sweat of perspiration riddling the deep wrinkles of his forehead before exuding to coalesce with the chill morning air. The effort of leading the donkey cart exerted an ever-increasing strain upon his over-pumping heart, spinning spasms of pain through to the thin veins of his extremities. The others followed behind without much enthusiasm, all four felt a sense of the inevitable, that whatever might happen in the next few hours would bring little joy or enlightenment to their upturned lives. The solemn expressions of both Miryam and Salome said everything, they had the unenviable task of keeping the preacher alive when by their reckoning he should be dead. Nicodemus though, felt nothing, the emptiness of his thoughts reflecting the solitude of his mind given that, by now, both himself and Yosef of Arim'athea were far too deep into this deteriorating conspiracy against the Sanhedrin. But, for Yosef, the strain was beginning to tell.

Everything went around and around inside his racing head. When they reached the tomb to find the preacher still alive then what would happen next? Or, if Yeshua had died during the night, then where in heavens sake would they take his body? Yosef had solemnly agreed that any crucified remains would be taken to the disciples when released by the Romans, but because of Magdalen and what she had done, everything had changed. There was no possibility of the messiah being taken to Shem'ayon now Peter whether Yeshua was alive or not - if they did then he would be seized by the Sanhedrin, he would then be claimed by the high priest Caiaphas for whatever purpose the high priest ordained. What was more, if Yeshua had lost his fight for life, then neither could his body stay in the tomb, the burial chamber was the treasured possession of Yosef for his own burial and for those of his family when they died. And what of the archangel Gabriel? Did this glorious envoy of God have his reasons for claiming the life of the preacher? To add more fuel to the proverbial fire, was it conceivable that Yeshua *was* the redeemable spirit of God? If so, would the messiah ascend to heaven as many professed he would? In his pulsating mixed-up mind, Yosef thought this ironic – if the preacher did depart this world of ruthless men, then there was no doubt the terrible burden upon himself would be lessened. Whatever might happen, Yosef knew that his fate did not look good, nor was his destiny in his own hands. At this moment in time, he felt both agitated and uneasy - no less by the alarming rattle and commotion of the donkey cart, the rickety wheels of which created a disconcerting clatter against the uneven stone path that wound itself upwards towards the rounded pinnacle of Golgotha.

The disconsolate party made frustrating slow progress uphill; their long shadows created by the dawn-streaked sky receding as daylight crawled upon them. They neared the last of the steep bends which twisted to the right, away from the towering sun-bleached grey walls that surrounded the still sleeping city of Jer'usalem. Nothing stirred, nor was anything said between them. When they skirted the sharp bend the sullen skull-like mound of Golgotha stood before them, majestic in its supreme abjection. The bleak knoll had on many occasions witnessed ritual executions, the desolate hilltop again and again dealt death by crucifixion while baying hoards of unforgiving Judaeans trampled the stone ground into the dusty-grey grime that now rose to choke the nostrils of two desperate men and both fragile women.

But instead of continuing upwards to the rock of Golgotha, Yosef of Arim'athea veered, leading them down the far less used pathway to the left, retracing their unsteady steps of the previous evening. They continued without much enthusiasm towards the out-of-sight cemetery of the Sanhedrin, their route now taking them downwards which relieved them of the stress of their uphill climb. Yosef himself began to breathe easier, the struggle having vexed his ageing years to the point of near exhaustion. He paused, then turned to look at the others, they trudged with their heads bowed downwards to keep a keen eye upon their stumbling footsteps, Yosef felt a slight pang of gratification when he saw how they struggled for breath - belying their younger years of fortitude. The motionless early morning air still retained the sharp chill of dawn that cooled their exhausted efforts. Yosef paused his stumbling progress to express his feelings.

"My thoughts are that whoever spied us yesterday evening has given up and left," said Yosef between inward breaths to no one in particular. "With luck and hope, they saw us leave then decided there was nothing more to witness."

"What if they are still there?" asked Nicodemus. He was the second youngest of the four, which gave him a distinct advantage in that he was able to recover his breath.

Yosef did not answer, he knew that whoever it was who witnessed the hard-to-believe events of the previous evening, they may not have fallen for their ruse of leaving the tomb. It had been a gamble, but then all four of them needed rest and a night of sleep. They had not slept for the first two nights - in the same evening of the execution Shem'ayon now Peter had begged them to collect the messiah's body from the Romans which meant they had slept nothing at all. Then on the day before the sabbath day, they had to entomb the torn-up body of the preacher only to discover that he still lived. Without doubt, the out-of-this-world apparition of the sacred Gabriel had then changed everything. With sadness, the sabbath day itself was a day of morbid retribution followed by a night of extreme anxiety after their decision to leave the cemetery of Golgotha. Little wonder the extraordinary events of the last four days were now taking their toll, thought Yosef to himself. Two days before the sabbath day, three condemned men were crucified in barbaric circumstances on this desolate cranium-shaped hill, one of those men had somehow survived his atrocious wounds which, in Yosef of Arim'athea's racing mind, could only have happened by some divine intervention of God.

It occurred to Yosef, as more time passed, that a spiritual Yeshua might just be the child of God, given to the world by the Lord in heaven to perhaps, in some way, save mankind. The uncanny appearance of the angel Gabriel only served to reinforce Yosef's growing conviction that tumultuous events were descending upon them, that Caiaphas and the Sanhedrin might have played a bad hand against the one adversary it could never hope to defeat. What would the consequences be to the Yehudiish people if they had crucified the one son of God?

Yosef stumbled around the small bend in the pathway, then froze. A sharp intake of breath behind him meant that Nicodemus also came to an abrupt halt. Both Miryam and Salome stopped in confusion, their vision of the view ahead obscured by the still-loaded donkey cart. On the trail not more than a few paces forward of them sat four men staring in their direction, alerted by the ruckus of the cart on the rock cobblestones. Yosef's mind descended into turmoil; it was not unreasonable to come across someone even at this early hour in the morning, but it was the shock of the unexpected. The four men sat opposite each other on scattered boulders, they were ensconced as if they were waiting for events to happen. With consternation flooding through his inner being, Yosef realised with dread that two of the men ahead wore the imposing uniform of the Sanhedrin special guard.

Nicodemus felt panic overwhelm him. Until now, he thought that no one had associated himself with the disciples, with Magdalen or with Yeshua of Naz'areth but this confrontation would have bad consequences for his wellbeing. He saw that two of the men were Sanhedrin guards. Then straightaway he recognised one of the two men who sat with the guards – he saw the blind storyteller, the old beggar who told stories in the corner of the marketplace.

Like Nicodemus, Yosef thought he recognised the blind beggar, though the storyteller stared showing no signs of blindness. With unwelcome foreboding, Yosef knew who the two guards were. One he knew by name, Bazeus of Heb'ron Al Labinda, he was one of the more moderate of the Sanhedrin guards who he presided over during sabbath temple prayers. The other guard had been around for a long time, but Yosef did not know his name. The remaining older man, who also sat with the guards, he did not know.

"Yosef, what shall we do?" breathed Nicodemus in a low whisper, there were nervous undertones in his voice.

Yosef's mind again raced, it whirled like a spinning top not unlike a child's whirlpoint made to spin by a fast-whipping line. This immediate confrontation was not going to go well. Yosef thought quick, their only hope was to bluff their way through but in the back of his subconsciousness Yosef realised that something was not right, why would two of the Sanhedrin's elite guards be here on the pathway accompanied by two old beggar men from the marketplace?

"I think providence will be our one salvation right now," whispered Yosef, replying to Nicodemus.

"We cannot turn back Yosef," said Nicodemus, "We will look like foolish rats caught in a trap."

Yosef tried to think with rational reasoning, realising that it was not unusual for him to be visiting his family tomb. Perhaps he could bluff their way through, but this would depend upon how much the two Sanhedrin guards knew.

"Let us keep going," said Yosef. "Show no sign of the reasons why we are here, we are proceeding to my family tomb to prepare for a burial. There is nothing unusual in this."

Miryam and Salome gasped in panic when they saw the four men ahead.

"Lord upon us," uttered Miryam under her breath. Then to Salome, "It is the Sanhedrin." Salome did not reply. The four of them drew up to the four men, who eyed their approach with clear suspicion.

"Shoh-lehm ah-Leh-khem to you Bazeus of Heb'ron Al Labinda," Yosef offered the traditional Yehudiish greeting to the one Sanhedrin guard he knew well, who stood to greet them. The still breathless priest sensed unease in the guard's demeanour.

"Yosef of Arim'athea, Shoh-lehm ah-Leh-khem to you my friend," replied Bazeus. "What tragedy brings you to the cemetery of the Sanhedrin at this early hour of the morning following the sabbath?" As Bazeus spoke the second of the two guards rose to his feet in a way that suggested he might well intervene.

"We go to my family burial tomb, Bazeus," replied Yosef with conviction, knowing that he was telling no lie. If there were to be repercussions or should he ever be brought before Caiaphas, then Yosef could at least claim that he told the truth. He looked down at the other two older men who both sat squatted upon the smooth rounded boulders. Yosef noticed the blind storyteller staring straight at him, in a way suggesting the beggar could somehow discern his thoughts. Yosef felt uneasy.

"A family tragedy is the ill will of God my friend, may our Lord in heaven be with you," replied Bazeus, who had no desire for confrontation with more priests of the Sanhedrin - seeing that Nicodemus bore the low rank of temple priesthood. This unexpected encounter was a disturbing distraction. The shimmering heat of the rising dawn had not yet risen to its full morning intensity, there was still the chilling residual coldness from the long dark night of disparity, there existed a raw frigidity that created an atmospheric conclusion to the sabbath day just passed.

Yosef of Arim'athea turned to Miriam and Salome. "The two of you must continue ahead to the tomb. Take the donkey and the cart with you, Nicodemus and I will deal with this matter." Yosef spoke low in a whisper, if the two women continued to the tomb with little haste, then they might not raise too much suspicion. In any event, it would be good manners for himself and Nicodemus to converse in an informal manner with these guards from the Sanhedrin. But Yosef still sensed that something was not right.

"Why are elite guards of the Sanhedrin here in the sacred cemetery of the esteemed temple?" enquired Yosef to Bazeus without trying to raise suspicion. "What business of the Sanhedrin brings you here?"

As he spoke Miryam and Salome stumbled ahead, continuing along the rugged pathway, Miryam taking the reigns of the donkey from Yosef. Neither of the women passed any look or marginal glance at the four men beside the pathway, they kept their heads bowed downwards to steady their feet, not wishing to raise any suspicion of intent or to give any impression of why they should not be there. Under her dark hooded cloak, Miryam shook with nervous fear, her shivering not helped by the chilling sting in the morning air. There was still some distance to make before they once more climbed upwards to reach the desolate tomb entrance, the rock cave where the suffering messiah still lay on his stone slab. Yosef was right, thought Miryam, the two of them could tend to the wounds of the sacred preacher if he had in some way managed to survive through the long night. She and Salome could at least continue their intensive care, then they would wait for Yosef and Nicodemus to join them.

Miryam gathered her resolve, she stumbled ahead. The blind storyteller Celidonius, though, watched them pass, there was something afoot that did not fool him, he felt uneasy - with the deep suspicion of someone who felt his destiny at stake.

As the two women continued onwards Yosef of Arim'athea stared at Bazeus waiting for him to reply, nothing came forth from him about why the guards were there. Then it occurred to Yosef that something was wrong, it dawned upon him that these four men on the pathway were as uneasy with their presence as he was with theirs. It appeared that neither he nor Bazeus wished to declare the reason for their presence in the cemetery of the Sanhedrin. Celidonius, the blind beggar, broke the fragile impasse.

"It seems the Sanhedrin has much interest in this place of the dead," he drawled. "What can it be that brings all of you to this graveyard of the rich and powerful eh?" Celidonius offered his searching question to no one in particular, he still sat squatting upon his bony haunches. "Can it be there are more sacred souls buried here than you care to declare?"

Yosef eyed Celidonius with deep suspicion. His thoughts turned on the double, his mind charged like a raging bull, his eyes danced between each of the four men before him. He remembered that Salome had earlier informed him how elite guards had been killed, that it was said in the marketplace how the guard captain himself suffered sword wounds inside the temple of the Sanhedrin. If this was true, there must be a link with the four men who now barred his way. And was there any news of Magdalen?

"I have to warn you Yosef, the high priest Caiaphas and the Sanhedrin general guard will soon be here," volunteered Bazeus, sensing that he had no choice but to tell the truth, he knew that both women with Yosef were part of the dead preacher's close band of followers. Why were they here with Yosef of Arim'athea? "They know from the Romans the holy preacher from Naz'areth who was crucified might lie somewhere in this cemetery."

"The Romans?" Yosef gasped. His mind staggered. Peleus the Roman centurion knew that Yeshua was not yet dead. Did Caiaphas know this also?

"The Romans search for the witch woman Magdalen," added Bazeus. "Do you know where she is? The Sanhedrin want to find this woman, it seems she might hold the key to these misfortunes that befall the Sanhedrin."

"Bazeus, I know nothing of this woman's whereabouts. What has happened inside the temple of the Sanhedrin? Please tell me," probed Yosef. "I know nothing of this."

Yosef could see the worried hesitation in the eyes of Bazeus, he saw there was an uneasy glance between the two guards. There was something they did not wish to say. It was Celidonius who once more interrupted.

"Our two illustrious friends here who wear their uniforms of remorse, they are now Sanhedrin renegades also," he chortled. "Caiaphas searches for the Magdalen woman and for ourselves. The list of enemies to the Sanhedrin grows by the hour."

"Does Caiaphas search for the dead preacher from Naz'areth?" asked Yosef to Bazeus, ignoring the blind storyteller squatting on the tallest rock.

"No, he does not," replied Bazeus. "The preacher is dead; it is the living that Caiaphas fears. The Sanhedrin searches for the Magdalen woman and for the traitorous Yehudas Isca'riot, the informer who turned in the preacher from Naz'areth."

"Why does he search for Magdalen and Isca'riot?" asked Yosef.

"I am a simple Sanhedrin guard Yosef," said Bazeus. "I am not party to the happenings within the hierarchy. I simply follow orders. But three guards are now dead by the hands of this woman."

Yosef felt breathless, a riptide had ripped through the Sanhedrin since he had led Nicodemus with the two women to collect the body of Yeshua from the Romans as agreed with Shem'ayon now Peter. But, with a sigh of inward relief, although he was wrong, it seemed that no one might yet suspect his involvement in these astonishing events, nor that of Nicodemus though it was clear Magdalen was exacting her revenge in a way that he, Yosef of Arim'athea, never dreamed possible. Yosef thought hard, he needed to make an immediate decision about what to do next.

The morning twilight had long passed, as he stood there disconsolate on the stone path it was easy for Yosef to see over the imposing city wall. The distant hanging rooftops hidden amidst twisted stone spires were discernible, the imposing red-tiled roofs glistening under the first rays of cascading sunlight that created an illusion of exploding colour, a dramatic spectacle that would soon fade when the sun rose higher into the cloudless spring sky. Jer'usalem was stirring, the last sabbath of Passover had passed, in a short while the bustling crowds would be going about their business like busy ants in their uncountable chaotic thousands. The dust and foul stinking stench of the city would soon begin to fuse with the rancid azure, it would create impenetrable barriers to the intense sunlight of the morning - meaning that few of the Judaean people inside the walls would ever know that fate had played yet one more cruel hand in the blood-ridden annals of the Yehudiish chosen people.

Yosef realised that he and Nicodemus could go no further, to do so would endanger the life of the near-dead preacher. To continue would risk the dramatic news of the messiah's still fragile suffering to spread - the two renegade priests of the Sanhedrin must in some way draw away these four men who, for their own reasons, wished to discover the whereabouts of the preacher's crucified body. Little did Yosef realise that these desperate renegades also searched for Magdalen, they had little hope but for her to save them. There were prying Romans close by, if the centurion Peleus was hereabouts then he would no doubt descend upon them in angry retribution, the vengeful centurion would deal yet more Roman justice. And Yosef could not risk feeding the fiery anger of Pontius Pilot; never must the ageing priest have sole responsibility for drawing Roman wrath against the Sanhedrin. To make matters worse, Yosef of Arim'athea knew that soon he would have to confront an unforgiving Caiaphas, the supreme high priest of the Sanhedrin who would deal his own form of retribution.

It dawned upon Yosef with growing dread that Miryam and Salome would now have to suffer the awesome coming of the spiritual archangel Gabriel alone, they would need to make their own accord with the reverent messenger of the Lord while at the same time offering care to a dying man. And what if the preacher had died during the long night? What would Miryam and Salome do then? How would their fragile emotions cope with that? Yosef's tomb could easily be their own if the full might of the Sanhedrin, the Roman Empire and the all-powerful Gabriel descended upon them - all at the same time. This, Yosef realised with self-induced panic, was now a rapidly deteriorating disaster that sat squarely upon the shoulders of the one ruby-cloaked woman that no one could find.

It then hit Yosef like a blind thunderhead that these four men here confronting him were also running. From their uneasy demeanour and worried glances, he could see they had no wish to be caught by Caiaphas or his Sanhedrin guards. What total devilment had unfolded inside the temple? How was it that Magdalen, a mere woman who carried a strangeness that he could never fathom, could wreak such havoc and destruction? What unfathomable link was there between her and the seditious messiah who it was claimed by many might be the long prophesied descendant of the great Lord above? And what had driven this preacher from the small settlement of Naz'areth to make such a wild confession even if it had been extracted under the extreme duress of bloody torture by the Sanhedrin?

One more doom-ridden thought pressed to the forefront of Yosef of Arim'athea's confused mind. Where in the Lord's name was Magdalena, where was Magdalen during this extraordinarily difficult time?

"Where are we?" asked Yehudas. "I do not know this place."

"We are at the Gihon Spring, the fountain of the virgin, it brings water to the pools of Siloam," the old woman replied. "This is a sacred place."

"Why is it sacred?" Isca'riot looked around, in the prevailing darkness he could not discern much. He could hear the trickling of running water mixed with the eerie clatter of nighttime crickets. The two of them were standing amidst ancient man-made rocks, the sound of water emanated from somewhere within the thick mulberry bushes to his right.

"The pools of Siloam is the reason that you men first came here, it is why this stinking city of Jer'usalem exists," replied the old woman. "It is sacred because here the virgin concubine Tabitha broke the will of the Yehudiish King David. Men, in all their endeavours, need water to survive." The old woman maintained her expression of indifference in a way that suggested some other preoccupation.

"Why are we here?" asked Yehudas.

"We need rest, the morning will bring a day of great remembrance and bloodshed, perhaps more death."

The water woman sat herself down upon the remains of a crumbling grey wall. For the first time, Isca'riot noticed that she wore the same ruby cloak though it was much faded and torn, her attire seemed to have aged in the same way that she too had morphed.

"You must tell me. Are you the same Marusya Magdalen? Do you carry the child of Yeshua?" He asked his question knowing that he would not get an easy answer. Yehudas sat down a short distance opposite, he felt the dampness of the stone wall seep through his ragged cloak, sensing the wet moistness of rancid green moss that now stained the worn-out fibres. He did not care.

"No. I am not the same woman," the old water woman answered his question. "The woman whose name is Magdalena, or Magdalen as you say, is a figment of time inside your mind. She does not exist."

"Then who are you? I do not understand"

"I am the same. I draw breath only within the power of your imagination."

"This is strange talk," declared Yehudas. "I can see no sense in what you say. This new confusion is beginning to hurt my head." Dim starlight lit the wrinkled features of the ageing water seller. She eyed him, Isca'riot knew that he was sinking to some depth that lay well beyond his rational reasoning.

"No woman or man can transform, no one human has the power to change into another human," she replied. "Even so-called gods or goddesses cannot do this."

"Do you carry the child of Yeshua inside you?" Yehudas once more asked, thinking he could perhaps force the water seller into saying something he could at least understand.

She paused to choose her words. "The child grows in her own inhuman way. She cannot transform from one birthmother to another, nor can she be changed in her destiny."

"Tell me what you mean," urged Isca'riot, his confused frustration beginning to reverberate in his voice. "Does this mean that you do not carry the child? Are you saying that Marusya is not elsewhere or in another place?"

"No, she is not. But her infant grows inside me, the child has done since the night she was conceived."

"But you tell me you are not Magdalen," pronounced Yehudas in uncensored annoyance, he felt his mind once more beginning to tremble.

"I am not the Magdalena nor am I the old water seller woman you see now. I am something you cannot imagine in your vivid dreams." A strange hint of twilight struck the eastern sky, the first reckoning of a towering dawn that would be some hours yet. The crickets continued their rhythmic beat, a timeless rhythm that in some way synchronised with the heartbeat of a despairing Yehudas.

"What are you saying?" he asked.

"The minds of men see what they want to see, they believe what they want to believe," said the water seller. "It is easy for me to be not who I am. The history of men is full of make-believe and untruths, twisted lies and a myriad of things that never happened. I have no real name, only names written by medicine men in their ancient scribes and old tablets. Magdalena, Eve, Lilith or Hyvah, which do you prefer?"

Yehudas couldn't think of anything more to say. Not for one moment did he understand what the water seller said. He sat and watched the old woman gather a few sticks of firewood from beneath the mulberry trees, checking each one for dryness and no moisture. Then she stacked them within a ring of cobblestones she formed up between the two of them. In an instant the sticks burst into flames, Yehudas saw and wondered to himself how she did this, but the warmth of the small kindling fire was quick to spread through his shivering body - it smoothed his restless mind.

"You should sleep, Yehudas," the old woman suggested. "We are safe here, no one comes to this place," she confided. "Remember this Gihon spring, it is where you must come when the time comes for you to honour the promise you made to Magdalena."

"To take her bones?" he asked. "Is this where she will die?"

"Yes, this is a sacred place."

In the gentle heat of the fire, Yehudas lay down to his side to rest his tired head. He watched the old water seller; he saw flickering flames creating an illusion of alluring shadows dancing upon her expressionless face as she stared without emotion into the burning embers. The nearby crickets lowered their incessant tempo, suggesting they knew another time for mankind was dawning. Then, for some reason, for a few moments, the crickets were altogether silent. An eerie total silence. Isca'riot felt his eyelids closing, for a few seconds he tried hard to resist the creeping weariness that devoured him. In the end the comforting fire finished him, he was gone, lost in a sleep that offered no real respite to his uncompromising spirit.

Isca'riot did not know when he dreamed the dream, the timeless dream that he would forever remember. For the rest of his traitorous life. First, he saw the old woman standing amidst the flickering flames, she stood with her arms raised level to each side creating the image of the sacred cross that shaped her whole body. She upturned both her palms, then her unlit face to the starlit sky, the fire burning around the bare flesh of her womanly torso that bore angel-gossamer wings lit by the dim glow of the fire. Then he saw the Naz'areth preacher, who kneeled then prayed to her in subliminal worship. The renegade preacher whispered his undying love, the ruby-coloured robe that cloaked her then burned away to reveal her reverence. She stood naked, her bare breasts heaving and alluring, the so-called messiah paying no attention to her woman's body. Yeshua seemed lost then once more found. Isca'riot saw the terrible wounds that covered his one-time friend's wretched body, lacerations of pure blood that no normal man could withstand. Yehudas saw two gaping spear wounds that holed Yeshua's left side, then the appalling punctures to his mangled broken hands. There was no excrement of death nor the relentless foulness that permeates every man who suffers violent suffering, he was cleaned and cared for as best that someone could; a Yehudiish woman touch that Yehudas had never experienced, not in *his* life. Then, without warning, the endearing dream of Yehudas Isca'riot ended, he slept the fitful sleep of the redeemed traitor.

In the morning the sun rose sharp, the residual heat of the long-dead fire was cold and burned out, leaving flakes of ash blowing skyward in a gentle whispering breeze. Yehudas had missed the flaming dawn, when he awoke it was already the fullness of a magnificent new day. He sat himself up, shaking off his slumbering sleep and the shocked residual feeling of his inspiring nightmare dream.

The old woman was gone, Isca'riot was alone and shambolic, he sat bolt upright in his bewildered reverence.

Both Miryam and Salome heaved at the rounded stone that kept the family tomb of Yosef of Arim'athea closed. It took all of their combined efforts to move it to one side, but once they had an amount of movement the stone began to roll easier. Late morning sunlight flooded into the cramped interior, the wild darkness inside wrenched aside by the intensity of the bright new day. Once more, the pungent smell of the dead raced out to greet them, rancid air that fouled their nasals to make both women wince in revulsion.

It took a few moments for their eyes to adjust to the changing of the light but once inside Salome stood frozen with instantaneous, shuddering shock. Miryam too began to shake, out of control, as they both stared at the empty stone slab before them. Neither of them twitched a muscle or moved, they could not, in the few moments it took for the terrible reality to overwhelm them their immediate senses failed. Yeshua was not there, nowhere in the tomb revealed his presence, nor any sign of how he had been able to leave. It was as if he had just vanished into the air. Neither of the two women knew what to do; both Salome and Miryam stood motionless, unable to reason their disbelief.

Outside the tomb Gabriel approached, striding his long strides that gave him his strangeness that dispelled any doubts that he was anything but angelic. This time there had been no magnificent in his coming nor any spectacular displays of resplendence, he did not wish to draw further attention from anyone who might be around. Gabriel just wanted to get this done, he wished to snare Magdalen, destroy her child then make sure this false prophet lying in the tomb was dead - the preacher would die a mortal human death. It might not happen in this instant, but he knew that while the preacher lay near to death then Magdalen would soon make her appearance. He was sure of this. For now, all Gabriel needed to do was use the two women to keep this delusional preacher alive.

Gabriel had spied Miryam and Salome in their approach, they had indeed returned to the tomb three days after the burial of the preacher in the way he had demanded, but he saw that both Yosef of Arim'athea and the Sanhedrin priest Nicodemus were this time not with them. There was no sign yet of Magdalen, but it was only a question of time. The tomb had not been disturbed since the four humans left the night before, Gabriel was sure of this, he understood why they had left because he also caught sight of the watching Romans. The Romans did not concern him, it did not matter if they witnessed the final destruction of Magdalen or the ultimate death of this preacher, Gabriel's only concern was to once-and-for-all end the immense danger of Magdalen's child being born. The dealings and history of mankind was then their own affair, his dominance of this race of men over everything else was well underway, it could not be challenged. Everything rested upon Magdalen and this preacher coming together here at the cemetery of the Sanhedrin - and his trap was now well set.

Miryam was the first to stagger outside the tomb. Salome still stood devastated inside; her thoughts were at last coming together. She began to apply logic to this bizarre situation. The messiah had been left near to death, lying on the stone slab in front of her unable to move or able to do anything for himself. Salome was well sure of this. It was not possible that he could in some way, by a miracle, recover then climb from the slab to roll open the stone doorway from inside. Therefore, whoever watched from the opposite cliffside must have opened the tomb then taken the mutilated messiah. It was the one logical explanation.

Salome walked out of the tomb to seek out Miryam. Salome knew it would be pointless to get any sense of logic out of Miryam, she could see her friend convulsing in tears of absolute despair. Salome sat down on the rock next to her, trying to think with rationale about what they should do.

Poor Miryam, she had reasoned her own logic about what had happened. The messiah must have recovered through the divine intervention of God his father during the night, then ascended to heaven with the help of God's angels. Right now, this resurrection was the one reasonable explanation, certainly this would be affirmed by the archangel Gabriel who, as promised, would appear quite soon. He would then tell them what to do. This is what Gabriel had before instructed, to care for the preacher until the third day following the crucifixion. The night just passed must have been when the resurrected preacher ascended to be with God his true father. This is what Miryam was convinced had happened. It all made uneasy sense.

On the hillside opposite the tomb Peleus and his Roman guards watched all this. He saw the two Judaean women roll back the stone doorway to enter the tomb. He watched as they both ran outside a short time afterwards. There was still no sign of the woman in the ruby cloak who, his guards said, would return to the cemetery to be with the crucified preacher from Naz'areth. Peleus felt agitated, something was not right. He saw the distress of the two women, straightaway he assumed the preacher must have died during the night; their tearful grief was easy testament to this. Peleus and his men had not approached the tomb during the night, the Romans had once before given up the broken body of the crucified preacher to the Judaeans, Peleus had no wish to take him back. Neither had anyone else visited the tomb since the two men and the two women left the previous night. He was sure of this too.

The centurion's growing apprehension made no sense, his gut feeling was to take his men down to the tomb to take control but if the preacher was dead then there was nothing more the Romans could do. Another sixth sense then kicked in, he would wait for the appearance of the Magdalen woman who would change everything, then he and his men might descend to the tomb if there were any signs of trouble. Little did Peleus realise that he had just a short time to live, soon his life would end in terrifying circumstances. He would be dead before the sun reached its nascent high in the coming midday heat.

Gabriel stood with splendid adornment before Miryam and Salome, he once more took the magnificent form of the resplendent angel. His gossamer wings were covered by the white cloak of fine woven silk that left nothing to the imagination. He was the messenger of God, he wanted anyone spying to be well aware of this. His short fire-blade sword was well hidden. Miryam and Salome in one swift moment fell to their knees.

"Women, pay your penance to your God then rise to your feet," commanded Gabriel. The archangel did not pay much attention to the human race unless he was dealing with a priest or high priest of order.

Both women climbed to their feet in reverence, silent in their demeanour except for the whimpering tears of Miryam. Salome stood frozen with fear.

Gabriel at once saw outward dread in their tearful eyes. Something was wrong, in an instant he determined the preacher must have died during the night. He bent low to enter the tomb to see for himself the calamity that had occurred. Then, Gabriel stood rigid with absolute shock horror.

The empty stone slap confronting him said everything. Gabriel tried to suppress his rising anger, he looked around to see no other way out of the tomb except the one entrance, there were only small vent holes to other tombs that contained their own rotting dead. The dreadful implications of what he saw began to dawn upon him; there was no preacher from Naz'areth, no seditious messiah who was born from the tramp of a woman in Bethlehem. There was no worm of a woman who they called Magdalen nor, Gabriel grasped, would she ever be here with her wretched unborn child. Gabriel knew that she would never appear, once more he had been deceived. Outwitted. His temper rose to a crescendo like an exploding volcano.

Gabriel strode from the tomb in tumultuous anger. No longer did he possess the appearance of an angel, his folded wings had dissipated along with his angelic aurora complete with its prickly crown of thorns. Now he stood tall and imposing, sort of transparent in his natural existence. The long fingers of his spindly boneless hands held his fire-blade sword that was no real sword, he held it upwards towards the deep blue sky where the sun hung suspended at its supreme midday peak. There were no fluffy white clouds to dissipate the intense noon heat, there was just the glare of the shimmering motionless air that carried the stench of the stinking city up to the forsaken hill of Golgotha.

"Zamora the true God, hear this," cried Gabriel, imploring to the wide open sky. "I know you seek this man who was crucified. I tell you, he is not here, for he has risen."

Gabriel, with all his might, struck his fire-blade staff deep into the ground. The earth, all of a sudden, trembled. He raised his sword once more to strike violence into the hard rock hillside, shocks and tremors began to shake the core of Golgotha. Miryam and Salome stood in shear shock and horrified horror, the world beneath their feet beginning to shake and contort in wild madness. On the cliffside opposite, the

Roman centurion Peleus felt harrowing dread and intense trepidation, never before had he experienced the deep feeling of creeping fear that enveloped his muscular powerful body. Gabriel struck his sword into the rock-ridden ground a third time, the earth began to tremble. The hollow roar of destruction exploded upon Golgotha like the shattering of a mountain, the shockwave of ruination spreading outwards in waves of surfing oceanic mayhem that drove heartbreak and death before it. The travelling earthquake of destructive maelstrom would find her, Gabriel was sure of this, but he knew deep within his stone-cold heart that it would never destroy her.

Salome was the first to die when the crumbling doorway fell upon her, in the split-second it took for the heavy round stone to fall she saw the terrified tears of Miryam of Bath'uma, whose own mixed-up mind succumbed to the vengeance of her loving God. Salome died with the vision of those who loved her foremost in her mind: she was never enthusiastic in her desire to aid Yosef of Arim'athea in his gruesome task but she died under the falling stone nevertheless. The centurion Peleus died when the crumbling cliffside tumbled: his brave instincts that always served him froze when he perceived the unrolling disaster that enveloped him; he died when his broken body fell into the chasm of rising dust that rose high into the sky to claim him. The high midday sun mocked his wretched fall by reflecting sunbeams of bright light that flashed like flames of fire from his polished centurion's armour. The centurion's terrified guards died right beside him, their piercing screams that no one heard echoing into the silent obliqueness.

Back on the cobbled roadway, Celidonius, the blind storyteller, saw with terrifying clarity the strange riptide of destruction that descended like a wave upon them: then he heard the roar of exploding madness that claimed him. Before he died a beggar's death he smiled, knowing the woman in the ruby-coloured cloak had once more claimed him: he remembered why it was that she cured his years of blindness. But he never got to tell the one story he always wanted - the agonising story about how he would forever relish the pure joy of his sightless freedom. The old bean seller beggar man, he died also, he died without even thinking.

The Sanhedrin guard Bazeus tried to run in blind panic with his torn tunic tangling between his bare flesh knees, when he ran as fast as his legs would take him. He saw the tortured face of his grief-stricken sister sibling - the slaver's knife wounds the heartbreaking scars of her destruction. Bazeus reached out imploring her to save him, but death descended when the breaking ground beneath absorbed him. When Bazeus died he cried tears that were never destined to save him. Yosef of Arim'athea died when he tried his best to reason, while he tried to fathom the horrible injustice of his affirmation: he died a high priest's death without anyone around to forever condemn him. He realised at once that running away would serve no purpose, because the delicate eulogy of his ageing years would strike him down long before this cataclysmic earthquake caught him. Yosef of Arim'athea died in peace, with his head tilted in the pose of tragic all-thinking contemplation.

Nicodemus, he lived, he remained alive in confusing fashion that would forever, for the rest of his life, torment him: in his irrational mind he could not see why it was this tragic earthquake did not kill him. The other Sanhedrin guard, he died while staring with stupid stupefaction at the running Bazeus, he died when the stone rockslide fell upon him. The same rockslide that claimed Yosef of Arim'athea, along with the disgruntled guard Bazeus, surprised the approaching Caiaphas and his Sanhedrin guards when the roadway to the cemetery vanished in the avalanche of falling rocks that fell all around them. Caiaphas, he lived, his surviving guards pulling and heaving him squealing like a demented pig from under the rock-strewn madness. He stumbled to his feet in utter confusion, shivering in whimpering fear before he blasphemed to the guards who saved him.

Miryam of Bath'uma lived, she survived the death-dealing chaos because of the mumbling prayers of her salvation. She survived, because her God in his overwhelming good sense saved her: he heard her desperate pleas of devotion then decided it was not yet Miriam's time to meet her creator. Gabriel's God above was no fool - he desired a lucid voice to tell the world of callous men the twisted story of the messiah's resurrection. Gabriel, in his supreme wisdom, saw there was at last a way to create yet one more mesmerising prophet.

"Tell us what happened," demanded Shem'ayon now Peter. Miryam cried in tearful confusion. She raised her lowered head to tell them her vision of what happened – though just four of the twelve self-declared apostles sat there before her. Creeping nighttime shadows heralded the closing of the dreadful day of ground-shaking retribution. Outside the city, mayhem still reigned in the aftermath of the earthquake that had destroyed the desolate hill of Golgotha.

"You say you saw everything?" demanded Johan, his face grim with ill-concealed unease.

"Yes, but you must give me some time," protested Miryam, trying hard to stem the flow of her streaming tears. "You have known the messiah longer than I though you have not seen what I have seen." Miryam looked the Baptist straight in the eye, for all his proclamations of loyalty and straight talking he had been conspicuous by his absence when the situation became threatening. In her mind he was not to be trusted, she every time felt discomposed in his presence – she had the notion that Johan first and foremost was concerned only with himself. Perhaps it was a woman's instinct, but Miryam did not think high of the so-called Baptist. Where had he been along with the rest when Yeshua, the true messiah, was in desperate trouble? How was it that these men who were Yeshua's chosen disciples had forsaken him? In Miryam's mind, this whole pack of devotees, Isca'riot included, followed the messiah like dribbling leeches. To make matters worse, they showed no regard for the women who tried to include themselves in Yeshua's band of believers. The followers of the prophet held their own inner council like the covetous devoted band they were.

As ever, Miryam knew her woman's place. Into this turbulent mix of quarrelling men had come the defiant Magdalen. Miryam, for selfish reasons, did not adhere herself to Magdalen who, in her own way, changed everything. Along with Salome, Miryam had agreed to bring back the messiah's body because of her mutual respect for Yosef of Arim'athea. And now, where was Yosef? Was he dead too? And where was Magdalen now?

"Our messiah still lived when his body was returned by the Romans, each of you must not tell anyone this," Miryam implored. "Gabriel the angel showed us how to keep the messiah alive, he demanded that we tell no one, not even you, his disciples."

Johan looked displeased; he did not relish how he was beholding to this woman. "Describe to us again what happened. Is Yeshua dead or alive?" The Baptist did not seem in the least sympathetic or even open-minded towards Miryam.

"Yes, he must have died, now he is risen," answered Miryam.

"Where is the messiah's body?" interrupted Shem'ayon now Peter, he appeared agitated, to Miryam there was no doubt that Shem'ayon now Peter was keeping something quiet. The sheepish look in his eyes hid nothing.

"I tell you, there is no body, our messiah was gone, he is risen," Miryam reaffirmed to them once more. "He was lying close to death when we left him in the tomb in the evening of the Sabbath. We returned after sunrise to find the tomb of Yosef of Arim'athea empty. Yeshua was not there, yet the stone entrance had not been opened."

Shem'ayon now Peter looked at Johan in agitated discomfort. Johan himself was now close to tears: they did not seem to be tears of compassion, to Miryam they were tears of sudden guilt and shame. Didymus sat in the corner silent, the shock of what Miryam described was too much, he could not find words to speak; he felt sorry for Miryam. Ya'akov, who was the younger son of Alphaeus, still slept, his sleepy drunken stupor overwhelming his shabby regard. He was laid out on the stone slab that served as a communal bench - the dim candlelight of the room offering an easy place for him to hide.

"You tell us he is risen," gasped Shem'ayon now Peter. "How do you know this?"

Miryam, nervous, paused - to one more time find the same words.

She felt uncomfortable with this hostile questioning, it was as if they disbelieved her. Miryam looked from Johan to Shem'ayon now Peter.

"I have told you, I know this from the blessed Gabriel's own revelation," said Miryam, "I tell you again, he proclaimed aloud to his own Lord in heaven, before our own eyes - to our own God. Gabriel said, 'You seek this man who was crucified. He is not here for he has risen.' These were Gabriel's own words to the Lord, these were his words, do you not understand what has happened? You are disbelievers, you disciples should know that Gabriel's proclamation is written in the blood of those who are now dead." Miryam, in her resolute mind, remembered everything. Gabriel's passionate declaration to God was etched into the fragile soul of her sanity. One more time she wept, her tears flowing free when the tragic memory of young Salome's death came flooding back into her mind.

Shem'ayon now Peter was slow-witted, but he was no stupid fool. He listened with ascetic concern. Before the crucifixion, Yehudas Isca'riot had revealed to him the dreadful secret of Magdalen carrying the unborn child of their messiah: to Shem'ayon now Peter, Isca'riot was not the much maligned traitor that everyone made out. The two of them had argued long into the night about what they should do, how it would be best to deal with this devastating news. In the end, they agreed that no one should be told, the situation then deteriorated when the Sanhedrin learned of the unborn child, more so when they realised the terrible consequences. What Shem'ayon now Peter did not know was that it was Isca'riot himself who had informed Caiaphas, the high priest of the Sanhedrin that Magdalen carried the messiah's child. Caiaphas was quick to understand the reality of Magdalen's legacy and the danger of the infant she carried. In the event, Shem'ayon now Peter had taken upon himself not to reveal the existence of the child to his fellow disciples and, he now realised, Miryam of Ba'thuma had no knowledge of the child either. Shem'ayon now Peter felt relieved, Miryam was not about to reveal this devastating news to the disciples as he feared: this would have placed him in an extraordinarily difficult situation – more so with Johan the Baptist whose terrible temper was well known.

While listening to Miryam of Ba'thuma's tearful recital of the incredible events on the hill of Golgotha, Shem'ayon now Peter's mind lurched from thought to thought. The flickering light of the room, dim candlelight that offered no warmth or even a semblance of comfort, created an atmosphere of oppressive misery that was both disconsolate and doom-laden. The sobbing tears of Miryam coupled with the drunken snoring of the horizontal Ya'akov only served to dampen the pervading mood even further. Shem'ayon now Peter looked at Johan, who was trying hard to maintain his composure. Shem'ayon now Peter knew that soon the Baptist would break, that the heavily bearded disciple who epitomised the inner souls of the followers of the messiah would not be able to deal with the news that his convictions to the uniqueness of the messiah were right all along, that their preacher from Naz'areth was the prophesied son of God who was now risen to be with God his true father. In the mind of Johan, the empty tomb and the proclamation of the archangel Gabriel as described by Miryam of Ba'thuma was enough proof of this. Shem'ayon now Peter saw the inner guilt that tormented the Baptist, who was not the only disciple to disown the messiah to save his own skin. When the guards of the Sanhedrin came in the dead of night to the garden of Gethsemane, to hunt for the promulgated son of God, not one of the inner circle of disciple friends had intervened to save him. It was not only Isca'riot's shame that prevailed.

Nevertheless, in the deepest part of his heart, Shem'ayon now Peter was not convinced by these extraordinary revelations revealed by Miryam of Ba'thuma. Knowing what he himself knew about the unborn child, he was convinced that Yeshua had not risen to his heavenly place in heaven. Perhaps there occurred some devil's supreme trickery, maybe there had been yet one more unbelievable miracle. Was it possible, was it conceivable, that the proffered high priest Caiaphas and the Sanhedrin had made a grim mistake - that Yeshua, the Magdalena and their unborn infant had deceived everyone?

In the ponderous mind of Shem'ayon now Peter, the complicated pieces of the puzzle began to fall into place. Their sacred prophet Yeshua was made to confess under duress, the baying clamour of Judaeans who claimed he must be the seed of God had made the messiah a marked man, he must have known that he would be tried then crucified for blasphemy at the hands of the Sanhedrin for not dispelling such a claim. He was executed for the heretical act of taking the Lord's name in vain, but more so for the seditious crime of high treason – for creating the likelihood of being proclaimed the new king of Judaea, the saviour of the Yehudiish people. Yeshua would have known that Caiaphas and the Sanhedrin would tolerate neither blasphemy nor sedition, nor would Pontius Pilot and the Romans. But if Yeshua was executed for rebellious treason then, without question, the Sanhedrin would ensure that Magdalen and her child would be murdered also. Shem'ayon now Peter realised that, if Yeshua was crucified for being the prophesied seed of God without anyone even suspecting that he fathered a child, then Magdalen and her newborn infant might stand a chance of survival. This made sense – Yeshua had made a false confession to protect Magdalen and their infant child, perhaps Yeshua and Magdalen always knew he might in some way survive the crucifixion on the stake – this must be why Yeshua had made a false confession to being the son of God. The more Shem'ayon Peter pondered, with the bright light of enlightenment flooding his mind, the more he realised the prophet Yeshua must have decided that he would not die, that he must in some way survive being nailed to the stake – to then disappear into the mist of time accompanied by the Magdalena.

Shem'ayon now Peter smiled to himself in satisfaction. Could the messiah have, in some way, performed his ultimate miracle and not died? Might he have lived so that he could stand by the side of Magdalen and their child? Could it be that Yeshua the messiah and the woman, who some Judaeans rumoured might herself be a descendent of Adamah's Hyvah, may now be somewhere together with their unborn child? Was it possible that everyone had been deceived? Led by the hand? To Shem'ayon now Peter – Yeshua and Magdalen may have made the perfect escape. The messiah's crucifixion could have been a wonderful means of hiding from the persecution and death of his soon to be born child.

Both God and Shem'ayon now Peter decided the same thing at the same time. The so-called disciples, the dedicated band of followers who worshipped the cultish prophesies of the renegade preacher from Naz'areth must now transform. From this day they would become the Saviour's apostles, they would go out into the world of men to teach how God gave his only son to save them from the evil sins of mankind. What both God and Shem'ayon now Peter together realised, what they both concluded without any shadow of reverence, was that never should the real truth be revealed. Never must the tragic world of men know how the renegade preacher was in his own way a true prophet, that he was the chosen one - but chosen by neither Gabriel nor his Lord. He had faced death in its vicious form. Never must it be written that any son of God had endured the ravaging of his soul to endure the survival of his unborn child. Nor must anyone learn that Yeshua was crucified to protect the woman who had, since the beginning of time, nurtured the inner soul of the human race.

Yehudas Isca'riot knew that never again would he set his eyes upon the old water seller, nor the scourge of a woman whom he would, one day, know as the blessed Magdalena. When he awoke at dawn on the morning after the Sabbath, the feast of Passover was done. The sun shone bright, it shone in the exact same way the world had known for more than four billion Earth years. Isca'riot realised that his nighttime dream of the sanctified preacher ascending to be with the woman who changed everything, was a normal day just like every other day. Time would never change, neither would his transcendental dream - the dream that was never the perfect dream.

A long time from now, Isca'riot would find it within himself to once more return to the Gihon Spring, the hidden fountain of the venerated virgin. Beside the slow-moving water, he would discover the rotting remains of the woman he feared, he would scoop up her bones to begin his long journey to the white frozen north - to bury her ashes deep beneath the hard granite monolith stone inscribed with strange hieroglyphics that no man save one would ever fathom.

Isca'riot would write down his own words, he would transcribe every-thing that had happened. He wished it made known that he was never a treacherous traitor, that he should not be condemned in the minds of men who did not know the truth. In his unread writings, the Gospels according to Yehudas Isca'riot, the world would learn how he tried to save the soul of the renegade preacher, the prophet from Naz'areth whom he revered with every shred of loyalty a man could possess...

6

O paque, bright yellow wing tips merged with deep crimson red, attracting the admiring attention of no one. There was no sentient lifeform anywhere close by, the vast silent forest wilderness was complete. The effervescent, joyful butterfly settled on the sun-lushed side of the flower bush, a small distance beneath the deep blue petals that by nature's design lured the butterfly to be there. The butterfly did not move, not for some considerable time, content to stay twitching its thin gossamer wings as the sun cast its warmth around the small woodland glade.

After what seemed like a thousand years, the butterfly flickered its delicate antennae spikes as if to launch itself into chaotic flights of fantasy, but for some dark, selfish reason the butterfly's instinct was to remain, to soak up the radiant heat that teased the flamboyant lepidopteran into an insensible sense of security. The sun inched its way across the untarnished, blameless sky; with beams of intense summer heat that fed countless wilting trees before an irregular white cloud drifted from the east to temper the haze by casting intermittent shadows across the grass-covered forest floor. This was one more summer in uncountable millions of silent summers in this untarnished garden world of Hyvah's Erewhon.

The butterfly was content to stay, to savour the beauty of its short life, safe in the knowledge that it would perhaps survive the whole day. Twice in fractional moments of time the same song thrush that had before eyed the resplendent coloured butterfly flew close before suspecting that an attempted meal might end in foolish failure, the bright colours of the butterfly a stark warning of gluttony danger. The thrush flew by, into the top of the sycamore trees before flying onwards towards the deepest part of the forest; the silence of the greenwood was now both deafening and serene.

The day, like every other day, had begun with the noisy melodious dawn chorus with the sun's heat building into its daily cascade. By a small measure of circumstance, the butterfly perched alone in the glade seemed to sense its solitude; no longer accompanied by the sweet songs of songbirds that by this time flew soundless through the gentle swaying treetops. For some self-serving reason, the butterfly did not leave the flowering bush, it stayed for an appreciable, almost insane amount of time. By mid-afternoon the summer sun reached the zenith peak of intenseness, all insect life within the vast northern forest soaked the vital rays of warmth into their delicate fragile forms – such was the importance of life-sustaining sunbeams that danced their way through open gaps in the green foliage canopy.

Then, without warning, an unexpected change; subtle enough that it was impossible to detect. A gentle breeze drifted from the open south with enough strength to disturb the rustling trees; swishing leaves whispered the breezy song of creaking branches. The gust passed, undetected in its significance by the meaningless life within the forest... except for the rainbow-stained butterfly. Sensing the immediate catastrophic meaning of stupendous change, it flickered its wings in alarm, suspecting the uncertainty of its own life, feeling that momentous events would soon unfold in the sleazy world of predatory men. The butterfly decided now would be the right time to leave – by launching itself into random chaotic flight, appearing first to fall towards the grass-covered floor but was caught by the strengthening breeze to soar high into the tops of the surrounding sycamores. Unable to determine its journey, the butterfly accepted the path of life chosen by the wind, carried along through the woodland not against its will; or even by nature's logic that meant it might yet survive. Nothing could detect the weak submission of the butterfly – the erratic manner of its flight gave the appearance of a free independent spirit though its terrible northerly direction was always the same. The first swirling winds of the approaching storm laughed their way through the forest trees, heralding the tumultuous events that would soon unfold.

Tens of thousands of leagues to the south, far away from the northern woodland glade, the two decrepit cities of Sodom and Gomor'rah burned. The almighty Gabriel, he had decided how the devious disloyalty of these men would end, the angel paid no heed to the screams of slaughtered women nor their wide-eyed children; Gabriel looked away when men slashed with their swords then revelled in the joyous butchery of those who were weak, untrained or too frightened to fight. Gabriel smiled with appeased delight when the city walls tumbled, when rampant fires ravaged the tortured squares with their glorious orange trees, when the gaily coloured balconies fell – when desperate preachers on their bloody knees begged Gabriel to take his leave.

Then the Lord's avenging angel, he crowed. "Woe to you, you who conceal the traitorous unrighteous in your midst. Remember what I did to Sodom and Gomor'rah, whose lands now lie in the ruins of fire and heaps of ashes. So will I do to those who have not listened to me, see how these men defile and rape their fellow men? I will burn these cities in tar, I will seize these women for the tribes of Israel, I will enslave these children from you." Both cities burned with fire, they were razed until no stone would ever be found by more gentle men.

On the highest hilltop to the west of Gomor'rah, in the flickering glow of burning fires, a pair of womanly eyes perceived in pain the death of every innocent man, woman and child who had no cause to face God's powerful vassal. Her hair fell before her eyes; when she tossed the strands away with the angry flick of her femininely right hand...

Andronikos Karahalios

Cleomenes showed his extreme displeasure. Within three days of the celebration of the Feast of Gestedes, he summoned together each of his governors, fearsome generals of the formidable Spartan army. King Cleomenes would have no choice but to bend to the utmost will of the gods, to march on the infamous citadel of Athens. Hades, god of the underworld and the dead, smiled in self-satisfied anticipation - his chthonic wife Persephone would be torn between her love for the worldly Cleomenes or her other mortal lover Patriach, citizen-general of the mighty Athenians. The scheming Hades had succeeded, this time he did not counsel with any of his compatriot all-powerful gods of Olympus, there was no need, his cunning plan had worked beyond his wildest dreams. Hades reached over to pat the head of his three-headed monster Cerberus, who whimpered with sublime pleasure from his master's unadulterated attention.

Hades knew that Persephone, esoteric daughter of the goddess Demeter, would react with defiant outrage - but what could she do? The one way Persephone could prevent the attack by the masterful army of Sparta upon the once ascending but now decadent city of Athens was to intervene, to plead with Cleomenes to temper his terrible anger, to show him how the deliberate incarceration of the youngest of his daughters was a cunning trap set by the gods. But to confront Cleomenes, Persephone would have to take her indigenous mortal form, she would need to reveal her inner being, the true origins of her hidden self. *This* is what Hades desired - because the devious blood-drinking god of the dark world had long suspected that his consort wife was not who she avowed to be.

Under the watchful eyes of the authoritarian gods of Mount Olympus, the intriguing drama enveloping the world of earth-born men unfolded to the gods' utter fascination. On the dry dusty plain that led to the imposing city gates, Cleomenes halted his fast-moving Hippias cavalry. The distant Athenian walls were now in view; the hot summer haze made the ancient city dance and leap in the shimmering heat of the afternoon breeze. Behind his horse-mounted cavalry, the king's exhausted foot soldiers paused, relieved to at last rest their tired bodies wearied by their heavy loads of sweat-laden armour. They laid down their pointed spears and battlefield shields for which the undefeated Spartans were famed, now they could drain the last of much-needed refreshing water to satisfy their life-threatening thirst. Though trained to the highest fighting perfection known throughout the heralded world of the terrible gods, the stamina of these warrior men had been tested to the limit by their long relentless march - never before had they been force trekked in this fashion, driven by the driving generals of the revengeful Cleomenes determined to confront the treacherous Athenians. The lagging entourage of camp followers, the supply wagons and womenfolk who were all less able to keep the pace were by now strung out many leagues behind. In a little under seven days and six nights, the magnificent Spartan army had arrived before the city-state of their long-standing rivals. Mighty, dominant Athens.

Cleomenes eyed the distant walls with a strange sense of unease, a feeling inside that warned him this might be a conflict more difficult than he first thought. Seeing the closed gates and imposing battlements, the taking of the city and the release of his hostage daughter was not going to be easy. King Cleomenes was sometimes a fool, maybe, he conceded inside his middle-aged, sometimes paranoid mind, he might have allowed his uncontrolled anger to get the better of him. He spied the daunting task that lay before him, the Spartan king began to question his over-impulsive judgment. Perhaps diplomacy might have in the end prevailed, but the love of his now captive daughter drove everything. During these last moments of their frenzied march from Sparta and the debilitating punishment he had forced his army to endure, hidden doubts played inside his mind. As he and his men drew closer to the powerful city of the dominant Hellenic states, the much-vaunted king of the Spartans needed to recover his composure. He turned to his second-in-command, the redoubtable Andronikos who sat mounted upon his black stallion deep in his instinctive thoughts.

Andronikos, the experienced ageing cavalry general, tried hard to hide his exhaustion from the long ride from Sparta. Each night when they stopped the army to rest, he made excuses to retire to his tent to recuperate as best he could, careful not to reveal to anyone the aching hurt he felt inside his weary, creaking bones. He refused to participate in the usual late-night entertainment, the drinking of wine, the wily women offering temptation, the dancing whores and the showcase fighting of young warriors not yet blooded. It was important to Andronikos to drive his men hard, he was proud of his ability to be one step ahead so that he could lead by extreme example, to display his infamous toughness so that he could command the army in the one way he knew - but now, his sixty-two years was beginning to hurt. On top of his tired weariness, his intuition was also laced with unease. It was not the thought of battle with the Athenians that nagged Andronikos, the Spartans would defeat the city of Athens, he had no doubts about this - it was the strange sequence of these events that troubled the old general. And he was certain his old friend, the battle-scarred Cleomenes sensed the same unsureness, Andronikos saw this much within his king's much-lauded deep brown eyes - this whole escapade was clouded in deep uncertainty.

"Tell me your true thoughts my faithful Andronikos," Cleomenes surveyed the towering city walls that stood like a straddling bulwark across the dust-hazed plain - he spoke with disguised unease. Cleomenes knew it would be pointless to ask nothing but a direct question to his trusted general, who had won every bloody confrontation the Spartans fought during the last ten score years. In his mad rush decision to march on Athens, Cleomenes had not until now sought the inner convictions of his most valuable ally.

Andronikos deliberated his answer, the proud general had long pondered when he would be asked.

"My king, you should know my feelings. This is a fool's errand though we can finish this quick," Andronikos paused, eyeing the same imposing granite walls. Before their eyes was the formidable barrier that needed to be stormed before they could claim victory. "These Athenian walls are tall, they are built strong though it is no secret their city is garrisoned by men who swim and dance in their own wine," the general tried to sound upbeat, forcing as much optimism as he could. "Athens makes war with clever treaties and devious trade, it is a long time since their armies fought with true blood and valour." The grey-haired Andronikos had little respect for any show of weakness, he thought for a moment to ponder the empty scene before him. "Their gates are locked closed; these sons of bitches are forewarned of our coming. I fear our task to break down these gates will be hard, perhaps beyond our will if we give them time to prepare the defence of their stinking city." Andronikos wanted to get this nauseous deed done, he did not relish the thought of a long siege for which the Spartans were not prepared. The Spartans were feared by their enemies in the fields of open battle for good reason, even when defending in the mountainous ravines of their homeland, but the act of laying siege in the open plains to the largest city of their rivals was an unfamiliar tactic, a form of warfare Sparta had not attempted for countless years.

Cleomenes looked long and hard at Andronikos, he pondered his friend's heartfelt reply. He noted the plains surrounding the city, they were desolate, empty of any significant activity except for the hurried flight of the few remaining farmers. Hardly a soul, it seemed, had any business outside the walls, there was not the usual hustle and bustle of hundreds coming and going through open gates or the normal signs of the day-to-day activity of a thriving city, nor the panicky flight of Athenians fleeing to safety behind the citadel walls – a situation the Spartans expected to encounter and had hoped to take advantage of. Everything was quiet and still, just the shimmering heat endorsed by the buzz of ten million irritating flies - blood-biting pests attracted by the festering dung of a thousand horses alongside the sweating, unwashed bodies of the Spartan army fatigued by its long march. The king of the Spartans sat upon his white stallion, weighing up his options without much more said. For a few moments he sat thinking, he recalled in his mind everything that had happened, how this imposing disaster had unfolded.

Only one half-moon before the strange-looking eunuch, an emissary from the southern kingdom of Thessaloniki, had announced himself as the personal messenger of the scheming king Aleminis. The quiet-spoken ambassador, with the strange grating high-pitched voice that he was infamous for, appeared with two henchmen by his side while Cleomenes and his entourage were hunting wild boar in the high mountain forests above the city of Sparta. The Thessalonian ambassador brought to Cleomenes alarming news, disastrous news. Cleomenes's youngest daughter Elenoras, the emissary informed them, was now held captive by a band of Athenian skirmishers. The princess had been taken while her entourage was en route from Thessaloniki back to Sparta, returning from their goodwill visit at the invitation of King Aleminis. The emissary told how the column of heavily laden caravans had been attacked, with the surviving women and children shackled as slaves. Both of Elenoras's cousins, Cleomenes's nephews Felipas and Cregoreas, had been killed in the encounter. When told of this by the eunuch ambassador, Cleomenes was stunned, he felt violated, then unconditionally outraged.

In the long-distant past, there was history of violent encounters between Sparta and Athens, more so when the dominant Athenians began building their large fleet of ships which, when completed, threatened the shores of Sparta from a new direction. In those far-off days, neither side claimed final victory, there had been relative peace between the two states during the years since, a compromise peace that had brought growing prosperity to both Sparta and Athens. Sparta used their mushrooming wealth to enlarge its already formidable army, to train its men to new heights of preparedness - the borders of Sparta were all the time threatened by a multitude of enemies. The Athenians, on the other hand, revelled in their fattening wealth, preferring the luxuries of easy living fuelled by flowing wine. It was said the gods of Olympus themselves were to be found in the luxurious Athenian palaces, savouring sacrificial offerings, pleasures of the flesh and good portions of fine fattening food.

When first hearing the mind-numbing news about this Athenian outrage, Cleomenes without hesitation ordered the rapid assembly of the more feared of his troops - his revered Hippias cavalry with their legions of fearsome mounts. Within eight days of the kidnap of Elenoras, the king began his frenzied march in the direction of distant Athens. Meanwhile, Andronikos himself oversaw the gathering of the remaining Spartan army, the well-trained foot soldiers whose formidable reputation preceded them far and wide. But Andronikos, the sharp-witted general who had served two Spartan kings in his time as supreme commander of the army, was troubled.

Andronikos sensed from the beginning that something was not right. The Athenians, the most dominant of the city-states, would not act like this without good reason. Why risk a war with Sparta when both states were in their prosperous ascendancy when they were no threat to each other? The vicious Persian wars of the past, of thirty years previous, when Athens secured their status of dominance and cemented their freedom over the invading Persians were not forgotten, those wars were these days talked of in solemn song and verse. Sparta and the other Hellenic states had at that troubled time allied with Athens to rid themselves of Persian domination - but since then Sparta had asserted their growing independence through the sheer bravery of their fearsome army. This many times led to bloody confrontations between Sparta and other kingdom states – and the Spartans in each and every encounter were victorious. The Athenians themselves were never in doubt, they were well aware that final victory over the invading Persians was in the main achieved by the infamous warriors of Sparta, citizen soldiers trained and drilled from a young age to fight victorious wars. It was common knowledge that young boys born in Sparta who were deemed too sick or never fit to become proficient swordsmen or archers were put to death by sacrifice to Ares, the towering god of war - and Ares was known to have rewarded the Spartans well. Until now, there was a beneficial peace between the Athenians and Sparta, a grudging respect for each other's power. Why attack the travelling baggage train of the Spartan king's daughter, why put to death all of the men then take the Spartan women and their children captive? To Andronikos it did not make sense.

"It is now late in the afternoon," said Cleomenes. "We will make our camp beside the Kifissos River so that we have fresh water to cool the horses. Our womenfolk will have an easier time to cook and feed their men. We must recover our strength before we tear down these walls." Cleomenes spoke with decisive authority, he needed to reaffirm his leadership over the men who perhaps sensed his outward uncertainty, his unease that an impossible task might lay ahead.

"Perhaps it is best that we call one more council of war my Lord," Andronikos suggested, knowing the answer.

"Yes, Andronikos. Summon each of the generals, have my compound set beside my night camp. By sunrise, with the will of Ares, we will have a good plan. In two days, after all our men have rested, we will begin our attack against the city. I wish to be long gone from this place; I wish this fight to be settled with speed."

The angry fire was back in the eyes of Cleomenes. The thought of battle stimulated the king, he was himself a renowned swordsman bearing the bitter scars of many encounters. In all his forty-two years he had trained in the same way as every other man in Sparta - to fight for the army, to defend Sparta. When his father died in the penultimate battle against the Corsicans, Cleomenes was ready to become king. He took the throne and Sparta thrived, growing stronger, ever more prosperous. Cleomenes was well respected by the over-demanding Spartans, he commanded his army with revered authority. To say he was loved would be an overstatement, because Cleomenes could be cruel like every other statesman king but he endeavoured to rule fair, the fierceness of his command was how all the kings of Sparta ruled - but it was the Spartan king's unadulterated love for the aberrant goddess Persephone that troubled many of his clear-thinking generals – as always with powerful kings and exuberant royal princes, good reason and common sense sometimes disappeared like sunburned mist.

"My Lord Cleomenes, let us not dally long with these Athenians. They are weak, they cannot be prepared. The longer we give them the more they will be ready. I believe that we should begin our attack now, *this night,*" implored Andronikos.

Cleomenes was taken aback, surprised, a radical attack had never entered his mind. For a few moments, he considered what Andronikos said but attacking now was out of the question. The most experienced of the king's generals was victorious in all of his bloody battles by using unconventional means, by ignoring sound reasoning, by disregarding the advice of the more cautious army leaders. His impulsive instincts, the much-vaunted leadership and the skills of Andronikos were valued by the whole Spartan army – so the redoubtable advice of Andronikos to attack before the next sunrise bore heavy upon the mind of Cleomenes – adding to the king's general unease. The king tempered his thoughts, he forced himself to think with logic; there was no way his men were yet ready, nor would they be during this day or the next, the foot soldiers were exhausted from their long forced march.

Andronikos, though, thought with an alternative mind, Cleomenes knew this – without doubt Andronikos would not hesitate to attack, giving no thought to the tiredness of the army – this was how his venerable general operated, how the Spartan army was conditioned to fight to their death for victory no matter what circumstances they faced. But Cleomenes could see the tired weariness in the eyes of Andronikos, eyes that compounded his creeping sense of something not right. Andronikos wore the stooping gait in the saddle, that distinct air that he too suspected events were being controlled by the gods in a way the Spartans did not yet understand. Cleomenes continued to stare at his second-in-command, perhaps the ageing general was not the formidable fighter of past years, but it was his trusted ally's vast experience of war that Cleomenes needed right now. The evening sun began to set, the vast redness of the sky forewarning of tumultuous bloodletting violence, the tinge of crimson streaks that meandered towards the flat horizon before disappearing into the dark depths of nighttime seemed to have been painted by the feasting gods. Ahead lay the long night that would feed the devious work of Hades, the god of death who sensed that soon he would possess the souls of many more dead men.

"I value your instincts, my dear friend. No doubt you are right. But even you are beyond the power to climb those towering walls before the sun falls," Cleomenes warned. The king looked away, he worried that Andronikos would see his agitated expression. "A war council of my generals after we are well fed, wined and fornicated, this is the best way to plan this madcap escapade."

"My Lord," Andronikos interrupted, exasperated. "The Athenians see our army has arrived. They know we are tired and will rest beside the river for two or three nights. They expect we must prepare and make plans. These Athenians know the logical way, that our army is strong, but they believe their walls are stronger. They know how to defend their city, never before has it been taken or defeated. Why not attack now, in the darkness, during the night, when the Athenians are resting in their beds thinking they are safe and how we are tired? We will take them by surprise, we will have their city in our hands by sunrise."

Cleomenes sat upon his horse, he once more stared hard at Andronikos, there was logic and reasoning in the old general's advice. It occurred to Cleomenes how Andronikos had never lost a battle. There came the nagging doubt in the back of the king's mind, the unworldly feeling that perhaps his revengeful dreadnought army was not the righteous righters of the wrong he believed.

"Tell me what bothers you my good friend Andronikos, there is trouble in your eyes. Do you think we might walk into a lion's cage?"

Andronikos sat silent upon his stout black stallion, whose own armour inched down its brow in ominous dexterity. The old general did not reply.

Patriach looked out over the plains from the highest tower of the formidable fortress that was Athens. The sun rose over the distant plains, the coming day would be arid and dry, the hot air turning the throats of desperate thirsty men into curdling rasping cut-throats. The general surveyed the scene in despair, the Spartans had arrived outside the city from Sparta in a little under one-quarter of the moon's phase, their campfires being well established during the preceding cool night. The Athenian general had known the Spartans would arrive, he had known this since the previous afternoon then watched their army emerge from the direction of the Taygetos Pass like a swarm of ravaging locusts seeking to lay waste to the thriving farms and lush vineyards lying outside the city walls.

Patriach had learned the previous sunrise from outlying bands of scouts that sightings of the approaching Spartan army were being reported, that Cleomenes was fast nearing the borders of the Athenian domain. Awaiting the Spartan army, Patriach ordered the city's main gates closed, he commanded all the lesser gateways to be guarded but open to allow farmers frightened with panic to retreat inside the walls fleeing for their lives. All through the previous day, in the back of his mind, Patriach had feared a swift move during the night by the Spartans to take the city by surprise, a disastrous attack that his men would not be ready to defend; he was ungrudging, relieved to see Spartan campfires burning through the night - a feeling that gave him a welcomed respite from his unease. Patriach needed more time, it would take this day and the next before the best of his enfeebled out of shape army would be ready - by then he could make the city walls impregnable in their extreme.

As a precaution Patriach issued orders for everyone entering the city to be searched, their wagons checked when they came in from the riverbanks and fields - the general was well aware of the cunning reputation of his adversary Andronikos. Patriach long remembered fighting the invading Persians alongside the lionhearted hero from Sparta, back then their mutual respect bound them in uncommon bondship, a friendship that neither of them wished to break. Patriach thought he might get at least six days of preparation before Cleomenes took the dreadful bait forced upon him by the abduction of his daughter Elenoras, a move against the Spartans that Patriach never assented to. Athenian skirmishers were often a law unto themselves, they were not under Patriach's direct command, they followed the orders of the Akropolis priesthood and even this could be fickle. The Athenian general, who was by default governor of Athens until the infant King Thebes was of ruling age, did not desire war with the Spartans though he was grudging in his acceptance that another way did not exist. The complicated issue of Persephone must be settled, the hold of Hades over both himself and the citizens of Athens could not be tolerated much longer – many brave men would die to appease the more vile of the mountain gods.

Looking down from the tower Patriach's mood was sombre, his confidence now tested to the limit. How had the Spartans managed this incredible feat? How had they raised such a formidable army, a coming together of formations so well prepared and armed that it was able to march to their gates in such a short time? But, he thought to himself, all was not lost, the Athenians themselves would have enough time to prepare, they would have two or three days of daylight before the Spartans were ready to attack. In his mind the general took stock of his own depleted forces.

He possessed just four detachments of his more reliable troops. The rest, more than nine large formations, were unfit, not well trained and no match for the Spartans - but the general had the awesome defences of the city at his disposal. Patriach might have no more than four of his best contingents available – but he knew he would need just two to defend the city. The remaining two could be kept back for the unconventional plan he had in mind, a fallback situation that he would no doubt need as the vicious fight wore on. Patriach knew full well he could hold the Spartans back beyond the walls for long enough, there were abundant food stocks in the city, the water wells were full - and the citizens of Athens were fat from their times of gluttony, wine and debauchery. Would Cleomenes have the stomach for such a long siege? Patriach, convincing himself in his mind, doubted that he had.

Like Cleomenes, Patriach was no fool. Patriach understood how both he and the Spartan king were woven into a spider's web of intrigue, how they were caught in a game of scheming conspiracy. This was to be a vicious confrontation anticipated by the bloodthirsty gods of Olympus. Human blood would be shed to appease the god of the underworld Hades, who was determined to pit both Athens and Sparta against each other in spiteful revenge against his wife Persephone.

The slim advantage that worldly Patriach held over Cleomenes was that he knew of the devious foulness that Hades had unleashed, Patriach also understood the mind-twisting reasons why - the tall, silver-haired general had long realised they were small pawns in the dangerous tragedy that crept upon the unsuspecting race of mortal men. In time past, Patriach himself had succumbed to Persephone's mesmerising draw, he knew his terrible part was written, that he had no choice but to perhaps die in the final confrontation unfolding within the strange, inhabited world of surreptitious gods. This was the deadliest of games, the battle to save Athens from its fate was of small consequence in the conflict that would decide events far greater than two armies of fighting men.

Persephone was not who she claimed to be, Patriach had long suspected this. The ghostly goddess of Olympus whom he worshipped and adored, the unearthly woman who tormented his besieged mind in ways unimaginable to the ranks of lesser men - she would be the one who in the end paid the highest price for this game between Athens and Sparta, between himself and Cleomenes. This was Patriach's nemesis, burned inside his mind since he was a young boy lost in the mountainous wilderness, from the time when the beautiful goddess of sunlight discovered him being stalked by lions, long after the night his young half-brother was slaughtered by the ghastly three-headed beast that Hades kept leashed in chains of strongest bronze.

Persephone that night saved his life, Patriach knew this. Then she nurtured the young orphan throughout his young adulthood, she gifted him skills he would not have learned of his own accord, Persephone guided him, moulded him until he rose to command the greatest city state the civilised world of men had witnessed. The ways of Persephone were complex, harsh - alongside her loving protection for himself, for her own reasons she also cherished his now bitter rival, a powerful king - Cleomenes of the Spartans. Patriach stood tall on the tower searching the ranks of the distant Spartans to see if he could spy on his unwilling adversary. Patriach became morose, he peered over the rapidly heating plain spreading southwards from the walls of Athens. He suppressed his anger, his resentment of Hades, the hatred he felt that was stoked and cultivated by the goddess he adored. To complicate everything there was Elenoras, the daughter of King Cleomenes who, Patriach knew, was born of Persephone herself. The sunken well of intrigue and revenge was deep and dangerous.

Andronikos was the first to see the approaching horseman. Without hesitating he sent his aide-de-camp to wake King Cleomenes. In the meantime, the sun inched above the flat horizon, the yellow hot disk of fire driving away the first-morning haze in clouds of shimmering dust. Soon the distant shadowy mountains not quite lost in the dancing mist would be hidden, they would fade into the haziness of the day to become blue-grey smudges of blur that would play no part in the ravages of the looming blood-strewn conflict. The high rounded hills would simply merge into the nothingness of the dry hot day of intense heat. The dark clouds of meaty flies were back in uncontrollable swarms, drawn by the foul excrement of five thousand Spartan warriors who began to dig their festering latrine pits in the hardness of the stony ground on either side of the slow meandering river. The silverish water stayed clean and refreshing, its distant source an unspoiled interlude of serenity snaking its way through the Spartan encampment. Andronikos, rising at his usual time of daybreak, had decided to stand himself upwind of the stinking horse-dung odour of the camp, this was why the horseman galloped into his keen-eyed vision, moving at a fast pace from the direction of distant Athens - the rider creating their own rising dust cloud of ominous distraction.

Andronikos, surprised by how quickly he was joined by the still half-sleepy Cleomenes, who at once became wide awake when he too spied the approaching horseman, felt a feeling of apprehension. The king was still dressing in his regal robes as he tried to decipher this dawn intrusion. The king's aides were keen to attire their lord in his full regency décor, but Cleomenes dismissed each of them in irritable temper.

"Who is this Andronikos, do you know?" demanded Cleomenes puzzled, staring out towards the distant rider who now closed fast.

"I do not know my Lord. This horseman rides at some speed from the side gate of Athens," Andronikos turned towards his aide-de-camp; a worried frown etched upon his face. "Bring me my horse," he barked to his aide who was quick to disappear following his commander's instruction. "And be sure to bring my sharpest sword," added Andronikos as his aide departed.

King Cleomenes had by now summoned his horse, his entourage of six mounted personal guards joined him, armed and clad in their armoured helmets that displayed the typical arched top-sway of gaily coloured feathers stiffened with sticky pine pitch. It was important to make an impression upon the approaching visitor.

"Let us ride out to meet this horseman," suggested Cleomenes in a muted tone. "What daybreak trickery is this, we must be on our guard."

The small band of Spartans, with Andronikos at its head, proceeded at a half trot towards the approaching rider, who turned towards them when it spied the gathered entourage of nobility. Behind, back in the Spartan encampment, the king's Hippias cavalry were coming to order, gathering together their arms to meet the potential threat of unforeseen conflict, perhaps unexpected trouble that might arise from a simple trap - or maybe a bold assassination attempt upon their now vulnerable king. Andronikos and Cleomenes rode a short way out onto the flat open plain then stopped, they saw the rider swerve to approach them still galloping at high speed. When the horseman came up close, Andronikos's draw dropped like a stone-dead weight.

The rider pulled up their horse a short distance before them, close enough to make the king's guards draw their swords in hostile precaution.

The rider rode a magnificent stallion of grey powder, the horse bore no armour or battle shield, giving the distinct impression of swift speed and brute power. The stallion snorted its defiance as the rider brought the horse to an abrupt halt, ignoring the mounted guards who closed together in threatening formation.

Andronikos was the first to see the rider was a woman.

"Greetings," ventured the rider with no signs of unease. She eyed the Spartan guards with mean-looking disdain, seeing how they closed ranks in sinister threat. "Tell your guards to sheath their swords, or they will be dead before their stinking bodies hit the ground," warned the rider, her low-cut voice laced with outright menace. "The god of the underworld forever desires more souls to dwell beside his fire pits." There followed a long pause of stunned silence.

Cleomenes was the first to reply, he spoke with caution, with distinct unease. "And what if you decide to take my life?" he ventured. "Are my men not allowed to protect their king?" Cleomenes stared at the rider, he saw that she carried no outward visible weapon. He took note of how she worked hard to keep control of her horse whose power was impressive - but she had the mastery of the stallion in a way that ingratiated a display of unexplainable subtleness, that she was not to be trifled with.

"Do not fear Cleomenes, you are safe enough. I am not here to draw your blood," mocked the rider with a smile of contempt.

When he saw that she was unarmed Andronikos signalled to the guards with a nod of his head, they sheathed their swords with a deferent show of defiance, displaying how they might draw them once more at the slightest hint of aggression.

"Who are you and why are you here?" snapped Cleomenes, he was anxious to control his anger that threatened to erupt over the way she spoke without any show of respect or reverence. His long greying hair blew wild in the rising morning breeze - like a lion's whipping mane.

"Who I am is of no concern," the rider replied, studying Cleomenes as if she were unsure if he was even the Spartan king. "I am here to warn you." She paused, noting the hostility in the eyes of each of the men who faced her, eyes that drilled into her like spikes of hot iron. "If you begin your attack against these walls then each one of you mounted in your Spartan saddles will die," she waited, to let her hard-hitting words sink for maximum effect. The sun by now was a little higher in the sky as the last embers of dawn transgressed into the bounty of another scorching day. "And your captive daughter Elenoras, she will be put to death at the command of the senate if you attempt to breach these gates. She will die on their sacred altar, in appeasement to the inglorious gods whom you men worship in mindless reverence."

Stunned silence descended, the morning breeze grew then blustered harder, whipping dirt and tiny grains of soil into a small whirlwind that danced in outward warning. The sun beat down in its relentless dogma, the day's heat began to build.

The long pause of disbelieving stillness was broken by Cleomenes,

"Look behind me. Five thousand of my best Spartan warriors are gathered. My Hippias cavalry are armed to their teeth, their valour knows no bounds. We Spartans have not lost one battle in fifteen hot summers or cold winters, my army of men will each give their lives to my cause, they are willing to die for Sparta. Why should we heed these strange warning words you speak? Do you expect that we will turn around and go home?" Cleomenes glared in angry defiance, sweat beads formed along his deep-wrinkled brow. His horse, sensing his master's distaste, huffed and reared until controlled by Cleomenes pulling hard on its leather reins.

Andronikos, mounted by the side of Cleomenes, was unmoved and silent. He knew who the rider was, he had recognised her the moment she pulled up.

"It makes no difference. If there were *ten* thousand of you, it would mean more Spartan deaths," the rider answered.

"Why do you say this? What makes you think we will be defeated?" demanded Cleomenes.

"You Spartans have been lured like vermin bait," the woman glared. "You do not realise that you have been fooled." The breeze caught her raven-dark hair, casting it across her eyes in a way that she whipped it aside with a casual toss of her hand, making Cleomenes catch his breath without much thought. "Your daughter Elenoras was taken by Athenian skirmishers because they had no choice," she continued. "Athens will be destroyed by fire and lava, their destruction will be wrought by the revengeful Hades if the Athenians do not bend to his will," the rider looked away to scan the Spartan encampment. By this time the Hippias cavalry were mounted and waiting, she surveyed them in the distance with squinting eyes before turning her attention back to the king. "The gods demanded that Elenoras be held captive to entice you here, then sacrificed to the appeasement of Hades and his bloodthirsty gang as atonement for your sins against the gods. The Athenians buy the favour of the god of war Ares, Ares will fight against you. They will pay Ares for their victory by giving him your daughter Elenoras to do as he will before her sacrifice is done. You cannot defeat these powerful walls, not when they are defended by the gods themselves. You will die Cleomenes, in the way that Hades intends."

Cleomenes sat bolt upright in his saddle, shocked. He had for a long time suspected that something was not right. He looked to his left, seeking the support of the redoubtable Andronikos. Even the guards saddled behind looked at each other with distinct unease.

"I know who you are," interrupted Andronikos, speaking for the first time, he sought to parry her stupefying strike from out of the blue. He stared hard at the rider; Andronikos could not hide his agitated unease.

"Ah, yes, the redoubtable Andronikos Karahalios," the rider turned to stare at him, like a hunting insect eyeing its prey, "I see you still have that look of your mother in your eyes."

The perplexed expression etched upon the face of Andronikos changed to one of incomprehensible shock, shock that flowed through his body in a spasm of rigidity. His breathless alarm came under hegemony only when he calmed himself down, even then he felt sweats of perspiration erupt without warning from beneath the pores of his skin. His mother had died in childbirth. She had breathed her last breath when Andronikos was born into the world under the mulberry trees in the mountains north of Sparta.

Andronikos had never known his mother – this horsewoman had cut him to his knees in one single instant, she had sliced his mind in two with a piercing thrust that made Andronikos aware that it was a deliberate act of incapacitation.

Andronikos fought to regain an element of rationality. On the outside, he tried to remain calm but when he saw that she continued to scrutinise his anguish through the full blaze of her preying eye he wiped a bead of sweat from his brow. It was not just her sword jab remark about his mother - he remembered this horsewoman well - how could he ever forget? It was a time since he had last seen her, but she did not seem to have aged one year. With her flowing dark hair and deep sunburned skin she was no slothful city dweller, this much Andronikos was certain - but from where had she come? Meanwhile, his mind continued to race though he began to recover his composure, Andronikos took her blow like the fighting warrior he was, he rallied himself in the timeless manner that made him the supreme combative fighter of men - he must not let her master him – this woman, she could not have known his mother.

Cleomenes, sitting motionless and rigid, had no words he could think of to say. The rider had ridden towards them from the direction of the side gate of Athens, even though no one had spied the gate being opened. The king was the first to break the long pause that threatened to hurl the Spartans back to their camp in confused retreat.

"So, you ride up, tell us to break camp and turn around to head back to Sparta in defeat," said Cleomenes after a few moments of silence. "You tell us that Elenoras was kidnapped by Athenian skirmishers because their senate was given no choice, they were made to do this by the god of the underworld or Athens will be destroyed by Hades. You say Elenoras is bait to lure the Spartan army here to destroy Athens, the Athenians will then sacrifice Elenoras to gain the goodwill of the gods to defend Athens and defeat this undefeated Spartan army who camp behind me. Am I right in what you say?"

"Yes," the rider answered without a hint of compassion. "Except it is not the Athenians or the Spartans who are condemned to die. It is yourself,

Cleomenes, and Patriach, you are both expected to pay the debt to Hades with your blood for cohorting with his wife Persephone."

"I do not understand what you say. Why Elenoras? Why did these Athenian wine swillers take only Elenoras? How do you know all this? Why is it that you are here?"

The rider studied the king in deference, her sharp-witted eyes pierced into him like burning fire-tipped skewers.

"I am here before you by the will of Persephone, whom you know well King Cleomenes," the rider exclaimed. "If Persephone takes her human form to warn you then she will be slain by Hades. You alone know why Elenoras is more precious than any of your Spartan subjects realise," she added with an element of distaste. "When you slept by the side of her birth mother to ferment the birth of your daughter, you were deceived. Your mistress Persephone did what she needed to do, to unpick the deed done to her a long time ago even though it meant your undoing. In siring your sibling daughter, you sowed the wrath of Hades and his unworldly scum."

Cleomenes again sat unmoving and grey-faced, dejection crept through his veins like a plague of vermin scurrying from some unknown dark place, driven by a firestorm of rampant flames. Cleomenes looked hard at the rider, she seemed all-conquering but showed no sense of victory or even mercy, she held him in her hands; hard-skinned hands that Cleomenes saw gripped her horses' reins like a vice, hands that Cleomenes knew were never the hands of reverent compassion.

Andronikos stared in confounded torment, then his facial expression once more set hard, the stone of realisation dropped in dry-mouthed revelation, his mind reeled in thunderstruck mayhem, heaven and earth merged into a blur of inconsequential quagmire when it dawned upon him how easy the Spartan army had been lured.

The mightiest of all the gods Zeus, who from time to time took the form of a winged angel, was agitated and concerned. Why had Persephone, the so-called queen of the underworld, set about cultivating both Patriach and this king called Cleomenes in such a sagacious way? In some ways the half-goddess was exacting her revenge against Hades, she had done this in a precocious and calculating manner which meant the master of the gods must now keep a watchful eye upon how this unforeseen conflict between the two powerful city-states was unfolding. Zeus knew the reasons for Persephone's vengeance, but not why she had singled out the Spartan king and the Athenian general. Hades had acted in his deceitful way by not revealing his secretive plan for the abduction of the Spartan king's daughter, nor had he made known his reasons why he desired the Spartans to turn against their allied Athenians - now Athens and Sparta were about to face each other in a bloody siege because Hades saw to it that they would. Zeus was aware that great numbers of brave men would perish.

Hades had turned the tables against his wife Persephone in a manner that made Zeus think the god of the underworld must harbour complex deep-rooted motives for his reprisals. Zeus also held no doubts about why offering the life of the young princess Elenoras would please Ares, the god of war - Ares would revel in this glorified worship, because of this cardinal sacrifice Ares would without hesitation see to it that Athens did not fall to the Spartans. Moreover, Zeus knew well that Hades had played his hand in a cunning and underhand way - the taking of Elenoras had caused this king of the Spartans to march his army to Athens yet the gods themselves would side with Athens.

Hades was shrewd, he was lining the gods against the much feared Spartans - by promising that Ares would fight on the Athenian walls the bloodthirsty gods would relish the ritual sacrifice of the same princess the Spartans were marching to set free. But something was not right, the mighty Zeus smelled more, perhaps Hades in his extreme deviousness was himself being outwitted - it may be that another hand was involved, someone whom the king of gods Zeus knew would take the opportunity to strike if the occasion arose. This thought grew within the majestic god's powers of reasoning like a creeping paralysis. Zeus, for his own reasons, felt the ominous shooting pains of concern – might this war created by the shadowy master of the underworld turn inexorably against the Olympus gods? What if his monstrous foe herself should intercede? What if she sided with the Spartans? What if she were to pit her considerable might against the powerful Ares? Zeus knew if this was so then it would be a short one-sided contest.

A long time ago Zeus had allowed Hades to abduct the irresistible Persephone, Hades was besotted, he was infatuated with the half-goddess in a whimpering way that made his fellow gods giggle and make fun. Persephone, Zeus knew, would never be a true blue-blood queen to Hades because her mother, Demeter, goddess of the harvest and self-declared saviour of all enslaved women who laboured in the fields, often cohorted with men of the land, they worshipped her with reverence whenever their crops were good - but when the rains were not forthcoming, through the meanness of the gods or because the gods were angered by men's lack of respect and poor sacrifices, then love for Demeter could be fickle.

Demeter adored the adulation of men, their harvest offerings pleased her, their grains would grow tall and fruitful leading to the wondrous celebration of all – the time when the crops were gathered in. The harvesting of the wheat and corn was when men worshipped Demeter the most, when she took full advantage in the one way that Demeter knew how. Therefore, Persephone's true heritage concerned Zeus, her vague ancestral bloodline disturbed him - what if Persephone's origins were the one thing that mattered, what if Hades had been a fool? Was it at all possible that Persephone might be descended through the one bloodline Zeus feared? To Hawwāh herself?

Perhaps Persephone was *not* the daughter of Demeter? But then who was Demeter? What was Demeter's line of blood? With these thoughts turning in his mind Zeus decided that he could not take this considerable risk, he must side with Hades, he must support the underworld god of death to make sure this unweaving disaster worked to the securest of all conclusions. Persephone must not, under any circumstances, be allowed to prevail - Athens could not fall to the revenge of this Spartan king, it would be more agreeable to the wellbeing of the gods if Persephone herself vanished. Nor should this troublesome king Cleomenes be allowed to survive, nor his determined adversary Patriach of the Athenians - because

Zeus could not take the remotest chance that both men were cast in some form of intricate web woven by Persephone for her revenge – and there was the unsettling prospect this abducted Spartan princess might herself be born from the womanly womb of Persephone. But what of Demeter?

Demeter did not want Hades to take Persephone as his consort wife, Demeter hated Hades, she would not countenance the young Persephone becoming queen of the underworld or the dead. Demeter was the goddess of all things good, the freshness of the vines and crops, of sunshine and the harvesting of food, of the fruitful celebrations that men adored and revered – death and the underworld were feared if the daughter of Demeter became linked with death and the drinking of blood then the wholesome ethics of good hard-working men might begin to fester, Persephone must not become the cohort of Hades under any circumstances. But Zeus decided otherwise, Zeus forever needed to cultivate Hades, Zeus needed to keep Hades close at hand, when men died fighting their bitter wars of hate, when they slaughtered each other in unimaginable ways then the spirits of men became slaves to Hades in his burning world of fire and brimstone.

When Zeus agreed that Hades could have Persephone for his wife, Hades hatched the first of his devious abduction plots. Persephone was gathering flowers in the green fields beside the fast-flowing river which cut through the realm of the god of love Adonis, who dwelt with Artemis, goddess of childbirth and the sister of Apollo. Artemis was the true offspring of Zeus and his consort goddess Leto, who herself resided with Pallas, daughter of Triton. In the fading evening sunlight Hades burst through a cleft that opened in the ground to take Persephone against her will. When Demeter learned that Persephone had disappeared, that she was nowhere to be found, she searched for one whole summer to no avail. During this summertime, in the depths of her despair, she forbade the earth to make crops, she made it that nothing worthwhile would grow. Mankind floundered; men, their wives and their children began to starve.

Helios, the god of the sun, he was the one who told Demeter that Hades had abducted Persephone to be his wife, Helios had seen everything during the long sun-dripped days as summer unfolded. In this way, Demeter learned of the trickery of Hades, that Persephone was now the uncrowned queen of the underworld, who would be reviled and feared by all men who bared their living souls to the gods.

Persephone and Demeter would one day have their revenge, Zeus had long realised this, but the womanly gods must know their place in the same way that womankind in the world of men knew theirs. Hades was driven by adoration, his desires for Persephone were his divine rights, lust played its evangelical part in the same way gods demanded whenever siren women taunted them with their irresistible lure. In this new war of attrition between foolish proud men, Zeus sensed the hand of Demeter, he suspected her part because he knew of Demeter, it had been made known to Zeus that she possessed intimate ways her earthly lovers understood. Her siren offspring Persephone was also an unknown seed – what concerned Zeus more than all the sorrows of the gods was that he was unsure of both their bloodlines, if their seed was one or they were not of common blood. Now Zeus was faced with some hatched plot of revenge that either Persephone or, more likely Demeter, had set in motion. Zeus understood why Hades desired Cleomenes, Patriach and Elenoras all dead, they were the lovers and the bastard daughter of Persephone, her infidelity in revenge for her abduction by Hades. It was a clever plan by Hades derived from sound reasoning, Persephone would learn her lesson by the will of her master. But Zeus needed to know more, much more.

Hades had threatened the Athenians with the destruction of their city by fire and lava if they did not abduct the princess of King Cleomenes, this was why the war between men had been unleashed. Though it pleased the senses of Zeus and his fellow gods that one more bloody confrontation between men would unfold, that a worshipping ritual sacrifice would be made to the gods to gain their favour, Hades had set in motion more than just a way to stock his underworld kingdom with the souls of dead men, Hades felt he had been wronged – Hades was seeking vengeance, his retribution was directed at those who were making to strike a reprisal blow for their cause. The gods were all-powerful, they could not be brought to task by mere women who saw themselves as goddesses, or by warring men who dwelt in the boundless dominions governed by the supreme immortals lorded by Zeus. Little did Zeus know that in this he was wrong, Zeus was concerned but he never in ten million years suspected how much the realm of the ancient gods was not the mighty brotherhood he thought it to be.

Patriach saw the same rider depart through the small western side gate that must have been opened for good reason. He caught sight of the commotion, spying movement in the corner of his eye while he scanned the sunrise scene for some clue as to what might happen next. Patriach was alarmed, just about everyone outside was trying desperately to get inside the city walls for their safety, no one wanted to be outside at the mercy of the blood-curdling Spartans. What in the name of the gods was happening? He watched the horseman ride away at speed, he saw the same dust cloud kicked up by galloping hooves that caught the keen-eyed attention of Andronikos. The rider rode in the direction of the Spartans, at the same time giving the impression this was no panic-driven escape, Patriach sensed an element of confident mastery by the horseman over this unexpected turn of events. In time, he saw, at a distance, the small party of Spartan nobility ride out to greet the rider. What devious trickery was this?

An apprehensive feeling of gloom descended upon Patriach; he watched the distant gathering for the length of its duration - suspicious that some form of dispiriting parlay was being done. He did not understand what drove this new sense of uneasiness that grew inside him, he felt a perception of inward desperation, a warning of extreme danger that filled his veins with dread like a creeping paralysis. His sense of the impossible began to reach the inner regions of his determination to see this thing through. The horseman leaving the city in itself did not signify defeat, not on any level, but it confirmed his sickening suspicions that this whole charade of warfare with the undefeatable Spartans would in some way lead to his inevitable doom - even if Athens did survive the Spartan onslaught. The fate of Athens might more and more rest with the desperate offering of the captive princess to Ares, the immortal god of war.

Patriach tried hard to comfort himself, he built himself up one more time in his mind – he tried to convince himself that his extreme unease with the sacrifice of Elenoras to the gods was unwarranted - with Ares on their side then there was little doubt that Athens would be victorious. Deep down, his gut feeling instinct told him that with two detachments of reliable guards to defend their walls, with two more in reserve, they should be able to hold their own against any attack even without Ares standing beside them. Patriach did not desire the ritual death of the Spartan princess, he saw no reason for this bloodthirsty finale that would bring no lasting resolution - except to feed the gods with more exhilaration.

Patriach had given orders for his remaining battalions of pathetic, unfit and drunken troops to police the city, to gather together all the stocks of food – and to ensure there were no Spartan spies loose among them. Something had gone wrong, the horseman was an undercover mole of sorts, helped by traitorous citizens who had no faith in his abilities to hold the city. Without doubt, he thought, the rider was in the pay of someone, there were devious negotiating forces of surrender at work, some plan of deceit and deception that could undermine all of Patriach's hurried preparations. Powerful Athenians within the city realised that Hades would wreak their destruction if his terrible demands were not met, they would try anything to preserve their easy way of living.

There were those who demanded that Elenoras be offered as payment for victory, also those who feared the prospect of a long war if the princess was put to death. Patriach himself saw no good in the death of Elenoras. Where the hell was Persephone during this troubled time? The wife of Hades, the uncrowned queen of the underworld, was the cause of this conflict, she had used him to wrong Hades – Patriach was under no illusion that Hades would not hesitate to exact his revenge against him and the whole city if the Athenian senate did not bend to his will. Patriach now had no choice, he needed to defend the city against King Cleomenes, because he knew that Cleomenes had committed his own violations against Hades – but the unjustifiable death of Elenoras would enrage the Spartan king. Patriach smiled to himself at the irony of the situation, a smile that was brief, for it was not a smiling moment.

"My lord general, the Akropolis senators, they grow impatient." The expressionless face of Patriach's aide-de-camp was grim. Patriach peered one last time at the distant horseman, then at his tough-looking long-standing aide. Patriach's wrinkled expression lied about his deceptive middle-aged years, he was younger than his compatriot King Cleomenes and his old mentor Andronikos, but all of these Athenian troubles weighed him down like a dead weight. The ills of the world seemed like an overwhelming burden upon Patriach's shoulders.

"Let us go to meet with them," replied Patriach to his aide-de-camp. "Where are they gathered?"

"In the lower chamber of the Akropolis temple, my lord general."

"What is their latest mood?" demanded Patriach. They both turned to descend the stone steps from the battlement walls. They walked into the cooler shadows of the big city gate.

"Not good my lord, they are scared like frightened rabbits," replied the aide as they strode across the main courtyard square. "They argue and fight, the majority demand the quick sacrifice of the young princess Elenoras."

Patriach tried to think. There was not much he could say to the elders right now, his inner instincts told him that any dangerous sacrificial offerings must be delayed, that this savage course of action should be halted until he had time to consider these fast-turning events. But the wine-swilling, pig-eating elders demanded the all-important sacrifice done, they wanted the surety of knowing the god Ares would be on their side. Patriach saw that his aide looked troubled.

"Do you know anything of this horseman who left through the west gate?" asked Patriach.

Again, his aide appeared uneasy. "Yes, my lord..." his aide paused, holding back.

"What?" Patriach stopped in his stride, he turned to face his aide-de-camp, whose facial expression once more did not look good. "What has happened?"

The air between them was tense. "Two guards at the gate, they are dead," replied his aide. "I am told they died in a strange way, without any wounds to their flesh," he added. "They apprehended the woman, but she somehow took the best of their cavalry horses then escaped," he said with a hint of mordancy, as an afterthought that might bring the wrath of his general crashing down upon his head.

"Woman?" Patriach froze.

"Yes, the guards tell me the rider who left through the gate was a woman," the aide confirmed, "I do not know anything more."

Patriach turned and marched on with purpose in his stride, it was a long half-hour journey by foot to the Akropolis. Together with his aide-de-camp, they reached the lower chamber which bustled with the argumentative uproar of over fifty of the city nobles, Patriach in an instant saw that, this time, all of them were there. They were the rich elite of Athens, the ones who would lose everything should the Spartans rampage through their city or if Hades wreaked havoc through his threat of revenge.

Their noisy commotion died when Patriach entered the Akropolis chamber, he stood with an air of supremacy while surveying the scene before him, feeling the strained atmosphere driven by an overwhelming prophetic taste of hostility as they all glared in his direction.

"By the gods, our supreme general has deigned to come among us," sneered the portly Belus with thinly veiled contempt, his long red robe of velvet a sure sign of his supreme wealth and high standing - he was in the middle of a long inflammatory speech to the council when Patriach and his aide appeared. "And what news do you bring of our Spartan adversaries, do they yet attack with that swine king Cleomenes at their head?" Belus turned to face his baying supporters in the chamber, "I do believe our general here might offer up our finest wine and leanest feasting meat to our Spartan enemy. Or are we to give up our glorious freedom to eat like pigs ferreting their noses in shit swill," he paused for maximum effect, the murmurings of his audience rose in uproarious support. "We are not *you*, lordish Patriach, never did any of we lie between the sheets with our heads upon the bare breasts of a god's queenly wife, we Athenian nobles choose our mistresses more wisely, *we* know a good mistress when we see one." There was unrestrained laughter from a large number of Belus's avid council supporters, until they were shouted down by the more moderate members of the council who would never countenance the pot-bellied oligarchs' attempt to dominate the senate.

Belus was in a belligerent mood, Patriach recognised this in a split second. This was not going to be easy he thought to himself. The bellicose air in the Akropolis chamber continued to fester, it began to build into a crescendo of noise a short mark below outright mayhem. Before he spoke, Patriach turned to his aide-de-camp, "Go. Find out what you can about this horsewoman rider who left through the west gate," he looked grim. "Find out who she was, I want to know what she was doing inside the city. I must know everything." His aide nodded then turned to march out, leaving Patriach alone to face the hostile chamber music.

"Let the general speak," roared Thorne, leader of the more middling element of the senate. "LET THE GENERAL SPEAK," he bellowed with more resolve - the hustling noise lessened though it did not die away into complete silence. Patriach stood with purpose on the stone slab podium. The citizen general knew what he wanted to say though he was unsure of how to say it. Never had he cohorted in any mistress relationship with the unworldly goddess Persephone, of this he was in no doubt, no doubt whatsoever – but malicious chamber rumours whispered otherwise. When the back-handed knives were out, they were sharp and uncompromising. In truth, Persephone had singled him out, she had saved his life, she had favoured and countenanced him in the many ways that had made Hades jealous. Persephone every time came to him, she came when he was alone hunting in the mountain hills, she would shine bright in the glorious way of the gods, they would talk about what Patriach must do, how he could lead Athens to its former greatness. She warned him that one day Hades would strike against him, she claimed that a more redoubtable soul than herself would someday save him. Patriach often thought who this might be, what had Persephone meant by this?

"The Spartan king Cleomenes does not yet attack. His forces are weary from their march from Sparta," Patriach began his address to the assembly with as much conviction as he could muster - but with a sense of misgiving in his deliverance. "We have three days, perhaps four, before his army begins to storm our city." Patriach looked around the temple chamber, there were many hostile eyes upon him, there were also pleading eyes as well as helpless eyes with burning fear like scared rabbits. Patriach had decided that it was not Belus with his large band of sycophantic followers whom he must deal with first, it was the row of seven holy priests who sat silent and menacing on the highest of the stone benches. Behind these powerful temple ministers of the gods stood the magnificent stone pillars that had taken a generation of skilled masons to build, this was the priesthood's domain, their territory of exquisite marble statues of towering gods adorning the stark plastered walls of subtle domination. Patriach felt uneasy, he felt uncomfortable in this wild confrontational environment, he could see how the hard-nosed priests were out for blood, both his blood and the blood of Princess Elenoras, they had whipped up the rage of the senate who now demanded a victim, someone to appease the mighty gods in the temple Akropolis built on the highest hill in Athens. Patriach had placed himself at the centre of the cauldron, the fire of retribution flared around him, it tortured his convictions in twisting sinews of determination that now threatened to desert him - right now he was unsure whether he might burn himself alive or survive long enough to die another day, either by the hand of Hades, by a Spartan sword of revenge or devoured by the hostile assembly of nobility who themselves could with ease finish him. The congregation of truculent half-sober aristocrats now waited in silence, they were desperate, they wanted to know who it would be that saved them.

Of course, none of the rich and powerful of the senate assembly had ever set eyes upon the god Hades or the beautiful Persephone - the gods were the preserve of the elite high priest of the Akropolis. Only through the esteemed clerics of the temple did any of the gods speak. Persephone came to Patriach in his more vivid of dreams, she came when he dozed or rested in the mountains, or when he slept alone during the long Athenian nights in the hard scabbard bed of his humble city dwelling. There was no rich living for Patriach, no slumberous times of debauchery and drunkenness, just the dark hours of the night and short periods of cooling mountain shade when the goddess of the underworld confided in him.

That Persephone had singled him out was clear to Patriach, that she had steered King Cleomenes into his cauldron of fire to inflict some form of retribution against Hades was obvious. Hades had created the conflict between Athens and Sparta for a reason, and the more Patriach thought about the band of high priest's demands for the executional sacrifice of Princess Elenoras, the more Patriach suspected that both the Athenians and Spartans had marched into a miserable god-driven trap. Patriach needed time, time for something to happen that would change everything, but what would this miracle be? He could not see a way out, not yet, though in the meantime the Athenians must not do nothing, because nothing would ever come from nothing, later they could escape the lure that had been set by the most terrible of all the gods. Patriach had his eyes set firm upon the impatient and militant assembly of Athenian nobles, but it was not they who held Athens in their hands, Patriach turned to face the solemn row of holy men who sat side-by-side aside the towering stone pillars.

"Senators and you holy priests of the Akropolis," the manner in which he stood made it clear that Patriach was addressing the high priests, not the noble elders. "The Spartans prepare their assault upon us, they camp beyond our gates because we hold the daughter of their king," he took a moment to look down at his own, white-knuckled hands gripping the granite stone bannister. "Our skirmishers abducted their women; they killed the cousins of their king. So why is it this senate assembly quakes with fear when the Spartan army marches to our city gates to exact revenge?" Patriach looked around at their solemn faces, he noted they were all silent, there was no nervous bickering or argumentative fightback, but he could feel the hostile tension against him.

"I do not know if the Spartan king yet knows how you holy men plan to sacrifice his youngest daughter. You tell us we must do this, you tell

us we must appease both the god of the underworld and the god of war to
save our city," Patriach eyed the holy men with deep suspicion, "I suspect
their king at this time knows of this sacrifice, because a horseman rider
left this city to parlay with the Spartan king and his general Andronikos a
short time ago. Gentlemen of the senate, we all know Andronikos well, he
and his Spartan army drove back the Persians from our borders, his hand
handed you the gluttonous wealth you nobles consume each day. Now
Andronikos and his king are here to take it back, because you high priests
who speak with the gods give the Spartans no choice." Patriach searched
their upturned faces for clues as to what he would say next, he could see
their uncertain hatred mingled with their fear - distrust of himself, their
fear of both the gods and the supreme general of their enemy.

All Athenians knew of the fearsome reputation of the Spartan commander - Andronikos and the Hippias cavalry had helped save the day at
the battle of Thermopylae when the allied Theban army of the Boeotia
alliance broke and ran before the Persian onslaught. Three hundred
dismounted Spartans with their long shaft-like spears and bronze shields,
with Andronikos at their head, had held the vast Persian hoards. The
Boeotia league states then rallied, Patriach, who at that time was a low
commander of a small troop of Athenian swordsmen saw his general fall
dead in the Athenian retreat when the Thebans were put to flight by the
Persians, Patriach also saw the charge of the Hippias horsemen led by
Andronikos and the Spartan king Leonidas, he saw how they blocked the
mountain pass of Thermopylae then slaughtered the Persians army in
their many hundreds.

Patriach himself had rallied the dispirited Athenians to charge into the
Persian rear to avoid outright defeat, he was followed by the few Thebans
who survived the first route and by Helot archers - who were out-of-
the-blue joined in the victorious charge by the seven hundred Thespian
Hoplites led by an unknown female warrior who seemed to appear out of
nowhere. Later it was known their nameless leader called herself Phryne.
Phryne had at first wavered in her support of the Boeotia federation but
joined late to turn the battle when King Leonidas of the Spartans was slain.

Though the Persians could not be stopped at Thermopylae, it was the beginning of the end for the Persian invasion and a change in fortunes for the Boeotia alliance. Both Patriach and Andronikos rose to head their own armies, and the conquered states of Thrace and Macedon were later freed from the Persian yoke - with Patriach and Andronikos becoming revered heroes in their kingdoms. What became of the extraordinary Thespian warrior Phryne no one knew - after the long and eventual defeat of the Persians, when Phryne cut down the Persian king Xerxes, she disappeared.

At this moment Patriach, for some reason, remembered the beguiling Thespian commander who changed everything, he brought to mind the words Phryne had last spoken when she warned that it was always enemies you could not see who wielded the traitorous axe, not the valiant foe with a fighting lance or a sharpened sword. She had chosen her time to join the Boeotian federation stand, in a way that she decided who would be the victors in the Persian war, but this Phryne's stark warning now played havoc with his hot-wired thoughts, his mind raced with self-preservational instinct like a bulging wide-eyed sphinx. Patriach half turned to address the revered supreme cleric who led the seven priests of the Akropolis, who had said not one word since Patriach had arrived in the temple hall.

"Horus, you do not speak, you sit there quiet and say no words," said Patriach. "Tell me, what is it these gods say to you? What do *you* say?"

Horus, the small, wiry skin of a man who dressed insignificantly in simple saffron silk ropes, stared back at Patriach in stubborn silence. His complete lack of body hair looked in character with his pale skin face, in a way that he was forced to give the impression of aloofness through his impenetrable bond with the power-crazed overlord of the gods - his yellowing teeth a hallowing testimony to his habitual prayer smoke addiction. Horus took time to choose his words, knowing that every pair of riveted eyes in the chamber were now turned in his direction. The momentary stillness inside the senate was broken by the ticking of time as the greatest of the gods sensed a moment of monumental confrontation.

Zeus looked down upon the Akropolis senate, he folded his angelic wings around him, a feeling of intense fortitude descended upon him.

"The gods are all-knowing Patriach, they know the minds of all men," croaked Horus. He stood, then turned to accept the nodding acknowledgement of his six fellow priests who sat in a line of solid patronage. He did not add anything more.

"Then tell me, what is the will of the gods? Do they read my mind?" scoffed Patriach, the strain of passion in his voice enforced the silence of the noble elders.

"The gods see you in the same way the wolf sees its foe the lynx," said Horus, "or the great lion of the plains sees its enemy the hyena." This was now the final head-to-head confrontation that had been building to a crescendo, a festering clash between the steadfast general and the hostile senate who were under no doubt the survival of Athens was at stake. The holy priests, more so Horus, had long held the nobles in their mealy hands like a snake curled around its victim. "This is the dark time, the god of the underworld demands blood and the god of war *smells* blood," warned Horus. "Your blood, because you are the one the queen of the underworld covets. Have no doubt how the gods know your mind Patriach."

Patriach stiffened, he acknowledged the challenge. "Then tell me, what is your mind Horus? And are the minds of your sycophant priests addled by the mystic smoke they inhale in the same way as you yourself?" Patriach was in no mood to take prisoners, he was fighting for his survival, his existence as the esteemed leader of the Athenian army - though he knew there was no other venerated general to take his place, no one who could command the army and fight the enemy in the way he could. All the senate assembly, the holy priests included, were aware of this - which added to the senate's extreme unease and disloyalty.

Horus narrowed his eyes; this was his moment. "My mind is that Athens wallows in this dire situation because of you, my dear Patriach. You dishonour the gods, they demand your blood, they desire the blood of all Athenians if we do not fight the Spartan king. To win this victory the god of war desires a high sacrifice to feed his passion, he wants the blood of the Spartan princess so that he will take up his sword for Athens," Horus hissed. "If we have Ares on our side then we do not need you, Patriach."

The long day of dark traitorous retribution wore on, no one in the chamber of the Akropolis sensed that midday was now approaching, there was no news from his aide-de-camp, Patriach stood motionless on the senate podium. This was the tragic moment, thought Patriach, this was when he must make his fateful challenge for supremacy over both Horus and Belus, when he must test the resolve of the nobles who were split in their loyalty towards him. Patriach was aware of who his principal enemies in the senate were - their driving hostility was clear; they drove the senate before them.

"There is another way," Patriach proposed with newfound passion, "I believe there is a way to hold back the useless slaughter and decimation of this city. Do you want your wives and daughters ravaged by bloodthirsty victors if the god of war fails to defeat these Spartans? You all know the will of the gods is forever uncertain. What if your illustrious god of war decides to side with Cleomenes because the Spartans fight with more valour? The gods are fickle, they side with no man, we all know this. Do not put your trust in the god of war, do not bend to the demands of the underworld god of the dead just because he thinks he has been wronged by his consort queen." Patriach looked around at their upturned faces, he was near to being there, he was close to turning the undecided, there were those in the chamber who were faltering, some who feared the consequences of enraging the Spartan king. "Let us not kill the princess, let us give her back to the Spartans and get this dreadful deed we committed put right. We have no quarrel with their king, we have fought side-by-side against our Persian enemy, we have grown rich in our victories. Why do we men fight this vile war because the gods demand it is what we must do?

There was a ripple of discontent, Patriach sensed the will of the senate turn against him. "If you are not with us, then you are against us," Belus at once rose to his feet then fumed, mass bedlam broke out as nobles rose to their feet with shaking fists. With worrying disquiet, the ones who were with Patriach did not rise to defend him, they stayed silent and sitting. "Let us be done with this nonsense," Belus roared, his face red with rage.

"This sacrifice must be done before the day is out. With Ares by our side, we will ride out to send these Spartans slithering back to where they came from. The whole of Sparta will then fall before our victorious armies." The noise in the Akropolis temple rose to a vicious crescendo, a smiling smirk spread like a creeping stain of delight over the pale white face of Horus.

Patriach once more stood motionless. Appalled. His thoughts raced, out of the corner of his eye he saw Horus and Belus nod to each other in some form of prearranged signal, three Akropolis guards standing behind the largest of the stone pillars drew their swords upon some agreed command then moved with menace towards him, in an instant Patriach realised how this had all been contrived, he had walked into a trap of the senates' deliberate making. What should he do now, he could not escape, the way out was barred, by now the whole assembly wanted his blood, the more moderate of the nobles on his side were quick to realise their own fate was more important, they rose in defiance against him. The swordsmen guards were near, Patriach could not run, there was nowhere to hide, his fate was irrevocable and sealed, his mind tumbled into the abyss. On the highest peak of the god's Mount Olympus, Hades of the underworld smiled in seeming satisfaction.

In the complete mayhem of bellowing confusion, no one in the temple saw the lone sword bearer appear from a location unseen. In a few fractions of a moment, the unknown assailant lurched from behind the largest pillar nearest to the fist-waving priests. Before the temple guards reached Patriach to arrest or assassinate him the unknown attacker pointed a menacing silver blade direct against the bared throat of Horus, the sword tip threatening the pronounced rigid bulge in his scrawny neck. Horus stared wide-eyed silent.

The senate in an instant fell hushed, like the unforeseen deaths of a pack of baying dogs. Patriach's mind reeled, his life all of a sudden not on a knife-edge precipice. His mouth fell open when he realised who the assailant was, her long flowing dark hair and battered battle armour failing to hide her piercing eyes as she stared with menace into the horrified ice-white face of Horus. Horus, shocked, knew who his hostile attacker was.

476

"Call off your wolves Horus, or I will take your head," everyone froze, including the assassin guards. In that instant Patriach pieced together the vision of the woman with piercing reality - she wore the same ragged tunic and armour breastplate as the horsewoman rider he had watched ride to the Spartans earlier in the morning. Seeing her close he smiled. Of course, he without doubt recognised her, the same woman, the same womanly warrior who had led the Thespian Hoplites against the Persian invaders, the same mystifying woman who cut down the Persian king Xerxes years ago. Patriach gaped, aghast, confused, she had not changed or aged - it was as if she had just delivered herself straight from the war against the Persians - she was graced in the exact same way.

Patriach realised in an instant that she was here for himself. He did not know why but he was taking no chances. He leapt from the podium towards the Akropolis exit. The whole senate stood transfixed, the noisy rumpus now ice silent, the three guards who had moved to arrest him stood motionless in their absolute indecision. No one told them what to do. In the meantime, Patriach's redeemer held the blade of her sword rigid against the throat of Horus who began to recover his composure, his eyes darting around those nearby to demand assistance or some form of retribution. No one moved.

"You know who I am Horus, no one here or any of your precious gods is going to help you," she hissed. "Patriach will leave here with me and you will come with us." She half-turned to Patriach, without taking her eyes from the terrified priest. "Take your leave general. Your aide-de-camp is waiting. He knows where to take you."

"What about the princess? We must free Elenoras," blurted Patriach in passionate confusion.

"Why would we want to take Elenoras?" questioned Phryne, with a sly half-smile that said nothing.

Horus was frozen rigid; he knew who Phryne was - even the gods themselves spat venom whenever her name was broached. The devious plan of Hades was beginning to unravel, Horus felt himself shaking, he shivered in the warm late morning air like the verminous rat he was.

Andronikos sat upon the large, rounded rock half buried in the hard-packed earth outside his stinking goatskin tent, he did not care much for the luxurious luxuries of his fellow Spartans. The terrain beside the river showed that water had once flowed a different course, the smoothness of the stones a testament to their longtime erosion. Andronikos thought he could see signs of an old riverbed, one now dry and disused, not like the fast-flowing water now cutting its way through the dry flat plain of Athens. The afternoon sun was becoming hot, he saw how the river was full of naked men bathing their fatigued bodies while their women camp followers laundered their men's clothes, seeming unperturbed by the throngs of male stripped-bare bodies in the river. The women filled great clay jars to take water to the shoreline then waited for their menfolk to heave them ashore into the scattered camps that smouldered under the steady drifting smoke of hundreds of cooking fires.

The Spartan general watched his army preparing, in less than two days they would be ready to lay siege to the city. He turned his attention back to the dried portion of the riverbed, he thought to himself how long it must have been since the water had flowed a different course, it would take an extraordinarily long time for a river to cut a new path – perhaps the gods were wrong when they said the world was made by the great father of Zeus in just seven days. Time, something was wrong with time, time did not add up, there were many signs that time did not conform to what the scriptures said, time was twisted and convoluted – because when Andronikos had stared at the horseback rider in stunned disbelief, he realised with shock how she had not aged since he last saw her.

He had grown from the young virile warrior who could lead his men in battle, his muscled lean body able to wield a lance or sword in ways that made his enemies fear him. Now he was long past his middling years, his wrinkles of age defied his distant youth – like the old riverbed, his life would soon dry up to be bypassed by younger men, men who would one day take his reigns to lead Sparta in their own way. This uncalled-for fight against Athens would be his last battle.

Now he was old and wise he thought to himself in worrying sorrow; but not wise enough to figure out why he felt agitated with hints of fear. He had last seen this same woman among the camp followers, the women who followed the Spartans in battle, the wives and children who marched in the army's rear setting up camps for their warrior men because they had no other life when the army was gone from Sparta. He remembered, he had seen her late in the evening wrapped in a full-cloaked blanket, when she took water from another nameless river far away many leagues to the north. This was a long time ago. Her dark hair spilling from her hood, she had flipped it back with a subtle toss of her hand which, even now, for some reason, Andronikos still remembered to this day. Her stark grey eyes had pierced him in the same way, in the way that made him hurt right now.

Andronikos knew her name, he knew who she was but then he did not. Four times in his long withering life she had messed his mind in a way he could not fathom, she appeared then disappeared, without logic, offering no sane reason why she was there.

The second time he saw her was more spectacular, more insane – out of nowhere she led the Thespian Hoplites in the magnificent final battle charge that split the royal Constantinople Persians in a way that King Xerxes had to fight hard to salvage. Xerxes had strived to cut her down, he cornered her with the best of his guards while the Spartans stared transfixed. Xerxes died, he did not die a king's death, he died in a way that none of his men could understand, in a way that ended the war that saved the Thespians their city. But this was not the first time Andronikos had encountered this woman, who in the war against the Persians was called Phryne. She was not called by this name the first time he saw her. The first time was long ago, long before the great Persian war, during the slaughterhouse battle of Marathon against the first Achaemenid king. Andronikos, then a young brave Spartan warrior, wounded, delirious, near to death, given up by the camp women who tended him during his high fever and fight for life - in his feverish state he was incoherent, raving, babbling, deranged. From nowhere she was there, by his side, from someplace unseen. Sometimes she was alone, other times she was two, sometimes three, sometimes she became all three in one, his fading consciousness could not decide. She was in some way a goddess, perhaps like Persephone and Demeter, a beautiful woman with dark hair and pale grey eyes like no other eyes he had seen. Then she was gone.

Now Phryne, or whoever she was, was back. This changed everything for Andronikos, this whole conflict was now different. Andronikos sat quiet upon his sitting rock thinking over what had happened. Nothing added up. This appearance by Phryne signified to Andronikos that it was clear there was a strangeness unravelling, a subtleness he could not even begin to imagine - this was much more than revenge for the abduction of Elenoras by the Athenians or her simple recapture from these scoundrel dogs - these indescribable happenings must be the work of the gods. What bothered Andronikos, what played upon his mind more than anything, was the way in which Phryne had stared at him within the Spartan encampment that time many years ago, this was linked to everything that was happening now. When he last saw her, for the third time, in the wayward guise of one of the Spartan army's band of camp followers, he had ordered her brought before him - but once more she proved elusive, she disappeared like a strange ghost playing for time in the mists of cascading water. What was more, she had given him the exact look earlier in the morning, when she without warning rode out to them from someplace unknown. Sitting forthright, he remembered her words. 'You have the look of your mother in your eyes.'

It was a remonstrance, a striking blow against his invincibility, Andronikos was sure of this. Phryne had singled him out, she was no brazen fool, she was here for a reason, there was a purpose for her to return.

A noise startled Andronikos from behind. It was Cleomenes.

Cleomenes was in modest dress, he turned to his two accompanying aides. "Leave us," he ordered. The old general and the warrior king sat together alone.

The king was attired in his simplest cow-skin tunic, it was lightweight and close-notched, most of the time he wore it beneath his warlord leathers. Cleomenes cut a dashing figure for his middle years, though his grim facial expression said it all. He offered Andronikos a cup of wine.

"This wine is like river water; it is the offering of life. It feeds and replenishes us," said Cleomenes. There was a distinct unease in his voice.

Andronikos watched the swift-flowing river for a fraction of a moment. He was surprised to see his king.

"Yes, the cool water revives the men after their long march," replied Andronikos, almost as a matter of fact. He turned to face Cleomenes, taking the wine in half-hearted gratitude. He took a small sip; the full-bodied redness was bitter and wholesome with a complex crossover of flavours. It was good wine; it was king's wine. "Is she gone? I did not see her leave."

"Yes, she left," answered Cleomenes, "I watched her ride back towards the city. Before she left, she said something strange."

"Uh, whatever she said, it would not surprise me," exclaimed Andronikos, with a halfway smile. "It bothers me that she has business with the Athenians," he frowned. "What is this strange thing she said?" Andronikos felt uneasy with his king, the general still felt they had missed their chance, how they should have attacked the Athenians when first arriving the evening before. They should have fallen upon the city when least expected, there would have been no time for the sacrificial death of Elenoras; this dirty complicated business could have been done quick. Now their best chance was gone. It was difficult to imagine what events were now occurring in the Athenian city. Andronikos stared into his stone goblet of wine. Cleomenes watched the flowing river.

"She said there must be no attack by the Spartan army. She said our army is already defeated," Cleomenes replied.

Andronikos looked up, surprised. He felt for something to say, if Phryne had said this then she showed a deep perception of what was happening. Was she taking control?

"Andronikos, we must talk," said Cleomenes. "I think we have been marched into a war not of our making."

Andronikos sipped more of his wine. He saw that Cleomenes's goblet was left untouched. The king was troubled.

"You must tell me more about Persephone," said Andronikos. "I believe this is where the troubles for Sparta begin."

"Yes, you are correct my wise friend. I have made a mistake, I have not acted in a kingly manner," said Cleomenes. He took a large gulp of his wine.

Andronikos looked at Cleomenes, he did not reply.

"I am the first of Spartan kings never to take a wife. I offer no queen for Sparta," said Cleomenes. "I take my love from concubines and harlots." He paused, silent. He looked out over the river, many more of his men now bathed in the cool water as the afternoon sun grew hot. By their sides the growing hordes of women still worked relentless, not for them the relaxing pleasures before the coming conflict, their blood would not be spilt by the thrust of a sword or an enemy's lance. Their bodies would be defiled in a different way if their men were defeated, this was the price *they* would pay thought Cleomenes.

"I fought for another king long before you," said Andronikos. "Leonidas, your father's half-brother, we fought together at Thermopylae where he died. His queen Gorgo, she was no beauty, but she was loyal. And one more king before you, their son Pleistarchus, he was a weak ruler with no woman by his side until he took a brothel woman for his queen, he took favours from Xerxes of the Persians until your brother Agesipolis deposed him. Your father, the first overlord called Cleomenes, lost his kingship to Leonidas because he left no heirs, no one to take up the crown for Sparta. This is why we Spartans fight for you, your daughter, the princess Elenoras, is descended by blood from your father Cleomenes the First, from Leonidas and Queen Gorgo. Elenoras will be our next queen, the man she betroths our new king. The army is loyal to you and to Elenoras."

Andronikos had fought alongside every one of these deposed monarchs, he knew the army was loyal at best to himself, long before any sworn loyalty to whoever was king, kings were interested in being kings. Andronikos sensed a moment of truth, he felt a feeling of dread. No one was sure who the mother of Elenoras was, though this was never an issue with Spartans – concubines and whores were the mothers of many of Sparta's best fighting men. But Andronikos was conscious of more.

"I know all this, Spartan kings are like all kings," replied Cleomenes.

"We dig deep to justify our heritage; we fight wars for our sons to descend us." Cleomenes paused, he looked deep into his general's eyes. "You sometimes ask about the goddess Persephone? Well, there is something about Persephone you should know my friend."

Andronikos stiffened, this was the moment of expectation, the time for which he had been waiting when this whole escapade would become clear. He half knew what Cleomenes would say.

"The goddess Persephone is the mother of Elenoras. This is why the gods are against us," declared Cleomenes without emotion. "This is why the god Hades detests us, why these Athenians are driven to sacrifice the princess to seek the favour of Ares to fight against us." Cleomenes watched hard to see how Andronikos would react. "This Phryne who rides her mount to warn us, she is right when she says our army is already defeated," he added with deep tones of remorse. Cleomenes felt the same old despondency, feelings of guilt creeping through his bones.

In the far distance, the indistinct greyness of the featureless mountains disrupted the horizon of the flat plain. The heat haze that built in the middle of every afternoon now began to distort the glimmering vista, the far-off landscape was even more dry and desolate than earlier in the day, there was a flickering deadness in the vision that reminded Andronikos of his dry-mouthed ambivalence.

Andronikos thought to himself in contemplative silence. If what Cleomenes said was true then this war could not continue, the Spartan army could not be victorious because there was no victory to be had, just the useless slaughter of valiant lives to satisfy the powdery will of the gods. How perceptive was Phryne, how did she know all this? Was she aware of the ways of this goddess Persephone? Did she know that Elenoras could herself be descended from patronage blood? Elenoras. Elenoras, over and over again Elenoras. Sparta could be defeated because the princess daughter of their king was the fateful spinal cord in some complicated fight between hostile gods - what had Sparta done to anger the gods in such an efficacious manner?

It then occurred to Andronikos that Phryne, not Elenoras, held the key, that this was not the first time she had grasped his fate in her hands. Everyone talked about the legend of the Spartans at Thermopylae, but it was Phryne with her Thespian band of freed ragtag slaves that saved the day, she had bided her time, she had waited in a way that suggested she was undecided if she would deem to intervene or not, then something had happened, something had stirred her in a way that changed everything. Phryne turned her Thespians upon the Persians, the Athenians under the young unknown warrior Patriach had rallied behind her which then bought time, time enough for the Boeotia alliance to withdraw in good order. Andronikos asked himself again, who *was* Phryne? How did she draw breath in this world of warring kings and squabbling gods? Was the same hair-splitting intervention by this strange warrior woman happening all over again?

One more thought occurred to the old ageless warrior, he finished his wine in one last gulp. He sensed that Cleomenes was waiting for him to say something, but he could think of nothing worthwhile to say. The grumbling thought inside his mind grew rapid as the meandering river water flowed from east to west in front of his perplexed eyes. What was the strange link between Phryne and Persephone? If Elenoras was the daughter of Persephone, then for what reason did Phryne appear on horseback to warn them of the imminent execution of Elenoras? This war, thought Andronikos, was out of Spartan hands, Sparta was about to be dragged through a vicious siege it might well lose.

"You keep your thoughts to yourself Andronikos, why do you not say what is in your mind? Tell me your thoughts Andronikos..." the king's trembling voice faltered.

Andronikos remained silent, trying to decide his words. All the kings of Sparta worked in their mysterious ways, they were forever twisting and manoeuvring to protect their dynasty, there were always threats, intrigues hiding behind corners which made Andronikos long ago decide he would never be party to any plot against a Spartan king - this was why he had risen to lead the army; he could be trusted, he would be loyal whatever.

"My lord," said Andronikos. "You must drink your wine and be thankful.

You have this magnificent army behind you, the day after tomorrow we will begin our siege of Athens, these Athenians will quiver on their feet when they see the mightiest Spartan army march to their gates. We are not already defeated. Sparta has never been defeated so easily. If we fight against gods, then we will defeat these gods. This is my thinking my lord king." Andronikos lied, he lied with conviction. These were not the thoughts of Andronikos at all.

The truth was that Andronikos could see no way out. It was probable that Elenoras was by now dead, executed in the magnificent Akropolis temple to appease the truculent god of war. Andronikos decided, at this moment, in his mind, that tomorrow he would ride alone to the gates of Athens adorned in his finest battle attire, he would ride on his magnificent white stallion horse with his longest spear and sharpest sword. He would demand to speak direct with Patriach or whoever was now leading these devious Athenians; he would call for the release of Elenoras, he would threaten the destruction of their city if they did not. This was the one stupid plan he could think of, Andronikos did not believe for a single moment that his plan would succeed, the scheming gods had decided the victors, soon one more Spartan king would be dead because this was what the gods of the underworld demanded. Cleomenes was a fool, a stupid wooden-headed buffoon to be seduced and twisted by the scheming goddess of the dead. Hades was clever, his fellow gods would relish watching the destruction of the king of Sparta's army, they would revel in the death of Cleomenes and Elenoras. Ares would be in a bloodthirsty mood; the Athenians would be victorious over their bitter longtime rivals - and no doubt Persephone would be banished or burned in the fires of Mount Olympus. All because a foolish king had declared his undying love for the scheming goddess of those who were dead.

Their one last chance, thought Andronikos, was Patriach. Patriach was a virtuous man, a brave warrior who could not be twisted with ease. The Spartan's last chance, their one chance, was to negotiate with Patriach. Patriach controlled the Athenian senate, perhaps the Athenian general could be convinced to make his mighty senators see good sense, the gods would not be so ruthless to destroy the whole city just because one god was wronged by his wife. The gods were whimsical, but never before had they been so devastating in their morality - though their justice could be incomprehensible, vicious and bloodthirsty when driven to the extreme; perhaps the gods would not destroy the power of the city because the god of the underworld had decided it should be so.

While Andronikos sat beside the mind-calming river, beside the now silent king, he never for one moment suspected that Patriach had fallen for the same intricate charms of the scheming underworld goddess, that Hades desired the death of the Athenian citizen general as more payment for the worldly rituals of his unfaithful wife. Neither did Andronikos realise that all the gods were intrigued to their absolute delight, that they were gathering in joyous celebration of the most wondrous form of distraction that Hades could ever have dreamed up. Hades was lapping up their praise in lavish style, his three-headed beast Cerberus revelled in the playful attention of his devious master. All the gods that is except Zeus, Zeus was no fool, Zeus realised something more, Zeus knew full well the hidden hands of this intriguing game that might threaten Olympus had not yet played out.

Andronikos sat beside his contemplative king, whose mood was one of subdued acknowledgement of his deteriorating predicament. There was an unexpected commotion behind, both men turned to see the king's senior aide who was flustered to the extreme.

"My king, you must come quick," the aide blurted, the veins in his brow close to bursting. The day of Spartan retribution turned inside out. "The horseback rider, she returns."

Both Cleomenes and Andronikos stared at the aide in astonishment, there were a few moments of shocked silence before the storm of real-isation broke. This was unexpected, one more twist in the bewildering appearance of the renegade queenlike nymph dressed in her well-worn breastplate armour.

"Yes, we will come," Cleomenes spluttered in surprise. "Calm yourself man. Why in the god's name is she here?"

"My lord, she is not alone," replied the aide, hurrying his words in jabbering confusion. "The Athenian general Patriach and a druid priest are with her. The priest... I think the priest is their captive."

Andronikos looked up towards the wide open sky, a single cloud drifted from nowhere, a lone warning of how the day might yet hold strange destinies in its hands. He was careful not to cast his one squinting good eye upon the burning afternoon sun.

Zeus looked down upon his captive world and he saw. He saw the rider he feared ride from the main gate of Athens, opened by a frightened guard who could never begin to understand. Two mounts with a third tied behind, they galloped away in a calm unrushed manner that Zeus knew meant trouble of the worse kind. Zeus alone spied this, the other gods were fornicating and drinking their debauching wine. Nor did Ares see, he was busy donning his silver armour while choosing his finest fighting battle axe. Zeus looked on, seeing Ares preening and grooming himself in vain self-satisfaction. Zeus watched Hades drinking deep red blood - not for Hades weak fruity wine or unclean pig meat, Hades satisfied his hunger with the finest animal flesh before reaching out to caress the smooth breasts of his latest mistress consort - one more kidnapped concubine for his deviant desires. Zeus sensed all the god's noxious moods, the pentaprism excitement of anticipation, of war and spilled blood between feuding men. Zeus saw there was no Persephone, nor her mother god Demeter - where were Persephone and Demeter while the earthly sun rose in the god-given sky? Persephone, Demeter and this dreadful menace in the world of men called Phryne.

Zeus turned to gaze one more time at Hades who by this time had his tongue upon his naked woman's navel. The disgusting beast Cerberus lapped up the spilt blood from his master's goblet, but Zeus paid little attention, because everything, for Zeus, began to fall in place. Zeus stood up tall, he strode with defiance to sit upon his mountain, he had no slave or worshipping consort, no woman to offer her open legs or womanly flesh. Zeus reached out to take his simplest short sword, a sharp-bladed blade he had never before used, he tied it around his angelic waist in a way that did not hinder his enormous white wings curled and furled under his mystic tunic of fine white-woven silk. This war, the battle threatening on the great plain of Athens was now significant, though it was nothing compared to what might soon begin. Zeus looked hopeless and grim, the worried frown upon his ageless face belying the intenseness of his deep concern. Hades was a stupid fool, Ares an arrogant dullard who did not stand even the remotest chance of survival. Zeus looked down upon the drooling monster Cerberus and smiled, he smiled a tarnished grin that hid the depth of his unease, when Cerberus cooed and sought the compassion of the greatest of the gods Zeus stood tall. Cerberus then fell under the forbidding shadow of two unfurled wings of magnificent whiteness and whimpered, the foul stench of his three salivating mouths dripping saliva that mixed with the congealed blood of the tipped-over goblet, a gift from the god of mankind. Zeus looked on and thought hard. Of course, it now began to fall in place – Persephone, Demeter, Elenoras and the despicable one these men called Phryne. Zeus tried to think decisive of how many more. His eyes then froze in abject shock, a rigid sickness spread through his mind when the rock-hard stone of realisation from nowhere struck.

"Tomorrow will not be another tomorrow," whispered Persephone, her fragile voice struggling to overcome the piercing mountain silence. "The day will change, so will all days. I hope for a sweet wind to ravage the scourge of these buggering gods." The dense, drifting grey mist half hid the mundane unblessed sky of the late evening sun. Persephone, in excruciating pain, lay prone upon the rough bed of tussled grasses that softened the stony ground.

Demeter looked desolate, the redness in her eyes her testament to tears of outright despair. Tomorrow might be tomorrow, but today was today.

"Before, when I played in the name of a captive slave, I dreamed that one day we would both be free," said Demeter with extraordinary grimace. She sat quiet, painful, kneeling on her haunches between the prickly bushes dried and withered in the waterless wasteland of the arid foothills. Demeter reached once more to hold the lace-white hand of her daughter, the ravaging wounds inflicted by the wild disgusting beast Cerberus would never heal, the poisons in the monster's salivating drool were by now congealing within Persephone's blood. When Persephone had transfixed her human form, Cerberus struck, he knew when to strike, when Persephone would be at her vulnerable point of homosapien indecision. For the enforced goddess of the dead, there was not long left.

"I am not free; I am held in fear by every mortal man who lives. I am the captive queen of that vile underworld, when I die will I be gone from the frightened fears of all these men," Persephone whispered, the weakness in her voice the frightful stamp of death.

"Save your strength, do not concern yourself with the lives of these men. This is not your war, it is a longtime war now in your name. The seeds of revenge sown by Hades has stirred the terrible retribution against him, against each of these gods; this time not just between men..." Demeter's voice wavered.

Persephone lay quiet, she despaired of this worthless conflict between Cleomenes and Patriach, she wanted to warn Cleomenes, to help Elenoras in her fearless task. She felt the pain of Hades desiring the death of Elenoras, the thoughts of her ritual slaughter tore the last ribbons of hurt from her heart. Her task of ultimate revenge against Hades was failing, the odds were turning wrong, Hades could now pick each of them off one by one.

"I remember the time in the long wet summer when we picked purple flowers in the green grass meadow," lamented Persephone with death flowing free within her blood.

"You were a small child. Those days are treasure days." Demeter could see Persephone growing weaker. Her ravaged wounds across her breasts, her abdomen torn open was beginning to fester, there was the stench of putrid puss in the still evening air. Demeter's hatred for Hades and his vile beast reached its zenith, it sent shivers of desolation through her desperate body. She loathed Hades, she despised him with an intensity she could not measure. Demeter felt the desolation that threatened to overwhelm her, the total devastation of her soul that could soon play havoc with her balance of mind, the feeling of overwhelming pain creeping through to her inner sanctuary where the intense love of siblings by their mothers lies.

Woeful Persephone, she had turned to Cleomenes in distress, not for revenge, she did not seek green shoots of love or the treasured companionship of a loyal consort, his grace would be a way she hoped might ward off the cruelty of her captive life with Hades, Persephone cultivated her friendship with the king of the Spartans knowing this would give her power against Hades. Elenoras was born not from love but from the hereditary necessity of her survival, for her sense of revenge for being cast as the dark queen of the underworld when in fact she was a kidnapped slave. Persephone had gambled and lost, she took a razor-thin chance that Spartan invincibility would in some way save her, but Hades was always two steps ahead, he schemed to make her life a miserable existence. Then came sibling love, her love for Patriach grew from nothing, it blossomed like the wild purple flowers she remembered from her childhood, it grew then withered like the coming of winter in the summer meadows, it was always an unrelinquished sisterly love when she realised that Hades once more would take his evil retribution. Persephone had underestimated the power of the gods, how they could band together like thieving thieves or fight in petty futile feuds.

Persephone died, she died in the parched dust lands of the nearest hills where nothing grew sacred, her life flickered then slipped away in that instantaneous transformation when light turns to darkness. She died in that tiny fraction of one moment when Demeter did not know she was dead. She died in silence, when life is extinguished in the minutest of an unmeasurable fragment in time when there is no light.

In that same despairing moment, Zeus felt a fugacious tick of unease, before it was quick to pass. Hades, for some unknown reason, looked down, perturbed, at Cerberus curled like a monster beside his feet, before stroking him with contemplating gratification - with a sublime feeling of happiness he could not fathom. Ares held his battle axe with a firmer grip without ever knowing why.

Demeter shook like a shivering leaf caught by an out of nowhere gust of cool breeze that had no sensible reason to blow. She took Persephone's hand in her own, then she held it to her breast in the vein hope that she might breathe life back into her lifeless child in that way only disbarring mothers know; then she turned her ashen grey face to the sky and wailed, she howled the mournful cry of pain, one that mankind in its desperate insecurity had never heard. Zeus pricked his ears, he listened with shock. In this instant he realised this frightful game of charades would soon end; the earth shook, and there was a danger unleashed which he had long known would one day come. Hades, in his blood-dripping domain, shivered, he trembled in ill-defined fear when Demeter's stricken voice cut the air in woeful pain, when he knew he must confront the same grieving revenge of a desacralised mother for a second time.

"Aaahuooo," sang Demeter, her chilling cry split the evening night. "Aaahuooo," she wailed in tune, her rising voice telling the whole world how the one nearest to her had died. "Aaahuooo," she wept, her unwilling teardrops staining the ground a colourless blue. Demeter's cry was not a wolf-like cry, it was a melodious song of discontent, an acknowledgement of the cruel world of gods who slew the innocent, a selective plea to someone who might listen.

The blueness of the sky intensified though Demeter did not know this, the thick swirling mist enveloped Persephone's lifeless body with Demeter kneeling over. Demeter climbed to her feet in forlorn dejection before walking to the tall, white, leaning pinnacle boulder nearby, she began to remove the rocks and stones in the cool shadow of the boulder stone, then began to hollow the ground with her bare hands. In her days as a captive slave, she had dug many shallow graves, Demeter knew what depth and shape a good burial pit should be, how deep a dead slave should be buried. In the cool evening, when Persephone was dug into the ground in lasting peace, Demeter leaned back against the pinnacle rock exhausted and drained, her tears were finished, she had no sorrow left, the shock of the awful day had wrenched her apart. As the sun began to fade into the dreadful night that Demeter knew would come, she sensed a movement from the direction of the towering boulder stones to her right.

Out of the scrub rode four horsemen. It took Demeter a few moments of frightened uncertainty to see they were led by a breast-plated tunic-clad woman. Behind her were a packhorse and two grey-haired heavily armed men, who in turn led a dejected-looking man shrouded in a cloak of rough brown hemp - whose hands were lashed tight together in front.

Both Cleomenes and Andronikos raced back alongside the aide-de-camp. True to the aide's word, Phryne squatted beside the cooking fire in the king's inner camp. With her was the Athenian general Patriach - their adversary in this new emblazoning war. Andronikos did not recognise the second man, but from his cloaked dress, he was without doubt a holy priest from the Akropolis temple. The cleric appeared dejected and tired, he looked held against his will.

Patriach gazed at Andronikos in ill-concealed embarrassment. The Athenian acknowledged Andronikos with a subtle nod of recognition, a straight indication of his extreme unease. King Cleomenes and Patriach had never before set eyes on each other, there was an unsure silence between them when Patriach realised who the king was. Both Patriach and the miserable-looking Horus stood in extreme discomfort behind Phryne, who busied herself picking food from the king's clay pot hanging above the flames.

Phryne looked upwards to the Spartan king. "We renegades are hungry Cleomenes, will you not share your food with three esteemed visitors?" The king's two cooking maids stood back in silent indecision. Cleomenes paused, uncertain. He looked to Andronikos, who nodded in affirmation.

"Make the food table ready for all of us here," ordered Cleomenes to his kitchen maid. He saw Phryne glance at the two maids then follow them with her eyes, then she looked over to Cleomenes.

"Are your two servant maids women of freedom? Or are they slaves?" Phryne's question shook Cleomenes.

"Perhaps they were slaves, a long time ago," he answered, unsure of the right answer. "Now they are here of their own free will." Cleomenes did not feel that he should elaborate.

Phryne looked long and inquisitive at the king. She did not believe him. Andronikos interrupted. "Both these women are from the island kingdom of Ithaca," he felt the need to diffuse the situation. "Their men fought with the Spartan army against the Persians, those men were mercenaries who were killed in the field of battle, their women then chose to stay in our land. There are many such women in Sparta." Phryne glanced at one of the two maids, who nodded a subtle nod to Phryne in affirmation.

Andronikos turned to Patriach, he thought it best to break the impasse between Phryne and Cleomenes, also the awkwardness of this unthinkable moment. "It is good to see you again Patriach. It is a long time."

Patriach did not know what to say, his thoughts raced about how to reply. He recalled the code between enemies, that Sparta and Athens had until recently been allies.

"It is my honour to eat with you again Andronikos, I wish these were better days," Patriach replied.

Cleomenes gazed at Phryne. "Are these two men your captives, your hostages or your travelling companions?" The Spartan king growled his question, Cleomenes was confused like everyone else present, he could see many men of his army gathering outside his regal compound, staring inside towards them in bewilderment and curiosity. Phryne's arrival with the enemy's commander-general and the Athenian priest had not gone unnoticed, it had caused a rapid widespread stir.

Phryne did not answer, she continued to poke a spoon ladle inside the pot, stirring the contents.

"Is this surprise visit a parlay or a begging of truce?" asked Andronikos, sensing the growing tension between Cleomenes and Phryne. He knew that Cleomenes would not agree to any suspension of hostilities without the deliverance of Elenoras from her Athenian captors.

Phryne still squatted by the fire, she seemed more concerned about what was cooking inside the clay cauldron. After a while, she looked up to Andronikos, ignoring Cleomenes.

"Horus is here against his will, he is my hostage," she answered. "Take heart, I do not think the Athenians will sacrifice the king's princess while Horus is here." Phryne then turned to glare at Cleomenes, "Patriach is my honoured companion, he is under my protection, you and your men will not harm him."

"He is our enemy, he is inside my camp, his men kidnapped my innocent daughter," barked Cleomenes, an angry tone in his voice. "It is my choice to decide what we will do with these two men."

Phryne picked up a nearby poke. She poked the embers of the fire, there was an outflung flickering of flame when air blew into the dying embers. She gave Cleomenes a momentary stare, seeing the look of defiance in the king's eyes.

"You will decide nothing, King Cleomenes."

"Why are you here?" Andronikos again interrupted, the situation was becoming dangerous and tense.

"I am here for you Andronikos, I have a task for you, you must come with us, a task in which you have no choice," Phryne answered.

There were gasps of surprise, Andronikos stood silent.

Cleomenes, standing in the forefront, thought quick, he was losing control. He gazed at both Horus and Patriach who stood expressionless and resigned, as if they knew the fate that awaited them. From nowhere this whole war had changed. Without doubt, thought Cleomenes, with Patriach and Horus no more in Athens, this was the Spartan's opportunity to attack. Their enemy would be leaderless, confused, unable to fight back. There would not be a greater chance of victory to free Elenoras. Then he saw Phryne glaring at him, in a way that she knew what he was thinking. Then he thought some more, more rational. the Athenians would never free Elenoras without a fight, there were no guarantees that Elenoras would be saved. Then, it occurred to Cleomenes, there was Ares, would the more savage of the gods still fight on the Athenian side? Hades and Ares together? Perhaps even Zeus himself? Cleomenes began to see that his hands were tied. What forces had this abominable Phryne woman unleashed?

Andronikos broke the king's stunned silence. "Come with you to where?"

Phryne turned her attention away from the fire. "Hades will soon wield his destruction upon Athens, Ares also senses blood. If you Spartans attack then you will be defeated, many of the lesser gods will fight beside Ares. If the king here thinks now is a good time to attack the city, then he is mistaken," warned Phryne. "You cannot win, you Spartans are gripped in the fist of Hades." Phryne saw the expression of grim acceptance grind itself into the face of Andronikos, the reality of the situation was plain. "You must come with us Andronikos, we will go to the mountain citadel of Olympus. Either the gods will descend upon Athens, or we go to the gods."

Once more, with an air of bewilderment, there was stunned surprise - this time with complete silence. Shock horror froze the expression of Horus, his horrified face said everything. Patriach stood rigid, it was plain that neither men had no prior knowledge of what Phryne intended.

Cleomenes let his thoughts tumble into confusion, his numbed mind tried to fathom what Phryne meant. Mortal men never dwelt in the absolute realm of the gods.

"If Zeus suspects that I myself might ascend upon his citadel kingdom, then bloodthirsty Ares and his fellow gods might not be so quick to defend Athens," continued Phryne. "They will stay to fight for Zeus. Elenoras and Athens will not be harmed, Elenoras is well able to take care of herself, that is unless I am put to death by Hades or that disgusting beast he covets."

Andronikos was dumbstruck like the rest. There were a few moments of awkward silence. Cleomenes broke the trance-like state.

"What? Are you saying that we Spartans should march on the gods?" he blurted, the exasperated disbelief in his voice plain.

"No, Cleomenes. You and your army will stay here. You will do nothing. Andronikos and Patriach alone will ride with me to the gate of Olympus. And this snake Horus, he is the key to the Thessalon gate that guards these gods who deem to call themselves gods," said Phryne.

"I find you reprehensible. What you say is madness. You are a simple woman," scoffed Cleomenes, his voice incredulous.

Patriach, standing motionless behind Phryne, remained silent, his expression dour. This was now a deteriorating situation that had gone wrong, he realised how the many twists and turns had created a dangerous game. What appeared to be a god wronged by the goddess kidnapped by force to be the scheming god's consort wife, now threatened to mushroom into a conflict far more deadly than any war before - it would not take much to ignite a far greater battle, a war between rampaging city-states allied to either Sparta or Athens. It was a matter of time, thought Patriach, before the pillars of fragile peace tumbled. King Cleomenes was out of his depth, this woman, Phryne, whoever she might be, was the master of this king. Patriach realised with increasing unease that Cleomenes would not tolerate this situation for long.

Horus, who looked beyond miserable, spoke up.

"You are all fools. Stupid fools. The gods play with you like children's toys. The mighty gods do not fear mortal men. Do you think they quiver and shake in fear of you? The gods will rally to the god of the underworld, he is one of their own. The gods are immortal, they are for the rest of time immortal."

Everyone, including Phryne, turned to stare at him.

"The gods are *not* immortal," remonstrated Phryne. "The gods are a creation of Zeus, Zeus took Olympus from the Titans in their long hundred-year war. This conflict you see now was a savage quarrel long before you were even born Horus. It is you who is the fool."

Horus looked horrified. "Are you saying the gods are fools?" he hissed in contemptuous shock, "Zeus? Apollo and Poseidon? Hera and Hermes?"

Andronikos and Cleomenes, their rounded eyes bulging in rigid astonishment, said nothing. Their mystified expressions said everything. Again, there was silence. No one answered Horus, this was uncomfortable ground, unanswerable ground. Phryne looked on with disdain, unmoved, the contempt she held for Horus was plain. Cleomenes turned to Andronikos.

"We must talk, come with me," said Cleomenes in plain voice, after an implausible pause of hushed hostility. Phryne turned her attention back to poking the flames of the fire, seeming unconcerned. Patriach sat himself down, far apart from the miserable-looking Horus.

Both Cleomenes and Andronikos departed to sit alone in the king's adorned goatskin tent. They left Phryne, Patriach and Horus to consume the contents straight from the cooking pot, the eating places set by the two serving maids unused. Before leaving, Andronikos noted that Phryne did not eat.

Once inside the king's tent, Cleomenes looked pensive.

"What do you make of this strangeness?" he asked, the sober tone in his voice making a sound like a waveless quiver.

Andronikos did not reply, he was unsure of what to say.

"This woman is not a woman," continued Cleomenes. "No woman can take men down like this, she must be some demon for what she has done."

"I have seen this woman before," Andronikos responded, choosing his words with unease. "I have seen her lead men like a fiend, men who would have followed her into mountain fires of hell." Andronikos did not elaborate, nor did he tell Cleomenes that he had twice seen her in Spartan camps, that she had in the past saved his life, that he believed his destiny was linked to her fate - more so as this drama unfolded. Andronikos believed that she stalked him for a reason, that her intended confrontation with the gods, confounding as it was, was meant to happen, that he was sure to be immortalised in the ballads and fireside tales that would one day be written.

"Do you not realise who she is? She is the same woman who slew King Xerxes of the Persians," Andronikos added, he did not mention that each time in his life when their paths had crossed, she had not aged one year, nor did Andronikos feel like elaborating upon his concerns about Phryne's open hostility towards the king.

Cleomenes regarded Andronikos with a perplexed expression, it took a few moments for him to acknowledge what Andronikos had said, he knew the campfire stories of the woman who led the Thespian Hoplites, he was desperate to try to piece together all these mind-bending events. "When she first rode in from the city, she mentioned your mother. Tell me, how did she know your mother?"

"I do not know why she said this," Andronikos lied. Cleomenes was beginning to tread on unsteady ground.

Cleomenes saw the evasiveness in his general's expression, the king began to suspect he might be losing the loyalty of his trusted ally. By now Cleomenes realised this ill-thought siege was turning into a dreadful disaster - he felt his uncertainties, how his kingship could be under threat, that at some point he would face a revolt – a not unusual way in which kings ended their reign in not just Sparta. "What are we to do?" he begged.

"We have no choice," replied Andronikos. "You and the army must stay here; you must do nothing. There is now great unrest within the Athenian senate, the general of their army and the holy priest of their temple have both been abducted. Who is now their leader?"

"Without a shadow of doubt, now is the best time to attack their city," said Cleomenes, he thought it ironic the tables were now turned, how it was himself urging a surprise attack, not Andronikos.

Andronikos paused apprehensive. This woman Phryne had changed everything. He felt fear, a fear of being unable to control what was happening, they were like pawns in the ancient Bæctrian battle game played by old men. If Phryne could snatch Patriach from the senate, and take this Horus priest prisoner, then why had she not rescued Elenoras when inside the temple? There was another nagging doubt circling in the old general's mind, it took a few moments of whirlwind thoughts before it clicked. The skirmishers, the Athenian skirmishers. Why was it skirmishers who had attacked the travelling wagons returning from Thessaloniki? The Thessalonian king Aleminis, his weasel of an ambassador, the eunuch who turned up when they were hunting in the hills to tell them the train had been attacked, something did not add up. The Athenian skirmishers were notorious mercenaries, they were thieves rumoured to be in the pay of the prayer-smoking Akropolis priests - they were truculent fighting men not to be trusted who themselves trusted no one, they were men of different ethnic origins – there were even renegade Spartans who fought among these skirmisher bands. Why did the skirmishers bother him? Andronikos squatted, he looked up.

"Do you not see?" said Cleomenes, "I tell you; the tables have been turned. Now it is me who demands we attack without delay."

Andronikos stared into the king's watery blue eyes, his mind still turning, "I must talk man talk with Patriach."

"Yes, you are right," agreed Cleomenes, "I will summon my interrogator, we will make Patriach talk, now that we have him he will tell us everything he knows."

"Torture under pain?" blurted Andronikos. "If you try this then Phryne will kill you, she will drive her sword through you if you even think of it." Andronikos saw that Cleomenes was shocked, not expecting this outright insolence. "Do you not see? Patriach is *not* this woman's prisoner."

It was the turn of Cleomenes to look worried. "We have to know what is happening, our army cannot stay here swimming in this soiled river and feasting out of their cooking pots."

"We have no choice," said Andronikos. "This fool's war is ended. I must talk with Patriach."

Cleomenes froze. "What you say is tantamount to treachery," he barked. "Only me, the king, has the authority to make parlay talk with our enemies."

Andronikos reacted in an instant, ignoring the formal bond between them. "The supreme general of our enemy is here in this camp for insane reasons neither you nor I understand, Patriach is not here to make peace nor to surrender. He is here because he knows we are not his enemy," Andronikos paused to calm his growing anger but could not stop his stupefaction. "These Athenian pigs have never been our friends, but my mind tells me right now there is no victory to be had. To win this war we should have stormed their city the first night our army arrived, if we had done this then we Spartans would be in control of our own destiny. Now there is no way we can win; this brazen woman is right when she says we are defeated."

An interrupting voice. "There is only one way to win."

Both Andronikos and Cleomenes turned together in startled alarm. Patriach stood in the doorway. He was alone. After an uneasy pause, the Athenian general walked to squat beside Andronikos. Cleomenes sensed the hair on his back beginning to bristle. Andronikos was struck silent.

"Do you not see how we Athenians and you Spartans are caught in a god-driven trap?" said Patriach. Both Andronikos and Cleomenes stared. "Phryne is right. We must go to Olympus, the domain of the gods, it is there where this battle must be fought."

"Our esteemed enemy deems it fine to just walk in and join us," Cleomenes glared. What had all this come to, the strangeness of the situation was overwhelming. The king, for a brief moment, considered taking Patriach by force regardless of what Andronikos had said, this Athenian general was the man who ordered the kidnapping of his daughter. But Cleomenes was quick to rationalise his thoughts, he calmed himself down. "Now that you are here, tell me this. What have we Spartans done to you Athenians to deserve this injustice?" the king fought to contain his anger. "We marched our army here because you Athenians took my princess Elenoras captive, you killed both my nephew kin then enslaved the whole wagon train who survived."

Patriach waited a moment, to let the king's anger dissipate.

"Let us talk rational, King Cleomenes, please sit beside me in bondship," Patriach beckoned to the ground beside him, he saw the extreme unease in the Spartan king's expression. "Let us talk temporary truce, we can discuss how we have both been unwise, why we must trust this Phryne when she says we should go to Olympus."

The god Apollo suspected nothing. He lay back upon his golden draped couch, listening to the soft singing voice sung by his nymph-goddess Daphne. The mesmerising music made Apollo relax easier, which is what Daphne in her murderous mood intended. Outside of the stone arched hallway lay the dead python which by now festered and rotted in the intense red hot heat of Olympus, killed by the one hundred arrows fired into its long twisting body by the god Apollo himself - the favourite son of the mighty god Zeus. Daphne knew she needed to be wary, lurking somewhere outside in the laurel bushes was Artemis, twin sister of Apollo, who knew the danger for her beloved brother that lay ahead. Artemis had pleaded in vain with Daphne, she had begged Daphne to spare Apollo even though she knew this could not be done.

"Bring your harp closer, then remove your robes," demanded Apollo to Daphne, "I wish to love your body in the way the two of us know well." The sun, worshipped by Helios from his domain sky high, dipped towards the rugged horizon hewn by molten lava and burning fire. Daphne paused, then continued to play, she made no move to obey Apollo's wishes. Now was near to being the right time.

Daphne knew she must wait, the silver-tipped blade felt less cold now that it had warmed against her flesh, it was the special four-million-year blade, honed and blessed by Hawwāh herself. She saw the anger begin to burn in Apollo's eyes when she did not obey him; this time she did not care, she would take his dreadful beating with the soothing knowledge that everything would soon change; the gods of Olympus would burn in the making of their own hell. Time. It was only a matter of time. Time that would soon descend then come.

In the Athenian hilltop Akropolis there was uproar. Mayhem reigned supreme when the stupefied silence broke into a thousand shattered dreams. The devil-woman had left, with her went both Patriach and Horus, no one had moved to prevent her. Chaos held sway for an uncountable period of time, the destruction of a sense of abnormality complete - no one in the Akropolis temple could begin to comprehend how they had been dismantled and torn down.

After a good while it was the portly Belus who was first to his feet, followed by his baying hordes of sycophant senate followers - even in the inconceivable riotous heat it was clear the senate was confused, they had no understanding of what to do. As a collective it was unruled panic - but a measure of order was restored when Belus bellowed with his booming voice above the madhouse mayhem.

"CALM," roared Belus. "WE MUST HAVE CALM." At first, there was not a great deal of calmness, not one bit, the wild madness was not an emotional moment for sanity. "CALM," he shouted once more, faces wrought with hysteria then turned in his direction. The redness in Belus' cheeks began to grow, his blood vessels ridden by crimson wretchedness spiked with pressure from his fast over-pumping heart. The Akropolis temple grew less chaotic, eager for any form of leadership that might in the late afternoon turmoil prevail.

As the pandemonium subsided, Belus was able to make himself heard. He looked around over two hundred upturned faces wrecked with fear, he sensed this was his crucial moment.

"Senators of Athens, you must listen to me," he implored at the top of his masterful voice. "Now is not the time for defeat," even as Belus thundered, he knew that Athens had been dealt a deadly blow. Both of their charismatic leaders were gone - even if they were about to battle with each other - a victor would have been able to lead them against the Spartans. Now there was just one way out. Belus himself would save the situation, Ares and the gods must be drawn in great haste to their side. The sacrifice of Elenoras was now more crucial than ever it was before.

"Let the gods know we worship them more than they ever desire," howled Belus. The was an abrupt silence in the senate. "We must offer Ares the life of the Spartan king's daughter, then we will have no need for this Patriach or his spineless ways. Our priests who are still here can speak for Horus, let us draw the will of the gods to fight beside us."

As he pleaded for support it dawned upon Belus that nothing that much had changed, in fact, his two greatest adversaries against the senate control he desired had both been forever removed. He right now saw the Athenian assembly there for his taking, the offering of Elenoras on the altar of sacrifice became the deciding factor, everything seemed to have been delivered to him on a plate. Belus began to feel good, his newfound good luck and scheming wherewithal seemed to entwine together, it began to show in his demeanour of growing confidence before the senate - and the senate in their blind oblivious panic, began to take note.

"Bring her now, let us get this deed done," Belus bellowed. "Bring her, bring her NOW," he contorted his face with venom, he sensed the senate beginning to bend to his will, his booming voice echoed above the din of rising support. The two assassins, whose original task had been to bring down Patriach, standing without any cohesion or purpose now that Horus had been taken, at once disappeared with sudden eagerness, they disappeared in the direction of the Akropolis dungeons. Both men descended the stone steps leading underground, the dank-dark air of obscenity rose to greet them as they neared the bottom of the winding stairway, they turned to walk quick, almost at a run, along the dimly lit tunnel cut through the sandstone hill upon which the towering Akropolis stood, the bedlam noise from the senate chamber above subsided into silence. The two guards came to the stone doorway, behind which the captive princess was held guarded by two more permanent dungeon custodians. One assassin guard banged on the door to be allowed entrance, but there was no answer. He banged loud one more time, using the hilt of his sword to maximum effect - perhaps the men inside feared an armed rescue attempt and would not respond - but then the guard saw the door lock already unlocked, he pushed the prison door open.

Both guards stood aghast. There was no Princess Elenoras, only two motionless bodies lying on the cold floor of the dungeon. The guards walked with their swords raised towards the flayed-out lifeless men, they examined each of them and found no visible wounds or signs of how they had died. They saw that one of the dead displayed prominent marks on the side of his neck, two thumbprints in the shape of a rough cross. They turned over the body of the second dead guard, there were no marks or wounds, just the incomprehensible terrified expression etched upon the man's face, it was as if the guard had died on the spot from pure fright which, of course, he had.

Both assassin guards turned to leave, they once more froze dismayed, frightened when they saw the doorway was barred. There was no exit. There was no doorway. There was a blank wall where before there was a door.

In the senate temple chamber, Belus waited with impatience, he had the senators on his side, but the row of priests sat silent. There was still chaos, the Athenian seminary shouted and bayed in eager anticipation, their earlier fear had turned into a frenzied scene of bloodthirsty poison, red wine and pig meat was being passed around from man to man in celebration of their crazed victory. Belus felt an uneasy feeling, he could hold this wild senate in his hands for just a short while, he looked at the priests who stared at him in abject horror, they had not succumbed to his bellowing rhetoric. Where were the two guards with the princess? As the moments ticked by the senate elders drank more wine in uproarious celebrations, Belus began to worry, something was wrong, he felt a sickness grow inside his rounded girth, his ample body trapped inside by the purple robes of high rank. Where were the guards? Where was the princess?

Belus saw the terrified expressions descend upon the faces of the priest sitting a short distance away, the rampant noise of the frenzied senate straightaway subsided into stupefied silence. Belus turned. Then he froze.

In the large open galley that formed the main Akropolis entrance, between four towering rock stone pillars hewn from the mightiest Thessaloniki granite, stood a magnificent god adorned in shining silver armour, his yellow-white hair massing in ringlets that fell from beneath his close-fitting fighting helmet. His tallness was the size of two full-grown men, his round shield of jewelled bronze equal to the greatest shields that the strongest of mortal men could carry. His deadly sword was held in his right hand, pointing downwards towards the floor in defeated submission. Ares, the mighty god of war, stood defiant and bloody, the appalling wound upon his contorted face plain to see. His spectacular polished chest plates were covered in streams of his own blood, the flesh of his right arm shredded in cuts that oozed red wetness, the redness of which was not unlike the rich red wines flowing from jug to jug of the now hushed senate. Ares said nothing, he had nothing to say, not before he could stand to face them no more. The god of war fell to the ground, falling in a heap like a helpless tumble of proud useless life drawing its last breath. Ares fell dead, the great god of war defeated in some forlorn last battle he never thought he could lose.

Belus felt the utmost dread that each of the senate elders and the sycophant priests sensed also. A stillness descended upon the defeated assembly, a morbid feeling of intense doom when you know your enemy will in time kill you, that your life will end in the flash of a moment you will never recollect. The great Akropolis of Athens grew striking pigmented pink and magnificent, the setting sun cast its resplendent shadows upon its tallness built to honour the invincibility of the gods, the intensity of the sunset threw myriads of colours between the enormous pillars of stone. The gloriously carved statues of both gods and all-conquering men, of goddesses and demons of unknown origin stood motionless and unassuming, their thoughtless expressions casting no illusions as to how the citizens of Athens might one more time suffer. The sculptured idols of cold staring stone provided no answers.

"It is going to be a long ride," said Patriach.

The four horse riders made their way across the flat featureless plain towards the distant mountains. It was a slow journey; they picked their road through the rough rocky landscape as the midday sun beat down with relentless remorse, their furrowed brows caked with dirt-burned sweat. Soon they would need to find shelter from the mid-afternoon sun. Horus seemed to be struggling most, he was used to a gentler way of living; he was not coping with the bone-rattling horse ride to where he knew they were heading. Andronikos paused every short while to make sure Horus drank small sips of water. It was not that he was worried about the priest, it was more an instinct honed from making sure his men were fit for fighting battle.

"Yes. Nightfall will bring rest," agreed Andronikos. "Though I worry about how this god-talking friend of yours will make it."

Patriach's expression hardened, "Horus is no friend of mine." The memory of his close call with disaster inside the Akropolis still caused him emotional unease. There was a hint of bitterness in his voice.

Patriach thought about how much he could tell Andronikos, the reasons why Horus was not the priestly overlord who bent to the will of the Athenian senate. Andronikos was his one-time enemy who time and time again probed for more information about what had happened in the temple chamber. Patriach decided he must first test the water before jumping headlong into the quagmire of comrade friendship.

"Did I tell you that my life hung by a thread until the arrival of this woman who now leads us?" Patriach kept his gaze fixed ahead, Phryne rode onwards but Patriach was conscious they each needed to keep a keen eye on the vague outlines of the trail - it was a little used sidetrack. Dust kicked from the hooves of the priest's mount caught the breeze, blowing into Patriach's eyes. He felt apprehensive, Andronikos was his outright enemy though riding alongside him now it did not feel this way. It was a long time since they had fought together side-by-side, twice before they had battled the same Persian enemy - though the chivalrous pride was evident between them even now. Right now, Patriach felt a feeling of comradeship, a grudging friendship; he rode in silence while he tried to work out if their bond was strong enough for the two of them to talk. Because Patriach needed to talk. Little did Patriach know that Andronikos felt the same, the Spartan was anxious to offload in the same way.

"No, you did not. Perhaps it might be the right time for you to say," answered Andronikos with perception, hoping he was correct. Only through talking to Patriach could Andronikos learn what he needed to know. "Perhaps you and I are here for the same reasons," probed Andronikos.

The two grime-encrusted warriors rode together as a conspicuous pair. Not far ahead, choosing the dusty trackway, was Phryne who seemed to be sure of the road towards the distant rising mountain peaks of Olympus. The four mounted riders continued at a slow to moderate pace, Horus in the centre looked miserable, in his way beaten, the temple holy man was convinced the rounded hills on the nearer horizon did not get much closer even after several hours in the saddle. Phryne led the packhorse, she deemed it important enough not to let their supplies risk being lost.

"Yes, it is not common for enemies to join together through common cause in the same conflict," agreed Patriach, "I said to your king, we are all three woven into some freakish web. I believe we have been drawn into this dubious war by a vengeful god for his own reasons... l did not know you thought this," Patriach gripped his horse reins less tight, the tension between them eased. Patriach relaxed.

"I do, though I do not think it is one rogue god. This whole debacle is a strange war of twists and turns, it slithers like a serpent's tail," said Andronikos, half staring ahead. "The god woman who caused this conflict, Persephone, she plays with emotions like a jester without mercy."

Patriach fell silent. Andronikos spoke the truth. Patriach remembered being ripped apart by fires of envy, a gut-wrenching jealousness when he learned of Persephone's bond with the Spartan king, then when the rumoured birth of the king's daughter reached him Patriach was torn, he could see no sound reason why Persephone would give herself to a king who was not a dashing prince or a young regal monarch. Patriach knew Persephone, she would only be willing to give herself up to achieve some meaningful destiny - for revenge against her abductor. Patriach had been in no mood to see reason, he had acquiesced to the abduction of Elenoras when deep down he knew it was wrong, that nothing good would come of it. Within a short time, Patriach realised he had listened to Horus without good sense, the holy man had convinced the Athenian senate it was the will of the gods that Elenoras should die – then Patriach learned from Horus that Hades of the underworld was orchestrating against himself as well as the Spartan king, because of his closeness to Persephone - though never were his affections towards the goddess intimate. There were complex reasons why the Athenian senate had turned against him – Patriach was convinced that Hades and Horus had made it so. More than ever Patriach realised this whole charade was being contrived – and now they were embarking upon a fool's errand, a dangerous venture that would see them all dead.

For what reasons they were making for the mountain realm of the gods Patriach was not sure - but Phryne knew, he was certain of this, she knew what evil was unravelling in the complex world of men. Patriach now rode in deep reflection, his mind turning over long and hard. Patriach thought Andronikos was perceptive, the Spartan general was no fool. Persephone, Elenoras and Phryne? Patriach asked himself - why had

Phryne not attempted to rescue Elenoras when she freed himself from the blood-seeking senate and seized Horus? Perhaps this tragic war was not caused by a vengeful Persephone stirred by her hatred of one god. A nagging thought hung inside his mist-fogged brain, a notion that had no meaning or made sense. Demeter - from his whispered talks with Persephone - things she had said - there was Demeter. A little-known entity among fighting men, a simple undemanding goddess who each year made the crops grow.

"Tell me what happened inside the Akropolis," Andronikos interrupted the flow of wild thoughts remunerating inside Patriach's confused mind. There was an unrestrained germination of friendship in the way Andronikos asked - Patriach, in his confused state, hesitated.

"It is... it is difficult for me to tell you. You are my enemy though I feel there might perhaps be a bond between us," Patriach paused.

"You and I have moved beyond being enemies," said Andronikos. "We are drawn together in comradeship; this battle ahead is far beyond any war with Persian invaders. This war between us, this war drawn against our wiser judgements which we both know is wrong."

"The war or our judgements?" Patriach smiled. He slowed his mount to increase their distance between themselves and Horus, he thought it best to be well clear of earshot. Phryne had drawn further ahead, she seemed unconcerned about Horus.

"Wise judgement was never my strongest virtue," said Patriach. "The morning your army arrived I saw the rider leave through the western gate, then gallop to your camp. Then I learned the horseman was a woman, she overcame two of our guards to escape. At first, I feared this woman was Elenoras herself. When I reached our senate temple to face the mob I sensed the turn of mood in our senator's demeanour, there was a general feeling that we could not win, I saw a fear in their eyes, fear they could not hide," Patriach saw that Andronikos listened with riveted astonishment.

Patriach continued, "The senate had been turned, the fat pig Belus held them in his hand. I intended to propose the release of Elenoras, though I was worried how this would incur the wrath of the gods. Through Horus, the god of the underworld threatened the destruction of the city if Elenoras was not seized, he demanded that she be sacrificed to seduce the goodwill of Ares and his fellow gods, in this way the god of war would defend Athens against you Spartans. But we did not need the fighting sword of Ares, with my best men we would have been victorious against you, I have no doubt of this, but the citizens of Athens were agitated and fearful."

"This war between us is something worse," Patriach kept going, the floodgate had opened, "I think this futile war is a war between resentful gods of the underworld, a war of revenge against your stupid king and myself. Elenoras was salicylic bait to lure you Spartans to our gates, so that both your king and I would perish and our armies diminished by conflict. Both Sparta and Athens would learn not to defile the gods or lay claim to their women. When I learned that Elenoras was the birth child of Persephone's false love for King Cleomenes then I succumbed to Belus and this devious plan of Hades. But I could not countenance the sacrifice of Elenoras, if she is the daughter of Persephone then I could not hurt Persephone like this, I could not deliver Persephone and Elenoras into the evil hands of Hades. Nor could I give up my own life to these gods who desire me dead."

Andronikos was silent, Patriach's description of what happened, from what little Andronikos knew, was true.

"Did you know the horseback rider you described leaving your gate was Phryne?" Andronikos asked, seeing Patriach flinch.

"No... no I did not," Patriach faltered.

Andronikos paused, then decided to ask. "What happened inside your senate? Why did you ride to our encampment with Phryne and Horus?" He tried to make his tone of voice conciliatory, he did not wish Patriach to think he was being interrogated by his enemy which, of course, he was.

"As I said... the senate had been turned, they demanded your king's daughter be sacrificed quick, they wanted to make certain the god of war would fight by our side... they also blamed me for turning Hades against Athens." Patriach struggled, his voice echoing the rampant chaos in the temple embittered with uncertain passion. "The whole charade against me... it was preordained. Then everything happened as swiftly as a chariot's horse, in the blink of an eye."

"What? What happened?" grilled Andronikos.

"She appeared from nowhere."

"Who?" demanded Andronikos, "Phryne?"

"Yes," said Patriach. "The guards moved against me; they had been ordered to detain me. Then she was there, out of nowhere, with her sword at the throat of Horus," Patriach looked Andronikos straight into his eyes. "No man I know could do this. No enemy of Athens could walk into the senate then leave with mighty Athen's two leaders made captive... and she is a woman. Who is she Andronikos?"

Andronikos was silent. What Patriach now described left him agitated and uneasy, almost stunned. His memories of Phryne came flooding back, the vicious war against the Persians, how he had spied her in their Spartan encampments. How she had singled him out. How, in the beginning, she had saved his life.

"We both saw what she did... we both know how she turned the battle of Thermopylae leading her Hoplite warriors..." said Patriach. "And then... the Persian king... this is the same woman who drove her sword into the throat of Xerxes when the Persians thought they had her cornered."

Andronikos did not know what to say. Patriach was right, whenever anyone spoke of what Phryne of the Hoplites did against the Persians, they then fell silent, with an incomprehension that any woman could do what Phryne had done. Andronikos decided to press Patriach more.

"What did this holy man Horus make of being taken prisoner?" he questioned, with a more concerned tone in his voice.

"He knows," Patriach answered. "He knows who Phryne is, there was pure dread in his eyes, dread that was not from the point of the sword at his throat."

"Yes, even now he fears her, I see this. He trembles whenever she speaks with him. His manner is revealing."

"If you talk to him, he might tell *you* something," Patriach yanked on his reins to slow his horse, he desired not to pull ahead of Andronikos whose own horse seemed more in control. Patriach's mount was not his own, it had been provided to him from the Spartan camp, it was more restless and impatient to gallop but they were now all four moving at a slower pace in the scorching afternoon sun. Andronikos offered him a sip of lukewarm water.

"If he recognises her then this tells us something," Andronikos was intrigued, deep in thought. Phryne was closer to the gods than he realised. Her attitude to the gods was without doubt hostile. It niggled him that Horus might know something he did not. Patriach was right, he would do well to find out what this holy priest knew.

Patriach took the water offered to him by Andronikos, he sipped a small mouthful noting that it offered no refreshment, soon they would need to rest under shade but there was no immediate respite from the debilitating heat. Phryne, still riding ahead, did not seem concerned but Horus sat lower in his saddle - he was near done. Patriach felt a growing concern, they must ease up or Horus would not make it. For some unearthly reason he still could not fathom, Phryne needed Horus.

"How is it that you know something of this woman?" probed Patriach.

Andronikos continued to look ahead, unwilling to reply. To answer Patriach would be an acknowledgement of their deepening friendship which for Andronikos would be against his natural instincts. It was unwise to trust your enemy. But Andronikos knew he was treading on unsteady ground, hallowed ground, he felt a bond ship with Patriach, to reveal the truth to him would signify an inner level of camaraderie that Andronikos never gave light-hearted... how was it that Phryne knew his own mother?

"Our paths crossed before Thermopylae," revealed Andronikos, deciding that trust and comradeship with Patriach would be the best way out of this predicament. "She saved my life. I was wounded by a Persian spear on the Marathon plain, in my delirious state I was marked out to die. In my fever I saw her, she for some reason decided it was not my time to cross into the kingdom of Hades, for it is to Hades that I will lose my soul."

Patriach listened, what Andronikos said seemed to make sense - without Patriach understanding why.

"Then, a while later, after she slew Xerxes, I saw her in our Spartan encampment. She was dressed as a camp woman, taking water from the river,"

Patriach listened astonished. "Where? Are you sure? Do you know it was her?"

"Yes, I am sure. She flaked her hair in that strange way she has. When she saw me," said Andronikos, "I believe I was meant to cross paths with her."

"How did she flake her hair?" Now it was Patriach's turn to feel alarm.

"This mannerism she has is beguiling, it is difficult to describe."

Patriach was now more startled, he knew what Andronikos was trying to describe, he knew what Andronikos meant.

Their conversation came to a natural end, during the quiet interlude that followed Andronikos spurred his horse ahead to draw alongside Horus, who looked even more in a bad way. His conversation with Patriach had bothered him, he felt agitated, concerned that he had lowered his guard, the barriers to his inner soul. Horus did not look up when Andronikos pulled beside him, Andronikos offered the priest his flagon of water, Horus took it then drank more than his fair share. Andronikos watched concerned but did not take the remaining water from him.

"You know that we ride to the gates of Olympus," said Andronikos, determined to know more. "Do you know this way? Have you been there before?"

Horus turned to stare at Andronikos, his face death pale, it took a while for him to answer – his tired efforts to control his mount over the rough terrain had taken its toll.

"No, I have not. No mortal man that I know of has been to these gates," croaked Horus. "If we do not die along the way then we will die impaled before the Thessalon gate."

Andronikos pondered about what Horus said. "Perhaps not holy man, maybe our swords will protect us from whatever it is we find there."

"Ha! You are still a fool," sneered Horus.

Andronikos did not flinch, maybe he was a fool he thought to himself.

"Patriach has told me what happened inside your temple. It is interesting how easy you were seized." He said this with deliberate provocation.

Horus did not answer. He cowered lower in his saddle.

"What do you know about this woman who made you her prisoner?" grilled Andronikos one more time.

The priest remained silent, continuing to stare ahead.

"She singled you out for a reason, not just to rescue your commanding general from his own senate. You know something, something that Patriach and I do not."

Still, Horus did not reply, he gazed in the direction of Phryne, who seemed concerned with their unyielding route ahead. There was clear hostility in the priest's mean appearance, a look of intense hatred. What Andronikos did not see was that there was no absolute loathing between Horus and Phryne, it was more a deep mistrust.

"So, you will not talk, perhaps I will leave you to fend for yourself, perhaps you will die of thirst and exhaustion without my help," Andronikos warned.

The effect was immediate.

"I doubt my abductor will allow me to die so easily," hissed Horus. "She needs my help to show the way through the Thessalon gate, without my help we all perish, not just me alone, she has made me her prisoner for a reason."

Andronikos paused, Horus had a point.

"And yes, you are right in what you say," continued Horus, "I think you are a jackass; I know something of this woman that you and your new friend do not. If you wish to know then it might be wise for you to see that I survive."

Andronikos would not be drawn, he realised Horus would reveal nothing of what he knew because this information could perhaps keep him alive. Andronikos thought he would try again later when the toughness of the ride had worn Horus down a little more. Andronikos pulled on his horse's reins to pause, he waited for Patriach to draw up alongside.

"You are right, your holy man is woven into this web and knows more, but he will not say. Perhaps when his tongue is dry, he will talk," said Andronikos.

"Once a snake, then always a snake," Patriach replied.

They rode side-by-side in silence, both of them deep in their thoughts. The afternoon heat began to build, Andronikos himself felt tired and worn, once more the tenacity of the journey tore at his limps and joints in ways he never experienced as a younger warrior – not unlike the punishing march from Sparta to Athens. It was imperative that his three companions did not see how much he was fatigued. He was desperate for nighttime rest just like Horus.

After a long distance, it was Patriach who broke the informal quietude between them.

"When I was a young boy, I dreamed of one day living with the gods in Olympus."

Andronikos smiled. "Many children dream this, it is the same in Sparta," he said. "The boys are princes and the girls princesses. We each have our favourite gods who we worship."

"Perhaps this is our problem, we allow the gods to take privileges to which they should not be entitled," said Patriach. His thoughts drifted back to Persephone.

"Maybe any god that demands worship should not be trusted," said Andronikos.

"Do you think Phryne fears gods like we men?" asked Patriach.

"It seems to me she fears nothing..." Andronikos trailed off, he struggled with the concept that a woman could be more adept than the best of any Spartan warrior. He was troubled, the thought of her for some reason stalking him through his years made him shudder.

"Oh, she has fears," said Patriach. "I talked with her last night, I asked why it was that you and I should be dragged along in this wild conflict against Olympus. She told me, in no uncertain terms, that our two swords would be the thin line between life and death against the three-headed monster Cerberus."

Andronikos gasped, then pulled up his horse, he was at once startled.

Patriach continued to trot ahead, Andronikos was quick to catch him up. "Cerberus?" he gasped. "The three-headed beast of the underworld? It does not exist, Cerberus is folklore and hearsay, that myth is just fireside stories and not much more."

"I think you are wrong my friend," Patriach replied, "Persephone herself warned me this monstrosity exists, it is the plaything of the god Hades, he is its master when it is chained. The monster plagues the underworld and, I tell you now, Phryne fears it."

"And you think we must fight it out with this monstrous Cerberus?" Andronikos was uneasy.

"Yes, it is possible when we reach the Thessalon Gate or maybe before. Horus also believes this, I can tell. Something troubles Horus, I know this man well."

There was a long silent interlude, both men tossed their thoughts around in the cauldron of uncertainty. The afternoon air began to thin as the ground began to slope upwards, but neither of them took much notice of their growing fatigue.

When the sun at last set below the horizon, they had left the great plain behind, they were now on more rugged ground - though they were some distance from the tallest range of the fabled mountains. Andronikos believed it would take them at least another two or three days before they reached the Olympus foothills, but at least they had completed the debilitating journey across the flatland plain where the sun was at its perilous worst. As the ground rose, the midday afternoon temperatures would ease, there would be much-needed shade from the mulberry tree forests through which the little-used trail they followed passed.

In the evening they rested, it was sticky warm, but they lit their cooking fire nevertheless. Nearby a small creek provided much-needed water. Both Andronikos and Patriach bathed themselves in the refreshing cool tributary which originated somewhere in the far-off hills, to rid themselves of the days' grime. Horus took himself straight to a flat rock to lay himself out spreadeagled, his dispirited body wrecked beyond repair. He began his ritual evening chant to, it was assumed, the gods, hoping for help and salvation - until silenced by Phryne.

"Cease your worthless prayers, the god to whom you pray has more to worry about than your obscene troubles," warned Phryne. She was wrong, high on Olympus, Zeus was marking his time, he knew Phryne was coming, that each rising dawn would bring her closer to the gate of his mountaintop citadel. Zeus knew it was not to him that Horus prayed.

In the meantime, Andronikos wondered what they would eat, his meagre supplies of trail food, rice and dates, were running thin - soon they would need to hunt. The salted pig meat he had brought along was beginning to fester in the daytime heat, there was enough to share for one last nighttime meal.

He saw Patriach eyeing him with hunger. "This is the last of our pig meat, it is on the edge of edible. The dates will marinade the poor taste," he told Patriach's hungry eyes. Andronikos turned to Phryne. "You do not cook Phryne, not like the camp women. It is rare to see you eat."

Phryne regarded him with a degree of suspicion, she was not in the mood to be chided. It took her a few moments to respond to his half-hearted challenge.

"I consume my own sustenance, I take what the soil grows, I will not eat the flesh of living life," said Phryne, almost in rebuke. She returned her attention to the cauldron of water that began to boil on the flickering fire. "You men hunt, then your women cook the animal flesh you have killed. You slaughter your cows and pigs, your chickens and goats, you prey on beasts in the same way a lion stalks its victim on the great plains long to the south," Phryne emptied a muslin bag of beans into the pot hanging over the flames, Andronikos did not recognise the beans, nor did he know why she added in the fresh leaves he had seen her taking from hanging mulberry trees as she rode by. Phryne mixed in the dates he passed to her from his own dwindling supplies. What Phryne produced looked good, both Andronikos and Patriach looked on with slight pangs of hunger, they did not relish making their own evening food – and Phryne never offered to prepare it for them. Horus declared that he had no wish to eat. Their packhorse that Phryne led would make their last big meal in the hungry eyes of Andronikos, but Phryne had other ideas.

"Surely you consume meat?" queried Andronikos.

"I have never tasted animal flesh," Phryne answered, "I do not think it right to consume an entity that has life in its veins, all life has the freedom to live."

"Is this why you take leaves from trees and choose plants?" asked Patriach, joining the conversation with keen interest.

Andronikos looked doubtful. "Meat is sustenance, eating the flesh of a beast or bird gives you its strength into your heart," he said.

Phryne stared with distaste at Andronikos. "Forests and foliage are my heritage; my birthright is pure. My forebear came down from the trees to walk tall in the high grass of the grasslands. I eat only what grows from water and rain," said Phryne. "You sapien men hunt, we neanderthal live from the soil."

"What is this strange talk?" demanded Patriach.

There was silence.

"No man came down from the trees... none of our ancestors did this," Andronikos was astonished. "We are told, every one of us, the first primordial deity called Chaos gave birth to all primordial gods, Zeus, Gaia, Tartarus and Eros. We all know this. They created more gods, the Titans, who gave birth to the Olympians, you know this," there was extreme certainty in his eyes.

Patriach nodded in agreement, appearing ill at ease.

"If you believe this then you are naïve," answered Phryne.

Horus, lying spreadeagled upon his rock of stone, listened, then rose to censure. His thin-skinned resolve gave way.

"We both know you have never tasted flesh meat because of the right to life, yet you kill men without compunction," said Horus.

"Yes... and you will be lifeless if my sword finds your throat," hissed Phryne.

Both Andronikos and Patriach sat motionless.

"Does... does it thrill you to think you would be the cause of my death...?" Horus countered, his voice faltering.

"It would be no loss to this world," Phryne remonstrated. "You know much, I know you despise me. I know of your life Horus."

Again, Andronikos and Patriach squatted on their haunches riveted; uneasy in their extreme. Andronikos began to eat his food in resolute silence.

As the half-moon climbed into the star-cluttered sky, small clouds formed that drifted unseen in the insipid dark moonlight. By now the usual swarms of hidden crickets clicked their rhythmic clatter that was quick to build into a crescendo of vociferous mayhem. Andronikos paid no attention, it was as if the ritual choir of the night paled into insignificance when compared to the wild thoughts racing through his mind. Patriach sat in subdued silence – there was little that could be said in the way of meaningful conversation, the hostile atmosphere creating an air of bland disparity. Horus shivered in fear, the night was warm, but his body shook uncontrolled in the shadow of the mental breakdown that threatened to floor him.

Phryne eyed the nearby python, the leathery reptile that had for a long time hidden itself in the remote darkness. The snake was feasting its rounded unblinking eyes upon the ineptitude of the disjointed group staring flat-faced into the flames of the dying fire. Phryne was under no illusion, she knew the tongue-lashing snake was not a leather-bodied reptilian in the real sense, it was a demon of the gods sent to mark their approach to the distant citadel of Mount Olympus. The snake's eyes saw everything though Phryne's quiet calmness bothered the python, which watched Phryne watching it. In time, as the moon climbed higher into the black sky, the snake slithered into the scrubby nighttime grass, glad to be gone from the probing eyes of the woman whom the snake knew would be the cause of endless pain. As the python twisted its way along the remnants of the dried nearby riverbed, it came into its mind who the woman might be.

A long time later, dawn announced itself by way of a hurried flash of colour. The sky was indistinguishable from the surrounding darkness, then, in an instant, it was laid bare. As the sun sneaked its way upwards towards the horizon, the spying snake was caught in the open, it was devoured by the mongoose that stalked it, sensing the smell of the snake's slithering slyness.

The swiftness of the dawning sunrise caught Andronikos by surprise, he was not the first to be awake. Patriach lay under his sleeping blanket with his eyes closed tight, he was still fast off recovering from the intense fatigue of the previous day. Horus was buried deep under his own covering shroud, curled in the foetal position that seemed to ensure his nightmare survival – as yet he had no inclination that a new miserable day had descended upon him.

At first, Andronikos saw no sign of Phryne, but then vague movement in the shadows caught his eye. He spied her bathing in the cool waters of the meandering creek, he caught his breath in uncontrollable fascination. In the less than half light, the silhouette of her slim naked body stripped away any resourcefulness that made Andronikos rise each morning with determination to see the new day. He saw that Phryne portrayed no muscular form; he was surprised that she did not possess the warrior physique that made her so lethal. Andronikos gazed upon a beautiful young middle-aged woman, a woman whose body did not seem to be ravaged by time, her form did not set out to lure any man that he could think of.

Andronikos also noticed that Phryne's sleeping place had not been slept in, then he realised with stark surprise that perhaps she did not need to sleep in the way he and his fellow male travellers did. Andronikos squatted on his haunches to poke the embers of the night fire, it stuttered into life to which he then added a few sprigs of wood. The fire burst into a flamboyant flame to boil water for their communal breakfast, the first meal of what could be an exceptional hard day.

The day was pretty much a repeat of the one previous, except that Andronikos spent more time keeping Horus from dropping from his saddle. Phryne led the way with Patriach close behind holding the reins of the packhorse, whose load was lessening as time went by. They picked their way through more hilly ground as the great plain receded far behind.

Time passed slow, Andronikos noticed the smiling conversations between Phryne and Patriach, undoubted there was some unenforced solemness growing between them, a form of budding camaraderie that Andronikos guessed had arisen from Patriach's survival through Phryne's precocious intervention in the Akropolis temple. Their bondship was there - and Andronikos felt slight pangs of envious jealousness, a feeling he could not fathom until he dismissed it with irritable contempt.

During the slow hot afternoon Andronikos once more drew up alongside Horus, he passed the priest a whole flagon of fresh water which Horus drank with his usual abandon. Andronikos had by now given up on the idea of making Horus talk, the holy man was a stubborn mule who would die before he revealed what he knew about Phryne. Horus passed back the leather jug empty - it was good that Horus was drinking thought Andronikos.

"You know she is only half human," croaked Horus unexpected. His voice seemed forced, tinged by his fight for survival.

Andronikos looked at Horus, surprised, unsure how to respond.

"She is a curse against the gods," Horus added, after taking a few more mouthfuls of water.

The two of them continued to ride alongside, a tense silence between them.

"So, you know this woman," interrogated Andronikos, breaking the awkward moment.

Horus paused in deep thought, he at last sensed that his life expectancy might be in the hands of Andronikos. "Yes, but we have never before set our eyes upon each other," he whimpered.

"Then tell me what you know," demanded Andronikos in a cajoling voice.

Horus once more became hesitant...

"If I know what you know, then perhaps I can help you," said Andronikos.

"Do you think I am an idiot? You, you cannot help me..." Horus stuttered, he held his horse reins tight. "You are my enemy, why would you help me?" Horus for some reason appeared less resentful, there was a subtle pleading in his voice.

"Right now, we are not enemies. We ride together into the jaws of adversity," suggested Andronikos.

"Do you see ahead? How easy they are together?" said Horus, teasing.

Andronikos again saw Phryne and Patriach in relaxed conversation, Horus had made his point with persuasive accuracy - like an arrow hurtling direct to its intended target. But Andronikos was not to be baited.

"Almost like half-brother and sister, eh?" Horus left his suggestive comment hanging in the air. He straightaway saw the uncertain expression set itself deep into the brow of Andronikos. His arrow bolt had found its mark.

Andronikos froze. The incredulous thought remunerated around inside his consciousness. There was nothing he could think of to say, what Horus said did not make sense. Or did it? Perhaps it did make sense. Something else also... Andronikos was all at once thunderstruck by an instinctive notion that for some reason made him feel sick in the pit of his stomach. Persephone? Once more her invoking name hung inside his reeling awareness.

Then, in the blink of his eye, something half clicked. It came together like a million pieces of a tantalising broken mirror - with a few pieces still missing, a reflection cascading into a time-shattered pattern upon the uneven stone ground – a mirror that tumbled together in a rough perfect form to reflect what should have been obvious from the absolute beginning.

The evening began to turn into the third night as the four riders twisted and weaved through towering boulders of the sun-torched badlands. Neither Patriach nor Andronikos had been in this hostile terrain before, the mountain foothills were unfamiliar to both of them because never had either Sparta or Athens coveted this sparse land of nothingness. Horus himself never wandered far from the mighty walls of Athens - but this had not always been the case.

Andronikos remained in contemplative silence, preferring his own company since the taunting remark by Horus. He fell behind the others, his concentration often wavering and waning – more than once he had to pick his way back to the thin-marked route that was visible in places due to his travelling companions treading the trail. Meanwhile, his mind turned over and over like a stone wheel spinning of its own accord. Everything might now fall into place, every single significant event since the Persian war that involved himself, his king and the formidable Spartan army. What cretins they had been, he thought to himself, he had suspected that something did not add up. Now the mists of divine revelation were clearing, Andronikos needed time to think, he must decide what to do. First, he thought to himself, he must talk with Patriach because it dawned upon Andronikos that Patriach was bound in some familiar bondship with Phryne. It did not take long for Andronikos to work out why his adversary had little idea there was a riveting reason why Phryne had intervened in the Akropolis to save his life.

Then, from nowhere, there was an abrupt startling cry that split the sunset interlude. "Aaahuooo..." The melodious wail over and over was like nothing Andronikos had before heard, parting every hair on his tired perspiring body. His spine shivered in the shimmering heat, trembling like a reverberating stone hammer struck against cold iron. All four of them halted in stupefied alarm, Phryne's pinpricked ears vying in vain to locate the direction of the sound and the perpetrator of the tragic voice. Her face was awestruck by intense panic - as if she was aware of what the painful cry of grief meant. She cajoled her mount forward, quickening its pace though still on the same faded trail that led upwards through the ancient rockfalls of the tumbled cliffside. Patriach followed though Horus paused, hesitating until overtaken by Andronikos who goaded his horse to follow Patriach. Horus then followed in the rear, taking the reins of the forgotten packhorse almost as an afterthought. Phryne pulled ahead, picking her way, then she paused. Phryne seemed near to panic, fighting to regain her composure.

Andronikos, Patriach and Horus caught Phryne, each of them could hear gentle womanly sobs close by, behind the boulders to their right. Phryne led the way. They rounded the tall rocks to find an aged woman kneeling in the twilight of the rising moon, she squatted over a mound of new-heaped stones which to each of them was without doubt a burial grave. The woman cried, wailing in tears before realising the riders were there. The woman saw Phryne, Phryne dismounted to run - to take the emotional woman in her arms.

The three men sat quiet on their mounts, unable to comprehend this unexpected event. They were each mesmerised by the whole scene laid out before their perplexed eyes, to Andronikos it was clear the two women were known to each other, but who was it that had died and was then buried in this badlands wilderness? There was just enough rising moonlight for the shadowy assemblage to break the nothingness of the long past sunset, it would be a long and difficult night for which Andronikos and his two male companions were unprepared.

For Patriach a feeling of dread enveloped him without him at first knowing why. A gut feeling of fear invaded his consciousness, an awareness of impending doom spread through his bones when he saw Phryne turn to stare at him in horror. This was a different Phryne, a Phryne who straightened herself erect in defeated dejection which in the gleaming starlight delivered a moment of intense sorrow. Patriach dismounted, he climbed down from his mount in the same dispirited anxiety, giving his horse reins to Andronikos. Before Patriach walked the short distance, he was struck with dread, his suspicions grew even greater when he guessed that it was Demeter who kneeled facing the rough-dug grave of heaped stones covering the slave-like burial mound. The way Phryne gazed at him, deep in her anguish could mean just one thing.

"A family burial eh," whispered Horus to Andronikos, who spun his confused head to glare at Horus.

Horus sat in his saddle with an expressionless air of non-existent concern. The intense fatigue that wracked his whole body prevented him from saying anything more, but there was nothing more he could say. Horus was not sure who had died and was buried, but it did not take much thought for him to guess. The gods had taken their first-cut revenge, of this Horus was certain, because he could see the distressed anguish that beset Demeter and Phryne. When Horus saw Patriach fall upon the grave of heaped-up stones, when he saw Phryne tell Patriach whatever it was she said, the Akropolis priest watched a thin expression of insane dread spread across Patriach's parched split lips. It was not an appearance of revengeful hate - it was a look of deranged foreboding when the Athenian general realised everything was now way above all their heads. With Persephone dead, it could mean just one thing - a head-to-head conflict far beyond a simple war between two squabbling armies of men.

When Ares, the god of war, fell to the ground with his godly life extinguished, Belus and the senate stood like statues in their stupefied shock. The thunderless silence of the mass gathering of men was like the empty solitude of sun-charred wilderness, where not one thing moved to make the smallest sound, where nothing scurried or ferreted around in the dirty grime of conquest. Their senses reeled in abject horror when they each saw their one hope of salvation lying dead before their bulging frog-eyed eyes. When the mist of their inept bewilderment began to fade their trembling fear intensified and stiffened, the senate then froze in confusion when they saw the princess Elenoras standing upon the marble sacrificial alter defiant, her whole right side and short-bladed sword smeared in the thick red blood that moments before had flowed through the pulsating veins of Ares. The mighty god of war lay slumped, dead and defeated, his victor young, hostile and victorious.

"This city-kingdom of Athens is mine," Elenoras echoed loud in menacing rebelliousness, the hushed silence offering nothing in return. "You are in my bastard hands Belus; this senate of spineless men belongs to me."

There was a moment of movement, a momentary fraction of hope when the Akropolis guards attempted to respond, their trained resolve being the first element of bravery to recover from the fearfulness of these unscriptural events – but from the double-doored entrance, more armed men burst through. Athenian skirmishers. Straightaway the ragged ragtag skirmishers disarmed the Akropolis guards, threatening each of them to drop their weapons while forming a protective circle around the triumphant Princess Elenoras. The guards were no match for the band of merciless mercenaries and disloyal insurgents, men who right now bore no allegiance to the disenfranchised senate.

In the time it took for the sundial to make a shadow that timed a tiny fraction of daylight, the victory of Elenoras was complete. The mercenaries strengthened the ring of sharp steel around her, their swords pointing outwards on the smallest chance that Athenian swordsmen might themselves try to intervene – but nothing happened. Each Athenian commander throughout the city was under the same threat of a skirmisher blade - the Athenian army's supreme commander Patriach was nowhere to be found; skilfully removed by the warrior of unknown origin called Phryne – the headless Athenian army was no threat, the senate leaders now a blunt instrument of frightened rats. Athens, in the blink of an eye, had fallen.

It did not take long for Andronikos to realise that Horus was his one debatable ally. Patriach, Phryne and now Demeter seemed to be bound in some mystifying human attachment, they had cemented an alliance that was quick to solidify as nighttime ticked by. Horus, reacting in his usual devious way, reached out, determined to touch the raw open nerve.

"Now it is just you and me eh," he mocked with a disparaging smile.

"Quiet," barked Andronikos. "You will not snide me with your com-ments." Andronikos, though, took in everything he saw - events were turning beyond his realm of comprehension.

"The wheel of fate is turning my Spartan friend, I fear you will soon learn more than you bargained for," sniggered Horus, curling his lip with contempt. "You will see."

Andronikos ignored the denigrating remark by Horus, he had no choice. "Who is it that lies there buried?" He felt himself shudder, Andronikos was disturbed that Patriach and Phryne were in deep shock.

"The wrinkled woman kneeling beside the burial mound is the goddess Demeter, though I have never seen her in this human form," breathed

Horus, keeping his voice low. "She is the mother of Persephone, also the mother of Phryne who is the bane of my life." Horus expected this hammer-like thwack to strike Andronikos well under his belt.

Andronikos spun around incredulous. "Phryne?"

"Yes," smiled Horus. "Did you not know this?" The shock that froze the horrified expression of Andronikos confirmed to Horus that he did not. The holy priest was beginning to relish his mastery over his Spartan captor - this might be the unforeseen opportunity he could exploit.

Andronikos sat in his saddle in clouded confusion, despite that, in his mind, it all added up. Unknown to Horus, Andronikos had suspected an intriguing link. In fact, Andronikos, after the initial shock of Horus telling him that Phryne was joined by blood to Persephone, felt more assured; the Spartan felt that his whirling instincts had not let him down - his wild haunches were proving correct.

In the half moonlight, Horus feasted his spear-like eyes on the stricken grief of Phryne, Patriach and Demeter. "Seeing their overwhelming heartbreak, it appears that someone we know is buried there. It might be Persephone herself who is laid in this grave of heaped stones."

Andronikos stayed silent. He did not know Persephone, he had never laid eyes upon her but, if it was, then a catastrophe of enormous magnitude was now unfolding.

Phryne, Patriach and Demeter were in deep emotional conversation by the graveside. Patriach appeared both serious and grim. Now and then, every once in a while, he held his head in his hands. Andronikos decided it was best to leave them alone, he did not relish any involvement in these matters that grew more complex and difficult by the passing hour – he suspected that his budding comradeship with Patriach was compromised.

Patriach stood, then strode over to join Andronikos and Horus. The night was now past midnight, no one had much desire for sleep.

"Andronikos, I think it would be good for you and me to talk," said Patriach, in the darkness, Andronikos could see his Athenian adversary was ashen-grey faced.

"What about him?" replied Andronikos, pointing to Horus.

Patriach paused, thinking.

"I have no concerns if Horus hears what I have to tell you," said Patriach. "I suspect this dog knows much of what I will say."

Horus interrupted, "I am not a cretin... we all know who is buried there. And that is the goddess Demeter who grieves alongside the stone grave."

"You are in no position to offer your opinions," snapped Patriach. "No one here is interested in what a snivelling priest has to say."

The offended look on the priest's face showed his displeasure. "You think so? Well, think of this while you at last learn what is happening... perhaps my guards in the Akropolis were there to spirit you away, not to seize you..." Horus let his comment dangle.

Patriach looked at Horus, the Athenian general did not admonish him in a way that signified defeat.

"Is this true?" Andronikos turned to Patriach.

"I do not know," Patriach replied, "I suspect soon we will find out."

"What is happening?" Andronikos demanded. "Who has died and is now buried? Who is this woman who grieves? If we know this then perhaps we can fight our way out of this plight, then we can talk about what happened in your Akropolis temple."

"There is no way out Andronikos. We are in something far greater than a squabbling war between Athens and Sparta. This is not a simple fight to the death demanded by the god of the underworld Hades because of the abduction of some king's daughter."

Andronikos knew that Patriach was right, these complex chains of extraordinary events were linked.

"Uh... First, I think you should tell Andronikos everything, not just what you choose to say," grunted Horus to Patriach.

"Yes, I will," Patriach responded. "But how much do you know first." It was not a question, more of a pointed accusation - Patriach looked shaken and death faced.

"Did you know that Persephone was of Demeter's blood?" demanded Patriach to Horus.

"I knew our crops did not grow for one whole summer when Persephone was taken by Hades. Demeter did this, she was the goddess consumed by grief," Horus answered.

Patriach studied Horus, he had, with skill, evaded his question. "Demeter's grief is not grief, it is more anger and warlike," said Patriach. The nighttime fire began to take hold as Andronikos fed it more tinder-dry wood, it flared in defiant rebellion. Patriach once more pressed Horus, "Do you know why Persephone cultivated her bond with King Cleomenes?"

"Yes, for revenge against Hades. And because Elenoras is no simple princess of their lovemaking," Horus was endeavouring to give Patriach a difficult time, his self-protective instinct came to the fore. "I will tell you this, it is Demeter who commands the Athenian skirmishers. That loathsome band of mercenaries did not seize the young princess, not in the way you both believe," Horus glared at Patriach, relishing the perplexed expression that appeared on his face.

"As you know," Horus continued. "When Hades threatened the destruction of Athens it was first agreed by the senate that a company of Athenian cavalry would seize the Spartan king's daughter, I myself suggested to Belus how the skirmishers might be the wisest choice. This god Hades is a stupid fool, but Belus and his senate are more stupid. Hades has the power to destroy Athens, he made promises to Belus that Ares would fight by their side if the senate saw to sacrifice Elenoras. Zeus himself wanted Elenoras dead. Hades and Belus were lured into this idiotic threat, they were easily tricked into bringing the army of King Cleomenes to the gates of Athens. Hades demanded the seizure of Elenoras in the exact way that Demeter and Persephone knew he would, how they planned all along. Hades was deceived into thinking that you were the lover of Persephone, he does not yet know you are linked by stronger bonds than simple love. The fat fool Belus, he ordered the skirmishers to seize Elenoras when the skirmishers were already in the pay of Demeter. I knew this... does this answer your question? Elenoras is the daughter of Persephone, Persephone is the daughter of Demeter."

Andronikos' face contorted with shock; the final pieces of the broken mirror were beginning to fall into place – though not all. Yet more revelations of which he and his magnificent army of Spartans were unaware. It dawned upon Andronikos that Cleomenes had been deceived, the king did not know that his daughter Elenoras was never taken by force. Her two cousins died in their attempts to save her. But why? And then there was Phryne...

"What about Phryne? Do you know more of Phryne?" barked Andronikos to Horus.

"Only that she is the daughter of Demeter, the sister of Persephone."

Patriach and Andronikos, with open mouths, stared at each other. Andronikos of the two was dumbstruck, Patriach less so, Patriach himself knew more but to Andronikos this was a sinister development – and Horus was quick to note the deep uncertainty in the Spartan's eyes.

"Why does Phryne always threaten you?" demanded Patriach, he knew that if Phryne was the daughter of Demeter, then this opened a dreadful pit of worms. He tried to steer his questioning away from Phryne's origins.

"Phryne's hostility towards me is long and complicated my friend. I know Phryne's and Persephone's heritage when Hades does not, also that both are of your blood. And do you know what this means? Have the two of them told you?"

Andronikos, listening, realised the horrible truth, something close to what he had suspected all along. He sat beside the crackling fire motionless, with his head now buried in his soot-stained hands. Patriach was related by birth to Persephone, he was not the rival lover that Cleomenes believed and often talked about. For some extraordinary reason even Patriach had not known he was blood linked to Persephone, he had learned of his patronage to Demeter only a few moments before - when talking with Phryne and Demeter beside Persephone's grave. This was why Patriach looked like death, why his face was contorted with deep pain. His life had fallen apart.

It occurred to Andronikos how the armies of Sparta and Athens were being used to fight not each other, but to fight the gods themselves. Sparta was by now under Persephone's control, this realisation by Andronikos raised just one question - how could Athens be defeated with Ares and Hades by their side?

"What is your part in all of this Horus?" Patriach demanded. "Explain to both of us sat here now what you know," the extreme trauma was beginning to wear Patriach down.

Horus looked dour, in a way that he wanted to avoid the conversation. Phryne and Demeter watched from a distance; they knew the talk that was taking place between the three men. Phryne's stern expression left Andronikos in no doubt that she was not pleased with this turn of events, Demeter seemed distant, her fearful distress strewn across her face. In the dim moonlight, Andronikos thought she looked human, not in any way a goddess of the gods should look, she oozed grief in a way that involved no tears, the wretched meditative look of a woman whose daughter had been slain.

Horus remained silent for a good while, longer than he wished - in a way that showed he was trying to decide how this fragile conversation should go.

"You ask what I know, I will tell you," he said. "From the beginning you should have known what I will explain to you, perhaps then you will understand what is happening. I am not on the side of the gods, nor the side of Demeter and Phryne. I am on your side, we are all three caught between two hardstone rocks," Horus twisted his hands together in an uncertain reaction; a reflex mechanism upon his body ravaged by physical abuse on this endless journey, coupled with his life of unforgiving sobriety living as a holy priest. By nature's rules, he was thin and pale - now he carried the weight of the wretched world upon his bony shoulders.

Horus raised his eyes to look up to them both, his voice was hesitant. He had not planned this, but these two naive fighting warriors would soon be at the mercy of unredeemed powerful gods. If they survived, then his chances would be improved.

"This world of gods and devils was formed in a way you cretins cannot imagine," began Horus, knowing they would never believe him. He would shake their beliefs to the core. "The world you think you know was not made in seven days, nor in ten thousand days, the making of mortal existence took an unthinkable forever. The whole world, the moon, the sun and the stars in the night sky were formed not by one god, but from pulsating gas and lava, the world was made from the fire of a thousand volcanoes and of a hundred million earthquakes. The beginning was not like ancient scriptures tell us, men were not created in the image we see now," Andronikos and Patriach listened, both tried to look sceptical, but they were for some reason spellbound. Horus was well aware that both their minds would challenge what he would tell them. Andronikos, trying to appear nonchalant, added more wood to the fire, at the same time half noticing that Phryne and Demeter were making some form of ritual prayer over the grave made by Demeter – it seemed to him they were in a distant trance-like state. Andronikos then glanced at Patriach, whose face was drained - his emotions were trying to come to terms with the naked truth that Persephone was now dead. Patriach was deathly pale though he glared at Horus in disbelief.

"Who told you these untruths? How do you know this lie you tell us?" Patriach challenged, what Horus claimed did not make easy listening - more so since hearing the mind-twisting revelations about his birthright. "This is not what the gods and you holy men have us believe."

"You must first understand your heritage," said Horus to Patriach. "Then you will know who the gods are and how they behave. The gods are not who you believe they are."

"Tell us more," urged Andronikos. "You must tell us who you are, then we will listen to what you have to say."

"Look at me. You see I am unlike you fighting men," replied Horus, "I am not like you." He fidgeted; he again twisted his hands in nervous anticipation. Patriach, opposite, sat rigid.

"Look at them," Horus pointed over to Phryne and Demeter. "What do you see," Andronikos and Patriach continued to gaze at Horus. "You see two women, two women who are unlike any woman you have ever set your eyes upon," he said, "I tell you; both are not like any woman you know. Both are the same blood-root as me."

"I do not understand what you say. What do you mean? First, tell us why they despise you," Andronikos threw down his gauntlet. He needed to know everything.

This time it was the turn of Horus to look ashen-faced. "Like I say to you, look at my skin. It is pale and white," he said. "This is because my ancestral origin originates from the north, this is why my skin is not like yours. Because I come from a forest land of ice and cold. Demeter, and more so Phryne, are wary of me because I see things, I see their past, I see their future... in ways you cannot imagine. I know their heritage, because in the land where I was born there is a great stone, a written tablet stone, a monolith that was formed at the beginning of time, when the world was only fire and water. It was there, there in this place the heritage of Demeter came into being, where she first walked upon a new land of soil and water. She was never called Demeter then, she is only Demeter now, because she has used many names. First, the Neanderthal men called her Hawwāh, or in the far-off lands of Abraham and Moses to the east, Havah, Hyvah or Eva. One day men from the north will call her Eve."

Andronikos and Patriach began to feel overwhelmed, Andronikos tried to think, but he did not know what to say. All of his beliefs, his understanding of the gods, his reason for existence were threatened with every lying sentence that Horus uttered. He felt himself shrinking back towards the flickering flames of the all-consuming fire.

"Listen to this, I tell you, Demeter and Phryne, they do not despise me, they are afraid of me," Horus continued, seeing the dazed eyes of Andronikos and Patriach. "I know Phryne's birth... and I also see her death," he declared after a nervous pause, "I know her life, I know how she will die. Like Persephone died, who was torn apart by the monstrous beast that Hades keeps by his side. Like Demeter's first daughter Lasonas once died, at the hands of one savage god who did not wish the female child to survive. I know who Demeter is. This is why I am here, why Phryne seized me with her sword at my throat from the temple."

"How do you know she will die?" demanded Patriach. Andronikos was silent, everything Horus said seemed to make no sense. But for some reason, it all felt real.

"Because female births descended from Hawwāh, they do not survive.

They are hunted down like vermin, like rats," Horus answered.

"By whom?" demanded Patriach. There was fear in his eyes... if he was the half-blood of Demeter then...

"By the god Zeus, except Zeus is not Zeus."

"What?" exclaimed Andronikos. "What are you saying?"

Horus began with what they might know, the fortitude of the occasion meant there was an improved chance of his survival...

"Zeus created this world of the gods when he took Olympus from the Titans, then he gave each of the Titans patronage favours," said Horus. "Zeus is Gabriel, Gabriel is the vassal of the Lesser Lords, Lords who took this world from Hawwāh. Both these lords and Zeus fear Hawwāh, they fear her heritage who have the will of mind to ravage the world that Zeus creates.

"Other men like you, a long way to the east, believe their Lord created this world in seven days before making man in his own image. Their prophets teach that from the rib bone of a man they call Adamah this lord created woman though it was never like this," Horus continued, the sweat on his brow glistening in the growing moonlight. "In other more distant lands men believe in different gods, each one procreated by Gabriel to spread his dominance through menkind. The truth is different, the truth to you is frightening, it is too fearful for you to behold."

"What is this truth?" demanded Andronikos. Andronikos listened, Andronikos knew what the truth would be. Andronikos began to suspect that everything he believed was wrong. He did not know who he was.

"Races of palaeolithic peoples, they were the primitive seed from Hawwāh, four-limbed beings who descended from the trees to walk biped in the grasslands. They changed, they evolved, they conquered the land by living from what the land grew. The neanderthal were the strongest, they were the more numerous of the prehistoric peoples in a way that Hawwāh nourished them. When Gabriel came to this world, he nurtured meat-eating sapiens who killed for their meat, he made it that his people vanquished the neanderthaloid by cultivating sapien savagery, they took neanderthal women to procreate their race through domination. Gabriel conquered the world for his Lords in this way,"

"Who are these ancient people, where are they?" asked Patriach, his thoughts in rampant full flow.

"These palaeolithics died, they were wiped out by the violence of sapien men. Few pure descendants of Hawwāh survive."

"Are these descendants only women?" asked Andronikos.

"Pure descendants, yes," said Horus. "They exist, they have learned to evolve their form, they know how to survive. There are men who carry the blood of both, these men are few but they are good men. My tribe of northern men are less pure, we have not their strength or will of mind, but we know the ways of these palaeolithic people. We try to protect their heritage though we do not worship them."

"Where are these men with this blood within them?" demanded Andronikos, he stared hard at Patriach.

"Two are here now, they sit beside this fire," declared Horus.

"Me?" Andronikos gasped.

"Yes. Why do you think Demeter saved you? When you lay wounded in your cot at the battle of Marathon," Horus answered.

Andronikos sat open-mouthed astonished. "But that was Phryne... it was Phryne who cared for me," he blurted.

"It was both, Demeter came to save you then said to Phryne to watch over you," replied Horus.

"Why?" Andronikos gasped.

"Why?" answered Horus, "because your birth mother was pure palae-olithic, your father was a sapien god. You have the warrior strength of your mother, the piercing eyes of your mother, not those of your father... your father was a much-feared god, he was no neanderthal, he never had good blood within him."

"Why were the wounds of Andronikos cared for in this way, why was he saved by Demeter?" interrupted Patriach, suspecting the answer.

"Because we are here now in this place for one reason, to defeat the gods. Demeter and Phryne have the will to destroy Olympus."

"What?" exclaimed Patriach, Andronikos though remained silent.

"Gods will fight men, men fight men," said Horus. "Your swords are the best, the most powerful Demeter can wield against them, more so against this terrifying beast Cerberus. Hades is a fool; he does not know what revenge he has unleashed."

Andronikos did not speak, he was in deep thought, his mind tumbling over and over. What Horus said made him feel nauseous, though every-thing made eerie sense. He was the strongest warrior in Sparta, something which made him stand out among the many fearsome fighters Spartan culture produced. He knew he was different, why he had risen through the legions of men to command the greatest Spartan army.

His thoughts raced back to the day when Phryne had ridden out of Athens to confront the Spartans, when she had glared at him in that intense way that was now the curse of his life. When she had said he had the familiar look of his mother. Of course, she had said this, her words were meant to defeat him, to deal him a knockout blow before he could intervene. It had worked, he suffered a debilitating blow far worse than any sword strike – and Phryne had said this because she knew his mother. What Andronikos did not know was that he was wrong, Phryne had no wish to defeat him, she had no desire to force him to the ground in confrontational conquest. His mother never did die in the process of childbirth. His mother had been savaged, raped by his brutal father Cronus, violated before her act of giving birth – Demeter herself had delivered Andronikos from his dying mother. Horus knew this - but Phryne would pierce his throat if he breathed one word to Andronikos.

Andronikos once more sat with his head in his wretched hands. The fire roared in rampant flame from the excess of wood that Andronikos had thrown upon it, an uncontrollable reflex action from listening to Horus relating uncomfortable, rational explanations of how the world and this war were so. The rampant glow of the blaze spread wide from where the three of them sat, at the outer rim of flickering radiance Phryne and Demeter talked, the two of them shielding the piled-up stones of the burial grave. Beyond the ring of firelight, there was complete darkness, the moonlight was lost in the ripple of flames, the uneven landscape of boulders and escapements created its own intrigue in terms of shadows and hidden chasms.

In the far distance, the foothills began to climb higher until the majestic peaks of the Olympus range broke through the silvery nighttime clouds. Here Zeus stood defiant and disturbed, he knew that Demeter and Phryne were coming; he knew why, feeling a degree of uneasy satisfaction that when the new day came the terrifying three-headed beast Cerberus would be lying in wait. Cerberus had by this time torn and savaged the fearful goddess wife of Hades, but Zeus knew how Persephone's death alone would not be enough. Tomorrow, Cerberus, concealed in deadly ambush, would complete his task.

Phryne stood, then walked over to where Andronikos, Patriach and Horus sat beside the roaring fire. A little of her belligerent swagger had gone, right now she seemed more womanly female, a degree of worrying compassion replacing the outright bellicosity that sounded in everything she said and did.

"Andronikos - Demeter and myself would like to talk," Phryne made it sound like an empathetic impassioned request.

Andronikos stood without saying anything, then walked with Phryne the short distance to where Demeter sat, he had never before set eyes on Demeter. The ageing general was shocked.

Demeter's eyes were her first physical feature to appal him, they sent his senses reeling. A deep, deep greyish blue, they were unlike any human eyes he had set his own eyes upon, even in their blueness they projected fire animalistic in their intensity - intelligent primate-like eyes were his first instinctive thoughts but, even so, they were like no primate eyes Andronikos had seen. Demeter was pure goddess - but then she was not, Demeter was something else. She looked deep into his face, then her snake-shaped forked tongue lashed out like a serpent's flicking tail, probing him, sensing the atmospheric vibrations around him. Then, right before his eyes, she softened, Demeter transformed herself in a way not unlike a chameleon lizard, she metamorphosed herself by recasting her entire image, turning herself into something more subtle and appealing.

Andronikos stood transfixed, he felt his blood run cold.

"Come. Sit..." urged Demeter. Phryne squatted beside her. Andronikos moved to squat beside Demeter.

"It is going to be a long night," said Demeter, "I have good reason to tell you why you are here."

Somehow Demeter appeared less radical in her appearance, there were hints of great age but even this was fading. She was dressed in a loose grey robe, in the time it took for Andronikos to relax his disposition Demeter became more human, she took the form of a gentler woman, but she retained her palaeolithic aurora that impressed Andronikos with its subtle power and strength. "Relax, you have nothing to fear from myself or Phryne."

Andronikos sat beside the pile of stones that formed the burial mound. He could still feel the heat of the roaring fire a short distance away, he saw Patriach and Horus even now in deep argumentative conversation, Patriach using his hands to emphasise some point he was trying to make.

"We have talked with Horus," said Andronikos, beginning their conversation with a good deal of uncertainty. "He has told us much."

"Do not believe the lies he tells," Phryne responded, the flickering light of the nearby flames formed small shadows upon her perfectly featured face. "He is in the hands of Zeus, Horus always wishes to know what you know, he will tell you untruths to get it. Do not even begin to trust him."

Andronikos studied Phryne and what she said, it did not make sense, making everything more confusing. "What he has told us about where you came from beggars belief, it cannot be true," he answered.

"Then do not believe it," replied Phryne.

Andronikos ignored her, he had no choice. "He told me about my mother, about her bloodline," Andronikos became forthright, feelings of determination began to well up inside. The moonlight emphasised his craggy features and his grim outlook.

Phryne looked angry, Andronikos saw her stiffen, he had touched a raw nerve. He decided to press on, he needed to know more.

"Horus told me you both knew of my mother. You must tell me the truth;

how can this be possible?"

There was a silent pause, Phryne looked across to Demeter who sat stiff. Demeter spoke. "Two of my dearest daughters are dead. One who is dead lies beneath these stones, my other raped and butchered in childbirth. My one who did not die sits here beside me now," said Demeter, she left her thought-twisting comment dangling.

Andronikos froze when he realised what Demeter was about to say.

"Persephone was slain by Cerberus, the beast of Hades, Lasonas by the half-god Cronus who once ruled the Titans, Cronus was Zeus' god of power and strength. Lasonas was a good woman and your birthmother, she was my eldest born to this world when I took this form of Demeter. Cronus was an evil god, you have his violent fighting blood within you, in revenge this half-god Cronus was driven through by the sword of Phryne, my youngest who sits beside you now. You are of my blood, I know you do not know this," said Demeter.

Andronikos sat silent.

"There is more I should tell you," continued Demeter in her low drawling voice. "Your king, Cleomenes, he is dead. He was not long since killed inside your Spartan encampment by the god Ares. Ares chose to fight alongside the Athenians, though Athens has now fallen. Ares was slain by Elenoras, she put her righteous sword of retribution through his devil heart and scrawny neck. Elenoras is now queen of Sparta, also of Athens, Elenoras is the blood of Persephone who is of my blood – that part of this war is over, it is finished." Demeter waited, she knew how much Andronikos was reeling.

In just *three* days the whole world of Andronikos had changed. Andronikos was no longer Andronikos. He was now a renegade warrior who at last, after waiting his whole life, knew his impossible heritage – the final piece of the broken mirror had fallen into place. The image of himself he saw in the shattered shards did not look good, he saw a broken man, a commanding general who at this moment in time commanded no one. Three days before he had stood before a formidable army, beside his king, ready to attack Sparta's greatest adversary since the defeat of the Persians.

Sparta had been wronged, Sparta's army marched to the gates of Athens to right an unforgivable wrong, to fight for the king's princess daughter seized during a time of peace and prosperity. It never did make sense in the mind of Andronikos, only now did Andronikos know why. The old general knew he had no choice; he knew he had been drawn into a conflict that he did not understand, he knew for certain that ahead lay the destructive battle Spartan warriors expected and were trained to fight.

"Tomorrow," continued Demeter, "we must fight the most dangerous of foes. Cerberus is the salivating beast that guards the Thessalon Gate. Cerberus is the deviant prehistoric freak that still survives from the three hundred million years when beasts alone ruled this world. Cerberus is tied to Hades, a baksheesh gift from Zeus that he stole from the Titan gods. Cerberus prowls the underworld where he feeds off the cold blood of the dead... this beast of monstrosity can smell the breath of we palaeolithic encroachers who threaten the world of his godly masters. Tomorrow will be a day of blood; it might be that we will all die.

Andronikos felt fear, not for the first time in the last three days he shivered and shook.

Zeus turned to face Hermes, who looked grim-faced and concerned. Hermes did not relish his task of informing Zeus of the deaths that had begun to shake the foundations of the great mountain citadel. In the grand hall of the palace chamber, with its floor of pure gold, the nubile slave girls sensed the impending moment of crisis, they lost no time in making themselves scarce. Hermes thought it wise to be blunt and straightforward, there was little point in hiding the truth.

"My Lord Zeus, there is grave news from the Athenian city of Athens."

Zeus remained silent, his current mood was unpleasant and hostile, he was by this time aware of the worrying death of Apollo - whose throat had been slit by his consort wife Daphne while he slept peaceful in his sleep. Zeus did not answer Hermes – he waited for the uneasy god of prosperity to speak more. There followed an awkward short pause.

"Ares... he is slain by the princess daughter of Persephone," continued

Hermes, halting in uncertainty.

Zeus already knew of the death of the Spartan king Cleomenes, killed by Ares, but not that Ares himself was dead. Zeus stood stupefied and speechless.

"This princess woman has declared herself consort queen of both Sparta and Athens," said Hermes. "Both armies are united, I am told they now march here against Olympus."

Hermes was not sure how much Zeus knew - three days ahead of the army of Elenoras, a renegade band of three men and two women were approaching the Thessalon Gate. The anger of Hades, when informed of this, had been overwhelming, he had once more unchained his salivating beast Cerberus - who two days before had slain his traitorous wife Persephone. Cerberus was eager, uncontrollable in blood-drooling anticipation - his pungent breath a blood-curdling warning of how much the creature smelled more death.

The gods were in turmoil, they were beginning to turn upon Hades in anger. It became clear to them that Hades had miscalculated, that his masterpiece plan of retribution against Athens and Sparta for the unfaithfulness of his wife was nothing more than a trap he had been lured into, a clever ambush that had been turned against not just Hades but the full realm of the gods. Gods were now dying in their beds and palaces; gods were dying at the hands of their abducted consorts in some related and coordinated act of revenge. Unease was beginning to spread, the gods now turned to Zeus to intervene.

Zeus was prepared, his fireblade sword slung hidden beneath his grey tunic of silk. He unfolded his gossamer white wings to their full extent, causing Hermes to step backwards in astonished alarm. Zeus realised that if Ares and Apollo were both dead then there was no doubt the conflict he dreaded had begun - it could no longer be prevented. The whole disaster hung upon Cerberus guarding the gate – if Cerberus did what Cerberus existed to do then Demeter would never get to threaten Olympus. But deep uncertainties troubled Zeus, there was this formidable Phryne and the two fighting warriors from Sparta and Athens – what if these two men were not who he assumed them to be? What if both were the blood of Demeter? The priest, Horus, was with them though he had been silent since losing control of the Athenian senate. Just when Zeus folded his wings back beneath his cloak, the crisis facing the mighty Lord of the gods got worse - more gods were all of a sudden dead.

Dionysus, the gaiety god of fruitfulness and wine, lay poisoned and slumped, his crumpled body lying beside the fountain of youth he so embellished. His slave servants could find no clues to what had happened - nor could they find his consort wife Ariadne. The pungent smell of death in his half-drunk goblet, the dribbles of blood from his gaping mouth left them in no doubt that his debouching wife had in some way dealt him a deadly blow. But there was worse - much worse. Poseidon, the all-conquering mighty god of the sea, was nowhere to be found. High on the mountain top the sun god Helios watched the god of flying birds, Icarus, fall from high in the sky with the wax that held his wings melted, wax interchanged for useless animal lard by the slave girl he over desired. Hephaestus, the god of fire, lay dead in his burnt-out fire pit of virtuous retribution.

Zeus, agitated and concerned, turned to stare into the voluminous mirror of eternal life. He saw himself grand and magnificent, his reflection both appalling and enchanting. What Zeus saw made him shudder, he glimpsed both his destruction and his victorious parade of conquering vanquish. He did not see his death, not yet, only vestiges of defeat and victory in the shining misery of his mirrored self. In this instant Zeus would have to make the fateful decision, he foresaw the crumbling fall of Olympus - he saw the rise of new empires - the rise of Rome and Jerusalem. He saw prophets and kings, he saw white-skinned men in northern lands wielding swords and shields of silver, in the south he beheld the tears of black men shackled in chains – enslaving neck rings unbreakable in their terror. Zeus saw the chains that broke their spirits, the chains that made good men fall in dried mud then die.

Zeus turned back to Hermes, saying nothing. Mount Olympus would rise or fall on the victory or destruction of Cerberus - the evil blood-licking creature that survived the unyielding wipeout extinction of the tyrannosaurus-megalosaurs, the salivating monstrosity that for one hundred million years had butchered the palaeolithic children of Hawwāh.

Andronikos rode with Phryne, they travelled alongside towards the cloud-shrouded peaks of the mountainous massive. The morning sky was this time covered in a thin covering of wispy murk, preventing the vague perceivable sun from breaking through to warm the new day. Andronikos tried hard to think of a good way to open the conversation.

"The day is cooler the nearer we travel to the Olympus mountains," Andronikos said. Andronikos had learned many truths since arriving with the Spartan army before the gates of Athens, but there were still unanswered questions. For example, his mother was a distant memory, but he knew nothing of his father. It seemed ironic that Andronikos was ageing in years, only now was it important to him that he learned more, that he knew everything. He was agitated, the woman riding by his side knew what he needed to know, but his intense unease in asking Phryne to reveal more of what might cause him great pain weighed heavy upon him.

"Honoured generals of fighting armies talk about the daytime heat when they wish to delve into something more," said Phryne, she was not so easy to prize open. "Ask what you wish me to tell, Andronikos."

Phryne's directness every time uneased Andronikos. At the same time, he admired her forthright honesty, even though he felt disturbed. Their two ponies snorted in some form of communicative unison.

"I did not know my mother, my father even less," Andronikos probed. "From what has been said, and everything that has happened, you knew both," he surmised.

"What I will tell you might unnerve you," replied Phryne. "You are a strong man in body because of your blood heritage, but you are set in your ways in your old age. You Spartans talk about honour and truth, yet you are trained from youth to pit your strength against your fellow men. Your patronage ideals do not allow for treating your women or your slaves equal." For the first time, Andronikos saw that Phryne was emotional.

"Last night you learned that your mother was not who you thought," Phryne continued, "She was my half-sister, I watched your mother die, I saw her life drain from her soul in childbirth, your birth Andronikos. Lasonas did not die from her act of delivering you into the world, she died from the savagery of your father Cronus who tried to prevent your birth, the Titan god suspected who you would be, but he died with this secret inside him, he died by my sword."

This time Andronikos kept his control. He had prepared himself for the blow. He stood firm. "This makes you and I related by blood."

"Like I told you, you have the look of your mother in your eyes," said Phryne. "Persephone set out to draw King Cleomenes to Athens, which is what the stupid fool Hades desired, she did this to bring you and Elenoras together under the eyes of Hades, she delivered you to Patriach who is your blood. Do you not see?" Phryne turned her gaze from the roadway ahead to look Andronikos in the eye, "Zeus knows we are coming, Zeus realises that Hades was tricked and lured, how the stupidity of Hades brings the wrath that Zeus fears. You and I Andronikos, with Patriach, seeking vengeance. And three days behind is the strongest army you Grecians have yet seen - lead by Elenoras and her band of warmongering mercenary skirmishers."

Andronikos was silent. His whole being was reeling but he did not react. The first implication he realised was Phryne's great age, so too Demeter's and Persephone's. What about his mother Lasonas?

"I know what you are thinking," Phryne interrupted his chain of thoughts, "I have been in this world a long time, longer than you can imagine. Your mother also. But not you Andronikos. It is the female blood-line that carries this blood," Phryne smiled, she saw the instantaneous look of bewilderment in his eye.

"For your great age, you still carry much beauty," Andronikos replied.

"Ah, that old man's trick. Tell a woman how beautiful she is when you do not mean it," admonished Phryne. Again, she smiled, this time with a flush of well-concealed embarrassment.

Ahead, the trail turned slight to the left, to disappear behind a tuft of trees and tall boulders, to the rider's right a towering rock buttress climbed to the plateau of the first of the mountain tops of the Olympus range. Not far was the infamous Thessalon Gateway, a magnificent tower hewn from granite that precipitated the steep pathway that wound itself skyward like a meandering tangle of road stone. This was the perfect place for an ambush thought Andronikos, instinct and experience made him grip the hilt of his sword, but as they rounded the bend, with Demeter and Patriach leading the way, nothing happened. Andronikos slackened his sword grip.

Andronikos relaxed. Horus led the supply-laden packhorse, his mount walked at their combined slow pace between Patriach and Demeter at their head, with Andronikos and Phryne in the rear. The ground now was much steeper, the five of them picked their way upwards conscious of the lessening heat as they climbed higher into the foothills. The sweet smell of pine trees and mulberry blossom permeated the cooling air, bringing a freshness of mind to Andronikos whose confused selfness still made him feel tired and slightly out of breath...

Patriach died almost instantaneous, but not quite. In the fleeting second before his throat was ripped open, he spied the one pair of slathering jaws that slashed his neck, jaws that pounced from behind somewhere unseen. The Athenian general fell to the ground dead. More jaws, one of three heads, snapped themselves around the midriff of Horus, but his horse's saddle in some way saved him. His horse raised itself to its hind legs in abject fear then died as the carcass-stained teeth of the colossus slipped from closing together with Horus between, severing the terrified horse's jugular when the half-open jaws slashed downwards. Horus lived, but his blood began to saturate the stone ground, mixing inglorious with horse blood in a way that could not be determined which was human blood and which was not. The gushing red stain spread, to forever mark the spot where Horus fell. The salivating monster by now barred the entire path, its height of three grown men offering no way forward. The third head of the behemoth eyed those who had not died or been mortally wounded, the beast glared in a way that signified absolute victory, a death-dealing triumph of spectacular conquest that ceased as quickly as it had begun. All three heads poised themselves for the second strike, the one that would complete the monster's deadly attack.

Pure impulse made Andronikos roll out of his saddle, at the same time pulling free his sword from its scabbard - ingrained instinct made him fall to one knee with his sword raised, angled skyward, pointing in the precise direction of the next attack - his kneeled posture deliberate in presenting the smallest profile to his sudden attacker. At the same time, the leather-scaled creature launched its strike, one set of jaws lurching each to Andronikos, Phryne and Demeter. The super-quick first reaction of Andronikos caused one neck of the leviathan to fall upon the Spartan general's raised sword, which penetrated deep into the beast's neck flesh due to its momentum. The grotesque brute drew back, wounded but by no means struck mortal. Then came the stand off, the three-headed reptile held back hurt, its blood dribbling to the ground to mix with the bloodied sand surrounding the lifeless body of Patriach and the rigid Horus who, with his usual cunning, played dead. Andronikos leapfrogged backwards over and over, creating lifesaving distance between himself and his adversary, then he raised himself to stand full height, his sword still pointing outwards in instinctive defence. This gave Andronikos time, a few moments, to get the measure of what was happening – and what he should do next.

Andronikos straightaway saw that both Patriach and Horus were down, one glance told him that Patriach was dead, no man could survive wounds like that, Patriach's head was at the wrong angle for his spreadeagled body. About Horus, Andronikos was not so sure, but the priest was beyond immediate help, there was nothing that could be done in these first moments of the ambush. Andronikos looked over to Phryne and Demeter. He was shocked.

Both Phryne and Demeter had morphed, they had changed, no longer were they womanly women who moments before had been riding at a slow horse pace following the upwards curving pathway that, from nowhere, became the bloodstained road to death. Andronikos saw two humanoid forms, powerful built hunters that he could not define as woman or man. They both wore no clothing, which lay strewn against the rocks, instead, their muscular animalistic manifestations crouched ready to strike in hunter-like poise. Andronikos looked away, his mind could not deal with this in the heat of the death-dealing attack.

The dragonian beast was threatening to attack once more. Phryne, the younger of the two, leapt to the top of the largest boulder to the beast's right, it was a phenomenal leap in height sprung by muscular legs found on no human. Demeter remained on the ground, probing forward with a sword that glinted silver in the mid-morning sunlight. The flash of reflected light caught the right eye of Andronikos, he saw Demeter probing forward like a predatory huntress who knew what to do, showing no fear. Seeing this, Andronikos moved to the left, creating three diverse targets for the beast's three heads, the wounded head of Cerberus followed Andronikos around, its limpid green eyes piercing deep into his soul. The beast held back its attack, sensing that it was being provoked by Demeter in the centre. All three heads salivated and slathered, the foulness adding to the chaotic mayhem.

"Beware," warned Demeter to Andronikos at the top of her voice. "The saliva from those mouths will burn if it falls upon you. It is pure acid. The same with the monster's blood, do not let its saliva or blood touch you." Andronikos saw dripping blood drip down onto the lifeless body of Patriach, Patriach's flesh gave off whiffs of smoke as the stench of burning flesh permeated the fresh morning air. Andronikos felt worrying fear, all three of them could be killed with ease if one more of them fell.

The beast launched itself, all three heads attacking at once. Andronikos smelled the stinking breath that almost overwhelmed him as the beast's nostril passed inches from him, huge lashing teeth attempted to crush around him - but Andronikos was swift, he lurched leftwards at the same time lashing downward with his sword into the same wound in the beast's neck. His sword again cut home, but Andronikos lost grip of his sword which remained buried deep in the creature's neck, the neck that recoiled back and upwards as Cerberus retreated in pain. Andronikos felt more fear, now realising that he had no weapon, when the next attack came it would be his end. For now, he leapt backwards to avoid the spray of saliva and blood bursting from leathery nostrils. He looked up, he stared in awe.

In the flash of a fraction of one single moment, Phryne lashed downward with her sword from high upon the boulder on which she crouched. Then she stood triumphant, her sword raised pointed to the sky. She had done her work, her sword strike struck central between the creature's eyes, at the same time that Demeter leapt forward to drive her sword into the bared scaled chest of the three-headed tyrannosaurus monster - which then reeled backwards in more pain and confusion.

Cerberus retreated a short distance back, defiant and alarmed that he had been defeated. In the few moments before Cerberus crashed to the ground dead, he saw what he had always feared. He saw Hawwāh in her two billion-year incarnation, he observed her stride towards him without fear, he listened to her warn him in her own tongue that he was about to die...

"Kkaweenā hẹnneah Cerberus, vin deeeesinï Persephone eann Patriach." Demeter probed deep into the mind of Cerberus. She was quick to pick out an endless chain of evil evocations, too many to take note of – she recoiled in shock. In disturbed distress, Demeter expunged every evil memory from the monster's soul in the moments before the great leviathan died, Hades' one remaining survival chance lay dead upon the dry-parched ground.

Andronikos ran to where Patriach himself lay heaped upon the ground. The ageing Spartan, the veteran warrior of many deadly wars, was horrified. The wounds inflicted by Cerberus were overwhelming, Patriach's throat was ravaged to the point of decapitation. The rest of his body was covered in the blood and saliva from the unworldly beast, it burned and burbled gently in the still morning air.

"Aaahuooo," sang the palaeolithic being that was Phryne, she stood tall upon the rounded peak of the towering boulder upon where she pointed her sword skywards, her voice raised to the stark blue sky. The sound was like the melodious haunting of bitter victory, the final melody of the shocking dead. "Aaahuooo..." joined in Demeter, in tuneful harmony, a lamentable lament of grief. "Aaahuooo..." they sang together in unison, a chanting song of two differing octaves that cut through Andronikos, who turned towards where Horus lay breathing in desperate straights. "Aaahuooo..." came the answering chorus of more than ten thousand unseen distant voices, voices that were never in this world.

Zeus heard and listened when he realised his endgame was final. The task lorded upon him by his masters was spent, around him were the frightened eyes of panic-strewn gods.

Hades died a surprised and vengeful death, he died when he was overwhelmed then slaughtered by the embittered souls of the countless dead, dead no longer constrained by the monstrous beast Cerberus. Hades died with red-heat fear in his eyes, when it dawned upon him who his butchered wife might be, when in an instant he grasped how easy Demeter had claimed her rightful revenge.

Around him, in the crumbling citadel that was once all-conquering Olympus, more Titan gods died, they died unassuming deaths they did not expect. The mighty god of the sea Poseidon, who had somehow escaped from his incarceration beneath the Adriatic sea, died drowning in his own watery citadel. Poseidon died when his faithless wife Amphitrite filled his chalice with amniotic fluid - an odourless, tasteless, colourless saturate drawn from the foetal womb of his unwilling mistress who had died a tortuous death in tearful distress at the hands of Poseidon's son Triton - who himself feared with envious eyes his unborn rival heretofore undelivered. Triton died with stark terror in his terrified vision, in the darkness of the night when his unseen assailant stabbed her womanly blade of revenge through his jugular - he saw her shadowy form in that fractional fleeting moment before his life ebbed into the void of incomprehensible darkness.

Tartarus, the deviant son of Hephaestus, died in his father's white-hot furnace fires, the delinquent god of the abyss and the mining of bronze was slain when forced into his obligation to feed his father's all-consuming flames of iron - Tartarus was deceived with false promises of passion offered by the last of his suffering virgin concubine goddesses. The god of molten bronze stood proud beside his greatest creation, the shining armour of the invisible Achilles before the irresistible flames of destruction claimed his last breath in wide-eyed desperation. Tartarus died a coward's death, his withered ashes leaving no trace of the evangelical revenge of Demeter.

Meanwhile, Zeus sensed his defeat, like a wounded mountain lion he glimpsed the final moments in the ultimate fall of Olympus, the collapse of the kingdom realm he had stolen from the ancient Titan gods. Zeus knew his survival rested on his opportune escape, he harboured no desire to once more face his billion-year adversary on such detrimental terms, the shepherdess of men who had this time chosen the humanoid form of Demeter. Zeus unfurled his white wings of flight, flaunting his angel appearance to fool his onlooking enemies who might try to prevent the frenzied bolt of his moonlit freedom. Making his way through tumbling pillars of collapsing granite, Gabriel saw the easy opportunity for his backhanded exit – until his path was barred by the sword-bearing Phryne. Phryne stood tall, proud defiant, poised like the hunting panther who had found its prey, her task to halt Gabriel's flight by cutting him down. Phryne saw just Zeus, she did not see the Gabriel reincarnation for who he was, mighty Zeus was the masterful mastermind behind the destruction of her world, the destroyer of everything she held dear in the name of all the goddesses of fear.

"You have not yet paid your debt in blood, almighty Zeus," hissed Phryne with deep hostility, the hatred in her voice twisting the curling sinews of airborne mist. "You shall not pass, not while my blade bars your way." Phryne's sword was raised, pointing skyward ready to strike. Gabriel stopped halted, visibly shaken.

Gabriel stuttered his pace, knowing that his adversary was capable of his destruction - he knew full well who she was, that she was the vile seed of Demeter, that somewhere within the collapsing mountain would be Demeter herself, perhaps in her original transformation. Gabriel drew his burning sabre, his sword of fire that no human could master - but Gabriel discerned that Phryne herself was not human. Gabriel saw the powerful she-woman of neanderthal procreation, he saw the steely blue eyes of the huntress. He poised, striding forward with his threatening menace.

Their clash, when it came, was at first a tentative cat-and-mouse confrontation, both knowing their adversary was capable of dealing death. Phryne morphed back into her humanoid self, clearing her bitumen auburn hair from her blue-grey eyes with a casual toss of her brow. Gabriel at once gasped in abject shock – straightaway he realised that he must finish her, that she could not be allowed to live – her survival would endanger his master's emblazoned crusade. Phryne was the first to launch, she pounced forward with her blade aimed expertly at Gabriel's throat, the tip drawing his blood a fraction of a second before he stepped sideways. Straightaway, she sprang upon him once more, but Gabriel was unlike any warrior she had before encountered, he thrust downwards with his sword - at the same time revealing his hidden dagger held in his free hand. Gabriel's knife swiftly found its mark, the game was over with Phryne's adrenaline-filled heart pierced by his precision-placed blade. Phryne died a tragic death, a pure virgin maiden's death, she died in a futile way that was in the end always going to happen.

Zeus did not linger; he knew his time for survival was short. Facing Demeter would be one more enormous confrontation, the devastating death of Phryne would change the dynamics of any head-to-head encounter with Hawwāh's Demeter - Zeus was under no illusion that he was now in incalculable danger, that this was the final moment in the crumbling citadel of Olympus - he had seconds to make his escape.

The sudden burning pain that engulfed his right shoulder incapacitated him immediately. Zeus felt the piercing sword thrust deep into his flesh like a white-hot shard of iron, the searing stab continued when the blade hit hard upon bone. Gabriel turned to see Andronikos, the Spartan warrior incandescent with rage and determination. Andronikos raised his sword to deal the final blow, but Zeus reacted with instinct. Peeling to one side, though still unbalanced, Gabriel avoided the downward strike that would have split his skull. The sword blow missed by the merest fraction, Andronikos saw his sword tip ricocheting off the crumbled granite column that saved Gabriel from his untimed death. But Gabriel was struck, the burning wound to the right side of his body threatened to engulf him - it meant that his capable adversary could finish him, even when it was not yet Gabriel's moment to die. Never at this instant in mankind's existence was it Gabriel's juncture, not yet, his death was not written in time or history, it could not happen. Andronikos learned this when he launched his sword strike for the third time, the strike that should have finished Gabriel did not happen – because Gabriel was not there. Gabriel vanished in the guise of Zeus in the tiniest fraction of the smallest second, Gabriel was gone, returning to his own dimension in time to lick the gaping wound that came near to finishing him. Andronikos stared, astonished. In the instant of his overwhelming victory that would have settled the score, his enemy had disappeared.

It took a few moments for Gabriel to recover his composure. Here in his master's time-space, he was safe, there was nothing worldly humanoid to threaten him. The swirling mists of nothingness engulfed him in incomplete silence, this strange dimensional world bridging both the real and unreal elements of his existence. Here Gabriel could rest. Gabriel could bury himself in the ice-white misty fog knowing that he could not be found, here he was hidden for eternity, here he was unseen until he could perceive the moment when he could once more launch himself back into the incumbent world of man to inspire them to domineering victory. Here Gabriel could tend his mortal bloodless wound, he had escaped his doom by the thinnest margin; it would now take time. Time that he did not have, for it was in this instant that Gabriel realised with shock horror that he was not alone.

Andronikos sat back on his heels, he squatted in contemplative silence for one or two moments endeavouring to understand what had happened. Zeus was there for the final death-dealing blow, then he vanished. Andronikos rued his missed opportunity, his desperation knew no bounds, Phryne lay dead, her spreadeagled body crumpled lifeless in the corner of the wrecked passage where the unseen knife-cut of Zeus had severed her heart. Andronikos knew there could be no act of revenge, Zeus had delivered his crowning victory of which nothing could be done, the Lord of the gods was gone, he had escaped with his life while his crumbling empire domain collapsed in ruins from the unseen earthquake deep within the earth's bowels. Many of the gods who had not been assassinated by unseen hands were beginning to rally, knowing their combined might could overcome the renegade band of rebellious warriors who had somehow forced their way into their grandiose mountaintop kingdom. The destructive earthquake began to subside, the insurrection seemed to be over – but where was Zeus?

It dawned upon Andronikos that he was alone, there was no Demeter, Phryne was dead. Right now, he was in mortal jeopardy, he was fearful that he needed to find his escape. Making his way downwards seemed to be his one option, downwards meant down the mountain and out of danger. He crawled his way through the fallen columns of granite, the dust and darkness offering some semblance of inconspicuousness if he could maintain his stealth with silence. There was no one around to challenge him. Like Zeus, Andronikos asked himself where was Demeter?

Aniketus and Alexiares, the two godly sons of Heracles, they considered themselves the unconquerable inner gatekeepers of Olympus. The muscular and sinewy Titans had never tasted defeat, now they were the first of the panic-stricken power gods to rally. When the distraught brothers learned that Heracles had been slain; poisoned in his sleep by his conspiring concubines Megaera, Omphale, Deianira and Hebe, the two half-gods grasped how easy the realm of the Olympians had been ravaged. This was no unexpected assault on their mountain citadel, what they both realised was much worse. When they discovered the terrifying beast Cerberus, his lifeless body festering in the intense late afternoon heat in his cesspit of saliva-burning blood, Aniketus and Alexiares began to prepare, they began to compose themselves ready to fight their final fight - to the death if need be. They glared at each other with unease, aware of the peril they faced. The brothers knew that a far greater disaster lay ahead; they were conscious of how many of their compatriot gods were dead, but it was the way they had died that angered them. What was happening was preplanned and deliberate, it was a thought-out and calculated strike against Olympus – whoever was the mastermind behind the conquest had victory in their grasp. But not yet, not quite, not while Aniketus and Alexiares still lived.

The brothers were quick to rally the few surviving gods, together they might battle their way to survival, perhaps salvage their rightful ruling realm that had stood for over five thousand dog-eared years. A good number of still loyal goddesses stood beside the two twins - Aphrodite, Artemisia and Eileithyia among them - they feared the consequence of violent rape once the power of their godly masters was broken – not for the first time the gods would punish their women once it became known how the legions of ungodly consorts had turned upon and slaughtered their overlord rulers in this unprecedented act of aggression. The citadel mountain palaces had crumbled in the coinciding earth-shaking earthquake, drummed from the deep by the revengeful Demeter in her overpowering form – for Demeter possessed ascendency far greater than making the earth yield crops and grain. The gods and goddesses, they now gathered in a self-protecting circle knowing their unseen enemy would soon strike the final blow. One lone man, his greying stubble splattered with sweat-ridden exhaustion, his sword bloodied and unsheathed, descended from the ruined shambles that was once the mightiest kingdom that Gabriel had created.

"You gods who still live, lay down your swords and spears," challenged Andronikos. "No more blood should be spilled in this pitiless war."

Aniketus looked hard at his desperate brother Alexiares, unsure of how to react. In his heart, he knew the battle was lost, but both had vowed to each other to fight to their death. It was the goddess Artemisia who decided to intervene.

"You are Andronikos Karahalios of Sparta, we know who you are," she declared out loud. "You men of Sparta, you never demand the surrender of your enemies," her eyes burned with indignant passion, "I know you put enemies to death then defile their women. Every rampaging army since the beginning of time defeats their foe like this."

Andronikos felt pained. Artemisia was right in what she claimed, but this conflict was vast and different, this was a war for the freedom of the oppressive enslavement of women, their penultimate release from the dominion of men.

"This is not a war of men against men, this is not a war, it is not the same, it is more than man fighting against man," bellowed Andronikos. "I tell you, the time of you gods is finished," a surge of decisive pursuance flowed through the Spartan's blood, "Demeter is not the goddess of all things you believe, Demeter is the custodian of this world, your world, this unjust world ruled by the overpowering power of you gods," Andronikos saw the wavering indecision in the demeanour of Artemisia, also of the other Olympian goddesses who glanced at each other with unease. "Zeus has fled, he is gone, your powerful gods who were the bones of your lives, they are dead. This is no victory for Sparta, it is one conquest, the same unworldly confrontation that has existed from the beginning of time."

"Where is Demeter?" responded Artemisia in despair, demanding near the top of her voice. "Bring us Demeter." The swirling mists of confusion created an atmosphere of desperate gloom. The sun burned incessant; a deep glaring yellow.

A new voice interrupted, from somewhere at first unseen, "Demeter is not here. She has gone from this world." Andronikos spun his head in astonished surprise.

"She is departed, Demeter's unearthly task here is finished," the commanding voice of Elenoras filled the air, she stood proud on the nearby boulder peak overlooking this last-ditched stand of the surviving gods. Behind her was the rag-tag army of itinerant skirmishers, armed to the teeth with their glinting swords and pointed spears – hostile and threatening defiance.

The gods were dumbed silent, at last visualising their final defeat. The godly brothers, Aniketus and Alexiares, they were the last who refused to acknowledge the end, their imposing muscular size the height of near two grown men. Aniketus hesitated, then charged up the gradient slope towards Elenoras, his giant-sized sword raised pointed towards the sky in death-dealing threat. Alexiares, seeing his twin brother act with reckless bellicose, leapt after him with his flint-tipped spear poised towards the imposing form of Elenoras and the grim-faced skirmishers.

Neither of the two gods got far, Aniketus was the first to fall, falling to the ground in a crumpled heap with a sliver-tipped sword buried deep into his throat, launched through the air like a missile by Elenoras. Alexiares held back, stunned, his face fixed by anguish, his lunging brother lying dead beside his feet. Uncontrolled rage seized Alexiares, his madness death flashing before his eyes even as a hoard of skirmisher spears penetrated his bloodied armour - bringing him in an instant to his knees. Alexiares died beside his dead brother, their last breaths being the one remaining legacy of the once infamous gods of the mountain citadel of Olympus.

There followed a long silent pause, everyone present gathered their whirling senses, the whole world stood still as the reeling unreality of these momentous events hit home. The remaining goddesses, standing dejected in a muddled group, saw the futility of their once proud cause - with obedience serve their godly menfolk in the demeaning ways demanded by Zeus. The remaining gods now lost their will to fight, without a cause or the driving adrenaline of Aniketus and Alexiares, and the commanding presence of Ares, Hades and Zeus himself, there was nothing left to fight for, the revengeful victory of Demeter and Persephone was complete – though only victorious Elenoras was there to claim the momentous prize – but victory was to be a short-lived emotional prelude to her utter despair...

"Elenoras - I have to tell you, Persephone and Phryne, they are slain, they both lie dead," Andronikos cried out sensing that Elenoras could not know this. Andronikos saw the immediate transformation in Elenoras, the deep-eyed distress that contorted her womanly expression into painful pain, the rigid panic that swathed her whole being as Andronikos speared her heart; felling her with instantaneous grief - torment that threatened to overwhelm her. Her demeanour changed, gone was the victorious charade of confident victory, the momentous moment when the ultimate struggle of this conflict was complete. Her dear mother Persephone was dead, so was inglorious Phryne, indestructible Phryne, Phryne who had never tasted the bitter-sweet tinge of defeat. Elenoras had earlier reeled from the death of Cleomenes, her king and earthly father, killed by the bloody sword of the mighty god of war Ares.

"Patriach also," Andronikos added, lamenting the death of his bitter rival. "Now, there is just you and I to lead Sparta in this time of hallow victory."

"Tell me, how did they die?" Elenoras pleaded in desperation.

"Your mother, she was slain by Cerberus, the beast unleashed by Hades," Andronikos tried to voice his words with compassion, but his warrior upbringing created a moment of tearful pride. "Persephone was buried in her grave by Demeter, back in the Arberus foothills. Patriach was killed by the same slavering behemoth before it was slain by Phryne. Phryne was killed by Zeus, she lies there in the same place in the tower of Olympus, in the granite stone chamber of this defeated shit hole." The weeping maiden tears in the limpid eyes of Elenoras said everything that needed to be said. "We must return to Phryne, to burn her body," Andronikos finished.

Andronikos saw her regal tears staining her dust-strewn cheeks, tears that left faint pathways of desperate hope in tracks of unrelenting forlorn-ness.

"Yes," Elenoras paused before she answered. She turned her head upwards to gaze at the unblemished blue sky.

Zeus, who was Gabriel, he hid in the darkness that was his master's endgame kingdom. His deep wound, inflicted by the revenging sword of Andronikos, threatened to overwhelm him. Gabriel had suffered an inglorious defeat; of this, he had no doubts - the Titan gods had fallen and the empiric domination of Olympus was finished. Demeter was triumphant in her victory, but Gabriel knew it was to her terrible cost. It every time was.

In the corner of the nothingness where Gabriel lay he was desperate to be safe, here he could not be pursued by Andronikos though he had limited time with his wound beginning to fester. Gabriel needed time, time to be alone but this was not to be. He sensed rather than saw the dark shadow standing motionless in the complete blackness. Gabriel could not judge the distance; the gloominess of his hidden surroundings gave him no comfort when he had hoped to be safe. He froze in terror when he felt the tip of a sword against his throat.

"Tomorrow, I will take a new form, this existence of me is ended," said the voice, a voice that this time was not Demeter. "To the east, where the sun rises, there is a new foulness, where menkind worship your masters." There was a deadness to Hawwāh's tone of voice, here in this in-between place there was no echo.

Gabriel lay back propped upright, his ragged wings furled away hidden. He had not the strength to fight back, the sickness from his septic wound spread incapacitating weakness through his limbs, he had lost his fireblade sword in his desperation to flee Olympus. The hopelessness of this new defenceless situation threatened to overshadow the satisfaction of his escape; Gabriel expected his enemy to finish him.

"Make my death quick," breathed Gabriel. "Finish me, reclaim your world."

There was no fatal thrust of Hawwāh's sword, she did not need any weapon of steel to kill Gabriel – she could take his mind; she could impose her thoughts and will of force into his brain. Hawwāh did neither, in the intense pitch-black darkness she reached out with her hand to feel the bloodless wound that itself would finish her immortal adversary.

"This Andronikos sword-wound is no manly wound. It is a wound made by my bloodline, the son born of my Lasonas," whispered Hawwāh, who again was Demeter. "It is right that you die by this blade."

Gabriel said nothing, he could not think of anything meaningful to say. His defeat was complete, the masterful God he obeyed was nowhere to be found.

The penultimate God worshipped by war-driven men did not possess the ultimate power to vanquish this world, not while its custodian curator wielded her will of force to counter the domination demanded by his overlord. The sturdiness of motherhood was too powerful. The mightiness of man to sow his male seed inside the woman's womb empowered men to dominate their women enough, but this remnant palaeolithic female species was strong, they wielded a force and strength of will not seen in simplistic animal existence. Through Hawwāh, who was now Eve, every woman possessed female potency, the energy that made men weak-willed, driven to violence when they encountered dominating goodness in their women, when they suffered the emotion-driven by women that men called love. Devotion was a spiritual adoration demanded by his own master, a worshipfulness that was not intended to exist between a man and his woman.

Hawwāh, who was now Hyvah, placed the palm of her hand over Gabriel's lacerated gash. She felt the core of his wound, the split imbalance of calcium-carbon composition of shattered broken bone that had been penetrated by the pointed tip of Andronikos's sword, a despairing blade strike made in one final desperate attempt of revenge. Hyvah's sensitive hand found the congealed poison oozing from Gabriel's torn flesh, a wound not cleansed nor cleaned by free-flowing blood-red blood. She smoothed the shattered nerve ends, working in the way that a caring woman would. Hyvah, who was now Hawwāh, healed the wound in the manner Hawwāh would - in the same way that Eve, in the beginning, resurrected Adam.

"In the east, in the desert lands and olive orchards of Judaea, the seeds of the prophets you sowed there begin their infantile ascendancy," said Hawwāh. "You and I must make a new war there Gabriel, your fledgling ancestors of your Ab'raham and Mo'ses write scriptures there, they make stone tablets that describe the lying parables of your unholy prophets. Take note, Gabriel, there I will be the undefeatable Magdalena, I will be the wildflower of the storyteller who will bring down your blaspheming prophets before my bones are buried beneath the granite stone where I was created. Only in my cold northland can you defeat me."

Hawwāh did not turn her head upwards to gaze towards the sky, here in this strange place there was no sky, nor life-bearing sunlight to turn to. Instead, she turned her back upon the confused emissary of his masters who by now knew that he would survive. Hawwāh pursed her lips, lips that were not the humanoid lips she sometimes coveted. She drew her warm breath inwards, then breathed outwards to form the time-woven song chords of immortal hope.

"Aaahuooo," sang Hawwāh near the top of her voice, there were no clouds to drift across the cosmic star that men called the sun, not here in this dark nothingness place where Gabriel's healed wound would not now kill him. "Aaahuooo," responded Megaera, Omphale, Deianira and Hebe, the consort cohabiters of the fallen god Heracles, they each cried tears of hope. "Aaahuooo," sang Amphitrite, the enslaved concubine of the poisoned god Poseidon, Amphitrite the subjugate goddess who was now free. "Aaahuooo," sang Ariadne with melodious sadness, the enforced worldly wife of the dead god Dionysus. "Aaahuooo," wailed each of the silent slave girl assassins of Icarus, the soaring sun god whose waxed wings melted with inglorious contempt - also the arrogant god of bronze Hephaestus, who died burning in his slave pits of fire. "Aaahuooo," cried the one who did not die, Elenoras, whose desperate tears streamed into the dry dirt ground. Hawwāh tossed her hair from her moist eyes in the enchanting way that once more crucified the sweeping sadness of Andronikos. The one hundred skirmishers listened, they, at last, laid down their bloodied swords and long-lance spears to pledge their everlasting allegiance. Hawwāh heard no answering melody from Lasonas, Persephone or Phryne, redoubtable Phryne, who only one time was defeated.

Andronikos smiled half-hearted, he was bitten with overwhelming awareness when he listened - his grief hidden beneath the scaly crust of expressionless gaze under which all fighting men hide.

7

Gabriel slept his usual restless sleep. The Lord's angel knew he would dream the dream he feared – the dream of how his extravagant splendour was spent. She would come, alluring, seductive and dangerous, enticing him in the way she always did when his mind was curdling in turmoil. Lilith the demon, Lilith the lover, Lilith the heartless enchantress, Lilith who was Hyvah.

The misty haze began to clear, the uncertainty heightening Gabriel's awareness, his tensile sense of peril; she was there, she was waiting, Lilith beckoned him towards the same death Gabriel knew well...

"Why are you here?" cried Gabriel, almost in desperation.

"You know why I come," whispered Lilith, though now she had taken the form of the dreaded Hyvah. "You will not command me," Hyvah stared, she kneeled to breathe into his angelic ear, her snake like tongue probing the deliciousness of his unearthly skin. In the icy mist, once more she became Lilith. Lilith's soft-cusp breasts pointed chillingly naked, "I am here, you are mine, in time I will destroy you."

"No, not like this," gasped Gabriel helpless, "I cannot let you take this world from me, this is my Lord's world, this world is to be the world of my prophets."

"Listen to me," hissed the deadly Lilith. "I am your Lord, I am your God who demands worship, I made you," Lilith's lava eyes burned liquid fire. "Your breath will always be the breath of my breath, your blood will forever be the blood of my blood. But this is not your world. This world belongs to my kind, to me, in this world I am the goddess Hyvah."

Gabriel turned away desperate for Lilith to be gone. Lilith the good and Lilith *the bad. Gabriel's tears flowed, the Lord's angel could not take this. The first of the prophets was already sent, it could not be undone, Adam the thief, Adam the taker. Adam with his big pearly drum.*

Lilith faded into Hyvah, Hyvah again became Lilith. Tall, lithe and transparent. The tempestuous fire of this new world was driven by the hot burning maelstrom, tumultuous gases, gigantic rings of God-making volcanoes. From the firestorm of creation came Lilith, Lilith the maker, Lilith the creator, Lilith whose seed weaved into the ghostly form of Hyvah.

Gabriel awoke, he smiled, he sniggered, Gabriel remembered – the drum, the undefeatable big black drum...

In the Beginning

Hyvah pricked her ears then looked out over the threadbare treetops, down towards the horizonless plain below. The high mountain cliff descended beyond the line of desolate vegetation, falling away steep to the waterless desert that spread eastwards towards the heat of the rising sun. Hyvah sniffed the air sensing the strangeness that was wrong, that during the long hours of darkness there had been a subtle change, a subconscious difference that caused her a premonition of foreboding. Hyvah's first instinct disturbed her, agitating her in a way that caused her a perception of danger that remunerated deep inside her mind. Driven by troubled inquisitiveness, Hyvah weaved through the trees until she sat hunched upon her hind limbs, squatting just above the dense forest floor.

Then, without warning, in the dewdrop morning dawn, the shimmering heat reverberated from a new sound, a deviant rhythmic drumbeat that drifted serene in the gentle cooling breeze. Hyvah became alarmed, frozen in indecisive uncertainty; in bewildered confusion she retreated backwards to conceal herself in the denser cover of the lower vegetation. She listened for a while until her outward curiosity induced her to climb higher to the highest point of the tree line to see what she could see. Hyvah could see nothing, not anything that would reveal this surreal thing that was happening in her singular tree-dwelling world. For an indeterminate time she deliberated this unearthly intrusion, this unexpected phenomenon that toyed with her ascendant supremacy. Hyvah sat squatting upon her haunches, out of sight between two converging boughs while she considered her options of what she should do. Meanwhile, the drumbeat continued to grow more intense, the beating rhythm taking hold of her senses making her aware that she was being drawn into its magical embrace. Deep down in her subconscious self, Hyvah did not want the rhythmic beat to stop.

Forcing a measure of composure Hyvah decided to wait, to be careful, that her self-preservation was more precious in her world in which she reigned supreme. Later, when nightfall came, she would change into her intrepid self, her ground-dwelling self, her lowland hunter-predator form that would enable her to search out this new strangeness - this sharp intrusion that had descended into her world of domination. Hyvah's first instinct was one of hostile curiosity driven by a deep-down uncertainty she could not hope to suppress. As time crept by, Hyvah sensed she must in her own way control the emotional unease growing inside her, her inner self that succumbed to this freakishness she did not yet understand.

The hot day passed without cessation of the rhythmic drum. The yellow-white sun moved relentless across the deep-blue cloudless sky, giving no respite from the intense heat that began to rise from the scorched desert scrub a long distance below - to Hyvah, the day seemed to crawl before the nighttime darkness descended like a creeping tide of doom. In the growing dark shadows, she leapt through the trees, weaving with nimble subtleness from branch to branch using her agile limbs to zigzag her path as her instinctive choice of defence – aware that she might herself be hunted down. Hyvah's actions were reactive; a feeling of being stalked by unseen danger. This air of uncertainty was strange - there were no lifeforms in her garden world capable of high sentient being. Through the tense twilight hours, an awareness of primitive instinct ingratiated her soul, a primordial feeling that originated in the deep dark recesses of her mind. As darkness descended, Hyvah's resourcefulness served to ignite a tremendous energy inside. With the ending of the long hot day, she realised how this unexpectedness was meant to happen, that some predetermined fortuity was unravelling to threaten her means of preserving her commanding world. Hyvah decided that now was the time to morph into her other self.

Hyvah dropped from the lowest curving tree branch, she landed with stealth on the dark dank ground before sniffing the air to check the well-used wildlife trail, sensing nothing to alarm her. Hyvah cleared the tree line then raised herself to her hind legs to walk biped, her head just above the tall dry grass that bristled and rippled like whispering waves in the darkening cool breeze. She peered in each direction to be sure that no threat could endanger her existence.

Hyvah sensed nothing except for the relentless alluring drumbeat that originated from below the cliffs to the east. As full darkness descended, Hyvah became another Hyvah, she donned the dark naked humanoid skin of the earth - not the free-swinging tree dweller she preferred. Hyvah was the predator, the palaeolithic half-human neanderthaloid who bore the stalker instincts of the merciless nighttime hunter.

Hyvah decided a circular route, one to close upon this freakishness that lured her inexorable in its direction, once more she chose not to make a direct line because this might threaten her survival - Hyvah's immeasurable time of evolution had given her every continuance instinct her world of *Erewhon* demanded. When her morphing change was complete, Hyvah quickened her pace - her powerful hind legs driving her to leap forward using every scratch of cover she could find.

The drumbeat drifted skyward, not far from the fringe of vegetation that for now concealed her. Hyvah thought hard, her uneasiness lessened, her hunter form giving her more conviction in the task she faced. Soon she would need to break cover to make her descent downwards to the great plain. If she was discovered, this thing that she did not yet understand might overpower her to destroy her.

Hyvah once more paused to decide her path, but when she reached the cliff edge the powerful rhythmic beat quickened and took hold, making her stop, then sway, in a strange gyration that induced a subtle gratification throughout her entire being. She felt sensationalised pleasure in her lower loins, between her biped legs; a feeling new to her in her long forever existence - the drumbeat grew more intense in its beating rhythm.

Hyvah concentrated, she broke the spell of the powerful trance that held her. She drove away the feeling of pleasure, the sensual captivation of entrapment; Hyvah knew the enchanting magic was attempting to overpower her, that she must in some way drive out the magical embrace from her mind. She stood tall, then crouched on her hunched all-fours to leap to gain height on the outcrop bluff from where she would see down to the great plain. From the bluff, she spied a concealed route down the cliff face, one that would hide her until she reached the dry parched desert scrubland a long way below.

She descended quick, at the same time marking her path with earthy pungent scent sprayed from hairless glands beneath the pits of powerful hind limbs, nimble, agile extremities that might give her a chance to outrun the lurking adversary attempting to entice her. Hyvah still did not make a direct line towards the drumbeat; she possessed the instinctive instinct of the wary hunter - though each time she paused the beating magic once more took hold.

The half-moon moonlight was enough for Hyvah to see her way down the massif, the silvery darkness concealing her as the shadowy nighttime luminescence deepened. Spindly shrubs and rocky outfalls hid a vertical gully, a scar carved through the cliffs by long-vanished rainfall – the perfect route down. Through Hyvah's steep descent, the drumbeat continued, she was being summoned, drawn into a trap though Hyvah's long evolution meant she was no easy adversary - if some unworldly being was endeavouring to seize her then she would choose her way to destroy it.

Hyvah leapt from the cover of the gully that descended to the parched dust-bowl wasteland, then she made her way from the cliff base towards the towering boulders that marked the beginning of the desolate horizon-less plain. Moonlight cast eery shadows, Hyvah realised the drumming beat came from within the bouldered rock formation not far ahead. When she drew close, Hyvah saw with sudden dread that whatever drummed this manipulative drumbeat, it had chosen its location with deliberate intent. She grasped how simple it would be to take advantage of the cover offered by the irregular sandstone formation that would, without difficulty, be defendable against her one line of assault. Hyvah had no option but to bide her time, to not be lured or disadvantaged in this wild confrontational dilemma - she would need to consider every option before making her move; this unseen power could not continue to captivate her in the sensual way it did.

Hyvah stayed still. The rhythm of the drumbeat, just like before, began to overpower her cautious sense of deliberation - she realised that resolve and quickness of speed were the two options she had; even when her foremost instinct warned her that she was being drawn into a purpose laid trap. Beginning her assault with unhesitating single-minded resolve, Hyvah made her way with cold-hearted stealth towards the seductive rhythmic beat. Darkness and her changed form concealed her presence, allowing her enough invisibility to close in on the rock formation without sound or outward sign that she was there. Her furtiveness-like substance was her final morphed self, there was nothing she now feared. Hyvah was prepared; ready for whatever might be unleashed against her.

She reached the outermost boulders with the loudness of the drumbeat invading every sense she possessed. Hyvah fought hard against its power though every short while, when she paused, the beating magic battled to overpower her. Each time, when Hyvah stood still, her body involuntary gyrated, she writhed in the enchanting dance that she could not, under her greatest will, make stop. Blocking the deadly pleasure from her mind, Hyvah climbed the tallest of the boulders from where she could see inside the outlying ring of gigantic boulders while remaining hidden. The moon reached its pinnacle in the sky, creating an easy silvery light that cast a bewitching atmospheric presence inside the rock-strewn arena; a setting, Hyvah perceived with unashamed shock horror, that was chosen with care to ensnare her. The long, tall being with his pearl-black drum, his charcoal-black skin and trailing yellow hair, had decided his location well.

The man-beast, whoever he was, peered straight to Hyvah's hidden location without interrupting the rhythm of his throbbing drum. He became her earthshaking powerful master. From deep inside Hyvah knew there was nowhere she could hide - she raised herself to her full biped height while still standing on the pinnacle of the tallest rock. In the majestic silver moonlight, Hyvah cast herself in her most glorious form, writhing her body in the gyrating tempo she could not resist. Hyvah danced the cruel dance of enthralling dances, she danced the dance of the beholder, she danced the dance of the sensual temptress, the dance of the stalking hunter, she danced her contorting limbs in perfect time with the relentless beating rhythm; her arms held high towards the beast's moonshine heaven. He drummed his enchanting drumbeat faster - until Hyvah offered her soul to the seductive nerve-end drum.

Hyvah possessed no lance of light; she held no weapon or sword to defy the man-beast who drummed with his life to seduce her. Hyvah swathed and swayed in gyros gyration knowing she must fight back, from deep within her loins she felt the surge of sensuous fire, an unrealised sensation of empowering gratification. Passion. In her growing tenacity of single-minded purposefulness, Hyvah sensed the man beast's inherent weakness, that he could be captivated by her insane beauty, that she could arouse his coital instincts - his erotic self she could expose then tear and ravish. Hyvah danced to pierce his heartless heart, she danced long past the midnight hour, she danced until he crumbled in desire for her wild tempestuous body.

Hyvah towered triumphant and defiant above him. She stood tall and translucent, transparent in her final heavenly form that kissed in time-past visions of two sleek and slender platform starships. The man-beast lay down defeated - knowing this was the time he was vanquished, when his nemesis would rise in the same way the serpent-Lords ruled hi timeless heaven.

"You are not of my world," she breathed deep in her reverber .ng, guttural tongue. Hyvah stood victorious over the man with the d ated drum. "From where did you come with your magical beating dr n?"

The man drew one deep breath at Hyvah's naked form, he l ed in the leering way that forced his submission. "In Gabriel's glorio name, I am Adam. I came to claim your world for my world." In the m onlight night, the air was resplendent silent, the tune of rhythmic be ost to Hyvah's biorhythm.

"Your bones, they are the bones of my bones. Your flesh is the flesh of my flesh," said Hyvah to the man who said he was Adam. 'Your blood is the blood of my blood, your light for all time will be my light, your eyes will see this world through my eyes. This world belongs to me."

Hyvah tossed her primogenital hair from earthen neanderthaloid eyes with the flick of her long thin hand. The matriarch of earth's evolving creation stood steadfast defiant - but Hyvah did not see that she was wrong, Hyvah did not see her downfall defeat nor the danger from Adam's magnificent drum - or the rhythm that delivered Hyvah writhing and numb. The subjugating power of man was done.

In the beginning, the timeless scriptures said, there was no light. From the maelstrom storm of creation came light but the light was not good light. Then from the burning white lavas of tempestuous EREWHON came HYVAH and HYVAH was HAWWÂH, who was LILITH and EVE. Hyvah made the light good light and from the light of Hyvah came all light. Then from the darkness of the heavens came A'ADAM who was ADAMAH who was ADAM. In the GARDEN of all life, Hyvah said to A'adam, "Your bones, they are the bones of my bones, your flesh is the flesh of my flesh. You shall be called 'MAN', for the sake of all men who will be born from the eternal womb of 'WOMAN'."

On the light years distant moon of *Rios*, orbiting the dead world of *Affebiar IV* in the star system of *DRU Meir*, the granite stone cenotaph described the *rise of man* and his predatory kind, how Gabriel would rule in his *Lordship's* name. For eight billion earth years the *Rios* obelisk stood silent, tarred by no wind nor rain or watched by alien eyes. Not for Hyvah an epitaph of fame.

An incalculable distance beyond, on the wild untamed frontier of the star constellation *Mu Arae*, the creators of all life self-marked the monument moon guarded by two lifeless guardian sentinels - cold steel horrors prescribed from their own unworldly conscription. This moon's granite stone, left by the lithe, transparent matriarchal makers of all life who called themselves the *KATTII*, paid homage to the great starship wrecked within the timeless cavern buried on the same dead moon, the mother moon that shepherded the raging storm ravaged twin planets made of pure chemical ore. The unholy obelisk left by the *KATTII* told more and more and more besides; for all sentient life to take note. The *KATTII* forewarned of the coming of Gabriel with his slaves of men, the souls of mankind – and the fearful rise of *HYVAH, HAWWĀH, LILITH,* of *EVE* and *her* revengeful female kind.

No obelisk told of Gabriel's irreplaceable love, his ungodly love towards the one he tried with his might to subdue. The goddess with the flaking hair and animal blue-grey eyes – unearthly womanhood whom his Lords feared and would one day rue to despise.

About the Author

There is much to say about the author D.D. Did, suffice to say this is not Did's real name. It is a pseudonym, a pen name, the *nom de plume* used to hide the author's identity. Did's wish is to be considered an accepted and innovative storyteller, you might say a habitual spreader of artistic untruths, or a colourful artist of lies.

In the madcap world of media & magazine journalism, Did unmasked is an established writer and editor of some note, published in both traditional print and the worldwide web. Magdalena's Bones is the author's initial sally into fictional full-length writing so hiding behind the ubiquitous mask of anonymity protects Did's usual day-to-day bill-paying activities. The author's list of freelance writing credits is long, they are exemplary and widely accepted - in the journalistic world they are well respected.

In time the truth might prevail, Did may well be exposed for accusatory censure or for the golden grail of plausible publishing plaudit.

NOTE FROM THE AUTHOR

I would like to say one big thank you to those of you who downloaded the reviewer's free beta-read copy of Magdalena's Bones, I am grateful for your help. I am also indebted to my partners in storytelling crime - my development editor, my proofreaders and my book-cover designer, each of whom is credited within the manuscript's credits. Due to the subject matter in one or two of my storylines, those who assisted me in production have chosen to use alias identities in the same manner as myself. To those of you who have read Magdalena's Bones, I hope you found each of the storylines intriguing and entertaining. Nearly five years hard graft has been an enlightening experience not without its publishing pitfalls and writer's setbacks. I acknowledge that Magdalena's Bones might be considered a complex read, but endeavouring to entwine historical fact with sometimes dubious myths, ancient legends and established doctrines of religion was always going to be tough cookie - more so while maintaining my absolute right to creative license.

My eventual decision to take the self-publishing route is largely down to finance and subsistence reward – the number of working hours has been astronomical given the time needed for plot development, drafts and rewrites before teaming up with my professional support. It was a great shock to then realise that handing over to a London-based literary agen and their publishing house would garnish me little more than ten percer of eventual book sales revenues – perhaps less than the national minimum wage when calculating all the hours of writing time involved. *So, my brave plan now is to try it alone.*

I hope you enjoyed or were at least thought provoked by Magdalena's Bones. Please remember, this novel is a work of fiction, the storyline plots do not reflect my religious beliefs nor do I make claim to know more than yourself.

Thank you for purchasing, reading and leaving your review. Your review counts, your review makes a difference.

The Author D.D. Did

Printed in Great Britain
by Amazon

43631983R00330